ASTRAL

D. W. Olivas

This book is a work of fiction. Any references to historical events, real people, or real locales are used fictitiously. Other names, characters, places, and incidents are the product of the author's imagination, and any resemblances to actual events or locales or persons, living or dead, is entirely coincidental.

Book cover art by Hussam Eissa.
Author photo by Margaret Saadi Kramer.
All logos created & owned by D. W. Olivas.

For information and permissions, contact the publisher at:
www.dwolivas.com

ISBN Paperback: 9798832923376
ISBN Jacket Hardcover: XXX
ISBN Hardcover: 9798832944548
ISBN eBook: XXX
ASIN Kindle eBook: XXX

TABLE OF CONTENTS

ASTRAL

"I think that getting what you want, it quenches the fire that got you there, often…"

-Rodney Mullen

PROLOGUE

1.0

TEN YEARS AGO...

Derek and I left the safety of the force field and took off after the girl in the parachute. It only occurred to me once we had left the blue light, unfazed in the slightest, what our Mom had said about being able to pass through it. That only the strongest could. And there we were, sprinting down the cul-de-sac, chasing something falling out of the sky, just turning that force field into a door.

Derek was not only perfectly matching my pace, but our feet were, impossibly, in perfect time and step. It helped that we knew our neighborhood from hurting ourselves over every possible inch of it: bikes, skateboards, bare feet, like I said, we were eight. The road dipped into a creek path on the right, next to a familiar mound of dirt that looked suspiciously like a bike jump, as the abandoned neighborhood street came up to our left. As we ran, I looked to the sky and did my calculations. There was a bit of wind picking up. I could tell by the deflating parachute that the descender would land… somewhere over there.

"Check it out Derek, she's headed right for all that nice, soft lawn—"

And came a light show with our names on it. BOOM.

The house in front of us exploded into a raging fireblast, we screamed and hit the dirt of the driveway, almost becoming part of the shockwave ourselves—if not for somebody's smoking, half-brown, half-golden minivan. I hadn't seen it in this neighborhood before, but that car had just saved our lives.

"James, you okay?" My brother called.

"Yeah, just bad luck brother… or maybe the opposite…"

We stumbled to our feet. We were shook, but not hurt. In the red and yellow lights I turned in horror to the sky, but by a miracle the parachute had not been burned in the slightest. And the lights made things easier. Thank you, explosion. The only bad thing, of course, was that all that nice, soft lawn was now a raging ocean of fire, with half the house behind it vanished, the other half smoldering, and the parachuter was headed right for the flames. But as she passed the tallest of the neighborhood roofs, she was finally close enough that I could see her eyes flickering. She was just unconscious. Thank—

"She's alive," Derek said, at my side again. "But headed right for the—"

"I have an idea. Get me up that porch brother."

“We should have stayed inside the blue light filter,” he said, looking up at the still smoking remains of the next house, and the long overhead balcony on top of the front porch of this one. Too bad.

We scrambled up to the roof of that brown minivan. Derek put his hands together, I got a good handhold on the burnt wood of the roof behind the gutter, took a deep breath, and pulled myself up. Then I ran forward, my eyes somehow torn between the girl in the chute and my feet not falling off the roof, until there was nothing else to do… but jump off the roof, into the air.

“THAT’S your idea?” Derek shouted as he scrambled off the minivan.

Yes that was my idea. I caught her (crashed into her limp body) by the back with both arms, and we were swung like a swing on the tethers of that parachute, over the worst of the front lawn flames and back towards the street. The ground still came up quick, and when we hit, it hurt. But thankfully nothing was broken, and by the time the line and parachute itself started obscuring my vision, I had kept my ground, taken the hit, and caught the girl. She wasn’t heavy in my arms, it was just the weight of her fall that took a bit of… re-grounding.

“That was a great idea!” Derek shouted again.

Then the best thing happened. She opened her eyes. I had to say something.

“Aloha.”

She blinked. “Where…”

“Safe,” I said. “I think?”

Then the lights went out, as the parachute had dropped over us on all sides and it was just her and me, and darkness. My hands were occupied, but I heard someone already pulling at the fabric—Derek. Another explosion went off in the distant city, and a red light lit up the inside of that parachute. She and I were both looking at each other weird, our eyes narrowed in the dark.

“I don’t know you,” she said. “But thank you. You can let me down now.”

“You’re welcome. I mean right. I mean, both.”

And she stood, but on unsteady legs, still holding herself up by my arm.

“Sorry… I can walk, I’m trying…” her voice shook as much as her legs.

“I don’t know you, but don’t apologize to me. It’s dark, take your time.”

Silence. Then, “My father… our plane… I barely… he… I don’t think…”

It left my young brain spinning. I didn’t know what to say. I just spoke.

“I’m James. And I’m so sorry.”

“Thank you James,” she said, letting go of my shoulder and wiping her face with one hand, and holding out her other to shake.

I did, gently. And that was when Derek finally ripped the large parachute over the tops of us and found us there, holding hands. Kind of.

“Alright, what’d he do?” Derek asked the girl in tears.

“He caught me,” the girl answered, on legs much steadier.

“He did that,” Derek said. “I’m Derek. Twin brother.”

“Thought I was seeing double.”

“Yep,” Derek and I said at the same time.

She shook Derek’s hand with a small laugh. We had made the mystery falling girl laugh. Success. She was definitely younger than ten. Still taking deep breaths, but she looked calm (if that’s what we were calling it).

"My name is Kira Command."

"Welcome back to Silka, ma'am," I said. "How can we help?"

"We can start with this pack brother," Derek said, his arms still laden with the parachute. "I cannot see where I walk, brother."

Right. I snapped out of it and together, Derek and I got her parachute folded up and cartable in seconds—but as we did, I nudged my brother and spoke low.

"Wherever she came from… I think her father didn't make it."

"No," Derek said. "That's… no. Where did she come from? Who—"

"That's just it," I said. "Let's not push it. I want to help her, and I know you do too, but we might have to do it without any answers. For now."

"Okay."

"Just like that?" I asked.

"You know I trust you. And we're not owed anything right now. I'm not the one who just fell out of the sky. As far as I'm concerned, she's in charge."

"Why?" Kira said behind us, making us both jump.

She had been listening. She had outsmarted the two boys whispering to each other only a few feet from her.

"Hey man," Derek started.

"You're pretty sneaky for a parachuter," I said.

She smiled. "I like you two. So this is what safe is like."

BOOM.

Another explosion went off in the airspace above the neighborhood, more of a dogfighter's disaster than a targeted firebomb on the streets we stood. But it reminded us of where we were, and what was happening. Literally, war.

"Don't say that yet," Derek said, his eyes up on the sparks and detritus about to come down on us. "Here's crazy. We've got ten seconds till fire rain."

Kira looked at me. "You know anywhere actually safe?"

"Yes Ma'am," I said.

And we were running home, with our driveway and that blue light force field coming up in the distance. We thought. We hadn't gone two paces when from our left, the ground started to rumble, shaking our shoes so hard we had to stop.

"You don't happen to have supernatural control over the earthly terrain, do you?" Derek asked Kira, who raised her eyebrows at the question.

"I mean, I'm a girl, so eventually yes. But right now? That's not me."

Then the ground opened up to the steel spiral of an armored burrowing tank, landing on dark purple treads in front of us, shaking the street it had come from. The battle had found us. And it wasn't kids versus super soldiers any longer.

"That's a TANK!" I yelled.

"Not fair!" My brother screamed.

"Not me not me!" Kira shouted.

We all but tore a hole in the universe taking off in the opposite direction of the purple machine behind. It seemed to be following us as it revved its engines, just a terrifying canon of machinery, as well as a machine of canonry (probably).

We had to MOVE.

"James, look out, there's something else coming out of the sky—"

He was right. It was a faint glow, growing brighter and brighter. Kira even paused as the light hit us, and so did the war machine drilling through the street. We all watched together, as the single light turned into twenty, moving in on our neighborhood from all sides like shooting stars.

It was the army. Infinite had arrived.

A figure flashed by us and slammed against the tank, quickly followed by two others, for the combined force of a triple assault. The machine was forced down the block, skidding powerfully enough to quake the earth one more time.

"Thanks for saving us mister!" I said, in my best fifties' comic voice.

Mom had taught us manners. But even at eight, life had taught us sarcasm.

"You're welcome mate," came a slightly Aussie accented reply.

The tank was turning back to us, but only until the soldier fired some kind of plasma ray out of his wrist at the tank that landed with a BOOM, fire and heatwave and all.

"Things are going bump here," he said, almost to himself. "Right now, you kids best, you know, what's faster than skedaddle?"

"You say," Derek said. "What's going on, Mister Person?"

"If I could answer that, I would," he said, sounding sincere about it, which was scary. "All I can say is, if you know a safe place, you should be there."

Behind the still circling tank, we saw the ground moving—literally, the rock and dirt and earth of my neighborhood was being pushed aside by soldiers in dark purple armor. Our Infinite savior saw us staring, and his hands lit up with cracking white bolts of electricity, even before he turned around. Cool.

"Speak of the reaper," he said, ominously. "I can't afford to see you to safety. If I don't jump in, there won't be safety this side of the hills. Are you good as?"

"We are good as," I said confidently.

The Infinite man nodded, and leapt into the air without another word. Just as silently, the other shooting stars joined him in the air, towards the growing mass of bodies on the other end of the neighborhood, where three more of those burrowing machines had grouped up, ready to face off against Silka City's best.

"We should have stayed inside the blue light filter," I admitted, as Derek threw his hands up. "But that guy was super cool."

"And making friends is dope," Kira added, perfectly on beat.

"And safe is boring," Derek concluded.

Though ironically, those were our leaving words.

"Three Infinite against an army, what say you?" I asked Kira as we ran.

She shook her head. "I wish I knew why they were fighting. Maybe we could help. That's what say I."

Derek mouthed the word wow. Whoever this girl was, she was something.

"That's the most adult thing I've heard tonight, including skedaddle," I said.

Derek and Kira laughed. We were somehow balancing the completely unacceptable adult war world around us with the fact that, again, we were only eight years old. The irony helped us block out the shouting and blasting from literally only a few houses behind us. And the volume did not get any less the farther away we got. This would be a race. Some kids versus… something.

For midnight on a December evening, the fires and smoke in the sky had left the world warm, and muggy, and for all the beacons of the fleets at sea and emergency lights over the city, it may as well have been daytime. And it was starting to smell like burning, everywhere.

"You don't happen to know why the island is attacking itself, do you?" I asked our new commander as we ran.

Kira shook her head, keeping pace with my brother and me without question. "It wasn't like this an hour ago. I was, my dad…"

"Sorry I didn't—"

"You don't apologize to me either," she said, leaving me reeling, as she took a deep breath. "It's okay. I… We were flying over the clouds and boarded by soldiers with weapons, in blue and purple armor. My father chose… to save me, instead of himself. But when he threw me out of the plane, I didn't see much. I didn't know about the fighting until the parachute was out. Then I was out."

"We woke up with the bombs," I said, trying to change the subject, just a bit. "Our mom is fighting for the city right now. We were watching the sky burning, when we saw you coming towards us, straight out of the—"

"The darkness," Derek finished.

Kira nodded as she ran, her eyes everywhere. "I guess… I did make it."

So we tore through the rest of the neighborhood without problem, because we didn't give the universe a chance to give us any. A few minutes later, we made the final push up our hillside driveway, running around the back of our house where the force field stood before us like the mere door it was.

"We made it!" Derek cheered/wheezed. "Firebombs… my butt…"

Kira looked around, nowhere near as winded. "You left this safety for me?"

"Yes," I said.

She looked at me weird. "Thank you."

"BOYS!"

And then there was another voice behind us. A hovercraft was descending right through that blue light before us, whipping the winds up inside the house's protection bubble. It seemed like some Infinite soldiers were about to land in our backyard, aboard some futuristic, multi-bladed flying hovercraft. Cool.

Derek looked at me, and I nodded. Double time. He ran right through the force field into our backyard to see what was going on above us.

"Who is that?" Kira asked, looking at the ship with fear.

"Infinite, they're here to help," I said.

"You know that?"

"I… think that," I said. "You think something else?"

"Kinda," she said, sounding off. "It's just a feeling. A strange one."

"Well I did crash into you pretty hard," I said. "My fault."

"Everything is not your fault, James," she said, still holding her head. "I can't explain… I don't think I'm meant to go through that thing."

"No problem. We do have a front door. Oh wait, that's behind the field too."

The front door taunted me, shut tight behind that blue force field, just out of reach unless we were willing to cross a line.

Kira shook her head. "It's bigger than that. I hear something. I swear it."

"JAMES!"

It was Derek, calling me in his serious voice. I was torn. Kira could see it.

"I heard that too," she said. "He needs you."

"He needs us," I said. "You trust me?"

Kira looked at me, almost sadly. "I shouldn't… but I do."

And she kissed me on the cheek, quicker than I could react. "So do I just…"

"You just," I said.

I walked (or maybe stumbled) backwards through the force field. Kira was looking at me with a smile as she walked up and disappeared into the blue light. Just before she fully crossed, I could see her eyes wide and taken by what she was seeing. Then the energy flared and I closed my eyes for the bright lights, losing the feeling in my hand, not knowing if Kira was still holding on to me. Then the energy flared down, and I opened my eyes to a world of white, blinking madly, until my pupils could adjust enough to see…

Nothing.

"How… where…" I said.

She wasn't here. Not turned to dust, not fried to bits, just not here. Gone.

What?

"Hey now," I shouted, looking around, my head feeling like it was being twisted in a vice, my voice shaking. "What just happened?"

I held my shaking fingers out to touch the force field. The blue lights fazed over me warmly, but I revolted at their touch, no longer enamored by my own ability to use it like a door when the ONE person I was trying to save hadn't been able to cross through. No force field for her. No ending to our rescue op. And she had trusted me. And I…

Wait the front door was open.

To my own house, to be clear. A red flag came up, seeing it ajar. It had been closed for sure a moment ago, I had seen it behind the blue light filter myself. The ashen footprints on the porch were new too, and tiny. Like, eight-year-old girl in a parachute tiny.

"K… Kira?" I asked, my eyes wild. I mean wide.

I mean both.

PART I

DEREK NITE

1.1

ARMOGAN

From somewhere under the sun, far, *far* southwest of the hundred-mile island of Ocarina, from somewhere over the ocean, from somewhere out of the Vempire, four flying teenagers could be seen shooting through the low hanging fog, the purple and blue lights behind them dancing across the clouds, leaving the ever-changing, never-ending land behind.

"No rest," Heather said, like it hadn't hit her yet.

"Not over," Lynn said.

She only poured on the speed, lightning ripping from her shoes as purple crystal wings beat faster and angrier. She was using all the ways of flying we knew—two. We notched ourselves up without question, rising past the clouds to shoot towards Silka like stars, or quite possibly meteors.

For the moment, I was a man with no future. My eyes were working, but I couldn't see the sky I was flying into, not when I couldn't stop thinking about what we were leaving behind. What was the opposite of flight? Falling, right?

"Ana," I started.

"Just don't," my brother said, and I could hear the lump. "We know. She..."

It was my brother James, the shield, his long black hair an airstream behind him. It was Heather Denien, born of the dragon, but her claws had softened for the days we'd spent under her wings. I'd like to say I had a friend in that dragon. It was Lynn Lyre, the storm, prodigal daughter of the Vempire, first to the light and a full half of the reason we were able to knock down the big stupid lock on the overland. The other half was me, the sword, and the Reapers who had given their lives for us—no, not for us. For them. That's all leader Balin had left me with, before Infinite had taken aim at first chance, while I had the luxury of being surprised by the blood, while Lynn's face was stone if I had ever seen it.

Stone.

"Mara..." I said, the word catching in my throat. "She..."

"She knew too," Heather finished for me, kindly, fully out of character.

I couldn't help it. I shouted/cried into the sky, scratching my throat, the anguish turning to coughing as I let it all out (not even). No one said anything. I wouldn't have cared if they did, I had no cool left to loose. Never had much of that anyway.

If I could have gotten out of my head, I would have noticed how our voices were all coming through my suit's communications, since the supersonic speed cone of sound was taking our spoken words away from us faster than they could get to our ears. We were flying, faster than ever. And yet, there was no joy in it. Walking would have done the same thing, gotten me out of here.

But there was no walking away from this.

"I know we're all feeling a bit… heavy," Heather said softly, her necklace glowing purple, the words entering my nervous system for the supersonics. "But what we just saw is expected, given the return of the Reaper. I hope you know we're not flying into the same city you left."

"Last time we left Silka on-route to arrest and return you to it, and we couldn't even do that on their terms," I said. "Now we're flying in holding hands. What will they—"

"They will think that you have jumped ship," Heather said simply. "You know how Silka treats outsiders? You're about to get it, in full."

"You don't sound mad," I said.

Heather shook her head, fifty feet away from me in the air. "I get the feeling that your privilege is going to kick in at some point."

"You think we'll buckle," James said. "You think we'll beg forgiveness—"

"No, I didn't mean—" Heather started.

"You didn't mean to be mean?" Lynn said.

Heather sighed. "New me is holding on for hope, but the old me… yeah, she thinks you'll play the orphan card, or the father card if that doesn't work, weird that you've got both. She thinks Infinite will give you the one thing people like me never get. Another second chance."

"You think we'll cave?" I said. "After sleeping in the dirt?"

"That was one time," she snapped.

"Watch us prove you wrong," James said. "A second time."

"I'd love to," Heather said. "Again. Wait, how the hell are we talking?"

"She's right," Lynn said. "We usually lose you in the air. What's changed?"

"Besides everything?"

"I heard that," Heather said.

"I bet you did," the Oracle's voice came into my head. *"I could be dramatic, but it's been a day, so here's a short answer for once. It's the necklaces."*

We were all wearing them, either proudly on our chests or tucked away under our super wired Infinite supershirts. Interesting.

"It must be the combination," Lynn said. "Infinite and Reaper."

"Sapphire and amethyst," I said, my brother nodding along. "I'd be more surprised… if I wasn't less surprised."

"You aren't surprised about a new team ability, given the gravity of what you are flying directly into? That reminds me, turn around."

"Can't," I said.

"But you can."

"If we do, we'll never do anything ever again," James said, unfiltered.

"If you don't, the same will happen."

And the Oracle was silent. That was it. Also, what was that?

"Who saw that?" Lynn said.

"I did," I said. "Who's throwing shapes?"

We were too high for shapes. We held a good height above even the clouds, the sky nothing but bright blue, a little blurry where the atmospheres met. There was nothing up here that breathed naturally, yet we had blown past some splotches of color.

"What's up here?" Lynn asked, curving quickly through the air, thankfully avoiding a bug on the windshield situation, and then the shapes were gone. "What's supersonic, around 800 miles per hour?"

"Whatever we just passed was going close to that," Heather said.

"Oracle, what the hell?" I asked.

"I will ignore the attitude, given the trauma," came the reply. *"It was a multitude of island birds. Peregrine falcons, golden eagles, and white swifts, the fastest flying birds in the world. They should be no match for supersonic."*

"You sure about that?" James asked, and I looked over to him holding his arm out for something that was moving so fast it was a blur.

A falcon had cut through our blast zone and landed on James' outstretched Superman flying arms. The thing pecked at its wings and shook its head, tiny eyes darting around at us.

"I'm sorry, how did that just happen?" the Oracle said. *"At its best, the peregrine falcon has been recorded at 250 miles per hour. You are—"*

"Supersonic," Lynn said, eyes wide. "That's a fast bird."

"Hi there," James said to the falcon.

Caw.

"Uh," Lynn said, eyes even wider. "Who else heard that?"

"We all did," Heather said.

"Did the bird say your name?" James asked Lynn, like it wouldn't even be a surprise.

"It…" Lynn said, far too slowly.

"How is a bird this high?" I asked. "Can it even breathe?"

"Nope," James yelled, wincing. "Ow, come on bird! No!"

The bird tipped sideways on his left arm, using every ounce of its strength to keep its sharp talons gripped around James' long sleeve. Right before the bird fell off and was lost behind us, I saw the fabric rip apart, leaving a long, curved line of a red stain on my brother's wrist.

"What the hell," James said in a stupor, holding his hand like it was broken.

He held up the shredded sleeve of his Infinite supersuit (at least the t-shirt part of it) as the body of that beautiful supersonic bird fell away from us, tumbling out of the sky with small beads of my brother's blood following it down.

"So this thing can take a burying, but not a bird?" I said, looking around the sky, suddenly on the lookout for shapes.

"That hurts," James said, one of his wings frozen, like it was too much to move even his shoulder. At least he had a jet boot backup, and it already looked like the suit was stitching itself back together. "We should turn back before another bite."

"Maybe we should listen to a bird," Heather said ominously.

"That's what I said!" The Oracle complained. *"Am I invisible to you?"*

"Yes," I said lamely. "But your invisible heart is in the right place, for a computer, and maybe a bird is too. Maybe—"

Nope. It was too late for maybe. The time for maybe had passed, supersonically.

As I was looking at Lynn like she was next to fall out of the sky, and James was looking down at his cut wrist with Heather like they were both thinking the same ominous thing, we all saw the first tips of the valley mountains jutting out of the clouds. We followed the biggest one down through the last layers of Olympus (metaphorically) and before we had thought about it, we had emerged in full view of the valley ridge where Crete's mechanical mansion stood.

We knew what was waiting for us at Silka, but as long as we didn't pass the literal divide between nations, we thought we'd be okay. That's why we had gunned for here, that's why we had come out of our supersonic cloud city expressway, because well, rest stop. Maybe coffee.

But the world couldn't even give us that.

We slammed on the air brakes as the pressure mounted in my head, the dread of knowing in an instant that a mistake had been made, and was about to be faced in full. Sand and Crete were nowhere to be seen. Neither was the mansion we came here to find. It was clearly engaged in its underground state. Good for them. Not good for us. The mountain was clear… except for one thing.

The army. They had not retreated into the city. They were right there.

"But we aren't even in Silka," Heather said, blinking.

"Turn back," Lynn stammered.

"Too late," James said, his wrist forgotten. "We should have listened to a bird. Or—"

"I tried to warn you."

Yep, missed the hell out of that warning.

Fifty fliers had the airspace around that small body of water, and fifty more stood the perimeter of that huge patch of empty grass where Crete's mecha-mansion usually was. The protective (yeah right) ring of water was only ten feet wide at most, not a problem for anyone who could FLY. They had seen us coming and now locked on to us from all sides, swarming us in a collective hum, while another fifty white suited, armored, laser powered soldiers stood all along the Valley peak, their heads to us, their backs to the Silka side of things. We were coming out of the Vema side, it was easy to see who was who.

Infinite. Back so soon.

"Enemies," came a shout from below.

"Agreed," Lynn said.

It was Hannah, optics expert and ex-camera operator for what used to be Infinite's omniscient super satellite. She was still limping, but still at the vanguard of her small army. For the second time today she eyed us as our superspeed was cut short, already close enough to hear their weapons powering on, the clinks of metal swords and short spears as they were leveled against us.

We held her stares until a full gunmetal helicopter hovered down into view, backing up the grounded soldiers.

"Derek and James Nite," came another familiar voice through the military helicopter's speakers, point of the airborne like Hannah was point of the wall of watchmen (and watchwomen). **"Lynn Lyre, Heather Denien. On behalf of the island, you are under arrest."**

"You must mean city," I said, full on frozen, like spinning beachball of death mode.

"I do not," the voice in the jet said, hovering closer to us. It was a familiar voice, but excuse me for panicking—I couldn't place it for the fear. **"Issaic Nite awaits your custody. Put your hands behind your backs."**

"Sure thing, skyboss," Lynn said, the point of us, putting her hands behind her back, folding her fingers down into a count that only we could see.

Three.

"Finally, a smart decision from the girl," Hannah said.

She motioned to a group of three agents who pushed off the mountain ridge and into the air, rising up behind that helicopter in a direct path to us. They kept close to the chopper, like the air was water and we were sharks, the weaponry and lights of the skycraft held on us as the soldiers got closer.

I touched my facial screen and that shimmering glass cockpit of the helicopter was suddenly transparent. Right. That voice. It was Alcyon Akoura himself, no co-pilot, and he frowned when I saw him. We had locked eyes a good football field away, and we both knew it.

Then my ears twitched.

"Is it true, about Agent Mara?" Alcyon asked us.

The voice was coming into my supersuit itself, and not out of the on-board speakers of a sleek war helicopter. Alcyon still had his finger on the trigger—of the communications board, apparently. There was a look of sadness on his face instead of the terror and tremors of the three soldiers advancing on us.

"You're talking to us," I said.

"Is she really… gone?" Alcyon asked, no games, no time for them.

"No," James answered honestly, looking my way.

"Why?" Alcyon almost cried into the comms.

"Ask your own," I said under my breath, bitterly.

"They did what they did," James said, as the girls frowned at us.

He was tapped in. They weren't.

"She's still dead because of you," Alcyon seethed, the tears in tracks down his face. "Don't get it wrong."

"Then help us make it right," I said, shaking my head, the fury so intense I thought my fists would break off, the feeling of pressure coming over me, I had to get out…

Lynn's fingers showed two. Got it.

"Whatever it is, ready," I said through teeth about to break off against each other, quietly as I could, hoping my suit would pick it up.

I saw the tiniest of nods from Heather and James, as Lynn's hand showed only one finger left, until the tips of it started losing visibility, only to us. Ah…

"Ready," Hannah said.

One...

"No you're not," Alcyon warned, at speaker volume again.

Alcyon sat unmoving in the cockpit of his helicopter, as Hannah and the vanguard approached, reaching out to us on trembling hands like we were about to bite them off... and right as the first was about to make contact, we disappeared.

"WHAT!" Hannah roared, watching us fade until only the shimmering purple outline of our foursome was seen.

"Told you," Alcyon said, the mountain ridge of standing agents rising up into the air as her troops joined Alcyon's. **"With me, on trail."**

On trail, yeah right.

We had mirrored Lynn into invisibility, watching the stunned expressions on those agents as she killed her wings, then followed her cosmic purple outline drop low and away, and fast, on the Vema side of the valley. We let invisi-Lynn lead, letting the free-fall take us away in stealth, already far away from the swarm—until we looked up to see a hundred agents at full blast, tearing over the valley and following us down like they could see us.

Like they could see everything.

"But..." I started.

"ON TRAIL!" The speakers blasted, Alcyon and his jet leading the way... to us.

"We got you this time," Hannah said.

She was looking straight at us while overcoming the other flyers, Alcyon and that military chopper by her side, a hundred agents right behind them in two formations, all bearing either sharp or bright weaponry, all aimed at us, not a single one guessing.

Uh oh.

"Chaos theory," Lynn's voice came from my right. "It's always either something, or everything."

She stopped looking up and hit her wings hard, now that terminal velocity had a new meaning. We followed the barely visible purple outline of her silhouette, until our fall became flight, and our flight became chase.

"How are they doing this?" James shouted in a panic, now that the gambit was up. "They can SEE US NOW?"

"Something can," I said. "Kinda breaks the charm on the invisi-thing."

"We can still run away," James said. "Are we there yet?"

"Maybe," I said. "If they can see us with their eyes, then yes. But if this goes deeper..."

"This goes deeper," came the unfortunate validation from the Oracle. *"You are being watched, traced, tracked, and followed. It is possible because of—"*

"Freaking lasers," James said, realizing.

"Our suits," I said, translating. "They're drawing power from somewhere, we saw it like wifi, neon beams of light."

"I still haven't accounted for whatever happened underland, but back on the surface yes, you are connected to the source. Issaic Nite must have initiated

triangulation on your connection. It's already all I can do just to keep this line from interference."

"No duh Derek," I said, smacking myself on the head. "If Alcyon can talk directly to James and me, he's got us by the signals. Why didn't I see that?"

"Because being invisible is still new to you," Heather said. "If they've figured out how to trace your clothes, that probably means they can turn them off too."

I hadn't thought of that. "No way."

"Way," the voice came, reading my mind like the Oracle tended to do. *"You are trying to escape in the night, while glowing in the dark."*

"Then why wasn't turning us off the first thing they did?" I asked.

"Easy," the Oracle said. *"They are following you like a flame, in hopes that it will bring them to the light."*

I felt my body over for the nano-fabric that stitched together anywhere it touched, making the unbreakable bond between pants and socks, belt-line and super shirt. I was still alive and amplified. I was still repping both Infinite and Reaper technology, using every trick in the book to pull off my signature move—running away from a thing. But right now the very thing that was letting me run away…

"Because of where we are," James said. "They're following us to where we'd go."

"To someones, and someplaces," Lynn said, thinking fast. "Which means that's the last place we can go."

"Correct," the Oracle said again. *"Right now, I can't even allow Sand and Crete into your comms, let alone you into their house. If it helps, they are safe, hidden away under that mountain, and no breaches have been detected. You four, not so much."*

"It's always something," I said.

"Or everything," Lynn said sadly.

We were giving top tilt a new meaning. The army behind us was as fast as a speeding helicopter, and it was also led by one. We followed Lynn down in a curving, twisting spiral until we ran out of mountain, but then the sideways wall of granite fell away and we took to a tunnel, following a break in the mountains she'd found, jetting into the curvature of the massive rock on a dime. We followed, until suddenly the open air was nothing but rock, and the light went out as we entered some sort of cavern. That was the first time I realized I might be carrying a bit of resentment for the last few days without the sun.

"No, not here, I can't—" I started panicking, until James had his hand on my shoulder as we flew like madmen.

"You can do anything," he reminded me. "And have to."

Right. This wasn't the endless underland, it was just a mountain. I could take a mountain.

"Go, GO! All agents into the mountain! Cadet, hold the plane, I'm flying in."

"YES SIR!"

And the tunnels behind us were suddenly much louder and brighter than they'd been a second ago. We started flying under the low hanging stalactites and through the mountain's inner pass, but we'd passed about thirty different tunnels in five seconds, and Lynn stopped.

"We gotta go now!" I shouted.

"I have an idea," Lynn said, thinking fast. "Heather, pick a tunnel."

"What?" she shouted. "I'm not leaving you, I just found you!"

"You have to," Lynn said. "They're tracking our every move, but just us, just the Infinite part of this. We're compromised, we're as good as collared. But you're not. You're Heather Denien, there's no locator collar on you."

"Never," she said.

"You can be our breach," Lynn said. "When we need it. And it's not now."

"I…" Heather said, trying to find a problem with it, but she couldn't. She only nodded. "I like it. But having friends is going to get me killed."

"Not if we can help it," Lynn said. "Stay close, unless you don't."

"Okay bye," was the last thing we heard from Heather.

"Don't die," Lynn whispered as she left, so quiet I almost didn't hear it.

Heather certainly didn't. But thankfully, not a single Infinite broke rank, not a single flier changed course as Heather made her great escape, by flying off sideways and watching the hundred agents pass her by without a single one sensing the gambit. Her outline of purple shimmer must have been something you needed a necklace to see, but even to us eventually her diamonds faded into the diffused tunnel version of sunlight.

"She'll come back to us," Lynn said.

"Unless she doesn't," I said, my head heavy.

"Don't think like that," Lynn said. "We just went through something. We're still going through it."

"But where are we even going?" I asked.

"What's the point of hide and seek when they've got us chipped?" James asked under his breath.

"No point," Lynn said. "We're giving Heather a proper sendoff. She'll be fine, as long as we give her a decent…"

"Distraction," I said sadly. "That's all we are to you girls."

"Pretty much," Lynn said. "As for us, I think we came shooting in to Silka on the words of another girl. I need to answer that call."

"But what if… the call is already ended?" I said.

"I'll have to see that for myself," Lynn said, her eyes as narrow as I'd ever seen them "Maybe it's the nostalgia of Alcyon chasing us down behind a big giant military ship but… I can think of one way in that's worked before."

"No," I said, my mind blank. "Not that. Anything but—"

"But exactly what those people chasing us want too?" James said, sadly. "It's a perfect storm isn't it?"

"There's no such thing," Lynn said. "We either lose our minds, or our freedom. Easy choice, right?"

"Is this one of those go with dignity situations?" I asked, terrified.

Lynn sighed. "It might be. If we truly want to catch them off-guard, a proper distraction would be… the exact opposite."

And in that moment we saw the Infinite, and they saw us. Immediately we were surrounded, above and below, as a hundred agents encompassed every possible escape route. In a single move we all moved from the air to the ground, the invisibility given up upon the first step back on dirt. I saw the looks. Every single eye in the cavern turned to us in the same second. They had us. But… didn't we have them too?

"Where is the Reaper?" Was the first thing we heard, from a young, bearded agent with deep blue eyes and no hesitation in the hands aimed at our necks.

"Gone," Lynn said.

"How convenient," a voice came.

"If we're headed back, let's take the scenic route," I said. "One wave before prison?"

"How about no," came a gigantic voice.

It was Geran the axe-man, walking up to us wearing something that wasn't the usual slimline armor of Infinite. This was an actual bodysuit of thick, protective material, with patterns of reinforced and contoured metal all over. It wasn't fair. He was already big enough.

"So what is it," I asked, hands up. "Fight or flight?"

"I think… neither," Lynn sighed, then did something I had never seen her do.

She held her hands out in surrender.

Geran immediately yanked some sort of glowing fabric over her wrists that automatically snapped together; Lynn cried out in pain as her arms buckled and her elbows connected, as the handcuffs forced her hands up to her chin and the fabric expanded, lashing her bound hands to her neck. Hannah did the same to James and me, and my funny bones collided, as my bound fists shoved into my neck. Some sort of handcuff necklace, add it to my drip. But my hood came off in the squeeze, which meant the facial shield did too. James was the same.

Talk about vulnerable. Or, as I used to call it, normal.

"You good brother?" James asked, the look in his eyes all I needed to know.

"Second time in my life I've been in handcuffs," I said. "I'm starting to sense a pattern."

"So are we," Hannah said.

Then she turned to Lynn and backhanded her across the face, in what looked like the hardest hit a twenty-something year old woman was able to throw at a teenager. That turned quick.

"HEY!" I shouted.

But Geran's huge foot on my chest kept me from moving towards her. Lynn was knocked off both feet at once, and with nothing to stop her fall, she landed on her butt and back, the wind knocked out of her, as she twisted over to her side gasping for air, looking at me trying her best to mouth a single word in between the breathing.

Dis… traction…

"Can't get up?" Hannah taunted. "But I thought we were still fighting."

"NOT COOL—oomph!" I shouted.

I'd struggled a bit too much, only to get the handle of a glowing axe in the stomach from Geran right when I had emptied my lungs to shout. Not good. Instantly I couldn't breathe, I was gasping on the ground right next to Lynn, with half of my face numb and covered in dirt before I could react. I saw James hit the ground next, and suddenly we had gone from very much in control of a thing to well, not so much.

We were prepared to be arrested, again. We had done it before, the night we had first ever put on those speed shoes, when Alcyon's delta unit caught us outside a burning farmhouse. We had gone peacefully. We had weapons in our face, sure, but there had been no beatdown. Not like this, post coming up from the Vema side of things. There was no hold back now.

"We're... we were already surrendering..." I wheezed out.

"Can't be too careful with traitors," came the voice, as a gigantic foot stepped into the dirt beside my head.

"We saved you," I complained, like a cartoon.

"You buried and unburied me, that's it," the reply came. "You took a week from me. I've been waiting the whole time for this."

"Geran, let me handle him," came the voice of Hannah.

"You don't tell me what to do, glasses," he said.

"I guess I don't," Hannah said, sounding colder than ever.

And there was a blast of something above my head. Who...

I couldn't see, I couldn't turn my eyes or move my neck that way. All I saw was that gigantic foot hovering a foot off the ground, then it crumbled down with no thought by its bearer of control. The body of Geran slammed into the ground beside me with a small quake, his head making the loudest sound, leaving a ringing sound of dirt and metal, as the axe he had forgotten teetered on its hilt...

Right about to fall into me like a guillotine...

"I'm not even wearing glasses," Hannah said.

Her left hand was smoldering and glowing with the last of the laser discharge. She had fired from the hip, nary a fighting stance. The axe started falling, I started caterpillar-ing, but then the ringing stopped as Hannah took the axe in her ungloved hand, the other one standing perfectly still at her side, steady as the weapon it was.

"I should have let that fall," Hannah said. "Lucky your father wants you alive. The twins at least. As for the girl—"

"You touch her and no one leaves this cave alive," I said.

"Geran..." Lynn said, horrified. "What did you do?"

"GERAN!"

Two knees smashed into the dirt beside my head. It was Laurel Seagrave, desperately trying to haul Geran's huge body off the dirt. But by the way his body wasn't responding as she cried, I knew without seeing... it was bad.

"How could you," Laurel said, her feet digging into the dirt and moving towards Hannah.

"It was a point that needed to be made," Hannah said. "I'm not interested in anything but my every command going unquestioned among the Infinite. I answer to Issaic, and you answer to me. If you disagree, you die. The rest of you will find out soon enough how not kidding I am."

"He was of Silka!" Laurel shouted.

"And now he's of the ground. It's funny. I got Mara with the same move."

"Say… that again…" I wheezed, as my lungs were gasping, my stomach still convulsing.

"He's not the enemy, those three are!" Laurel shouted.

"Hence the super handcuffs," Hannah said, her voice growing darker. "Why aren't you in super handcuffs?"

"You don't tell me what to do," Laurel said, staring Hannah down, echoing Geran's words to her. "You never will."

"I guess I don't," Hannah said, just as intently as the first time.

All I could see was her hand twitch at her side, rotating in a flash to point her palm at Laurel's head. Then the light blinded me and the pain ricocheted around my head. I never even heard Laurel cry out in pain. She was already gone.

"NO!" Lynn shouted, her eyes on something over my head I couldn't see.

If I could un-remember anything in my life, it would probably be the sound of Laurel hitting the ground. The way… the sound… you just knew… I don't want to describe it. This was bad. Hannah's feet hadn't moved, and now the bodies of Laurel Seagrave and Geran Noel had joined us on the floor.

The worst part was, I couldn't move enough to see if they were dead or alive.

"What… what have you done?" My brother said, his eyes wide at whatever was happening over my shoulder.

"No…" Lynn said, her eyes finding mine, crazed, blinking, but holding each other.

"Ma'am," came the sound of a very scared soldier. "Should we… bring the bodies in?"

"Leave them," Hannah said. "They'll get up, or they won't. Does anyone else want to try my command?"

And the next worse thing was… no one did.

"Keep these three contained," Hannah said, eyeing us with nothing but hatred in her eyes. "They are more dangerous than you could possibly imagine. Our similarities begin and end there. Now let's bring them home to father."

Then someone grabbed me by the side shoulder and smashed me into the hard dirt headfirst. Lynn and James followed, though I didn't know it. Come on.

"AH!"

I reeled, seeing stars again, feeling like throwing up, until the tunnel vision came on and I was out. Darkness, only darkness… and a headache. Then—ow. I was back, my eyes shut tight as the pain in my head reminded me I was still among the living.

"Not cool…" I said, making sure I still had all my teeth. I did. Thank—

We were moving. We were out of that cave, we were flying, and coming down to the outskirts of a city I knew from a movie, or something. No wait, this wasn't a movie, it was real life, and this city was mine. My head hurt harder the more I thought, which was weird, probably no biggie. Then I realized we were hovering at the end of the historic downtown Silka City, with cars around us stopped to witness a hundred Infinite soldiers and their three prisoners walk through the last stretch of house-lined park, with the river and waterfall the only things in sight.

Those three prisoners were us. Myself, Lynn Lyre, next to me still unconscious, and my brother the same on the other side. We were held in some sort of airborne prison as the Infinite flew us down and through the streets as the people gathered wherever we went. Not a single soldier was looking at us, no one had realized I was awake. Barely.

"You… could have flown us over," I said, coughing blood.

"And miss the press?" Hannah replied, as we came to a stop. "You were so eager for the spotlight just a few hours ago. Now burn in it."

I picked my head up, dripping blood and sweat from the suit, dirt and dust from the caves. The three of us were wearing the day all over our clothes, while our guards and captors had the sleekest light blue suits, without a single scratch or blemish to be seen. It was easy to tell us apart, and that was before the wrist/neck handcuffs. But as I looked out, it was the normal city-wear that got me, the sandals frozen in fear on the curbs as army boots pounded through the grasses and streets, the absolute shock of seeing us come parading through. That's what reminded me where we were.

We were home. But not free. Not yet.

"I don't believe it," came a rushed, deep female voice, and it was only then I saw the cameras. "I'm live in downtown Silka between Third and Tower, where it appears that the Infinite Army has for the second time in a month made their appearance known. Does anyone care to comment on what's happened in the Vema Empire today?"

"Nothing about—wait, hey now," Hannah said.

She'd attempted to walk through the reporter, but the reporter was either a parkour expert or had been here before, as she ducked, weaved, and walked backwards, never giving Hannah more than a microphone's distance. If the crowd was an ocean of obstacles, the reporter was water.

"How do you already know about that?" Hannah asked.

"Ma'am, our weather radars are showing above ground activity and thermal readings from the Vempire we haven't seen in ten years," the reporter said. "In the same day, city security has report a loss of command over the perimeter force fields, and the entire historic district watched a hundred soldiers take off in the daylight like they were firing themselves off to war. We've gotten reports in all afternoon from citizens who've been contacted by friends and family they haven't heard from in years. Now tell us and don't lie, because we already know. What's happened?"

"Is it true," one woman cried.

"Are they back?" A man said, trying to grab the shoulder of a passing agent, who only brushed him off and kept walking.

"The Reapers of the Underworld, do they come for the city?" A kid shouted up at us.

Yeah. They knew.

"It is true they are back," Hannah said. "For ten years they have slept, and today, they woke."

"But… why?" The reporter said, blinking at the horror.

"Exactly," Hannah said, looking at the three of prisoners in the middle of the group. "I can't tell you if the Reaper is coming for us again, but we have already apprehended the three responsible for their return."

"But that's Derek and James, Teresa's kids—"

"They stopped a meteor shower from destroying the city—"

"And then they let the Vempire out into the daylight for the first time in ten years, while holding a team of seven Infinite agents hostage underland for seven days," Hanna growled. "Yes that includes me, yes I took my eyes off them and yes they went off mission unsupervised for a week, we're dealing with it. But as hard as this might be to understand, that's normal in wartime. We lose people, and give everything we've got to find them, all the time. What's not normal is doing what they did. These aren't kids you're looking at. They're scouts at least. Double agents. Liars, infiltrators. Spies, and possibly not even for Vema. What's most dangerous is that we just don't know. Hence the handcuffs."

The city looked at us differently now.

"They did…" the voices came.

"Teresa's kids did the…"

"…the worst thing a kid has ever done in Silka…" the reporter finished for us, the mic at her side, forgotten for what must have been the first time ever, as the crew behind her pointed the cameras at us without heart. "Is it true?"

The cameras were close, the lights even closer. But something told me not to talk. Maybe I didn't want the city to hear me like this, maybe I knew what I would look and sound like. Either way, it didn't matter. I didn't have to say anything. They already knew.

Then… boy, did we get booed.

Hannah made the motion and we were dragged away, through the shouting, through the cameras following us as our feet scrapped against the ground and our shoulders burned for the soldiers yanking us around. We must have looked bad. I wondered how many were watching. The people never stopped, not behind us, not in front of us, as a crowd gathered to shout as Infinite kept taking steps through the historic downtown, towards the bluffs and waterfall in the middle of the city, with the high rising cliffs and hills of the Engineerium District far above our heads. The crowd followed until the spray of water started hitting our skin, and the Infinite alone proceeded over the small river stream and towards the larger water.

I had my hands pressed up against my neck, which made claws a non-starter. I couldn't fly if I wanted to, by either of the two ways I knew. My supersuits were kaput with this neck/wrist lashing. I could barely breathe, which is why I'd been the slightest bit quiet lately. I only tried to get my breath back as I watched a fuzzy city roaring and shouting and spitting at me. No response, not yet, not there, not even as the water came down, bouncing harmlessly off the shielded, hooded heads of the agents around us, and then—

"AH!" James shouted for the three of us.

The waterfall was coming down hundreds of feet. I guess we had used a helicopter to get through last time. Now, our hoods weren't protecting anything, and we'd taken the water so hard on our head and shoulders that it had pressed us into the ground like pancakes in a blink.

"Look at the fish," came the taunts as the Infinite laughed, as we scrambled to get out of the way of the water that came down like canonry.

Were we the fish?

I found myself on my side, rudely splashed awake, my head in the worst vice it had ever been in. I had felt like throwing up for too long, and I finally did it, stumbling down to the rocky river water and unloading, excuse the term. I had no hands, I just laid sideways under the water, letting the waterfall take the bile and blood away. Why was there blood in my stomach?

"Clean the fish," Hannah ordered.

Which meant to drag me up and hold my entire body under the gigantic waterfall, apparently. It felt like a stoning, because it was water falling fifty feet in a dense smashing. Water was heavy man.

"AAAHHH!" I shouted, about to explode when—

They pulled me in.

"How'd that feel?" Hannah asked.

"Like you dropped the world on my head," I said, wincing.

"I could always put it through your head," Hannah said. "Someone get him some gum."

"Anything but Latin," I almost cried, holding my head, forced to follow the group, leaving wet, bloody footprints on the rough rock.

This sucked. I was dragged, half conscious and soaking wet down the main chute of the Infinite falloff, I guess that's what I was calling it now. I felt the weightlessness and got a bit of a dry in the air, but not enough. We landed and there was no Green Panel, no sitting down, no organization to the organization, they had met us at the door. Or the falloff. Or the atrium, if that's what we were calling it.

"Look at that," James said, his words a bit slurred from the pain. "Right where we wanted to be. Infinite. Back so soon."

"Why on earth would you…" Hannah started.

She looked at us like we were scum, but then her eyes changed. Maybe she was remembering how we usually came with big gigantic asterisks, no matter what we looked like. She bit her tongue, and looked at us one last time as the army crossed the room and started forming a unified rank before us. Then, just as I thought she had lost the thought—

"You either want nothing from this world or everything," Hannah said to us suddenly, quietly, under her breath. "I am scared of you. I don't think you know how much."

Then she left us there. The Infinite took the opposite side and folded their arms at us. Hannah became just another pair of judging eyes and bad posture, as we were dumped alone against a gaze of hundreds, with only a few Panel doors at our backs, and the entirety of Infinite standing in a half-moon before us, with a tall, clean shaven man in a blue suit at the helm.

He looked familiar…

“Well then,” suit guy said. “Long roundabout for a proper talk. Where’s the Reaper?”

“She has a name,” said James.

“I specifically sent the hunt for four,” suit guy said, ignoring my brother.

Real familiar…

“We only have access to three,” Odd said, walking up from nowhere (where he should have stayed). “The Reaper does not bear any of our technology, we have no trace on her.”

“She’s really just Reaper?” Suit guy said, looking puzzled. “Huh. I’ve had sixty years of the Vema trying to kill me and they always had help. She got closest, and all on her own? Now I’m really mad.”

Too familiar…

“She’ll come for these three,” Odd said. “You’ll have your chance.”

“That means I have to keep them alive,” the guy said. “Whose plan was that?”

And all the agents pointed to Hannah in the same moment.

“Strike one,” he said to her.

“But—” she tried to argue, then caught herself. “Yes Issaic.”

Wait a minute.

“Good save,” the clean shaven suit-guy in charge of Infinite said, as the bells FINALLY went off in my head. “Disagree and die, it cuts all ways. Now onto the fish. Can they stand? Or are we going to gut them on their knees?”

“We can stand, Issaic,” I said. “Took me a minute. I… liked the beard.”

“So did I,” Issaic said. “Thank you for saying that. I… like compliments.”

I heard the grunts of my brother and Lynn as we fought to find our feet. There was no way I was meeting my father in the fetal position. This was a beginning.

“All here? Finally?” Issaic Nite said. “Then how about we start with… Aloha.”

And with every soldier and weapon of Infinite aimed on us, we faced him on our feet.

JAMES NITE

1.2

HOPE MACHINE

Issaic Nite. Our biological father. The missing part of our family, but only by technicality. Here were all the things I knew about him. That was it.

With the lights of the army behind him, a line had clearly been drawn, and we were on the other side of it. For once, for the first time, we were standing face to face… but again, only kind of. I couldn't feel the heaviness of something I'd been waiting my whole adolescence for, not when the cop and robber part was playing out before me like a bad dream, not when my face was all red and bruised from getting pummeled into the ground by someone we had supposedly 'beaten' not even a few hours ago. I didn't feel like this was the first time I would be meeting my dad. I felt more like I had pissed off the sensei, and now the entire karate class had lined up behind him with their arms folded as the master had it out with me in front of everyone.

Because at least *that* would make sense.

"Aloha," I said.

"That's the first thing your brother said to me," Issaic said, in a deep voice with a bit of a rasp to it. High and low, at the same time. At least he was a walking contradiction, just like us. "In the name of courtesy, I'll return it. Aloha, sons of Teresa."

"For lots of reasons, let's keep that distance," I said. "Issaic."

He nodded, no problem. "James Henry Nite. Derek William Nite. Named after Teresa's grandfathers, and two old friends of mine, we couldn't decide."

"What happened to distance?" I said.

"I'm sorry, did you want me to stay a world away from you for the rest of our lives?" Issaic asked.

"You never had a problem before," Derek said slowly.

He was right. I used to ask my mother the questions. Her answer was always the same. One day, we'd know everything. It was never a good enough answer, so I just kept asking. Then one day, I'd found her crying in bed after I'd been especially… demanding. I'd made my mother cry by asking about my father, and that was all a six year old needed to know. I could honestly say that for the next twelve years… I'd held on tight to nothing. I felt my eyes sting at the memory of my mother, that house, that hill. This was all back when I had everything—what was a tiny bit of nothing to the luckiest kid ever?

"No," Issaic said, his eyes shimmering with something. "From your perspectives, I suppose not. Where are we starting this time?"

"With the cloud you came from," I said. "We saw you fall, we caught you. We could have let you drop into the ocean."

"But you didn't," Issaic said.

"Where did you come from?" Derek asked.

Issaic looked us over, carefully. "The distance."

He looked at us like we had the answer. Almost testing us. Seeing what we knew.

"Why?" I asked.

"You think you know me," Issaic said, shaking his head. "That's going to—"

"You're going in circles," Lynn cut in. "Where's Ana?"

"The doctor?" Issaic said. "The one put in the hospital by the same Reaper who tried to kill me? She has succumbed to her injuries, she died days ago. And yes you missed the funeral. You were busy, letting the world's greatest killers back out into broad daylight. Remember?"

That's when the karate class—sorry, I mean a hundred Infinite soldiers standing in a crescent moon behind 'dad' started shouting and screaming at us from all angles, all at once. I saw every face I had ever put a name to down here and more, and they did not hold back a word. The quiet ones were Odd and Hannah, their arms folded smugly on either side of Issaic, but even quieter than them was Iliad, the younger brother of Benjann, who sat with his eyes wide and heart absolutely broken between a screaming Eve and raging Jemeni, their younger voices cutting a higher pitch through the crowd. They both had all sorts of grown-ups arms around their shoulders and necks, clearly holding them back from bolting at us, but I heard the things they called us, I could feel the absolute pure hatred coming off those kids, the orphans who called the Blue Panel bunkers of Infinite their home.

All I could think was… sorry.

I was so, so sorry. For… I couldn't. For everything, leave it at that. They were wrong to boo us, but were they? It sure felt like they weren't. Lynn made no sound. I could hear my brother's breathing in the bellows of that atrium, until Issaic held up a hand and the shouting stopped. All that was left was my heart beating so hard I could feel it in my throat.

"All sentiment for the fallen doctor aside," captain Troy said beside Issaic, wearing all black in contrary to the light blues and whites of the others, quiet but posed, like a snake. "We're starting from the part where four children loosed the ancient threat of the Vempire back onto the surface of the island. We can probably count the days before they rise against us again on one hand, which means what happened to Ana is only the beginning of their reign of terror."

"Reign of terror, they're EATING for the first time in a year!" Derek shouted, his blood boiling at the injustice, or maybe that was me. "What if everything we've ever seen contradicts everything you think you know?"

"Then I would laugh at your eighteen years of so-called life, against my forty," Troy said. "And you owe me those years, boy. Ten years ago, I was holding back the Blitz with my Silka City brothers and sisters in arms, while you were cowering in your bedrooms, letting your mother fight your battles for you."

"I thought no one here remembered Teresa Nite," I said.

"We do not greet strangers with every ounce of information we possess available," Troy said, looking down at us. "I think the feeling is mutual."

"Look at that, we agree on something," Derek said, his rage turned down, but still simmering. "And I thought we couldn't change anything."

"And yet you just did," Issaic said. "Tell me, how were four children able to do what you just did? Apart from the part I played, of course, let's be honest."

"We all saw them trick you into it, sir," Troy said.

"And how terribly easy that was, sir," Lynn said, mock saluting.

Issaic ignored her. "A lot happened before the barrier came down. A lot for children. I think there's something else behind these three, some mysterious benefactor, some forgotten part of the past that a better me would have figured out by now..."

"It's just us man," Derek said bitterly.

"It's literally not," Issaic said. "Else the Reaper would be here too."

"She HAS A NAME!" I shouted, not even for the first time in this solid marble headquarters. "It's Heather Denien, and she is of Silka. The funny thing is you've got Vema in front of you, but you don't care about the logical side of this."

"When has tribalism ever been logical?" Derek asked rhetorically.

"You pronounced fascism wrong," Lynn said sadly.

"You are Vema?" Issaic said, his eyes landing on Lynn. "Well thanks for showing up in handcuffs, they fit you as well as they do my... them."

"We aren't your anything," I said loudly.

Issaic ignored me—the only time he would.

"This isn't about the past," he reminded himself as much as us. "This is about the present. And presently, I have a decision to make about three children who caused more damage to my city than I've ever seen a team of supervillains do—and that was before they woke the Reaper."

"A team of what now?" I asked.

"Yeah you can't just drop that, and on us..." Derek said, blinking harder.

"My agents say you were inside this headquarters not even two weeks ago," Issaic said. "They tell me you came in with fake names and mustaches."

"I mean," I said, feeling the baby fuzz on my upper lip. "Bad ones..."

"You have caused chaos since the moment you were met by the Infinite Army," Issaic said. "Your presence directly caused the decommissioning of our Echelon satellite. Not to mention the death of Mara Stone, the first Infinite operative casualty in seven years."

"Be very careful about what you say next," Lynn said, in a low, hushed tone that screamed bring it.

"Not to mention Ana Brooks, medical practitioner in the making," Issaic said slowly. "You have the deaths of two very powerful women on your hands, little girl. How does that make you feel about the side of man you have chosen?"

And that did it. Lynn roared at Issaic and the purple glow started like a whip even in her chained hands—until she caught herself and allowed the black wisps of light to break against the Infinite, no harm, only the shocked looks of every agent in the atrium. Except Issaic.

"Logical to a fault," he said to Lynn. "Just like a Lyre."

He hadn't even blinked. He had seen the situation as Lynn had. One completely impossible for a little girl to overcome with fighting alone. I hope that didn't sound sarcastic, because right now, it was just true. Lynn only glared at Issaic, her fists still held to her own neck. She would never fight a losing battle. Me, well I didn't exactly possess the zen to think such profound thoughts while monsters of emotions were levied against me from all angles. I was more of a reactionary. Lynn was not. She knew how to pick her fights. I did not.

Hannah stepped forward with her backhand raised again, Lynn didn't budge an inch, but Issaic held back his commander from my friend.

"For the sake of love commander, you can't hit a woman," Issaic said.

"I'm a woman," Hannah said. "Are you telling me what I can and can't do with my own body?"

"Oh," Issaic said, backing off from Hannah, shrugging at Lynn. "I tried."

"I'm on her side here," Lynn said, licking her lips at Hannah, daring her to do it (again). "Come on Polly Pocket. Hit me with your best shot."

"I… hate both of those things," Hannah growled, trying to sound tough while looking at Lynn like she was crazy. Or like she was afraid of her.

"Don't kill her, that is an order," Issaic said.

"Yes sir," Hannah said, bound by duty. Issaic seemed pleased at the loophole.

"It's okay Lynn," Derek said. "She's just looking to even the score. Don't give it to her. No fight, no flight. We're here for reasons."

Lynn nodded to him, the light in her hands receding. "Sorry."

"You are about to die. It would be weird if you went quiet," Issaic said, with what sounded like the smallest bit of respect for her.

"You can't do that until you've gotten everything out of us," I said, logically.

"Oh?" Issaic said. "So you think me incapable of necromancy?"

"Are… you not?" Odd asked, looking at Issaic like… demons.

"Of course not," Issaic said. "The kids must live. For now. Until I devise another method of keeping those barbarians from ever posing a threat again."

"They DON'T!" I shouted.

"Tell that to MARK AND COURTNEY!" Issaic shouted at us. "Killed by the Reaper this summer. Tell that to ex-interim captain Mara Stone, a traitor to our city yes, but an Infinite, killed by the Reaper this summer. Tell that to the never doctor Ana Brook, killed by the Reaper, this summer. Tell that to the Echelon. Tell it to the Observatory. Get the pattern? What would you call four deaths and all this mystique in two weeks, would you call it NORMAL?"

Lynn laughed, turning her back on Issaic to wipe her eyes, not giving him the satisfaction. The atrium of agents held their breath, watching us, waiting for our response. But laughter—

"She's laughing at murder," Issaic said, frowning.

"She's laughing at you," Derek corrected.

And that beat belonged to us. The atrium was a vacuum.

"Wanna explain that one?" Issaic finally said, dangerously.

"You're oh for four, dad," I said, my words drawn out, the anger not hidden by danger. "Odd killed your elders for personal gain, your army dogs killed Mara as she was saving thousands, and you can be damn sure we've got it out for the duo behind Ana. That's why we're here. We delivered ourselves to you like a man on crutches opening a prisoner's door in the darkness. For that one, we're back, back again."

With him standing the closest of all the Infinite to us, none of his agents saw the look on his face, and with Lynn turned away laughing at not-murder, she missed it too. But for a moment, we had spoken Issaic's language. It went farther than letting him know we knew about Odd. We had just let them both know that we knew what happened to Ana. For the second time this summer, we were facing down the Infinite from within their own little hideout. For maybe the tenth time this summer, we had forced them to stop everything they normally did and pay attention to us instead. But for the first time in forever, I saw Issaic flinch. And boy, if silence could get quieter.

In that moment, Issaic was realizing we might not be something to sneeze at. Unless you had to sneeze, that was okay. In that moment, in that single flinch, I could tell one thing for sure. He had seen us for the first time. And he wasn't scared of us, but he was wary.

He should be.

"Yeah," Derek said, trying to sound intimidating. "More than meets the eye."

"That's from..." Issaic said. "No. My son just quoted transformers to me. That's a failure on all systems. I need to think, take them straight to solitary."

"To what?" Lynn asked. "The part where you're going to torture children?"

"I said solitary, not the stretch table," Issaic said. "Should I rephrase?"

"Never let them out," came a quiet voice.

The voice was of the absolute youngest kid in here, who couldn't possibly have known what he was saying. Iliad. And it pushed any fight I had left out of my heart. I was done. A handful of agents came up to us, two adults for each kid, and grabbed us by the bound wrists. We were wrenched sideways but I didn't even mean to go limp and make them fight for it. I was numb. Eyes blurry, ears ringing. Why did Iliad have to say that...

"Solitary confinement has been proven the worst torture a social mammal like humans can endure," Lynn said. "Don't pretend not to be a warden."

"Go quietly, children," Odd said. "Don't—"

"Don't forget to break down the door on the way back?" Derek said, low.

It landed. The look on Odd's face was worth the fog lifting for. He and Issaic were clenching right now, I could see that too. Then the guards were taking us through something called Pink Panel, and down a sloping incline to the prison district of Infinite. Funny, it was probably geographically the center-point of our city. I was getting more used to the concept of an entire city settled above and around a secret underground world virtually the same size below as above.

"That might just have worked," Derek said. "How about that?"

"How about you shut the hell up?" the guy on my wrist said.

It was a freckled, red-haired agent I didn't have a name for. He was a few inches taller than me, and had no problem handling me in one hand and Derek in the other. We came to a side door in the dark that opened on sliding treads to a tiny, quarantined, white walled processing room. There was a single table with three sets of blue clothes that looked like medical scrubs, and three small empty bins, as the lights baked us from above.

Burning in the spotlight.

"You will take everything you have and put it in those bins, including the attitude," Freckles said. "Then you will put on the blues. Change."

Two other guards came in behind him and closed the door—one smaller, standing with his weight back and arms dangling, like a wrestler ready to take us down six different ways, the other the tallest in the room, his face hidden by the shadow of some offset hat.

"You forgot the dressing room," Lynn said.

Freckles made a motion, and the material around our hands and necks released. Finally. We threw the handcuffs to the ground the first chance we had, great, but then we turned to the table and… no way man. The three of us could go butt-to-butt, but that still left two guards and whoever knows what-else to watch three underage kids get naked. Not cool.

"No," Derek said. "You try to make that teenage girl strip in front of you, and I promise you don't live to see it."

"But you're so small," the red-head said, not sounding too worried.

"We'll find a way, even without our clothes, which if you hadn't realized, your own leader already turned off," Derek said. "We're useless in jumpsuits, but in these clothes we're trackable, and traceable by your own organization. In these clothes, you control us more than you could ever by putting us in orange—or blue, I guess."

"You want us to take off the thing that let Issaic find us in the first place?" I said, coming to his side only when I knew what to say—this time. One for two.

Freckles blinked. His taller, shadowy partner nudged him.

"It's true. Check your prism view."

Freckles touched the side of his head and nodded. "You're right. Nothing in, nothing out. No trace, no connection. No powers. And you're sure the only way to turn them back on is—"

"Is me," Issaic's voice said over the comms. **"It's true, I have the control to their hope machines right here, my finger on the dial, the dial on zero."**

"Hooray for symbolism," Derek fake cheered.

"However… I was just thinking how stoic they've been," Issaic continued, ignoring Derek. **"Thinking something along the lines of how you can't take the fight out of the fighter. Then I started thinking, well, you *can* take the laser out of a laser guidance array, leave the tracking and tracing alone but crippling the cannon, so to speak."**

"And?" I asked, dreading the answer.

"I think I am going to need your superwear after all. I think we can

learn as much from the clothes on your back as we could from opening up your chest. And the plan is to have you here for a while so... let's begin."

Freckles and Skeletor (not their actual names) cracked their knuckles, the blue lightning crackling around the two of them as they aimed the weaponry of the guard upon our prisoner heads. I didn't need to consult with my side—the losing side, let's be clear—to know what we had to do. Now it really was our lives, or our clothes. And damn if she wasn't consistent, Lynn made the right call first, her face screwed up in hatred as she tore her shirt off in anger, standing before us in just a sports bra before—

"Derek, grab that bin," I said.

And as Lynn angrily threw her clothes off and changed into a form-fitting pair of blue scrubs, she looked up to see Derek and I standing with our backs to her, those blue bins held together, making a person-sized cover. The guards really had never looked away. They would have... yeah. And we weren't given many options, but we'd done our best.

"You are the best two people that have ever been people," Lynn said to the backs of our heads, buttoning the clearly medical wear up, throwing her clothes across the room for the agents of inappropriateness to pick up themselves. "Bins down."

"Ma'am," Derek and I said at the same time.

Without even consulting each other, we both spun and flung those blue bins as hard as we could at the Infinite guards who had stood and watched. Of course they didn't so much as flinch. The bins only clattered off the supersuits and down to the ground like they were ready for this exact situation.

"Good bins," was all I said. "But these are scrubs, not prison garb."

"We don't get many prisoners in paradise," the freckled guard said, as his goons kicked the bins back to us, skidding to a stop at our feet. "Not anymore."

"Our turn brother," Derek said to me, with one hand on his pants.

"Back to the butt to butt life," I said sadly. "Lynn don't watch."

"No man tells me what to do."

"I can literally see you peeking, right now," Derek teased.

"I'm not!"

I almost smiled. Lyre.

I disrobed, literally, but it was more than pants I was giving up. It was the craggy, mechanical gloves that extended into curved claws, gone. The moving, living chainmail suspenders that housed those crystal wings, surrendered. The chained, amethyst necklace that was both my unbreakable Reaper armor and a gift from a really cool girl, both just as important for survival—that one hurt to hand over. Then onto the Infinite, the slightly humming, surprisingly crystal clean pink supershoes hand-given to us by Sand aboard his personal jet. The slim, space-age watch that had once put our communications, sword, storm, shield and supersuit in the same container. For all the multitude of half-explained superpowers, those communications had always been our biggest asset. The ability to talk a thing to death, while running away at the same time... that was us at our most basic— now even that was on ice. Finally, and most unwillingly, the physical armor on top of all the gadgets—the long-sleeved shirt and hood, the slim joggers (stretchy pants), the socks, everything that gave us a single, unbroken line of defense from head to toe. The thing that had taken meteors, cave-ins, underwater adventures, seen the depths of Eclipso, all of that went in stupid blue bins. And I thought that was bad, until—

"Boxers too," the guards said.

"Overkill," I complained. "Come on."

"You come on," Freckles said. "We just watched you take off about fifty different ways to kill us. We aren't taking any chances over exploding trousers."

"Wouldn't I be the one taking that chance?" Derek said bitterly. "Lynn, what are you doing?"

"I got you," was all she said.

It was her turn to hold up some bins. Aw. Two pairs of bad boxers later, we were now three kids in thin pants and v-neck blue elastic scrubs, not an underwear in sight. Not sexy.

"Doctor," I said, nodding to my brother.

"Better," the taller, still shadowy, creepiest prison guard of all time said. "First Nite, let's go."

"No wait, that's not how we do things," Derek said.

Too bad. The agent grabbed him by the wrist and lead him away and around the corner in a blink of an eye, his feet almost lifted off the ground again.

"Derek!" I shouted.

Too late. Freckles took my hands and the smaller wrestler yanked Lynn away from me, both of us shouting and fighting against arms and elbows that weighed tons to us. There was no fighting that kind of grip.

"I… have feet…" I grumbled.

"Funny, you don't use them much," Freckles said, moving too fast for me to keep up, especially when his hands were digging into my wrists that were still sore from being bound. "Let's GO Nite—"

"Ahh!"

And that was it. The next thing I knew, I was thrown headfirst across the jagged, dirty floor of a tiny stone cell with iron bars on the ceiling and walls with only one barred window, the rest of the space taken up by a tiny toilet and two opposing bunk beds. It was just me in the room, except for the smell. The feeling that something was on top of that top bunk.

"How's that hope now?"

"What have you done?" I asked, horrified.

"What you have made us do," he said.

Freckles was taunting me through the open doorway as he saw me react to the smell. There was nothing but fury in his voice. No remorse for what we both knew was up there. I closed my nose, and took hold of the first ladder rung. I only had to climb up a few feet. I didn't even get a good look, but just a glimpse was enough, and it hit me in the soul and stomach like a train. I fell off the ladder and threw up. It had been on my mind since Derek at the waterfall, and once you think a thing too much, then find a dead body in your room…

My body chose exodus via stomach. Sorry. Yak.

It was the dead body of Noah. Last name unknown. Again here lay the body of a person I hadn't even gotten the chance to know, not nearly well enough. He had been an obstacle for us, in so many small, stupid ways, but then he wasn't. Back in… were we calling it the Battle for Reaper? The Fight for Light? The Vemascension? Sorry, just spiraling in the dark. After Derek had found his way past the entire air-force and army, the very last thing in his way had been Noah and Mikael. Just two Infinite agents who hated the Reaper because of kidnapping reasons. The last to stand against the cause—our cause, and for real reasons, not perceived reasons, like the other Infinite. But when the time came to decide once and for all if we meant them harm, they stepped aside. No fight, no flight. No drama. Just… a choice. The choice for light.

Side of life.

Like Mara Stone, the story of Noah and Mikael was fleeting, at least to the lives of James and Derek. But it had included a small, meaningful act of defiance against suppression, and the Infinite (or…) had deemed it worthy of a death sentence. For the simple act of stepping out of my brother's way, for letting us initiate the breakdown, Noah had given his life. Or more accurately, Infinite had taken it. How was that right?

I was still on the floor when I heard the laughter from the guards. I was uncuffed and the door was open, but I was broken, and they knew it. They laughed as I crawled on the floor, their laughter only grew when we heard two cries in the distance just like mine. One a young male, the timbre and accent just like mine even in scream, and one a young girl, like she had found Mara or Ana in her bunk. I hated that my brain was able to fill in the holes, but I didn't have to imagine Derek finding Mikael in his bunk like I had found Noah. I just knew that had happened, by whatever power of being a twin, or maybe just a person.

Finally the door shut and those distant voices were cut off. Maybe they weren't so distant. Or maybe I was alone, in a room the size of a shoebox, with a gross toilet and a dead body. My arms wrapped around my knees and I was truly in the fetal position, on the ground stained dark with something… probably exactly what I thought it was. Damn it.

The hope machine was losing power.

"How… how do we end up here?" I said, catching my breath as it tried to get away.

"Unprepared… usually," came the response.

That was hope. The voice of family at my lowest point, that was my definition of hope. That was my brother. Like a man who had forgotten what sunlight was, I turned to the window and ran for it.

"D… Derek?" I said to the world.

"On your left," his voice came, as well as a small clickety clacking coming from what must have been his own bars. "They've got a very liberal definition of solitary."

"Maybe the window guy messed up?" came the voice of Lynn to the right.

I grabbed the metal and shoved my face as far through as it would go. I only got to my cheeks, but it was as close to them as I could get. Even though I knew it was solid metal, my hands were already pulling as hard as they could to try to get through them, but of course nothing I did moved an inch of metal. I knew a girl who could though. My muscles relaxed as soon as I had that thought. I had no place to go, so I stopped resisting, really looked out the window, and saw that we were not in the center of anything Silka. If I had only opened my eyes the sight alone would have done me some zen. So I took a breath, cheeks pressed against the bars, accepting the finite. For now.

"Are you seeing this Derek?" I said, still unable to see him. "It's an ocean."

"It's the ocean," he said. "We've only got one. The island, you know?"

"I… used to," I said.

I almost cried, in relief, in anger, in disgust, in peace. That's how my mind worked. All the emotions, ending as usual, with the fact that we were still alive drowning the rest of it out. But… was this life?

My cell faced the open eastern ocean, in a cell that was clearly built far into the farthest cliffs of the Engineerium district, the ones with the last port shore to their front and the open cliffs of the oceanfall to their backs. The smell of the salt water, the ocean spray on my face was the literal antidote to being locked in a room with blood and vomit-stained stone floors, oh and a dead body. I had never been so relieved, and that was just the physical. When I realized where we must be, what was right over our heads…

"What's he laughing at?" came Lynn's voice, to my right.

"Ironically, this is closer to home than anything so far," Derek explained.

I only nodded in between those beautiful voices, my eyes to the ocean, to the horizon that was as perfect as I had ever seen it, to the open air right outside my fingertips, so close but so far. And even though I knew Derek and Lynn were only a cell away, I couldn't turn enough to see them. I was looking at paradise and hearing their words come out of it.

"Do we all… have roommates…" I asked, regretting it the moment I did.

There was silence.

"Yeah," Lynn said. "It's Ana. Her message is confirmed. She's… signed off."

"So are Mikael and Noah," Derek said, not even waiting for my validation, just like I hadn't waited for his. "They didn't deserve this."

"Neither did she," Lynn said, sounding like she had already been crying. "The way Issaic described it…"

"Let's all agree to take a hard pause when it comes to things that guy says," Derek said softly. "He's been word-manipulating things since the moment he opened his mouth. There's a difference between someone trying to get a rise out of you, and someone trying to get a ruse over everyone. I think Issaic is both."

"You know he can probably hear all of this, right?" Lynn asked.

"Correct," Issaic said, his voice coming over the speakers.

And somehow, I wasn't surprised. There was usually at least one disembodied voice watching us at any given time, right?

"Of course I know that," Derek said. "Why else are we here? Why did he put us side by side facing the ocean, a single rock away from being together again? Who do we know that can take a rock and move it like butter?"

"Oh damn," Lynn said, faking realization. "We're bait. For… whoever comes to rescue us. For whatever it is we've got planned, oh no…"

"We're the temptresses?" Derek said, angry. "No man makes a damsel out of me. Right Heather?"

And the world was silent, as... nothing happened.

"If she was here, she would have agreed with me," Derek said. "She would have said same, or rage, or shut up James."

"Sounds like her," Lynn agreed.

I threw my hands up, then remembered they couldn't see me.

"You're lucky she's not here," I said. "We all are."

"If she was, we'd be doomed," Lynn said. "Sorry Issaic, won't be that easy."

"For a moment... I thought you would be," came the slightly annoyed, slightly proud voice from the ceilings. **"You're in a prison cell, stop playing games. Troy, switch to video only."**

"Just trying to cope man," Derek started. "As long as we're trapped in—"

And the speakers clicked out.

"Should have done that first," Lynn said to Derek.

"I'm just glad no one saw me try to wink just now," he said. "You're right, like always. What next?"

"What's next is Issaic can't kill us, we're bait, and what he wants to catch is worth keeping us alive for," Lynn said. "So we'll stay here..."

"Facing the ocean," I said, blinking.

"With probably the entirety of Infinite on ready alert, all weapons aimed at us for the first semblance of breakout," Derek finished sadly. "Or even worse, in this context... rescue."

I sighed. The worst part was, Heather was probably already on her way to save us. Right?

"So as long as we're forced to keep our noses out of the window for the corpses in our rooms," Lynn said. "Since we can't talk about anything related to our master plans to take over the island. That's a nice sunset. That's some nice water we've got here on this little world of ours."

"You're being sarcastic about taking over the island, right?" I asked.

"I'm being what he thinks I am," Lynn said. "Island to ocean, I'll take it all."

"You ever think about what's on the other side of the ocean?" Derek asked.

"Only all the time," Lynn said. "James, you?"

"We're not doing that," I said.

"Doing what?" Lynn asked.

"In every story set on an island, you always find some young scrappy, romantic, raft-building, adult-defying, wanderlusting kids talking about all the things that could possibly be on the other side of all that water," I said. "We're islanders, not idiots. The answer is either nothing, or more people and less land—or maybe the opposite. Either way, boom. Now you don't have to daydream."

"But what if I wanted to daydream?" Derek asked.

"You've been hanging around Heather too long," Lynn said.

"I want to be wrong," I said.

"Well then maybe you'll like my actual answer," Lynn said. "Of course I've thought about it. I just don't have to wonder, because one day I'm going to find out. And it won't be on a raft, I can promise you that."

"Find out what?" I asked.

"If what we've been told our whole lives is true," Lynn said. "If there really isn't anywhere else on the planet to live. A whole world and this is the only dry land left? I think I'll be the judge of that."

"Lynn Lyre against the world?" Derek said. "You'll need a damn good map."

"There is no map, we have to make it," Lynn said, sounding excited. "That's the best part. An honest, actual adventure, with no ulterior motives or mysterious benefactors behind us. Once we get our wings back, of course."

"Of course," I said. "You think the supersuits would work a hundred miles out over the open ocean?"

Lynn paused for a moment. "True. We can always build a raft."

"But you just said—"

"I said what I said," she laughed. "I'm just kidding. I know the island is all we've ever known, but you do realize there is something completely absurdly ridiculous about being able to fly on jet boosters, about controlling rocks with necklaces, or never-ending plasma force fields, right?"

"I don't know, I read a lot of comics," I said, folding my arms.

"Anything's possible," Derek said.

"It's NOT THOUGH!" Lynn said, half laughing, half serious. "There is something on this island that makes all those clothes we just took off worth more than the stars in the sky. There's a good chance everything that makes this island what it is would be lost by leaving it. In other words—"

"The real world literally couldn't handle us," I said. "If there was—"

"If there was a real world left at all," Lynn agreed.

Then the speakers clicked on again.

"Which there's not, let me remind you," Issaic said through the comms. **"All we know is all we know."**

Yeah. This island, that was it. Unless everything I had ever been taught in primary school history class was a lie. No way, right?

"Then where have you been?" Derek asked the world quietly. "Before and after the Blitz. You owe us two answers."

"I owe you nothing."

And quiet.

That tended to happen when you levied the weight of a world lost against a teenager. Also when the guy who gave you the greatest gift of all told you he owed you nothing beyond that, not learning to walk, or talk, or how to shave, how to ride a bike or even drive, that had all been our mother. At least we'd had her. I missed her more now than ever, for some reason.

"Why are we talking about this?" I said, snapping out of my own self-existentialism.

"Because we're distraught," Lynn said. "It's normal to question the world when the world throws you in a torture chamber. And I can't think about what's in that bunk anymore so please don't stop talking."

"I'm hitting roadblocking on the talking," I said, looking up to wherever the speakers were built into my cell. "This guy's got something against family."

"Well too bad for him, because you were never really without it," Lynn said. "Purely out of spite and defiance and boredom all at once… tell us something about the family you did have, Derek."

And the feeling came over me. Sure there was a shadowy figure in our family portrait, but Lynn was right. I had a home, I knew it anywhere (before it got exploded). I had a family, a mother, a brother, and me.

"I could," Derek said, his voice already calming. "I could tell you the story of the sea conch, that is if—"

"As long as I get to interrupt you every time you tell a lie," I said.

"James, a lot of people saw the bare naked truth that day," Derek grinned.

"I will END YOU!" I shouted, before catching myself, and Lynn and Derek were laughing their heads off. "You knew those trunks didn't fit me."

"You wanted to see the reef brother!" Derek said through tears of laughter.

"Yeah well you didn't say anything at the time," I scowled.

"I was the CAMERA GUY! You told me not to talk!"

"But you could laugh!" I countered.

"I'm still human," Derek said. "Anyways we're out looking at the reef, ooh pretty, when a wave set comes in from nowhere, and the underwater pressure hits us a second before the actual water starts arcing."

"Don't," Lynn said, on the verge of dying laughing.

"If I could harness that power, I could make guns obsolete," I admitted. "My pants went flying off so fast it was like a cartoon. All I could see underwater was a beautiful half-domed sea conch, right there in the sand. I grabbed it and next thing I knew, I had washed out."

"I was on my way with the surfboard for decency," Derek tried.

"You were laughing too hard to tow a beachball, you liar," I said.

"Was there any… decency?" Lynn asked, trying to hide her laughter.

"Not from my angle," Derek said sadly.

"I had a sea conch, and a choice," I said.

"Wait," Lynn said. "The one you picked up from the incredibly fertile, life bearing coral shores of Silka City?"

I winced, the memory landing hard, as I was standing on that beach, the blinks of a hundred people, most of whom I knew by at least one degree. I was naked but for a conch, hiding behind it like the best shield in the world but that was the problem. The conch moved. The shield was compromised. A tiny claw was snapped. And the beach heard the scream of a young teenage boy who had just willingly flung the only protection he wore away, as a sizable hermit crab emerged from it and dove back into the water.

"Agrghgfhhhaaaah!"

And the beach had laughed so hard, they forgot about all the nakedness. A lifeguard came up and threw me a towel from a distance, then fell into the sand laughing. I couldn't blame him.

"Did you lose a—" Lynn started.

"NO!" I shouted, and Derek laughed harder.

"Then what happened?" Lynn said.

"The lifeguards radioed for the boy's mother," Derek said, wiping the tears away. "And when everyone saw Teresa wheeling herself over the sand, the laughter stopped. She came up to us right there on the shore, and when she laughed, the entire cove lit up again. I've still never seen her laugh harder."

"That was almost worth a scar," I said, eyes low, a cell separating us, but it didn't feel like it. "I'm glad my suffering brought so much—"

"Utopia," Derek said.

"Where scar?" Lynn asked, curious.

"Too far," I said. "Let's just say… I really hate stitches."

"Okay," Lynn said. "I know you can't feel it, but every second I get you talking about family, my heart beats slower. You're a natural come-down."

"You calling us boring?" Derek said.

"I'm calling you wonderful," Lynn said. "I think as long as we can hear each other talk, we're alright. Right?"

"Right," I said, letting the idea of her relief become my own.

It was true. We were in jail, or island prison, or whatever you wanted to call it. It wasn't supposed to be nice. It was horrifying, and don't get me wrong, every part of this had me horrified. Not only where we were and what we had just talked about, but for the first time we were in a place designed to strip us of all hope. Hope that we were here wrongly, nope, right now we were Silka's most wanted. Hope that someone might rescue us, nope, that's just what Issaic and the Infinite were waiting for. Hope that we could survive by running away no matter what, well we'd only get so far without supersuits. Hope that some Silka City deus ex logica would swoop down on us, that the right would prevail over the wrong just because it was supposed to… well Infinite's supermax treatment included psychological torture and extreme physical duress targeted at certain teenagers—and death for others.

It had certainly taken more than a few scars for this 'utopia' to come to be.

"What kind of perfect world builds prisons?" I wondered aloud.

"They don't," Derek replied. "A world with any sort of prison is not perfect. So this isn't either. Right?"

"It's complicated," Issaic said through the speakers. **"But the easy answer is… it depends on which side of the prison you're on."**

He was listening. He was watching, and he wasn't doing it to help out. He was learning, studying us, listening to us talk about our mother and our childhood. And he was right about what side of prison you were on. Before we had seen the barrels of the Infinite aimed on us, we had thought differently of the city that saw us through kindergarten, elementary, middle and high school. We had loved this city, and like every kid, had grown up believing it was perfect, that if anything was wrong then it was our job to change, not the city's.

But what if that just wasn't true?

I wanted to believe. I needed to. I was too young to start contemplating the idea that nothing mattered. My whole thing was optimism. Just be nice, just behave, just believe.

And that's when the bird landed on the iron bars, those long talons digging into even the metal.

"Oh no you don't," I said, whipping my hands behind me.

I was still bleeding from the first bird, the one we'd lost somewhere over the mountain.

Caw.

"Hi bird," Lynn called.

"Damn James, something out there likes you," my brother said.

I shrugged, looking at that island bird perched sideways on the bars, its tail feathers wrapping around like the tail of a dragon to help it stay upright. The bird had a sleek white underbelly and different shades of browns and blues for the wing. Its head was a dark blue bobble, with black eyes and a small ridge of brown feathers like scales on a dragon down its neck. The beak was sharp bone, and the claws were too.

"She's a beautiful hunting falcon," I said.

Caw.

"She's… not a hunter," Lynn said. "She's a… refugee."

"My mistake," I said. "Brother, can we get someone to check on Lynn? She's clearly lied about having that meltdown."

"I have not," Lynn said. "I'm just hearing the bird's cawing like normal human words. It's not that crazy, when you consider the… when you…"

"When you can't finish that sentence," I said, nodding.

"Okay sounds crazy," she said.

"Not any more than talking to some thick rocks," I said. "But what's up with you today?"

"I don't know," Lynn said. "I can't talk to animals right now, that's too much, I already had too much. I was going to tell my father everything. Now I've just got… more everything."

"Sorry you didn't get the chance," I said.

"Don't be," Lynn said, her eyes hardening, looking up at the ceiling where Issaic's voice was coming from. "It's just… clearly not the time to take a guard down."

<u>JAMES NITE</u>

1.3

SAND & SEA

Me again. Still stuck in that cell. Only difference was, I'd been here so long, the moon was out now. A different light, ooh.

We had spent the sunset hours on those bars, leaning shoulders and knees against stone and metal. It was beautiful enough to stay, but it had broken us enough to eventually retreat to the horrible, scratchy cots that awaited us. The lights were gone but for the moonlight, and I had finally fallen asleep, on the bottom bunk of the unit opposite the body of Mikael. I don't know who lay stiller, the dead or the living, the claustrophobia working its way through my mind like the odor was digging into my physical body. How could I sleep here?

That's when the alarms went off. Not long, clearly. I woke up with a start and banged my head into the underwood of the top bunk, immediately.

"Damnit!" I roared in head-splitting pain, seeing stars instead of prison.

"The under district, the caverns where those stupid kids used to play stupid ball in!" Issaic was calling over the speaker system. **"All agents go!"**

"What's going on?" I asked the stone ceiling like it was alive.

There was movement in the hallway, but it was hard to see through a three inch slot of light, when I was half a room away.

"Your Reaper is here," Issaic's voice came into my cell. **"She's attempting to blast her way in through an old underground entrance, the same one our cameras caught her coming through last time she was here. You know, when she tried to kill me."**

"Heather's where?" I said.

"We'll stop her," the voice said. **"There's no way she's your escape, and there's nothing you can do to make it so."**

Then the wall to my left moved. It was either a craftsman's detonation or someone with a certain ability to move stone and rock; either way, there was barely any sound. I froze, seeing the motion outside my cell door as the agents rushed by. But not in.

What in the dark earth…

The speaker clicked off again, Issaic's voice faded away, and so did the motion blurs outside my cell door. I was fixed on the motion happing around that hole in the wall, watching someone (or something) as it crawled one limb at a time into my cell. It was humanoid, until it was obviously human, until the dark shadowy figure of a girl had her hand out to me. Eh, none of the guards were paying us any attention anyways. I took the out. I jumped to it, and followed the girl out of the cell through a coffee table sized hole in the wall, my legs dangling out over nothing, when—

"Sir! Anything wrong?"

I looked back to see the eyes and nose of Alcyon Akoura pressed against that three inch slot of light and metal built into my locked cell door. He stared at me, with half my body outside the cell, clearly about to escape. I froze.

"All good here," he shouted into my cell, still blocking the view from the soldiers behind. He slapped a dark cover over the door bars and left me to it.

"Alcyon," I said. "Still making up for Victoria."

"He'll spend the rest of his life doing that," Heather said. "Focus James."

Right. The cliffside. Except—

"I can't fly," I said to the figure. "Did you bring wings?"

"I brought rocks," was her answer. "You trust me?"

My answer was to push myself fully out of that escape hole. I was instantly free-falling, gravity taking me in a moment until—I wasn't falling any longer. My hands were suddenly full of something, two small rocks the size of a football, with handholds. I held onto them, and Heather held them suspended in the air. But I was weaker than I wanted to admit without that suit.

"I can't..." I started.

"You can," she said. "Give a girl at least a minute, damn."

I felt something smack against the bare sole of my foot. It was clay, a rock plate that molded to my foot, and as soon as it did, the weight on my arms went away. It felt like I was standing on the world's weirdest upright bike. Though for the shock, I was flying. And it wasn't either of the usual ways. This was new.

"Thanks Heather," I said. "I mean it."

"I know you do," she said.

I saw Lynn and Derek joining us, looking like they had been frozen in time climbing a rock wall (probably just like me) as Heather threw us around at will.

"You never did this before," Derek said, suspicious.

"I never needed to," Heather said. "We gotta get out of here."

Heather Denien shot up into the stratosphere on those tinted crystal wings and we came up after her, leaving our cells in the sheer mountain face empty, the detritus from three small holes in the cliff-rock still crumbling away into the ocean waves lapping at the base of a thousand foot drop.

Supermax, my ass. We were free.

With the mud on our feet it only felt like we were on an invisible elevator, but in reality we were trusting Heather Denien to hold us thousands of feet in the air. She was all that stood between us and a cold, hard plummet into the center of the very city we had left behind, and she had already put a huge comfort blanket of clouds between us and the Infinite. Issaic had been distracted with a false alarm (?) in the underground, as Heather did the thing he had been waiting for us to do from the start.

"Can they trace you?" we heard her shout over the crazy winds.

No, she wasn't invisible. We couldn't see Heather anymore for the simple reason that without an Infinite facial visor, Lynn, Derek and I were all flying blind. It was all we could do to hold on, head first, eyes closed, literally. We didn't know where we were going, we only felt the g-force building, the cold, heavy cloud air stinging our cheeks and neck.

"Are you asking if any of us selfishly kept any part of our Infinite superwear?" Lynn finally managed to shout back, her voice somehow tiny and huge against the winds. "Because no! Also PULL OVER!"

And suddenly the world was trying to break against our faces less. I opened my eyes, and even though we were a world above a world, I was instantly calmed. I had been up here before, and almost on stranger tides. Almost.

"I forgot," Heather said. "You just did 3 Gs without letting go."

"It hurt my face," I said honestly.

We were alone in a part of the world few would ever know—good old cloud city. Heather had us hovering a few hundred feet above and among the clouds. Below us was an ocean, above was everything else. It was beautiful. Again we'd been here only once before, but it still took my breath away. Until—

Wait a minute, I literally couldn't breathe.

"Can't…" my brother said it all, throat closing up. "Actually… dying…"

"Damnit!" Heather shouted, kicking herself. "Hold on!"

We weren't as free as we thought. She dove us down below the clouds again, already flying over the plains, far away from the downtown lights of Silka and headed for the endless northern jungle of the island, already almost at city limits,—then the light-headedness passed and the chill in my bones went away.

"My bad," Heather said. "You're just kids, forgot about that. You—"

"Haven't kicked that oxygen, no," I said, breathing deep. "I kept nothing."

"Same," Derek said, throwing his hips around for the proof. "All the clothes, all gone. None of it gets me except for the—"

"The necklaces," I said at the same time as him.

"I'm sorry Lynn," he said, avoiding her eyes.

"I'm no different," she said, scratching at some small red marks in her skin where her amethyst necklace, the living rock of the Reaper, usually was. "My father gave me that necklace. We've officially surrendered every single step of progress we've ever made—this month."

"Good," Heather said, phasing into focus by our side. She had been there, just vibrating too fast for us to see. "Means we can actually start over."

"What is it you think two teenage boys and I can bring to this?" Lynn said.

"You? Everything," Heather said. "But maybe not right now. As for the boys, I'll give them this. They've got wheels."

"We've got what?" I said, blinking.

Heather pulled the brakes. We came to a stop in the air, right before something came flickering on in front of us like… wait. As we hovered, the air in front of us started shimmering, like something fizzling in from the fourth dimension. Turns out that's exactly what was happening, because in a blink, just as Heather was grinning at us trying to figure out how we were going to get out of here alive, unseen, and breathing…

Beep.

"Hell yes," I said, the feeling of relief washing over me even before the concept had settled in my brain. "YES!"

"Well now I know what hope sounds like," Lynn said, amazed.

Our flying, self-piloting, land and sky vehicle was back. The golden (brown) Honda CRV, our first car, handed down to us last summer by our Mom, the one that had already broken our asses out of about six different impossible situations. This must have been the next save point. Damn my video game brain.

"Get in."

"I love that sound," my brother said.

Heather moved us towards the door, the Oracle swung the doors open while our hands were full of rock, and the rock only melted away to dust as we took hold of the metal frame of the car, and one by one ducked in. I sat in the backseat, Derek slammed up against me, and Lynn against him, in that familiar car that ten years of soccer, martial arts, gymnastics, and music gear cartage had torn up. There were scuffs on the leather, scratches in the plastic, and dirt all over the carpets from the car's time underland. We had come so far.

"I hate the middle seat!" Derek complained.

But we were still us.

Heather shut the passenger door and we all breathed a sigh of relief. The AC clicked on and we cheered, but then Matchbox Twenty started and Heather's finger shut that down before three steps.

"I thought we were friends!" I shouted, ready for war—

"Stow those sighs of relief," she said. "We aren't done with anything."

Right. No rest. Not over. The part where—

"We were in prison ten minutes ago, straight lost," Lynn said, frowning. "And now we're found…"

"I thought the Oracle was tracing us through the Infinite connection," I said. "How did you find us? We've gone unplugged."

"I've noticed," the Oracle responded in a quiet, cool voice. *"I was instructed in the undergrounds of Infinite to meet you here."*

"I haven't given orders to any talking cars today," Heather said.

"Are we missing a teammate?" Lynn asked, looking around. "Boys?"

"I didn't… think so," I said, patting myself down. "Oracle, who are you talking about? None of us were underground. Heather—"

"Was able to touch base with Sand, Crete and my dad inside the mecha-mansion, before gunning here and following Hector's instructions and locations as to the Infinite's definition of supermax," Heather said. "I could have used a flying car. But I didn't."

"You got through to them alone?" Lynn said. "Did anyone—"

"No Lynn, I know how to watch my own back, that's literally what I do best," Heather said. "I saw no one but some mountain people. They wish us the best. Crete was well aware of the Infinite presence over his mansion. The three of them were packing their emergency bags and retreating to an address they say only Derek and James will know. My question is are we safe enough for them to disclose it?"

"You are," the Oracle said. *"I'll prove it by not making anyone say it. We are on route to the regrouping that I ordered a full week ago. Freedom and Magellan await."*

"Don't forget my dad," Heather said.

"Hector Denien, the ex-Arcana, will not be present. Neither will Luthor Lyre, as was the original plan."

"The ex-what now?" I asked, blinking.

"The original what now?" Lynn asked.

"And the killer super soldiers who put us in jail aren't right behind us?" My brother asked.

"Not in the slightest. Infinite hasn't yet discovered your empty cells. Wait. Yep, bad timing on that answer actually—"

From out of the windows, and far below and behind us, we heard the bells.

"You are found out."

No duh.

Those were warning bells that I had only ever heard unloosed on Silka twice in my lifetime. Once when I was eight, during the Blitz, when the island had woke to bombs and blaring warning bells, shaking the city out of its sleep and the Infinite to the defense. And again, a few weeks ago, when Odd's toying with the Infinite super satellite ended with the entire thing broken out of orbit and crashing down in flaming pieces over my city. Both times Infinite had heeded the bells, at the very least for the people of the city. There was good in that. Just quit it with the nationalism and I could see an Infinite one day that actually did what it should. But then the image was gone, and I was reminded that the current collective of Silka City supersoldiers were rising up in dark shapes, on bright jet trails, as they shot into the sky down there in that tiny downtown district and started spreading out over the city.

"They are all about finding and killing you now," the Oracle said, like it would help. *"Particularly... the Reaper."*

Heather sighed. "She has a name. But talk about kicking an Infinite after I've sent him to the hospital. I have thrown away my freedom, and my mercy. I am a dead woman walking."

"Pretty much..."

"Stop not helping!" I said. "Well damn Heather, I guess we'll just have to pull out all the stops to keep you alive in strangerland. Oh wait, that's exactly what you just did for us for a whole book."

"Week," Derek offered.

"A whole week," I said. "What goes around comes around. So get ready."

Heather just looked at me weird.

"The boys are right," Lynn agreed. "The whole reason for putting us in such a rescuable state... they wanted to track the rest of our side down, like they weren't able to at the valley."

"Wait, really?" Heather said. "I know my father helped build that prison sector, and he's even bad at time-outs. Never once grounded me, there's no way that man's good at prison."

"What good man is?" Lynn said, and Heather nodded.

"Issaic basically admitted this," I said. "He put us on the side of a mountain knowing very well that all of our friends can fly. Their definition of supermax included an open window with rock walls and metal bars, nothing for a Reaper. We were there for hours and they didn't even give us water. They knew—"

"Then why wasn't he there when we did exactly what he knew we were going to do?" My brother wondered.

"Infinite had a breach, and Issaic rushed it with all the king's army and all the queen's men," the Oracle said. *"If it really wasn't Heather who came shooting into the underground, triggering all the physical failsafes and silent intruder alarms, then who was it? Am I missing a teammate?"*

"That's what we just said," I said, blinking.

"The only friend we've made since the Vempire was a bird," Derek said.

"That is concerning," the Oracle said. *"Did the bird talk to anyone?"*

"Uh oh," I said, looking at Lynn, as her eyes dilated in wonder, then her eyebrows came down in worry. "What if… maybe?"

"Of course," the Oracle said, almost sighing. *"It's never easy with you four."*

"I mean, I'll take easy the moment I see it," I said. "But not now."

"Now we sometimes talk to birds, apparently," Derek finished for me.

"As well as rocks, caves, cars, watches, weird metaphysical girls in the darkness…" Heather said, her fingers shuffling over quick.

"Point made," Lynn said, like it made her feel better. "But why…"

"Why you?" I said. "Let me break it to you, be ready for that to go unanswered for a while. Also get in line."

"Right," Lynn said, her eyes even wilder than usual.

"Lynn, you just went from the world's most unstoppable warrior to a cute lil puppy who can't even breathe in the troposphere," Heather said. "That would break any timeline, you ending up with bird-powers is only logical."

Lynn laughed. "Okay, officially dealing with it. Thanks for making me feel better sister."

And now it was Heather's turn for her eyes to go wide, brimming up.

"Soo cute," the Oracle came through. *"There are places on this island home to the most advanced animal trainers in the old world or new. What you heard might be more real than you thought."*

"Hooray," Lynn said, her face trapped between a thing, worry versus wonder.

"Are we going to any such places?" Heather asked.

"No," the Oracle replied. *"Those places are long forgotten, long claimed and re-lost by the northern Jerico Territory. We are not going to Jerico."*

"Good, because I don't know anything about Jerico," I said.

"Then stop talking about Jerico!" Heather shouted. "Talk about what's happening. Look at this place. You and your brother know where we're actually going right? Well your crew doesn't. If you trust us and the Oracle, tell us where we're going and what to expect."

That was fair.

"Okay," my brother said. "We are… damnit, James, where are we?"

I was looking out the window. I had a thought as to where we might be heading, and my view confirmed it. I had flown this path before. I had looked out this very window on this very path before. Something about our trajectory, about the forest treetops, as we left the city on a northern path in our flying car, leaving everything we had ever known behind.

"Back where it all began," was my answer.

"Could you BE more ominous?" Heather said.

We didn't stop flying until we reached a part of the city I had almost forgotten. The part that wasn't any city street we knew of. Rather, forest. The flying CRV dived low, gently passing through a small green foliage that was more than a few stories tall, nothing on the Jerico apparently. But we were enveloped in forest greens and dirt before we could realize how lost in the forest we were. Or just maybe…

"We're here," the Oracle said.

Heather frowned and looked around. "Where?"

"Something something something street," the car said, mysteriously.

"This address is a parallax!" Lynn said, confused.

"I've had this conversation before. Just... look up."

Then the lights appeared, on either side of what was clearly a lamp-lined pathway, a slightly paved and graveled road through the dark midnight jungle.

"Quickly," the Oracle said, as wheels touched down. *"And... you know... best of luck..."*

"Thanks," I said.

Derek opened the door for me, Lynn right behind, Heather next, stepping out of the passenger seat into the calm, relaxing green leafy world of quiet—

"Okay anyone else hearing that?" Heather said, her body low, ready to run.

She wasn't wrong. The forest was alive, sure, with the white noise of the wind over branches, frogs, crickets, but there were much fewer natural noises coming from far up in the sky. They sounded far away, but fast, like the Infinite were flying at maximum speed all over the blue sky looking for us anywhere there was a place to look. Eventually that would include this place. We weren't completely safe, but relatively…

"Trust us," I said.

Lynn and Heather shrugged to each other, then followed us up the path, the lights on either side built atop long bamboo stilts sticking out of the forest that now had a bit of claustrophobia to it.

"I hate to say it," Heather said, keeping close. "But there's nothing here."

"I mean, you say that," I said, pointing up to the large, very ancient looking mansion that was only now appearing through the woods, and Heather gasped.

"Boom baby," Lynn said shakily, beating me to it by an inch.

It had appeared out of nowhere, a blind corner and an entire grove in the middle of the forest opened up. A mechanical whirl sounded above us, and the door opened without a second's hesitation.

"Still trying to figure you boys out," Heather said, nodding to us as we ran up to the big ol' front door. "You're so weird most times. Then you go and do…

stuff like this. What's your secret?"

"Gonna assume you weren't followed," came the voice from inside.

"Scout's honor," Derek said quickly. "Let's not fight to the death over it?"

"Just this once."

And we dove inside without contest. Somewhere back in that beautiful midnight grove, a flying car again turned invisible, and somewhere within the amber wooden walls and old oil paintings, we found some comfort. The old, original start to the city Silka, now reclaimed by the island's own fertility. A mansion in the woods, a place so secret that our mother had made us eat paper to keep it safe. The door slammed behind us and we rose to a sight, alright.

333 Drine Street. Sand's house, the Sandcastle. That's what we called it.

"We calling in the superfriends?" Heather said.

"No," Sand said, looking down at us with pride. "We are."

Touché. Sand Freedom stood tall before us, shirtless for some reason, holding brilliant escrima sticks sparkling with electricity. But that wasn't it.

"No way," Lynn said, her eyes lighting up.

"So way," Crete Magellan said with a smile.

He was standing beside Sand in a suit that I could only describe as… tight.

"Are we… all welcome?" Heather asked gingerly, looking at the way we were all looking at each other.

"Yes my very scary young old friend, we are," Crete responded. "Sand?"

"Doors shut, all safety perimeters deployed, we are secure," Sand nodded.

"Then one time, can I get a HELL YEAH FOR THE UNBURIERS?" Crete shouted, throwing his head back and yelling at the top of his lungs. "HELL—"

"Yay?" Derek and I said meekly.

"YEAAH!"

Heather and Lynn had more than made up for our lackluster efforts. They drowned us out without even trying.

"Beanbug," Crete said.

He walked forward to hug Lynn but she danced two feet back in preemptive defense, we had learned it from a week alone in the Vempire. Crete's face fell.

"Okay not gonna lie, that hurt, but—"

"Sorry buddy," Lynn said, she unfurled, and hugged Crete. "You know my dad and I can never thank you for what you did for me."

"You and your…" Crete said, eyes brimming up.

Lynn nodded. "He's alive. He's fine."

"Then it's a family reunion," Crete said smiling. "Except—"

He froze, looking at me and my brother.

"We'll allow it," I said, smiling honestly. "Soo cute."

"You pronounced weird wrong," Lynn said, now leaning on Heather like she was her bookshelf. Heather didn't budge an inch, making a pretty reliable bookshelf to lean on.

"A thing can be both, or neither, sister," Heather said, sounding pretty at peace with it. "You taught me that."

"Cuter," Derek said.

Heather turned red and shoved Lynn's arm off her shoulder, only to be lost to my sight by a man stepping up in front of Derek and me—

"Boys," Sand said slowly. "You have no idea what you just did. Or—"

"Undid," I said with a smile. "We know a bit."

"Then tell me what you know, and I'll respond in kind," Sand said. "It's time."

"It's beyond past time," Derek said. "But we live on a take-what-we-can-get basis."

"Be careful what you wish for," Sand said. "Welcome h… to here."

"Thanks for not saying home," I said honestly.

Family reunion, if that's what we were calling it. Now *was* the time to let a guard down.

We let the guy lead us into his ancient mansion in the forest. We walked as a group of six down the halls we had been through only once before, the day of the observatory explosion. This was a place we had been meant to find, and it seemed that our mother had helped us find it—first the note, tucked away in that telescope, and then the car that brought us here, not just once.

"The plan was Crete's place, wasn't it?" I asked as we walked.

"Crete's place is kaput," Sand said. "There's been guards day and night for a few days now, just looking for a way in. Now that you validated that watch, even if they can't get the doors open, they'll be there."

"That's what we told Heather when she popped into the panic chambers like a ghost, before speeding off to save you from cliff jail," Crete said. "She got the secret tunnel entrance from you beanbug, right? Please tell me I'm right, and don't lie."

"I actually… no," Lynn said, blinking. "I forgot to tell her about the secret tunnel. She is Heather though."

"I am, and I know my rocks, sir," Heather said. "I can detect the slightest magnetic imbalances in the dirt, like a secret tunnel built into the crag a hundred meters down, only accessible from the Silka path, an entire mountain ridge away from these three tiny heroes and all their distracting."

"Do you people always think twenty steps ahead of everything?" I asked.

"What do you mean you people?" Heather said, with the snap of a single sharpened claw clicking into place.

"Ah! I meant nothing but Reaper," I said. "Sorry."

"Sorry?" Heather said, with a smile. "Yes our people have thought endlessly about what we might do, once back upon the surface. My people have lived to make those thoughts come true, thanks to your leading. In the words of my ancient ancestors… we cool."

"So the Vema Empire is finally freed from ten years of suffering," Crete said, sighing in relief. "Just saying the words makes the burden—I mean the guilt—I mean the weight of it… you know what I mean."

"You responsible for it or something?" I asked, eyebrows high.

"Are you?" Crete said, eyeing me.

"Oh," I said. "I get it. We weren't, not directly. But we're related to it."

"Exactly," Sand said.

"Wait," Lynn said, frowning. "Does that mean you are too—"

"Crete," Sand interrupted.

"What?" Crete said, wheeling on Sand like Heather usually did on us. "We still half-assing everything from them? Or did you miss the part where they unburied a whole ass world?"

Sand and Crete stepped towards each other, like Derek and I had done a thousand times. They were us.

"A world I should be helping cradle," Crete said. "Because of these four, that's possible. I've already gone the first two weeks of this summer thinking I would die before getting the chance to tell her why. I won't lose another second. I can't take it."

"You have to," Sand said softly.

"We deserve to know," Heather said, taking Lynn's side because of course.

"You will," Sand said, looking around to us. "I am very fond of each and every one of you. You don't have all of me yet, but you do have my love. If that comes as a shock, or for the first time, too bad. But I have a saying. Love by loving, and trust by verifying."

"Aw," I said.

"One is not the same as the other," Sand said, shooting me a look.

"Oh," Derek said.

"I can love you with all the risks that come with that," Sand said. "I'd rather die than not feel things—believe me, I've tried both."

"How?" Heather asked.

"There are some things in my head I can't even trust Crete with," Sand said. "It's not just you. It's not because you aren't worth it. On this island, under these skies, we aren't as free as we think we are."

"Then what the hell is the point of your last name?" I said.

"You clearly haven't been paying attention," Sand said. "You still want to know everything?"

What.

"All I want," I said, speaking slowly, thinking. "Is our mother. She had the worst birthday ever man. I just want… her. For all the people who survived the blast… no offense to your father, Heather."

"None taken," she said. "You saved a nation with a notebook, kind of a proud moment for a room full of scientists. I'm sure he's on the level."

"Okay great," I said sadly. "So how has that not brought her home? How are we not exactly where we're supposed to be? How is this STILL not the answer?"

Sand looked at me sadly. Then he slapped me. Not hard, but hard enough to remind me that we were in regular clothes, with no Infinite superwear to protect us. We were only human.

"Yo!" I said. "The absolute—"

"I did that so your brain would remember this," Sand said. "This island is an ocean. Your questions are keeping you afloat. But you'll know the answer when you see it like a ship at the bottom of the sea."

Heather looked at him in wonder.

"There's a lot to unpack there," I said.

"So where do we start?" Sand asked. "Above water or below?"

"Our mother," I said. "You said she was alive. You said she wasn't dead. I went an entire week without making a thing about myself but I can't take it any longer. If she isn't dead, why isn't she here?"

Sand looked at me true. "She isn't here... so we might have a chance."

"At WHAT?" I asked. "A fair answer, for once?"

"I told you," Sand said. "There's a thousand questions you could ask me, that I would love to answer. Your supersuits, the full potential of a connection to the source, the reason you and your brother seem to always get more done together than apart. Yet you always find a way straight through the easy questions and right to the impossible. When it comes to Teresa Nite, I will repeat. You'll know that answer when you see it, and not a moment before. Should I slap you again?"

And that was it. I blinked, waiting for more. But there wasn't any.

"You can't be serious," I said, shaking my head at Sand. "I get it, there are some things you can't tell me. But my own mother is not one of them, period, end of sentence. Do you think differently?"

"I do," Sand said. "Seeing as I've known Teresa Nite for forty-six years, almost three times what you've got. If it's easier for you to just think of her as dead, then by all means, save us the burden. But if you have such a thing as hope, then hold onto it like a rope, and trust us. Trust her. Or don't, I'm just the guy steering you towards a ship at the bottom of the sea. That makes me the farthest thing from a good captain you'll ever know. Or not."

Metaphors. We were having metaphors—I mean problems.

"The twins are just tired," Heather said, sensing danger. "We all are. We haven't slept more than four times in the last week."

"Yet you are only among safety because of us," Sand said.

And he stared at me. Like it was a test. Soldier or sarcasm. My mind was swimming in—damnit, yep, more metaphors. But even though Sand was challenging me like an alpha to a superbeta, it wasn't out of pride, or ego, or violence. He was trying to beat something into me, sure, but it was almost like his intentions behind it were... good.

"Yes sir," I said.

San looked at me, trying to decide. It was tough. I wasn't even sure which one I had given him. He deserved respect, but the situation deserved sarcasm.

"I told you," Sand said. "It's a long road. But we're still on our way. Until we make it, don't even think about hugging me. We're still mad at each other."

"No we aren't..." I said under my breath.

"What was that?" Sand demanded, smiling.

"Oh you heard me," I said.

Sand winked at us, like he knew we weren't really fighting. And wasn't it a sign of respect amongst kids and elders when they had arguments, instead of blindly co-existing without questioning any part of the other's world? Was I still in existential mode? I wondered...

"Okay then about our mother," Derek said. "Because let me tell you, we met our father. And all things considered, sending us to you first... I still thank Mom for it."

"I do too," Sand said. "If it's gone unsaid."

"You mean untrusted," Derek said. "Or what did you say, unverified?"

"I want you to know everything," Sand said. "I really do. But the island doesn't. Raise your hand if you've been imprisoned and tortured, not matter how mildly, by Infinite this week."

Facts were facts. Only Heather and Sand had their hands down.

"We're counting Odd," I said to Heather.

"And Luthor, and Hector too," Lynn said.

"And you wonder why I have no one to talk to," Sand said, sounding lonely.

"Even I am guilty there, old friend," Crete said, coming up next to Sand. "They got me good, it wasn't just the kids. But speaking of them, and I hate to pile on when I'm at fault of the same... we also trusted them with the finest supersuits I've ever spun. They literally took over three hundred hours of nano-stitching apiece. I don't suppose they're tucked... deep away?"

"No," I sighed. "The Infinite prison goons took it all."

"Case in point," Crete said, like it hurt him to admit it.

"Yep," Sand said, cold as ice.

"You don't... happen to have a backup handy?" My brother asked.

My heart rose. Could it be so easy?

"Nope," Crete said sadly. "Our last two pairs of supershoes, our hand-made watches, and the suits your mother and I worked for years on. We put everything into them, and you have managed to lose it all."

And my heart sank. Course not.

"Prison sucks man," I said, quick with the excuse.

But I felt the cut. Like a kid who had messed up in front of the adults. That part of me was not gone. Sand and Crete were fifty-something year old men, we were eighteen, and angry at them for not sharing the secrets of the universe with us. That was ridiculous. That wasn't fair, especially not after the way they had dared the Infinite headquarters to meet us in that guest room and do their best at communicating a huge future chaos plan to teenagers. Also yeah, we had lost something important to them, and to us. Or had it taken away. Same thing.

"You aren't perfect, neither are we," Sand said, sounding like he was trying to comfort us. "We are what we are. I'll take it."

"Hey man," Derek said, smiling.

"Your father," Sand said. "What was he like?"

Derek stopped smiling. "I mean... evil. That's the whole takeaway, right?"

"Evil?" Crete said, blinking. "That's a cartoon word. Issaic Nite is anything but a cartoon. I once saw him juggle four elephants at once—on fire."

"Him or the elephants?" I asked, bewildered. "Wait, this wasn't a cartoon?"

"I don't know what you call the will to let an entire race of people die out, but for me, evil works," Heather said.

"What was on fire?" I demanded.

"He's the most dangerous man on island," Sand agreed quietly, ignoring me.

"Now who's talking in cartoons?" Derek asked, a hand on my shoulder. "For us it's a bit more complicated. I still don't think we've met him. Not in private, not one on one."

"That's actually true," I said. "He's been surrounded by eyes and ears since we caught him. Wonder if it's all an act for the omniscience of Infinite?"

Sand frowned.

"Wonder not," Heather said. "It's no act. I'm still the first Reaper to ever take a shot at him, miss, and live."

"True," Crete said. "Kinda makes her a living legend, no?"

"Say no and lose a finger," Heather warned us.

We said nothing. Until—

"It's a very simple question," I said quietly.

"Oh for—Issaic was on fire, happy?" Crete said to me. "Trying to conquer an island is evil, setting elephants on fire is satanic. Not even Issaic would—"

"I'm glad we're so concerned about imaginary creatures," Heather said.

"Elephants are real," Sand said.

"Not in the Vempire," Heather said.

"Go north, you'll find elephants," Sand said.

"We're north enough, especially after last week," I said.

"I don't agree," Sand said. "Wise travelers, to come so far, and find nothing."

"Well you can't even ever tell us what the mission is, so how do we know it's not over?" I asked. "We did your job. We did Hector's and Heather's as well, no hard feelings there by the way."

"No objections either," Heather said.

"It is true, you've done everything asked of you and more," Sand said.

"Yeah, because you don't ask, you just point us in a direction and pull the trigger!" I shouted. "For all the buildup, we're a pretty lousy bullet. And for all the mystery, I haven't seen you in action yet Sand."

"You are saying you haven't seen Silka City's most wanted helping to defy the pawns and patrolmen?" Crete laughed at us, no mercy. "That is a puzzle."

"You are children, and I am excommunicated," Sand said. "You also happen to be related to one parent who is undoubtedly respected within Infinite, and another who is revered in Silka. In the same situation, you cannot simply replace me with the two of you."

"So that's your plan of attack, in all things full tilt and half-explained?" I said. "Us?"

"When has it not been?" Sand said.

"But what do you want us to DO?" Derek asked. "Why are we here? Why did our mother send us here? What's with the superfriends, and why don't we just get a normal summer? Who ARE YOU?"

Sand looked at Crete, and Crete nodded.

"They deserve that," Crete said. "At least… the short version."

"Even the short version would take days, brother," Sand sighed. "How about the elevator version?"

They looked at us. I sighed.

"We'll take what we can get," I said, staying true to my words.

"We aren't Infinite," Sand said. "We aren't Reaper. We don't stand for any single city on this island. We stand for the island."

"Does the island really… need you?" I asked, head spinning.

"Good question," Sand said. "The idealistic answer is no. Of course there shouldn't be a single central stronghold of power that governs the sovereign island from shore to shore. There's far too much power in that sort of, let's call it what it is, omnipotence."

"However, in another time, one without us," Crete said slowly. "There are parties on this island that would gladly take that mantle."

"You think Infinite wants to take over the island?" I asked, frowning.

"No, never," Sand said.

For a moment, I was relieved. But then, I remembered sarcasm existed.

"I think Issaic wants to take over the island," Sand said in a clear voice. "Or at least, be in charge of it, on a certain date in the future. The very near future."

What.

"Cartoons…" My brother said, faintly.

"Evil exists," Heather said. "I've seen it. I've taken a shot at it."

"At our father though…" I said, blinking. "Holy xenocide…"

"There's nothing Issaic has ever wanted more than to have Infinite go unchallenged from east to west, from north to south, as long as he commands that reach," Sand said. "It's clear the burying of the Vema was because he sees the Reaper as one of the only island threats to Infinite. It's easy to see why he's so angry at what you did, it's because he's scared. Good."

"You want him scared?" I asked, scratching my head.

"I want him back," Sand said, angry and sad at the same time. "The Issaic Nite I knew… he would never have done those things. Sorry, elevator version, let me rephrase: Silka City was always a beacon, but you don't get to paradise by razing other cities into your foundation. Or maybe that's the only way to utopia, and we've already seen how it doesn't work for all sides…"

"You said elevator version…" I said, blinking.

"Right, sorry," Sand said, clearing his throat. "Utopia, dystopia, both are stupid, neither work, either way I'm fighting something."

And that we couldn't unhear. That stuck. Almost like… wait, was that what an elevator pitch was? I thought it was what you would say if you were in an elevator and it snapped and you only had a moment to get it all out regardless of your own self, certain death meant the story had to be bigger than you…

"You're all fighting…" I said, looking around at the adults.

"You said you founded Infinite," Derek said, simply.

"I did," Sand said. "And as someone who literally imagined all it could be, let me promise you, what we've got is as far from that imagination as possible."

Lynn thought on it. Heather was silent, watching us get knocked around the ring by the very secrets of the universe we had pursued so belligerently.

"You're not Infinite," I said to Sand, again, simply. Just to be sure.

"I am what Infinite should be," Sand said. "And maybe… so are you."

Sand held his hand up and something came shooting from the living room couch into his hand as we passed it. It was my own backpack, the one I had left in that room next to Lynn's, back at the mecha-mansion. They had grabbed our stuff before coming here, how thoughtful, but Sand had also just telekinetically moved the backpack by waving his arm, objectively insane. Sand had his hand in my backpack before I had blinked once, and came out holding a picture, one that I may or may not have stolen from Sand's guest room, our first day here.

"Your turn," he said. "Explain yourselves."

"Not a chance," I said. "A certain date? What did you mean by that?"

And Sand only held my eyes. Thinking about whether or not to trust a kid with what he said next. He must have decided for it.

"Sand," Crete said, and how the tables had tabled.

"Okay, here's a taste of the long version," Sand said, seeing our guilty but wondering looks, ignoring Crete. "This island is all we know. But what if I told you there was a way off? What if I told you there was more out there?"

"Sand…" Crete said, his eyes not on us now, but there was no stopping him.

"What if I told you that everything we've ever done on Ocarina has always been about biding our time, surviving, until the day a return to the world outside this island was possible?"

I only stared back. Lynn was frozen. Only Derek had the nerve to speak.

"No… no rafts?" He asked.

"No rafts," Sand promised.

"Sand!" Crete warned, a light coming out of his body just in time for—

Then the universe decided it didn't like us discussing its own secrets, and the material world caught up with us like someone had thrown it against my face.

They had. Boom.

The redwood behind Sand burned redder than it was ever designed to, and the yellow and black busts of fire and flames followed. The explosion sent the world of walls sideways, blowing the picture out of Sand's hand as the house from ground to ceiling to wall to armchair was thrown sideways. Crete was suddenly standing between the four of us kids with a blue holo shield extending around us like a protective force field bubble—hello trauma, thanks for the save.

"SAND!" Crete shouted.

He didn't dare to move for his best friend, choosing to save us instead of anything else. But he needn't have worried. It was true, we hadn't seen Sand fight anything yet, save for us. But for standing in middle of a storm of wooden shards, poisonous black ash clouds, smoke-bombs and fire-blasts, with flying chunks of furniture bouncing off him like his skin was made of metal, Sand Freedom didn't move. As his house burned around him, he weathered the storm without his feet leaving the ground, his fists only clenching harder in the tempest, turning slowly to see who had fired on him.

"Uh oh."

1.4

WHO CAN'T BE BROKEN

Boom.

The situation had exploded again, with no warning, rhyme, or reason. In a blue tinted field of plasma we saw the carnage happening all around us, as that first blast was followed by another farther to the left, the explosions changing directions like the tide. The blue light filter over us danced around Crete's bare hands, no watches or devices to be seen. He was holding the field, maybe he was the field. One moment we had been deep in conversation, the next we needed somewhere to run. And I had thought we were done running. Guess not.

"What happened to warning?" I shouted, the world breaking over my head.

"I think that was the warning," Derek said.

We were shielded from the debris in a glowing blue sphere, but out there Sand was engulfed by it, the fire and smoke licking against his bare arms until it swallowed him, until finally the bombing stopped and the lights came on, the dust still swirling with such a current it was like we were underwater.

"Uh oh."

It was hard to see through the blue tint and the ashen air, but eventually I saw a single figure standing between us… and all the other figures. It was Sand. He wasn't burned, he wasn't even fazed. He held his ground in an ocean of chaos, as through the surface emerged the flying figures. Sand was still in the shallows, he had enough of a smokescreen and all the time in the world to get himself out. In that time I wondered what he would choose: his own sacred anonymity, or us. He didn't make a move but to clench his fists, so tight we heard the crack.

He chose us.

"He's… fine," I said, not believing it.

"Don't reduce a man to his looks," Crete said.

"I don't believe it," came the first of the airborne voices.

"I do."

Through the debris we could see the swarm of agents surrounding the Sandcastle, surrounding the entire forest grove actually, now that the roof was gone. But here in the house, only three dared to get this close to us. Odd, in a new buzzcut, wearing padded white armor that was no longer any sort of slim. This one had sharp edges and pieces of body protection that folded into each other, like a living coat of chainmail. He hovered in the air with a green sword at his side, face frozen on Sand. Hannah was beside him, her hair noticeably cut short too, wearing dark armor similar to Odd, but without the sword.

"Issaic," Hannah spoke into her watch. "We've found them. It's as Lu… as our agent said, as exactly you feared."

"Both of them?" Issaic's voice came out of Hannah's watch.

So that's where he was. Not here.

"Both," Hannah said, looking at Crete and Sand. "Can I kill the boys now?"

"Derek and James, yes," Issaic said. **"But the legacies, no. Now that we know what kind of tree is behind the teenagers, they are no longer useful. Cut the leaves down, but leave Sand and Crete alive. They owe an old friend some answers."**

"We owe you nothing," Sand said.

"I've… missed that voice," Issaic said, sounding like he might mean it.

"Enough," Odd said, coming down out of the air swinging his sword at Sand.

"LOOK OUT—" I started to shout.

But Crete had his hand over me. He wasn't worried for a moment.

The blade broke apart on Sand's shoulder. Let me say that again. Sand was shirtless, and Odd had come down out of the sky swinging his sword like an axe. The glowing green sword, of an origin we still knew not of. Yet instead of cutting Sand in two, the blade had broken apart into a thousand pieces. Not a cut, not a drop of blood. It was fire and smoke all over again. Somehow, they couldn't touch Sand.

"What are you?" Odd shouted.

"Whatever I need to be," Sand said.

"I literally just told you to leave him alive," Issaic said.

"You didn't see what we just did," Odd said. "He took the rocketeer missile on his shoulders. And a sword."

"I literally saw everything. Odd, dismissed. Leave the rest to Hannah."

"I take it they gave your armor an upgrade?" Odd said, still looking Sand's skin over for something, a break in the mail, a shimmer, anything.

"I was going to say the same," Sand said, equally admiring the combat edges and padding all over Odd.

"The best Infinite has to offer," Odd growled.

"I'll remember you said that," Sand said.

"Odd, last chance, we can't help you if you won't—"

And Sand stepped forward in a horse-stance, hitting Odd with an open palm in the middle of the stomach. Odd was blasted backwards so far it was comical, honestly he was probably flying over the city, after taking a hit from such a super force. It wasn't human. The shockwave from where Sand's open palm hit the Infinite superwear shattered the hardwood floors and blew us backwards. Hannah's shoes lit up to counter the force, fighting through the airwave just like she would a water wave. So that's what it was like seeing Sand fight. Just one question. The usual question. WHY?

"You still want him alive?" Hannah asked, a new level of respect (and fear).

"How many times..." Issaic sighed. **"It's the last time I'll say literally. But it was LITERALLY the first thing I said. For your own safety, not his. Whatever you think's happening, you are in more danger right now than you've ever been in before. We just firebombed the house of Freedom."**

"We still have the ultraviolet," Hannah said. "And two more shots."

"Who took the first?" Sand asked slowly, suddenly. "You?"

And the air froze. He looked up at Hannah, or through her, and through the agents still behind her in the air, until his eyes settled on the airship, hovering at stasis only a few hundred feet in the air, with no regard to the trees it had trampled to get down here into the forest.

"I guess it doesn't matter," Sand said. "I'll take the second."

"Abandon the ultraviolet. Pilots and all crew, GET OUT NOW!"

And suddenly a mechanical whirl sounded out, as something cracked out of the wreckage. It was that mechanical camera that stood at the front doors of the Sandcastle—or it had, before the front doors had been blown down. But as from the detritus the camera emerged, the mechanics began re-aligning themselves, and in front of our eyes it grew until it was less of a camera and there was a different kind of barrel aimed at that jet.

"No, everybody out, I get it now!" Hannah shouted behind her.

Boom. A blue laser the size of a small house exploded the jet into pieces just as the last crew-member jumped out and into the sky.

"Issaic, cut them off!" Hannah shouted.

"I already did!" Issaic's voice came through the watch. **"This isn't the kids, it's SAND FREEDOM! I don't have that dial, I never did!"**

"That doesn't make sense," Hannah said.

"I don't have to," Sand said, facing his sword-breaking body towards her. "To me, you don't make sense."

"THAT doesn't make sense," Hannah stammered.

She was afraid. For once.

"I could have lived here in peace," Sand said, walking towards her. "I didn't want this."

"But you did," Hannah said, not backing down. "You once tried to give the island a pass for almost trampling Silka City into detritus. We didn't let you then, and we won't let you now. Sand Freedom, stand down."

"Or what?" Sand asked.

"Or... you'll have to kill us all," Hannah said. "Starting with me."

She swallowed the fear in her throat and signaling for the army to advance. She herself took the first step, the agents in the sky behind her shaking as they gladly let her approach first.

And funny enough, Sand seemed to respond to that one.

"I don't want that," he said. "Good stratagem, Hannah. I won't do that."

"Then do the right thing for once in your life. Stand aside while we arrest those four," Hannah said, coming closer, her palm lasers getting brighter...

"No," I said, the word coming out on its own, the bars of Infinite prison coming back into mind, the smell...

"I can't do that Hannah," Sand said. "Crete, get these kids out of here. Now."

"But—" Crete started.

"NOW!" Sand roared.

It happened again. One moment I was watching Sand stare down an army, the next thing I knew, someone had punched all the air out of my body. Once again the world was spaghetti, once again the blurred shapes and colors were all I could see. Crete had heeded the call.

Zoom.

My head whipped back into a cushion, body strapped into a familiar jet, my brother looking around wildly in the seat next to me, Heather on one side and Lynn on the other. Time flies when you're out of your mind.

Unzoom.

"Hey!" Lynn shouted.

"What in the jet!" Heather cried.

We were in a jet. One I thought had been exploded into a thousand pieces by the valley Reapers of yesteryear (book one). Sand's relic, the same ship we had learned to free-fall in.

"Why is this jet not in a thousand pieces?" I asked.

"We call this jet the Refugee," Crete said.

"Foreshadowing," Heather complained.

"You want to know how to be free or BE FREE?" Pilot Crete called back to us, pressing all the buttons from underneath a new leather helmet. "Hold on!"

"What about Sand?" I shouted.

"I'd worry about the army," Crete said. "At this rate, they'll both catch up."

"Holding on," I said, giving up (for now).

Crete didn't waste a second. The jet powered on and thundered down the marble stone cavern, the underground takeoff tunnel. The wheels lifted off and Crete expertly took the curves of the cavern all on his own, the jet going faster and faster until the light shot through us, and we shot through the ground.

"Stop that plane!"

Of course Hannah had seen us, she had already caught our trajectory and countered it, flying up towards us on a path to collide—until a shirtless blur arced past and knocked her straight down to the ground, her jets only saving her fall at the last second, and we screamed past the intersection point, saved by the bell. But the bell had been wrung, and in Hannah's place the swarm was on, not even that far behind us, as a single shirtless old man took on soldier after soldier.

"Where are going?" I shouted to the pilot.

"Wherever they aren't," was Crete's only answer.

"Let me help!" Heather shouted.

"There's too many!" Crete said. "We have to get you out."

"To WHERE?" I shouted. "We have a home, just get them to stop fighting and we'll go there!"

"Correction, I have a home, you have a bunk bed, and what do you think Sand is doing right now?" Crete shouted back. "He is sacrificing himself for YOU!"

The ship was hit by something, some kind of laser bolt that chipped away a baseball-sized chunk of the Refugee.

"And maybe a bit for us too," Crete said. "I've got a bad feeling about turning home. Any ideas?"

Heather growled, trapped inside the ship, but still willing to help. She made a fist, and the baseball-sized chunk of Refugee rocketed back the way the laser had come. From inside the windows, we watched the grunt out there take the thing straight into his chest. Right. If a thing was made out of minerals, then somewhere, a necklace was going to be glowing purple.

"Gonna have to teach me that one, Denien," Crete said, both hands on the steering mechanisms as he took the plane on a full tilt evasive maneuver.

"I could teach you lots of things," Heather said. "But right now I want to know how they found us."

"You swear you weren't followed?" Crete roared.

"We weren't," Lynn said. "Oracle, you want to back me up on that?"

"It's true," the voice came from overhead. *"I detected no Infinite signatures on the route to something-street."*

"The island is not only Infinite," Crete said, steering the ship clear of another trio of fliers, up into the air and down again, all we could do was hold on. "What about Reaper?"

"You think Sand can take a sword on the shoulder, but got followed from there to here?" Lynn said.

"A bird got through my armor," I said, quietly, but it landed.

"But it's insane," Lynn said. "They were inside the mansion. There was no way in, we made sure—"

"We did," I said, blinking. "But we weren't the only ones to take the long way all the way to something-street."

"I cannot account for the readouts surrounding Heather Denien during your latest... distraction. She may have been followed by any number of Reaper agents. A thousand or one, I would have no way of knowing. I am... sorry."

"Don't be," my brother said. "But that... would mean..."

"They had us from the start," Lynn said. "From the moment we broke the valley, they were counting on Heather splitting off. They followed her to the mansion, and saw Crete and Sand all the way here. It wasn't us. Not this time."

"But who?" Heather said. "We accounted for the Odd Squad..."

"All but one," my brother said, his words heavy. "When a thing fits, it fits."

"One scout won't be enough to flip the script," I stammered. "Lu..."

"Luthor?" Lynn asked, surprised. "As in my father, that Luthor?"

"That's not what I was thinking," my brother said.

"Thank the underland," Lynn said. Then it hit her. "No. It can't be. Lukas?"

"Finally."

A voice came from behind me, in the empty row, and I felt the hair on the back of my neck stand up. The blades came quick, and I would have lost a head, if Heather hadn't extended her Reaper wings at the last moment and thrown us aside with the weight of their deployment.

"LOOK OUT!" Heather shouted at us.

Slash. Not the rock star. The air melted, Heather's wings took a huge gash, and we were on the floor. Heather had her claws out and behind her in a blink, and though the enemy got through her wings, they didn't get through her claws.

"One scout won't be enough..." a voice said, from the empty air Heather was struggling against. "I never stopped hearing those words, Derek."

As again I stubbornly got to my feet with James and Lynn, the air warped around something new, something clearly locked in the jet with us. It was familiar, but barely. So much had happened since. I had truly forgotten.

"Lukas," Heather said, blinking. "You... how long?"

"Long," he said, looking at us with some sort of insanity in those blue eyes.

And my stomach turned upside down. No. He was bluffing, he hadn't been following us invisibly, just out of reach, not saying a word for weeks... there was no way... right? His blonde hair was dirty, like frayed and burnt dirty, and his armor was chipped and cracking, like he was a Reaper who'd slept in the dirt a few too many times. But his eyes said it all. He'd done it for a reason. For this.

"You tried so hard to give us a good distraction," Lukas said, firing himself up the more he watched us clench. "I'll admit, counting on Heather is usually a safe bet. But she didn't count on me."

"I let you in the mansion..." Heather said, blinking.

"You did," Lukas said. "I learned a lot in that place. I burned even more."

"And there's the bad feeling," Crete said. "You little..."

Crete put the plane on autopilot and dove at the Reaper, but Lukas only kicked off the ground so hard the plane shifted in the sky, and suddenly the ceiling had slammed into Crete. We all buckled but Heather, who had one wing frame fluttering just enough to give her some autonomy, her claws coming forward like a whip. Lukas caught them sideways with his own claws, and they both blew away from each other, Lukas to the farthest back of the plane, Heather into the cockpit—but she must have slammed into something, because the plane pitched down and started trying to kill us even harder than Lukas.

"AAAHH—"

"Taking autopilot," came the Oracle. *"Should I be concerned?"*

"Only the usual amount," I said.

Crete pulled himself up, Lukas grinned a bloody grin before disappearing.

"Not even," Heather said.

Her necklace flared up, and sharpened pieces of her shredded wingsuit flew from her, peppering the back of the craft at her aim.

"AH!"

The cry came from an invisible part of the ship, where there were little pieces of rock and fabric sticking out of the air, like they had been embedded in Lukas's armor, or chest. Ew. But we had a target.

"James, get back," Heather said, not feeling the same. "I'm not your savior."

"Listen to the girl," Lukas said from the unseen world, and then those pieces of rock were moving towards us.

"You're no Reaper," Heather said, angrily.

"I've got this," the Oracle said.

The ground under Lukas lit up in blue electricity, but we didn't know where he was, only that he'd met the charging world with a sound like a whip cracking around us, the dark radius spreading out like a blade, and as we leaped back to avoid it we felt something dashing through us and exploding out of the cockpit. When I opened my eyes I only saw Heather's open hands glowing purple, in a successful (?) attempt to shield us from the literal coming darkness.

"I hate that," my brother said, standing his ground.

"Thanks Heather," I stammered.

"Where is he?" was all Heather said.

Then the wind hit us, and it was easy to see why—there was a gigantic X shaped hole where the giant cockpit windshield should have been. Where all the controls should be. They were all gone. Both pilot's chairs were sliced in half at an angle, and in the brief moment before our nose pitched own again, Lukas made himself visible outside the plane, holding himself hovering in the air on purple wings that had burst through what looked like the remains of an old, tattered Infinite supersuit.

"I'm no Reaper," Lukas agreed. "It takes a monster to kill a monster."

"Why is he…" Heather said, thinking. "Oh for the love of—lookout!"

Lukas's wings beat like a cannon as he came back through, claws wide, ready to take us out—until something punched through the bottom of our already broken ship and expanded into a yellow patchwork of electricity, an open space for Lukas to fly through, and his metal claws caught against the edges. It had caught him spread eagle in the air by hands and feet, like a magnet.

"What?"

Crete Magellan flew in through the open cockpit. Right.

"Let me—ah!"

Crete punched him square in the mouth, then grabbed his jaw and forced something that looked like a capsule down his throat. Lukas started to shout in protest until Crete kicked him in the stomach and clapped him on the ears in the same blink. He held Lukas's mouth closed until he swallowed.

"What… what did you just do?" He coughed at Crete.

"Nothing but a nano-bot tracker system," Crete said, staring Lukas down. "You got me by surprise twice. Now you're back to cause my kids harm. Clearly the pattern is the ability to avoid detection. Let's see who you are without that."

"Did an old man really just drug me?" Lukas shouted.

"Yeah, well you shot me into space," Crete said, like he was still mad about it. "Now a boy comes with a tiny tracker, and goes with a big no."

Crete made a motion with his hand and the magnetic net that held Lukas buckled, reversing polarity and shooting him literally so far away I was worried he would fall into the ocean—on the far side of the island.

"NOOOoooo!"

Lukas screamed as he shot out of frame. Kind of like he was—

"Blasting off again," I said on autopilot.

"I mean," Crete said, looking around. "You think he went farther than Odd?"

Then we really started falling. All sides were compromised, all parts of the plane that usually kept it up in the air were falling down. Heather did something and I felt a padding of minerals smack into my feet again, and felt the world pulling against me as my feet stuck to the ground.

"Give me back my zero gravity!" Derek shouted.

"Not now!" Heather roared, not trying to hide her terror.

This was the full Humpty Dumpty. Not even Crete was going to be able to fix this plane now. Unless…

"This is a nightmare!" Crete shouted. "Not even I can fix this plane now!"

Damnit.

"Then your *PLAN SIR?*" I shouted.

"Parachutes," Crete said. "Let's start with parachutes."

"You could fly us out of here, let's start THERE!" Derek shouted.

"I could, if not for this nonsense," Crete said.

"I wasn't talking to you," Derek said. "Heather, give us those floating rock handholds one more time."

"You see any rock up here?" Lynn asked.

"Use the plane!" Derek shouted. "You can do it right?"

"I can't," she said. "Not… not all four of us, not without wings myself."

"Parachutes it is," Lynn said.

And as the falling airship found a steady rotation, we looked up out of the busted open cockpit just in time to see the sky full of stars. Except those weren't stars, they were fully booted and armored Infinite super soldiers, shooting towards us, faster than we were even falling. Right. The part where this wasn't just about us. At this rate, we wouldn't even get the chance to go down with the ship. They would tear us apart in the sky quicker than we would explode on dirt. There was nothing between them and us…

Except for two old men who I still knew next to nothing about.

"Sand and I will hold the fliers," Crete said. "The parachutes will get you down. Heather and Lynn will get you safe."

"To where?!" I shouted, asking for the third time.

"To safety," Crete said.

We could almost see the end of the island, at least the northern edges of it.

"Wherever the Infinite aren't?" Lynn translated.

Crete nodded. The thought settled in his eyes, as he accepted the fact that this was a retreat. That we couldn't go home, there was no home to go to. Or maybe that was my realization, and I was just projecting it onto Crete. Seeing myself in him, if just for a moment. Trying to be as calm as he was.

"This is nowhere!" Derek shouted. "We don't know where we're going!"

"Yeah but look where we're coming from," Heather said, pointing out the window, or the cockpit, same thing.

"She's right," Lynn said. "Can't go home, can't stay here."

"That's just the kind of thing Sand says before we do something way too deep for teenagers," I said sadly.

"That means… you're learning," Sand's voice came over us one last time through the crackling speakers of the dying, free-falling airship.

"Sand, I'm so sorry!" Heather shouted into the void. "I didn't know Lukas was… I brought him straight to both your houses…"

"No time for apologies Denien," Sand said. *"Forget about houses. You need*

to get out, we'll hold Issaic off."

"Don't you mean you'll hold the Infinite off?" Derek asked, his voice faint.

"No," Sand said, before the speakers started to crack too much to hear him. *"Wherever you land, we'll follow. So... please land."*

"What he means is good luck to all..." the Oracle said, her voice fading.

"But I don't know how to parachute!" I shouted. "What if it malfunctions?"

"Then you'll have the rest of your life to figure it out," Crete said, taking me by the shoulder, one last time. "I hate goodbyes."

And in the silence, Crete shoved me into the others. We fell back without a wall to grab onto, and as our feet left the Refugee, we were struck down by the air like we'd hit some sort of reverse Mario Kart speed panel.

"AAAHHH"

The three of us did our best to stay together, as hard as it was to keep our eyes open, and talking was impossible. Free falling had a way of sending a heart into overdrive, but after the initial adrenaline, we remembered falling was nothing new. The craft that had carried us this far melted away. Even Heather was freaking out a bit, with the shredded framework of her wings shaking in the wind, wrenching her shoulders in random directions. But speaking of—

"Now?" Derek shouted.

"NOW!" Lynn answered.

I pulled the cord and the world tugged me upright, my armpits were on fire, I was suddenly much less worried about Heather. It was like someone had caught me in a glove like a baseball, there was an impact. Damn, air.

"Ow!" My brother.

"Ah!" Lynn.

"Oh come on." Heather.

But those were real words, heard by ears. No more communication systems. Suddenly I was drifting. The world slowed down, but I could still tell I was falling, and faster than I'd expected. We were three parachutes in the sky, as the falling body of a jet missing a cockpit plummeted down through us and carried on down to the almost ocean-like canopy of dense, green jungle growth below.

"Ground control to major plane in... now," Lynn said sadly.

Boom.

We covered our eyes. The jet hit the forest in a brilliantly horrible explosion of reds and yellows, like a small sunset. The green sea around the small spherical blast was shredded, rippling like a wave. But though a fire started to burn, it didn't start to spread. The green canopy rebounded, swallowing the blast and putting out the colors, without the ground below burning—and believe me, we'd been there. The explosion was contained, the forest had straight up ate it.

"Terrible first impression," Derek said.

"It was either that ship or us," Lynn said.

"I've heard that before," I said. "Every time we choose us, things get worse."

"But you're still alive," Lynn said. "How could the alternative be worse

"Teach me to parachute in the next thirty seconds and I'll chill," Derek said.

"I can do that," Lynn said. "See those two straps? Pull one to go in that direction, pull both down to go up. You'll need to pull down right before hitting the ground to get them angles. Like an airplane, not like a hot air balloon."

"Got it," Derek said. "Surprisingly sufficient explanation. Chilling out now. Wait, why am I chilling? What happened to the army, why aren't they—"

It was true. The Infinite were watching the same movie, but they'd held back as we passed through into this farther airspace. We were deep out in the (green) ocean, and they had stopped at the shallow reef, if the reef was the metaphorical spot where the last of the voices in our heads had died away. A hundred lights in the sky hovered, less like stars and more like a shiny, miniature asteroid belt, but they were a good thousand feet away, and we were only drifting farther.

"They aren't following," I said. "The enemy is getting farther away."

"So are the stars," Derek reminded.

Right. Also Sand and Crete were gone, so wherever we were headed into, it was a place we could finally be alone. Did I want that?

"We're coming fast, don't chill too hard," Lynn said flying sideways as we came up on the chute of Heather, Lynn's left hand pulling that left strap down about half an arm. "Look where we are."

"The place we weren't supposed to talk about," Derek growled. "This is Jerico Territory. We shouldn't be here."

"Tell that to the currents," I said sadly, letting the wind whip me about as it pleased, as we came up on Heather's parachute.

"Finally, I didn't want to shout and alert everyone—come HERE," Heather whisper/shouted as we were all together again. "I couldn't, Lynn, I tried to fly instead of stupid parachuting, but even if Lukas hadn't shredded it open, my wings don't work, they NEVER DON'T WORK! Where are we? Are we in—"

"We are," Lynn said, frowning. "What's wrong?"

"You brought an underlander to Jerico!" Heather shouted.

She reached for her neck and pulled out an amethyst gemstone that wasn't glowing, not even a single lumen. The rock was dull, and lifeless. I checked mine to see if it was the same… only to find skin. Right. Prison sucks.

"My wings don't work here Lynn, I CAN'T FLY!" Heather panicked.

"Does that go for the Infinite too?" My brother asked.

"Is that why they're hanging back?" I asked. "Are we worse off for trees—"

"Doesn't matter, trees are here!" Lynn shouted.

She meant the ground—the ground was here. We were flying faster than I'd realized, sideways and down, and I was ready to crash into the tops of those canopies when at the last moment we hit a grove, like the trees had opened up for us. Either that clearing hadn't been there before or we were going too fast and too low to have spotted only open space in ten square miles. The leaves weren't rustling as much as speeding up towards us too fast to look for branches. We weren't going to have that airplane landing strip. But I didn't count on losing the light as I came shooting from the sky to the grove, and with the trees overhead and a parachute too, the sun was gone.

"I can't see—" Derek shouted.

"The ground, look up, pull up!" Lynn yelled back.

For some stupid reason, all my brain heard was up. I pushed on my wires up, instead of pulling down, and it wrong, all wrong. My chute folded and I plummeted, some part of the tree caught my chute and ripped it away from me with the feeling like a house had broken off against my chest, I bounced and coughed once, and then the straps ripped away to dump me the remaining twenty feet to the ground. My body smashed into the ground and I blacked out for a moment. A bad moment. That was quick.

"JAMES!"

"Don't move, James don't…"

Derek, Lynn, and Heather hit the earth softly, making life-saving use out of less than twenty feet of a landing. There were three bodies standing over me, the clicks of parachute backpacks hitting the floor, already forgotten. I saw parachute fabric at least a hundred feet up the trunk of the nearest—

"Trees are moving," I said, in shock.

"You… did hit them pretty hard," Derek said, sadly.

That's not what I meant. They didn't look away from me, from the cuts on my arms to the ankle bent at a weird angle. They couldn't see what I saw. We were already in the darkness of twilight. So when the canopies of the grove overhead moved together again, cutting off the break in the canopy we had used to land, I was the only one to see it. It was so dark down here it made little difference at midnight, but I had seen what I'd seen.

"The trees are—" I tried again.

"He pulled the wrong way," Lynn said.

"His foot's the wrong way," Derek said.

And that's when it hit me. Not the answers to the unexplained universe, the pain. Something was wrong. I was in shock. I had never felt anything like this. My ankle was broken. Or my foot, or my leg—I didn't know, I just couldn't feet my toes, I couldn't bear an ounce of weight on the right side, from the hip down.

"Uh oh," I said, looking down, ready for the worst…

But not for that angle. Ew. I was about to throw up or cry for the pain, squeezing my eyes closed and feeling the full force of a broken leg bone at once. The leg bones were the biggest bones in the body, and I was a ten year old kid in that moment. The pain was closer to the ankle than the knee, so maybe there was some luck there—some dark luck of course.

"I got you," Derek said, his eyes wide. "You're good man, there's no bone, nothing sticking out…"

"Promise?" I said.

"I promise," he said. "It's just the ankle brother. Bad."

"I was only trying to land," I said, my breath even hurting the leg, I felt like swearing. "I just… forgot how important landing was."

"Don't move," Heather said, leaning over us and holding her hands out.

But nothing happened.

"Not a good time for issues," Lynn said softly.

"This has never happened before, I swear," Heather said, blinking, holding her hands out for the purple glow and the magical healing. "Oh come ON!"

"Heather," I said. "I'm about to say some things… it hurts… please…"

"I'm trying James," Heather said, her eyes wide, brimming up in frustration, locked on mine, especially after the please. "I'm sorry James. It's not working."

Lynn looked her hands over, and there was nothing. No yellow storm, no purple glow. She found Heather doing the same, both their eyes wide, facing the cataclysm of not only being a stranger in a strange land, but also losing everything she depended on to keep her alive…

Now why was that so familiar?

"WHAT IS HAPPENING?" Derek roared. "You can't fly, my brother can't walk, where ARE WE? And not that I don't know what it's like and not that it's about damn time, but what is this place to take your Vema living rock abilities away? We could REALLY use a quick heal right now. We don't have time for casts and crutches."

"Then make your goodbyes quick," Heather said, still rattled.

Derek only folded his arms at her. "That's not sarcasm, is it?"

"We're in trouble," Lynn said.

"We are," Heather said.

"I'll… I'll take a crutch," I said gently, the right side of my body aching.

"Not until I know where in the floating world we are," Derek said.

"Welcome to Galan Town," I said through my teeth

"What?" Heather asked.

"Showing up ready to help is… harder when your swords and speed shoes don't work underland," I said, my voice labored for the pain. "When it's—"

"Just you," Heather said. "I get it. I'm a teenage girl and nothing more, we're finally the same."

Boom. Roasted. Derek hung his head, either laughing or wincing.

"Just give a brother an answer," I said. "Give it to me straight."

"I'll give it to you gay," Heather shot back. "Sorry. I'm very combative for some reason. But it's simple. We've landed in the northern jungles of Jerico."

"Hooray for places, how does that affect your magnetic field?" Derek asked.

"It's storm season," Lynn said ominously. "I've heard the stories. I just… thought I'd be special."

"Me too," Heather said.

"If it helps you're special to us," Derek said. "But what doES THAT—?"

"This part of the north gets hit with magnetic storms, all year round," Heather said.

"But it's summer," Derek said, blinking.

"You've never heard of June Gloom?" Heather said. "The worst storms of the year break during the summer, all summer."

"That must be why the Infinite are staying out," Lynn said, realizing. "Their suits will literally fail to function if they cross the line between Silka and Jerico, just like they did on the falloff between Silka and Vema."

"For a group called Infinite… they've sure got a lot of limits," I said, trying not to let my voice crack.

"I already told you what to think about a man-made thing," Lynn said. "Everything ends, one day we'll all be skeletons, welcome to the club."

"No club, just a loop," Heather said.

"Well we just found our hiding place," Derek said. "A place Infinite can't get to, sounds perfect. Is it really that simple?"

"My leg, brother," I said, now trying not to cry.

"Right," Derek said. "Not simple. Hell brother, I don't know what to do."

"I do," Heather said. "We need to relax, and get somewhere safe."

"You just said the Infinite couldn't come down here," Lynn said.

"They can't," Heather said. "It's the locals I'm more worried about."

"The Jerico?" Derek asked.

"Yeah," Heather said. "Because forget about storm season for a second. That's not the only reason those agents won't cross into Jerico Territory. The locals are protected from the rest of the island by the strongest understanding a traveler can possess, whether it goes spoken or not. You do NOT cross into Jerico without permission. I can promise you the entire nation knows we are here, and are deciding right now what they are going to do about it. We already might as well have knocked the imaginary gates down."

"And onto my leg," I whispered.

"Okay so do we survive, or prepare to be arrested again?" Lynn said. "Both are very different mindsets. I need to know which mode—"

And a single tree branch fell between us, with a shuffling sound from above. Only I wasn't surprised. The others looked up, cautiously, to see…

"Understood," Lynn said, narrowing her eyes. "The trees are moving. Why are the trees moving?"

1.5

LIONHEART

James was messed up, man.

I don't know if you've ever broken a bone. I don't expect anyone who hasn't gone through that to understand. I hadn't stopped looking at him in pain since it happened, we hadn't even packed our parachutes. But that tree branch had come down quick. I knew then there was something alive in those trees, something waiting for us, watching us. The only question was… human or animal?

"You know of us."

Words. Good start.

The voice preceded four sets of barefooted figures smashing down into the dirt. Two men, two women, all over six feet tall with arms like tree trunks, each with the same untamed, long, dark hair and no shoes, no clothes except for matching tan wristlets all around, and the same leathery fabric around their hips and chests. Three of them took up martial arts stances against us, while one approached with his hands behind his back, like a tall, tanned, shirtless monk.

"And we mean you no harm," Heather stammered, the only one of us to talk.

"A lot of good that kind of soldier does," the monk said.

"Don't get it wrong," I said. "We can hold our own. When the time comes."

"Prove it," the monk-man said without moving a muscle.

"No offense," Heather said. "This isn't the time. We have wounded."

"A forest watched him fall," the guy said. "Who were the two others?"

"Sand Freedom and Crete Magellan," Lynn said, before we could speak.

She hadn't asked for permission, she just answered the guy, right in the face, assuming we would understand enough to not contradict her. But… why not lie?

"They are of the territory," the figure nodded. "Send word, let them live."

"Sir," one of the tree-women agreed.

That's why. Apparently. Before I could see how, she was back in the canopies, sprinting away faster on those tiny branches than I could have flown.

"Let them… okay damn," Heather said.

"Your knowledge of our territory is correct, except for one factor," he said. "We do have more than imaginary walls. You are in our land yes, but not our home. Home is only the strongest. Home is that way."

He held his arm up into a section of forest, and the world bent around that leather wristlet. Trees, trunks, grasses, and branches all moved aside in the wind, and through the forest basin valley, we caught a fleeting view of a wooden wall, hundreds of feet high, keeping the north safe from farther north.

"What in the jungle madness..." I said, gazing through the eye of the world.

"I tried to tell you," James said, through the pain. "The trees are moving."

They were. The trees snapped back together, shaking a small cloud of leaves loose, almost elastic with the force. Wood was snappy, we knew this from skateboarding. But right now it was my knowledge of skateboarding versus this warrior monk's ability to part the green trees like a red sea. I was silent.

"Prove yourself," the spirit of the forest said. "Arrive at our gates without desecrating any more of our forest, and we will decide what to do with you."

"My brother has a broken leg," I said. "He can't walk, he can't stand."

"Then leave him," he said. "Jerico is only the strong. Seems simple."

"Not to me..." James wheezed, trying to stay conscious for the conversation.

"You can't be serious, we need actual medical help here," I said, but the guy only shot upwards and back into the foliage. "Oh COME ON!"

"You come on," the voice rang out in stereo, swinging circles around us. "Get to the gates, and you'll prove at least one thing."

"Which is?" Lynn shouted.

"That we made the right choice letting you live," the voice came, ominously.

And the monk was nothing but wind in the leaves. Gone.

"Don't leave me..." my brother said.

"You know that's not happening," I said, feeling the leaves around us move.

"Okay cool thanks, just checking..."

"Where did they come from?" Heather said.

"Where did they go?" Lynn asked, whipping around.

"Where do babies—" I started, but Lynn cut me off with a finger. "What?"

And as we fell silent, I could hear the movement around us, the whistling of the trees, the ambient sounds of living nature, all around. This wasn't the city. There could be more than plants nearby.

"To what?" I asked.

"To all the other eyes on us," she said ominously. "You can't feel them?"

"Not even," I said. "But we'll trust you, until an easier answer comes up."

"It will," Lynn promised.

"How... cute..." James said from the ground.

"Call us cute again, Nite," Heather dared him.

She held her hand out to levitate James up by the mineral magnetic powers of her Reaper necklace—before remembering where we were, and sighing when nothing happened.

"This is going to suck," she sighed. "I'm down to claws."

"Still better than us," I said. "James, stupid question, how we feeling?"

"Terrible," he said. "But I'm okay for a bit. It's the shock. The idea of dying in the grass, just how much we need to not be here, adrenaline is crazy. I've got a crash coming I can feel it."

"Could you walk?" Heather asked, gently.

"I could crutch," he said, holding back more pain than he cared to admit.

"We need wood," I said, blinking. "You can make anything out of wood."

"I'm good with rocks and dirt," Heather said. "Living things, not so much."

"We're not underground anymore," Lynn said. "Help me with this tree. No, too healthy, I'd hate to cut a root. There's enough timber for us to…"

"And a shorter one for the handle, you got a hair tie Lynn?" Heather asked.

"Is that even a question? Here's a hundred…"

And when Heather threw a pile of sticks at us, it was actually helpful.

"Right," I said, looking around for anything else we could use to help a brother out, finding nothing but my blue shirt. "Does it get cold in Jerico?"

"It's the middle of summer, and the closest part of the island to the equator, so no," Heather said. "It can only get hotter from here."

I took the shirt off.

"I'm always right," she said, looking away. "But I didn't mean—"

"It's necessity," I said. "Unless you would volunteer your own."

"I would not," Heather said, blushing just a bit. "Although I do appreciate being considered equally. Little strips?"

I nodded, threw her a dirty blue button up, and she caught it on a single claw. I didn't know wood-shop like Crete, but I had ideas. Lynn found a few curved walking sticks, Heather filed some grooves in the tops, and we connected them with a small stick for a handle, cutting notches in the timber to really get those hair ties in place, reinforced with blue strips of my once-shirt.

"The service in this jungle," my brother winced as we pulled him to his feet.

"That's what having friends is," Heather said. "Go easy on these, I'd hate to see you crash and rash, slip and trip, flail and impale, you get it—"

"I've been on crutches, thank you," James said. "I can tell you haven't."

"How?" Heather said.

"If you don't wrap the handles in something, I'll scrape my armpits off in an hour," James said. "That's the worst part. You know, after the broken leg part."

"So sensitive," Heather said, rolling her eyes, but still she clawed what was left of my right pants off to the knee in a single slash (not the rock star).

I was startled, but willing.

"You can't use your superpowers to take people's CLOTHES OFF!" Lynn shouted. "This isn't even the first time, what's wrong with you?"

James laughed. Heather bit her lip as she helped James with the last of our (my) blue fabric, making a soft padding under each arm instead of bare wood.

"Better?" Heather asked, almost like she cared.

"Perfect," he said. "Thank you Heather. You do it all."

Lynn and I held our splinter-covered hands out in protest.

"Yes?" James asked, blinking to us.

"Something distracting you from all that pain?" I teased.

"Not really," he said, shrugging—

But then the crutch slipped off a rock and he shouted in pain as he fell—almost. Heather caught him by the back of the shirt before his foot got anywhere close to hitting the ground, her claws retracting at the very last second, none of us even that worried about it.

"Okay, I'm going to need her close for a while," James said.

"You can't afford me," Heather said, putting him down right-side up.

"Oh," I said to Lynn. "See I was just joking around. But they might..."

"Yep," she said, holding her hand up in between us.

"What's that for?" I asked.

"I'm trying to stay focused, thank you very much," Lynn said. "As adorable as your six chest hairs are..."

"I forgot," I said. I was shirtless, and red in the face about it. "Sorry."

"Don't be," Lynn said, again looking at me while not looking at me (somehow). "You didn't have abs two weeks ago."

"Kind of happens when you don't eat for two weeks," I admitted sadly.

"Ah, true," Lynn said. "We need to get James out of the jungle."

"Well, we're oh for two on the Sandcastle and mecha-mansion," I said sadly. "Also a hometown would probably throw us in prison before a hospital."

"What about Vema?" James asked. "We just made a whole bunch of... not enemies there. If there was anyone who could give us harbor—"

"And lead the army right back to my land, with the perfect excuse to cut it in half again?" Heather stood her ground. "We're not putting this on Vema."

"Then there's nowhere to go," I said.

"Not true," James said. "But going home is hard when you don't have one."

I thought Heather would snap back. She reached out to James, but he was too far away so the claws came out like she was going to slice him in half—but she only gently put a single razor sharp point on his shoulder, and it didn't even break the bare skin. Comfort from afar, by claw. She could be very... steady. Not gentle. I wasn't going there.

"You have a home, Nite," she said. "Right here. A sharp knife, and us."

"I'm crying," Lynn said. "Heather, you're the best thing since jet boots."

"Since you," Heather said.

"Behind is known," Lynn said. "So what do we think about the unknown?"

"You're thinking of..." James asked, pointing out into the open arbor.

"Finding you some sort of doctor is our only option right now, until Sand and Crete decide to show up and save our asses again," Heather said (and I didn't disagree). "If there's a settlement somewhere around, wouldn't they have an easier time finding us there instead of in the literal middle of nowhere?"

"True," Lynn said. "I guess I'm asking... what do we all think about—"

"About the prophetic coordinates of a mystery tree-person?" I finished.

She touched her nose, then my nose with a very sharp walking stick, and I again I didn't even bleed. Not gentle, more like... stable. We all thought on it.

"Well, like the grandma I never knew used to say—" I started.

"To always do it, right in the face?" Heather asked.

"Wouldn't know, never met her," I said. "But I'm imagining she was a maverick, so yeah. I'd say, onwards, us mediocre excuses for teammates."

"You mean friends," Heather said.

"He does, actually," James said, smiling (through the very obvious pain). "We've come too far to not see how far we've come."

"I said that," Heather said.

"I know, I remembered it because I thought it was poignant," James said.

"Okay thanks for paying attention to a girl, not a lot of guys do," she said.

"Ah—puddles!" James cried, as Heather led them straight through a small puddle of water. "You should be paying attention to puddles."

"I'm not from here! I don't know these stupid un-hallowed grounds."

"Then learn them," Lynn said. "That goes for all of us, and all grounds, hallowed or not. Show strangerland some respect."

"Yes Ma'am!" The three of us said in unison.

"Then to the gates of Jerico, ready go," Lynn said.

And we went. Deep into the forest, somehow finding a path through the trees and a wall of them at the same time. We could only travel as fast as James. We were like kids at camp, when just a day ago we had been… well we hadn't been superheroes, but we had been super something. What would you call that?

"One more… one minute," James gasped, collapsing onto a trunk.

He could only go about ten minutes at a time. Not super.

"We're sure this is a path, and not just—" Heather said.

"Someone's walked this way," Lynn said. "The only question—"

"Human or animal," I said, while still keeping a good forty percent of my attention on my brother. "Where are we, what do we expect?"

"We're north," Lynn said. "Farther than expected, kinda happens when you fall and flee for your life into the jungle where none leave and none enter."

"That was… scarier than expected," I said.

"Too bad, I'm r-ready," James said. "Time for pain. Let's GO—"

We continued to put one muddy blue foot in front of the other. It was like walking in slippers, I would have complained if James wasn't in earshot. He was the one having a hard time here, I was the one who hadn't broken an ankle on that landing. Talk about irony. There were a hundred times where we hadn't been sidelined, where we'd been thrown head-first into a thing and expected to hurt ourselves, and James had lost a leg to a parachute. Was someone supposed to have caught him? Was that symbolic? A shoe for a house, the old saying went—the one we made up, at least. My question was, without the ability to run away from anything… what in the world were we doing here? Making our own path? That would have been alright if there was nothing to run from—but just as I had that thought, the path split in front of us. A crossroads for strangers, who didn't know this tree from that. What would you call that? Randomness or fate?

"What in the…" I said, as we came to a stop.

"Try the wizard of oz thing," James said. "But take your time. I need—"

"We don't have it," Heather said. "Sorry James. I like this one."

"Don't," Lynn said, and Heather's foot froze in the air. "You hear that?"

"Hear what?" Heather said.

"The growling," Lynn said.

It was my turn to freeze in place, the wind of the leaves against my skin, the humidity of the jungle on my face, the smell like there just might be water around, or maybe something in the water. But I couldn't hear anything.

"You're right, she is getting scarier," James said, speaking for all of us.

"I heard animal spirits," Lynn said. "There's something watching us."

"Well tell them a girl can change her mind," Heather said, and she put her foot back down behind her. "Better?"

"Actually yeah, real quick nobody breathe," Lynn said.

We stood closer and stiller than ever, even James keeping his lips pressed together listening around, above, behind, all of it. All directions were covered, which was ironic, because we only had directions in front of us. The question was, which one? I didn't know. But Lynn did—apparently. She leaned towards the fork in the road, listening to the wind. She took a step towards the rightmost path, and… nothing happened.

"Follow me," she said. "Apparently."

We followed her. No questions asked. None of us had heard anything. But when a girl like Lynn says she hears growling in the jungle, you either bring superpowers, or listen to her. And we were all out of superpowers.

"You alright in the head, hun?" Heather asked.

"I'm sane," Lynn said. "I just know this is the direction we weren't supposed to have figured out. I just know we're supposed to walk right into… this."

And she stopped in time to see the blur of something melting down to the ground in front of us like a mirage, landing without a sound. I'd never seen bigger muscles or claws on four legs. The whiskers were a foot long from end to end, and the giant green eyes were locked on us, head low, teeth bared.

Leopard.

"Follow you," I said quietly. "My—"

But the leopard didn't kill us, at least, not immediately. It looked at us. More accurately, it looked at Lynn.

"You," Lynn said, blinking.

"Uh oh," Heather said. "We lost Lynn."

The animal walked towards us, its back rolling with each step, nothing but muscle, a good four feet off the ground, the eyes only a head below Lynn's. This was a three hundred pound animal before us, bigger sideways than any of us were tall, with dusky black fur and sharp white spots, down to the claws and paws that blended into the dirt like a killer shadow walking.

"I found Lynn," Lynn said, as Heather threw her hands up.

But she wasn't talking to us.

Without fear, Lynn held her hand out for the animal to smell her. She didn't have to crouch down, this wasn't a baby. This was a hunter, an alpha who responded to betas by eating them. Bowing to something like this was already surrender. Meët it as an old friend, just as crazy. But that's what Lynn did.

The leopard came right up to Lynn… and pressed its nose into her hand.

"Kitty," Lynn said, her eyes wide.

It took all five fingers for Lynn to scratch behind a single, massive ear, but the leopard licked her arms when she did. Then the thing purred, rolled its eyes up, and straight up nuzzled its neck into Lynn's body and arms.

"Ow!" Lynn laughed, her whole arm red and from the sandpaper tongue. "No come back, it's okay, you're worth it. Hold on. What in the hell…"

The leopard licked her again, but Lynn slowly put her hand inside its mouth, freeing what looked like a small bracelet with a single, smashed green stone in the middle of it. Lynn wiped the leopard slobber off and pocketed the thing, as the cat turned away and started down the path. Lynn was a step behind, before remembering. You know, us. What in the—

"Coming?" She said, to our open mouths, dropped jaws.

"You… that…" James said.

"She's beautiful, no?" Lynn said.

"She's gorgeous," Heather said. "But how—"

"I don't know how," Lynn said. "But I hear something else in my head when you hear caw—I mean growl. You understand I have no choice in this, right?"

And the worst part was… of course I did.

"That's in your head?" Heather said, just a bit unbelieving.

"Lionheart," I said. "She done went elemental on us."

The leopard nodded. Literally. I would have thrown my hands up and laughed if I wasn't so terrified of making sudden moves. Okay so… okay.

"I've always been me," Lynn said. "I promise you this is new. The island's on some new stuff as of, like, a day ago. I wonder what changed?"

"Um, only everything," Heather said. "We opened the door to the underland. Who knows what came out?"

"We did," Lynn said, thinking hard. "And I barely understand myself."

"Good point," Heather said, shaking the disbelief off. "Lead the way, lions."

The leopard pawed at its face and turned on us again, walking off. We looked one last time amongst ourselves, and to a very confident looking Lynn. I guess I trusted her about as much as I trusted myself. So we let Lynn and the cat lead us into jungle land, because here in the Jerico, that was normal. The path was quiet, but only because we were terrified of that beautiful, impossible to understand creature leading the way, the one who had dropped down into our lives and taken charge without question. The leopard had us scared too.

We walked a path unpaved by any definition, following the slightest marks of treading through the dirt. There were always trees, even when we came across an incline, where the path got too steep to walk over our heads, so we kept to the lower grounds. Now we had trees to our left and a natural rock wall to our right. The jungle came and went fast around here (like I knew a damn thing about a jungle). The dirt got muddier, the humidity set in, the last of the light disappeared, and the green started turning into other colors. Red flowers, purple vines descending down from yellow and blue colored accents to otherwise brown and green trees. There were vines bearing strange fruits, there were berry bushes, and dried leaves of all colors on the ground.

"Hold," Lynn said.

The leopard took a few more steps and stopped at one of these colors, her nose sniffing at something in the ground, a neon blue fairy ring of mushrooms.

"How is it speaking to you?" Heather asked. "I wouldn't ask if it weren't so… impossible. Boys, how are you just watching this happen?"

"Easily," I said. "It's a good movie. Why?"

The leopard sneezed, used its front paw to dig around the dirt, and carefully took the mushroom with its teeth, careful not to pierce the thing. Then, with all eyes on her, she placed a neon blue mushroom in my brother's hand.

"Th… thanks," he gritted his teeth, always the gentleman. "I love flowers."

The leopard looked through my brother's fake etiquette and down to the leg. For such a big animal, the small sound she let out was the gentlest thing I'd ever heard. Somehow, she knew we had a cub in pain. Her front paw came forward like a cat about to investigate/smack something, but she was gentle. For now…

"The mushroom is for the broken," Lynn said. "It is safe for all stomachs, cat and human, local or foreign. It might make you see strange things, but it will put an end to your pain. After that, it's on the pack to get you to safety. That's us."

"Strange things?" I asked. "How strange?"

"How about we start with that second part, no one needs to stick a root—" Heather said. "Wait a minute. Lynn, you're not on my side here, are you?"

Lynn looked at her sadly, yet proudly. "I am not."

"Well, that means I'm on the wrong side," Heather said.

She sat down and held a hand out to the leopard. Sophia let Heather run her fingers across her ears, both pleased by the acceptance. Then she saw our faces.

"What?" Heather asked. "I can't change a decision that's not mine. Right?"

"A hallucinating James is something everyone needs to see once in their life," I said with a small smile.

"See?" Heather said, as the leopard licked her leg through her torn jeans.

"Here's the thing about me, I'm not very easily convinced," James said. "Although in this case it seems like a good idea. You promise it's safe?"

The leopard took a break from Heather's knee and nodded like a person.

"It's the closest we're getting to medicine?" I asked.

Another nod.

"The science checks out," I said, turning around to— "What, you're done?"

"Myup," James said, his tongue glowing bright blue. "Hope I don't die."

"I would have taken more a second to think about a thing, before eating a radiated jungle mushroom," Heather said.

"But you just said—" James shouted.

"We solved the radiation problem," Lynn said.

"Says who?" Heather said.

The leopard smacked the ground with her huge tail.

"Says her," Lynn said weirdly—like there was another way to describe a human interpreting a leopard.

"Oh come on, I'm just thinking survival," Heather said.

"So is she," Lynn said. "I can't describe it. How you feeling James?"

He was staring down at his leg. "Better. Instantly. I can't feel my leg."

"And you're not hallucinating?" I asked.

"Absolutely not, talking rainbow," James said, as his pupils dilated in front of our eyes. "Now it's my turn to ask the answers. Where is the pot of gold? I need it for money reasons."

"We lost James," Heather said.

The leopard made a sound that sounded like laughing. James looked down at his crutches, and the ankle that we had wrapped in what was left of my blue prison shirt. He easily pulled himself up on one foot and two crutches.

"Who feet?"

"You broke your foot," I said, trying not to laugh. "All you have to do is keep on those crutches brother. Just follow me."

"But it isn't even rocks," he said. "When did the Vempire get green?"

"We're in Jerico, James," Lynn said.

"Well then half of you is home, Lynn," was his answer, his head moving around like he'd already forgotten what he'd said.

But Lynn's eyes narrowed. "He's right. At least, that's what—"

"That's what flying, metal Mom said," James said, reeling on the spot, fully gone now. "That's why you couldn't open the door. Not from Silka, Nora."

"That's my mom's name…." Lynn said, her eyes locked on my brother.

"That was the Oracle's voice coming out of a minivan, brother," I said.

"Hey," he said, turning to me on a delay. "Our minivan is a CRV, and it can fly. Don't tell me what's possible, just show me where the gold is."

I joined Lynn in staring at him, wondering if the mushroom had opened his third eye or something else.

"Oh no, sheriff," James said, squaring off against the leopard like he had just seen it. "Derek, lend a smarter brother your sword."

"I don't have it," I reminded him.

And the leopard fell to the ground making some sort of purring sound, definitely laughing its beastly head off.

"I've got this guy," Heather said, keeping a hand on James' shoulder, one he hadn't even realized was there. "Lynn, we staying the night or what?"

"I think…" she said, the leopard coming up to her side again. "As far as our forest guide goes, this is it."

"She brought us to a pot of mushrooms, not gold," James said.

"She did, for you," Lynn said. "She helped us when the Jerico didn't."

"Oh," James said, the eyes of the leopard still on him. "Then thank you."

And the leopard bowed to my brother, in such apparent graciousness I couldn't even take it. Again, I had the urge to throw my hands up. But this time… it wasn't fear that kept me from it. That cat had my respect. We were on a sir and ma'am basis, bows and all. It was always something.

"She says for her, she has the forest," Lynn said. "For us, there's no place to go but everywhere."

The leopard made a sound, like they were deep in conversation.

"Not everywhere," Lynn said. "Up. No place to go but up."

"But we… we just…" I said, sensing another fork in the road.

The leopard growled, almost sadly, non-threateningly.

"Do you have a name?" Lynn asked.

The leopard circled Lynn, rubbing its cheek glands against her one last time, then it was gone. It arced up into the trees a good twenty feet over our heads, in a jump that should have been impossible. Then it was gone.

"What'd she say?" I asked, swallowing every ounce of sarcasm in my body.

"Sophia," Lynn said. "That cat knew her own name."

"Thank you Sophia," Heather and I echoed, without even thinking twice.

The cat nodded, bowed to Heather, and was gone.

"She said… welcome back," Lynn said, one last time.

"Who saw that?" James said. "That person had four legs."

And from high above us, from somewhere in the endless green and brown canopy of colors, I swear I heard the purring.

"We go up now, don't we?" I said, looking at the lost expressions on the girl's faces. I hadn't known either of them for long, but I had never seen them that deep in conflicting introspective self-thought. Welcome to the—

"We go up," Lynn agreed, her eyes in the skies. "And then everywhere."

"In that order," Heather said, backing up her new friend. "What she says, that's what goes. Also what I say, that also goes. James, get on your brother."

"Score," he said.

"No wait—AH!" I shouted, as James had bellyflopped onto my back, and I took his weight on mine as Heather lashed his hands together with more fabric from my pants, quickly becoming shorts. "Oh come ON!"

"Up, boys," Heather said, smiling as Lynn was lost in her ascension up the cliffs, like the leopard was waiting for her and her alone.

The rocks were slick and wet with the rest of the rainforest, but the ledges were big enough to scale, and not straight up, more like a steady hand and feet climb, maybe a sixty degree slope—still deadly scary. Heather and Lynn were a few feet up already, scouting out the best paths to take. I was trailing a bit behind, or below them. Tends to happen when you lash a brother to your back and suddenly have to ascend vertically with double your body weight.

"Who's boat is this?" James said into my ear. "We hitting turbulence!"

"It's clear skies damnit," I panted, and pushed up to the next handhold with a grunt. "Keep that leg clear brother, and hold on. That's your only job."

"And what's yours, being so close to me I can EAT the body spray?"

"Yep," I said. "And not leaving. Now count my hair and hold on tight."

"Will do captain," he said, and I heard the sniffling as I was trying not to die.

Heather's hand slipped off a crumbling part of the cliff and she darted sideways on her long claws before she was lost. We stared at her.

"All good," she said. "Don't go left."

"Finally, a shower," James said, taking the landslide dirt and rocks on his head, not even noticing the ones that left red marks on his nose and cheeks.

"Derek, don't use your brother as a shield!" Lynn shouted at me.

"I'm... that's his... I'm NOT!" I shouted, holding onto the wall for dear life.

"My tongue tastes blue," James said. "Anyone else?"

It wasn't funny any longer. At least he wasn't in pain, but he was talking like he'd just come out of surgery with the loonies of anesthesia, but none of the actual benefits of surgery. I tuned him out. All he had to do was hang on. All I had to do was scale a mountain with someone on my back.

I was more worried about me.

"Step by step Derek," Lynn called to me, encouraging.

All positivity aside, what came next was an absolute gauntlet. I climbed about sixty feet of nearly vertical cliffside, I also might have said some things about my brother's weight that should never be repeated. Thankfully he was out to lunch for most of it, gasping at the wonder of the world, never questioning why he was holding on for dear life. Some survival instinct. Finally I felt hands on my shoulders—it was Heather and Lynn pulling James off me as I dug my hands into the final handhold, solid ground. My own weight was nothing compared to what I had just pushed straight up, and when I threw myself forward onto the ground, I had never been happier to slam.

"Land!" James said, balanced perfectly on one foot over me, looking into the trees like a sailor looking into the sunset.

"I think… sleep…" I said.

"No rest," Lynn said, and she pulled me to my shaking feet. "We need you."

"You've… got me," I said, groaning.

"Land!" James said again, excitedly.

"Okay how about next time, we don't climb like leopards," I said. "When life tells you there's nowhere to go but up, you find a ramp."

"Absolutely not," Lynn said. "That's literally the worst thing I've ever heard you say. Next time… we just find a way to fly. That's your way isn't it?."

"That's my way?" I said.

"We need it to be," Lynn said, with a look that said *don't lose hope now*.

"LAND!"

"That's it, wait. Look!" Heather said, turning on a dime.

Lynn and I turned to see what James had been stuck on repeat about. Land. It made sense, if you were on mushrooms. For the forest we were already in, we were facing a world of wood. A gate, a wall, same thing. The dirt, mud, shrubs and trees continued up to the thing on all sides, until they reached a line in the grass, an unmarked, uniform distance from what we had just found in the forest. The path was the unplanted part, extending from the forest to what looked like a giant wooden ringed wall, here in the middle of the shrubs. This wood was different. This was man-made. This was a gate. Did I have to say it?

"Where?" Heather blinked.

"From the forest, through the madness, farther down, until the gates tower over all," James said ominously.

Okay, my brother was still there, but so was this nonsense.

"Any way to turn the creepy down on this guy?" Lynn asked, as James used his crutches to dig strange letters of arcana into the ground, no big deal.

"Not when he's on mushrooms, not ethically, no," I said, breaking the circle he was clearly trying to carve into the earth.

"You really care," James said, looking at me with tears in his eyes, stepping all over his very important carvings. "Are you, by chance, my daughter?"

"What were you drawing?" I asked, ignoring him.

"A map to hell," he said blankly. "Why?"

"It kind of looked like our house," I said, turning my head sideways.

"Movement," Lynn said. "The gates—look out!"

A blur of movement among the trees. The rustling of all the leaves, all at once. Other cliches that came with literally being surrounded by trees.

"Something's out here," Heather said.

"Everything is out here," came a voice that shook the trees. All the trees.

And feet hit the ground before us faster than I could see where they had come from. There was no mechanical sound, no flurry of wind, just the weight of something landing and a single figure before us. She had spoken. At least we didn't have to worry about talking trees. It was a tall, barefoot woman, here in the middle of the forest, with the closest tree a good twenty feet away. Whoever she was, she hadn't even ducked and rolled, she had taken that far of a fall on her feet. Impressive, but not surprising, because warrior woman was all muscle. She stood at least six feet tall in the dirt, red hair but real ruby red, no freckles, no sunset ginger, and sharp, small features from the face to the wrists, where she too wore a familiar leather arm band on her left hand, more of a sports strap than a bracelet or wristlet. But the eyes, black as the cosmos…

They were Lynn's eyes.

"You kids are giving lost a new meaning," she said.

"Could be worse," I said softly, the three of us facing the newcomer with all the caution, while James was holding a finger out to catch a butterfly.

"We aren't lost," Lynn started.

"And we aren't kids," Heather finished.

"You're something else, alright," the warrior woman said.

She wasn't a big woman, just tall, and on the *far* side of toned, and we were on her turf. With no actual way of presenting a fight. And she knew it. She wore no weapon, in fact I think that was the gambit. She wasn't wearing any actual shirt or jeans, just a length of tan fabric wrapped around her waist and down to her knees, and a x-pattern of the same around her neck and chest. It was modest, for a warrior in the humid rainforest this far north. And in storm season.

"And what are you?" I asked, before I could stop myself.

"Fair question," the warrior woman said. "I am sister Ollux, daughter to Jerico, soldier of the Astral. I gave you my name, you give me yours."

And suddenly it wasn't just us in that small patch of forest. I saw the movement at the farthest edges of my vision. They were staying out of our sight, but they were there. Ollux wasn't alone. Wherever we were, we were already surrounded by whatever kind of people lived in this part of the island.

"My name's Derek Nite," I said. "Meet you Lynn Lyre, and Heather Denien. And this, well, this is my brother James. He broke his leg so we made him these crutches, but then he ate some jungle mushrooms that are making him hallucinate something awful. It's hilarious, but also not, and I don't think you're quite going to meet him here, so I'm just going to have to shake your hand and apologize on our both behalf."

"Don't get ahead of yourself," Ollux said. "Why are we meeting?"

"Well," I said honestly. "We're kinda hoping you've got a space-age hospital behind those gates."

"I know why you're at the gates, I asked why are we meeting?" Ollux asked. "And if you don't know the difference, I hope you know how to turn around."

"It's complicated, but okay," James said, stalling. "My first memories were of the girl in the parachute. It was also the night my mom turned into a superhero. But I remember first—"

I had a hand on his mouth before he could get us kicked back into the jungle. The same hand I had used to dig holes in the mud and climb up a mountain with.

"He was saying?" Ollux said.

"Issaic Nite is returned to Silka, and he's taken command of Infinite," Lynn interrupted over my shoulder.

"Issaic is returned to Silka?" Ollux said. "Before or after you opened the door to the Vempire?"

"During," Lynn said. "Our first stop was always Silka. But that was…"

"Before you saw handcuffs waiting," Ollux said darkly.

"Before we broke out of them," Lynn said, rubbing at her throat again where that necklace usually hung from her neck. Or maybe it was leftover burns from our neck/wrist handcuffs, because I had those itches too. Phantom cuffs.

Ollux looked impressed by Lynn, then she looked at me for confirmation, her hand going to that leather wristlet, like it too was more a manacle than jewelry.

"We couldn't have less of a home to go back to," I said, trying to say it all.

"And you thought your home wouldn't be able to track your supertech here, even if they couldn't pass the border?" Ollux asked, calmly.

"I've been Infinite," I said honestly. "And I've been Reaper. I've flown into space, I've been buried alive, both times I came back. But right now you're looking at two brothers with three legs. A good sized snake could take us out, so your perimeter guard isn't really necessary. We come bearing nothing. That's coming from someone who used to have everything."

"He still does, brother," James said to me.

I was touched. James even reached out to pat me on the shoulder, but it was in the completely wrong direction, and he was patting air. Still touching.

"I would say good answer, but here, honest is the only answer," Ollux said.

"That was a test," I said, realizing.

"Yes. You'd be dead by now if we had detected anything with a connection to the source. Right Crete?"

"Checks out," came a voice as familiar as they came. "The Infinite source cannot reach here. Just babes in the woods."

Excuse me.

"They are less than that to me," Ollux said, folding her arms as our mouths dropped. "They are more like… four legs of a ghost horse, walking aimlessly through the forest. They are an honest ghost horse, at least."

"CRETE?" Lynn yelled, her mouth open. "Is that you?"

"It might be," that familiar voice came again. "Why?"

A part of the green leaves parted by the gates, and from over the shoulder of Ollux, the unmistakable figure of Crete Magellan waved at us. He was standing on a tree trunk, holding onto a perfectly positioned branch with his left hand.

"You know the wayfarer?" Ollux asked. "Did you help them here?"

"Absolutely not," Crete said, smiling.

"He didn't help at all," I shouted, my eyes darting between them. "YOU dumped us in a forest, and YOUR people told us to leave James behind. Why are we going through all this when you're right THERE?"

"Wow, you take the long way home one time and come back with anger issues," Crete said. "Let me ask, did you maybe *learn* anything in the jungle?"

I only stared at him, my fists clenched, as the girls watched me fume.

“Is Sand here too?” Lynn said.

“Maybe,” came another voice through the trees.

“So you do know the wayfarers,” Ollux said.

“Where are we?” Heather shouted. “Sorry, I’ve been trying to wait my turn.”

“You should know, Lady Denien, offspring of the ex-Arcana,” Ollux said.

“You could call me Hector’s daughter,” Heather said. “I’m just a girl.”

“The girl who orchestrated the ascension of an entire people?” Ollux said. “You are history, Heather Denien. That’s not a threat, that’s a statement.”

“You know—” I started

“Everything,” Ollux said. “Words precede you, but not by more than…”

Crete shrugged. “About an hour?”

“Damn,” I said. “Your eyes in the trees figured us out faster than Silka’s weather satellites.”

“Eyes in the what?” Ollux said, blinking.

“Like the ring of warriors around us right now,” I said. “Those two on that giant redwood tree. The four behind us, way up there in the thinner branches. You got twenty soldiers on us, don’t you?”

Ollux blinked. “Even if that were true. Is that not enough for you four?”

“No,” I said. “Speaking from previous experience… today.”

Crete put a hand over his mouth to stow the laughter. As he doubled over, he silently gave me the good old thumbs up from behind Ollux’s shoulder.

“My perimeter guard is supposed to remain unseen at all times,” Ollux said.

“Well it’s us, so don’t feel bad,” I said. “I thought you already knew us?”

“I do,” Ollux said.

“And an ancient, hidden civilization in the forest already knows us because…” Lynn asked.

“Because we are hidden, to an island,” the woman said. “But an island has never been hidden to us. I still won’t shake your hands—not just yet. But I understand why we’re meeting, and I agree to it.”

“Which is code for you deciding not to kill us?” Heather said. “Again?”

“Look at you,” Ollux said proudly. “Just paying attention.”

And behind us, the gates boomed. They were opening. Why’d they have to boom? Couldn’t they just open like normal doors?

1.6

GATES OF JERICO

Normal doors opened. These two-hundred foot maple gates didn't just open.

There was no knocking, there was no giant handle. The construct itself of giant, individual stripped wooden spikes just started moving, all two hundred feet of them, to reveal an entrance the size of a city block. I was expecting light and the sound of harps to come pouring out, but no, it was the same part of the darkened, damp jungle, just behind a big wall. Still, this was something.

I had lived my entire life on this island, in the schools, baseball fields, shores, surfs, and backyards of Silka City. I had been witness to an entirely different culture in the Vema, and to be honest, I was still too young to do that adventure justice. But I had once before seen the world move around me, and now it was happening again. What had we said about waiting for Crete and Sand at the nearest civilization? What if the civilization was already waiting for us?

Were we meant to be here? Other cliches? My only question was the usual.

"But… why?" I asked her, the two guys in the trees, the universe in general.

"Because if we're not inside by nightfall, the cats will eat us," Ollux said.

"Eh," Lynn said, with a shrug. "We've made our peace with cats."

Ollux laughed. "You pet a territory cat in front of me, I'll cook you dinner."

"Is that a promise?" Lynn asked, holding her hand out.

"It's a bet," Ollux said, turning around to shake. "I'll remember you fondly as having two hands."

Well, I knew what we were doing for dinner.

We followed Ollux through the gates, leaving behind the endless colors and trees of the north behind us to come upon like weary travelers…

"Is this a joke?" I asked

It was just more forest. The doors that weren't doors boomed behind us and the lights didn't even change. We were still in the rainforest. I guess within the interior, they had removed the lowest hanging brushes and foliage, the ones we had been trooping through and jumping over for a few hours back there in the denser jungle. Here lay a barren tanbark floor of dark, amber dirt, only decorated by the most massive tree trunks I had ever seen in my life. And that was it.

"This city is a sham," I said, eyes up, hands out. "Do we fight?"

Ollux shrugged. "If you say so."

"We don't need to fight," Heather said. "Our friend is injured and we need help, not another struggle through the trees."

"Careful," Ollux said. "My life is a struggle through the trees."

"My brother needs help from an actual adult, not a mystery prophecy—excuse me, ANOTHER mystery prophecy," I said. "Why is this not a hospital?"

"Trust, Derek," Ollux said slowly. "You are bravely defending your brother, noted, but right now you need to trust the advice and wisdom of the wayfa—"

"Don't, that's just so stupid, they have names," I said.

"Names Jerico knows," Ollux said.

"Either way, we're still mad at each other," I said.

"No we're not," came the echoes from above. It was both of them.

"I see you very much know know Sand Freedom and Crete Magellan," Ollux said. "Right now, none of this is about them. It's about you. We've heard your names. We've heard what you did to the Vema Empire, what no one in seven years has been able to do. All by simply... looking... up."

We turned to the sky and all registered it in our own time (James was last).

"What in the socks," Lynn said.

"Awesome," Heather said. "Derek..."

"I seen it," I said, my eyes softening just like they'd done seeing the bunk beds waiting for us in Crete's mecha-mansion.

Treehouses. There was just something about treehouses.

It's hard to describe how tall the trees were in here. Outside the gates, the trees and shrubbery started all over the place, from the ground up, and there wasn't any real start to the low hanging leaves and vines. You were whipped in the face by three fruits and a flower and a six foot branch all at once, or at least I'd been, countless times just today. Out there the way we came, if you looked up, the inner canopy blocked out the true height of the tallest trees, and there was just no way to see scale from the forest floor. But inside the gates, there was no inner level of foliage to block the scale, we could truly look straight up.

For a few hundred feet.

"I guess you weren't kidding about the leopards," I said, almost stammering.

"They're the best climbers in the natural world," Ollux said, nodding. "But even they tap out around a hundred feet straight up. The forest—I mean the island—is full of enemies. We have always lived with them."

"I get it now," I said, humbled by the sight.

"Me man," Ollux said, miming me. "Life larger than me. Must appreciate."

I still couldn't see the sky or sun for the tallest world cover of green leaves intertwined as dense as the jungle. But starting about three hundred feet off the ground was the network of conjoined and bridged settlements carved into and around the trees, reinforced all together with moving wood planks and ropes. There were decks as big as soccer fields, houses that looked normal in every way except the fact that they were built into the trees, and the entire city was moving slightly with the wind, with no one giving it a second thought. I saw small dots of moving people all over, and that was all from only the ten trees in my immediate view. I saw the settlements and treehouse constructs continuing in all directions from this small portside place.

It was a world of treehouses, and I was a teenage boy. My day was made.

"Now that's land," James said.

"Keep on crutching friend," Ollux said, nudging us forward lest we stop and stare all day. "See that hut with the red roofing, right next to the banana trees? There's your space age hospital. And yes we're going up, and now. And no, don't worry about ladders. We've got you."

I could finally breathe. I could be patient for something I wanted, but when half of my brother didn't work, you were getting obnoxious, relentless Derek. I wasn't sorry. They said good things came to those who waited. Well for all our waiting, something was finally coming straight for us. We still couldn't see the sky. Again, why? Why again? What part of rest and relaxation didn't the universe understand, you can't just throw the same group of friends from one adventure straight into another! Kids needed sleep, food, and some of them needed a bathroom right now. But whatever we had expected, it was not a home.

From such great heights, some sort of platform on four ropes came down from the trees above, landing with a soft thud on the dirt at our feet. Nice—

"Oh I'm sorry," Ollux said, putting her arm around James. "I was misheard. This is for our broken boy soldier. But for you three… we have ladders."

"You can't be serious," I said

"Pick a tree, strangers," Ollux said, eying me without a worry in the world.

And with a smooth, quick start, the platform was lifted off the ground on four ropes as long as the trees were tall. James managed to smile and wave us goodbye with his left hand, the bandages oddly reminiscent of the thick leather band Ollux wore on her left wrist. She glared down at us, but I saw the concern. She finally shook her head and pointed at something over Lynn's shoulder.

"Pick that tree, strangers!" she called back, before disappearing.

And they were gone, lifted up at blinding speed, covering hundreds of feet in seconds. My brother had been taken into the tree. I had not stopped the tree.

All that breathing easy was kicking me in the butt right now.

"Bad Jerico," I said.

"What just happened?" Lynn said.

"We lost James, that's what just happened," I said, seeing a systematic carving of ledges into the trunk that was so massive, I was basically about to climb up a flat surface. The dugouts were angled in our favor, it was secure.

"We just climbed up a mountain, that wasn't enough?" Heather said, as she threw herself right into the tree with me, and we climbed.

"I'd climb a thousand if I had to," I said.

"A little action hero macho don't you think?" Heather teased.

"No, I just don't know why I didn't…"

"Throw yourself at the platform and bring it down with all your muscles that are definitely bigger than hers?" Heather said.

"No!" I said. "We're playing by their rules. But the second those rules include harming my brother or using him for evil ways, those rules are gone, and I'm going to need you to understand if I go off the rails a bit."

"If you make the top without us carrying you, you can do whatever you want," Lynn said, looking at me with all the worry. "You might not make this. What happens if we're two hundred feet up and you hit a wall? Should we rest first? Go back down and make sure we're ready?"

"We're ready," I said, my eyes set. "No wall, no fall. Not right now."

"I believe," Lynn said. "Stay close, let us know the second you get scared."

Okay, no action hero macho but… come on. I was worth more than that. Did she actually believe me? Or was that the first lie a girl named Lyre ever told me?

As the anger over that comment built, I realized where it came from. I hadn't given the girls any reason to believe I was an alpha. I had thought and fought and plotted my way out of most things, or supersuit and sword had done the work. Right now I was just a kid who did some high school sports. I wasn't a man, that was just a fact. I wasn't a fighter, I had yet to throw a punch in my life without sparring gear or a supersuit. But what non-super Derek had, well that was all I had left. So when I said I had no problem with the climb, I meant it.

Because who needs superpowers to get up a LADDER?

We climbed for a half hour, using legs instead of hands whenever possible. For origin reasons, Heather had no problem rock climbing, it was Lynn and I who traded off calling for breaks. Yes it was hard to look down and see the ground moving in the wind. Falling was no longer an option. We had to be nearing three hundred feet.

"Eyes up from here on," Lynn said.

"Metaphors," I said in agreement.

Then we saw the light not twenty handholds from us. A big surface, like we were coming on the undercroft of some huge platform, the size of a small colosseum, the tree built straight through the center of it, with enough room for us to climb straight through.

"I'd be excited, if James were here," I said as we neared the top end.

"He is," came a voice from the trees. "I'd be more worried about… you."

We were done with ladders. The lights of something much brighter than forest caught us hard, and we pushed off that last rung to find a surface world up here in the trees—a flat stadium floor, the tree continuing straight through the center of it, our tree-ladder still running higher up to the next few hundreds of feet of leaves before the sky-blocking canopy started.

"I thought you said you'd heard about us," Heather said, sounding pissed.

Ollux grinned, full tiger eyes. "I have. Put up your hands."

And as hard as I was clenching… she wasn't talking to us.

Boom. Our ears were split, my head was ringing, but that was no explosion. It was a human sound, and that meant… people. A cheering ring of people on all sides. This stadium-sized platform was in fact a wooden amphitheater, the size of a small soccer pitch, with multiple levels of wooden bleachers high in the air, full of tall, shirtless, tan tree people yelling and cheering. This was new.

"Strangers at the gate!" the crowd cheered.

There were a thousand eyes on us, more than we had ever seen in Infinite, only rivaled by the Reaper Den…

"I thought—" I shouted at Ollux.

"Wrong," she said, alone with us on this side of the grandstands. "Most don't survive the forest, let alone the gates. We watched one of you do it with a broken leg. To come this far, you must have been accepted by our ancestors. But to go any farther, you'll need our acceptance. The gates of Jerico only reveal themselves to the strong, but when it's an unknown source of strength, then I would speak for us all when I say… it's your turn to reveal yourselves."

"Sounds like you want a show out of us," I said, eyes low, looking up to my brother, you know, the one who couldn't even walk straight, let alone fight.

"I want everything out of you," Ollux said, her knees bending slightly, her weight shifting back. "More than just your names."

"Be careful what you wish for," Heather said, the first to put her hands up. "You just might get it all, and then some you don't want. Damnit James—"

"Prove it," Ollux said, glad about it. "Honor our traditions like adults and we won't treat you like children—or the devil spawn of the xenocide."

"You mean our father don't you?" I said, groaning, there it was (like always).

"Are you saying he controls the weather?" James asked, aghast.

"Of course not," Ollux said. "Well, maybe. I wouldn't bet against it."

"What the hell Sand," I said, under my tongue.

And like my brain had already seen it, I realized who the two men standing closest to James were, up there on that center-field platform. It was them. Sand Freedom, still without a single scratch on him or the raggedy white shirt and brown adventurer (cargo) pants he now wore. Crete Magellan had a long-sleeve rash guard and tropical shorts on, wearing dark sunglasses.

"Haven't you been here before?" Sand asked me. "Imagine a thing, being challenged in combat on your immediate arrival to a place, all future welcome dependent on your response to action. Even if you aren't fighters…"

"We are survivors," I said, blinking hard.

"Hey, it's just like the first day we met," James said, then his face froze. "Oh. So you're home too, Sand?"

"Kind of, friend," Sand said, holding my brother's unblinking eyes, watching him put all the weight on those slapped together wooden crutches, even for the bandages on his left hand, no longer loose in the wind, like someone had tightened them for him. "And we've got you, James. You know that right?"

"I hope that," he said to Sand. "But who's got Derek?"

"That we're less sure about," Crete said, frowning from the safety of the box.

"Here's the show," Ollux said, grinning from the danger of the field. "I'm going to attack you. All three of you. You knock me down once before I kill you, and broken boy soldier over here wins a doctor."

"What if we don't die, and we take you down first?" I asked.

"Then I'll make you dinner too," Ollux said, but somehow she had made that into a threat, as she took a step towards Heather. "You first dear. If you need a minute that's okay. You're going to get blood all over those cute gloves."

"You're right," Heather said, her hands up but her claws stowed, without an ounce of giveaway. "I am."

Ollux stopped smirking. The wind rustled, the audience fell silent, and Ollux leapt forward, her hand a flat disc arcing into the side of Heather's face—but

Heather wasn't there. She dodged the open palm and Ollux stumbled to a stop, turning around quick to catch Heather's sidekick just before it landed on her face. They had traded places, each had sent and stopped a blow, all in a second.

"Nice," Ollux said, as Heather landed on one leg, as the crowd erupted in cheering, going crazy at the surprise attack. What were they cheering for?

"Give me back my foot," Heather said, as stoic as possible.

"Sure thing," Ollux said, and yanked Heather's heel sideways.

I watcher Heather bite down on her lip as the ankle rolled, before Ollux let go and Heather went tumbling. No mercy, and no letup from the crowd of cheering tree people either. I saw middle aged men doing a group chant, slapping their knees and shoulders in unison, I saw small children with sticks in their hands shouting in a different language, one I couldn't understand. We weren't the youngest of them, we weren't the smallest, we were just the most dressed. Was this what Jerico was, or what Jerico was supposed to be?

And regardless—why were we already fighting?

"A little help friends," Heather said as she tried to get to her feet, but slipped on the wood, landing hard, not a good fall.

"They'll get their turn," Ollux answered, with a look that said *don't move.*

"Can it be now?" Heather said sarcastically. "Not you, don't you help me—"

Ollux's answer was lifting Heather up and throwing her to the ground like a big potato, no problem for arms bigger than mine would ever be. Heather hit hard but though she stayed on the ground, she slid away like she should have last time. Wait. It was an act. She knew how to fall as well as anyone. She'd never needed our help to get up before. As soon as I realized it was a trap, Ollux had already dove on top of her again.

The crowd cheered.

"HEATHER!" Lynn shouted.

"Stay out of this… Lyre…" Heather got out, before Ollux slammed her knee into Heather's chest and her elbows buckled, her back hitting the ground hard.

Boom.

"Don't worry," I said, my eyes wide seeing Heather take the hit. "It's a…"

Her head snapped back and Ollux was already hitting it again, twice now her head almost broke the wood. Boom.

"It's gotta be a…" I said, but the faith was fading. "Come on Heather…"

"Derek, whatever you're thinking, you're wrong!" Lynn shouted.

"Who will you be when the lights go out, Lady Denien?" Ollux said, darkly.

My brain was broken. We didn't survive an empire to be lost in the forest. And thankfully, both Lynn and Heather thought the same. Lynn moved beside me, so I did too. Heather's skinny, teenage arm that had been lying motionless in the dirt came up like a cannon. It took Ollux two hands to stop it, and she sneered down at Heather, until she saw the blood on Heather's gloves. Realized both her hands were occupied.

"I'll… be… me," Heather said.

That's when she hooked the leg and rolled Ollux over, shoving her away with her feet into the air—where Lynn and I came like lightning, from the opposite direction. Together we jumped into the air and side-kicked Ollux at the same time, sending her tumbling over into the wood, crashing and burning, us completely out of balance and falling over for the momentum to join Heather on the hard wooden floor.

The crowd was silent. Ollux was on the ground. But so were the three of us.

"Let's get one thing straight Lyre," Heather said as we got up slowly, all eyes on Ollux. "Derek knew I had a plan, he just forgot that you had one too. Derek, open your eyes out here—when you make a plan, don't forget to consider the factors you haven't considered and Lynn; don't you EVER doubt him again."

"I like this movie!" James yelled down at us, tapping his good foot.

"We could use a working James right now," Heather admitted.

"Whatever I'm thinking… I'm wrong?" I said, looking at Lynn.

"Sorry…" she said, her eyes wide, caught. "Good job team?"

"Not this time," Heather said before I could.

"She's getting up," I said, not looking at Lynn.

A few feet from us, Ollux was stumbling to find her feet, until Heather pulled her up by the back strap of her chest fabric—not that there was a lot of it.

"You…" Ollux said, not understanding. "Take the shot."

"Can't hit a girl on the ground," Heather said, bringing her fists up, raised knuckles like her claws were about to come out. "That was a team-up, I'll admit. But this one's all me."

She stood Ollux up just long enough to swing back and unloose a right jab all the way across the face. No claws. Ollux took the blow like a warrior, wiped the blood off her lip, nodded once at the Reaper, and swung back. Heather took it, licked the blood off her lips, and nodded back.

It was on.

"For VEMA!" Heather shouted.

"For ANA SUN!" Ollux shouted back.

"Who she lady?" James called, his hands around his mouth for volume.

Oh James.

This wasn't like watching Lynn run circles around Hannah. Heather and Ollux were both at full tilt, neither holding anything back, neither afraid to take the cheap shot. I saw Heather barely deflect a kick from Ollux that would have broken my bones. I saw fingernails make contact with skin and dig in, leaving red burn marks—both of them. Ollux was taller, but Heather was quicker, and could get two good hits in before Ollux would grab her, and it would take all four of Heather's limbs to break her out of even a single wrist hold. It seemed Ollux picked up on how Heather was using the stadium to her advantage, because she decided to shorten the stadium by navigating Heather into that huge tree in the middle of the court. But Heather wasn't watching what was behind her, that was usually our job. Her head hit wood and she started, and looked back—Ollux took the opportunity to send her fist straight for Heather's head. Her face was pressed into the bark before she ever saw it coming.

Boom. I saw red in the tree.

"You didn't take the shot," Ollux said to Heather.

"I could have," Heather said, glaring at her, gently touching the back of her head. "That's gonna need stitches. Maybe I should have."

"Then do it," Ollux said, lunging forward again but—

With her back to the wall (tree), Heather deployed her razor sharp claws, holding them steady in front of her without actually weaponizing them yet. It was a shield strategy, a scare tactic. And it worked. Ollux registered the steel and came to a screeching halt with razors like kitchen knives at her throat in one hand, and slender claws as long as extra arms already reaching around the back of her neck in the other. The claws were clean, but there was blood all over the gloves, and not all of it was Heather's.

"You had those the whole time?" Ollux said softly.

"Yep," Heather said.

"You still hit me without them?"

"I don't need to take the shot," Heather said. "I'm always capable of it. But the world is usually bigger than, you know, stabbing. Right?"

Ollux looked at her… and as she nodded. "Right."

Then some sort of weird bell rang out over the crowd of people around us, and something even weirder happened. The people started cheering her name.

"Stranger! Heather! Stranger!"

"Why?" Heather stared around, still breathing heavy.

"Next," Ollux said.

"What do you mean by—AHH!" Lynn shouted. "I get it now!"

Ollux turned to Lynn, leaving Heather completely forgotten behind. She melted down the tree trunk, exhausted, her claws retracting in a flash, her hands holding the back of her head as I ran to her, tearing yet another piece of my pants away from the already knee-low cuff.

"You good Heather?" I asked, as she slumped backwards.

"Apparently," Heather said, raising her hand, trembling. "Girl though…"

Yeah. Lynn tumbled away in some sort of back handspring that was more panic than grace, and dodged the follow up combo.

"We've died and gone to the thunder-dome," I said. "Or I'm still asleep."

"Either way not good," Heather said, holding her head.

"Hold… still… just go to bed…" Ollux was stumbling over her words and punches, not able to land a solid blow on Lynn. "You fight like me."

"You fight like me!" Lynn countered.

I made a move to run to Lynn but Heather had her hand locked in a vice-grip around my wrist, her claws threatening to come out, like a wounded cat.

"Let her," she said. "She's ten of you."

"Ouch, but accurate," I said.

Heather's head bandage fell off. I sighed.

Lynn fought a bit more technically than Heather. She easily blocked Ollux's killer blows from those same three stances I remembered from Hannah. Ollux was towering over Lynn, squared shoulders, weight back, daring her to approach, ready with all the body's power to defend. Horse stance. Lynn had her body sideways, cat stance. All power in the back foot, sideways to present a smaller target, calculating the perfect chance to swipe. And that's exactly what happened—only the other way around. Life, right?

Ollux roared out of her defensive stance and shot sideways at Lynn, propelled by something more than human. Lynn squared her shoulders, stood her ground, and found a way to turn Ollux's pummeling into a perfect head-first takedown. In a blink, Lynn was in the air above the reeling, watching Ollux flailing into the ground like a skateboarder bailing a bad simile.

"Who taught you how to fight like me?" Ollux gasped, on the ground like potatoes for the second time.

"My mother, technically," Lynn said. "My father… and then my interim father, they both always said the same thing. That my mother never wanted to fight, but she knew how, and well enough to pass it down. If I was to learn to fight, it would be her way. The old way."

"The only way," Ollux blinked at her. "You remind me of… me, Lyre."

"I am just a normal girl!" Lynn shouted.

And from above us all, a leopard roared as loud as thunder, shaking the trees, sending James almost to his face. The thing was a blur as quick as the day was long, and that same animal friend from before was suddenly by Lynn's side, clearly ready to defend her against Ollux.

The crowd gasped—literally, all of them, all at once.

"A normal girl with bad timing," Lynn corrected, still holding her head up.

The leopard purred at her, then was back to a war stance, fangs bared, shoulders hunched. Lynn was suddenly deadlier than ever, if that were possible.

"Hi Sophia," I said gently, smiling at Ollux. "You were saying, about this place being too high for enemies?"

"I was," Ollux said, frowning at us, trying to figure us out for the fifth time. "You gave that jungle creature a people name?"

"Nope," Lynn said. "She told me her name."

"We all seeing that tiny elephant?" James asked. "Am I too wide to ride?"

Lynn held her hand out, grinning, watching Ollux's eyes go wide with fear as her hand hovered over the creature's eyes. The crowd was silent.

"Don't you dare," Ollux said. "I just cleaned the kitchen."

"But I need you to take me seriously," Lynn said, shrugging, and then her hand made contact with Sophia's fur. "Bet."

Sophia kept her war eyes locked on Ollux, but we all heard the purring, the back foot came up and everything.

"My dinner, not yours," Lynn said. "Sorry girl. Yes I know landing from that high is bad for the knees, how could it not be? You've got four of them, you're fine. Hell yeah it was badass! Okay you too, stay close, see you soon."

The leopard growled once, nuzzled Lynn's leg, bowed to the terrified audience (including Ollux) and leapt back up thirty feet into the air, leaving on the branches of a nearby system, disappearing into a moving ripple among leaves, like watching a shark swimming off into the darker waters. No less than six guards leapt out of the canopy as the motion passed them, swinging on some sort of mechanical vine contraption in their palms, shouting their heads off.

The colosseum stared at Lynn.

"I'll take back that normal thing," she said again with that half smile, the one that meant she knew she had a way out.

Lynn Lyre, ladies and cavemen.

Ollux stopped blinking, eyes frozen on Lynn as the bell sounded to a stunned, silent audience. Then those kids in the front row went crazy.

"Did you see that? It was a cat! She pet a territory cat!"

"She didn't even get eaten!"

"What a day!"

And as the bell went off, the kids did too, and the crowd followed, clapping nervously, then cheering, then standing up and shouting her name, some still turning over their shoulders to the canopies to look for more falling cats.

"Lynn! Stranger! Lynn!"

"Okay, you're good too," Ollux said, laughing to herself a bit. "Good to have some girls around. You wouldn't believe how many adventurers, journalists, geographers, cartographers, zoologists, and scientists are men. It's getting old."

"It's been old," Lynn agreed. "There's a Teresa Silk to every Alexander Veman."

"A Mylo Ocarina to every Ana Sun," Ollux said, agreeing.

But all we heard was a stab in the heart.

"Ana," I said.

"Teresa," my brother said, his eyes dilating, like his heart was fighting the psychoactives.

"They're both just names," Heather said, one hand on her head. "Although yeah. That's going to make things…"

"Not confusing," I finished.

"Trust us, it's purely symbolic," Heather said, rolling her eyes. "Ollux, you on salary or something?"

"Right," she said. "Sorry. But next…"

"That'd be me, wouldn't it?" I asked.

"Afraid so," Ollux said, now as afraid of me as I'd been of her the entire time. "Your mother bears the same name as the woman who founded Silka City, four hundred years ago?"

"Seem so," I said. "Never really thought about it. But now, with both mother and motherland gone, I tend to wonder."

"I do too," Ollux said, her eyes flashing. "Who will you be in the dark, Nite?"

"I won't be a redundancy, that's for sure," I said. "I was more wondering… who's left? You? I can deal with you."

And the crowd oohed. They were on our side now. That, or it was all in my head. Either way, I was just going out the same way I had come in. Sarcastically.

Ollux sighed, and moved faster than I was ready for. My defense of sarcasm was hit with something like a train… station. Bam. My hands were wrenched sideways with a hook kick, followed up with a full on spinning backfist to my wide open face, and a foot to the bare chest to finish the combo, sending me blasting backwards until I hit that tree in the center of everything. Boom. Thankfully it wasn't the part that led to the ladder. This part of the platform was built straight into the trunk, carved and curved within a hair's distance of perfect. I felt the tree with my back, then the platform with my butt. Ow.

My head and the world were pulsing, my vision black and white for some reason, my ears nothing but piercing sound and then silence, until I looked sideways and saw Heather breathing hard beside me.

"Hey."

I couldn't hear her, that's just what her lips had said.

"Hey," I coughed out, hearing the words just a bit, through the dense ringing.

"Should I kill her?" Heather mouthed.

"No… maybe later," I shook my head, making an x in the air with my hands.

Heather only stared at me, then she turned to Lynn. "He's delusional. Should I kill him?"

"You sure on that, boy wonder?" Ollux shouted out, her words coming in hard from behind me, as Heather's eyes widened. "Had enough? Ready to die? Or are you going to show me what you've got?"

And the ringing was gone, my vision back, the pulsing had whipped into focus and I got to my feet, shaking, holding my hands up as hard as I could. Heather was reaching out for me, but I left her hand hanging as I took a few steps in a circle, taking Ollux's attention off that center tree, keeping it on me. Not on Heather.

"Wasn't… planning on dying," I said. "I was just analyzing."

"Analyzing what?" Ollux said.

"You," I said, wiping the blood off my mouth. And nose. And neck. There was a lot of blood. "Talk about redundant. You really think you're going to do the same thing three times without one of us picking up the pattern?"

"What pattern?" Ollux asked, innocently.

"You're going to beat me so bad I start to fear for my life, right?" I said. "That's when people really show you what you're made of. Isn't it?"

And the crowd was absolutely silent. There were no cries to continue the fight. They were close enough to hear my words, they were part of this too.

"Derek," Heather said, blinking at me.

"Brilliant," Lynn said, proudly (I hoped).

"How did you—" Ollux said, the first to break the cadence.

"I'm no fighter," I said. "But I'm no dummy. I'll take a hit if you need to throw one, but we aren't here to fight you. My eyes are open. I saw your guard and I raise you two me's—isn't that right James?"

"Absotutely," he said, full confidence, no regrets (not even a single letter).

"What he said," I grinned. "Congrats on being the last to learn not to mess with Heather and Lynn, now welcome to me."

I put my hands up and started towards her. Some sort of aura was coming over me, some confidence that all I needed was my own two hands and my words to get me through any situation.

"Now that's badass," Heather said.

"What happened to action hero macho?" Lynn said.

"I never said that was a bad thing," Heather said. "It's all in the context. Derek look out—nevermind… ouch, that turned quick… right in the macho…"

I'd called her bluff, but she called mine harder, right in the ear. Her fists came first, and I was once again getting pummeled. Her knee caught me in the chest and I felt something go out, either my lung or my rib. Again, ow.

"Is this redundant enough?" Ollux shouted at me.

"You shouldn't have to ask what my greatest weapon is!" I shouted through the pain. "If you were smarter, you'd already know."

I fell to my knees and somehow just knew her foot was coming, so I put my hands out and caught her by the ankle and death-rolled like a crocodile. I spun her off her feet by pure chance, for a blink of a moment she was on her back in the dirt, her hands flung backwards—and two crutches came flying in like javelins and bounced point-first off the ground on either side of her neck. They hadn't stuck, because this was wood and so were they, but the aim was too perfect. I stopped. She did too. Her eyes were wide, while James stood perfectly balanced on one leg, smiling as the shirtless guards ran to grab him, far too late.

"You're using my brother as some sort of third party manipulation over us," I said, getting to my feet as she lay frozen, her throat far too close to the chips in the wood on either side. "That means I will actually die before letting you get away with it. We both will. That's our default mode, Ma'am. Till the end."

"Is someone talking about me?" James asked, not looking our way at all. "Wait, even better—is someone talking about... tacos?"

"Always, brother," I said. "I'll get you out of this mess, just hold on. I think I've cracked this gambit."

"You call it a gambit," Ollux said to me from the dirt. "I call it... four for three. Put up your hands."

"But we just DID THAT!" I said before realizing—she wasn't talking to me.

And just before the crowd went crazy, I heard two pairs of hands clapping out. That bell rang out twice, right beside Sand and Crete, who were looking at us proudly, with nothing short of relief on their faces, and they nodded me up as the cheers rang out. The cheers for me. Right?

"Nite! Nite! Nite!"

"What happened to stranger?" I asked.

"Exactly," Ollux said, clapping her hands.

"They're happy about... that?" I asked, confused.

"About new friends, and family in the territory?" Ollux said. "You are alive. That is the best show we could hope to have."

I had thought that faceless crowd was here for normal colosseum reasons. But to know the ring of unbroken eyes and muscles around us could applaud a bunch of people not dying... I was almost tearing up, man. These were my people. Not literally. Actually not at all. Why had I thought that? Because I had nowhere left to go? I was spiraling. But I was grateful. Or was I just alive...

"You psycho," I said, to Ollux or to myself I didn't know, but I grabbed her hand and helped her stand nonetheless. "No fighting."

"No fighting," Ollux agreed, turning to my brother. "All good up there?"

And the six guards who were about to tackle James... didn't, leaving him standing on one foot in full zen. My brother only nodded as they backed off, then Crete waked up and handed his crutches back to him.

"No harm done?" James asked us, like he was channeling Ollux.

“I guess not,” I said. “Did they mess with you brother?”

“You’re asking me?” he said, pointing at me. “YOU just faced down death and said hey… not now man.”

“Apt,” Ollux said, trying not to laugh at James, for respect reasons.

The crowd was gone. It was the five of us on that stadium floor, and Ollux walked us to one side of it, away from the tree three of us had climbed up, thank you ladders. As she led us off the field and straight into a break in the stands, my eyes only honed in harder on all that was outside this weird colosseum. It looked like land. But it was tree.

It was both. The stadium was literally only a stadium from inside, and we walked out amongst the increasingly towering support beams of the last rows of the bleachers, clear of the construct quicker than we expected. Looking back it was a framework outline of a stadium, with all the supportive wooden beams clear as day, exposed for modifications and checkups. A living stadium, literally. But what we saw looking forward… was everything else.

“Aloha, my new brothers and sisters,” Ollux said, as Lynn and Heather stopped moving, and I audibly gasped. “Welcome to Jerico Territory.”

A world awaited. A full platformed world, with small and large houses and huts carved straight into the trees, the connecting path a never-ending walkway of not only perfectly sanded wooden ground but also fruits, shrubs, trees and actual grass lawns, enough to make you completely forget that we were three hundred feet in the air at least.

“Thank you flower child,” I said sarcastically, finally free to be. “Just one question, the usual one. WHY—”

1.7

MAD HONEY

"A whole new—"

"No," I said, slapping James out of his song. "That's copyrighted."

I was reminded of standing on a certain stone, looking out at the vast underland of the Vempire. I was that guy again, just on a tree this time. A lot of trees, vertical trunks from here to heaven, like the entire place was a roman cathedral of godly pillars. As a skateboarder and a guitar player (and single for some reason) I preferred wood to almost anything. I owed my favorite hobbies in this world to trees. But this world owed its world to trees.

Up here, the platform exterior of the colosseum seemed like the ground. But we had climbed half a tree to get to that ground, and it wasn't even real ground. Outside the colosseum, that was proven only a few meters away by the wood under our feet ending without warning, without rope or barrier. It was only continued in other places by walkways and bridges, some just lashes of long half-logs following a natural branch, some suspended high by vines, ropes, and wires, leading up and down to other platforms like ours, built around and through every giant trunk in sight. Some were big enough to hold a soccer field.

Tree world. Or just farther down.

"This was here the whole time?" Lynn said. "I've lived my entire life thinking I already lost everything. But the finds lately. Damn."

"I'll second that damn," Heather said, looking out onto the new world.

"Southern Arbor, as close to the edge of Jerico as you can get," a voice came.

Ollux had led us to a floating bridge with no safety ropes or edges to it. Waiting for us there was a guy who looked a bit like Ollux. Tall, not dark skinned but tan as hell for not seeing the sun yet, muscles on his muscles, and a face that was all smile. He fell in step beside Ollux. They walked the exact same, and I saw some similar features in their noses and ears.

"That was the best welcome we've seen in years," the guy said. "I am brother Astor. Allow me to shake the hands of warriors?"

I was barely keeping myself centered, but I nodded—but Astor turned around to walk the bridge with no balcony backwards, holding his hand out to

Lynn and Heather as he did, bowing his head like he was about to shake hands with goddesses. He was, but I was here too. Don't look down Derek…

"Astor and Ollux?" I said. "Sounds like you're both missing something."

"Missing what?" they asked together, full innocence.

Nevermind.

Heather and Lynn were walking the very center of the bridge, their arms around each other for balance. Heather cautiously held her free left hand out to Astor, and they shook awkwardly.

"The velocity, your combat style," he said to Heather, still walking backwards. "Is that technique common in the Vempire?"

"Physical combat is not that common, no," Heather said. "We have other ways of moving our wills around."

"Like magic?" Astor asked.

"Like rocks," Heather said. "Like a magnetic control over the mineral world that died at the border, just like the Infinite supertechnology does. I assure you that's where my similarities with all things Silka end."

"Fascinating," Astor said, nodding. "Storm season, bad timing."

"That, and Reaper swarm from the air," Heather said, suddenly all talk around the taller Astor, with what looked like a twelve-pack, and if we thought his sister's biceps were insulting. "What you saw was me going cavewoman."

"We all start somewhere," Astor said, winking, and turning his attention to Lynn (which seemed to infuriate Heather). "And you, Lyre. You know our stances. You have the blood of the jungle in your heart, something tells me this."

"My mother was from here," she said softly. "Or at least… I was told that. By… those who didn't die giving birth to me. What a burden."

Aster bowed his head. He got the message.

"If life is a burden, then we are all bearers," Ollux said. "I wish your mother was here to see you win your way back into her world, Lyre. She would have been so proud, but scared of the leopard like we all were, and rightfully so…"

"That's… kind," Lynn said.

"She was a kind lion," Astor said. "It is an honor, to meet the lion cub."

He about-faced, his stride matching Ollux's to the toes, both barefoot, and the smallclothes didn't leave much to the imagination. Lynn and Heather laughed weird as he turned around. I had one hand on my brother's back, and Ollux was with it, sweeping fallen leaves and twigs away before we got there, for fear of his wooden crutches slipping a brother off the tree bridge. Nice touch, new person. I wondered if there were safety nets below us. I wanted to believe…

"We'd have burned brighter, if we'd known it was a game," Heather said.

"But only Derek knew that," Astor winked over his shoulder. "Am I wrong?"

Heather sighed honestly, and shook her head. "No…"

"I didn't even, I just saw a line, and wanted ice cream—" James started.

"I'm going to cut you off there, sprinkles," Ollux said. "I've been through enough ceremony to know strangers usually die a lot easier than you four—I meant that survivors usually have some resentment towards me, no idea why."

"No idea?" I said, my eyebrows high, the move reminding me that there was still blood on my face and in my hair, from someone, somewhere. Was it mine?

"Derek," Lynn said, looking at me trying to wipe it off before anyone saw.

"Lynn," I said, trying to play it off, and turning my attention to Ollux. "I figured the answer, I get the goal. But what's the question? What's the game?"

"Jerico is only the strong," Ollux said. "Now you have the entire Southern Arbor witness to your strength. You may have noticed that I haven't technically said the words welcome yet, because you weren't. Now you are."

"Because we fought good?" I said.

Ollux laughed. "Some of you did. But strength isn't fighting. You explain."

"Not much to explain," Astor said. "You don't kill us, we don't kill you, and we all accept that the other is capable. The real strongest learn to fight only so they may never need to. You went four for three on that one, so come on in."

I could have been sarcastic, but it was one of those times where it was so strangely applicable, so coincidental, that I couldn't even make fun of it. I had heard that before.

"We've heard that before," James said, looking at me.

"How before?" Lynn asked, cautiously.

"Our mom told us that," I said. "Right after our first ever sparring session."

"Mixed martial arts?" Heather asked, curiously.

"Tae-kwon-do," I admitted.

"That's DANCING!" Heather shouted.

"The mixed martial arts came later, promise," I complained.

"How much later?" Ollux asked, grinning.

"You still took dance classes, I've got that on the books," Heather teased.

"Fine," I said. "Well after all the patterns, we would spar. We were kids, first punches and foam padding, and I never got too hurt but still, I hated it. I didn't understand why I had to get punched in the face for after-school activities. Mom only said that to learn why fighting wasn't the answer, we had to learn to fight."

"So she wanted you to learn how to take a punch," Heather translated.

James put his finger on his nose.

"Maybe," I said. "But we got older and the pads disappeared. I'll never forget this—a few years ago, I was against an instructor, he had a good foot on me, I think he was in college. Maybe he was trying to teach me something. We were circling, I was blocking the jabs, but I was wild, and he told me to calm down. Stop bouncing. Stop looking at my hands and feet. Look me in the eyes."

"Oh," Heather said, sounding like she approved again. "Did it help?"

"Absolutely not," I said. "I stared him in the eyes with everything I had, and he kicked me across the face. I didn't see it coming. I wasn't looking at his feet."

Then something funny happened. Nobody laughed.

"You were looking into his eyes," Heather said. "And he did that to a kid?"

"I walked into that ring," I said. "He got me fair and square."

"Maybe he did teach you something," Lynn said.

"That's what I was trying to put into you when I… hit you," Heather said.

"Again, walked into that ring too," I said.

"You can take a hit," Heather said. "I'll give you that… and an apology. I can feel it, the old still-sorry versus trying to move on ratio. You know?"

"The old pain to learning things ratio," I said. "Too well."

"Too much," Lynn said, quietly. "That doesn't excuse what I did."

"Maybe not," I said, still stung by Lynn's distrust more than Heather's feet would ever hurt. "You didn't think I was thinking. I'm never doing that."

"But you're still not…" Lynn said, confused.

"Oh come on, just say it," Heather said. "He's still not a fighter, you're still worth ten of him. Don't feel bad about facts. Right Derek?"

"I mean…" I said, looking at Lynn. "I'm no Amadeus. But I shouldn't…"

"Shouldn't need two girls to fight your battles for you?" Heather said. "Swords cut both ways, so does truth."

"You think that?" Lynn said, looking disgusted. "Now? After everything we've been through, suddenly your ego can't take me standing up for you?"

"It's not that," I said, my mind spinning. "It's… just once… I can't say it, it would come out wrong."

"What would?" Lynn asked, not understanding.

I clenched my fists. I wanted… just once… I couldn't say it.

"See?" Heather said. "Not a fighter."

"We don't need fighters," Lynn said.

"Well…" Ollux said, raising a finger. "The boy says he has fight experience. We would of course be willing to have him in the cadet program. Derek, I don't know if learning to fight is something you've ever thought about—"

"I'll do it," I said, before blinking.

"You'll do nothing," Lynn said. "We're in pain right now. The pain of not being what we want, the pain of not having as much freedom as we'd like. But at least we can all be in pain together. That's how we fight, Derek. Look at what we learned right out of the ground for that together pain. A book of people."

"You mean the Vempire," Ollux said, her expression softening.

"I like them," Astor said to his sister. "They fight like family."

"Thinking we won't kill you is going to get you killed," Heather said, all danger. "We aren't family, we're… more… than meets the eye… damnit."

"I don't believe it," James said. "My own son just quoted Transformers to me. That's a failure on all systems. Take them away, now, please."

"That's something your father said," Lynn said, shocked. "Word for word."

"How did he do that?" I said, looking up at James, the bad feelings all back. "Isn't he hallucinating hard enough to block every nerve receptor in his body?"

"He is," Astor said. "He is one with the blueblood, his mind and body have been flung farther than the sun, to return with the moon."

We stared at him.

"It's twenty four hours of bliss, with a gradual return of mental and physical function, including the nervous system," Astor explained. "Means it'll wear off by nighttime. I have to say, I'm offended you didn't assume I was a doctor."

"Are you?" I asked.

"Of course not," Astor said.

"We didn't ask the cat that either," Lynn pointed out.

"Well if I'd known it was called the BLUEBLOOD!" I said to Lynn.

She growled at me. Like a cat.

The bridge was finally ending. We were somewhere far from the colosseum, heading for a circular platform around a thirty-foot-thick tree trunk. Going with the theme, I saw a single, circular house built into the side of the trunk, wood for the foundation and fabrics, pelts, and giant leaves covering the roof. It was a round robin treehouse in every sense of the word, just giant, and when the jungle bride ended, we followed Ollux and Astor right inside. Walls, roof, windows, it had it all, for a treehouse. The air was slightly smoky, as the single fire in the center of the thing filled up the wooden frame with an aura.

"It's a bug thing," Astor said. "I know there's no windows, that's on purpose. It's just the small bugs in here. The big ones—"

"Let me guess, they have their part of the jungle, you have yours?" I said.

Astor blinked at me. "Again, this guy."

"How did you know that?" Ollux said. "Have you been here before?"

"Metaphorically, absolutely," I said. "Why?"

James crutched down to us, and leaned against Ollux's shoulder. Uh oh.

"Speaking from the astral plane," James said. "We're good on the blueblood. It led us here. You can say all sorts of scary things about the Jerico, and you can say we were treated as strangers all the same, but don't deny that when the world gives you a teenager limping through the forest, you feel just a tiny bit of a call to heart. So thanks for helping a brother out. Sincerely. I sleep here?"

And it was the sanest thing we had heard from James yet, until he let go of his crutches and went to faceplant on the floor. Of course Heather caught him, slapped him twice, and put him back on the crutches. His eyes were still up in the clouds, avoiding us all. He probably thought he was talking to butterflies.

"You're delusional," Ollux said. "Derek, control your brother."

"Impossible," I said. "James, why do you hold onto quotes so hard?"

"Because you're not the only one who wants to be a writer one day," James said. "I'm still trying to figure out what makes something memorable, or not."

"I didn't know that," I said. "Did I ever ask?"

"No," James said, and I thought there would be more to it, but… no.

"Well… damn," Heather said.

"I know you're in there… but you're in there, right brother?" I asked quietly.

"Total recall, total honesty," Ollux said. "I'm not much for superstition, but I did wake up to voices this morning telling me to patrol the gates. Now I know for absolute certainty… that I'm still asleep."

"You aren't though," Heather said slowly.

"I'm getting a tribal, military-state mentality kinda vibe here," James said, whipping his head around. "Where feet?"

Circles. We were going in—

"Okay, we could use some help here," I said to Ollux and her brother.

"Welcome to the conversation," Ollux said. "James, on the ground. Astor, you got some leaves, a bucket of leftover banana peels, anything for his foot?"

"Um, I have blankets and pillows, like a regular person," Astor said, throwing a quilt at James. "Everyone sit down. If you want my help then I need yours. I need you to hold hands, and I need you to drink this."

"Yes have some," James said, reaching out for nothing.

Lynn smacked his hands away.

"We're not taking—" I started.

"It's rain water," Astor said. "It's traditional, something about it out blues the blood. It does taste like shoes though. James is the lucky one, he's still got a half-day of taste-bud blocking shroom-juice in his blood."

"Why you gotta say it like that?" I said, blanching.

"It's also blocking every pain receptor in his body," Astor said. "Worth it?"

"Yes but I'm angry about it," I said.

"And everybody knows," Astor said, a hand on my shoulder.

I simmered down, and Ollux's brother handed us all small clay cups. Heather grabbed his and switched it with hers. Astor smiled and drank first from the cup that would be Heather's, no hold back, no surrender. I was planning on holding out, until I saw James had downed his before I could knock it out of his hands.

"James," I sighed.

"What'd I do?" He asked, looking at me so innocently…

"Nothing," I said. "You good brother?"

"Good brother," he said, turning away, his eyes back in the sky. Or ceiling.

"This is on you," I said to Astor. "We've never needed this before. He's not himself, he's not connected to the truth of the universe, I'd know it."

"But you wouldn't know it," Astor said.

"I would," I said. "I'd figure it out. I'd ask him something neither of us know. James, which one of us is older?"

"I know," James said. "I heard Mom talking with Ms. Roberts about it in first grade. I just forgot it. Should I remember it?"

What.

"No," I said, almost stumbling away. "No, d-don't remember it."

"Okay," James said simply, eyes back in the sky (ceiling).

"For Vema?" Heather said, testing the room, eyeing me the entire time.

But I only saw Astor. Because I hadn't stopped staring at him. What in the…

"On you," I said, holding my cup up for his.

He switched with me without a word, just a nod, his face never faltering…

And we both drank. Bleh.

It did taste like water, just water from old shoes. And just as it was my turn to fall down, some weird energy came over me, flowing from my brother on my left to Heather on my right, and through Lynn on her right. Ollux was tumbling away from us in fear, but Astor had thrown his hand out to Lynn's on the hard wood… before something deflected his hand away at the last moment.

"Um… they're glowing," Ollux said. "Are they supposed to glow?"

Apparently the four of us were… yeah.

"The circle is complete," Astor said, mesmerized. "But it's not. I was supposed to bridge the final gap."

"Then explain Lynn and James both having an empty hand," Ollux said.

"I can't," Astor said.

"We're missing a piece," James said. "Easy answer, someone's razor—"

"James…" I said. "How could you forget which one of us is older?"

"There's other stuff in my brain right now," James said. "But... we were six. Things were lost early, brother. You know this."

"You can't just drop that," Lynn said, blinking, even Heather had her hands over her mouth. "Derek... are you okay?"

"Are you serious?" I said, completely locked onto James. "Can I trust you like this? This is worse than drunk brother. I hate this. Astor get him out."

"I can't," Astor said, the aura in the room spinning. "You started the journey without me, now I can only help from the outside. But from my non-glowing perspective... there's something here more important than learning to fight, more important than the Vempire, hell, even more important than the Jerico—at least, to James."

"Is that true?" Lynn asked.

"Of course it is," James said, his eyes blank, but his body strong.

I froze. This day, I swear to tree...

"Enough," I started. "This isn't about our mother. And this isn't about—"

"Derek," James said, his voice like a prophecy writing itself on my face. "Can you remember every detail of our lives back in the first week of us turning eight? Can you remember everything that happened that night?"

"I mean..." I said. "No. I'm almost nineteen. That happened over ten years ago, and there's a layer of trauma over the trauma. Why, can you?"

"Yes," James said, ominously.

"You wanna go there?" I asked him.

The group waited for his answer. But what we got... was it that?

"I am James," he said.

That was no answer. I held back tears. I didn't like this. We had a throughline to my brother's inner conscience, and we were pulling on that cord blindly, trying to get answers out of the only one of us incapable of doing the only thing I'd want to do in his situation. Run away.

"What is he talking about?" Lynn asked gently.

"He's talking about the girl in the parachute," I said, racking my brain, the memory super fuzzy for some reason. "He's talking about the thing we don't bring up in front of James."

"Well James is out to lunch at the moment, bring a memory up," Ollux said.

"NO!" I shouted. "I'm ending this, it's not going down this way! Unplug my brother RIGHT NOW, OR I'LL—"

"It doesn't work that way," Astor said. "You can try to stop the wave and crash upon your brother like rocks, or you can ride this one with him."

"I'm okay," James said, and the tone of his voice was what got me. It was completely content. "I need the fear to be in the past. I want this."

"I..." I said, shook. "I'm here for you brother."

"You weren't that night," he said, out of nowhere.

"The night of the Blitz?" Astor asked.

"You're paying attention," James said, saluting Astor with his left hand, the bandages over his wrist clear to see.

Everything stop, full stop, all stop. What was happening? I hated this. I wanted a way out. Please, someone stronger than me, stop this.

"My first memories were of the girl in the parachute. It was also the night my mother turned into a superhero. But I remember first waking up with the explosions. Boom—"

And like the universe had heard me, the flaps to the tent flew open and Crete Magellan stood poking his upper body into the circle, seeing us on the floor of a drug-hut, holding hands and glowing all sorts of weird colors. Thank—

"WHAT ARE YOU DOING?" he shouted, stunned, holding his hands out.

I was more relieved than ever before… until the shame hit.

"Arcana," Astor said quickly, bowing his head. "You honor me."

"Honor nothing, kids, what am I seeing?" Crete demanded. "When a guy has a broken leg, you don't go to the spirit shaman, you go to the HOSPITAL! Stop glowing this instant. I said stop it."

"I don't know how!" Lynn cried, waving her arms.

"You have their host's apologies," Ollux said. "I am charged with showing them through our city. Brother Astor is our temple expert on psychoactives. He's doing for James' mind right now what the doctors will do to his body in less than an hour."

"I appreciate the outreach, but let's switch those two," Crete said. "That way, James will have some conscious say over a bunch of hands inside his mind. You know all about consent, right doctor? And speaking of proper doctoring, whose idea was it to stick a radiated jungle mushroom in the twin, Derek?"

"A leopard told me to do it," I said, wincing.

"You LET a leopard tell you to do it," Crete corrected. "Just like you are LETTING these two tell you not to go to the hospital."

"The job of the pack," Heather said, hanging her head.

The logic was solid. We had a responsibility to James, and well, it hadn't gone great so far. We picked our guilty asses up and gravitated towards Crete in the doorframe. Ollux tried to join us but Crete held up a hand, then walked all four of us out of that round robin. He made a quick finger to the lips motion as we walked out on that wide radius of a tree platform. The possibilities were endless. High, low, swinging vines in between, paths were paths.

"Man, I was just about to tell them everything!" James complained, loudly.

"That's exactly what they wanted," Crete said as he stormed us over to a wooden walkway facing a grouping of massive multi-leveled structures carved into a collection of trees to our right. "We don't even know everything going on in that head of yours, and you wanna give it away to tree people? In this state?"

"Which state?" James asked. "Cal… California?"

"Don't mention California in front of me. James, keep your mouth—and brain—closed for one second. I can't believe you would eat something so foreign. I can't believe how mad I am. I also can't believe how hungry I am."

Crete took a weird lumpy piece of red fruit out of his pocket.

"Double standard," I said, pointing at the strange fruit.

"This is an apple," Crete said, taking a bite. "It goes in, it comes out. What you've done to James… here's a hint. If a plant is BIOLUMINESCENT—"

"We know, that's why we're headed for help," I explained. "They say we won a doctor, they didn't say what kind."

"I forgot teenagers always think they're invincible," Crete sighed. "You lucky bones are lucky bones heal on their own."

"Hey man," Lynn said (for me).

"We're in Jerico!" Crete said, hands in the air. "You just HAD to land us in the garden, didn't you?"

"You dumped us out the ship, we did what we had to!" I shouted, a bit hot.

"I get that," Crete said. "I get most of what you've been through. I'm just confused as to your decision to take decision from a talking leopard."

"How do you know everything, after doing nothing?" Lynn complained.

"Wow, doing nothing, okay—you know what, I'm letting that one go," Crete said, folding his arms. "Secondly, OF COURSE I KNOW EVERYTHING! We all saw it. I can only assume the cat found you in the forest, took pity on James, and led you to the animal version of homeopathy and a shortcut to the gates. Oh, and Lynn developed a strong bond with it along the way and saying goodbye was harder than she thought it would be. Am I wrong?"

"Nope," Lynn said, blinking fast, almost sucking the tear back up into her eyes. "You catch up fast. And you never do nothing. Sorry."

"You don't apologize to me beanbug," Crete said. "Alright, Zack and Cody. What do you know about a garden?"

"Nothing," I said, then I blinked. "Wait."

"Roasted," Crete said.

My hands went up. Lynn and Heather laughed their heads off as we walked.

"Sorry not sorry," Crete said. "We had to pull every favor left to keep our heads after the Refugee crashed. Your welcome ceremony was peanuts of what it should have been. The crutches went a long way, good looking out James."

"Helping!" he said, as optimistic as a kid on crutches could be.

"It wasn't planned," I said.

That was an understatement. I looked at my brother on hair-tied wooden walking sticks for crutches, on a rough wooden path on the upside of a TREE TRUNK, keeping up with us like this was normal, all hundreds of feet above the ground because reasons. This was not normal. This was either jungle madness, or I was more of a city kid than I realized. I think it was that thought, the sleepless city, that made me realize.

"There's no lights," I said. "Not in the colosseum, not in that round house, not here, nowhere."

"About time," Crete said.

"I thought it was storm season," Lynn said, not understanding.

"Storms end," I said. "But..."

"Tis but another city, no?" James asked.

"Not exactly," Crete said. "I thought you knew."

"Knew what Crete?" I asked, a pit in my stomach as deep as the Vempire...

"That for as long as we've lived on this island, the Jerico people have lived without electricity," he said, simply.

"For the whole summer?" I asked.

"For the whole year," Crete said. "Every year."

"Without electricity..." I said, blinking, my hands on my head. "I never knew there were people here living without…"

"The sun?" Heather said, sharply.

"I thought I fixed that one," I said, like I had touched a nerve. "I suppose this is where you tell me my father is behind the thunder and lightning too?"

"This part of the island pre-dates him," Crete said.

"Good on you though," Heather offered, white in the face.

I growled, but I was grateful to be on the sidelines for once. Maybe we wouldn't draw all the attention this time. Maybe, just maybe, we wouldn't find out that the burying of an entire nation was our father's fault, again.

But let's be honest we probably would.

"So you know the Vema powers don't work here, because… neither do you," Heather asked, like we were being watched (we probably were).

"It's not a secret," Crete said. "You think saying the word microwave will break the spell? These people don't chose to live here without electricity. Well some do actually—"

"I thought, you know, season implied a change of season," I said, logically.

"Nope, all time, everyday storms, welcome to Jerico," Crete said. "The only good thing is the worst thing. The Infinite source can't reach our sensors. The Reaper crystal cannot read this magnetic map. We are powerless, but safe, if that's what we're calling it. The only power that remains in Jerico is the Astral."

"The Astral," I said. "I've heard that thrice now. What is it?"

"A strong story of long people," Crete said. "Switch those. Let's see how much we can get through before Sand finds us. Should I start at the beginning?"

I could have cried. "That's… all I've ever wanted. No distractions, just go."

"Great," Crete said. "As you know—JAMES!"

He was faltering on his crutches, as a weird vibe came over his movements. I could see it coming, it was a shutdown. He collapsed forward, falling face-first towards the hard wooden planks like he had in front of Heather ten times already today, but this time, she was farther away than I was. I was the only one to see what was happening, too far from my brother to catch him this time…

Until Ollux appeared from the underside of the tree and caught his head in her hands, taking a harder slam than James had, but keeping a brother's head from whiplashing into the ground. She winced, checked James to make sure he wasn't dead, just unconscious, and looked up at us from the ground.

She gave a thumbs up.

"Thank you," I said, always polite.

"Maybe you were right about that hospital," Ollux said. "Red roof, go!"

1.8

A SENSE OF COMMAND

Into the ocean.

That's how I'd felt ever since the mushroom. My body knew enough to stick around those blurry shapes of friends, but my mind was stuck on a view of the blue, only marred by the giant, iron bars that blocked the wide window.

My body experienced the things they took me through—Derek climbing up the cliffs with me on his back, the gates that rose higher than anything but the trees, that dumb colosseum game—but the entire time, my mind was stuck in supermax. Pink Panel. Whatever Infinite called the only prison I'd ever been in. I could feel the others by my sides, but I couldn't quite see them, couldn't really communicate with them, just like that cell. I was blocked by some dark curtain of what was and wasn't real, by whatever midnight hands put me here. The worst part wasn't that I couldn't tell the difference. The worst part was… I had been here before. My mind was open, farther than usual, and the last few times this had happened, something had gotten in.

I was starting to be afraid.

I had seen and heard too much in the last month. I had grown accustomed to talking to the artificial intelligence program in my car. That was weird. I knew what it was like to hear my friends in my brain, not my ears. That was crazy. I had heard the dark earth of the underland say my name, realizing now that it was a cautionary warning from the triplet siblings controlling those dirt drones—even crazier. I'd say impossible, but I had heard something else in the Vempire, something leader Reya the Red had called the ancients. The dragon eyes, the disembodied voice in the cave. The statues of all those people, glowing different colors for reasons (probably). And then the girl in the middle of it all. Breaking down that wall between over and underland… it had done more than open one side to another. It had taken more. There had been something in between. Something forgotten. Something… ancient, maybe only to me. What would you call that, if not insane? If insanity wasn't the answer, if all those things were part of the question then… what on earth kind of answer would it take for this to make sense?

While my body made its way to Jerico, my mind was searching for the answer, but all my eyes could see was prison, only a single answer away from the ocean—yet the moment I thought that, a big island bird caught itself on the bars, wrapping its talons and tail around the iron. There was blood and light blue fabric on one of its daggers for fingers. My blood.

"It's you," I heard myself say. "It has to be you."

This time when I reached for those prison window bars, they disappeared, and the bird latched back onto my left hand. I felt the pain, right where the bird had cut me for real. But I winced, manned up, and held steady.

"Sorry," I said. "I meant… caw."

"Good," the voice in the dark replied, because of course.

No, it wasn't the Oracle.

"It's time. Where are you?"

"She asked, like I have any physical control over what's happening to my body right now," I said sarcastically, channeling my brother.

"You have all the control of the mind," she said. *"Use it. Look around."*

And suddenly the view outside those bars changed. The iron was still there, vertical obstacles, but I caught a look through to what must have been my physical body, barely held up between Derek and Heather, as Crete and Lynn were shouting to others on various branches and bridges, watching tall, bronzed warriors land from swinging vines into what should have been bone-breaking jumps left and right. They took me from my brother and Heather, holding me amongst at least four of them, with another two just for my broken foot, towards a building with a big red roof.

"That's going to hurt to face," I said, warning myself.

"Most broken things are," the voice came. *"But you can't heal from something that didn't hurt you."*

"She says, to the boy having an internal conversation with his ten year old trauma, still very much unresolved," I said, again sarcastic.

"Well we haven't faced each other yet," the voice came. *"You can handle me, right?"*

I took a breath. "I think the answer you're looking for is… yes?"

"Yes James. Now where are you?"

I turned back out the window, looking past the bird, and watched my procession down a bridge that expanded as it descended until coming to an eight sided building, doctors and nurses running out with what looked like a gurney. Not a tree-made one, I saw metal, there were rubber wheels and clean blankets and everything. And right beside the tall nurses, there was a younger girl running with them. A girl with blonde hair, kind eyes, the worry and ability clear as day in her eyes… she was definitely a doctor. She even looked like Ana.

But I knew it wasn't her.

"Jerico Territory," I heard myself say. "Look for… a big red roof."

"See you soon. Make sure they're ready for me."

"I can hardly tell an entire civilization what to do," I said, again sarcastically.

"You've done it before," was her answer. *"I kind of need you to keep doing it. That is, if you still want to be friends."*

"Girls," I said, shaking my head. "Always projecting their astral forms through impossible distances, asking teenage cavemen to help outsmart cities."

The voice laughed. *"You're not a caveman, James. You're the opposite. You're the future."*

That was too much. I felt too much. Wait a minute, I could feel my legs again, and the PAIN—yep, this was gonna suck.

The prison cell warped, the images beyond that window were rushed into me and broke against my face. I had left the mind prison and was slowly entering my own body again or something, it was very physical. The hallucinogens were wearing off, and the pain was coming back. I was in a weird limbo, able to duck back into the psychoactive side of it for just a bit longer, feeling the ability to block out the pain of my own body. Was I a demigod? No, I was just on pain medicine. I hated things messing with my brain, but I hated pain too.

I didn't want to stay in that mind prison… so why was I holding on to it?

"You don't belong here," the last words of the girl in the parachute spoke to me. *"Go. I'll find you."*

"Again," I said.

Instantly I was back. I had a headache and a weird, fuzzy memory of my brother and friends in some dodgy opium den—wait, that couldn't be right. I was on my back on some sort of rolling bed, and there were three hands on my two shoulders. My brother, and friends—except not, and it was just pillows. Weird. My brain knew to feel for it before the nerves knew to fire… but once they did…

"Why foot?" I said, groggily.

I winced at the raging pain in my leg—that was only half as bad as last time. There was a small white splint around it, and it wasn't even propped up.

"Hold on," came a voice on the opposite side of the room.

I turned left to see Sand and Crete sitting at a small coffee table next to a window. They had a chess set in between them, and Sand was staring intensely down at the board.

"Hold… on?" I asked slowly, blinking.

"It's check," Sand said.

He'd spoke without even looking at me, eyes digging burrows into Crete's, and he moved his queen without looking down at the board either. Crete shook his head and moved his rook sideways, without breaking eye contact with Sand.

"Now it's checkmate."

Sand roared and there was a glint of metal in his hand, as a small sword swung across the board, cutting every chess piece perfectly in half. The tops of the pieces hit the board like rain. Crete didn't look surprised, he only took his half of a rook and knocked over Sand's already cut down king.

"I'll take care of it," Sand said.

"You… pieces… of…" I said, each word a whole thing.

"Hello James," Sand said, sword stowed, all manners back. "You survived."

"Shengcun," I said through clenched teeth.

But as the anger rose, it withered, because just then Derek walked into the room and tossed something at Sand.

"Here's the superglue, mister princess. Still don't know what you need it for, you're just lucky this hospital is stocked as—"

Then Derek saw me sitting upright in the medical bed. "Shengcun."

"Just happened," Crete said. "If you take the honors… I can keep sitting."

"He's back," Derek said to himself, then he wheeled on Sand and Crete. "You've been very lax about our mortal coils ever since we escaped from super prison. James, hell yes. Everyone else GET IN HERE!"

And as Sand bent over the chessboard with his very important superglue, everyone else arrived. I struggled to sit up, Derek ran to lock the gurney upright as I did. His short shorts were gone, replaced with a slim tan shirt and long pants, the same material I had seen those tree people wearing in my coma dreams, but he still had leaves in his hair. I probably did too. Then Lynn and Heather ran in holding scissors, wearing the same, although it looked like they'd been in the middle of some alterations. A sleeve hung half-cut from Lynn's shoulder, and Heather's shorts were different lengths on either side of the knee.

"Are you still in loonyland?" Heather demanded. "Say something normal, right now."

"Coffee," I said, yawning without moving the right side of my body. The pain was sleeping, but if I moved, it woke. "This day has been a long week."

"He's back," Derek said.

"Rage," Heather said, her eyes doing something weird. "I'm not sure about the service in this jungle though."

"This jungle? Where kona coffee grows?" A tall, tan warrior woman standing behind Lynn said. "I could drop four hundred year's knowledge of the bean on your head, but James has been through hell, so I'll be civil. Hot or cold?"

I frowned at her. I realized there were people in this room I did not know personally, but that I recognized from the window I had watched my body through. I think that was the same young woman who had taken my friends on, one on one. The one who had only stopped trying to kill Heather once the claws came out. Who had gotten Lynn at her absolute worst, only for Lynn to find another way to bend nature around her. Who had my brother dead to rights before he had wielded his mind instead of a weapon, and not out-smarted, but definitely out-thought Jerico's welcome party. The crutches were only meant to be a weapon for Derek to use; after all, he'd made them. Turns out the blueblood made you a pro at spear throwing.

"Ground control to agent Nite?" The woman asked, frowning.

"I'm not an agent," I said, blinking.

"He means three of each, just to be sure," Derek cut in for me. "Thanks."

The woman I thought was Ollux sighed, bowed to us, and left. Sand and Crete hadn't even reacted to her either. I was missing something. Like, a day.

"Who was that?" I asked.

"No?" Heather asked. "Dig deep Jimmy, find us a brain blast—"

"O… Ollux?" I said. "Our Jerico host, and also mortal enemy number one?"

"Nah, we're done fighting," Derek said. "That was just a test. Like the day we met Sand, remember?"

"I remember," I said. "Derek, am I going to die in treehouse world?"

"We live three hundred feet up, you think a broken leg's a first? Really?"

The confident voice had come from a younger woman coming into the room. She was semi-dark skinned, wearing an open white hospital gown, nothing but that brown fabric in strips over her chest and waist underneath. Her brown hair was held back in a ponytail by a thin, ornate wooden block.

"Ana," I said, seeing the doctor we had lost in this one, just for a moment.

"I'm flattered," the doctor said. "But no. I'm no Ana Sun."

"Different Ana," Derek said quietly.

"Oh, well I'm an ass," the doctor said. "I'll stop assuming, if you do too."

"Fair," I said, nodding. "Do me right, doc."

"I already did. I just told you to stop assuming, literally two seconds ago."

"Oh you're good," I said.

The doctor smiled. "You managed to fracture your ankle connector, the lowest part of the fibula. Technically that's a leg bone, but the break was localized, and all we had to do was set your foot so the bones will fuse naturally—in the right direction now, of course. I've applied a local morphine, and due to the complete lack of protrusion, only a soft splint is required, no chemical casting necessary, the nerves in your foot will thank you for that. You won't run for weeks, but recovery is guaranteed, up to ninety-nine percent of the original function."

"Talk about good news for once," Derek said, sighing in relief. But—

I was shook. Ninety-nine percent? What had I just lost one percent of? ME?

"I won't run for weeks," I repeated, making sure I wasn't still in loonyland. "And that's good news?"

"Your leg will heal," the doctor said, looking at the bandages on my left wrist like she was proud of her work, or something. "So will that. Next time you parachute, you should think about someone catching you."

"I always am!" I cried, the thought too close to home.

"You're gonna be fine," Heather assured me. "And if you're not in pain, can I ask what exactly your problem is with parachutes?"

"NO!" I said, too distraught to see the look Derek was shooting at the girls. Or maybe I did see it and just didn't know why.

"Okay then can we at least laugh about all the things you said on mushrooms?" Heather asked.

"What are you talking about?" I frowned.

"Oh nothing," Derek smirked, but seemingly glad to change the subject. "Just one question. Are you, by chance, my daughter?"

"What?" I said. "Who said that? I said that?"

"An animal in pain is no laughing matter," Lynn scolded us, shooting daggers to the doctor.

"He was hilarious," the doctor said. "I know that's unprofessional… too bad. Bring him back in a week, other than that, the bones will heal no matter what the rest of the boy does, except walk. I believe these are your new best friends."

And the doctor moved aside so I could see two wooden crutches waiting for me by the door. I grimaced, thinking of all the ways we had seen a half-explained, super-convenient healing technology deployed in front of our stupid teenage faces. Now they were all just gone? Really? NOW?

"No shortcuts," the doc said, reading my brain like braille. "You need time to become complete again, James Nite. But it's a beautiful day, so do it outside."

"Thanks doc," I said. "You remind me of a good person I used to know."

"High praise," the doctor said, bowing to us one last time, the first to duck out the door. She took one last look at the slapped together wooden sticks for crutches. "Also who made these?"

Lynn, Heather and Derek put their hands up.

"Not bad," she said. "I'm Claire, by the way. Just wanted to let you know that I've got a name, a backstory, a favorite color and everything. It's—"

"Thanks Claire," came the us chorus.

Claire was gone. Heather closed the door and picked up the crutches.

"As a new old friend says, we go, and now," Heather said, throwing me the crutches like the soldier I was.

I caught them, one of them at least, gave her a nod, and pushed my feet off the bed—and instantly regretted everything.

"AAH!"

I (sort of) gracefully braced for the pain that seared from my ankle to toe (all of them), every part of my leg, up to the knee. It was just pressure. Unrelenting, building, impossible to ignore pressure. My eyes only saw darkness, because they were shut tight. I waited it out and the building stopped, the wave releasing, just far too slowly. Finally my eyes opened, and I realized I had clenched up like a clam in front of everyone, my fingers making dents in the soft, still wet wood of the crutches. The room was staring at me.

"Okay, we go, and slow," Heather said, correcting herself.

"So besides all that… how we feeling?" Derek asked.

"I'm all here," I said. "Only… I don't remember getting here."

"What do you remember?" Lynn asked.

"Besides everything?" I said, sarcastically. "I'll start and end that with a glowing blue mushroom."

"Well we got what we paid for there, didn't we?" Heather said. "Lynn didn't even have to twist your wrist. You were a hungry boy."

"I just wanted to not be in pain," I admitted, looking down to the bandages on my wrist, the memory coming back—a bird tearing through what I'd thought was an impenetrable suit of Infinite super armor and making me bleed at ten thousand feet. "Nice. But—"

"Ten stitches," Lynn said, smacking my hand as I reached for the bandages. "Don't look, let it set."

"Ten—blast you, bird!" I said, outraged, then not so much. "Whatever. That scar better be symbolic."

"It probably is, our track record, you know," Lynn said, nodding, Derek joining her, his face emotionless. Facts. "Didn't Issaic break your hand on the force field? I thought I heard something crack."

"You did," I said in disbelief. "Whatever you and Heather and the Vema did to us was so effective that I forgot about that. Now I'm going to be out for the rest of the summer. It's funny, I didn't wake up today thinking I would give up the ability to walk."

"You didn't," Heather said. "Derek watch that side, James get up. You can walk without superpowers, I'll force it out of you."

"I believe you," I said with a smile.

Now that the weight of my leg was already vertical, I took up the crutches and pushed myself upright. I felt more of a burn from where I could tell the stitches were, both on my wrist and ankle. They'd done something through skin, I could tell, and not in a good way. It was all the wrong kinds of pulling. Ew.

"You've still got that big brain of yours," Lynn said, trying to help. "We aren't giving up anything. We're safe. For now."

"For here," I said. "Jerico, the place we didn't need to talk about?"

"To be fair, you missed a bit," Derek said, scratching his head. "And we were about to get a bit of a catchup out of Crete when you toppled like timber."

"Okay so here's the part where we pick it all up on our own leisure," I said, not understanding the problem. "Didn't we come all this way for—"

"Yeah Crete, back to it," Derek said. "As we know—"

"That was four hours ago," Crete said. "Now, well we have an appointment."

"With what?" Derek asked. "Who do you owe anything to more than us?"

"How about the king of Jerico?" Sand said, finally joining us.

"You say that like it's not… stupid," Derek said.

Sand shrugged. "You're right. No one calls him king, it's capo here. Right?"

We looked around, each wondering if Sand was asking us.

"I brought coffee," Ollux almost sang as she came back into the room, pressing a cup of hot (or cold) black and tan coffee into each of our confused hands. "What'd I miss?"

"That's the best damn coffee I've ever had," Sand said.

It was the truth.

"Rosebud cocoa… and underwater truffle?" Crete said, sniffing his glass.

"Two out of five," Ollux said, nodding. "I tell you more, I have to kill you."

"I won't die for beans," Crete said.

"And we'd hate to keep a capo waiting," Sand said, bowing.

"Caput," Ollux said. "We aren't mobsters, we are what James calls shengcun, in human form. You are Kapyushon, a french word for the hood."

"You just spoke Latin, French, and Portuguese right there," Lynn said.

"I speak six languages, most here do," Ollux said.

"And without the internet?" Lynn said, amazed.

"What is internet?" Ollux asked.

We only stared.

"I'm kidding," she said. "But also not. I hope you see by now that Jerico is not a digital space. We are a single family, made up of every kind of person there is or used to be. We are survivors, living among the forest for the good of land and man, guided by our commanding family Caput Manus."

"That translates to The Head of the Hand," Crete said, looking down at the three of us kids. "I can tell no one brought gum."

"What's gum?" Ollux asked.

She was hard to read.

"I knew I forgot something—the caput is going to have to meet you tomorrow. He was called to help subdue the forest fires caused by what I believe you arrived in—or tried to, at least. You will meet the survivors of the Ravenna crash site tomorrow. I'm here to show you to—"

"Let me guess, the guest house," I said.

"Yep, nailed it, follow me," Ollux said, turning out the doorway, but seeing the coffee table and the chess board with a sword slash through it. "What happened to chess?"

"I fixed them," Sand said.

"Yes but you've glued the tops of dark pieces to the bottoms of white pieces," Ollux said. "Who's going to be able to tell one side from the other?"

"I like them better this way," Sand said simply.

It landed like a challenge. Ollux glared. Sand did not care.

We walked outside the hospital—meaning the group in front of me walked, and I continued to crutch, my armpits suddenly very aware of how sore they were. Still, it was only day one. I knew by day three I would have the muscles and calluses I needed, like a reverse sunburn. We emptied out in front of that huge red roof, and for some reason, the first thing I did was tilt my head back and stare up at the canopy. I was expecting something. I saw nothing. That didn't mean there was nothing up there. I smiled to the unassuming forest.

"Soon," I said to the sky.

"Should we turn around?" Derek asked.

"No need," I said, bringing my eyes down. "I'm good."

"No more pentagrams in the dirt, and I'll believe it."

"I did that?" I asked, blinking.

"You did a lot of weird stuff," Derek said. "You also... said something. About which one of us was older. Do you remember that?"

"I remember that the answer was right there," I said. "It was like a light, at the end of an ocean—or the bottom of the sea, same thing I guess. I remember... all the things that were left to remember. I couldn't latch onto much. But when I heard your voice, it directed me straight to the part of my brain that held the answer to what you wanted to know."

"I didn't know it worked that way," Derek said, blinking. "You said you heard Mrs. Roberts talking with our mother in first grade. What happened at the light at the end of the ocean?"

"I never got there," I said, sighing. "You told me not to, so I... turned back."

"I... didn't know it worked that way," Derek said, broken record.

"That's the truth, I'm not—"

"I believe you," Derek said. "I just asked the first throw-away question I could think of, and you turned it into another falloff. Do you care which one—"

"Not enough to go back in and find out, no," I said, honestly.

"Are you mad I kept you from it?"

"Are you kidding?" I said. "I'm keeping you from it. You aren't mad at me?"

"Never," Derek said. "We were kids. Come on man."

"Come on man," I said, nodding.

"You don't care about ways to reach into your brain in search of memories?" Sand asked as we moved.

"That can't be possible," I said, shaking my head.

"Have you MET me?" Crete said.

"Not really," I said honestly. "Not yet."

"Then don't doubt what a man of science can do, even in a world without it," Crete said. "Also, Odd was two seconds from using my super satellite to do the same, rest in pieces. Twice now I have watched manipulating forces try to get inside the memories of the Nite twins, sons to the founder of Infinite himself and Teresa, crippled in the Blitz under bizarre circumstances. Clearly Astor and Ollux are not the only ones on this island who want what's in your head."

"Right what was that?" I asked. "They tried to what, drug me? Again?"

"They didn't get far," Lynn said. "Crete went full nuclear dad mode, and understandably. You saw smoke coming out the window, the tapestries, okay we *were* sitting cross legged in a circle..."

"When was this?" Sand asked, immediately curious.

"I found them at brother Astor's hut, with their most gracious host Ollux."

"Oh that's no worry then," Sand said.

"It's not?" Crete said. "Ollux and Astor clearly brought them there to take advantage of the twin in a hallucinogenic state. They were willing to open the brain of James, after knowing him for only an hour, what kind of friend does that? Are you not even at all concerned?"

"I would be," Sand said. "If I were a matter of securing the territory."

"Maybe we are," Derek said, trying to be flip.

"Is that what you want to be?" Sand said, folding his arms at Derek.

"I... don't know," Derek said honestly. "Are you what you want to be?"

Sand's eyes softened. "Not even a little. But also, all considered, absolutely."

"Scarecrow," I complained, my hands both pointing in completely opposite directions. "So what's the deal? Are you and Crete from here?"

"Our mothers were," Crete said, sounding nostalgic. "Both of our fathers were born in Silka, both of our mothers grew up as not only friends in the territory, but warriors of Astral as well. They are our common denominator. And luckily, they were both as adventurous and fearless, living in a time on this island when the borders between nations were highways, not walls. I have been to Jerico a hundred times. Sand?"

"A hundred and one," Sand said. "It's been a while since I stayed the night, but I do remember the lake trips, the hikes, summer camp in the woods, the travel days to and from Silka, leaving all electricity behind at the magnetic fault lines... memories."

"So the internet's been down for how long?" I asked.

"All the long," Crete said. "Some say Jerico Territory was born in the magnetic black hole, being such an impossible option for the more modern settlers that they all gravitated to Mylo or Silka. But there were still those of the original settlers who wanted to start over, sticks and stones, a life without roofs, living under the stars you know? There were more people willing to throw their phones into the oceans than you would have thought."

"I would ask you to explain every word of what you just said," I said, blinking.

"Then, there are those who say Jerico was as functional as the other parts of the island at maintaining electric currents," Crete said, ignoring me completely. "Some ancestors tell stories of the first hundred years on the island, and how Jerico was advancing faster than even Silka. Some say the city was about to be the first to reach total energy efficiency, when the dark clouds first came from the north. Some say it was the Jerico themselves who ripped a hole in the magnetic field of the earth by putting up a city so quick, some say it was the jealousy of the lightning city and a secret, ancient control over all things electric that was cradled in Silka and deployed in all lands beyond their city."

"Well which one was it?" I demanded.

"It doesn't matter," Sand said.

"It does if it's the second," Heather said, alarmed.

"The beauty of this place has surpassed its past," Sand said. "If you don't believe me…"

Then in answer, the world thumped around us. We all heard it.

"What on earth…" Heather said, her arms dropping to her sides forgotten.

"You will," Sand said, smiling.

It was eyes staring at us. I thought we had been hundreds of feet above the ground, but we had traveled into Jerico enough that the rising lands of the north started catching up with the perfectly leveled world of wood they had up here in the trees. We were only twenty feet above the ground now, thanks to the panther patrol for the warning, NOT—but it wasn't a panther in front of us. It was a wrinkled, grey like dead coral, and absolutely massive elephant. No tusks, just ears bigger than my CRV and a trunk that may as well have been a tree. Its eyes were the size of softballs, not exactly fitting the rest of the creature's dimensions, but it looked at us with something between fear and respect.

No one made a move. The elephant kept moving, down the trees and bridges, until it stopped at a woman laughing and leaning over a balcony with a stalk of grass like a fishing pole. The woman raised her cup and sat down, having breakfast with the elephant, leaning over the balcony for pets and everything.

"There's an elephant on my island," Heather said, blinking.

"A dwarf elephant," Sand said, nodding.

"Those are—" Heather exclaimed, too happy to hide it.

"They are," Sand said smiling. "Most living things grow at ratio to their environment. If these wonderful things just had a bigger fishbowl…"

"The jungles of Jerico are vast, but the island is bigger," Lynn said. "They have a bigger fishbowl. Why can't they use it?"

"Because that would require peace between nations, something called agreed upon diplomacy, or just a willingness to not kill each other for like a second," Crete said, pushing his imaginary glasses up. "On this island, all three of those are rarer than elephants, and likely to go extinct first."

"Damn," I said. "Way to start a thing with some doom."

"You were born to doom, you just didn't know it," Crete said.

"Damn!" I complained, Heather, Lynn and Derek joining me this time.

Even the elephant let out a noise like a small horn, like *come on man*.

"Yes Crete, what else would you like to tell them?" Sand said. "By all means keep breaking every internal safeguard the two of us put into place before we started on this incredibly perilous path."

"You were the one who cracked a bottle of champagne the moment we started, you said a thing will either make its way to a target or not, either way drink!" Crete roared. "I won't get far for superfriends if you keep insisting that two sixty year olds can do this without help."

"Do what without help?" Lynn asked.

"We can," Sand said, ignoring her.

"Can what?" Heather asked.

"Then why are they here?" Crete demanded, pointing at us.

"Us?" I said, pointing at my brother and me.

Sand looked us over. "Not just them. Infinite will have our faces pasted on every street corner. The City of Silka now has a most wanted list, and it stops at six. Us six. That's why we're here. We can't be there."

We suddenly were looking at the trees with a much more… permanent feeling in mind.

"I would say we should have stayed in Vema," Heather said, blinking. "But from a distraction—or dystopian—perspective… we were very loud about going north. Infinite know we're here, don't they?"

"They can't trace us, unless they can," Sand said. "But yes. They watched us pass the line. Not a single agent was dumb enough to follow. Unless they were."

"Come on man," I said.

Sand only looked off at that woman and the elephant having breakfast.

"We can't bring our problems here," he said. "We can maybe hide from them long enough to be ready when they come knocking, and believe me they will, but we can't afford collateral damage. Not here."

"You getting sentimental or something?" I teased. "Or is this that side of life, side of the island thing you were talking about?"

"Let's just say the Jerico live for their family, and die for no one," Sand said. "If we end up on the wrong side of this nation, in this state, we're done."

"Done?" I asked.

"Dead," Sand said. "I should have been more clear. For all our fighting, to this day there has never been a single Astral killed in action. The warriors here grew up without computers, do you know what that means? For every moment you ever spent reading of superheroes, they were outside climbing trees with their bare feet. In combat, Lynn is worth ten of a twin, but here, even she is only… whatever a warrior minus a leopard is. You will die here, James, unless you find a way not to. That goes for all of us. Everybody ready?"

"To… die?" Derek asked, blinking.

"No," Crete said. "For the opposite."

Suddenly there was something hitting us in the face. Sunlight. Kind of.

The sea of greens swatches and brown barks above us (an endless canopy, just think rainforest, EVERYWHERE) had a break coming up, one that would be impossible to see unless you were underneath it. That's where we were heading, and when we got there, the forest broke, our eyes adjusted, and we were staring down at solid ground below, clear blue sky above.

"Now that's land," Derek said.

"Big smiles," Crete said, almost cautionary.

We were somewhere. A civilized somewhere. As in…

"About time," Ollux called up to us fondly.

It was an oasis outpost city. We had found a city in the jungle, with paved roads and beautiful cascading terrace farms framing the rolling hills, huge wooden houses, temples, and craftsman huts everywhere. The break in the canopy was like an open window on top of us, with an infinite view in any direction except for the very northern side, where the inclined hill continued, rising high over the outpost. So as high up as we were in the jungle, this place was also a city at the base of a mountain as well.

It was easily the size of Silka's downtown, historic, and waterfall districts put together, but where we had the next level of hills and cliffs around us like a valley, here the trees filled that bowl role, with the wooden constructs like ramps, ladders, even scaffolding built straight into them. There were accesses all around the ring of trees surrounding this perfect circle of hills, wherever nature merged the gap between treehouse and solid ground. However we hadn't found a ramp, just a bridge through the trees that ended without fanfare, without a balcony or anything, not but ten feet from the green grass below us, where the heart of the Territory was waiting.

At least, that's what it looked like to me.

"So much for climbing what, three hundred feet?" Derek said, shaking his head, looking at the drop-off height between plank and grass, only ten feet. A bruise or a roll for sure, but compared to such great heights—

"At least it was macho," Heather said sarcastically, and Derek laughed.

That one I actually didn't have any memories about. Unless—

"Oh right, I took the platform," I said.

"You did," Derek said. "Give it up for ladders."

"No," Lynn said, simply.

My mind was racing. Derek was complaining about having to climb so high just to step off, but that meant wherever we were, this was elevation for sure, something taller than the tallest cliffs over Silka. This was the northern end of the island, and we had been traveling at an incline ever since we left sea-level Silka. And we were at the farthest ends of it—so far that we had seen the end of the northern island for a brief moment when we parachuted out of that plane. In all my so-called childhood, I had never seen that side of the ocean before.

But speaking of memories.

I was reminded of something I once called, in a moment of discovery, cloud city. I remembered how close those clouds hung to the mountainous ridges and peaks of the Valley of Edna, back when we had first been given the super shoes and a very undeserved green light. First thing we did with such freedom? We'd booked it, straight into those clouds. I think Derek had been following the girl with pretty hair at that point, while I had taken to that uprise at full speed and full tilt like the Flash.

But I wasn't the Flash. I was James. And I wasn't in Silka anymore. I looked up. Yeah. Those clouds weren't as big as cloud city, but they were definitely bigger than they would have been in Silka. That could only mean one thing.

We were getting closer to the stars.

1.9

MAELSTROM

"About time," came a familiar voice.

Ollux was waiting, her feet on grass, not tree, not platform. Good old land.

"I thought you said the rain was coming," I said.

"I did," Ollux said, pointing straight up. "Watch that rock."

We looked up to the only side of this new grove settlement that had anything but sky or canopy above it—the northern side, where the incline continued up even in that center grass, and the exterior of that part of the valley rose high into mountainous bluffs, towering over us and disappearing into the clouds like their own mount Olympus. Cool. Even cooler, about halfway up, still another hundred feet above us, a single figure could be seen walking out on a narrow rock. He was shirtless because of course, and standing over the city with a red horn in his hand. When he blew the horn, to say the word shook was an understatement.

"Sonic vibrations tuned to the natural frequency of a city," Crete said, his palm on the wood of our platform floor as the sound had rang out. "I felt that more than heard it. You took my advice."

"All did," Ollux agreed. "Now watch the trees."

"Which trees?" I shouted down.

She didn't answer. Crete had to lean in close and clear his throat.

"All the trees."

Truth. Something was happening all over the circular city. Though the terrain and altitude varied, the entire clearing was ringed by the same redwoods we already knew too well. From all the trees, like literally all of them, a system of ropes was being levied into the air. I looked closer and saw (shirtless) men and (mostly shirtless) women working together to hoist the ropes up, chanting together in song. On each downbeat, the rope rose up another few feet.

"Take a look at your clear blue sky, one last time," Sand said, pointing up. "Damnit. Sorry Heather, I didn't mean—"

"I'm… good," she said, torn. "This world isn't about me."

The sight alone was enough to humble a man, let alone a teenager. The sapphire skies had turned in an instant. This oasis city was something like a square mile wide, but something the size of a few titanics was coming up from the western edge. It was a dark grey shade, a length of unbroken fabric a city wide, being raised up on ropes, slowly throwing our new oasis grove settlement into darkness—just as the rain started.

"Okay let's go," Crete said, jumping down from the tree we'd come in on to the grassy ground only fifteen feet away. He landed with a thump.

"We... can't do that," I said.

"Fine," Ollux said. "Can I get a platform over here..."

A moment later, the edge of that platform had become a platform, falling out of the sky and halting at ground level without a sound. It waited for us. Beckoned even. But still.

"Why?" I asked.

"I mean, storm's coming strong," Ollux said. "You'll be safe down here. The arborists, well, treehouses don't always stay in the trees. Your call."

"We got this," Lynn said, a hand on my arm. "Together. Go team—Derek are you flexing right now?"

"Go team," I said quickly.

And we were swinging down on another one of those rectangular, four-roped platforms that had come down out of the taller canopy on command. I had no idea where they were coming from, or who was pulling the ropes here, but it was definitely human... I hoped. We were lowered down on to the grassy hill of something straight out of a midsummer, just replace the crystal clear blue sky with a raging torrent of grey clouds opening up with the thunder and rain of some very angry olympians...

Just as the gigantic canopy shade was locked into place, the fabric snapping taunt, the water smacking into it and cascading down in a single unbroken stream that grew into a huge waterfall at the north eastern mountains of the grassy hill, the lowest part of the fabric dipping the weight of the water into what looked like an open cave dugout waterway, disappearing into the mountain like the city was drinking the rain.

"Is that repurposed?" I asked.

My feet were on the ground now, as the group stepped off the platform to dig our feet into real, actual, solid ground for the first time since tree.

"Repurposed?" Ollux asked. "That is its purpose. It will be treated and fortified before running off to our terrace farms, irrigation systems, homes, greenhouses, and outposts in the territory. There's also a divergent built into the intake for a swimming pool that only fills up during active storms. It's too far inside the mountain for lightning, no worries. All the cool kids will be there..."

"You can miss one storm," Sand said. "Given the gravity."

"The gravity does weigh heavy," Ollux said sadly. "This way."

"Where way?" I asked.

The thunder rolled.

"Well, it's a storm, so higher ground," Sand called to us over the rain, his voice nothing against the sounds of the downpour. Not to mention—

And the lightning struck.

"Don't know how to tell you this," I shouted, looking around. "Where could possibly higher ground be?"

Sand only pointed up the hills opposite us, his body leaning back like a baseball batter at home plate, about to send the pitch out of the park. It had to be a joke, we'd already climbed too high for one day. Then his finger lowered, past the circular paths dug into the cragrock, down past the first canopies of trees, and to a small circle terrace with a single hut facing the circle of the common-ground. Like the batter had decided to hit a tiny lil infield blooper instead.

"It is a joke," James said. "Why are you in a good mood?"

"The storm, obviously," Sand said. "And a roof. That roof."

"Sand Freedom has never responded to anything normally," Crete said. "Then again, we are presented with a stronghold as far away from Infinite as possible, under more protection than usual, completely hidden amongst the comforts of not only strangers but old friends as well…"

"Yep," Sand said, and then he did something he'd never done. He yawned.

"Sleepytime?" I asked, sarcastically.

"I'm wary about the word home," he said. "I know you've given yours. But out here, lost in strangerland, holding on by the dugouts we carved years ago, stranded with a crew who can't decide who to trust… this is my home."

"Weird for a man named Freedom," Lynn said.

"And this is Jerico Territory," James said. "Half an island away from the closest of our homes. We can't stay here, this isn't actually—"

"Of course not, physically," Sand said. "But sometimes, home is more of a feeling. And right now, I'm feeling it, and I'm not apologizing for it. A man doesn't get many homes. An old man, even less."

"Also teenagers who's names are our names, lesser," I challenged him.

"Teenagers who accidentally contributed to the explosions of multiple homes," Heather said, grimacing.

Oh right. I wasn't the only one who… boom…

Sand nodded. "I know who I am. I know who I'm talking to. I don't have all your answers, but I do have experience. I understand that even though you are all much younger than me, you all think you know what it's like to lose your home. I would kindly suggest that… perhaps you don't."

We all fell silent on that one, as we walked an inclined crescent like we were at the beach, but this took us up and around the curve to the small hut Sand had pointed out. The terrace farms were everywhere, meaning that every few feet we climbed gave us a better perspective on just how much land there was, and how every inch of it was being used to the fullest. James was keeping up fine. The day was turning to dusk, the storm overhead was a constant barrage of sound, the humidity in the air was like nothing else. It wasn't stiflingly, just super tropical. This was elevation, I knew that, compared to what we were used to—let alone compared to a week underland. I still didn't know how deep we'd been.

"There's a word for kids with parents, but no home," Sand said finally.

"Right, the part where we apologize for the orphan thing," Lynn said.

"To whom?" Sand asked. "You had a world collapse between your parents, you too Heather. It was your refusal to accept it that brought you back together. You may not be orphans, but you are wards. Waifs. I think they mean the—"

"That's not fair," Heather said. "That means we got the thing that every kid wants, at least every kid with a lost parent... and the world chose us. Why?"

"I think you should ask Hector that, for as long as you have left," Crete said. "But we call it either change or growth, when a word no longer describes you."

Lynn only shook her head. She understood. Sure, words were words, they could change, but when you introduce yourself to those kids in Blue Panel as orphans, and they respond with the same... I felt like crying. Something like losing a parent, that didn't just change. That was permanent. I realized in that moment that I had walked through a door without knocking first, I had opened my mouth about something that I didn't have any real-world experience about, and I owed a universal apology about it. No excuses. No hold back. How could we face those kids now?

Don't ever let them out...

Oh right, we weren't going to. We'd gotten Ana killed, they wouldn't listen to us for the two words it would take to say *I'm sorry*. Iliad had looked us in the eye, and said something he truly wished for with all his heart—the heart Issaic (and us by proxy) had broken right in two. I'd thought... that no matter what, that had been Infinite, and we'd been in Silka. Those kids were as close to my brother and I as we were going to get. But though we were from the same city, we were not the same. Not right now.

"Here," Sand said, and suddenly we were facing another wooden door.

Please be normal...

"A house for a home," James said, somehow prophetically.

"A roof for a storm," Sand said. "Don't get attached. Shoes off."

"But you just said—"

"Shoes off or fists up, you pick," Sand said, feet and fists up (somehow).

So we took our shoes off and crossed most graciously into the hut—which was much more charming from the inside. A large hearth and fireplace awaited, with room enough for counters and tables on one side, built a step into the floor just like the polestar had been. Beyond that was a few barely separated rooms built underneath the loft that started halfway over the common area, ladders on either side. There was a water tanker in the corner, a set of tools on the counter closest to the fire, there were beds with pillows and blankets...

"Yeah, not getting that feeling," I said sarcastically to Sand.

"Can we speak freely here?" Lynn asked.

"Did you build this house?" Sand answered. "Can you tell me for sure what we saw outside is all there is to see?"

"Judging from this interior alone, I'd say no way," Heather said.

"Jerico does not make empty threats," Sand agreed. "If the times comes for us to be removed from this place, no locks or doors we see will shield us. Who knows how many soldiers, or spying ears can fit within these walls, even now?"

"Who could sleep after that?" Heather complained.

"Not all of us, and not at the same time," Crete said. "As long as we are within this house, one of us must remain awake, and fully. That means we can't half ass it, no chances, no rotations. One of us must be given up. One of us must become the night. You will sleep during the day, you will live a solitary life from dusk until dawn. Your only mission will be to rouse us during our slumber, if anything should chose to enter this house without permission."

"I thought we were headed back to primal times?" I said. "Surely sleeping through the night was figured out long ago?"

"It was," Crete said. "But you didn't even bring a dog, so that's probably why this house isn't a home."

"Right," I said sadly. "That's why."

The heaviness sunk in, but also a big shadowy figure slunk in, and my brain was broken trying to figure out which was more important. Suddenly an ashen, black and grey spotted leopard had entered the situation, walking straight up to Lynn and burying a tiger sized head into a girl sized stomach—but in a cute way.

"Sophia!" Lynn shouted, and the lightning cracked outside as the leopard made a purring, soft growling sound. "Crete, you were saying about a dog?"

"Or a cat," Crete said, smiling. "Let us have the day, every one of us. We've got our guard. That is, if she accepts?"

Sophia nodded, moving her head up and down while staring Crete in the eye.

"Best guard dog ever," Crete said. "Lynn, what is this technology?"

"I love that you think this is coming from me," Lynn said, as Sophia purred.

"It's not?" Crete asked, blankly.

"Of course not," Lynn said. "That's a clouded leopard."

"A clouded leopard?" James said. "That's so cool."

"They've got the biggest canine to skull ratio in the animal kingdom," Lynn said. "She's the closest thing left to a sabretooth."

"I'm sorry, what's the word for cooler than cool?" I said. "And why are you just saying this now? You already saw her, twice."

"My bad, I was either biting on tanbark to keep from screaming, or hallucinating hard enough to see through time and space," James said. "Give me a clear head, and I'll give you an answer, deal?"

Heather laughed, and punched James in the arm for some reason.

"I think it might be the opposite, brother," I said.

James frowned, and pointed at Heather. I shook my head. His eyes went wide as he realized the same as me—how it was the lack of a clear head that had gotten us closer to answers than anything yet.

"Sophia Sabretooth," Lynn said, looking at the territory cat.

"We got three beds up here," came a voice far above us. Heather had taken to the left loft stairs and was leaning over the balcony a good twenty feet above our heads. "Three down there as well. Are we going adults and kids?"

"How about boys and girls?" Sand called up to her. "Throw one of those beds down here. You and Lynn deserve some privacy."

"Why, because of sexism?" Heather challenged.

"No, because I already made Derek and James take their shoes off," Sand said. "And I don't usually have regrets…"

"We'll take it," Heather called down, dancing around the loft, clearly happy with the choice. "Get up here Lyre."

"Much appreciated," Lynn winked.

She and Sophia waited until a huge mattress and wooden frame came tumbling over the huge balcony, landing with a bang at Lynn's feet. It was built to drop, and still so intact that Lynn stepped onto it and jumped off onto the small staircase from it like a trampoline, while Sophia made the bound in a single motion, from downstairs to perched on the balcony of the loft, at least fifteen feet above the ground.

"I want that bed."

"I want that bed. Duel to the death?"

"How about a pillow to the FACE—oh you were serious? You can have it, I'll take the—Lynn NO!"

Bam.

And the loft was full of loud animal snarls and growls. Sophia only purred the whole time, her long powerful tail whipping around over the balcony, clearly enjoying Heather and Lynn beating the feathers out of each other.

"So," Sand said. "I think the first question we need to consider in this private moment between boys is... can James go to the bathroom on his own?"

James' stomach replied for him. He looked down, defeated. Or not.

"I have to try."

Sand only pointed to a small door at the very back of the house, and James was off on his greatest adventure yet—which meant I was alone.

I sat down on the first surface I could get to, the long dining table offset from the fireplace, one end pointing into the walled-off kitchen. I must have been doing my breathing exercises, because Crete looked up at me.

"Is that a sigh of relief to get away from James? Or are you just—"

"I'm tired man," I said. "It's been a summer."

"So you can be yourself around anyone, it doesn't matter?" Crete asked.

"I've never been anyone else," I said. "And after the last two weeks, and two hours, the bathroom's as far away from me as he's getting."

"That's... admirable, Derek," Crete said. "A lot of adults spend their entire lives trying to just be themselves."

"You're serious right now, aren't you?" I asked. "You've lived with Lynn for how many years, ten?"

"Ten years," Crete said.

"You know a bit better than Sand how to talk to a kid," I said, the compliment sticking in my throat for a moment, but only because I meant it. "Don't forget, that's what I am."

"Don't underestimate that man," Crete said, hands on his knees, sitting down on a bar stool, our eyes at the same height. "But yes. I've been through what you might call the teenage girl paradox. Even Luthor missed those years, and for as many things I could say about girls right now..."

"Be careful right now," I said.

"It was an absolute honor," Crete said.

"There we go," I said.

"I've read a thousand books, I've invented a thousand machines. I've traveled this island from stem to cape, I learned four new languages between ages twenty and sixty. But I... always wondered what kind of father I'd be. I'm still not. But what I learned from that kid, Derek, there's no word for that. For what that teaches you. It's something you won't until you… if you ever…"

"I know," I said. "I… wonder that too. Let me become a man first, damn."

"You aren't far off," Crete said, smiling at me. "You have your… well, I was going to say your mother's eyes, but hers were green, yours are blue. Derek, you remind me of your mother in every other way, except for the eyes."

"Thanks," I said, trying not to laugh. "I always wanted to be different."

"Who needs tv?" Lynn cried.

My eyes shot up to see Heather and Lynn leaning over the loft, both of their eyes all misty, sharing a blanket they were both using to dab their eyes.

"What's wrong with two fathers?" Lynn asked.

"Absolutely nothing," Crete said, smiling, as Heather and I nodded hard, agreeing. It was a nice moment. Then—

"I did it!" My brother exclaimed, the door to the outhouse slamming shut.

Moment over. Lynn and Heather laughed so hard they almost fell off the loft. My brother went red in the face and did the crutch of shame out from under the back half of the house.

"You didn't hear that," he said, forcing himself to look us in the face.

'It's all in the timing, brother," I said.

"Well… what are you guys talking about?" He asked.

Then the floor vibrated, enough to shake both crutches and, you know, everything else. I put a hand on a brother's shoulder until the sound and feeling stopped—the feeling like a horn had blown through the ground itself.

"James, what did you do in that—" Heather started.

"Storm's end," Crete said.

"I was… I can be sarcastic too," Heather said.

Sand appeared from the walled-off kitchenette, joining Crete at the open door of the guest hut. We followed. For the first time since we'd arrived, it wasn't shaking in the wind. No one had bothered to close it, but with the humidity, sure. Lynn, Heather and Sophia dropped down from the loft and joined us in staring, high up on the mountains, through the dusk, where we could barely see the horn-blower on his outpost again, holding a blue horn now. Above us the sheet blanket curtain started falling, and I realized it was being recalled. I saw the warriors on each tree around the quad, at least four hundred men and women all working together down to the beat of the song they sung. Then the curtain came down, and the sky was revealed. The darkness of the storm had passed, behind it came the natural dusk, a cosmic darkness that was much farther away than the angry clouds, only clear moonlight left in its wake—as well as a new light. A green light, a wave dancing over the world, moving a thousand times faster than any cloud I'd ever seen.

"That's me making the sun up to you," Sand said to Heather.

"That's the most beautiful apology I've ever…" Heather couldn't finish.

"Is that what I think it is?" James said.

"Well we are in the north, and they are lights," Lynn said.

"The northern lights," I said.

"Way to bring something to the conversation Derek," Heather said.

But there was no other word for it, we were looking at the northern lights. They were as real as they were cliche—I mean AWESOME. Clearly the maelstrom had shook something loose in its heavenly wake, the world lighting up in greens and pale pinks was only normal. The colors rose and fell, as light as neon, as dark as moss, but I was using worldly artifacts to describe the paranormal. There really were no words. For a moment, the break in the canopies of the territory filled itself back in with a calm, but raging emerald sky.

We weren't the only people coming outside to see. Around the circle, the small, flickering flames came on over the scattered porches, some moving torches, some stationary lampposts, and we could see families, couples, solitary soldiers, groups of friends and even more masses coming out to be hit with the last fleeting raindrops of the storm, to see the aurora flowing through the stars, the red fires of man no match for a light of such literal cosmic proportions.

It was beautiful.

"Stormy days make the most amazing nights," Lynn said, out of nowhere.

"Moonbreaker," Sand said. "Storm's end. The sky is spent, the clouds are dispelled, the electricity and water in the air stabilizes, moonlight is all that's left. You are hearing the best sound any citizen of Jerico can hear."

"I'm feeling it more than hearing it," I admitted.

"Sound is physical frequency, I thought you were musicians," Sand said.

"We are not, we play guitar," James corrected him.

"My mistake," Sand said.

"You can read music can't you?" Heather asked.

Sand shrugged. "I don't see a piano."

"Give me a few cables from the fuselage and half a tree," Crete said.

"I have neither of those things to give you, old friend," Sand said.

"Not tonight," Crete said. "There's a workbench in the corner and it's not even vice-gripping anything. We're wasting build hours."

"On pianos?" James asked.

"On anything," Crete said. "We can start with a giant litter box."

"Show me how?" James asked.

"You got it," Crete said, nodding at my brother. "I'll introduce you to Racket and Foe in the morning, they're friends as old as steel. Anything built to last starts in their woodshop."

"That actually sounds… good," James said. "Is that what we're doing? Hunkering down, setting up sleepaway home here, like this?"

"If it is, might as well make it comfortable and learn something from it right?" Crete said.

"There's the Crete I know," Sand said with a smile. "Let's get dinner started. I saw a chicken in the coldstone."

"You saw a what in the what?" I asked, confused.

"A chicken, in the coldstone," Sand repeated. "No electricity remember? The hunters make their rounds before sunrise."

"You're offering us dead, spoiled chicken?" Lynn said, her nose turned up.

"True, cured vegetables and meats don't last long without a refrigerator, unless you put them in a slab cutout connected to underground air vents, naturally supercooled by the sheer depth," Sand said, walking to what I'd thought was a long bench next to the kitchen, and lifting the top slab to a gust of cold air and a frost/mist dust cloud. "Yep, frozen solid. Who wants chicken but not for a few hours? Before you answer, remember it's better than nothing."

We all raised our hands, even Sophia pawing the air like she was listening to every word we were saying. I know it was a compete fantasy, but would there ever be anything better than a talking animal?

"Then start the fires," Sand said.

"WAIT!"

Sand froze, already facing the house. Crete had his back, and put a hand on his shoulder, letting Sand know in a single motion, to calm the hell down.

"It's only Ollux," Crete said.

He was right. She ran through the quad grass, looking back at the sun as she came up to us, admittedly almost at a full sprint.

"All good?" Crete called out, as Sand turned around.

"All… sunset… sorry," she panted. "Don't… don't cook that chicken."

"Something wrong with it?" Sand asked, eying her curiously. "Gone foul?"

"Not… funny…" Ollux said, taking a breath. "By thunder, barely made it. A bet's a bet."

She handed Lynn a full basket. I could see the heat coming off it. Sophia licked her lips.

"There's enough for the wayfarers, and Sophia too," Ollux said. "Right?"

Lynn nodded, and so did the clouded leopard. She understood. Normal.

"Then come on in," Heather said.

"I can't," Ollux said, again looking back at the setting sun.

"That's not the point of a homemade meal," Lynn said.

"Believe me I know," Ollux said. "Another night, I'm all yours. Tonight… fine you want me to say it? I've got a date."

"Yeah right!" Heather said. "Sorry, I said good luck wrong."

"Thanks?" Ollux said/asked.

"Wasn't talking to you," Heather said. "Double burn, boom."

"What—whatever, just get your strength for tomorrow," Ollux said. "Sand, save that chicken for another day."

"Finally, a win," he said sarcastically, as he walked inside.

Lynn and Heather ran in after him, Sophia pouncing along after the girls. Crete turned around, leaving us brothers behind, watching Ollux sticking to the long curved path around the quad instead of cutting back through it.

"You coming?" Crete asked. "The girls are in there."

"Very funny," I said. "Just gonna debrief with my brother if you don't mind."

"Hold on there Bond and Bonder," Crete said, the only one still on the porch with us, as the lights went on in the cabin behind. "I'd like to remind you that there is no such thing as teenage locker room privacy here. Sound carries over water, and this place is a sea of trees."

"Don't we have a guard cat for reasons?" I asked.

And on cue, Sophia walked out of the house, literally pushing the sliding door open with her huge snout, pawing the ground powerfully with each step. She came right up next to me, and arced her head up to the trees, scanning each one, her nostrils flaring in all directions. Then her eyes settled, and she gave the smallest growl I'd ever heard. But like Crete said, it traveled.

"No harm, no fowl, just leave before she comes up there," I said.

"Yep, thanks, we'll take it," came a voice in the trees.

And two figures darted off the roof and up to the branches over our cabin. Sophia growled, but stood her ground, not darting for the chase, lucky for them.

"They were on my roof," James said, pointing.

"It's not your roof!" Crete said, reminding us where we were for the tenth time. It hadn't quite sunk in. "Nothing here is yours, least of all this wonderful creature of the earth, so treat it all that way."

Sophia made a strange sound at Crete from a certain distance away, almost like she was agreeing with him… or afraid of him.

"I'm changing my mind about indoor cats," James said. "This madness might be the difference between survival and… the other thing."

Crete wheeled on us, walking back inside the house, leaving us under Sophia's protection.

"You…" I said.

"Aren't allowed to tell you everything, why would I expect you to treat me any different?" Crete said wisely, leaving us alone.

"Good man," I said. "What's up brother?"

"I lied."

I froze. Big words. "About what?"

"About Kira."

My face contorted, there was a weird twitch in my forehead. "She disappeared brother, you told me this. Couldn't cross the blue light filter."

"That's not what happened," James said. "It was the blueblood. I was trapped in my own mind and memories for a day brother. I remembered knowing that one of us was older, and I bet if I go back in I'd find the answer."

"You said you didn't care about that," I said.

"I meant it," James said. "But I've been remembering… more than that."

"Like what?" I asked.

"Like… something," James said lamely.

"Something?" I said, my eyebrows as high as they would go. "We've done a lot more for less. What something is it, brother?"

"It's an open door," James said, racking his brain. "There's something off, something about the fog covering the rest of that night. I remember something besides Kira disappearing. I remember… footprints leading into our house."

"Did you follow them?" I asked.

"That's the weird part," James said. "My brain goes blank there, like a flash of light, something that maybe I could explain now, but at the time, my brain couldn't. Then again… it is like me to follow a girl."

"That's true," I said. "So you're saying there's more to the prologue. Do we beat it out of you? Should I try?"

"No!" James said. "Though it's not for lack of trying, apparently."

"Oh," I said. Then it hit me. "Oh. You think you've actually got something worth killing for inside that big brain. I was joking, trying to get it out. But—"

"They will not be joking, the next time they try to get it out," James said, referring to a couple different theys. "I'm sorry if that ruins your summer."

"Summer's long dead," I said, honestly. "We're on guard. Permanently. Anything in particular you want me to do about it?"

He shrugged back. "Help me figure out what in the fourth dimension is calling me, and why?"

"Can do," I said. "It's not even the first time I've done that. Wait—did we ever figure out what was giving you superpowers underland?"

"Nope," James said.

"Then put them both on my tab. I'll get you through brother, don't fret."

"Don't remind me of my guitar," he said.

"You—ah," I said, about to say the same to him. "That's a double edged blade—or shield, actually."

"How shield?" James asked.

"Well… just because we lost our guitars, that doesn't mean we'll never play again," I said. "Right?"

"True," James said. "It's the skill we keep, not the thing. But we can't use the skill without the thing. Without both, neither exists."

"Build that piano, I'll show you," I said.

He laughed. It was hell to hear me clunk around on keys, but give me a guitar… and it got slightly better, still not great. But better.

"At least you didn't break your hands," I said, trying to change the subject.

"I'd give an arm for a leg right now," James said. "I can't walk without these… I can't defend myself. I… I need you. I don't mean to ask for so much."

"You never do," I said. "Leave it at that."

And we did. James put both crutches in the mud, making sure they would stick before putting his weight on them, and I put my hand on his shoulder as we slowly walked/crutched back up to the cabin. But something happened as we did. Something that even by our new standards was… weird.

We left the quad just as the last of the sun was setting in the distance. Our feet left the grass the moment the sun left the sky, and good thing too—because without warning, the grass suddenly grew sharp, small blades in uniform distance, each one sticking up a good six inches out of the lawn. Sophia snarled at the grass, loudly, for the entire community to hear through such silence. We looked back behind us, where our feet had been mere seconds before, and stared. Lynn and Heather came out running, both stopping at the porch where Sophia was perched, following the looks on our faces.

I couldn't believe what I was seeing, and I had seen a lot.

"The grass is swords," Heather said, blinking.

"Normal grass my ass," I said, narrowing my eyes at it, making sure it wasn't some trick of the moonlight.

Nope. There were really a hundred thousand small pointed, razor sharp blades sticking up where the grass should have been. Talk about a deterrent. Sand poked his head out the door.

"Sand what the hell is this?" James asked.

"Must be curfew," he said, not sounding that surprised about it.

"We've been welcomed in," I said, back inside the cabin, every door closed, every light on. "Is being welcomed out a whole other thing?"

"Walls can only hold back so much," Sand said, more ominous that usual.

"It sounds like you aren't that surprised to find blades sprouting out of the ground like weeds," James said. "Did you plant them?"

"That's ridiculous," Sand said, thinking hard, turning to Crete. "Or..."

Crete nodded his head sadly.

"That's not a normal thing," Lynn said. "It took Heather at full tilt to break us out of prison. Looks like she didn't take us as far as we thought."

"I was just starting to like this place," I said.

"And now you don't, because you can't lay out on the grass under the stars?" Crete laughed. "That's all it takes to break the spell? The stars will still be there tomorrow. Storms come and go. Did you think this was story's end?"

"No, but I thought we were... I guess I still don't know," I said. "There was a tribal charm to this place that feels a lot more stabby now."

"Keep off the grass seems simple enough to me," Crete said. "Are you going to equate any tiny obstacle with still being in prison? The laws of nature are that oppressive? Didn't nature just give you a house, and a bed, a bathroom too?"

"It did," James said sadly, looking down. "Sorry Jerico. I respect you."

"James stop narrating," Sand repeated. "Derek?"

"There's two sides to me," I said quietly. "The side that obeys rules, because that's how life works. But then there's the side that sees a no skateboarding sign in public, and suddenly I don't care how many people yell at me. Don't bother young children when they are skateboarding."

"That should be a quote," James said.

"It is, it's just from a really controversial figure who I don't know well enough to back," I explained. "But I really shouldn't talk about things I don't know. Oh wait. Damn..."

"So the concept does exist to you," Sand said frowning. "Why'd you have to put it into weird skate language to find the lesson?"

"That's how I've learned every one of my lessons," I said. "Except—"

"Girls," Heather said at the same time as me. "Okay good, awareness."

"Course," I said. "I don't know anything about girls, except they really don't care about skateboarding. Those video games lied to me."

"Well when we turn to video games and skateboarding to teach us about women, we GET WHAT WE PAY FOR!" Heather shouted.

"It might be time to kill the boys," Crete said.

"Which boys?" I asked, fists up.

"You were way too ready for that," Crete said. "You boys. We need the men. The boys got us here yes, but they might not survive. The men will."

"What about the girls?" James asked.

"They're doing fine," Sand said. "They can hold their own against almost anything. As Lynn says, full tilt. Right now, this is not full tilt."

"I'll say," Lynn said. "For all this stupid superhero story, we keep finding new ways to lose our connection to anything that could make us… super."

"You think that?" Sand asked.

"Metaphorically, yes," Heather said. "But literally, I suppose not. We've got each other, friends and family for the win. A sharp knife, and us."

"Good," Sand said. "Just making sure we're all still here, together on this side of storm of swords. A sea of blades, we should be united in our approach."

"So what, we don't question it, we just… keep off the grass?" James said.

"Depends," Crete said, folding his arms at me (us). "How's your rebellion to exhaustion ratio leaning?"

"Too tired to rage, by far," I said. "You got me there."

"Then we sleep, and dream of normal grass," Crete said. "Can you do that?"

I could do that.

THE ALWAYS SOLDIER

"Be exactly who you are every day," I said. "Heroes."

"Supermom," I heard them say as I took flight.

Nerds. They still couldn't even surf.

I thought of them as I took to the first of the ships, the closest access point to our homes in the hills. There were already twenty wooden leviathans docked, shattering the storefront pavilion in their beaching, and warriors were pouring out onto the sand armed in the living leaf of the Jerico. There were homes on the portside, but there was also a path up into the hills atop Silka, and I watched as every warrior made straight for the hills, leaving the homes untouched.

Good. Let it be known for the first time in centuries, Jerico had listened.

I could have taken each ship out with nothing but a command. I didn't, for obvious reasons. Instead, I left the ocean behind and soared low over the cliffs of the Engineerium district towards the downtown valley. I blinked through my radars until I could see straight through the miles of skyscrapers, to the back half of the city where the streets stopped and the farms began, and saw them. Vessels two stories tall bearing down on the outskirts of the town, already throwing glowing purple rocks towards a line of citizens half-dressed in white, doing their best at keeping the houses guarded from the oncoming. Then the world around me was a blur, and the voice circled me before I even saw the flier. Like usual.

It was Issaic. We had arrived at the end of the city together, the last paved line before the farmlands, diving down out of the sky towards a faction of Infinite soldiers already overtaken by a cloud of purple.

"They're swarming, dear," Issaic said, blinking.

"Call me Ma'am or die," I said.

"Sorry," he said, touching his forehead in sarcastic salute, as we air-braked and prepared for the sonic boom to catch up to us. "Ma'am."

The soldiers were terrified, we could hear them screaming at each other to stand their ground. Then speaking of sonics—BOOM.

"Issaic," a voice said.

We looked left, to see our old friend Todd Circus rising up in the air towards us, holding his chest with his non-bleeding hand. Circus coughed blood. He looked like he'd been crying, I couldn't blame him.

"It's... worse than we thought chief."

"Are they after us, or me?" Issaic said.

"It's not you, Issaic," Circus said. "It's not us. You know why they're here."

Issaic's face fell, and then so did Circus.

"No," Issaic said, his mind switched like a light. "No, they couldn't know... they couldn't possibly..."

"What is it?" I asked, desperate for the answer. "Issaic, what does he mean, how isn't this for you? How could it not be? Why..."

But Issaic had no time for me. Story of my life. He was a shooting star before I could see the actual stars, but in the direction of... no.

"I knew it," I said.

And I followed him into the blue, until we collided in hyperspeed, Issaic and myself fighting to knock each other out of our trajectories. Somehow he dodged two beams of light and kept flying, too much of a coward to even fight me for what we both knew was about to happen.

"You don't TOUCH MY FAMILY!" I shouted at him.

I was trying to re-cycle the energy in my palms but accidentally hit my jet boots instead of the blasters and rocketed towards him so fast I took him with me as our bodies collided. But then the lights in his eyes lit up, his hands turned superhuman, and as every ounce of my energy was spent holding him as close as possible, one punch was all it took.

One punch I wasn't ready for. From the man I had married.

"I will do what I WANT!" He roared at me.

I went flying, fast and hard, tumbling into the sky seeing ocean, then mountain, then city gridlock, then it happened all over again, and again, until I hit something and felt my back snap something awful. I'd hit the top of a building with my back and skipped off it like a rock.

"Oh come on, you know what to do," I said to my supersuit.

But the suit gave me nothing I couldn't reach my vitals, I needed someone to speak it to me. That actually wasn't the worst idea. So without any sort of help at all, with my back already broken, I fell, long and hard, until I felt the ground hit me so hard in the back I almost threw up. The lights blinked in and out, and the claws of the Reaper came in, slashing hard, taking me for an easy win, until my facial screen was shredded. Then every scout over me lowered their helms, eyes wide. Then I heard a familiar voice.

"It's her. Stand down, it's Teresa. She..."

I only remember my eyes rolling as hard as the thunder, and the darkness coming in as Mare held me in his hands. He looked down with horror, calm for the colors in the sky behind him.

"What have we done?" he asked.

PART II

2.1

THE GRASS IS SWORDS

I dreamt about dancing lobsters, because dreams were just dreams. They were only symbolic of what your brain feared. But at least I was dreaming.

I woke up to a chanting outside our guest hut. It was past sunrise, the grass was normal. I walked outside to see the cadets coming out onto a perfectly square pitch with a worn track in the grass around it. There were twenty of them, one middle aged guy calling the shots, and two helpers on either side. It looked like soccer camp. Hell yes. I walked over, until the guy in charge noticed me. I put my hands together in an obvious prayer, and nodded to the pitch. He nodded.

"Alright topline cadets, I want an entire lap of pancakes, don't take all day."

"I love pancakes," I said.

All I got were stares, as the soldiers gravitated to a section of worn down grass that curved in an oval around the field—wait, it was a track. They all took a pushup stance on the track, and moved forward in that position, their entire abs held clenched off the ground the entire time. Like a jumping plank. No.

"Do you like pancakes now?" One guy said as he hopping by me, his entire body not even a foot off the ground.

I sighed. This wasn't soccer camp, it was boot camp. Damn you pancakes.

It was a long lap. I had never been more awake five minutes after waking up. The pull of my muscles, the aches, the stitches, the cramps… I loved it, hence why I'm not allowed to get tattoos. James was always afraid I would like the pain. I didn't exactly disagree. In twenty minutes every cadet but one had finished. In thirty minutes I joined them, my arms and shoulders about to burst, my wrists good and cooked. But at least I was breathing.

"A reminder to the newbie that we ran a good six miles before this," one of the helpers said, a young woman, almost my age or even younger.

"I mean no disrespect, ma'am," I said from my back.

"Ma'am?" The helper said, looking down on me with the sweat dripping dangerously close. "There is a saying about a man who arrives to learn with already a full cup. Have you been through martial training before, *sir?"*

"Not like this," I said. "My cup is only full enough to stay steady."

"Then a cup tries not to spill," she said, pulling me up by the shirt.

The other helper came up, a young guy with a skinny face and sort of a British mop of blonde hair everywhere. He threw three red kicking shields out onto the ground, while the woman next to me leaned down for the first.

I should probably learn some names.

"Line up!" The captain shouted. "Power drills. Send newbie to the stars."

"I've already been to the stars," I said, picking up a bag.

"Words," the first trainee said, digging her feet into the ground like shovels. "Our feet are our greatest weapons, besides all our real weapons."

Bam.

My arms held strong as the sofa cushion sized pad was hit with a tree trunk, or that's what it felt like at least. Girl was strong.

"What's your name?" I wheezed.

"Zedta," she said.

"You people kick hard Zedta," I said. "Sorry for saying you people."

"We do kick hard," she said with a curtsey before joining the end of the line.

"You don't know anything about us do you?" a guy said, taking her place.

"Not a bit, no," I said. "And what's your name?"

"Brin," he said, as he reared back—funny enough, I did see stars that time.

"What did they teach you about us in school Derek?" The next girl said.

"Not this hive mind madness, damn," I said, my legs buckling, but forcing myself to hold her gaze, holding the pad down on purpose like I was waiting for something.

"Rosetta," she said, smiling.

She was taller than me. She had a ponytail whipping around in the wind almost unnaturally, until I saw a jadestone tied to the end of it. Then she shoved her back foot into the ground so hard the dirt carved away like she was a Reaper and I forgot all about jewelry. I gulped, but raised the pad.

BAM.

And for some reason the echoing was coming from above me. It made more sense when they picked me up off the ground.

"I've been duped," I muttered to myself, shaking my head, readying the pad for another round like I'd been born in the briar patch.

Then it happened. Not right away. Another few drills later, I started remembering real quick what each was capable of. Stocky gym dude (Dalle) with the white earrings hit the hardest. He only moved at right angles, even his jaw a block of brick. Ponytail girl (Rosetta) was the second worst on that list, her legs bigger than even Crete's, hitting with the power of Ollux—even though Rosetta was closer to my height by a foot. Then it was sideburns and half-shirt girl (a boy named Fawn and a girl who only went by Plain Jane).

"Why not PAIN Jane?" I cried, pulling myself off the ground again.

"That's actually better," she said, as I tried not to cry.

But then there was blue eyes, a girl with blonde bangs who always looked at me weird before shouting loud but not hitting that hard. Her name was Viridi Via. Then there was bandana-man Wren, who could only hit me half as hard as he could yell. The only two others wouldn't talk to me, but apparently they didn't talk to anyone, so I called them left foot right foot, since they came with opposite stances. They looked like they didn't want to be there.

In less than five minutes, I had read the line. I knew when to flinch, I knew when to relax. I could read each of them like a book, like they were the ones taking the turn on my sword. Yet by every definition in the world, this was a shield. For the first time, I found myself on my brother's end of the thing. For the first time in a while, I knew everyone's name.

"Derek, pads up," middle-aged blonde helper guy reminded me.

Damnit.

"Osion," he said, reading me. "Your training methods are unorthodox, but… not unwelcome. You've earned something. Would you like a break or a try?"

Interesting. They were all watching, seeing what I would do—and I had an idea. It was easy to hold the pad against a straight attack, just throw the body behind it and ouch. It was easy to defend against something coming down, just dig in. But something coming up… that was different. That was all arms. And what had Heather Denien taught us about fighting? Something about sideways?

I threw Osion the pad, and he caught it by the wrist straps. He smirked, but I had counted on it, and was already leaping forward.

"Nice try," he said, slipping the guard straps on at the last moment…

My feet gripped the pad and brought it up, the friction was enough to overturn the pad, and it arced up and over Osion's shoulder like a windmill to smash open into a thousand feathers across the ground behind him. His arm whiplashed with the loss of weight, the momentum already wrenching him all the way over. Thankfully helper girl Ivy was there, and she slid her pad underneath him at the last second.

BOOM.

Osion landed on his back, on the pad, in the grass, at my feet, gospel truth.

"Soldier OSION! The banana peel bollocks was that?"

The instructor had appeared next to us like Batman. Osion struggled to his feet, then collapsed back down and missed the pad. Ivy threw her hands up.

"I'm… kid knocked the wind out my…" Osion said, staring at me with a thumb sideways.

"Soldier Ivy, stand him up," the captain commanded.

But Ivy was frozen, standing with her hands out in a wonderful wind of floating feathers, absolutely taken by the beauty. For a moment they seemed to swirl for only her, and only around her, before they were blown away for the grass, or destined to drift off farther into the sky and trees. Even the cadets were frozen in their feet watching her, distraction.

"It's so beautiful," soldier Ivy whispered.

"What is going on today," the captain said, shaking his head, turning to me. "You said you were here with an empty cup. What part of that wasn't martial?"

"That was sideways," I said. "I can hold my own—where I'm from. But I think for where I'm going, I think I need to be more. I think I need to learn how to fight. I think you're going to teach me."

The captain looked at me stunned. Helper girl (Ivy) blinked, and came back to us as the feathers were finally gone, clearly completely lost and unsure what we were talking about. It was helper guy (Osion) who spoke first, into the grass, but loud enough—

"On behalf of the crew… we'd love to have ya…."

"Go on," he said, the captain staring at me. "We're not here to learn how to fight. You're looking at the summer topline shift, shipping up tomorrow. This is boot camp, and as much as it looks like we're preparing for war, it's peace that really takes the training. Now everyone, hand patterns, all fifteen, both stances. We've just gained a twenty-first cadet. Let's get him up to speed on the basics."

"SIR!"

"My name is Soltis," the captain said. "But you can continue to call me sir."

"Yes sir," I grinned.

Hours later, there was no way I could climb up that incline the same way I'd come down, so I took the long, sloping path up towards that cabin on the quad. It was day, the grass was just grass, and I confirmed it about twenty feet in front of the sliding front doors, right where James and I had stood last night. I was on my back, not gasping, just breathing deeper and clearer. I would just stay here a while. Then I heard something to my right.

"Thanks for the note at least," she said, throwing me a book. "Good touch."

It was Lynn, sitting down with a wooden plate in her hand.

"I thought so," I said, hit in the face with the same open pages I'd left on my pillow, a single word scrawled out in the notebook.

Explorin'!

"I was worried, for the first hour," she said. "Then I was wondering why you were there. Could you be… out making friends, meeting the locals, attempting to honor the customs and engraining yourself in one of the most prestigious warrior programs the island has to offer, all at 6am on the first day?"

"So you saw everything," I said.

"I'm not mad," Lynn said. "But I'm not bringing you breakfast again."

"I wouldn't expect it," I said. "Especially not if you come with."

"You don't want to keep me away while you're… developing?"

"First of all, how *dare* you," I said, covering as much of my body as two arms could. Lynn smiled. "Secondly, of course I don't want you far away, all you've ever done is help, why would I keep you out of anything? I don't know how to tell you this Lynn, there's no TV here—"

"I know," Lynn said looking at me weird again. "You should want me—I mean—you would want me away, if you were trying to speed-run becoming a fighter to prove some sort of masculine idiocracy to us. To make the change about the end result alone, to cut us out of any possible journey of humility."

"It's about the journey, a hero taught me that," I said. "And the story a circle.

"But what's even the journey?"

"You know how to defend yourself," I said. "You weird, yellow lightning having, storm-handed, sun-harnessing flying supergirl—all I want is to be as cool as you, that so bad?"

"I…" Lynn said, like she couldn't believe what I was saying.

"I'm bad with words," I said, taking a breath. "I just can't think of anyone better to be around."

"First of all… you're good with words," she said, in a hushed voice.

"Secondly… I thought you were mad at me."

"If I were you'd know it, and breakfast wouldn't cut it," I said.

"I brought you coffee too," Lynn said. "But I… drank it. Sorry—"

"Nope," I said. "I told you, don't ever apologize to me. I'm not mad at you. I'm mad at the truth, I haven't given anyone good reason why I'm still here."

"Maybe not in the last five minutes, but the echelon satellite, the gates of Vema, both came down, I was there too man—"

"I know what we look like," I said. "I know what we can't do here, the only thing we've ever been able to. I don't have a supersuit, but I can only see myself through your eyes Lynn. I know what you see."

"You sure about that?" She asked. "Or are you maybe talking about things you don't understand, again?"

I sat up in that grass that wasn't even swords. "Did you eat?"

"I was waiting for you."

"Then we're sharing this," I said, breaking a stick I had just picked up in the grass, half for me, half for her. She took it, and we both speared a piece of fruit.

"I love strawberry," I said.

"Me too," she said. "What's second of all?"

"Second of all," I said, suddenly my heart beating fast again. "Come with me tomorrow. To training—more like boot camp. It's gonna suck. You'll love it."

"It sounds like you're asking me on the world's worst date," Lynn teased.

I'm not, I swear I was about to say, but Crete's words came into my head at the perfect moment. Kill the boy. Right.

"What if I was?" I asked, biting my tongue, clenching down, praying my five seconds of confidence wouldn't end up with Lynn laughing at me.

She only bit her lip and looked at me weird, like I'd seen her do before. Then she did laugh. But it was almost… genuine.

"Then I'd say yes—but only to boot camp," she said, as cool as ever.

"Are you one of those people who goes to the gym on vacation?" I asked.

"I am," Lynn said. "Are you?"

"I will die before that happens," I said.

"How about yoga?" She said, standing up and stretching, and I followed without hesitation. "Sun salutations. You'll feel better after two. I want five."

"Yes Ma'am," I said, bending over.

I was already so sore from topline boot camp I could barely get my hands over my shoulders, but she was right. After standing up for the second time, I felt better.

"I said FIVE!"

"Yes Ma'am" I cried, hands up to the sky.

Finally the white spots cleared, and I picked up the plate on the grass on my way up from the last move. We hung there for a moment, just watching the trees on the edge of the small circle sway. My body felt better, my back didn't have that twinge for once, nice.

"This place is weird Lynn," I said, no holds.

She shrugged. "We made it though. To a place not many know. I don't know if your father will expect you here. We might actually be… safe."

From safety, I thought to myself.

Together we walked back inside the guest hut on the edge of the grass, some of us limping more than others, but I forced myself to walk right as James came literally crutching over, his right ankle wrapped in fabric.

"There they are," Heather said. "The man with the plan, to die."

"Spoilers," I complained, with a big grin.

"So how was black belt training?" James asked, all foreshadowing-like.

"It… was like that," I nodded. "How'd you sleep brother?"

"On a bed, for the first time since my bed."

"How's the leg?" Lynn asked.

"The pain is there but there's nothing I can do about it," James said. "I can feel it healing. We're out of the jungle, you got me out. Far as I'm concerned I woke up not in prison, it's a beautiful morning! Dance with me Derek—"

"I have less legs than you right now," I said, grinning, holding myself up against the wall. "Where's the coffee?"

"I drank it all!" James said, with one last cheesy grin. "I'll calm down."

"I knew you could take a kick, but that was a lot of feet," Heather said to me.

"And he took them, every one, right in the face," Crete said.

He even swiveled around in a wooden armchair too, big dramatic reveal, ooh. But unless he was holding, I wasn't—wait. I bowed, just something I had seen this morning, my brain was still on soldier mode—I mean autopilot.

"You gave every cadet at least one free shot," Crete said, as he handed over the carafe. "I saw it. You really have done this dance before."

"They're proper dancers, that's what's up," Heather said, smirking. "What exactly did you learn in dance class?"

"Karate," James said, pouting.

"Coffee," I corrected.

"It was sparring," James said. "And as for what we learned… fear."

A fear coffee couldn't overcome. I was back.

"He's right," I said. "Today was nothing."

"All that?" Heather said, pointing out all my bruises. "That's all nothing?"

"Every year for like, three, there was one day we'd meet the new class," James said, ominously. "Twenty kids, either all friended up already, scared to death, or trying to ignore their parents cheering for them to fight. That first day we'd form two lines. Even though there were ten kids on either side of you, you could be called at any time, sometimes back to back, sometimes not for fifteen minutes. The first day, looking around at all those people you didn't know, all wearing gloves and foot guards for only one reason, waiting was the second worst part. Hearing your name was the worst. And once you heard it, there was nothing else to do but walk up and see who the instructor would choose from the other line. Bow, touch gloves, and…"

"And what?" Lynn asked, as I trailed off.

"The rest depends on who you're fighting," James said.

"Yeah," I said. "If it's a kid my age, ten years old and we don't know each other, we come out swinging. If it's someone's mom or dad, you stick to technical points only, unless they give you that look, then good luck me."

"If it's your brother, he puts you in a headlock, sings opera into your ear, and you're laughing too hard to get out," James said.

"That was one time, and we both ran laps after," I said. "If it's that girl that won't stop staring at me, take my body and do your worst. If it's the college kid who's got it out for me because he's too old to admit he likes that girl staring at me, he kicks me in the face—we've been over that one."

"That story's getting deeper," Lynn said. "Wait who was this girl?"

"The point is for the rest of the year…" Crete started.

"I'd know everything about everyone I was fighting," I finished. "The strongest in the class, the ones likely to come in mad, the ones vying for top marks, the ones about to fail out, the ones who tried to help their opponent, the ones who used their opponent for their own gain. It took a while to catch on, but that first day would tell me everything. I just needed to take a hit from everyone in the class for it to sink in."

"You gave me a free shot once," Heather said to me.

"You needed it," I said. "But I took my notes on you back in that air vent. You didn't shoot us. You shushed us, and you're as terrifying as the dark earth you came from. Says it all."

"Thanks," she said, blushing, then blinking. "Wait. Says what?"

"That you liked us before you liked us," I said, only logically.

"YOU TAKE THAT—" she said, about to fly into a rage when… she didn't. She took a deep breath and nodded. "Fine. But speaking of people I like, what are the chances of Hector or Luthor paying us a very overdue visit?"

Crete wrinkled his face. "Bad chances."

"Too easy for the Infinite to follow them here?" I offered.

"No, designated survivors," Crete said.

"I'm sorry?" Lynn said, blinking.

"I'm kidding?" Crete said, blinking back at her, all sarcasm, no brakes.

"So what, I guess we're all just meant to be here, or somewhat?" James asked, leaning forward on his crutches, swinging both feet off the ground. He was balanced pretty well on crutch tips alone, after just one day. "Well I can't go far, so if I'm going to crutch around, it's gonna be here. Crete, what's the plan?"

"Depends," he said. "You ever made or been inside a pressure chamber?"

"Nope," I said.

"You're about to do both," Crete said. "Heather, I could use the extra… hmm. I was going to say hands, but—"

"I got legs," she said, nodding. "I also have plans."

"You have plans?" Lynn said, eyes wide. "In Jerico Territory?"

"I have plans to not spend the entire day inside," she said. "I understand if you think the unburying of my people is still about you."

"I don't," Lynn said. "Crete, pop the hood."

"Yes Kapyushon," Crete said.

He pulled on a cable running from the fireplace to the ceiling that definitely wasn't there yesterday. With a blast of noise and a sight like the ceiling was coming apart in two (because it was), the roof came apart at the apex and slid down tracks on the outside walls of the house like nothing. The loft was open to the elements, the sun came down on all of us. Last night we'd seen this place only by the light of the torch. Now… no way. Had James already had some sort of bonding moment with Crete, waking up early and creating some sort of roofing shelf system? That would be dope. But that would also be assuming.

"Upgrade!" James said. "Crete, you make that this morning?"

Thought so.

"Not at all," Crete said. "I thought you were going to stop assuming."

"Wrong twin," I said. "It gets tricky because we look nothing alike, I know."

"If it helps, you can just apply all lessons learned equally across both our characters," James said.

"What's the point of that?" Crete said.

"Um… so that there's no true main character?" I said, scratching my head.

"That's stupid," Crete said. "Whoever's telling the story is the main character, even if the story isn't about them."

"It's… the sun," Heather said, shaking her head. "Sorry. Old habits."

I looked to Lynn, only logically. "When did you get this done?"

"While the peasants were making breakfast," Lynn grinned. "Crete helped, he's teasing. It took a while though. Exactly what happened in that kitchen?"

"We cooked you breakfast that's what happened," James said.

"You cooked us bread and fruit, it took an hour?" Crete asked.

"It was… from scratch," James said, clearly trying to avoid it.

"You made strawberries from scratch?" Lynn asked.

Maybe it was the sun, I saw some real blushing going on. Foreshadowing…

"No worries," I said, pretending I hadn't noticed anything. "Easy answer—thank you for breakfast, and we'll rotate cooking duty tomorrow."

"NO!" Heather and James shouted at the same time, standing their ground.

"Whatever you want," I said, holding my hands up. "You want the sun, boom. You want the moon, soon. How about a star?"

"I've got a piece of a star in my wallet," Crete said.

And suddenly we were all looking at him.

"What?" He said. "Do you… want it?"

"We don't want your star, Crete!" Lynn said. "We… what do we want?"

"To not be seen as enemies of the state, to Silka or our father, so we can maybe return to the lands we grew up in without being hunted?" I said, heavy.

"To go home," Crete said. "Continue."

"But to maybe also see this weird vigilante escapee nonsense through, until it ends at the truth about where our mother is, why she's been gone so long, and for what reasons?" James asked.

"To have a home to go back to," Crete said, turning on the girls. "You?"

"To find out exactly why this stupid superhero escapee nonsense is even here, and how much damage has already been done that can't be… undone," Heather said, looking at us like we were something to her.

"To treat the world as your home," Crete said, nodding. "Lynn?"

"To find out if there's anything beyond the world we know," she said.

"That's so weird," Crete said, breaking the spell, and as we blinked he was laughing. "Sorry beanbug. I meant… to treat your home as the world. So that is what you want. I noticed no one has asked what I want."

"What do you want?" I asked.

"I want all of those things, for all of you," Crete said. "But as a wise woman who was married to Harrison Ford once said—you can have it all, but not all at once, and not right away."

"But she was married to… oh I get it," Lynn said.

"Me too," Heather said. "I love a man who's scared of snakes."

"You'll see a lot of coldbloods here," Crete said. "There's something about the jungle that filters the sunlight. With so much photosynthesis going on, I guess it makes sense. We're high up yes, but both warm-blooded and coldblooded animals can spend all day in the sun here. No sunscreen."

"That's the closest thing to paradise I've ever heard," Heather said. "Okay you got me. Lynn, I'm starting to like this guy. James, today you've got four hands. What's the plan?"

"We find four pop stars and slap them all at once," James said, no hesitation.

"I am IN!" Heather said/laughed. "What about you twos?"

"Dunno," I said, cool as anything. "Lynn, you trying to go somewhere?"

"I was," she said. "I'm going to the crash site, to help however I can. I was going to go off on my own for a bit, you know, the same thing you did this morning, clear my head, get some alone time to remind me why I'm here."

"Oh," I said. "Sounds important."

"It is," Lynn said, smiling. "But you invited me to your important thing. I guess I can do the same. You coming, flyboy?"

She held her hand out. The word came out before I thought about it.

"Always."

I didn't hesitate, I didn't overthink it. I reached for her hand—but she snapped it back before I could touch it, looking at me with something in her eyes that told me once again the confidence had worked. Kill the boy.

"It's a long way man, we aren't holding hands the whole time," Lynn said.

She called me man.

"Boo," Heather said very loudly.

Maybe it was the yoga, but Lynn's face was redder than usual. Same.

"You good without me for a bit brother?" I said to James.

"I'll manage," he said, Heather turning away behind him. "We can do a day apart, it's not going to—you know what, I'm not going to finish that sentence."

"Prove it," Crete said. "Prove it, prove it, prove it, prove it."

And we went our separate ways—if just for one day.

Lynn and I made our way through the quad, the grass that had been swords, now just a regular walk for two regular kids. Kind of.

"Should we be asking Ollux about this?" Lynn asked.

"I know where to go," I said. "One of the cadets told me, up the arbor, through the northwest pass, past the giants nest, around the devil's knot, and over the gates. Should take us half an hour."

"Look at you," Lynn said. "All prepared and sh…engcun."

"What do you think I meant by explorin?" I laughed. "I can't ask for favors when I'm already in debt. If we're going to get a second chance, it has to be a clean one. Otherwise we're just dropping our damage all over the city again."

"You say again, but the Vempire got out clean," Lynn said. "I hate to minimize it but yeah. That happened. Don't forget it."

"I won't," I promised. I could never forget that story. It hadn't even ended either. "Maybe we should have stayed underground."

We were at the other side of the quad in minutes. We found a low hanging platform close enough to a tree with some nice, thick branches, staggered low enough to climb up. There was a familiar ladder carving in the trunk too, but sometimes it was more fun to branch out. We helped each other up to the platform, and looked out at the almost stadium scaffolding that awaited.

"Start your maps," Lynn said. "Wait you're—I was kidding."

I already had the pen and notebook in hand. "No?"

"You brought your notebook?" She said.

"You threw it at me!" I said. "You wanted me here, doesn't matter, we go."

"And now," Lynn said, shaking her head. "Explorin'!"

"I mean everything I write," I said.

We left that circular city and sun behind. I noted every platform bridge and turn we were making with small marks on my page. This world was huge, the map had to be tiny. As we walked, Lynn pointed out plants and flowers she knew as we crossed between huge groves of trees that almost covered the entire pathway, only to walk through them and realized were on the edge of a whole community, on every altitude imaginable, a fully 3D system of circular disc platforms shooting out from the trunks, connected by branches and bridges alike, with all sorts of open and closed roof houses among them. It was beautiful. The colors, the natural minimalism, the absolute ingenious constructions, this was a world that shouldn't have existed. I was glad it did. There was nothing about this place that gave me pause—except for whatever that smell was, suddenly coming over us, it hadn't been there before. I looked around, trying to see what had changed. I found it.

"Hey Lynn," I said, stopping in my tracks, gritting my teeth. "Don't move."

Lynn's eyes shot up in wonder. "Giraffes. Derek, it's giraffes."

It was. There were the long splotchy necks of a few giraffes up here with us, their bodies nowhere in sight, just the yellowish, orangish hair and the dark brown spots, decorating all the way up to their necks and heads. Dinosaurs were real, and they smelled terrible. But I didn't care. One of them came close enough to lean his/her head over the pathway, and I realized from the chin to those two adorable nubs for horns, it was five feet tall. A face as big as a person. The pattern of fur, right down to the nose. That huge tongue that wrapped itself around the wood of the balcony, bigger than my entire arm.

Lynn had her hand out, walking slowly towards the thing, and the giraffe blinked at her calmly, but took his head back over the balcony before she could touch. He/she looked back at Lynn as he/she rejoined the rest of the pack, moving on without worry of us.

"I love giraffes," Lynn said. "Tallest mammals on earth since dinosaurs."

"I read somewhere that we learned space travel from them," I said. "Or maybe I'm thinking of comic books again. Giraffe-Man, anyone?"

"You're right," Lynn said, touching me on the arm again, always in the same spot. "Weightlessness is hell on the body. The first astronauts found out the hard way. Up there, the muscles, bones, and arteries weaken so much that it's hard to stand under Earth's gravity again. We learned lower body artery conservation by studying how baby giraffes are able to stand up almost immediately after birth."

"Giraffes helped us go to space," I said, absolutely amazed.

"I mean they weren't along for the ride, can you imagine the rocket?" Lynn said. "Science is just figuring out the universe as it already is. Maybe we shouldn't have made so many species extinct before figuring out why they were here in the first place."

"Imagine the problems we could have figured out," I said. "Power sharing. Total resource utilization. City parking. Aluminum deodorant."

"People who play bass with a pick," Lynn smiled.

"It's only for rhythm, which is what bass is LITERALLY—nevermind. A real sabretooth wouldn't be having these problems," I said, shaking my head.

Lynn laughed, and we continued down the path, just the two of us, but now following the backs of a whole pack of giraffes, clearly headed the same direction we were. But I had leapt to defend something like playing bass with a pick for a reason. A very familiar reason. Benjann. Why'd I have to think about him right now? Sure he'd been through hell and back with us, and subject to a fate almost worse than Noah, or Mikael, or for that matter Geran and Laurel, whom I'd chosen to just not think about at all until now. Was it possible they were all… back with Mara now? Could every single person from the last mission have ended up dead, besides Hannah, Benjann, and us?

These were all the thoughts that simply melted away from my brain, looking into eyes twenty times the size of mine, to such spotted fur, the ears that stuck up, those damn nubs. The eyes had me. They knew everything I was thinking, I knew it. And as soon as I was seen, I had no choice but to look back at that giraffe and think…

Yeah buddy. Doing okay, could be better, no lie.

The giraffe made a motion with its head, a slight one, but it was directly towards Lynn.

I know.

And my new giraffe buddy winked at me. As I could have faced all those deeper thoughts, as much as I could have brought them up with Lynn and believe me I wanted to… it was just too wonderful to ruin. I would ruin it later.

For one day, giraffes.

The Giant's Bed and the Devil's Knot turned out to be clearly marked pathways through the trees. We went from sturdy platforms with handholds four feet tall to branches with simple strips of lumber nailed in a level but narrow, precarious unaided tightrope walk up to the next platform. Some of them ended in ladder rungs, or ended in three foot falloffs to the platform below. This was a city built for people at least six feet tall, every one of them. Why was that? Was it the technology, or lack of it? Did they sleep hanging upside down from the trees like bats? Were they just better than us in every human way? I wondered without answers, as we followed the wood, up and down and around again until those huge wooden spikes started coming up in the distance.

"Made it, sans host," Lynn said. "You got the way back?"

"I do," I said, flipping through my notebook.

"Derek, those are just drawings of different giraffes."

"It's actually different drawings of the same giraffe, thank you," I said. "I need a name though, you didn't pick that one up did you? That one right there?"

She looked down to the pack. By now we were so far above them that they were tiny to us, standing thirty feet high yes, but we were hundreds of feet above the ground now, and those rising wooden walls had put an end to a world that usually went unobstructed for a giraffe. But as the others stared lamely, sadly at the gates, one of the pack tilted its head up and stared straight at us.

"Masai," she said without realizing she'd spoken. "I've got nothing."

I stared at her. The giraffe nodded to Lynn, and turned back to the walls.

"He wants to go outside," Lynn said.

She was slumped over the branch, her hands reaching down in the air, just looking at the giraffes. Then finally, as my eyebrows couldn't go any higher, it clicked. She pushed herself up off the branch and landed in a fighting stance.

"There she is," I said, keeping my distance.

"How did I know that?" she said. "The other stuff I read in zoo books, it's not like I just tapped into a full animal kingdom database in my head."

"No worries, another animal told you its name," I said, pen on paper, writing it down under my best drawing, a half profile with the unfinished hand of a certain girl reaching out from the edge of the page. I looked up and Lynn's eyes were wide. "What? Lynn, I wish I could say this was the first time."

"This must be how James felt all week," she said, sighing. "I'll be good."

We were so high up in the trees that we could look down at the Gates of Jerico and the world beyond them, the vast height of the jungle canopy spread out before us like a green ocean, as well as a certain very obvious and clear opening in the terrain, where the Refugee had crashed down. We were marveling at the sight when we saw movement over our heads. It was a wire, a cable line running from here all the way down to the clearing, taunt and bouncing around like there was a fish on the other end of it. We watched as a moving platform grew closer and closer to us, coming up like a ski-lift, over miles of open jungle, the weight of it nothing for how taunt the line was attached to the tree over us, a good fifty foot trunk. Then the platform reached us, and a small crew of six stepped off.

"Crash site?" I asked, only pointing down where they had come.

The guy closest to me narrowed his eyes at us, and nodded his head. He held the line of the platform until Lynn and I could step on, and gave a whirling motion to something above us. Before we could thank him, the platform had lifted off the ground, and we were on our very long ride down to the ground.

"Better than ladders," Lynn and I said at the same time.

The world was suddenly much less solid ground. We swung around a bit, until the thing leveled out, only a single floor and less than two feet of a raised edge to the thing, otherwise completely open to the elements. Lynn grabbed my hand here, no qualms about it. We both were laying down with our backs to the wood, our feet and arms cornered against the edges like that would help stop the platform from blowing in the wind.

"We used to FLY!" I shouted, more scared than I would be free-falling.

"And we were getting good at it!" Lynn shouted, laughing.

I wasn't scared after that.

The zipline held, the wooden gates were high above us again, and we were coming up on the much lower canopy line of the outside jungle surrounding the walled Jerico territory. I did my best to peer over the edge. It felt like we were being lowered into a hole at the bottom of the sea, as we passed through the canopy on a perfect angle to hit the ground at the far end of the clearing.

"You made it," came the voice before we landed. "Told you they would."

"Anybody could be in here," I said, still laying on my back in the thing.

The platform dug into the ground and the bodies of Ollux, Astor, and Sand came over us, finding us holding hands, white in the face, breathing heavy.

"You are through the arbor," Ollux said, blinking. "Did you have help?"

"We had direction, from the cadets," I said, shrugging. "I can make friends."

"Saw you out the window this morning," Sand said, giving me a proud look. "Didn't want to intrude on a good thing."

"You met soldier Soltis?" Ollux said, blinking. "I was going to introduce you both, once your brother was healed."

"No time for that," I said. "We're losing build hours, as Crete says."

Sand punched the air in victory. Seeing him in a good mood was interesting.

"We've come to help, didn't bring much but how bad could it—" Lynn said, standing up and seeing the site behind. "Oh my pieces of stars…"

Behind them was, well, I didn't know what I expected a crashed jet in the jungle to look like. The wreckage was a single piece, true, but the same could not be said for the jungle. The loss of four trees alone had created an open aired pocket in the otherwise seamless green canopies of the lower forest, a small soccer sized clearing where the sun could come through and light up what was usually much darker, and much denser. But the forest floor was uneven, the grass was untamed, with a thick layer of dead brown leaves and broken branches over everything, huge rips in the still standing trees around us in a single direction, and a deep trench in the ground through the whole thing, the dirt ripped to pieces, the bushes dug up and scattered, only stopping where the gigantic, hundred feet long and ten feet wide fallen trunks started, the sheer size of them disappearing into the wilderness on all sides.

"We cleared the detritus around the jet," Sand said. "Now we can get this thing gone."

"How?" I asked.

"Crete and I designed her as light as anything," Sand said. "It weighs in total, about half a car. Ten average men should be able to lift it. So in Jerico…"

"Bring me five men," one of the taller warriors commanded.

Five Jerico easily lifted the entire airship off the ground like nothing. The huge carriage settled on its side, the sleek design of the jet holding flat against their shoulders. Sideways. Nice.

"You flew in this?" One of them asked. "I've had horses that weigh more."

"Horses are all heart," Sand said. "This thing is technology. It's cold and empty. We've been all over the island together and she still does us this dirty."

"Will she fly again?" The guy asked. "You know... somewhere else?"

"That's the plan," Sand said. "That, or we strip her down to bolts. Either way, park her by the guest house. I'll help decide what parts of this machinery can help Jerico. I keep everything else though."

"Deal, but only the first part," the guy said. "We do have every natural resource we could ever need covered, but the jungle willingly accepts your tribute of such space-age metal. This belongs to the territory now. It's up to Racket and Foe's, what comes and goes. You knows."

"I knows," Sand said. "It's just... that's my favorite plane."

"Yeah well those were our favorite trees," the guy said, as they walked off with Sand's plane, and his higher ground too.

"Could use a hand," Sand said to me.

"You could use a hand factory," I said. "But we'll be enough. We got you. Let's get to work. Lynn, what do I do?"

"Ollux, what does he do?" Lynn asked, turning the question over.

"Three piles," came a voice that wasn't any of us.

So it wasn't just us in that grove. We turned to see a woman standing before us, a new face, a beautiful one, with long red hair and at least six foot five, wearing long white robes that screamed medical doctor. But then again Infinite had put us in prison scrubs. Maybe I just shouldn't judge a person by their clothes, least of all women? Nah, that couldn't be right.

"Seath, MD," she said, and in my mind, I threw my hands up. "First, a pile of feedstock for the livestock. Anything unscarred from stem to root goes through me, then to the farmers."

"So you can note exactly what was lost and replant accordingly, on top of properly utilizing every blade of grass as lifeblood to the herbivores," I said.

"What is alive, to be utilized by those what want it," the doctor said.

"Something's different about you today," Sand said, grinning at me.

"Second, a pile of anything charred, we don't want that in the feed," the doctor said. "We'll keep it for the next round of dark earth."

"Terra preta," Lynn said, turning all the heads. "One pile for biochar."

"What is dead, to be reused by those what need it," the doctor said. "You know of terra preta, who are you?"

"Derek Nite and Lynn Lyre, travelers without a home," I said.

"Doctor without a pen," Seath replied honestly, pointing to herself.

I handed her my notebook and pen.

"I like you," she said. "Give me a minute, let me unload what's already been accounted for today before I forget..."

"I thought you said you didn't bring much," Sand said, again impressed.

"I also said it would be enough," I reminded him, pretending to roll up my sleeves. "What's the third pile for? Wait who's that guy?"

"SAND FREEDOM!"

And as Ollux only yawned, and Seath only scribbled faster, Lynn and I looked up to see the man was already tearing his shirt off, coming at us walking like he was on his way to a boxing ring. Sand sighed.

"I'm sorry, and this is?" Lynn asked.

"Kit," the new guy said, throwing his brown half-shirt to the ground. "Sand Freedom, I challenge you in combat for crimes against the territory."

"Straight to the point then," Sand said, putting his hands up.

"WHAT—" I started.

"Relax, there's been eight of these guys already this morning," Ollux said, sitting on a log in the grass, just taking a break.

"You're condoning this?" I shouted.

"Every warrior of Jerico has the freedom to get wrecked," Ollux said.

Kit charged Sand, but Sand only dug his feet into the ground. Kit landed a much younger fist on Sand's old-man face, but the old jaw didn't move, and in fact Sand countered with a push kick against Kit's chest so hard that by the time the young fist hit the old face, there wasn't any momentum behind it. With a single move Sand brought his hands up like spears directly into each of Kit's flailing armpits and Kit whimpered instead of roared, his arms going limp in a moment. Then Sand pivoted him around with a shoulder twist and stepped on his feet from behind.

"Timber," Sand said.

"AAAHH!" Was the only response we got from Kit.

Sand set him up to fall like he would a tree—away from us (I hoped). With his feet trapped and arms useless, Kit wheeled forward in slow motion, unable to stop his landing, until he face-planted in the grassy ground in what we in the skateboarding (and trampoline) business call a scorpion. He slammed on his stomach and his feet whipped around so hard they touched the back of his head—then it was over, score one for the opposite of a broken back. But still… bodied. After taking that much force, all he could do was gasp for breath on the ground, his eyes fluttering, closing in pain, instead of rolling back in unconsciousness. Eh, he was fine.

"I know," Sand said, patting him on the back. "Just go to sleep…"

"How… did you do that?" I asked, unsure if I was excited or horrified.

"With great remorse, and hope that he will learn from one, instead of stumble through many," Sand said. "Put him in the third pile."

We looked sideways and saw a group of guys, at least six of them, either motionless or slowly groaning on the ground, all looking just like Kit, all with dirt on their faces. They were all confined to their backs, I hadn't registered them, I wasn't looking for people on the ground.

"THAT'S the third pile?" I shouted.

"I did not decide the rules," Sand said. "But they have not stopped coming."

"We'll never break you," Seath said. "Still formidable as the day you left."

Left?

"More would be dead if I had stayed," Sand said. "Why do you think I've been gone?"

Stayed? Gone? Words?

"To hide from your shameful past, to start again with those who don't know you, take your pick," Seath said. "You owed us before you owed us, Freedom. If you won't take a thousand lashes—and that pile seems to speak for itself on that one—then you will take a thousand miles. The kids are doing a good enough job excavating. It is time the penance of Freedom begins. Citizen soldiers, stop."

We had arrived to a broken field and two towering piles of already cleared leaves. While we had been talking, those piles seemed to be disappearing as fast as we could make them, and now we realized on the other side there was a constant stream of regular townsfolk, men and women and children too, all barefoot, all using nothing but short sling bags to carry two huge armfuls of debris each, walking up empty handed and away overloaded with sticks and twigs and leaves and ferns. They walked a single file path away from us, and I noticed on the way down, the kids would dart through the load-bearing path like little shooting stars, picking up any loose sticks or fallen twigs, anything that wasn't supposed to be there. When their hands would get full, they would run to the giant pile and throw it back. A perfect system, unless you were a child. There were no machines. There was nothing to put tread marks into such a forest, the path itself wound around nature as if to remind us why it was taking a village to clean up such a huge mess. Sand looked towards all that had gone into finishing the cleanup, just as the perfectly working line behind the disappearance of the piles stopped.

"Damn," Sand said.

"Each villager has walked a mile and back, some twice, or more, in just the light of this morning," Seath said. "They have shown up to help even when the cost of their labor is everything, and the consequence is not their own. From here on out, you will complete the pile, no matter how big it grows, no matter how long it takes. The bio-char drop off is a quarter mile up that way, and the feedstock goes just beyond, to a silver silo system at the base of the walls. You'll see it, trust me. Yes doctor?"

"Yes doctor," Sand said, sighing. "I understand. I accept. I would do anything to make this up to you."

"Does that mean you'll go easier on my warriors?" Seath asked.

"No," Sand said. "Let me still be useful to the territory in my own way, perhaps the only way I have left."

"SAND FREEDOM—oph!"

And before I'd even seen him coming, another young male warrior charging in was on his stomach in the dirt. His arms twitched by his sides; they had not been used to stop the fall, not even a bit.

"Are you just going to let them keep coming and going?" I asked.

"Yeah," Sand said. "I won't give up, not on myself, and not on Jerico. I am here for a reason. I welcome anyone to see for themselves if I've gotten too old for that to still be true. But when the third pile overshadows the other two, when the time calls for your strongest, do not forget who he is. He still carries the territory in his heart, and he owes you much more than three piles. He never forgot you. He never forgot… anything."

"Hope not," Seath said, looking at Sand funny. She was about his age after all. "You should talk like that more."

"I've talked enough for one life," Sand said, staring back.

The platform had landed behind her and she stepped on, leaving a much taller, muscular warrior guy in her place, growling at Sand. He sighed as the wind picked up and Seath sat down on the platform for stability, taking out a nice leather bound notebook and going over what looked objectively like a well-crafted, almost realistic sketch of—

Wait a damn moment.

"Give me back my notebook!" I shouted, running over the grass after Seath, who was traveling faster sideways than up at the moment.

"I'm sorry Derek, too far away, can't hear you…"

"You can hear me fine!" I shouted into the wind.

"Sorry but we need a head start on seedlings!" was all the doc said, the wooden platform raised a good six feet into the air, out of reach. "I'm taking this to the Zentri agriculture center."

"That doesn't… I thought the Zentri was underland?" I shouted back.

"Damn he's smart."

"See you CAN HEAR ME!" I said, taking a jump and swiping at the bottom of the wood, my fingers just brushing it before it was suddenly twenty, thirty feet overhead.

"I said sorry!" Seath said, poking her head precariously over the side. "I'll bring it back unless you know… science! Ollux, do more than sit on a log. What are all these drawings of horses for?"

And she was gone. I had run like a fool the entire clearing over, and had a ways to go before rejoining with the group.

"She took my notebook," I said to Lynn.

"We heard," she said. "Do you need me to teach you how to draw better?"

"I need you to teach me how to do everything better," I said.

She looked at me funny—but not the usual funny. This was different.

"No you don't," she said. "You just want me to."

"What's the difference?" I asked, my mind still not really there.

"Everything," Lynn said. "You can see that, can't you?"

"Nope," I said honestly. "I'm kinda occupied, trying to remember what else was on that notebook. It's the library computer all over again…"

"The what?"

"Nothing, you're not James," I said lamely.

"That's much less charming than the sea conch story," Lynn said, shaking her head. "Alright tell it to me straight. How many terrible emo punk rock songs have you written about this summer?"

"Four," I admitted, looking down. "But those I'm not ashamed of. It's more like the blueprints of our old house, the map from Galan Town to Cradlesong and back, both over and underland, any other secrets Hector may have hid in those pages, don't forget everyone here probably speaks Latin, the secrets of the satellite… oh, and possibly a few private notes from a much younger me that may include you, Heather, Crete, Sand, Trevor, Percy, Victoria, Alcyon, Odd, Issaic, and everyone else we've ever been in the same room with since… the start?"

"Of what?" Lynn demanded.

"Since... want some coffee?" I said.

She froze. "That was the first thing I ever said to you."

"That's why I wrote it down," I said. "I lost a whole novel on that computer."

"Don't lie to me, you're bad at it," Lynn said. "Derek... are you keeping a journal of our adventure through time and space?"

"I don't know how to answer that without saying yes," I said.

"So..." Lynn coaxed.

"Oh, yes, absolutely," I said.

"Can I read it? Once it's out of enemy hands?"

"Good idea, starting at opposite ends," Sand shouted to us over the clearing. "Leaves and dead leaves, let's go!"

"You can read anything I write," I said. "How about after this damage has been undone, we go steal the crap out of my notebook—or you know, track that doctor down through totally ordinary means and beg her for my drawings back."

Lynn smiled. "It's leaves and dead leaves then.

Sand didn't say a word as we got to work, lifting plants, checking them for damage, and creating two massive piles on the edge of the clearing. We cleared the place in the next few hours, leaving only two massive piles to be hand-transported up the hill. It took a while, it took a few stories about Lynn and her father, about James and my mother and me, about high school versus home school, the time Crete turned every surface of his house into a touch screen—but finally the forest was clear, the dirt and grasses just as they were, you know... before the jet crashed down like a meteor. We had the easy part. The piles of debris and detritus were huge. It really would take a thousand trips for a human with no tools to carry all that away. When we finally did get the place clear, we fell to the grass at the same time, exhausted.

Something whistled above my head. I looked up just in time to see the canteen falling down, heavy with—yes, that was water. I wanted to thank someone, but I also wanted to drink water. Then—

It was a little girl with purple eyes, standing not even tall enough to peer over the balcony, instead sticking half her body out of it to throw me the canteen. She pointed to Lynn.

Lynn looked over and caught me. "You—"

"Fine, here," I said, giving her the first sip.

The little girl in the trees nodded, as Lynn took a sniff, nodded like Sophia (our new semi-sabretoothed clouded leopard friend) would, drank half the thing and threw it back to me. I took a few sips and tossed the thing to Sand. He perfectly deflected it and it landed back in my hand. I looked up to the girl in the trees. She nodded. That was allowed, apparently.

I took another few sips, as Sand took out a slim flask from his waist.

"Water, don't worry," he said.

"Never do," I said.

"I appreciate it," he said. "Everything."

"So do we," I said.

He looked at us hard just then. Like he was seeing something new.

"It's after mid-day," he said. "I want Derek to be able to walk tomorrow, so I'd like you to leave the rest to me. There's a lot more of Jerico to see than this."

"Like giraffes?" Lynn said smiling.

"You saw giraffes?" Sand asked. "Pictures or it didn't happen."

"The doctor took my notebook," I said.

"You gave a doctor your notebook," Sand corrected. "It's a notebook. It can't much impact a plot. Anyways we already did that. I am here to carry these leaves up that hill. Fighting back is just burning daylight, so as long as I am here, I will speak the strongest language I can. If some would spread the word about how foolish it is to distract me from my burden, well that's only communication. Go back."

"Hell I will," I said. "I've been watching you stand a human shield against these warriors all day. They can spread the word. You keep taking them out, I'll keep taking notes."

"Without your very important notebook?" Sand said.

"I can remember things," I said.

"Lynn, talk some sense into him," Sand said.

"Nope," Lynn said. "We're not in this halfway. We didn't stop by so we could feel good about ourselves. We go home when you do."

"Damn," Sand said, smiling. "Okay, but leave the piles to me. Ollux, what's next?"

"Depends which one of them wants to learn how to cut a tree in half by hand," Ollux said, yawning.

"What if both?" Lynn and I said at the same exact time.

2.2

AT NIGHT IN DREAMS

The last time I slept this well on my back, it had been under the snowy caves of Vema, in a mound of dirt, and in my work clothes (the Infinite kind). This time it was because my damn splint wouldn't let me sleep on my stomach like usual, not if I didn't want the edge of it slicing into the back of my calf. Also this was the only way I could keep an eye on both doors, the one behind us that led to that side-hall and bathroom, and the sliding front door past the fireplace. I couldn't sleep facing away from a door, old habits. Yet somehow I hadn't moved all night, somehow my body had actually slept.

But my mind hadn't. I dreamt of the night it had all started. The blast that woke us up, watching Mom shoot up to the stars, flying for the first time. The girl in the parachute, an open door, some tiny footsteps. A voice, a single echo in the noises, nothing more than static but I heard it like words so real…

Dream boy…

Then I was awake. No blueblood to stop my body jolting awake from a good old fashioned nightmare. I wasn't eight, I wasn't in Silka. I was in—

Jerico Territory. Hello world.

"Wake up boy."

"Universe?" I said, looking around.

"No, Heather," she said.

I hadn't seen her. Actually, I still didn't. I only heard her voice from above. I left the bed behind and crutched out into the sun, staring up at the loft. Everyone else was missing, I didn't see anyone until Heather stuck her head over the balcony. Her purple hair was a mess, but her eyes were wide awake.

"You gotta see this," she said.

"You know I can't—" I started.

"We both know you can," she said. "I climbed a tree for you."

I dropped the crutches and took to the ladder with two hands and one foot. It took a few good jumps, but then Heather had her hand under my arm and she pulled me up, not only to the loft, but right into her arms. My foot… if there was any pain, something was distracting me from it, probably her hand still over my shoulder—and that was before she sat me down on her bed. Her blankets were clumped around us at the foot. I never made my bed either, I always forgot. But the blankets were soft. Like her arms, if not her hands.

"Wait you showered before coming up here, right?" Heather asked.

I groaned, looking back at the ladder.

"Kidding," she said. "I don't mind the dirt. I am the dirt, I can't be crushed."

"Flowerchild," I said. "Are you one of those charcoal for deodorant types?"

"What? Ew, no, there's a line, we're teenagers," Heather said.

We both sat on the end of her bed and I saw for the first time, there were windows up here. Through one of them I could hear the source of all that faint shouting I'd heard this morning. About thirty people, kids and instructors total, were exercising out on a field behind our cabin, away from the main quad and down a bit of an incline from us. It wasn't hard to spot Derek.

"He's gonna die," I said.

"Then he'll just come back stronger," Heather said.

"He isn't a demon," I said, frowning.

"You have one second to answer, do you wish you were out there too?"

"Yes," I said. "I can't sleep on my back for a month."

"You were out like a snoring light," Heather said.

"I was snoring?" I asked.

"Someone was snoring. Either way you slept fine, I can see it in your eyes."

"I… slept… eyes," I admitted. "But I can't do this right now."

"Do what right why?" Heather asked.

"I can't keep making it up the ladder on one leg," I said. "Not this ladder. I can't be a cripple in the middle of being wanted by one city, being trapped in another, and being forever entangled in the present, history and future comings of another. I can't do this to you. Not here."

"What are you doing to me exactly?"

"I'm asking you—how do you sleep while the city's burning?" I asked, letting my brain take over. "Sorry, I meant, where do you go when you can't go home? I mean, damnit, what do I do when I can't do anything? What would you do? What do I—"

"First we breathe," Heather said, taking her eyes off Derek, as he hit the dirt for the tenth time since we'd sat down. "Second of all, no city wants or doesn't want you that bad. Third, you aren't a cripple, you're James. Forth, aw, so cute. And fifth, I forgot to ask because I'm a terrible friend, how's the leg?"

"Whatever they did for the local pain hasn't worn off," I said. "I can't put an ounce of weight on the bones but as long as you don't kick me in the splint…"

"I wouldn't kick a baby bird in its wounded wing, I'm not a monster—"

"I'm a man Heather, a full grown—"

"Breathe," she said. "You don't want to be a warrior, you just want to help."

"Yeah," I said. "I don't know what a woman's relationship to work is, besides probably being better at it than me but… men work. We do things to serve a purpose or we don't get love, that's our curse. And even if that's stupid, and not appropriate to apply to just a single binary gender role, fine, whatever, but tell me what can a guy like me hope to—"

"Can you cook on one foot?" Heather asked.

"I… think?" I said.

"Then congratulations James Nite, you're useful again," she said.

"Because you're hungry?" I asked, incredulously.

"Because I think Crete and Lynn are outside working on some super-secret invention, probably the Jerico version of some stupid comic book troupe, instead of doing my laundry for me," Heather said.

"Then breakfast is on us," I said.

"It's on you flyboy. I haven't cooked since… since the day I lost the sun."

"That's a crime," I said. "That's the opposite of fairy tale. That's… perfect."

"What is?"

"I can help, and make you something nice, at the same time," I said.

"I can't have nice things," Heather said. "They just leave me alone underground with rocks. I can have rocks."

"I'm better than rocks," I said, smiling. "I know that for sure."

I was about to stand up on one leg when the bed opposite us pulsed, and the covers fell off the giant head and mane of Sophia, sleeping like a baby in Lynn's bed, completely oblivious to us.

"She's—" I started, but the adorableness beat out the fear in a blink.

"Perfect in every way, let a killer queen sleep." Heather agreed, quietly.

I nodded, pushing myself off the bed for just long enough to see that steep declining ladder, reminding me where I was. Um…

"Life is a ladder," I sighed, as humbled (not by choice) as a guy could be. "Can I get a shoulder, Heather?"

"Only because you begged."

And she took my arms and led me back to the ladder. Remember no crutches up here. It was hard to find a path through all the feathers. I climbed down to the first floor, fell to the ground to reach the crutches, got back up again, and headed to the kitchen. It wasn't anything but the far left corner of the cabin, separated by one wall running through a third of the living room. There was a small stove and sink but most of the space was taken by the huge wooden counters and cabinets all around us. There were tools by the sink and yep, the drawers were full of all sorts of metal and wooden pots, pans, utensils, everything we'd need.

"I don't even know most of these colors," Heather said.

She opened the big pantry door. It was full. Not hotel full, not guest room full. Like it had all grown here full. Fruits, vegetables, jars of bread starters, spices and seasonings, dried herbs, and a coldstone at the bottom full of meat.

"Well at least this prison has a decent kitchen," Heather said.

"Oh so that's hanging over your head too?" I said.

"We're not talking about bad clouds," Heather said. "You can talk to me about whatever you want. If you're wondering what I think of the sword grass and the initiation ceremony, I would tell you I probably think the same as you. This is just a different kind of prison. Unless…"

"Unless?" I asked, juggling three kinds of peanut butter.

She screwed up her face. "Unless this is exactly how you felt when we fell you down the falloff, thrust asunder into Vema on the plight of the Reaper."

"All I heard was asunder," I said.

Heather threw some sort of pinkish, green-tipped fruit at me, and three clay jars hit the ground as I caught the spiky fruit (thankfully the peanut butter wasn't compromised). I peeled back the skin and took a bite, or two. The inside was a white pulp, with black specks making each bite look like dominos. She was right about all the new colors, I didn't know what it was either. But it was good.

"Can I just say one thing?" I asked, throwing the fruit back to her like a football. "Did you just try to think like me?"

She nodded. Then she caught the fruit, took a bite, and her face changed.

"I don't know what that is either," I said. "Yes this is exactly how we felt, and yes that means this is much more than a trap. We're here for reasons. Maybe not family or home reasons, but it's still just a sharp knife, and us. That I know."

"I heard you," Heather said.

"I know you did," I said.

"No, I mean… I heard you," she said, taking a deep breath. "The day your mother… I told you we had the Observatory bugged. I heard your mother talking to Hector. I heard my father's voice for the first time in ten years, and then I heard you call him sir. I heard the way Teresa talked of my… of the other parts of my family I may never know. I heard your voices and I could feel the respect you were giving him. Giving us. Nite, I liked you before I ever saw your faces. And when I did see them, I wasn't expecting it. I thought you dead. I thought my father dead. Odd wasn't worried, he said any Infinite like Hector or Teresa would be able to escape death like taxes."

"Ew," I said. "Come on Odd."

"I didn't believe him, because he's terrible," Heather said. "I didn't know what he was talking about, until I saw you in that vent. You didn't have to speak, but I was about to. Then something in my brain put the face to the voice before I could. In that moment everything I'd ever hoped about the lightning city came true. In that moment I knew my father was still alive. You gave that to me."

"Oh," I said. "Didn't know my trick worked for other people."

"The ancient art of first impressions?" Heather asked. "That's not a trick. Sometimes it is. Sometimes all you need is…"

I carefully flipped a razor sharp kitchen knife around by the balance point and held the handle out to Heather. "And us."

"I come equipped," she said, ten claws sharper than any knife in her hands, the ones that so far today had only helped hold me up. I'd almost forgotten.

"I think the counters are made of wood for a reason," I said. "Only thing missing, the first thing I ever learned to make in woodshop. Cutting boards."

"Then I'll take that knife," she said, claws stowed, gloves off and in her pockets again. "Nothing dulls damascus faster than wood."

"Oh, backstory," I said. "I thought our days of precious metals were done."

"Oh, commentary," she said, and I laughed. Nicely done. "There's only one precious earthly thing I want right now."

"Pancakes," I said. "Am I right or am I right?"

"How'd you know that?" She asked.

"You talk in your sleep," I said. "Something about coconut pancakes. Not last night, the snow cave underground mountain dirt bed floor night."

"Which snow cave under—"

"Stop it," I said, and the impossible happened—she laughed. "Am I wrong?"

Her face was as white as the flour. "James…"

"Sorry, dirt bed, couldn't sleep, got ears."

"Don't be sorry for having ears," she said. "I was trailing off for sentiment—when a girl says your name in a crescendo, it's usually a good thing. Whatever you're thinking, keep going."

Was I supposed to be able to think after that?

"Well…" I said, avoiding *um* only with all my willpower. "Whose idea was the coconut?"

Heather's hand twitched, and she smiled. That was a yes. Again it was weird to see her guard down. She wasn't normal, it didn't take only empathy. Usually to win a moment with her involved respect, and reminding her we were worthy of it. To Heather, that was closeness.

"Mine," she said.

"Not even surprised," I said. "See, claws down, you've still got some pretty good taste. Anytime you have something to throw in the pot, I want to hear it. I'll let you know when that stops."

"And when we leave the kitchen?" She asked.

"Still listening," I said. "I wrote a song for you, wanna hear it, here it go. You've got a frieeeeeend in—"

She laughed and went to salute me but her hands refused to move, her body remembering it was holding a knife before her brain did. I saw it. I liked it.

"So you do have a hold back," I said.

"I'm a normal girl," she said, twirling the knife like she was trying to take her own fingers off. "How do you turn that into pancakes?"

"That's turning into butter glaze for the strawberries," I said.

"You can make strawberries better?" Heather asked/shouted.

"Not by much," I said, smiling. "Leave it to me. You just coconut."

"Yes sir," she said, looking at me weird as she started removing the outer layer of brown leafing around the fruit with that knife.

For SOME reason, Heather wasn't that helpful. She was following me the whole time, looking amazed at me turning simple ingredients into breakfast. We weren't even in there an hour, and I wasn't a masterchef like the mysterious and serendipitous Gira of Zentri, but Mom had taught us to make everything we'd ever wanted growing up. Short story, I could cook, and it seemed to surprise Heather. She stared at me when I set the first two pancakes on two round wooden plates, from the other side of a small kitchen island counter.

"James," she said again, making my name into more syllables than I'd ever heard before. Was that a crescendo? I couldn't read music.

She took a piece of pancake by her fingers, ripping it out of the rest. I did the same, then looked up see Heather silent in her seat, staring at the pancakes with one hand over her mouth, both eyes clearly welling up in tears. Her whole body was still. I didn't make a move. I watched as she reached out and poked the thing with her finger.

"It's real," I said.

Bad move. She blitzed out of her emotions with ten razor sharp claws inches from my face, the ringing of metal so close I could almost taste it.

"Sorry," she said, her claws still as steady as anything. "I'm… sorry."

"You have nothing on or under earth to be sorry about," I said. "Not to me."

"It's just, I'm kind of emotional about… pancakes," Heather said. "You can keep talking. If you really understand… pancakes, as much as you seem to."

I thought real hard.

"He's alive, Heather," I said. "These aren't closure pancakes, but they're damn sure victory pancakes. I know both of those sound too sweet to be true. But they are. Now pass a cripple a strawberry and hold the metaphors."

"Damn you," she said, shaking her head.

I thought I'd blown it. Then she put a strawberry in her mouth, and leaned over the table. Her lips were wrapped far more than halfway around it, there wasn't much room for… retrieval. I flinched, but she only looked at me like she was daring me. So more gently than I'd ever done a thing before…

I met her at strawberry. Our lips weren't touching until they were. Our eyes were open until she closed hers, and I did too, even if for just two seconds. Her hair smelled like coconut, I felt her breath on my lips, and she was… kissing me? Was that code for strawberry? I didn't know, that's all I knew. No questions, no answers, other than I was NOT ready for it. Then she opened her eyes, let go of the fruit, and sat back all cool on her side of the counter.

"I… choke on this now right?" I said.

"Please don't," she said, her face as red as the strawberry.

"Because pancakes?" I said.

"Because you," she said, the same voice, the same purple eyes staring me down. "One does not simply wake up in strangerland and make coconut pancakes. That means this isn't strangerland. You give me perspective, James."

"I make a good angle?" I said, not really understanding.

"You make more than that, to me," Heather said. "Do I…"

"Yes," I blurted out.

And only her eyebrows gave her away. Somehow, by not knowing exactly what we meant, it meant more than anything. Aw.

"I did that before you did," she said. "I did it halfway… so… so you could remind me that we have work to do. If it was the other way around… I don't know. I need you to say it. I can't."

"What if I can't either?" I asked. "Isn't that kind of a big deal?"

"Then why does it feel so… unimportant?" Heather asked, sadly.

It was a sad kind of true. She was right, this should mean more. It could…

"You just called kissing me unimportant," I said. "I'm offended."

Heather smiled nervously. "I didn't mean—"

"I'm not offended," I said.

And again, a lot of it went unsaid. The way we were looking at each other in the sun. How much of our lives had fallen apart in the first half of this summer. How much we brought out the best in each other. How people wanted both of us dead, or worse. How cool it was that her hair was naturally purple, remembering she'd bleached it white when we met, probably so no one in Silka City would know she was Vema, again for wanting her dead reasons. The fireworks going off in my heart, the actual bombs and explosions that had gone off around us (both had happened).

"Come on flyboy, say it."

"What makes you think I want to?" I asked.

She looked sad again. She didn't have to say anything, she was right. We couldn't have nice things, not yet. Rocks would have to do.

"I get it," I said, trying to control my eighteen year old heart (like that ever worked). "I think I do. Work to do?"

"Work to do," she said, blinking, backing off to her side of the counter with a sigh. She stared at me for a moment, then remembered her plate of pancakes and picked one up by hand. She bared her vampire fangs (joking) and took a bite.

"It's perfect."

I smiled. I could still feel her on my—no. Work to do.

"So we're not in prison, we're not in either of our home towns, and we're not even in strangerland," I said. "Where do you think we are?"

"I don't know this place," Heather said, admitting it. "Can you walk?"

"I can do anything," I said.

"Can you keep a secret?" Heather asked, looking behind me at something.

"From my brother?" I said, wincing. "Not for long."

Heather shrugged. "Do what you will, I'm not your boss."

"Yes ma'am," I said, and she tried not to blush. I'd learned that from Derek.

And speaking of—there he was, leaning on Lynn, walking back inside the cabin with some sort of limp, but I couldn't tell which side it was on. Copycat.

"There they are," Heather said, beating me to it by a second, smiling. "The man with the plan—to die."

"Spoilers," Derek complained, with a big grin.

"So how was black belt training?" I asked.

Foreshadowing achieved. A bunch of stuff happened here, but I think you already got that from my brother. We'll pick it up at... prove it.

Prove it, prove it, prove it, prove it—

We waved Derek and Lynn off with innocent eyes. Sarcasm. They weren't going off to war, they were going into trees, they'd be fine.

"I think Sophia followed Lynn into the arbor," I said, crutching into the sunlight, from soft wood to softer grass. "Heather, where's your talking animal?"

"I don't get it," Heather said.

"It's a storybook stereotype, he's making fun of you," Crete said.

"Are you calling me a princess?" Heather said, wheeling on me. Then she stopped, and her eyes welled up. "Wait. Are you calling me a princess?"

I held my hands up. "I'm just saying in the movies, princesses either come with flying horses or talking toads. I'm wondering what it says about you that we're stuck with the second one."

Crete stopped moving, I couldn't see if he was laughing. But Heather was.

"It says a lot, for a toad," she said. "Crete, what's the plan?"

"I got distracted," he said, wiping his eyes. "This way."

We followed a very shirtless Crete Magellan up the incline of the curving quad pathway, leaving our hut and the point temple of the Astral far behind us as we made for a part of the circular watering hole that lay underneath the large, looming mountains that carried on into… actually, I had absolutely no idea what was on the other side of those mountains. I could see this like I could see Castle Eclipso, a structure built into an underground volcano that rose so high and produced so much smoke that we had still to this day never seen the full scale of it. For all I knew, it extended up and out through the overland—wait. We'd gotten in trouble before for separating the over *and* under lands into two worlds. They were the same, like yinyang. No *and* required.

"So a whole city in the jungle," I said.

"More than one," Crete said. "But we'll start small."

"You call this small?"

We passed a very different quad than last night. We walked a long, uphill, curving path that led us in front of dwellings just like our guest hut, and more than a few family units who gave us the accepting (or suspicious) looks as we passed their kids playing in the grass, either in close knits on the right tree-lined side of the path or the open unity of grass on the left of it. Some kids played together, some kids played alone, but the option for both was key—such was life for an introvert like me. And it wasn't just the kids taking advantage of the huge, almost endless stretch of rolling quad grass. There was a group of elderly people doing yoga to our left, all balanced on a single leg with their eyes closed as we passed. It was incredibly hard to balance with your eyes closed—just try it.

"I call this a singularity, true, we are in the ancestral centerpoint of a nation," Crete said. "But they've got enclosures like this one as far down the island as a few miles outside Mylo. You passed a quarter dozen on your way in, you just wouldn't expect them so close to Silka."

"A quarter dozen, say three," I said, shaking my head a quarter dozen times.

Soon the endless forest on our right started to be overtaken by an inclining ridge system of small mountains leading up to the big one in the background of that northeastern corner of the quad. There, we came up on what looked like a cluster of homes all with outdoor studios, long workbenches and tools all around, scrap wood and metal all around us. There was a small fence we were about to cross, behind it were a few men and women working on different projects, one carving a tree trunk into a huge statue of a young woman, one fixing the lopsided leg of what looked like an upside down bed frame, one sitting in the middle of a thousand arrow shafts, testing each one against some sort of angle sextant device. But Crete stopped us at the fence and pointed down to a row of small metal things that looked like shoes.

"I thought the Jerico could climb the tallest trees barefoot," I said.

"They can, but a nail is a nail," Crete said. "Two places you really don't want to be barefoot, bathrooms, and woodshops. Put em on."

Heather took a pair. I only needed one.

"The woodshop is all yours," Crete said.

"I don't remember building it," I said.

"You're learning," Crete said. "Everything here belongs to the current overwatchers of the assembly, the master crafters Racket and Foe Zekyl."

"And they are…" I said, leaning on my crutches, head in a swivel.

"Hell if I know, I just got here," Crete said.

Bam. A window exploded from our right, over a small wooden house.

"Sorry!" Came a voice from somewhere above us.

There were three guys leaning out of an upstairs window, slowly lowering a huge contraption down to the floor with nothing but a plank and ropes. The two guys on the ground leapt away from the glass, and were now trying to help guide the thing into place—until we all watched it hit the house in another bang, another window exploding for the angle, and everyone danced away again.

"Safety first," Crete bragged, pointing to the shoes.

"It's giving way, help!" One of the ground guys called.

Crete and Heather were there before I could ask. I threw Heather my crutches, and together the four of them and two crutches got the thing under control enough for it to land with a boom on the front porch, no more busted windows required (they were all already broken). Heather gently danced out of the glass, as the guys stomped out of it. One guy had ended up holding both crutches; he looked around, and found me sitting on my butt on the ground.

"A lot of help you were kid," he said.

I like to watch, I almost said. But I only held my hand out.

"Holy hell," he said, running over and helping me up, instead of just throwing the crutch back to me. "You… did help."

"I fell over," I said. "That's all I did."

"But you did it so we could… stand up, little one."

"I'm not little!" I shouted, like an eight year old would.

He smiled as I stood on my own (kinda).

"Thanks Landis," Crete said, a hand on the new guy's shoulder.

The guy named Landis started, looked right, and his eyes went wide. "You!"

"Me," Crete said. "Shame about the windows."

"They'll melt," Landis said. "Magellan and guests; scary girl, one-leg-boy."

"Good to see you too," Crete said, a hand out to silence me and Heather."Safety first. Not second, not third. You can't go back and be safe after the fact. You taught me that."

"I don't follow, friend," Landis said, confused.

"He wasn't talking to you," came a voice from behind us.

"We taught you well," came another one.

And we couldn't turn around fast enough. By the time we did, Crete was engulfed in a two way, two-shaped hug, or tackle, depends on how you define love, with Landis scratching his head behind us. Then the three were wrestling, and then they weren't, because Crete had both guys in the dirt, a knee on either.

"I could teach you so much more," Crete said, grinning, fake punching down at the two guys he had on the ground.

"But then the circle would be complete," one of them said with a smile, his head in the dirt, so close to the broken glass…

Crete pulled the two guys up without an ounce of effort. The first was a tall, wiry guy with wild, sun-streaked brown and blonde hair. He was top heavy with a tiny waist, like he had been a world champion swimmer at one point in his life. Now, he was older than even Crete, which must have put him in his seventies. But he had a few inches on his height, and had taken the fall gracefully, laughing as he pulled himself up out of the dirt on rough hands, calloused fingers, barely covered feet still covered in sawdust, probably tough as nails even without the shoes. He reminded me of Derek.

"Racket," Crete said, and the guy nodded, putting one hand on the ratchet in his belt, another on his heart, and bowed to us. "And co."

"And Foe," the other guy corrected.

The second was smaller than me, wearing something I hadn't seen in years—glasses. Small, circular, wireframe glasses on a tiny head and small features, bald as anything, but a small, trimmed white beard on his jaw. He smiled up at Crete, no bows, all teeth, quieter than Racket but just as happy to see us.

"It's been years," Racket said, like an old friend. "How was the war?"

Crete gave us a look, before answering. "Every breath we take is progress."

"So it never even ended," Foe said wisely, pushing his glasses up. "You make a terrible destroyer of worlds."

"Never wanted to be anything less," Crete said, looking at me.

"What worlds?" I asked, looking between them. "What war?"

"It's a figure of speech," Crete said, giving Racket the evil eye. "You are starting to get a sense of the island as the more… desensitized of us know it."

"Old," Heather said, arms folded.

"Experienced, seasoned maybe, out of respect for your elders," Crete said.

"Old as dirt," Heather said, digging in.

"Fine," Crete sighed. "We're old. The others died young or just died. As young as you are, you're only starting to feel the weight of something as powerful as the Infinite Army, and what that might mean for freedom. To us, joking around about the destruction of the island is nothing new."

"So these are the kids who woke the Vempire?" Foe said, raising his glasses at me and Heather again. "The ones the sun temple can't stop talking about, the bells we heard from South Arbor. Were you surprised Silka didn't welcome you home as saviors of the very nation they've spent ten years refusing to help?"

"I'm starting to be less surprised," I answered honestly. "But when it comes to the Vempire, I still don't understand why it took us to do it."

"Because no one else ever tried," Heather said, sadly, and madly, all at once.

"You talking to us?" Racket asked. "The builder co? Those who give their lives for the good of the Jerico? Those who broke backs and legs laying the tree bridges and floating houses, those who cleared miles of trees and established the farms and trading paths that keep our people alive?"

"Heather right?" Foe said, a hand on his buddy's shoulder, taking over like I would for Derek. "Heather, I feel for your people, and I'm glad they are finally free of the 'natural disaster' that kept them underland since the Blitz. But you're talking to the territory equivalent of nerds in the highest order. When did nerds ever change anything?"

"Sometimes nerds can change everything," Heather said, not willing to let them off the hook, reaching out with her hand trying to smack me on the shoulder. I moved away.

"Someone should have told me that in high school," Foe said. "Here, trees is knowledge, and we're the books."

"We used to have time to future craft, to look ahead to a time where we could return to the total resource utilization of our ancestors," Racket said, looking up to where the stars should have been. "Now we can barely keep up with the little things, like working plumbing, uphill irrigation, ever shifting plates below the foundations of the circle cities, tube mechanics and what they mean for the strength of a three hundred foot tree, it goes on."

"Hmm," Crete said. "Truthfully I was here to ask for as many spare parts as you've got, for personal reasons."

"I miss when honesty was enough," Foe said, almost nostalgically.

"It's not?" Crete said, a look on his face I wasn't ready for.

Racket sighed. "If Crete Magellan asks for a piece of the moon, he gets it. That's how it used to be. Now, I'm afraid we have nothing that has not been earmarked for the territory."

"I'm not here for the territory," Crete said, his eyes sad, or dark, or something. "You know me."

"We do, unfortunately," Racket said. "The last time you asked us for supplies, we never got them back. You know I hate circles."

"That's why I don't borrow," Crete said. "I repurpose. You taught me how to build a machine without wasting a part, and the ability to take it all apart someday. Machines are not usually designed to last forever."

"Then what are you asking us for?" Racket said.

"The one you owe me," Crete said. "Not Sand, me. Remember Portia?"

"Of course we remember Portia, she almost broke the moon," Racket said.

"She actually did break it, I just fixed it—" Crete started.

"Blast you," Foe said. "What do you want?"

"Nothing that's been earmarked, old friend," Crete said, the three of them speaking some kind of code I wasn't familiar with. "You'll know what I want."

"We always do," Foe sighed. "Wait, I meant we never do, and are always completely unprepared for the magnitude. That's what I meant."

"What's going on with the dado bind on that x-shaft?" I asked, curious.

"A new kind of support block for an old platform on top of an even older mountain," Foe said, as we saw a group of men transporting a huge wooden something else, breaking no windows on their way through.

"We've done six foundation replacements with this new bind," Racket said. "It's stronger than butt ending, even if the hand-routing takes longer."

"But it's for a treehouse," I said. "That means the bottom is the bottom."

Crete looked at me curiously. "I helped invent this system. Any joinery stronger requires too many cuts for hand tools, and too much weight for—"

"But you're weakening the wood where all the walking's happening," I said.

"What's the worst thing that can fall out of a treehouse?" Foe shrugged.

"The treehouse," I said, in monotone.

I crutched to the thing and gave the corner edge a push with the butt end of a crutch. The split happened as soon as my crutch touched the wood, and both sides of the craft fell apart around the guys carrying it.

"This is one of those times where I'm right… but I'm not," I said.

"Kill the cripple?"

I didn't see who said it, but the workers were all looking at me with emotionless eyes as their construct fell apart, holding their hands in the air, the universal sign for *come on man.*

"What's your name?" another said, staring at me with something else entirely in his eyes.

"James," I said lamely.

"You're hired, James," the guy said, and the crew walked off, leaving the guts of their build scattered all over the floor. Wait—

"He saw that by seeing it," Foe said to me.

"You looking for a job James?" Crete asked, smiling at me.

"You aren't surprised that he took that apart with one hit," Heather said, blinking. "Why?"

"Well… think of Jerico as a wee bit more offensive than we let on," Racket said. "The arborists live in a high, walled, ring of trees surrounding our circle city. The ground is clear around the walls, but as the jungle inclines towards the mountain, it becomes impossible to cross. The only way into our quad is through the arbor. And since flying isn't possible here, even the most steadfast intruder would have to come through the tree platforms. So if there's ever an intruder… we need a quick way to take that tree platform away."

"You design your foundations to fail?" I asked, blinking.

"Exactly," Foe said. "Call it destruct codes, call it a deterrent."

"Call grass whatever you want, just keep off it after sunset," Heather said.

"You saw that, good," Racket said. "Expect everything here to either fall apart or stab you, we call that the level."

"Well damn, welcome to Jerico," I said, shaking my head.

"You can always leave and return to the lightning city," Foe said.

"No we can't," I said. "We came all the way from south Arbor. The wood was solid. Maybe you do know what you're doing."

"High praise," Foe said, sarcastically.

"Would you like to learn exactly what we are doing?" Racket said, while his buddy only scoffed, but didn't object. "Have a bit of a foundation, so to speak, before you try to reassemble something that took a second to destroy?"

"How about it?" Heather teased. "You said you missed school."

"I did say that," I said. "Is this school?"

"It is a place where we can teach you things yes," Crete said. "I agree. Given your one-leggedness, you could at least keep your brain active during these hard times. Maybe by the time you can walk again, you will run."

"Okay rage," I said, Heather smacking me on the arm for stealing her word.

I bent down to pick up a small hammer on the ground, and I was already upright and holding it handle out to Racket when we all saw what we saw. A shockwave spread down my shoulder, a bolt of static electricity as clear as day, dancing around my hand and into the hammer, disappearing into my skin with one faint, final… zap.

"OW!" I shouted, only feeling the thing at that last moment, like I'd gotten shocked from a door handle after risky business-ing all over the carpet. Damn you hammer.

"We all saw that right?" Foe asked, blinking, his glasses held to his forehead as he stared at me. "What was that? There's no electricity here, not even the buildup of static energy would have… was that what that… help me out Hatch."

"Can't brother," he said. "I suppose… he'll be hard to handle."

"I can handle anything," I said, almost red in the face, caught in the blame for whatever just happened, knowing with my whole heart that I knew as little as anyone else about whatever just happened.

Or did I? Did I just punch through the very logical thing keeping the superpowers from me, AGAIN? The entire problem with this territory was the lack of electricity, but if I was a lightning rod…

I picked up the hammer again and grimaced as I handed it to Racket, no weird mystical lightning this time, thank the thunder. Racket took his tool and looked at the burn marks down the handle, over the clear outline of my hand and fingers where I'd been holding the thing.

"I'm thinking we…" Crete started gingerly.

"Save this for study, and immediately," Racket said, speaking Crete's language for him.

Crete nodded. "As for the boy who ate lightning…"

"Welcome to build school city," Racket said, grabbing my hand off my crutch to shake. "By the second day of sanding, we'll know everything about each other. I'm very much looking forward to it."

"I'm… willing to work," I said. "But I'm not that good at talking."

"You say that like it's a worse alternative," Racket said. "But okay. You want to learn from us, then learn this."

"Hey!"

Foe threw a bag at me. I let it smack me in the legs/crutches, whatever. Inside were a few beams of hard rosewood, metal bracings, and a leather sack of what felt like either pirates coins or hardware. I was betting on doubloons.

"Come back on proper supports, we will have you," Racket proposed.

"Sounds like a plan," I said, nodding to the builders. "See you in three legs."

"Until then, Nite," Foe said.

And we were back at the cabin. Time flies when Crete carries a bag for you, and Heather drank all the coffee. We spent the next few hours taking those materials to task, and rebuilding / reinforcing the crutches I was about to spend the next four weeks on.

"Alright James, try this one out," Crete said confidently.

I hit the floor in a spectacular shattering of wood and sawdust and splinters, taking the fall on my good leg.

"Oh wait, I forgot to latch the support beams. Get up, let's try again."

And we did, though that wasn't the last time I hit the floor. But eventually…

"Once more time James, give us a go," Crete said, wincing as he watched me put all my weight on the crutches one more time…

And I didn't fall.

"Feels good," I said. "The model holds. Clamp city, glue it up."

"He won't walk for hours," Heather argued.

"Not true," Crete said, pulling out a chair by the worktable and helping me sit down. "You think I have the patience to wait twenty four hours every time I want to make a chair? No. For someone my age, the most valuable thing I have left is my time."

"Mine is my hair," Heather said, fingers running through her purple curls.

Crete put my newly reinforced half wooden, half mechanical crutches into two vice clamps built right alongside the edge of the worktable. He leaned over them with some container of a permeating white paint, and then held a torch over the thing, tracing each part of the crutches with fire. I could hear the sizzling, the chemicals coming together, and with such a simple application, it looked like Crete was waving his magic fire stick over a pile of wood and waiting for it to come to life. Because he was.

"Done," Crete said, throwing both crutches to me.

I caught them like hot cakes, but the glue had completely disappeared from the surface of the wood. The thing was warm, but also soft, sanded, and perfect.

"Great, we learned how to make a small wooden rectangle thing, what next?" Heather asked, and just as she did, there came a noise from outside.

"Same thing, just bigger," Crete said. "Woodworking is all rectangles."

I was the one to look out the front door and see the small caravan of Jerico warriors carrying the entire jet plane on three wooden planks. It only took six men to lift the thing that had sent us here, and there it was, on its side with a hole punched out of the cockpit.

"That's the one they owe you," I said, realizing.

"That's friendship right there," Crete said.

"Is it really friendship if it's based on who owes who?" I asked.

"That's what real friendship is," Crete said, grinning. "We've been owing each other for decades. Now it's my turn to keep this favor in mind, the next time Foe gets lost in the tall grass."

I smiled, but should I have? Tall people's jokes were short people's problems. Humility and empathy, the death of comedy.

"So this is why you weren't worried when we came home empty handed," Heather said. "This had yet to be earmarked."

"Yes," Crete said. "It's tradition that anything lost in the territory goes to the territory. I'm still expecting the head of the hand to demand it returned, and stripped for parts. Before that happens, we need to do something that isn't exactly cool."

"Well then it helps that we're not part of the territory," I said.

Crete shook his head. "We are here, eating from the hunter's harvest, sleeping under a roof built by the hands of the head. To do what we are about to is a defiance against the first rule of welcome. We cannot share this ship, so we must make it worth the conspiracy."

"Okay," I said. "How do we do that?"

"Every piece of the plane is a conduit," Crete said. "The more we can take apart the better, but it's the brains we really need."

"Okay so what, the engine?" I asked.

"It's a solar powered, self-sustaining and autopiloted skyship, James," Crete said. "There's no engine, only a miniature anti-gravity machine and the most powerful nuclear thrusters ever designed under three feet long. I need those devices, they contain five percent of my entire technological arsenal."

"Aren't they all cabled together?" I asked.

Crete laughed. "I haven't used cables since I was in third grade. Everything is conducted magnetically, this will be like taking a puzzle apart."

"Okay but how?" I asked. "I only see these weird seven point screws. I'm not seeing—"

Crete handed me a seven point screwdriver, taken out of a secret compartment in the jet.

"Yes sir," I said, as he handed another one to Heather.

"Sorry plane," she said, with a wince.

And it began. I sat at that worktable unscrewing anything Heather or Crete brought me, and in five minutes the jet was a pile of walls and floor panels, a pile of electronics ranging in size from a basketball to a desk, a bunch of soft, cushiony chairs (probably water buoyant), and the two thrusters and a spherical device that was welded shut. Those last three Crete had taken inside and hadn't even told us where he'd put them.

When he came back out, we realized he had been right the whole time.

"You never could sit still, could you Crete?"

It was the unfamiliar voice of an unfamiliar female leading point through the grass, gracefully pivoting over the loose metal debris. She was as tall as Ollux—another objectively beautiful and intimidating woman standing a full foot over my head, her muscles rivaling anything I'd ever seen on any man under six feet tall. Even Astor stood a hair shorter than his sister. But this new woman spoke softer. Her shoulders weren't tense, her hands didn't show any signs of leaping to the fight. She came with a carelessness, like she could afford it.

She was probably in charge of something.

Behind her a small delegation of warriors were walking up to us, as the eyes of the neighbors followed. I did see Ollux and Astor behind her, as well as a younger woman, wearing a sword on her hip with one hand on the handle.

"Cool sword," I blurted out, channeling my inner Derek.

Sword girl winked at me.

"Three piles Ma'am," Crete said. "Support structures, hardware, and electronics. Just wanted to make it easy for the acquisition squad."

"You mean you've already culled through detritus and decided for us what we get to keep?" she said, smiling. "Now how could that be one-sided?"

"Only easily," Crete said, admitting as much.

"How about I call it the one I owe you, and you introduce me to the fodder."

"Yes Ma'am," Crete said, bowing. "Meet James Nite, and Heather Denien. Fodder, this is caput Bombelle, leader of the Jerico, proprietary guardian of this little circle city, the best dancer you'll never see, the leader who united the warring militias of the jungle with an arm wrestling contest that she *technically* won, and a friend as old as time itself."

"Did you just call us fodder?" I asked.

"Did you just call me old?" Bombelle asked. She wasn't nearly as old as Crete, clearly in her thirties whereas Crete and Sand were sixty something.

"How'd you technically out-arm wrestle a jungle?" Heather asked.

"I taught a silverback gorilla the limits of breaking human bones, and named her my name," Bombelle said.

"I think I just found my spirit animal," Heather said, taking notes.

"I hear the other half of you has spent the day assisting in the crash site cleanup," Bombelle said. "I would like to pass on the thanks of a nation."

"I'll never know how to deal with that," I said, shaking my head.

"Just keep doing what you're doing, it's working," Bombelle said. "I'm here to make sure the superjet was delivered in once piece. What happened here?"

There was a gash in the side of the jet. A metal trail deep into the side of the ship, from when Heather had scooped it out with her bare will and commanded it towards a certain attacking Infinite agent. Memories… with weapons.

"Such is me without limits," Heather said.

"You did this to titanium?" Bombelle asked. "Cute."

"You think that's titanium?" Crete countered. "Cute."

"This is serious," Bombelle said. "Where is the rest of you?"

And talk about perfect timing. Or perfect writ—

Out of the setting sun behind sword girl, Sand, Derek and Lynn came almost limping up the small pathway by the gigantic grass quad, currently empty, and very much bladed up. The three of them started as silhouettes that even in matte black I could place any day. Then as they got closer I could see it was sweat giving them the world's most awesome hair, backlit by the sunset, their eyes catch-lit by the torches behind us, just starting to light up as the dusk came on.

"Took you long enough," I said.

"Took the far way," Derek said. "If you didn't notice, the grass is swords."

"If you didn't notice, we have sharper company," Crete said.

And Derek looked up at Bombelle, suddenly red in the face and doing everything in his power to keep his jaw from dropping. "You are tall…"

"I am Bombelle. Follow me. Willa, don't let Freedom out of your sight."

"Good to see you too," Sand waved, as Bombelle turned on him about as quick as she had warmed to Crete. Meanwhile, sword-girl was walking a step behind Sand, her neck craned up at him the whole time like *what you gonna do?*

"That thing you said yesterday about meeting the stupid king of the stupid Jerico," Derek whispered to Sand. "Is that happening now?"

"Yep," Sand said, under earshot of everyone except sword girl and me. "And that's his wife, so be cool."

"Sir," Derek said, wheeling away before Sand could smack him in the head.

We followed Lady Bombelle down towards the sun temple of the Oleander. She was beautiful, and her dress barely stayed together when she walked that was just an objective fact but honestly, I was looking up at the sun when I heard it, the turn of the wind, no longer whistling over the grass, now making sharp echoing sounds like air over a fine bottle edge.

"Wait," Bombelle said, turning back around to us.

"For what?" I asked.

"It is sunset," was all she said.

And not even at the middle of sun temple stairs, but already facing the quad from a nice elevation, we saw people all down the path getting down on their hands and knees facing the fading sun. They lined the outside of the path, not a soul inside the huge open grassy area that was reinforced something deadly.

"It is sunset," Bombelle said again. "When we can, the Jerico gather together to feel the last of the sun. You will notice the warmth start to fade in… now."

And just as she said it, something about the fading light from the world hit me right in the stars, in the fingertips, ears, everywhere private.

"It's colder than before," I said. "You come together to feel cold?"

Bombelle nodded. "Sometimes you feel something most only when it leaves you. That feeling should have a name."

"It does," I said. "What about the opposite? Do you ever get up early in the absolute coldest moment of the night, only to feel the sun come through?"

"Do you?" Bombelle asked.

"Right, but I'm a normal city boy, there's the catch," I said, grinning.

She stared at me. "That tradition requires coming at the great cost of an even greater victory. What we're doing tonight is ritual. The opposite, the act of which you ask… we have not performed the sundance in a decade."

"No great victories around here I take it?" I asked.

"No," Bombelle said. "How about around you, Nite?"

"Nothing that wasn't equally terrifying as it was victorious," I admitted.

"But you have solved the centuries-old puzzle of the founder's own creation, translating the secrets of their craft generations ahead, and could maybe possibly do it again?" Bombelle asked.

"What?" I said, blinking.

"Woah," Derek said, suddenly eyes wide, staring at Bombelle. "Maybe?"

"The time for maybe is over, Nite," Bombelle said. "That is your calling, the one you will answer if you wish to continue living in the safety of the Oleander."

"The what?" I asked. "This circular watering hole quad grass circle has an actual name, and we can finally just call it that?"

"You said relative safety?" Lynn asked, curious.

"You bet your relative ass," Bombelle said. "Put the Oleander to your backs right now. Forget about the grass being swords, forget about your cadet corps, forget about your build city apprenticeship. Yes I know everything about you. That's why I know you're needed elsewhere. I don't care if you believe me or follow me, as long as you do both. Now."

And oddly enough… I did.

2.3

POLESTAR

Sometimes, it was nice to be needed. This wasn't one of those times.

Bombelle led us up the rest of those stairs, her back to us, no fear. We passed a bunch of people, they stared at us, or ignored us, either way they were all taller than us and we weren't their bosses, they could do what they wanted. We must have looked to the entire temple like we were being called to the principal's office. I checked my shirt—no accidental profanity, not this time. True story.

"Give me a minute, I'll come for you," Bombelle said, as the stairs ended on a pantheon-sized pitch, with only the single wooden construct in the middle.

"Oh great, you're leaving us with the goon squad, and she's already gone," I said, watching the temple doors close behind Bombelle.

"Look what we've got here."

Two figures stepped in front of us, two guys about six foot five each, one skinnier with longer blonde hair, one taller with a few fade lines cut into a short red buzzcut, both wearing only a waist fabric wrap, nothing to hide the biceps, the clenched fists, the anger, the stares at us.

"You would challenge my host, Shane?" Ollux said, suddenly back to that low voice she had used to ask us what we would be in the dark, or when the lights went out, or whatever.

"I would," the skinnier one said. Shane, I guess.

He had light skin and long light blonde hair, and he kept flipping it back like his neck had a tick. He was giving off mad emo Tony Hawk vibes. I frowned, looked for the bruises on his elbows and shins, and yep, I found them. They were familiar injuries. And yet I wasn't a fighter. Hmm…

"They are welcome here," Ollux said. "They have the entire southern stadium witness to their acceptance."

"That would only make sense if you weren't walking," Shane said, sounding dangerous about it. "You were supposed to fight until the crowd intervened for your life, yet I don't see a single scratch on you."

"I'll have the stadium historian come orate you the replay," Ollux growled.

"We know you went soft on their acceptance," the red-haired friend of Shane said, getting right into Ollux's face.

"Careful Bryan," Ollux said.

"You careful," was the hot-headed, red-haired reply. "Why me careful? The plane took out three acres in Ravenna, now my trainees are out picking up sticks instead of making me breakfast! Who was flying?"

Sand waved to skinny mcshouty (Bryan). "We stayed until the fire was out."

"He means we are very sorry about what was on fire," Crete smacked Sand.

"Until the fire was out, did you?" Bryan said. "How good. But your plane uprooted four royal redwoods didn't it? Four living, breathing members of our territory, growing strong since before you were born. You owe us four of them, at a hundred years each. That's a big debt."

"It was mayday," Crete said. "We took a head on from the Infinite Army. I'm good, but I can't fly a bird without a head. It was our lives or those trees."

Shane folded his arms, matching Bryan, again, adorable. "What was it that took down such a ship? Flying cannonball? Airborne heat seeker? Giant arrow?"

"The entire Army, all at once," Crete said. "Fifty fliers. No material weapons, no guns, but they do have... um, the power of the sun in their hands."

"We know what palm-mounted arc lasers are!" Bryan shouted.

"I was told the ship was being recovered in one piece," Shane said.

"Like I said, I'm good," Crete said. "We called her Refugee. I built her to withstand anything overland, sky, or sea. I built her to always come home."

"Point... nevermind," Heather said with a sharp look from Crete.

Point Reaper. She was giving one up to Lukas, the creepiest guy I had ever been around, and for longer than I would ever know, but she was right. The only thing to take out Crete's ship had been an attack of the Vema, from the inside out. What a concept. But Crete had just told a different story—why? Was the story of Lukas too long, still yet unknown, and/or too boring to dive into right here, now? Was he trying to keep the Vema from immediate suspicion? Or was he wielding suspicion and story like a weapon and recurving it back to Infinite?

Was the answer to all three yes?

"You want blood?" Derek said, surprising even me.

Shane and Bryan growled at us. Less cute, slightly intimidating, no lie. Especially when behind them a good old fashioned crowd was starting to gather round. We'd run out the clock on conspicuousness. Hello world!

"A stranger talks," Bryan said.

"Ollux, you were right, all the cool kids are at the pool," Derek said.

Ollux's shoulders relaxed the smallest bit. But I saw it.

"Well don't stop now," Bryan said. "You wanna talk—"

"Awesome, permission, thanks man," Derek said, as Bryan froze. "First, I love that you'd actually send a person to retell the events of our welcoming. It's such a human touch. Believe me, I love movies, but there's nothing better than having a story read to you. You like Harry Potter?"

"I love Harry Potter," Bryan said. "My dad read it to me as a kid. It's one of my most cherished memories with him. He was the best dad."

"Same here, just the Mom version," I said.

"Hooray for adolescence, your point?" Shane said, his eyes low.

"Point is, we've already been through this," Derek said. "Nobody is going to fight anybody, not again. So secondly, we're going to have to think of some other way to force the tiniest bit of respect out of you. And THIRDLY, I call you out. I know what you want. You want blood. You want a physical price, since there's nothing else we can offer. Fine. I'm game, but you first. Do a kickflip."

And Bryan blinked. "What?"

"How'd you know?" Shane asked.

For once the universe was on our side. I heard it before I saw it. From fifty feet away, a fellow Jerico kicked a skateboard out to Shane. Even the wheels were wooden, retro, nice, but that meant it was LOUD AS—

"The shins, brother," I said, finally seeing what Derek was seeing.

"You're saying, we both do a skateboard trick and I'll let you into our ancient solar temple?" Shane asked, the anger overtaken by laughter, the others around him joining in. "What do we get—"

Then they saw Derek taking off his shoes.

"A blood debt, a secret tunnel, I've been here before," he said. "I'll pay."

"Is that… a normal thing in Silka City?" Bryan asked, afraid of the answer.

"Consider it tribute," Derek said.

"Consider this sandpaper," Shane said. "You don't know what it's like—"

"To give everything?" Derek said. "I'm not enough? Should I do it switch?"

Bryan stared at me. "It depends how you want to bleed."

"That was ominous just now," Derek said. "Here goes hope."

Shane took the board by his toes, flipped it around until he was standing on it, and did the best barefoot skateboard trick I'd ever seen. The entire thing flipped around at least three feet over the ground. Shane landed and looked him dead in the eye before stepping off and kicking the board over to Derek.

"You're going to get blood on my board," he said.

"Sorry," was my brother's only answer.

"I've got a spare," Shane said. "You land first try, you can keep it… you know, after it stops being symbolic."

They shook hand, and suddenly Ollux, Sand, and Crete were watching. We wouldn't have let two guys stop us from the ancient sun temple. But turning their anger into a handshake was… something better.

"This is so dumb," Lynn complained, folding her arms, but biting her tongue.

"This is about skateboards?" Sand asked.

"Be quiet, I want to see him Yoshi slam," Heather said. "James, you recording this?"

"No," I said lamely. "Derek… I'm not usually a negative person. But a man can't change the world with a kickflip."

"Rodney Mullen did," Derek said.

"I…" I said. "Okay, maybe he can. But… you can't."

The words had come out before I realized what I was saying. We'd never once told each other we couldn't do something, unless we were sure it would end in a concussion. I shouldn't have said that. Derek pretended to ignore me, as he switched his feet to the proper position, which meant up on the toes like a ballerina, then jumped and slid the entire right side of his foot up the sandpaper grip. The blood flew in a perfect line as Derek landed back on the board in one final, blurred sensation of stabbing on my right foot. Sympathy pain? Oh wait, that was the foot I'd broken, the actual pain was just coursing through in waves.

But I was still the first (and only) to yell out for Derek, the sound of pure joy.

"FIRST TRY!"

Skateboarding was about finding zen on something that could chaos real quick. I could tell he was too happy on the inside to really feel the pain. I looked down and it was about what I imagined, like someone had taken a single swipe off his foot with sandpaper. Yes it was burned in evenly across all five toes, but that's just because he'd done it proper. Yes it looked super painful, still nothing on me, sorry brother. The blood flowed into the wood grain of the board, the jaws dropped, Derek took a bow, stepped off, and fell over as the pain hit him.

"Lame," Heather said.

"Not really," Shane said. "Was… was that switch?"

"It was," Derek said honestly.

The doors opened and Bombelle was back. She eyed us suspiciously, and we stared at her all guilty-like.

"Did I miss something?" Bombelle asked.

"No Ma'am," Shane said, and they stepped aside, parting the crowd of fighters around them too, the doors of the dojo finally clear to us as—

Suddenly the tall men and women all around us had hit the ground, even Shane and Bryan were taking a knee in front of the man who now walked towards us. He had Bombelle on his arm by now, looking every bit as commanding as he was, and two guards behind him, both wearing a different kind of ornate fabric around their wrists and necks.

"Welcome," the man said. "Or should I say, welcome back."

Sand and Crete walked forward, squaring off against the guy, their noses almost touching. I wondered who was going to break first. Then the man laughed and opened his arms, and Sand smiled. They hugged, Crete piling on from the side to make it a group thing.

"Say hello, kids," Crete said. "Old friends don't get much better than this."

"Thanks for not saying older," Bastile said.

"You'll never meet a nicer man named Bones, unless you're meeting in battle," Sand said, grinning.

"Is this battle?" I asked, tense as—

"No," Sand said.

And before all our eyes he did a small shuffle, a dance you could say. I was concerned for his mental health until we saw the Jerico leader Bastile miming his movements, both of them circling on their heels at the same time.

"You stop that right now," Bombelle said, smacking him out of the rhythm.

"Ah! At ease."

It wasn't only us who felt the urge to salute—at the call, every fighter behind us rose up from their knees, standing with their hands behind their backs, us in their focus. It wasn't salute, it was attention. But really… that was ease?

Surrounding the new arrivals, creating an inescapable wall of bodies cutting us off from any chance at escape? Oh—their ease, not ours. Right. Rats. Trapped like rats. Again. Then we were through the ancient looking doors that towered over us, and the light dimmed.

"It's been a long time you two," Bastile said, holding Sand at arm's length. "You said you wouldn't come back without a plan."

"They have names," Sand said.

"What plan?" Lynn asked. "We plan?"

"Yes, you plan," Sand said. "Meet you Derek, James, Lynn, and Heather."

"Never heard of them," Bastile said, as I gave a wave of the crutch. "Why is being here worth your lives?"

"You're supposed to tell us," Heather said frowning. "I've heard of the Jerico my whole life, but never of a circle town in the north. You think we showed up unprepared, but the truth is we were shot here like a cannonball. We're lucky we landed. You, maybe not so much."

Behind him Bryan brazenly held up four fingers, for each of the trees it had taken for us to land. Right. Lucky us.

"Honest," Bastile said. "Few outsiders make it past the gates, and even fewer through the trees. It's been eight years since we welcomed anyone into Oleander, the garden hearth of the Jerico."

"You said there were explorers, adventurers, scientists," Derek said to Ollux. "You said there were too many men that came this way looking for things."

"I did," Ollux said. "I did not say what happened to them. Most of them."

Bryan again stood up behind Bombelle and mouthed—ALL OF THEM.

"You…" I said, starting to remember where I was.

"Are serious when we put up gates the size of mountains, yes," Bombelle said. "Excuse me, there's something in my shoe."

She took off a heavy wooden sandal and threw it like a boomerang at Bryan. He took the thing in his neck and collapsed instantly, for all the muscles, for however dope that fade was in his red hair, we all just tried not to laugh.

"Like I was saying, our people have lived on this part of the island for over four hundred years, and in those decades we have seen every nation of this island breach our borders in pursuit of their gain at the expense of ours—EVERY one," Bombelle said, as we all held it in. "For the last hundred years we have enforced the only thing that gave us the respect we require to live, the greatest detour the world has left."

Suddenly no one was laughing anymore.

"But… you also said the Jerico traded with other nations," Derek said.

Ollux threw her hands up. "Do you just write down everything I say?"

"I remember it!"

"What kind of man remembers everything a woman says?" Ollux said. "Is this science fiction?"

Good question.

"A host does not admonish their guests for questions," Bastile said, shaking his head at Ollux, who turned bright red. "Yes Derek, we trade, but not from this place, and not for currency. Our silk roads, so to speak, were established centuries ago, but still we tend to them like the garden that keeps on giving, even today, even in the storm. We only do business at the ends of those routes, on foreign soil everyone. That is the trade—our surplus for their respect. Our goods are delivered by the hand of Jerico. It's not a threat, it's acceptance. They accept they are not free to ask for more, and if they come looking for more, they will find the end of everything. Any other questions?"

"Damn," I said.

The two caputs (?) of Jerico stared us down from the front. The citizens who'd kept to their huts all day were suddenly here in mass, with almost no light left in the sky. I saw by torches and lamps the hundreds of bare feet on the stairs, crowding the path and staying off the grass as the warriors tried to keep at least the inside of the temple clear for us. Though that was just the back of us. In front of us was the so-called hand of Astral. And THAT was what had my heart beating all colosseum like.

"Introduce yourselves," Bastile said.

He was not talking to me. A young woman walked up and bowed. Wait—

"Wildfire Willa the killa, nice to meet ya," said sword girl.

This close up, I could tell she was about twenty (but so was I), with long red hair, her entire upper body and waist covered in suspender style, braided strips of canvas fabric, golden metal chains and slim bracelets around her arms and ankles. She was tying a thick green belt around her tiny waist, her armored pants held up by chainmail, and a half sheath perfectly balanced at her left hip. I didn't even see the sword until my eyes adjusted and yep, there it was, blade down into the earth, so narrow at the edge it had been invisible to us. It was a katana, with a minimal wrist hilt, just enough to catch at the sheath.

"Respect," Derek said.

Willa gave him a wink as she did a no-handed cartwheel (aerial), grabbed the sword with the hands that didn't even touch the ground in her cartwheel, and stowed it in her sheath at the same time as she landed. Derek was mesmerized. For some reason Lynn looked ready to kill a man with her bare hands.

"Relax," Heather said. "He wasn't looking at anything but the sword."

"You two really took Ollux down?" Willa asked.

"We did—" I started.

"Shh, no, girls are talking," Willa said, to Heather and Lynn, who nodded together as Willa punched the air in victory. "Friends who aren't boys. Finally."

And there was the rough laughter from something I had just taken this entire time to be a stone. One of the soldiers was standing almost motionless in the shadows of the sun temple next to Willa, a thick coat of dirt or paint over his shirtless torso, with dark leggings down to the bare feet that looked every bit as thick and protective as his chest was exposed. He was a big boulder man, hunched over and... praying? He was lost in thought and hadn't give an inch when we passed only feet from him, but now I saw his feet move with every step we took, like he was a seismic sensor. He walked out of the shadows and looked down us from two feet away... vertically.

"I am Xero the Champion, hello to know you," came a much lower, slightly Latin accent from the guy who was as relaxed as he was huge, his arms as big as two of me, no need for a fight stance with a torso the size of a wheelbarrow.

"Is it obvious?" I asked.

"I mean no harm to small things," he said, ignoring me. "If that changes I'll give you a head start—I mean, I will let you know."

"The honorable Xero the Champion," Heather said, only half sarcastically.

"Is it not obvious?" Derek asked, looking at me, getting ignored just as hard.

"Thank you," Xero said to Heather. "No shortcuts, no easy victory. I live for honor. That is life's mission, being born a behemoth, trampling all this nice dirt. When I'm dead, bury me at sea. That's my life's end. Until then, nice to meet you, small, wise, girl thing."

"Thank you, giant, honest, boy guy," Heather said, reaching up to take his one hand with both of hers, the two of them sharing a look. "I've always wanted to be wise. But I'm so young."

"You know what you are, that is a good start," Xero said to her.

"I can't take it—why don't we just call you Xero the Hero?" I blurted out.

Lynn's eyes snapped into place. "Thank you."

Xero shook his head. "Don't call me that. I don't deserve it. Maybe someday I'll live to hear you call me that, and know I've earned it, but not today. When my body sinks to the bottom of the sea, you can call me whatever you want."

"You don't have to get all dark about it," I said, reaching out to shake.

"Friends of small wise girl thing, you are—"

"I'm almost nineteen," I said, as I let him obliterate my hand in a handshake.

"I am thirty six," Xero said as I tried not to whimper, until he let go and I still didn't want to breathe, didn't want to feel the pain. "It is a wonderful age, the thirties. I trust you have already met the wonder siblings?"

"I mean… we're right here," Derek said, a beat before me. Nice.

"Their host is warrior sister Ollux Akoura herself," Bastile said. "They have met each other in combat, she should know them better than any."

His hand went out to the two other soldiers, but all I heard was that last name. If my beating heart could give us away, there wouldn't be a story. Ever.

"Akoura?" I asked. "Did I hear that right?"

"Did we not mention it?" Ollux said.

"You know it?" Astor asked, blankly.

Uh, yeah we knew that name, from a certain Infinite agent who had literally been all up in our faces from the moment we had started everything. Alcyon Akoura. Any relation? Did we actually know something they didn't? Or would this be another dead end? Wait a minute. It had started off a joke, but they really were missing something. A brother.

"No, just processing, trying not to forget something as simple as names," I said, trying not to telegraph. "Sorry."

And no one challenged me. I had made a decision, to do what Lynn had done. To take command instead of asking for it.

"Much obliged," Bombelle said, sensing no distraction (I hoped). "So… how was your first day in the Jerico?"

"It was just what we needed," Derek sang, honestly. "Until now."

"Until we need something from you?" Bastile said. "That ends your perfect day? Doing one thing not for yourselves?"

"Something tells me it's going to be a pretty big something," Derek said, shrugging in apology all the same.

"It is, good radar," Bastile said. "Derek, the Soldier Soltis tells me you had a promising first run with the cadets. He leads me to believe that with daily training, you could earn your wings as well as anyone in the territory."

"He... said that... about me, sir?" Derek said, his hand trembling.

"His direct quote was you take a foot to the face like every soldier on the front lines should," Bastile said. "Does that help?"

"I..." he said, suddenly white in the face as Heather doubled over in laughter, not trying to hide it. "This is no longer a compliment, sir..."

"James, the master builders tell me you possess an eye worthy of a craft apprenticeship," Bastile said, ignoring Derek's existential sundowning, moving on. "Foe has plans to teach you the craft, from the basics to the bombastics, and Racket wants to study your atoms under the microscope, so just a heads up, you probably shouldn't go to sleep—"

"Thanks?" I said, head spinning, literally as I caught my balance on those darn crutches. "That's big words for a little guy. But what—"

"What about the girls, I know," Bombelle said. "I was just getting there."

Bastile came up to us and put his arms around us both, holding us close and tight, just enough that it was on the threatening side of powerful. He looked between us both and said nothing as Bombelle carried on as if we weren't being chokeholded. Chokeheld? Did it MAT—

"Lynn, though you came in preaching about the future, your appearance at the Ravenna crash site was appreciated," Bombelle said, taking over from Bastile like it was routine. "I trust the cleanup to no Sand, but something tells me to trust you. Maybe it's the Nora in you, but..."

"Appreciated," Lynn said. "The future can't start until the past is cleaned up, or at least accounted for. I saw what was left outside the village, I understand the concept of penance. But what exactly is Sand paying for, or back, to you?"

"His redemption among the Jerico does not include you," Bombelle said. "If he wants to explain that particular ticket, that's his choice. Sand?"

"Publicly, I do not," he admitted. "I'll keep kicking the leaves, thanks."

"And that's all we ask," Bombelle said. "From you. From Heather—"

"Aw I'd hoped you forgot about me," she said, caught.

"Never," Bastile said. "Heather of Vema, daughter of the underland, speaker for the Reaper. I trust you are aware of the decades long contingency accords, agreed to by both our nations in case this day ever arrived?"

"Here's the thing about that..." Heather said, blinking, looking around at the three of us. "I hate to let you down. But I'm gonna."

I didn't blame her. Our things had made sense. Hers had not.

"I was somewhat joking," Bastile said, a knowing look on his face as Heather visible shuddered in relief. "But yours will be this role, whether you want it or not. Whatever you have to do to get yourself ready, do it. Your partners already are. Don't let them outfly you."

"I taught them how to fly," Heather growled.

“No you didn’t,” we said at the same time.

“Well, on the wings of the Reaper I did,” she argued.

“Nope,” Derek said, looking straight at Lynn.

“Then damnit Lynn, why don’t you speak for the Vema?” Heather shouted.

“That sounds boring,” she said. “What you really mean is…”

“Sorry,” Heather said sadly, already past the rage. “It has to be me. You may have been born there Lynn, but somewhere along the line, we switched places.”

“We switched places on the same day, at the same age,” Lynn said, frowning.

“We should talk about that,” Heather said.

“How about you boys, what do you remember of that age?” Astor asked suddenly, turning on us out of nowhere—it seemed.

But to us, it wasn’t out of nowhere. The only good part was seeing Heather and Lynn look at each other, like they were on their own agreeing that this was suspicious. Nice. I could have made something up. I could have lied, I could have told a tale that was meaningful and metaphorical. But I was tired. In that moment, laziness kept me to the code of Jerico, without me even realizing it.

“Anything before a few months post Blitz, I just can’t place,” I said, careful.

“We didn’t expect you to,” Bastile said, moving on like he wasn’t stuck on one topic—like Astor. “We don’t usually deal in history, not unless it breaks loose of the buried ground and bites us in the ass.”

“Did that happen?” Lynn asked gently.

“Of course that happened!” Bastile said. “We gave you a house in the storm, a safe haven from the Infinite pursuing you. What did you think it was for?”

“I thought we gave you a good first day’s work, given the storm,” I said.

“We are the storm,” Bastile said. “When it changes course, you follow.”

“Hope,” I said, the word blurting itself out of my body before I could stop it.

My brother laughed, us alone knowing what in the world had just happened. Internal red flag going off, check. This was no dead end.

Follow the storm.

“Did we miss something?” Sand said, looking at us.

“You’re actually telling us the truth, aren’t you?” Derek asked. “That’s why we’re here?”

“Everything I say, bare-naked truth,” Sand said. “That’s why I talk so slow.”

“Stop narrating,” Crete said. “We’re here because the kids turned a hometown into a throwing knife.”

“Right,” my brother said, shutting up.

“Your plan involved—” Bastile started, sarcastically.

“Drawing the attention of Infinite as far away from Vema as physically possible,” Crete finished. “The surviving Reaper had only just emerged. A follow up strike in the early hours of such a fragile state… it would have undone everything they waited ten years to gain. But now that they’ve had the time to escape, we’ll receive the first Veman envoy within the week, I guarantee it.”

Bastile shut up. We’d left a king speechless.

“I think we’re receiving her now,” Bombelle said. “You are Heather Veman aren’t you?”

"You said Veman," Heather said. "Veman, the founder of Reaper, that—"

"You know Hector and Elin are brothers right?" Sand said blankly.

Heather's jaw dropped to the floor. "Elin Mare?"

"Elin Mare Veman," Sand said. "Like Hector Denien Veman. Boom, names."

"Do you not know who you are, Heather?" Crete asked quietly, casually.

"Apparently not," Heather said. "I'm just processing… give me a minute before I… actually speak for a nation."

"You're literally a princess," Lynn said, her smile as wide as her ears.

"You take that BACK!" Heather shouted, Lynn dancing away laughing.

"There it is," Bombelle said, smiling. "Elin's an old friend, I can see the same fire in you. You are right to feel the weight. You will make a great leader, Heather of Vema. Maybe someday, maybe today."

Heather couldn't respond. She was clearly panicking.

"Do you need her to speak for the Vema for some reason?" I asked.

"I do," Bastile said. "And now I am serious. A long time ago we made a pact, Vema and us. Over what would happen when the day came. We knew they would rise. We knew what it would symbolize."

"And what's that?" I asked.

"The end of Infinite, or the end of the island," was Bastile's answer. "Depending on how we respond."

"Can… can I seek the advice of my counsel?" Heather asked, barely getting the words out.

"You can do whatever you need, to lead," Bastile said.

"Okay," she said, to us. "I command you to solve all my problems for me."

"As you wish," Lynn said, bowing low to Heather. "Boys, do whatever Heather says."

"Always," Derek said. "Heavy, but always."

"Come heavy or don't come at all," Heather reminded.

Yeah. Wherever we were, we'd come heavy, that was for sure. Then the storm reminded me how heavy gravity weighed. On cue, the lightning struck for the first time since we'd been here, and just as the sky cracked open again, Lynn her hand on my shoulder. I still flinched at lightning. I put my hand over hers.

"It's always so loud," Bombelle complained. "Make it stop."

"I will, I promise," Bastile said, holding his wife.

"I thought you said you were the storm," Lynn said.

"We were," Bastile said. "You're pretty smart for a bunch of—nevermind. You're here to learn, that's the point."

"Learn about what, whether or not the Jerico has or hasn't always lived the way we never knew they did or didn't?" Derek asked/shouted. "Why are we here? What can we possibly contribute to this? I've been here before haven't I?"

"Yep," Heather said, her arms folded, biting her lips. That last outburst was for us. I was going in circles. Or I was about to be asked once AGAIN for—

"Did Silka loose some kind of astrological center this summer?" Bastile asked. "Someplace where the city studied the stars and celestials?"

"I mean," Derek said. "Only if you're asking why we're here. The Silka City

Observatory, on the highest hill of the Engineerium district, over the waterfall… something tells me you know the one."

"I know the one," Bastile said.

"How?" I said.

Bombelle held up a notebook. Derek's notebook.

"Hey man…" Derek said, blinking. "That's mine."

He wasn't lying. I could tell by the song lyrics in the gutter margins, only he did that. But Bombelle was holding the book open to a page relatively close to the opening, and it was stocked full of notes and readouts and latitudes and star charts of something we actually were very familiar with. The Silka City Observatory. Remember that madness? I did.

"That's what you're after," I said, white in the knuckles on those crutches.

"I would like to know every single thing about this, if you don't mind," Bombelle said, like we had broken the first rule of being a Jerico—which we weren't, and hadn't.

"James, you okay?" Heather said, the first to notice.

"Yeah," I said, the confidence coming from somewhere. "But I do mind."

"I'd listen to him," Heather said, coming to my side faster than I expected.

Thanks Heather.

"We trusted you," Bombelle said softly. "You kept this from us? Why?"

"Because the first part of that story is the part where my Mom…" Derek said, unable to go on.

"Stop," Lynn said, but not to me, with her hand on Derek's shoulder. "Derek, you don't have to do this to yourself."

I was thinking she was right. We didn't owe them, or anyone this particular story. I don't think I'd even really shared it with Heather and Lynn. Bombelle wasn't angry any more. Then her eyes lifted, and she looked back to the notebook, like the answer was on the next page.

"Your mother?" Bombelle asked. "Teresa Nite, if that's what we're calling her? What does the Always Soldier have to do with the Observatory?"

"They were both gone in the same explosion," Derek said, putting it as simply as he could. "Ollux asked us not why we were here, but why we were meeting. The answer you're looking for is this. We never had a father, but until a few weeks ago, we had a mother. Now… as much as he's back, she's not. Still not. Still out there, somewhere, waiting for us to either accept she's gone or find her. Somewhere back down the road we came, or the one in front of us, she's there. That's the path we arrived on."

"I…" Bastile said, torn between anger and empathy. "I didn't know. I saw the writing on the wall and assumed you had a reason for keeping secrets. The death of a mother is… I'm sorry. We came in hot, that's our bad."

Astor was tearing up. Even Willa looked softer than before, her hands slowly falling to her sides.

"It's a sad song, this is true," I said.

"Well you never end on a sad song," Bastile said. "So this isn't even over."

"Rage," I said, nodding to him. "What else did you find in that notebook?"

"We were kind of distracted by the first few pages," Bombelle admitted, tossing the notebook to Bastile—damnit. "I don't want to assume, but that observatory blowing up might be the very thing that brings our entire territory out of the stone age. Does that make your mother's sacrifice less meaningless?"

"For the world, maybe," I said. "For us, no."

"Then why are you here?" Ollux asked. "Helping your friends, the wayfarers, capitulating to a long way home that only MIGHT include redemption for your mother? I say you miss her more than anything, but you have clearly chosen the world over her."

I looked at my brother. "Is… is that true?"

"I'll answer that one for you," Sand said. "You have attempted to steer us towards her every chance you've gotten. You have chosen her at every junction. It is the rest of us who prevent you from her. It is I who prevent you from her. You have been forced to put her aside in the name of helping the family that remains. That will forever be the hardest thing you'll ever have to do, and right now, I think Bombelle's asking you to do it again."

"I am," she said. "Brave boys."

"Scared men," Derek corrected her. "Same but different."

"You're going to be easy to work with," Bombelle said, scratching her head.

"You're not right, but what's even the job?" I asked. "You want us to what, stop the storm?"

"Yes," Bombelle said.

"You're not even joking," Lynn said, her face falling.

"I am not," Bombelle said. "You saw those clouds last night, they were darker than normal. That's the second maelstrom this summer, and they've raged. Usually the summer is more stable than this, and the weather allows for all the maintenance that goes into preparing for the winter. This isn't June gloom, this is mad season. Something's changed."

"Almost like a piece in the storm system has gone missing," Bastile said.

"Was that a stab in the dark?" I asked, blinking. "Or are you that familiar with storms?"

"The second," Bombelle said. "For a hundred years our magnetic detectors have responded the same to every storm we have ever weathered. But I'll bet you a pound of syrup that today—"

"Magnetic detectors?" Derek asked.

"Pound of syrup?" Heather asked, curious, maybe aroused, I didn't know.

"Come with me," Bombelle said.

We walked farther into the temple until we were at the single step of a lowered platform in the middle of the room, and we all stood around what was clearly a big clock carved in ruts and small radial paths into the ground. It was a good ten feet wide, so there was enough circle for hundreds of hands, like every second on the circle had its own line leading from the epicenter out towards a different direction in 360 degrees. There was a key written into the ground too, a big N for north on the side facing out the front doors, a S on the other side, farthest into the place. The sun temple faced due north, apparently.

Bombelle walked up to a clay pot that was full of metal shavings, like black sand, and she scattered a handful down onto the painting. For a moment the shavings dropped like a dust cloud, then they were sucked down into specific pathways, completely ignoring ninety nine percent of the potential carved directions, and sticking to just three.

"Woah," Lynn said.

When the winds picked up outside, the shavings shook. When the lightning struck, they danced, but always came back to those tiny ruts, so shallow that there was really nothing keeping them from bouncing out to the next angle. They just... didn't want to.

"Who built this?" Crete asked, looking impressed.

"I did," Bombelle said. "We all know the geomagnetic storm season over Jerico keeps anything magnetic from working on the surface."

"Obviously," Derek said, nodding right along, full sarcasm.

"Well my invention harnesses the magnetic field created by the underland."

"Elementary," Derek said again, pretending he was on the level.

"You built a compass in Jerico?" Crete asked, excited. "You invented a way to trace magnetics without magnetics? I thought that was impossible!"

"It was, until I did it, and I didn't," Bombelle said, looking at Crete like someone might actually appreciate her work (because I sure as hell didn't). "There were four readings last month, before the maelstroms started. This bottom one here, it had a parallel, even closer to straight south, aimed directly at your Observatory. All year this compass has pointed the same, always four, always in the same four directions. Now one is gone, and three are left."

"The Observatory," Crete said, the gears clearly turning. "Of course."

"Of course not, explain it right damn—" Heather started.

"I can't," Bastile said. "Not yet. It's just a feeling."

"What kind of feeling?" Heather asked, biding her rage the best she could.

"None alive today are to blame for the decision to trap a nation in the stone age, we always figured there was nothing that could be done about our... predicament," Bastile said. "However, given the return of the Reaper, and this new anomaly, as well as the presence of the ancestors of our founders themselves... maybe we will finally have our answers."

"I thought we already gave you answers," Derek said sadly.

"You gave us this," Bombelle said, raising up the notebook again. "A whole journal full of words, but no answers. I liked the songs though."

"How many—" I asked, sighing.

"Four," Derek admitted. "And counting."

"Unless you count the story a song, then five," Bombelle said. "You write small, and a lot of it doesn't make sense without context. I miss pictures."

"So you didn't learn anything too compromising about us?" Heather asked.

"Don't you dare," Derek said, a hand out to Bombelle, who grinned at his embarrassment... but didn't speak. "Why am I explaining an outline to you?"

"Because I'm not a writer, I'm a warrior!" Bombelle bellowed.

"Derek, did you really bring Silka City's Engineerium Observatory back online with those equations?" Bastile asked, blunt as anything.

"I did nothing alone, but also yes," he said. "We did everything, together. James, me, Hector Denien, and Teresa Nite, our mother, running the thing from a wheelchair, like always."

"What did it take?" Bastile said. "Remember, no power tools."

"Help me out brother," Derek said.

I thought hard. "No power tools. Screwdrivers… a bit of soldering…"

"Fire and metal," Bastile smiled.

"Then we're set," I said. "Even the homemade glue guns, that's just pumps."

"You fixed a particle tracking electroshield with pumps," Bastile said, shaking his head for a moment, about what I didn't know.

"Bastile," Sand warned, because he could see the future, or some such—

"Do you know what they say of your lightning city ancestor Teresa Silk, the mother of the east?" Bastile said, ignoring Sand. "The stories say she stole fire from the gods and used it to spark all life on this island. They say she alone kept the ultimate technology under her personal guard while the old world burned and/or flooded. She knew not what it would become, nor she. The technology that plugged Silka City in, launched the first airborne soldiers of Infinite, connected the Reaper to the mineral makeup of the underland, and keeps us under this cloud of energy, it's all the same."

"Fire from the gods," I said, just trying to understand.

"And you're sure such a thing exists?" Derek asked.

"I am," Bastile said. "I have seen it. I have bled for it. Most the island has."

"That's enough," Sand threatened, already close to violence.

"So that's the reason we can do… what we can do," I said. "There really is a source, as the voices in our heads like to call it."

"Are these friendly voices in your head?" Bombelle asked, concerned.

"Half and half," I said, shrugging. "But that's what I call the level."

"That is not the right level," Bastile said. "Is this a normal island to you?"

"It is, when it's the only one we've got," Derek said.

"I guess I can't fault that," Bastile said. "But that technology was meant to save humanity, not for us to come up with superhero names."

"Both of those are equally science fiction, where does normal even live on the island anymore?" Derek cried.

Bastile couldn't argue that.

"So the ever weather…" I said.

"Might just turn out to be another coordinated island-wide effort of focusing the power of humanity against nature," Bastile said. "What would you do to stop a storm descending on your people, Nite? Would you maybe send everything you ever had against it, in hopes that by midnight it would all be over?"

"ENOUGH!" Sand shouted.

"FINE!" Bastile shouted at him. "See, we can all get loud. Right?"

My head was swimming.

"I don't know," Derek said. "If you've got the wrong guy, no harm here. I'm just me. I don't know this place, and if I'm to do anything in real time, I'll need Lynn and Heather by my side. Long as I got that, I'm good."

"Good," both Bastile and Bombelle said at the same time.

"Why you smile?" I asked.

"Because, Derek and James Nite… we need your help. We—"

"You want us to follow some metal shavings in the dirt, possibly destroy an other astronomical unit, and see about maybe bringing the lights back on in the jungle?" I asked. "In return you'll treat us as royalty here in the Jerico, with not a single barrier between us and our every whim?"

"You're asking us to break the storm," Lynn said, frozen in place.

"Were we that obvious?" Bastile asked. "Have you been here before?"

"Metaphorically, yes," I said. "Isn't that why you're asking?"

"I guess… yes," Bastile said. "But don't seek to destroy anything that can destroy you. And change that second part to where we'll allow you to sleep through the night in our ancestral lands without cutting your hands and feet off in your sleep. But yes we are sending out a search party at noon tomorrow, you help us, you live. Let's start there?"

Bombelle leaned over and whispered low. "Your answer is yes sir. Say it."

I only sighed. We had been here before. Why didn't I see this coming?

"SAY IT!"

"Yes sir!" we sounded off, about as confident as a bunch of twigs on the forest floor. And that should have been it.

But outside, the storm was growing stronger.

Inside, we were scattered throughout that temple with a handful of nameless soldiers wandering around, some sitting cross-legged, some doing one handed pushups in the corner, while the leaders and the six of us stood around that platform clock in the middle of the room that reminded me of a koi pond without all the fish. I was still holding myself up by the crutches. I was listening to the leaders of the Jerico ask for our help with my fists about to break off those wooden support handles. They were looking at us and everything. They could see what we were—three kids, one cripple, and two old men. Why were they asking us for favors, instead of the other way around? We hadn't even tended to our own families, and they were asking us to help theirs? I expected Sand and Crete to step in. I expected the entire thing to be a dream, and to wake up in the bedroom I'd gotten up in every day for the past eighteen years.

But no. The world was boxing me in. The universal claustrophobia was creeping closer from all sides. I was trapped, not in this sun temple, but here. Trapped by circumstance and situation (arrest warrants and non-functioning supersuits respectively). Trapped by what strangers in the forest thought of me, which was probably more and less than I thought, both at the same time. At least we were somewhere familiar. It was the fork in the road, and we were expected to take it.

Again.

Sand only looked at Derek, like he was expected to speak for everybody.

"I…" Derek said, searching for the words. "I'm going to have to let you down easy sir. Don't get me wrong, I understand you. You want peace. But I can't give you what I don't have."

"You will give me everything you have, starting tomorrow at noon," Bastile said. "Until then."

He flung his hand out of the open doors, to the raging winds but mostly dry air around the center hills, the Oleander as Bombelle had called it. Most followed his gaze but I was staring at the magnetic lines on the ground, the clock, wondering how it worked, when just like that prison cell window, the image beyond it turned into something else.

What in the brain.

It was my own house, that front door I'd seen countless times growing up. But it was red. That's right, before the rebuilding that followed the Blitz, it had been red. We'd gone with blue accents ever after, but it was the same tall, sprawling two story house on the hill, right where the road leveled out and led down towards the creek on the left, the tall hill in our backyard and the cliffside falloff far down the right side of the front. It was just as I remembered it—but red wasn't the only difference. The entire thing was bathed in a faint blue light, like the memory of it was color bent for a reason. Wait. Blue light filter. There was a half-dome circle of blue light like a portable force field generator coming from the back of the house, the source of it past my sights. That didn't matter—what did was the door to my childhood home, open, even swinging slightly like I had just caught the motion before it stopped. The curiosity, the blue tint to it all. And then the tiny ashen footsteps leading up to a slightly ajar door.

I couldn't resist. I said the word I wasn't supposed to say.

"Kira?"

But of course, as soon as the image was solidified, it was gone, and the clock was back. I alone was watching those metal shavings in their ruts, and I swear I saw them vibrate, or shimmer, or something, and a good half handful of them slowly turned-cloak on their previous positions, forming a single file line down the rut most closely aimed towards... me. Not even. I took a step to the right. The minerals followed me, a good twenty micro-ruts over, even their momentum mirroring me pulling them, closest to farthest.

"Nuh uh," I said, blankly.

"What you doing over there?" Some guy called to me mid-pushup.

"Nothing demonic," I almost cried.

That wasn't true. I was personally freaking the hell out from the inside, without moving a muscle, and the others noticed nothing—so far. I was shook, and in my desire to get away from that clock on the ground, I almost crutched for the door. I was about to bail, to run away from everything happening. I even saw myself do it, only in my mind, a flight so fast I would have heel-toed and ate it, a single thought rattling around my brain, fighting for control.

Run home, James. Before the lightning gets you.

DEREK NITE

2.4

BONES' BRIGADE

My mind was racing, and there was only one thought on it. One single, world-deciding decision to make. It was all or nothing. Here and now.

"I should skip training, right?" I said to no one.

"But Derek, we're already here," Lynn said.

"Right," I said, as I stretched out on the grasses of that training field.

Yeah. I couldn't sleep. The excuse machine was just a distraction. There was no skipping training. To me, that phrase didn't exist. We had gone right to sleep after temple, some of us more than others. A few hours before sunrise, Lynn had heard me tossing and turning, and we'd come out here instead, the night black as anything, the sun just about to peak over the slightly swaying treetops in the distance. I didn't know who I was trying to please out here—the soldiers, their caput, or myself. Then, just as the very first ray of light came up over them…

We heard the footsteps. Twenty cadets came running up, holding towels and water bottles, looking at us standing alone on their field with the sun just bright enough to make us impossible to miss.

"We got homeless coach," the voice of Brin came, too far away to see my face, until he wasn't. I watched him flinch. "Derek. I didn't mean—"

"I take no offense to the truth," I said, stretching my arms.

"Hey look, newbie's back," came the voice of Ivy.

"Who's the legs?" said… Dalle?

"Ew, but thanks?" Lynn said. "I'm Lynn, don't touch me."

I laughed, but took a step closer to her, seeing so many army brats around. Then soldier Soltis saw us, and I put my hands up in prayer. The universal sign for *please.* He nodded, and stomped his foot into the ground once. The cadets dropped anything they were holding and formed a running wall of bodies, taking laps around the entire clearing, the whole roundabout about as long as a single track lap. I followed Pain Jane and Lynn followed me, all without a word, such was the nature of the world's worst date (aka jungle boot camp).

But that single lap never even ended. Lynn was fine, and so was I. Keeping jogging pace with the twenty of them was no problem, the only issue was seeing Soltis's hand wave us on every time we completed another go. After six, I gave in, and drifted closer to Fawn on my right, speaking low.

"How… many…"

"Just twelve man," he breathed easy. "You're halfway there. You got this."

"If… you… say… so…" I said, talking on rhythm, the soreness gone from my entire body—wait was that the point of running first thing in the morning?

I made twelve, and we all came into a rest. Everyone was taking small steps forward, opening their arms and breathing deep. I was the only one doubled over, hands on my knees, until—

"Stand up straight."

It was Soltis, and he'd kicked my hands out. I almost fell over, but forced myself not to. I stood up and looked at him. He stood up right, held his hands out, and took a single, emphasized step forward, breathing in as he did.

"Don't make work for your lungs. It takes the body to heal the body."

"Yes sir," I said.

Lynn casually took her hands off her knees and stood straight behind me.

"Sprint to the hills and back, now!" Soltis shouted to everyone.

"YES SIR!"

I came back out of breath worse than before, and my hands were about to hit my knees when I saw Soltis in front of me with his foot ready to lash out. I clenched my hands, and forced myself to stand up and breathe.

"Better," Soltis said, pleased. He dropped the bag from his shoulders, letting it spill open onto the ground. It was full of ankle and wrist weights. Uh oh.

"Everyone put on ten pounds, and do it again," Soltis said.

Lynn looked at me, for the first time with some worry. "Do what again, sir?"

"All twelve laps," he said, walking away to a cadet on his knees in the grass, already throwing up. "Is three miles all you can give to your country?"

"No sir! I'm good, just a big breakfast, my mistake, hold on, BLEH—"

"Worst date ever, achieved," Lynn said under her breath to me, before bending over for the weights. She grabbed my hand and strapped one to my wrist, then the other, then before I knew it she'd done my feet as well.

"I could have—" I said.

"But you didn't," she said, clinking her wrist weights together like Wonder Woman's wristlets. "Here's the deal. Stay close, I might die."

"You and I both—" I started.

But Soltis stomped his foot, and we turned back for the track. Every step was heavier than before, every muscle in my upper shoulders on fire from the arms, but every step I took reminded me of how James couldn't. Also every step reminded me of pain, and feeling bad, about everything, especially how hard my wrists and ankles were pulling with each jostle. But the jostling had just begun.

Turns out that was most of training, since it took a good hour for each cadet to finish another twelve laps. We were running in butter, or ice cream, that's what it felt and looked like, like an invisible wall was holding us back. After a break of silent stretches, it was a small relay of bodyweight exercises—handstand pushups, wheelbarrow carries, lock-legged sit-ups, your basic boot camp warm down. With everyone officially too tired to talk, during our actual finishing stretches, Soltis started saying things that I'd never heard before.

“Mastery in one’s career and consciousness growth simply requires that we constantly produce results beyond and out of the ordinary,” he said, walking around us with his hands held behind his back. “Mastery is a product of consistently going beyond our limits. For most people, that starts with a technical excellence in a chosen field; then, with a commitment to excellence, we can create miracles. When we speak of miracles, we speak of events or experiences in the real world which are beyond the ordinary. Stand up.”

We did.

“Repeat,” Soltis said. “Mastery in one’s…”

And we echoed him, sentence by sentence, twice.

“Tomorrow we will repeat this, again when your lungs are empty, when your brain is numbed. If I could brand that paragraph into your skulls, I would. See you all tomorrow.”

Then he looked straight at Lynn and me. “Unless I don’t.”

“Ominous,” Lynn said.

“Don’t die out there and you’ll be fine,” Soltis said with a wink to us, walking away. “You are welcome here anytime, Derek. And friends.”

“And friends,” I said, raw emotion, no strength in my face to smile.

Then it was over, and we were taking tiny shuffling steps back up the hill to our cabin, somehow both holding each other up and using each other to hold ourselves up. The sun was soaring, the wind was kicking up, the day was starting. But the pain…

“I’ve always hated handstand pushups,” Lynn said.

“I blocked out everything after the second three miles,” I said. “I don’t think anyone spoke after that.”

“Nothing but yes sir and no sir,” Lynn agreed. “Is that the point?”

“At one time it was,” I nodded. “If we’re talking swords, real samurai fought feudally. That means they obeyed a single leader representing their land without question. The soldier is by definition secondary to what is being protected.”

“Because such power comes with such reason?” Lynn asked.

“It should,” I said. “It has to. Otherwise it’s just another machine to kill.”

“So you’d only do it if a commander told you?” Lynn asked.

“No,” I said. “I refuse to kill a human being in the name of a government.”

“And I thought you were calling me Ma’am as a joke,” Lynn said.

“That will never be a joke,” I said.

“You… have a complicated relationship with swords,” Lynn said.

We walked up to our square cabin, the front door already fully rolled open, the roof pulled back letting the sunlight directly in, showing Crete and James bent over three wooden tables they had arranged in a triangle around the hearth, with buckets of spare parts, long cables of wiring, and a second desktop underneath the top one on every table, completely overflowing with tools and wooden planks, and few bulky, but still incredibly well built and designed things on another, like things you’d rip out of a supersonic Infinite jet plane.

“A bit unconventional, but I’m too hungry to argue,” I said.

“Don’t eat the engines,” Crete said, not even looking up. “Eat the trees.”

“Excuse me?” Heather said sleepily, joining us with a few clay cups in one hand and a huge steel carafe in the other.

"It's a song we used to sing here," Crete said. "You don't know it? I am not grass, I am the weeds, I eat the trees?"

"Never eaten a tree in my life," I said.

"Ah but you have," Crete said. "I refuse to make any more of this story about skateboards, but between that, notebooks, guitars, and woodshop, you owe half of your hobbies to trees. These trees, to be specific. We cut them, strip them, process every part, how is that any different from swallowing them whole?"

"Because I don't have sawdust in my teeth, that's how!" James said.

Crete blew across the top of the table and a fine layer of sawdust raged at us like a small dust devil. I put a hand over my coffee just in time, but my mouth wasn't so sharp. I had bits of wood on my lips, neck, teeth, everywhere.

"That was unnecessary," James said, through the sawdust in my teeth.

"Get used to it," Crete said. "This will all be a pile of sawdust soon."

"Speaking of making piles, where's Sand?" Lynn asked.

"He left for the crash site even before you two got up," Heather said. "What is he doing exactly over there?"

"Paying his penance to the territory, for reasons we know not of," I said.

"Well as long as we're consistently inconsistent," Heather said sarcastically.

"What are you doing with the gravity machine from the super jet?" I asked.

"Hell, Derek," Crete said, looking around. "Give us your inside voice, yeah? I don't need electricity to take my inventions apart. I don't need to test them to know what they're capable of. I've only been doing this for fifty years."

"Then explain James," I said quietly.

"I CAN'T!" Crete shouted. "But I'm trying."

"So you're just building blind over there," James said, shaking his head.

"Happily," Crete said. "James, I'll have to finish your arrays. Actually, in full transparency, I'm just going to re-do your arrays anyways."

"I thought I was doing alright," he said sadly.

"You were, for a carpenter attempting electrical engineering," Crete smiled. "We'll come back to it. It's noon."

"Right," James said. "The part where… whatever."

We were laughing as we got to our feet and made for the front door, and then we were walking with Crete across the normal grass of the centerhills within Oleander. It was daytime. No swords—not yet. In minutes we were at the bottom of the stairs of the Sun Temple. In another few minutes, we were at the top of them, and all sweaty for some reason.

"The fodder has arrived," Bastille said, standing just within the temple doors.

"Ignore him," Bombelle said. "I take that back—come in, now, all of you."

And so we did. I saw sister Ollux and brother Astor, bent over a table of devices and weaponry, both holding dark helmets under their arms, both wearing some slim mesh material over their upper bodies, like a fishing net for a shirt that draped down to their militant pants full of pockets. Jungle dark leggings, so green they were almost black, perfect for camouflage. We gave them a nod, and they went back to gearing up.

"So we're suiting up? That's what's up," I said, looking around the inside of the sun temple. "I'm trying really hard not to say dope. Oops."

"And why not?" Bombelle asked.

"Because your situation requires martial intervention at the risk of human lives, and that's nothing to be flip about," I said, owning my mistake at least.

"It is not," Bombelle said. "But that apology was dope. And seeing the Astral in full form is… nothing to sneeze at. Unless—"

"Unless you already had to sneeze," Heather said, trailing off. "The pollen in this jungle."

"We are headed to Titan Arum, our last arbor outpost before the mountainous divide between Jerico and Silka, get ready for pollen," Bombelle said. "Our records of the outside world are kept as physical as currency. You will find our astronomy experts there, and they will help you decide a path to the Planetarium outside Titan Arum. An excursion simple enough for your first week here yes?"

"Day here, sure," I agreed.

"And what did you do in a day, exactly?" Bastile said. "Did you, I don't know, set up character goals and logical next steps for each one of you here in the weird forest jungle cabin home life you're about to live? Did you make plans to justify avoiding the problems of the lightning city you've left behind us all like a chasing storm? Did you FORGET ABOUT THE THUNDER?"

"We did not forget about the thunder," Heather said, ominously.

"I know you haven't," Bastile said. "For you this is safety. You do have an open door here, until you close it. But a citizen of the Jerico is a soldier of the Jerico, and right now we need you. All of you."

"On a scale of big to worse, how bad?" I asked.

"We aren't asking," Bastile said. "That bad. The best I can do is explain. Lady Bombelle, please explain."

Bombelle nodded and grabbed a handful of the metal shavings from that ornate, ancient looking urn. She cast the metal dust cloud into the small cutout of the hearth, same as last night, and they settled into that fateful three for four that we had already gone over, the four navigational points that might point Jerico to the very things keeping it clouded in anti-electricity. Was that a thing—I mean, in other places than here? Was here crazy? Wait. I was thinking about this wrong. A city wide EMP wasn't crazy, it was just as impossible and energy-consuming as… flying.

"What did you take those lines for?" Bombelle demanded. "There were always four, until there were three. Three tethers keeping us… tethered to the world of the un-electrical. I'm not a writer."

"Fourth ones' back boss," came the wavering voice of Xero the Champion.

"I will end you where you stand," Bombelle said, dark as hell until saw the clear fourth line, carving a direct line between here and—

"I don't lie," Xero said, puffing his chest up. "None of the territory do."

"You don't lie, and still I don't believe," Bombelle said. "Did the engine of the island already counteract? My whole point was about the lack of a fourth line. Now I've got nothing."

"I don't know if this will help," James said. "But I can account."

"Speaking of what now?" Bombelle asked.

"Speaking of not keeping things from…" James said.

"What are you on about brother?" I asked.

"I mean, there's so much we've just glossed over," he said sadly.

He took a step to the right, and that forth line moved. Magnetically following him, while the other three held steady. To the stunned looks of everyone in that chamber, very much including me, he hopped around, retraced his steps, even crutched around the entire circle, and that forth line, the one that shouldn't have been there… only followed him.

What.

"Oh thank the jungle," Bombelle said, as relieved as we were confused.

"First, no circles," James said. "Second, and this is important. I don't know."

"But you must," Bastile argued. "It's happening to you, and no one else."

"I agree," James held his ground. "Still don't know."

"But you… must…" Bombelle and Bastile said at the same time.

"I said no circles," James shot back.

"James why is the dirt following you?" Heather asked, a beat behind.

He stared at her.

"Maybe for the same reasons the animals are talking to Lynn?" I said to Heather under my breath.

"Crazy bonkers reasons, got it," Heather said. She was catching on quick.

"So it's all wash," Bombelle said, sinking to her knees over that floor cutout radar map. "Our radars, the coordinates to whatever's been throwing so much interference at us for centuries… and a teenage boy can move the needle."

"You think this contradicts?" Heather said, blinking at her. "You are wrong, but only about being wrong."

"So I'm… not wrong?" Bombelle asked curious. "How?"

"Can we tell them?" Heather asked, turning on us.

"Of course," James said. "Thanks for asking. But we don't lie. None of the territory do."

"Teenagers do listen, sometimes," Xero said, sounding hopeful.

"Tell us WHAT?" Bombelle shouted.

"That teenage boy right there commanded the Infinite technology underland," Heather said.

"That's impossible," Bombelle said. "The source doesn't reach underland, storm season or clear skies aside."

"That's what we said," Crete said.

Bastile was suddenly paying attention, looking the old man over for a counter, but his eyes were set, and true.

"We don't know yet," Crete said, asking the question before it was asked. "But I can give you the peace of mind that Heather keeps smacking you with. Did you build that radar to detect the connection radiation of space-age technology, such powers as, I don't know, the Infinite?"

"We did," Bombelle said from her knees, looking up at us.

"Then you're the best builder I know," Heather said, stepping up next to

James. “Your machine works. It still points you towards four sources of virtually unending power. We still have hope of finding what you’re expecting at the ends of these pathways. Regardless of what you end up doing, wherever it takes you, you still have your map.”

“We are going to stop them from showing up on our radars,” Bombelle said. “Simple as that.”

“Search and destroy, love it,” Heather said. “I only ask we don’t treat James the same as these snip-end coordinates.”

“I would never,” Bombelle said.

“Here’s the problem, they already are,” Heather said, gesturing over her shoulder to—

“Oh come on,” James said, taking a crutch step towards Heather. “Wait just a damn minute, all of you!”

The front door and what used to be the empty atrium behind us, before every warrior in earshot started creeping towards him, all of them holding the same low stance, one hand at their hip, one hand held up in front of their faces like a forearm shield, definitely some kind of group fighting stance against a brother.

“STAND DOWN,” Bastile roared.

James caught my eye, and it was a blimp in the conversation, a single look among thousands. But it was a scared one. There were a lot of sharp edges around us, and just for a single moment, they had surrounded us with every intention of treating us the same as the Reaper had treated my father. They wouldn’t need weapons, not against us.

My only question was… what was the plan for Sand and Crete?

“Not your enemy,” James said, as the warriors backed off.

“You swear, it?” Bastile asked.

“I swear it so hard,” James said, looking him dead in the face. “I swear it on every bone in my very breakable body, the one that’s usually covered in nanofiber, head to toe.”

“I believe him,” Bombelle said, and she stood up, even if Bastile didn’t move. “Do you promise to use your words, bodies, powers and abilities, no matter how big or small, for the territory, James?”

“It won’t be for Silka, not with that noise,” James said honestly.

And that seemed to do the trick. Bombelle nodded, and Bastile threw a brown strap bag to our feet. It was familiar.

“Wait a minute,” Heather said, frowning. “Talking about trust…”

“Trust takes a lifetime to build,” Bastile said. “But it can be lost in a single moment.”

“That’s from…” I said, stopping myself.

It was a quote from an old superhero show. It was also just a fact, so I shook it off, rejoined the adult world, and picked up the bag that Heather had given me atop a certain underground mountain range overlooking Galan Town 2.0. It was heavy, hopefully with exactly what I hoped was inside, although it would take a few missing links for it to make sense. But when had that ever stopped us?

I opened the zipper and… yep. Links were missing. But other things weren’t.

“Where on earth did you find this?” I asked.

"Roof of the hospital," Bastile said. "You know the big, round, red one?"

"I know the one," I said. "James, can you account for this too?"

"I…" he said, trailing off at the best time to avoid lying.

I felt it. The opposite of hope, dread. He might just have that missing link I was looking for, but it wasn't something he wanted to talk about here. And even worse, he didn't want to lie about it. We were caught. Until—

"Okay you're both clearly sundowning, just give it here," Heather said, swiping the thing and dumping the contents out like they weren't fragile at all.

Inside the bag were three bags. Three huge, thick, clear plastic bags, each with big black letters clearly written across them. DEREK. JAMES. LYNN. They were big enough to hold our shoes and all sorts of other things.

"Please," Lynn said, like she'd seen a ghost.

And even before the flurry of clothes and ripped plastic settled, Lynn was on her knees, calmly holding her necklace up gently by the silver chain, her eyes rippling as she stared at the thing, before putting it on with a sigh of relief. It bounced against her chest once, just below her neck, and maybe it was the weight of the moment, but I swear I saw a flash of glowing purple, and I watched the red scratch marks on her neck fade.

"Yes," Lynn said, holding her heart. "Thank you Bastile."

"I don't know who you should be thanking, but it's not me," he said.

"How much you wanna bet they got ours wrong?" James asked, picking up the DEREK bag. "Lookit, them's my pants. My skate shirt, not yours."

"Good old trousers," I said, holding my black v-neck shirt and jeans up.

"I give those shoes top props," Bombelle said, looking down at the pink skate shoes that were cooler than anyone in this room knew. "But you're matching for reasons. What is the function of those superpowers?"

"To turn the three-dimensional world into an infinite number of ways to escape from anything," I said. "That's been, so far, our greatest superpower. Running away. Ending up somewhere cooler than where we came from."

"I don't know where we're ending up this time, Derek," Bastile said. "Titan Arum is past the border. It's possible you end up in non-incorporated territory."

"You mean Silka?" I asked.

Bastile nodded. "In that situation, you would have normal access to your… clothes. But deploying them would undoubtedly make your locations known to the Infinite source, and we cannot rule out the possibility of the lightning city immediately tracking my entire unit down through you. My question is for the three of you who possess such an ability. You're good without it, right?"

Damn.

Lynn looked down at her watch, ready to call for backup or send that SOS the very first chance we got. But if we connected, we would be traced and tracked, then followed and trailed, maybe even hunted. And not just us. Anyone with us, including the Jerico handlers. That call would doom us all.

James probably wasn't thinking about friends or goals or superheroes, he was staring at the pants and socks, which we knew by experience would heal his broken ankle in minutes, if we were able to get somewhere outside Jerico. All the pain, all those weeks of crutching ahead, it could all be over—unless that's exactly what Infinite was waiting for.

As for me, I held one shoe in one hand and my watch in the other, both shaking as I fought the urge to put them on the very first chance given, so ready to be at full tilt super stupid action hero again, the sword, the shoes… but if it solved all our problems, the cost was the cost, and it was too high.

"Say we go alone," Heather said to me. "Say we leave the matter of whether or not we care about Infinite finding us to… us? Does your answer change?"

She had me. Even worse, she knew it.

"You're thinking about it," she said. "If you're so willing to pony up, why don't we just go? You'll all get exactly what you want, and then maybe, just MAYBE, we'll even be able to shoot off into the distance and escape back into the territory before Infinite ever catches up with us. You willing to risk it all?"

"A call for help that may as well be our last will," Lynn said. "Not now."

"A single sword against an unbreakable shield," I said sadly. "Not yet."

"A leg for a cell," James said. "Not ever. There's too much to our… all."

"When did that happen?" Lynn asked, all bittersweet.

"Let's all remember this moment," Heather said, her eyes narrowed at us. "I think you cityfolk just showed a bit of something the rest of us were born with hanging over our heads. Did I hear you say that you were afraid of In—?"

"We didn't say that," Lynn said. "We said we weren't willing to risk another round with them. Not even with… just not right now."

"Same," my brother and I said at the same time.

"So we can go right ahead and stop thinking you have any kind of courage these people don't?" Heather asked, like she was teaching us a lesson.

"What do you mean, these people?" Bombelle barked at her.

Heather turned white.

"Just kidding," Bombelle said. "Good lesson. Thanks demon child."

"You got it…" Heather said quietly.

"You can't just give a man back his supersuit…" I said like a child (it actually was the second saddest I'd ever been), then I took a big boy breath, balled up the suit and watch and shoes, and shoved them back in the plastic bag.

"Fine."

"How'd you switch off the sadness at not being able to be a superhero?" Bombelle asked. "You went from super shoes to bare feet in a blink."

"We aren't going barefoot anything," I said. "I can make the switch when a situation needs me to. But until then, we go through."

"You mean around?" Bombelle asked.

"We go through," I said, holding her eyes. "Right Reapers?"

"So that's what you're on about," Heather said, approvingly.

"By my dark rocks and wings," James said, the revelation hitting him in the face. "We do have other ways of getting through, fighting, flying, falling—and healing. All without bringing the Infinite into anything. Right Lynn?"

"Right," she said, holding her necklace like a lifeline. "The amethyst."

"And here we were, thinking we'd figured you out in a day," Bombelle said.

"No man or woman has ever done that," I said. "I'll prove it. Secondly, Bombelle, why did you give these back to us?"

"You mean why did she steal them from us?" Heather said.

"No," I said. "Sand and Crete almost lost a plane, why didn't we lose our pants? Everything in the territory goes to the territory, right?"

"You're right," Bastile said. "Factory-made jeans are good fabric, but the stitching is invaluable. There are probably two hundred yards of sewing material in each unit. These should be in the hands of the village seamstress."

"No, these should be in the inventory of the Infinite prison complex," Lynn said frowning. "How did they get here?"

"Like I said, found them on the big red roof," Bombelle said. "Anything you wish to share about how that happened…"

"We'll deal with that later," I said. "I'm going to leave my future tech in the hands of Crete Magellan while we're away from the Oleander. But now that we've got some potential again, some good old fashioned, fashion hope, you can take everything non-super as our tribute to the territory."

"Derek, we discussed this internally," Bombelle said. "We agree that though custom dictates everything go to the territory… are we not wrong in saying these are your only worldly possessions left?"

"They are what you say they are," I said.

Our backpacks were still at Crete's mecha mansion, and we'd unloaded some of the car into the Sandcastle, but both of those places were right now either imaginarily exploded or at least partially witnessed to have been physically exploded. Fire hath no mercy. Also, like, where was the car?

"I'm with him," James said. "My jeans, my favorite skate brand shirt, take it, enjoy. Leave me the clothes that actually might do me some good one day. As for getting around, you gave me the shirt on my back, let me repay it."

"True," I said. "Look what we're wearing. This is thanks for returning to us the only worldly possessions left that matter."

"Pants are pretty important," Bastile said. "Thank you.

"Don't leave me out," Lynn said, tossing Bastile the shirt and black jeans that she had clearly borrowed from Heather before the Vemascension. Dumb name, sure, but it worked.

"Come on, those are mine!" Heather said, but she didn't make a move to stop Lynn. "Fine, take my favorite purple sweater…"

"One of the elderly ladies in my mother's care home thanks you," Bombelle said.

She patted Heather on the shoulder straps of her suspenders, the ones she'd had on the entire time, as we'd swapped our Infinite prison scrubs for actual browns scrubs in the Jerico hospital, and had worn nothing else since. Heather sighed and looked away as Bombelle took her clothes. We were left with our tree fabrics, either as made or all cut up in weird places (if you were Lynn or Heather). But now over them we all wore the belt and shoulder suspenders of the Reaper, the one that, once combined with those amethyst necklaces, would give us the powers of the earth, sky, and more—you know, once we were free of this infernal territory. And even better, the mechanical gloves that didn't require any technology to deploy into five razor sharp spikes from each hand.

"James don't—" I said, remembering at the last minute.

“I know,” he said, gloved up, still swinging on those crutches. “Go on.”

I couldn’t resist, and he knew it. My claws came out, same as Heather’s. They usually responded to my thoughts and whatever actions were required to them, almost like I was wearing their controller around my neck (I was). But right now, that controller was offline, so they were only as rigid as my bones and as light and flexible as my fingers. Still pretty useful, if you were me.

“We good?” Willa asked.

“Chaotic good,” I answered. “Is that what you’re looking for?”

“I’ll be honest… not usually?” Bombelle said, speaking truthfully at the very least, but with a new light in her eye as she looked over us. Could it be… hope?

“Hand, follow me,” Bastile said. “Fodder, follow the Hand. It’s time.”

“You’re going to stop calling us that sometime today, sir,” Heather said.

“Incorrect,” Bastile said, his green eyes suddenly darker than Heather’s underland purple. “You can take rear guard. Anything tries to sneak up on us, you’d better meet it head on.”

“What might sneak up on us?” Heather asked.

Bastile did not answer.

“We’re headed for Arum,” Bombelle explained for her husband, as we walked out of the temple, but the back way this time, through a long chamber and hallway at the far end of the thing, leading us already a long way from the Oleander. “Lots of things that prey on the weak, in Arum.”

“Have we a way for a brother to keep up?” I asked.

“Yes, but I hate it,” Bombelle said.

Before we passed out the other side of the temple, she grabbed the bloody skateboard off the wall and held it out by the trucks. I winced at the mall grab.

“We have horses waiting outside the gates,” Bombelle said. “Until then, it’s mostly flat wood for floors. Save your strength, catch a wave.”

“You were hallucinating about a boat,” I said, sitting James down on the skateboard and leading him by the crutch down the last of the hallway.

“Good tides today,” he said, trying to be positive, but I could hear the relief in his voice, and loved it.

We exited into the jungle, straight out into an inclined wooden walkway that led much farther up than the heights of the highest Arbor treehouse around. It wasn’t a problem to pull James up the thing, it was just such an obvious limit to the otherwise supergroup. Xero and Willa had raced up the incline, both of them much faster than expected. Ollux and Astor were talking with Bastile, only Bombelle had her eyes on us, making sure I didn’t drop James off the platform (I didn’t, not even once). Finally the buildout of the temple fell away below us, and the incline ended on a flat wooden walkway high up in the trees. We caught one last, faraway glimpse of the Oleander, that center hill circle watering hole, hell we could almost see our cabin over there on the right side of the slopes—

“You’ll see it again,” Bombelle called to us. “But not right now.”

“No more messing around,” I said. “You can skate on one leg for days. Just do that.”

And suddenly James was on one foot, using one crutch to crutch, the other one on the nose of the board. I kept an eye out for the floor, but it was sanded and joined so well that it really wasn't hard to keep him moving. Still, I was looking forward to the horses.

We didn't pass as many trunk platforms or structures around us on this road through the trees. This one was a single direction with nothing else of construct around, almost like a kingsroad, made of the snappiest, most beautiful bare maple wood I'd ever seen. There were even thick, single slab handrails that came up three feet, making the entire thing like a jungle version of rainbow road, if it came with bumper rails (blasphemy). Every ten feet or so, there were two lengths of heavy ropes tied to the sides of the rails, with big blocks of stone lashed to the ends of each.

"What are those for?" I asked.

"Let's hope you don't find out," was all Bastile said.

He passed us with an eye to the skateboard James was traveling on. The sound of those wheels rolling over wood… I'm sure it was annoying everyone else in the neighborhood but to me, there was no sound sweeter.

"Is this a highway?" I asked. "Is life—"

"Don't you dare," Ollux answered. "Also… yes. Travel within the gates is accounted for. Only beyond them will we have to walk the forest floor."

"Who built these roads?" I asked.

"These days the builder co of Racket and Foe see to every inch of our territory," Bombelle said. "But of course we inherited the infrastructure from past generations of Jerico. To be honest, we don't even know how many bridges there are. Every year we find more, either that, or the remains of them."

"So you don't have a perfect map either," I said. "I'm sensing a pattern."

"It's a big island," Bastile agreed. "All maps are still being made. Or found."

2.5

WHO CAN'T COME HOME

Though the canopy over our heads never broke, we could see the moving shades of light as the endless overhead swayed in the wind, maybe a hundred feet over us at the most. I knew the farther out we went, the higher up we were, even though our path was straight, like scary flat, almost perfectly level.

"What are those?" Lynn asked.

Some sort of pink hibiscus with a yellow stem was starting to make the perfectly sanded and routed road feel like the love canoe.

"That is oleander the killer," Bastile said, careful not to touch the thing.

"Oleander? We just left her!" Derek said, frowning.

"One a city, one a plant," Bastile explained, clenching. "Both one of the most dangerous flowers on this island. A single blade ingested is death."

"And you've got it just dangling over the kingsroad because why?" I asked.

"Because the grass is swords," Derek said.

"Because deterrent," Bombelle said, as she dipped down under a single branch obscuring most of the path. "Carefully. But come see this."

And after ducking under that branch, all thoughts of the love canoe left my—

"Snake," Heather said.

Correct. The body of a python rested with its head in a patch of pink flowers, its tail wrapped around the entire bridge. It was thicker than I was, and twenty feet long at the least. But that wasn't all. There was an elderly man beside the snake, cross-legged, a hand over its neck like he'd been petting it.

"That was alive?" Lynn said, taking a step back. "This close to—"

"Better here than there," Bastile said. "That's the biggest one this season."

"Snake season," my brother and I said at the same time, sarcastically.

"She was a mother," the old man said, without looking up.

"In another world her babies would live to eat us all," Bastile said, crouching down. "Sir. It's not safe here. You're on the road again. We've been over this."

"I wanted to see the world from up here," the man rasped. "Like she did."

He was in tattered clothes if that, a long dark shirt that was nothing like the tan fabric of ours, full of holes and dirt, pants that ended around the knee in a clear, but terrible cut. No shoes, feet full of blisters, wrinkles, I could go on.

"I thought you'd seen enough of the world for one lifetime," Bastile said.

"I've... seen too much to not keep going," the man said, standing up with Bastile's help. "When the animals bleed, the jungle does too. When you cry, we all cry. Tears of crystal. You can't put those back in your eyes."

"I hear you," Bastile said. "Now you hear me, before my perimeter guards mistake you for a threat. If you must live this life, allow us to live ours. Please."

"I... allow that they're waiting for you, not a few minutes out," the old man said, hunched over again, something not right about him, but Bastile perked up quick like he'd been given a very much appreciated heads up. "That's why I lied about the snake. I'm sorry, I didn't mean to—"

"To break the first rule of Jerico, to demonstrate exactly why we might have a problem finding you on this side of the gates?" Bastile said, sounding mad as hell—until he let go of the man's arm. "Thanks Owl. Like always."

"Turn back," the old man said, sitting down again. "Like always."

"Maybe we should listen to a bird?" Lynn said, blinking.

"We aren't turning back anywhere," Bastile said. "I wasn't expecting company so close to the Oleander. But I don't every time get what I want."

"None do babe," Bombelle said.

"We just moved down the food chain," Lynn said, an eye on the flowers.

"Help me out here big guy," Willa said.

Xero helped her drop the weight of the thing off the side of the platform. The sight of the tail whipping over the road and out of sight was unnerving.

"I wouldn't have done that," Owl said suddenly.

"Why not?" Bastile said.

"You don't smell that bear?" Owl asked.

We all peered over the edge to see (and hear) the thing hit the floor, a few hundred feet below us, a straight shot down to the forest tanbark. But that was a mistake. Because just as we peered over the edge, something was looking up from the ground where the snake had landed. It was a bear. A big black bear.

"Today, really?" Bastile said.

The tree closest to us started rustling. Bears could climb anything.

"Um, problem boss," Heather said, her hands coming up, the gemstone around her neck still unresponsive, the claws still stowed.

"No problem fodder," Bastile said. "Willa, four hundred pounds. Male. Climbing quick, clearly well fed, above average shape. Give it some extra."

"I was planning on it," Willa said.

Suddenly there was a drawstring on the tip of her curved blade, reaching all the way down to the base of her hilt. She had turned a sword into a bow, and by the time I'd figured out how she already had it notched and drawn, her payload more syringe than arrow, full of a dark green liquid.

"What's that?" I asked.

"Horse tranquilizer," she said. "You want some?"

"No..." I said lamely.

"Then leave me alone, there's bears," Willa said.

There was one bear, and he had already made it up onto the kingsroad, leaving claw marks as deep as sawblades. It roared at us, looked back at the pink flowers, then shook its snout and walked in our direction, coming to a gallop in two seconds flat. Everyone who wasn't us froze.

"The breakers, NOW!" Bastile roared.

Astor and Xero ran to opposite sides of the bridge, picked up one of those ropes with weights on the ends, and at the same time flung them hard out over either side of the bridge. They arced out and came up to hit the platform in the middle of its bottom with a crunch, as Astor and Xero dove back to us like there was about to be an explosion behind them.

"Oh I get it," I said.

"Makes one of us!" Derek said, pulling me back the way Xero had gone as—

A perfectly cut ten foot square section of the kingsroad fell away, crumbling from the middle, leaving a full on black hole in the middle of rainbow road. The bear caught itself as it skidded to a stop, claws hanging over the open air that now separated us from it. He (or she) roared one more time, licking its huge canines, spit flying from its snout, eyes darting around for the closest tree branch or trunk to get to us… but there was none.

"A little warning," Heather said, her claws as close to the edge as the bear's.

"Warning," Willa said simply.

Willa loosed her arrow over Heather's shoulder like a bolt of lightning. The bear blinked, looking down at its chest where the huge shaft of a wooden arrow was sticking out, a dark green liquid being pumped into the thing's chest from the spring-loaded syringe arrow.

"Can't have you following us buddy," Willa said. "Go to sleep."

The bear tried to fight the tranquilizer arrow still sticking out of its chest, coming dangerously close to falling off that high rise platform, a few hundred feet from the forest floor…

"Not frontwards, never frontwards!" Willa shouted. "Backwards, PLEASE!"

And through the trees there was a rip of air, of speeding motion, something like a storm cloud descending in a flash. Out of nowhere, a huge clouded jungle leopard came shooting out of the trees to land perfectly balanced on the bear's upright body, all claws retracted, even careful to avoid the arrow shaft. The weight of the cat's landing forced the bear backwards just enough for it to topple over with a massive crunch to the still holding platform in the trees, the bear landing on its back with the leopard on its belly, like it was nothing.

"How dare we," Lynn said, like she was speaking for the cat again.

"What a day," Heather said, like Lynn had gone crazy. "Hi Sophia."

The cat purred, we heard it over the bear's snoring. Sophia gently took hold of the arrow shaft in her teeth and pulled the tip out of the bear, then slunk gracefully down to the platform and pounced over to us, making the ten foot jump without even a running leap.

"Willa the Killa. Ironic," Lynn said.

But Willa's eyes only glazed over as the cat approached, with her arrow in her teeth. Sophia took a sit a few feet from Willa, who was clearly tensing every muscle in her small body to stand tall.

"Be brave, soldier," Bombelle said.

Willa held her hand out, trying her best not to tremble. Sophia put her massive underjaw straight onto Willa's hand—but because of the canines, the cat had to open as wide as possible to let the arrow loose. For a moment Willa's lip quivered as she stuck her hand into the literal jaws of death to pick up her arrow from Sophia's sabreteeth. Then Sophia closed her mouth with a yawn, and sat there, looking more like a statue outside a library than the three hundred pound killer cat she was.

"Me… what?" Willa asked.

"Ironic," Lynn said, coming up beside Sophia, but from a good distance, enough that Sophia could see Lynn approaching, instead of just coming up from behind an animal like her. "Your nicknames did not broadcast hold back, Wildfire Willa the Killa. But that bear is not yet dead."

"Never," Willa said. "I don't kill anything. Nicknames are psychological, especially when your position is to defend your homeland, and the only threats to my homeland are human. The name is for humans. It's—"

"Another deterrent," Lynn said. Then she shook her head (like she was done being possessed) and looked around. "Kitty!"

Sophia leapt at Lynn, pawing at her face with soft, unclawed cat paws, licking her gently on the clothes instead of her soft skin. She was learning. Young cat, all the tricks.

"In no world can you allow that creature near the horses," Bastile said.

"Wanna BET?" Lynn shot back.

Sophia stuck her tongue out, like she was laughing.

"I don't wager," Bastile said. "A man can plan, or gamble. I choose plan. If our horses bolt, it would be faster to turn around and come back tomorrow than try to make it through the Arum on foot."

"Yes sir," Lynn said. "Let her see us through the trees, at least."

"I was already planning on it," Bastile said, giving the cat one last look before turning his back on her. "Soldiers, stay close. We're coming up on Portia Pass, and we still haven't accounted for the fires last month."

"Arsonists?" I asked.

"Maybe," Bombelle said. "Or quite possibly cannibals."

"I was joking," I said. "I should stop joking."

"You should," Bombelle said. "There are things worse than bears and snakes around here. Things more threatening."

"Like people?" I asked.

"There are non-incorporated tribes in the outer area, yes," Bombelle said. "Occasionally they make their way through. But they stay close to the gates, knowing if they're caught here, the hand will drag them deep within our territory like a Venus fly trap, and never let go."

"You said that last part kind of loud," I said. "Wait. We're here with the literal hand of Jerico, the legendary team I'd lived my whole life never knowing about. Are you here for us? Or are you here because… this is here?"

"Nine o clock, two meters up," Bombelle said, suddenly, without warning.

So it was like that. In a blink, Willa sent an arrow flying on faith without looking, in exactly the direction Bombelle had given her. And in response—

"AHH!"

Clearly she could hit a target.

The shout came from closer than I was expecting, and as we flinched in place the lights shifted overhead, as six figures dropped down from the trees above us on wires, upside down, their heads aimed at our heads.

"Boys and girls," Bastile said, his voice turning on a dime. "Prepare to fight for your lives as hard as any Astral. Welcome to life outside the gates, which always included the potential for cannibals. You know what, I need you at top tilt, so screw it, welcome to cannibals."

"You're joking," Lynn said, her eyes shaking slightly, like there was a train coming or something.

"I do not joke about getting eaten," Bastile said. "For everything—FIGHT!"

He had us at fight, which was good, because it was the last thing he'd said. In slow motion, I watched the hand of the Jerico at work. I would never forget it. Bastile spun so fast he sent up sawdust with one foot and back-kicked a six-foot falling goon in the chest with the other, sending him spinning to the edge of the platform, where he fell down just in time to not fall down. One. Bombelle was even faster; she didn't call for backup, she didn't wait for Bastile. She only reached up, grabbed the two feet of the next descending figure, stepped back and swung forward, letting him take the entire fall unprotected on his chest and shoulders, no feet allowed. The platform shook with the impact, the goon bounced once and was still. Two.

"Sensing a pattern," Derek said, his hands up, ready for anything.

The Champion picked a bulkier, bald-headed goon off the rope and held him up only high enough to smash foreheads, one of them instantly unconscious (it wasn't Xero). The assailant fell to our feet, as the Champ gave us a thumbs up.

"Three!" he said.

Willa fired an arrow into the sky, severing some rope just as the goon sliding down it made himself visible through the trees, and he screamed the final ten feet to smash into the ground, groaning, not moving.

"Four," Willa corrected.

"Five six," Ollux said, joining us from the side.

She and her brother Astor had the last of the six. They struck together, head, neck, legs, then they smashed the dazed the goons together hard enough to knock the wind out of them.

"Nobody missed?" Bastile asked.

The warriors of Astral shook their heads. Bastile and Bombelle had retreated to Willa and Xero, making a four-cornered fighting unit with their backs to each other. I took a head count and smacked Heather on the arm, nodding to what seemed like the official Jerico fighting stance—of four. We put our backs to each other as Astor and Ollux moved around the fallen assailants with rope for handcuffs. The assault seemed over, but there was no letting our guards down—not quite yet, not when the trees were still rustling, the wind was still singing, not when the swift, black shape of something dropped down in front of me, and I looked up over my crutches to the toothy smile of someone wearing another definition of dirt for clothes. It had been a long time since I'd smelled worse.

"S…seven…" I stammered.

"JAMES!" Heather shouted.

At least one of us jumped to the attack. Lynn came in like there was a soccer ball between us, colliding into the legs of the seventh guy and sending him to his back—just as Derek followed him to his knees with an elbow leading the way, the words of Bastile loosing something within him he'd probably been holding back ever since he realized just how hard he could fight.

"For BALIN!" Derek shouted out of absolutely nowhere. Then—bam.

I had never seen him hit a guy that hard.

"Get back here," Bastile said, a hand on the back of my shirt, dragging me away so quick I almost toppled over, as Lynn did the same to Derek.

"Is he dangerous?" I asked.

"More than you know," Bombelle said, taking over for Bastile, her hand somehow on both Lynn and me. "Nice reflexes."

"We're not done," Willa said.

Her bow was drawn again, as she moved down the platform, a big tree in our way, until we could see on the other side of it—a final guy stood, a wooden crossbow at his feet, one hand pinned into the trunk of the tree by Willa's arrow.

"Who is that?" Heather asked. "Why did they—"

"Not right now," Bastile said.

"Don't not right now me," Heather said. "What's happening, who are these people, apologies for saying these people?"

Bastile stared at her. It was clear he wasn't going to out-alpha Heather Denien. Not now, not ever.

"You are stepping on people in front of a Reaper," Heather said, channeling something I'd honestly never once seen from her. Even in the Den, she'd caved to Mare. This was different. "If you won't explain, I'll ask them. Who are you?"

"True... Jerico..." one of the men on the ground said, hands tied behind his back, spitting blood out from his smashed nose. But something else was off about his voice. "Veterans of the great war, messiah of the everchange..."

"Veterans?" I said. "Of what?"

"Of the most losing attack this island has ever seen, the one that left us with nothing but dirt," the guy in the trees said.

"All I know is dirt," Heather said, not standing down. "What's your name?"

"Elyia Kyudo, zen archer, third guard," the guy said, going back to trying to raise the crossbow with his feet, but the thing was loaded, and it was a dangerous gamble.

"That's not zen," I said.

"I'd listen to him," Willa said. "The pressure will set it off long before you get the chance to aim at me. If you want an arrow in the foot, I'm right here."

Elyia growled, and lowered his foot, gently placing the crossbow back on the ground. He looked defeated, but then we saw him pivoting the thing in the bark.

"You don't tell me what to do," Elyia said.

"You're right, I guess I don't," Heather said, lowering her hands, standing as tribute, trusting the guy we didn't know, in the polar opposite mindset of someone else we'd heard use those exact words.

Elyia looked at her like she was crazy. Then he stomped down on the crossbow and an arrow exploded out of it.

"On GUARD!" Willa shouted, no choice, loosing her own arrow—

Heather screamed, her claws coming up but too late, the glint of metal about to tear her in half—

"NO!" Lynn yelled, beat by a single moment, not the only one.

It wasn't Derek. It was me. The skateboard came up quicker than Heather's claws. My eyes were stuck on that arrow all the way to board like a batter watching the baseball hit his bat. I took the blow without my arm moving an inch, the muscles and veins in my forearm bulging. All that crutching wasn't doing my upper body any harm. Elyia's arrow stuck into the seven-plied wood, and though my hand recoiled a bunch, the arrow was stuck—no ricochet, no breakthrough, no harm to Heather. I held the thing by the wheel like it was always made to be a shield.

Or maybe I was.

Heather's claws finally deployed. She took the arrow out of my board on razor sharp fingertips, so fine they bit into the wood only by the nanometers. She returned the arrow to the small quiver on Willa's back, the one we hadn't even known was there until her sword had become a bow. Willa was turning out okay. Then as she came back, Heather reached out and touched my face.

It said it all.

"Thanks," Willa said. "All good back there skater boy?"

"If you're talking to me… all good," I said, still shaking. "Heather, how about—"

"All good now," she said. "Change, no change. Stay close James."

"What was your purpose in the group before the injury?" Bombelle asked me. "The honeypot?"

"The shield," I said. "Why?"

Bombelle nodded. "That fits too."

"Need a plan here," Willa called out, not sounding surprised at all that Heather wasn't dead. Wait.

"You had the shot," I said. "You knew not to take it. You knew…"

"I have more faith in my team than stars in the sky," Willa said. "My team now includes you. I have faith that you wouldn't be here if you didn't belong."

"But your name—" Derek said, frowning.

"It's just a NAME!" Wildfire Willa the Killa shouted.

Lynn moved in on Heather, grabbing her and fixing her hair, as Heather's hand latched onto Lynn's shoulder and didn't let go. Good. We could use the reminder, we'd gotten familiar, in a place we did not know. A place of cannibals and outsiders. So much for photosynthesis and community.

"James I owe you a life," Heather finally said.

"This isn't a video game Heather," I said, as I skateboarded past her, sensing the heat even without looking back. "Sorry. We're even."

"Not even," Heather said, watching me.

Astor and Ollux walked past, I looked back, and they had already tied up every single one of the goons that had fallen upon us, with long stretches of rope that Xero continued to check, kicking any wooden shards or rocks away from the reach of the captives. He danced away from the pocketknife that one of the goons was able to open and stab at him with, using only his toes.

"Nice try," the giant Xero said.

Xero was graceful in the pivot, but with such sassy legs he kicked the captive's foot so hard the toes unclenched, the metal blade skid across the ground and took the plunge over the side of the platform, lost to the jungle floor a hundred feet below us.

"What's your name?" Xero asked.

"Officer Butts, four hundred and twentieth guard, newly single," the guy who'd taken a stab at him said sarcastically.

"I get it," Xero said, folding his arms. "Officer Butts, you've clearly undergone foot dexterity training. I'm thinking you're ex-corps, you should remember the entire four-hundredth guard was—"

"I remember everything about the four-hundredth, thank you," the guy said, suddenly dropping the attitude, back to blank stares, lost inside his own mind.

"Corps?" Derek asked, blinking.

"Ex-corps," said the guy, like a conditioned response—or a tick.

"Foot dexterity training, that explains crossbow over here, too," Willa said.

"You got that from feet?" I asked.

But we could all see that even with a hand and a foot pinned by arrows into the tree behind him, Elyia had already gotten dangerously close to reloading that crossbow again. Willa sighed and sent an arrow at the contraption, snapping the string and plowing into the trunk, not an inch from Elyia's free ankle. He sighed, and went to work re-stringing the crossbow, with a spare thread from a pocket on his right hip. All of this with one foot.

Lynn threw her hands in the air.

"I bought us a minute Lynn, what have you done lately?" Willa said. "Can't risk blowing that thing to smiths, not before we can figure out where it came from. Our friends in build city will be able to trace the… um, build, to the…"

"The city?" I offered.

Willa shook her head. "Thought it'd be less simple."

"You can be simple," I said. "It's more relatable, and it opens the doors to metaphors."

"How does one open a door to a metaphor?" Willa asked, puzzled.

"Metaphorically, of course," I said.

"CORPS?" Derek asked/shouted, his hands out for answers.

I frowned. "Were you listening to like, anything I just said about simple?"

"Metaphorically… no," Derek said, his eyes dead set on Xero.

"There's only one place in the world that teaches the kind of assault these men are capable of," the Champion said, looking down sadly to the men tied up on the ground. Each is a graduate of the Astral, a training process that utilizes the entire territory, infinitely more than topline training."

"Ex-military," I said.

"It's certain," Xero said, looking sadder than I'd seen him yet. "Means once, they were kin. Brothers and sisters, and nothing less."

"So why are they waiting on the kingsroad to kill you?" I asked.

“Because they are something more,” the Champion said. “They refuse the community, they came back from, they have decided to live the rest of their lives in defiance to the rules of civilization. They are still our brothers and sisters, but they are not welcome. Yet in reality, here they are.”

“That’s why Willa won’t killa,” Derek said.

Xero cringed. “You’re the writer?”

“It takes both of us,” Derek said, grimacing.

“That makes more sense,” the Champion said. “Write this down, little ones. There’s a part of me that would take that arrow in my heart before punching down on these people, sorry for saying these people. It reminds me of the only guarantee we’ve got in this world, that we won’t survive it. But then of course, there’s the only instinct we’re born with, which is to try.”

“What do you choose, in that situation?” I asked.

I was swinging back and forth on my crutches, trying to keep the blood going. Adrenaline was a hell of a thing. With my heart beating this fast, the raging pain in my leg was as quiet as it had ever been.

“Shengcun,” Heather said, coming out of nowhere. “If I hadn’t spied on all of that… I thought my life was over. Now I’m just sad.”

“Sad is helpful,” Xero said. “But these people need empathy, not sympathy. We can’t just feel bad about it, we have to figure out why they feel sad, and act on every list item we can come up with. That’s change.”

“That’s what people like you always say, in your world,” the voice came, from Kyudo. “But in ours, the head has found a way to bleed from the ground up. You cut us off from the heart and act surprised at the decay.”

“The ones letting you live, we did that?” Willa said, her arrow still notched.

“Curse you.”

“Curse us?” Bastile roared. “You sent that bolt at the woman who liberated the entire Vempire.”

But it wasn’t Kyudo who replied, it was Officer Butts. He laughed at us.

“You expect us to believe that? Jerico is held in the stone age by clouds, the Vempire was trapped underland by bombs, magic, and a mile of dirt—and they overcame first? Before the mighty Territory? REALLY?”

“Really,” Heather said, unapologetic for what she’d done, as always.

But all that got was spit, missing her toes by an inch.

“Our lives were never yours,” the guy said. “How can you still not understand that…”

And that was it. He put his head on the wood, his body resting finally, where it had before been wrenching against the restraints. Now he was calm, and crying softly, his eyes tearing up as he accepted the position he was in. I don’t know why I did it, but I was closest, now that Bombelle had moved away. I kneeled down (sort of), and saw his eyes register the newcomer.

“He’s dangerous James,” Bastile said to me.

“I want to help,” I said.

“The baby bird thinks he can help,” the guy on the ground said, laughing slightly, until he turned to face me and the sight of my face sent a lightning bolt through him. “Hey baby bird—”

"Hi," I said, in my best non-aggressive voice.

"Is…" the guy said, scrambling up, blinking at me. "I…"

"I what?" I asked. "Because I James."

"Is… Issaic," the guy said.

His face was shaking. Something wasn't right. Was it getting colder?

"James get back," Lynn warned.

"No," the guy said, somehow already up on his feet. "NO!"

"I'm not Issaic, I'm just his son!" I said trying to help, the only thing—

"That'll do it," Heather said, but she was past making fun—

"NOO!"

The guy was panicked, wrenching his shoulders, desperately fighting his restraints trying to block me out, but he couldn't. He was forced to face me, high on that platform, with no other options. But that wasn't true, was it?

"What's happening?" Derek asked, but answered at the same time, and as the guy turned to him, Derek slapped his hands to his face.

Too late. The guy only needed a single moment of my brother's face before he screamed bloody murder, ran for the knee-high platform guard rail, ran OVER it, and was gone.

No.

"NO!" Lynn shouted, the only one of us to actually run for the guy but…

It was too late. I didn't want to face it. I didn't want to describe it… but I had to try. He'd crashed top-heavy into the railing and easily gone over, his legs arcing up, his bare feet the last thing we'd seen. There was no noise at first. Then it happened. It doesn't get an onomatopoeia. The same moment hit us all, literally, as we heard it we flinched together. If you have to know what it sounded like… it was the sound of a book ending. One we hadn't even read yet.

"But…" Derek started, not even sure what to say.

"Don't," I said, my eyes welling up. "Just… don't."

2.6

JUNGLEBLOOD

"Can I cry, or will that give away our strategic position, captain?" I asked, the words hollow, the emotion just not showing up (I wondered why).

"Do what you want," Bastile said, every word a labor.

"Thanks," I said. "Here I go."

But there was no sound that left my lips. We were shaking. By that I mean on the verge of bawling, and I was the only one dumb enough to think talking would help. I had never felt this chill. This absolute sheer cold. We had just watched a man die, and it wasn't even the first time this week. I couldn't take it. I felt like the spectra of something skeletal was following me, some bad clouds, some wave of misfortune from the ether, swallowing my body for the towering front. In moments like this, I was the smallest version of myself.

"I feel responsible," Bastile said, taking a knee before us, cutting us off from the point where he… where feet…

"I said just—" James started.

"Don't tell me what to do," Bastile said. "That man clearly took one look at your face and saw Issaic Nite. He saw the father, the rest of us see the sons. Your faces are something you can't change, by definition of being born. That… was not your fault. Don't you dare think for one moment it was."

"He could have… done so many other things about it…" I said.

"You aren't anywhere near the enemy Issaic is," came the voice of the guy pinned to a tree trunk only twenty feet away—Elyia Kyudo, and he had seen it all. "He's destroyer. Some can still face it. Some are… tired."

"By definition we are all survivors," Bastile said, nodding to the guy.

"A bird did tell us to turn back," James said.

"What on island did this to them?" I asked. "The Blitz?"

"What else do you think he saw when he looked at you?" Elyia asked, harsh. "He saw the night the lightning city put this on our skin."

And even though his palm was impaled by an arrow, he curved all five fingers up to show us the scar on his wrist, below all the bleeding.

"That looks like a brand," James said. "I can't make it out, it's too far away."

"No it's not," Bastile said.

Bastile himself was now free from that wristlet all the cool kids wore. But below the leather, there was an insignia on bare skin, an enflamed, twisting scar, it looked terrible. It was a lowercase letter 'a' with either a lightning bolt or a feathered, winged shape behind it, burned into him. It was a brand.

"It's time," Bombelle said, uncovering her own wrist to the same sight.

Willa held the taunt arrow tip with her bow hand, her free drawstring hand shaking the wristlet aside—yep, she had the same mark in the same place, even if she never even took her eyes off Kyudo. Xero walked up and added his bare wrist to Bombelle's and Bastile's. The couple looked at him weirdly.

"I thought I was family," Xero said.

"That man put them on us all," Bastile said. "It wasn't Sand, it was the guy after him. An odd guy, honestly, or maybe that was just his name."

"Odd did this?" Heather asked. "He… marked you?"

"Did he not mark the Reaper?" Bastile asked.

"In other ways," Heather said. "He thought we'd be bombed back into the stone age within a month, it's the only explanation for seeing the Reaper home."

"You were," Bastile reminded. "You speak like you were there, Heather. It's true our envoys would have been different than yours. Geography, you know."

"Envoy?" I asked. "I thought Sand Freedom commanded the assailants be returned home safely, without envoy."

The three of them looked at me, and chuckled. I felt like they would have burst out laughing, if things hadn't currently sucked so much.

"He's not wrong," Willa said. "He didn't ask what Infinite commanded. He asked what Sand Freedom did."

"Oh," Bastile said. "Then yes, technically those were his orders, good memory. But let me ask the fodder; what kind of general orders the attackers of his own city home safely? What kind of man sees his ports and farms burning and spends the moonlight protecting the very assailants that set his city on fire? How do you think your father's lightning city took that?"

"I take it as… the command that lost him command," I said.

"Well said, still short," Xero sighed.

"We're the same height!" I cried, waving a hand to James.

"Then you're both short," Xero said, arms crossed over our heads.

"Odd did this…" I said. "That means that's not some ancient scar."

"It's a ten year old scar," Bastile agreed. "Still hurts though."

"Don't we know it," I muttered, and James nodded hard.

"We still exist, same island, same world," Bastile said. "What I do know is this: every soldier of Jerico that surrendered to the city, Astral, cadet, even the women and children that snuck along, they all bear this mark. Most made it home. Some got close. Some didn't. That's why we can't write these men off. They're just… survivors who can't come home. We've been through hell and back, but what we came back to, and with… that's where our similarities end."

"That's the closest you've got yet," said one of the foaming mouths on the ground, sounding lucid for the first time since the surprise ambush.

"I'll keep trying," Bastile said. "There's no word for the pain of having to close the gates on family. What… what was your friend's name?"

And right I thought it couldn't get heavier, the guy on the ground finally sank to his stomach, now the mark as easy to see as day… the same brand on his wrist that Bastile had. They all had it. Everyone had it. A literal scarlet letter.

"His name… was David…" a voice came.

Crossbow scarecrow boy. Elyia Kyudo. Zen archer, third guard.

Willa walked over, stowed her bow, and kicked the guy in the stomach with one foot. He coughed and doubled over, but as soon as his body weight dropped, Willa yanked both arrows out of the tree (and skin) by the feathers, shoved them back in her quiver (blood and all) and caught the guy's weight as he dropped onto her shoulder like a backpack.

"Thank you kind and handsome soldier," Elyia said. "Wait—"

She flipped him to the ground with the rope already in hand, and Killa had Kyudo in a hogtie before his body was done reeling from the fall. He struggled to arc himself up by the stomach alone like a seal—with his legs, wrists, and neck all connected, he literally didn't have a limb to stand on.

"Oh come on, we were talking," he said.

"You shot at my crew," Willa said. "How are you not screaming in pain?"

"I had that beaten out of me a long time before you," the guy said.

"That's a red flag if ever," Willa said, suspicious.

With a small medical bag (again from nowhere), Willa took to each hand in turn, sealing the wound with a goo like glue, stowing the blood with gauze and wrapping the entire thing with something like self-adhesive sports tape. Then just as Kyudo realized what was happening, Willa was speed-wrapping the part of his foot her arrow had gone through, same process—glue goo, gauze, tape.

"In all my life of people sending sharp things at me," Kyudo said, impressed.

"Don't thank me yet," Willa said. "Here's crazy."

Where had I heard that before?

Willa stepped away just as Xero came up, grabbed the rope between the guys arms and ankles, and hauled him over his shoulder like a human sling, the Astral warrior tall enough to make it work.

"How dare you, put me—wait did you account for my weight with Mylo's famous leverage knots?"

"Let us know if anything starts turning blue," Xero said.

"Will do," the human backpack guy said. "You… didn't kill me."

"We don't do that," Willa said.

"We still owe you," Bastile said, looking at Willa proudly.

"I still hate you," Kyudo said. "I will not be a peaceful human backpack."

"I would not expect you to," my brother said, again sounding like Issaic.

That made a walk silent, if anything. We left the men tied on the ground in the middle of the forest—heartless on the surface, I know, but I'd asked Bastile about it not five seconds out, and his exact response had been:

"Good question Derek. Who will help them? Who, whoo?"

I'd thought him crazy. Then I remembered old man Owl. After that, I thought Bastile wise and able enough to convey an SOS without betraying what might be another one of these (I hate to put it so blunt) homeless. Maybe Owl didn't need the others beating up on him for knowing we were friendlies. Either way, I hoped an owl would get to those men before a bear. And here in Jerico, all I had was my hope, some gloves, suspenders, and a necklace that didn't even glow anymore. But we were heading out into the fringes of the territory, which maybe meant the boundary break. Was there a chance this path would end in super powers?

I touched the Vema necklace, tucked deep underneath the Jerico shirt. We'd met a different kind of survivor in the Vempire, but it was starting to hit me… these were all survivors of the same thing. Two parts of the island so massive I couldn't possibly have known the truth, not even if it had been part of school. We weren't talking about a small group of freedom fighters anymore.

It seemed that the Blitz of Silka City had ended nations. Plural.

"You don't even look like him," Elyia said, reading my thoughts. "There was never hope for David. All he had were his hands, his service, and his sons."

"What division were his sons in?" Bastile asked.

Kyudo thought hard, twitching his head. "His oldest was in the vanguard. Gone long before the rest of us were given the 'chance' to surrender. The younger brother saw it all from the rear guard, and surrendered with the branded. He lives now. Within your rules—I mean your walls."

"I'm sorry, you're on which side of the Gates right now?" Bombelle asked.

"You were there, Bastile," Kyudo said, sounding ominous again. "You too, Xero the Champion."

"I…" Xero said. "I mean of course. I remember."

"You remember surrendering with the rest, the fear the same from the Hand of the Head to the thousands of barefoot soldiers we lost, and the hundreds that survived. You aren't power. David was power, he found the agent that killed his son, and he was on the sixth before they finally brought him in."

"Then what happened to power?" Bastile asked.

Elyia looked down. "They tortured him for years."

"Who did?" James asked.

"Who else?" Elyia asked. "The power that refuses concession. The looming darkness. The only person on this island who has been proven time over time to seek nothing but absolute control, at the sake of our absolute submission. The very thing we were fighting against when three out of four nations threw our next decade in the garbage trying to take a single step forward?"

"Issaic Nite," I said, the words of a ghost.

"This is bigger than one man," Bastile said. "The answer is Infinite. Technically, the Infinite of the last forty years. From what my own history of the world tells me, everything before that was fine. Wait a damn minute."

Bombelle sighed. "My husband, ladies and ladies."

"That's what I'm saying," James said. "He didn't say Infinite."

"He didn't say…" Bastile repeated, looking down like the words had triggered something; a red flag, a yellow flag, what did offsides even mean? "The literal prodigal sons of Issaic, here, what were we thinking?"

"We've already been over this," I said, sadly. "Honestly it was nice, proving our worth and being done with it. Isn't that what the Jerico welcome means?"

"Aloha means aloha," Bastile admitted, sighing. "No exceptions."

“Thanks cap,” James said, without any emotion behind it. “But are we even still going? We just watched… we just saw a man…”

Bombelle looked at him sadly. “Oh hun. We’ll take better care of you, but you’re asking the island’s most elite assault squad if we can handle a casualty. Don’t think me heartless, but we call this the level. Get on it.”

“That’s a ridiculous level,” I said under my breath.

Bombelle’s eyes flared at me. “I’ll give you that one, because trauma. But I swear it on the sky, I’m not always this nice. Be cool now, Derek Nite. I’m only saying that because we need you.”

“Sometimes it’s nice to be needed,” James sighed. “But this isn’t—”

“Which direction do I push James in?” I asked.

“Ahead,” Bastile said. “We’re an hour out. Once there, we can send word for the recovery of David’s body, and finally give his family some… closure.”

“You were about to say peace,” I said sadly.

“I was actually,” Bastile said, just as sad. “I wish I could have brought him peace. I know I can’t do that for his family. I have failed them all.”

We walked in a trance, and it wasn’t even the first time. I didn’t even realize why James had gotten so light until I realized Heather had a hand on his back, pushing as I pulled. She saw me notice her, then she looked down at James and he only blinked both eyes at once. She frowned.

“That was supposed to be a confident wink,” he said to her, as low as he could. “Only problem is, I can’t wink. Never could, watch.”

He winked (blinked) at her again. Heather looked at him sideways, her mind as heavy as the rest of ours. She frowned, registering the blink, and then she bit down on her bottom lip to stop from laughing. Then she gently slapped my brother across the face, her fingers taking their time across his skin, almost sweetly.

“That was supposed to be another kiss,” she said. “We’re both broken.”

“I think that’s putting it mild,” James said.

“Don’t you dare remind me of salsa,” Heather said.

“I can’t do anything right…” he said, taking a big imaginary kick at something, Heather only biting down harder.

“I’m sorry, did you say another?” Lynn said, her mouth open, just out of sight of Heather.

“Work to do,” Heather said, but when James looked away I saw her mouth *shut up Lynn.*

“What happened to just don’t?” I asked, hands out.

“A sharp knife happened, that’s what,” James said, blushing.

If you knew, you knew. We weren’t claiming victim. We’d gone through that story’s end together, and we’d get through it only the same. The four of us. The only family we had left.

“I’m sorry, I can’t just come back to this one,” Lynn said, coming up next to Heather. “Did you actually—”

“He made me pancakes Lynn, what was I supposed to do!” Heather shouted.

“AaaawwWW!” Lynn said, a full on explosion from fuse to blast.

“It wasn’t even terrible,” Heather said. “But it was a one-time thing, after which we immediately remembered the dangerous road we walk and agreed that to prioritize our focus towards survival is not a refusal of other paths that one day we might be more free to explore together."

"You're actually serious," Lynn said. "James, don't mess it up."

"Yeah James," Heather said, staring at him. "Don't mess it up."

"Why would I mess it up?" He asked. "How? How specifically?"

"Just don't mess it up James," I said, grinning.

"You're on my side," James complained. "Fine. I can read a warning sign when my best friends bash me over the head with it. Like I said. Focus. Or—"

"Or worse," they all said at the same time.

"Rage," Heather said.

Her eyes were set, her mouth a thin line. She was the strongest of all of us. Still, when James looked at her, she looked away. It was so cute I could barf.

But… I didn't.

Together, we walked—except no we didn't, we were here. The platform ended, the road was done. We had two trees on either side of the road, but that was it, nothing but empty forest and a three hundred foot falloff before us.

"Halt," Bastile said. "Elyia, how are the limbs?"

"Limber, yours?" The zen archer said, fully unknotted, stretching out on the ground right next to Xero, not a single of us had noticed.

"Blast it all, how—"

"I let it happen," Xero said. "He's been cooperative, I appreciate it."

"And I appreciate not being a backpack," Elyia said.

Bastile stared at him until he tried again.

"I meant… I recognize the size of this man as my ultimate undoing, sir, no need to humiliate me farther," Kyudo said, under the shadow of Xero.

"Allowed," Bastile said. "Simple, see?"

"None of this is simple," Lynn said, before we could.

"Rear guard is supposed to be," Bastile said, frowning at Heather.

"We were distracted sir," Lynn said, jumping to Heather's defense. "Apparently there's been some inner-group fraternization going on. We were only trying to get to the bottom of such scandal."

Bastile looked like he would blow up, but he only nodded, his teeth grinding.

"Telling teenagers to get a hold of their feelings, not the best idea," he said to himself. "Can we get back to work now?"

"Absolutely," I said, like nothing had even happened. "We're professionals."

Bastile sighed, but as he did we could all see something coming out of the air towards us. It was another square platform on four thick ropes, being lowered down from what I could only see must have been the canopy itself.

"Do you have people up there?" James asked.

"Obviously," Bastile said. "Topline duty is as dangerous as it is dangerous."

"So you do have people up there," James said, looking up to the ends of the rope (but none of us could see that far).

"I just said…" Bastile said, blinking at my brother. "It's a draft system. Every citizen works a month out of the year."

"Do they survive?" James asked.

"Of course," Bastile said. "There's three months of training leading up to that one, so we don't die. I believe Derek met our summer guard."

"So every citizen within the walls goes through that, once a year," I said.

"We do," Bastile said. "The Infinite are agents, masters of deception, each armed with an arsenal the size of a small hanger. The Reaper are scouts, infiltrators yes, but with only tools of creation at the end of their scopes Anyone can put on claws or jets. In Jerico, we are warriors by hand, every one of us."

"And today's the turnover," I said, blinking.

"You got through a weekend routine with Soltis and kept your memory intact," Bastile said, sounding proud. "At least one of you can put a face to the hands of Jerico destined to travel the line between land and sky for the next week. That's your topline unit. Don't forget them."

Lynn and I shared a brief look of alarm. Right, James had no idea what had happened out on that field down the hill from our most current guest house. That was back there, in the safety of the Oleander. Soccer camp had turned into boot camp, and the faceless cadets in our backyard had turned into names. Here, miles out on the kingsroad itself, I'll be honest, I wasn't expecting them to show up—but just as I thought that, I saw the thick wooden platform stopped at a perfect right angle, marking the final stretch of rainbow jungle road. Before us had landed a final platform from the trees, held adrift by ropes alone here at the sidewalk's end, the thing as wide as the kingsroad itself, enough for us all to comfortably step on, big enough that it didn't even shift around that much. It was a bit like stepping on a boat—not like I had much experience with that. I'd been on a surfboard more times than I'd ever been on a boat.

"I'd say goodbye, but I'd regret it," James said, placing the skateboard gently against the last tree trunk before the falloff, back to crutching.

"I'd say hold on, but you're in the hands of the Caput's personal topline, hand-picked by upper management," Bombelle said, smiling. "Did you even realize we'd started moving?"

"Holy crap!" Heather said, looking back up at the road, already a hundred feet above us. We were hauling.

"You've got the suspension down," I said, impressed.

"The ancient art of pulling ropes," Bastile said. "Just because something is boring doesn't mean it can't be mastered."

"Mastery is a product of consistently going beyond our limits," I said.

"Good, Derek," Bastile and Bombelle said at the same time.

"What the hell Derek?" Heather asked, as James narrowed his eyes at me.

The descent was quick. Before I'd even found something to hold onto, the wood had weeds around the edges. That meant we had hit the forest floor. Right.

"Hyper elevator," I said.

I swear I heard someone shout out *thanks* from far up above us. We were back on solid ground, back to an endless jungle behind us, and in front…

"The gates of Jerico," Lynn said. "Nice to see both sides."

"Not many do," Bombelle said. "Our reputation is more… kingdom come."

Again, ominous. Here in the open grass around us, with the first of the trees starting a good fifty yards behind, it was kind of impossible to miss what came next. Only as tall as the gigantic, still unexplored canopy of the jungle, the gates of Jerico moved as soon as we did, the individual titan-sized pillars of wood coming apart at the sides, as the team of us were witness to the forest almost blowing apart at the sudden pressure change.

"No superpowers here my butt," James said. "I've never seen anyone move the earth like this, except for an entire civilization, and the Reaper."

"She has a name," Heather said, but almost… sweetly? Was that possible?

"You heard that," James said, living for that moment.

Heather blushed and turned away—only for her jaw to drop in delight, seeing the horses waiting for us closer than anything on that side of the gates. There were six of them, two brown, two black, two patterned. I loved horses, and apparently I wasn't alone there.

"Hell yes," Heather and James said at the same time.

"Lynn, you want to introduce us?" James asked.

He was only halfway joking, but the horses all snapped their eyes onto Lynn.

"Have you met Lynn?" I said meekly.

She didn't balk, she walked right up to the herd and held a hand out. The horses eyed her, sniffed her, walked closer, and then jumped up and down with happiness. It was alarming, but Lynn held her ground, smiling, as calm as she'd ever been as thousands of pounds of animals all danced around her. Again, I swear I heard the sad, low growl of a jungle cat somewhere in the trees high above us. I had good ears but damn.

"Something like this," Bastile said, frowning, stroking his chin as he stepped up beside James and me. "You would call normal?"

"You know, a month ago… no," I said. "But now…"

Lynn lined the horses up by hand and turned back to us with a smile.

"I trained all the horses."

"You've known them thirty seconds," Willa said, stunned.

"One hop this time," Lynn said, her eyes flashing at Willa.

The horses all took a synchronized hoof swipe. Willa dropped her sword.

"You ride?" Lynn asked Heather.

"I do now," Heather said. "First thing on my bucket list for years. Escape the underland, find my father, ride a horse. It's going to hurt, isn't it?"

"How'd you know?" Lynn asked.

"Everything on that list has hurt," Heather said. "I want this one. Lynn?"

"Um…" Lynn said. "I think you should ride with James. He needs our best."

"And that leaves you with—"

"Sidebar," Lynn said, grabbing Heather, walking away from the rest of us.

"It's just horses," James said. "A simple rock paper scissors would have sufficed. You have that game here, Champ?"

"We have rock rock rock," Xero said. "Everyone gets ten seconds, and whoever holds up the biggest rock wins. Then they get to throw it at—"

"Culture shift, we are no longer talking about the same thing," I interrupted.

Willa crept up next to me. "I don't know if culture shift has anything to do with this particular team dynamic, but I think the underlander wants to ride a horse with you. It has the potential to be… cute. Don't mess it up."

"What do I do?" I asked.

"Absolutely nothing," Willa said, as serious as a woman had ever been.

And in a way, it was the best advice I'd ever got.

"Ready," Xero said, holding a gigantic boulder over his head.

"No, put that away," Willa snapped.

"Aw..." Xero said, turning away with the rock held high, as Heather and Lynn came back to the group.

"Game recognizes game," Heather said, nodding to Xero in approval, pounding a closed fist against her chest three times.

Before we knew if we could ride horses or not, we'd learned how. I was with Lynn on the brown-haired Seanderthal, Heather and James were on the black-bodied Ekapian, Bastile and Bombelle had the black and brown patterned Garunde, Astor and Ollux had the tan coated Quixote, Xero rode the albino Ufwelle all to himself, and Willa held Elyia onto Jeff, the runt of the herd.

"You good back there?" Lynn asked.

"I will be, as long as you teach me how to ride a horse in the next ten seconds," I said. "What happens if it... malfunctions?"

"Then you'll have the rest of your life to figure it out," James said to me. "Wait sorry, that's parachutes. If it... malfunctions, just hold your legs out to the side, try turning it off and on again, I don't know man."

"You mean city boy," I admitted.

James looked away (he knew I wasn't wrong) as his and Heather's horse walked up to ours. My brother was sitting at the reins, with Heather holding onto his stomach the way I was holding onto Lynn's. Heather was taller than James, and he was down another kind of foot too, so she wasn't gentle about keeping him upright.She even had her suspenders pulled over James' shoulders, physically lashing him to her, whether it was by necessity or... something else.

"Sorry to throw you around," she said, adjusting his legs in the minimal saddle, just a morphed piece of leather barely big enough for two people.

"I'm not complaining," James said. "Don't let me fall. Tell me what to do."

"Be less fat," Heather said.

James clutched his pearls, feeling his abs, his sides.

"Kidding," Heather said. "Anyways, it matters not what things look like. Matters who they are. Matters what they do, where they go, and what they leave behind."

I thought it was pretty symbolic—until I saw what the black-bodied Ekapian was leaving behind. Heather and James pretended not to notice. Ew.

"To Titan!" Bastile shouted. "Follow the pine trees, south, and above all stay close to—"

"Let's GO JEFF!" Willa shouted.

Elyia screamed and held onto Willa's waist for his life, as they rocketed off into the distance in wild delight, in complete contradiction to Bastile's orders.

"She'll break him," Bastile said, smiling, not seeming to mind so much. "Kids, be more like her. Horses, stop pooping. Everybody, follow me."

"We're not kids," Heather warned.

Her horse made a small noise too. Could neighs be sarcastic? Did horses know to speak softly when making fun of the boss?

Bastile's horse took off down the path after Willa. Bombelle was behind him, but she was holding on with only her legs. One of her hands dangled at her side, the other held the hand Bastile's had behind him, his other barely even holding the reins. Adorable, and intimidating at the same time. Something told me there wasn't a weapon those two couldn't fire from that horse at full gallop. They simply didn't need their hands to ride. What a concept. Kind of like…

"Prepare to gallop," Lynn said, and I watched her feet clench down gently at Seanderthal's sides. "Try not to talk, you'll bite your tongue off, starting—"

Lynn closed her mouth just as Seanderthal reared up and took off, the rest of the horses behind us following suit. Got it, starting now. No talking. For ONCE.

Soon enough our world was a gallop through the forest, the trees dwarfing us, the path narrow, the team barreling down on it like we were dirt bikers in a line, but that was just what was going on outside the ride. My body was at maximum effort, instinctually leaning forward, the absolute opposite of—I'm not going to say it. The only thought I had that wasn't about myself was a constant reminder to not squeeze Lynn in half by the simple act of holding on.

"Mmmm!" I mumble/shouted.

It was my first word on horseback. It meant: you think I'd done this before? Yes horses, but never a gallop this fast sans paved path! City boy, city boy!

The dirt and dust kicked up wherever the horses stepped but something else kept hitting me from up above, sticks, twigs, pieces of moss. With my mouth still shut tight, and careful not to get jungle in my eyes, I looked up and saw her—the slick clouded leopard Sophia Sabretooth, jumping from tree to tree, trunk to branch, even upside down for parts of it, keeping up with the horses on the ground just as fast from a hundred feet up in the trees. She was silent too.

"Mhmm," Lynn mumble/said.

It meant: she knew.

I felt like mumble laughing. The only parts of our bodies that weren't touching were the feet. We were pressed together for the speed, the balance on both of us. I had her by the waist like a safety pole in the storm. She had the reins, and she would lean straight back into me on curves and sharp stops, I had figured that out soon enough. My job was to not break my teeth off on her chin, and hold on. All things considered, not that romantic.

Then Lynn took one hand off the reins and wrapped her hand around mine, her fingers finding my knuckles and digging deep. She kind of turned her head back at me, but the ride was rough, and it demanded… focus. Right. Still, we rode that horse like we'd swam through a certain underland lake pond thing—together, her hands on mine, mine on hers, and suddenly it wasn't so rough. Suddenly it was better in every way, suddenly her back against my chest was the most comfortable thing I'd ever felt… suddenly I didn't want that horse to stop.

But all horses stop. Once again out of nowhere, just as we'd settled into the journey…

"We're here," Bastile said.

Aw.

"Dismount sir?" Xero asked.

"Not quite yet," he said. "I sense thunder. Be like lightning. Ready to bolt."

Ah. The old take what I could get. But then Lynn took her hand off mine to properly grip the reins. Rightfully so. I backed off, moment officially over. We weren't exactly in paradise, there were things in this jungle that wanted us dead. It wasn't the time for time. It was time for focus, or worse.

"Willa, keep within eyesight from here out, that's an order," Bastile said.

We'd caught up to her. She was high on her horse in a small clearing, with Elyia on his knees behind her dry-heaving into a ditch.

"Trouble keeping up?" Bombelle asked

"It's the stench," Elyia said. "Can't you smell it?"

"The corpse flower, we are familiar," Xero said, standing strong. "Unlike Silka, we are one with all of our world, not just the beautiful parts of it."

"Are you a writer too?" I asked him. "Should I have asked you that sooner?"

"Yes, and yes," Xero said, smiling at us. "Although… little ones, friends from afar. Can you really not smell this?"

"Allergies," I said, shrugging. "Ears, great. Eyes, awesome. But if I could cut my nose off for the sake of consistency, I would."

"You say corpse flower, I say thank the universe for genetics," my brother said. "Girls, what's your excuse?"

"What is wrong with you?" Heather said in a high pitched voice, and I saw how high her eyes were turned, both hands clamped down onto her nose.

"You too?" I said, turning to Lynn.

"It's like a new color but a dead one," Lynn said, holding her nose too.

"ALLERGIES?" Heather shouted at us in half volume, half pitch, full nasal.

"You don't even know," I said, half apologetic, half honest. "What's it like?"

"The corpse flower Titan Arum?" Bombelle said. "Imitating a dead animal is what that plant does best."

"I get it," Lynn said, even higher pitch than Heather. "You had oleander planted before the Oleander. So you planted titan arum before the—"

"We should form a team and forget all these losers," Willa said, looking Lynn up and down. "The world would crumble at our feet."

"I can't rule the world, not yet," Lynn said.

"You're hard to read," Heather said to Willa. "Are you a doctor or a soldier?"

"Yes to both," Willa said. "Where we are, you'll need both."

"Wherever anyone is on this island, they'll need both," James said.

Willa touched my brother's nose. "You just learned something skater boy."

That nickname probably wasn't going anywhere. We deserved it.

2.7

CALM (LIKE THE BOMB)

The first thing I noticed about Titan Arum were the colors.

I guess there was supposed to be a stench about the place too, but again, I had a complicated relationship with my nose. All I saw was a dusky grove with twisting tree trunks curving out of the ground only to arc straight back down, like a swamp city on land. There were all sorts of these low-hanging tree systems, creating a sort of gnarly, multi-leveled mushroom city in the forest.

"Anyone else getting mad Electrical Parade vibes?" Derek asked.

I kind of saw it. I didn't know much about this place, but it was spread out before us in a way that made me think I could actually see the entire town, like a small stop in a big video game. The light was stifled by some sort of light green leaves that were so plentiful on these branches, and from up here on the horse, I could move the end of one crutch over them like the blades of a feather, almost like a unidirectional armor for the trees. But as I did, the ends of the feathers exploded, small seedlings thrown around in the wind, some sort of defense mechanism. Well played, plants.

"I like how the first thing you did was fondle the plants," Bastile said. "First rule of Titan, don't touch it. That goes for the water, the dirt, even the air."

"Don't touch the air?" Lynn asked, her eyebrows high.

"You heard what I said," Bastile said.

I counted about twelve structures including a few small brown bridges over a few small ponds, the blues and greens from the glint of the lights, the reds and purples from the tall, towering plants that looked like a cactus spear had erupted from an upside down cage dress. It was as colorful and beautiful as it was terrifying. A plant like that, you couldn't help but think dinosaur times.

"That looks like death," Heather said, pointing to the sixth upside down dress plant we'd passed in the last minute.

"It is," Bombelle said. "Imagine that inside your bloodstream. Instant death."

So… not Disney.

"I didn't know this place was still here," Elyia said, a bit ominously as we walked. through the shadows, yet to see a person.

"Of course it's still here, why wouldn't it be?" Bastile said, as we stopped by a small hut with a quirky, curvy roof—again, mushroom houses was the best way to put it. "The reach of Jerico depends on the strength of our people. We can't all live under shields. From the sulphur mines to the crystal caverns, from the marshes of Bianjon to the riverbanks by the sea, the real power of the territory comes from having settled ninety percent of it. Wherever you see green, wherever there is water and trees, we are there."

Bastile opened the door. Even from atop a horse I couldn't move around on much, I could see the entirety of that hut. There was no one there.

"Hmm," Bastile said. "This is not expected."

"No shame," Derek said. "That's weird to us too. I don't even see dust."

"There shouldn't be dust," Bastile said, looking lost, even angry. "I thought corps would have at least one ranger stationed here. Actually it's been mandated, ever since the Blitz. By me. Now I'm wondering where my soldiers are—besides right here, of course."

"Aw," Xero said, touching his heart. Then he focused. "It's true. I'm getting goosebumps over here captain."

"Science with Xero," Willa said, smiling with her mouth but not her eyes.

It was a distraction in the heaviness, not a break to it. We all felt it. Something was off.

"We're here for the planetarium, honey," Bombelle said. "We can accomplish that with the crew we rode in on."

"I know, but I wanted to get Elyia and David out of our care," Bastile said.

"Right now we can't focus on that," she said. "Later we can."

"But—" Bastile said, trying to argue.

"We'll come back to it," Bombelle said, holding him by the shoulder. "I promise."

Why was that so familiar?

Bastile sighed, and touched his cheek to her hand. Heather and Lynn made a weird sound. I looked away. It was… sweet.

"Coming back to the issue of not finding reinforcements where they're supposed to be, at the most dangerous, poisonous, and important part of everything?" Derek asked, wincing.

Bastile shrugged. "And?"

"You started off on the wrong foot, we call it mongo push," I said sadly.

"Then the other foot it is," Bastile said, like it was touché—I mean simple.

We were back to the curving walkway, still making our way up the slightly sloping banks of electrical parade / poison ivy city. The reds and purples were so bright among the greens, words really didn't do it justice, except for knowing those colors meant don't eat me. I hadn't touched anything but the reins of a horse (and a horse) since we'd found Elyia and Willa waiting by the entrance to this poisonous place. Beautiful, and strikingly colorful, but damned all the same.

"Check it out," Astor said.

He was pointing something out at the base of one of the giant poison plants, a blue glowing mushroom that was familiar for some reason. Wait—

"I don't know how many bones I'd have to break before putting something like that in my mouth," Astor said. "But it's more than one."

Was that a joke? I didn't really get Astor and Ollux, I had kind of tuned them out ever since they tried to drug me for memories. But as I locked eyes with that plant, something happened. The curious part of me tugged, the brain blasted, and I realized I was looking at another open door to metaphors. Was there something in my head worth weaponizing? Had I really forgotten something so important it was worth fighting over, even ten years later?

"What do you say James?" Astor said, reading my mind, looking at me just a bit too casually for me to feel like he had my back. "Feel like opening that mind back up? Who knows what might come out, perhaps the answer to everything?"

"I..." I stammered, caught in the middle of an internal breakdown.

"Be very careful what you say next," Lynn said, her eyes fading a bit, speaking for more than just herself. And not to me.

The sabretooth must have been close.

Astor sulked away, drifting close to the plant with all those glowing bluebloods growing out of the base. I couldn't think of food right now. I was thinking deeper. Did I feel like opening that mind back up? Not to Astor, not if he kept being this creepy, of course, but what about to myself? They say the face mirrors the heart, and the eyes are the window to the living room, or something. Lynn must have seen through all the terrible upholstery.

"You went through something heavy, under the blueblood," Bastile said.

"I..." I couldn't say.

"Don't say a word," Lynn said to me. But then she gave a curious look to Bastile. "What... exactly happens to a human on something like that?"

"They are one with their body," Bastile said. "Some in the territory use it to recover old memories. To revisit the faces of their parents, to remember things they learned in school before more school overtook the brain space. Every brain in this world has something inside that the conscious mind would never have been able to remember until the day they died. It takes guidance, but if you think there's something like that in you..."

"I never thought about that until Astor told me to," I said honestly.

"Was that a lie?" Bastile asked.

My ground was crumbling.

"Fine," I said. "Maybe it was. I like you, sir, but Lynn told me not to talk, so that's all you get. Sorry."

"Thank you," Lynn said.

Okay fine, I'd been plagued by visions of girls in faraway dimensions lately, this was true. Under the blueblood, at night in dreams, I had seen something. That was a fact. I could keep avoiding it, or I could force it to make sense. So which was I doing? I didn't know. Probably neither.

"Have we still seen no one?" Bastile asked, pulling me out of thought.

"Not yet," Bombelle said. "There's been no word from Titan for a year. There's a chance they've moved on to Ravenna, guard changes this season."

"Well I know one old lady who I can always count on here, no matter the season," Bastile said, walking along the path as the rest of us kept to our horses, not touching anything, like he'd made crystal clear. "My godmother."

"The godmother of the caput lives in a poison town?" I asked.

"You can learn a lot from poison," Bastile said. "How it takes the body, what it does to the brain. Then, if you're her, and you've dedicated your life to immunology, you can start to account for poison. How do you think we know so much about neon mushrooms?"

"I thought your contact in Titan Arum was the astronomical expert," Derek said.

"She's a lot of experts," Bastile said, sounding proud of his godmother. "You really do write everything down."

"I read something," Lynn said. "How space travel was made possible by studying the world's most poisonous substances, knowing we'd have to account for a whole new world of mortal microbial peril on another planet."

"That's the second time you've brought nature into space," Derek said. "You trying to bail on this world?"

"No, it's just that, I don't know, maybe understanding this world might help us unlock the next one," Lynn said like it was obvious. "Why?"

"What are you even talking about?" Heather asked.

"Giraffes," Derek said, with a small smile.

Heather only stared harder. "Did you hit your heads on each other's heads?"

"It's called a moment," I said, putting my arm over Heather's shoulder, and for the first time, not just for support. "Just let them have it dear."

Heather looked at me, at the arm I had over her shoulder, and bit my hand. I wrenched an arm back in a combination of amused surprise and actual fear.

"Ah! I always knew you were an animal," I said.

"I am," Heather said.

"Your teeth are sharper than mine," I said, holding my arm up, studying the indents. "This doesn't add up."

"You don't add up," Heather said. "You were supposed to be cargo. You've saved my life more times than people have tried to take it."

"What are you talking about Willis?" I asked, looking past my wrist for once. "How is that possible?"

"You'll know," Heather said. "Until then, you touch me when I tell you to, or suffer fangs. Understood?"

"You're lucky I speak vampire," I said, then I saw the glare in her eyes and tried again. "I mean yes Ma'am."

"Better," Heather said, and she grabbed the hand she'd bit and held it.

"And I'm okay with that," I said, again no choice but to match the projected intensity of Heather Denien, if I wanted a chance with her one day. Wait.

I could have laughed. Here I was, thinking whatever embers were burning between Lynn and Derek were so original. You could make teenage boys do just about anything, you could train them to dive, to fly, to scuba and climb mountains, win gold medals against men in their thirties, even train them to save the world sideways, whatever. Teenage boys were capable. But put them within eyesight of teenage girls, and hello built-in destruct system. Thanks nature. I was starting to think we weren't as far from home as we thought we were. Or maybe the human experience wasn't something that only belonged to me. It went unsaid, whether it was out of fear or something else. But something else that had gone unsaid was… a bit harder to put into words. Without giving our feelings too much credit, without trying to compartmentalize them in an unhealthy way, I think all four of us recognized how much more important the mission was than any personal… missions. Not that we ever knew what the mission was, but right now it had landed us about as far from Infinite's good graces as physically possible on this island. We were wanted by the most powerful supergroup on Ocarina, and only headed farther down. In respect for ears of all ages, I'll put it as poetically as possible.

If there was ever a time to holster it, it was now.

That's why Derek didn't object when Lynn pulled her hand away from his, and Heather didn't either when I did the same to her. As much as I didn't want to, as much as I wanted to steal every single moment possible… I was no thief. These moments weren't mine. Not yet.

We continued down the path, and it was beautiful, with ornate, decorated wooden twisting guard rails around a few small ponds on either side. The walking area was wide enough for two horses side by side. It was dark too, and the forest had never been so close, kind of a poison ivy lair, nowhere near the size of any so-called city we'd come up against so far. The ground sloped up and down, or maybe it was just the trees coming in at weird angles, but finally the leaves opened up and we came to a one story wooden cottage on the side of the road, at the far end of the grove. It was cozy, with a curved (mushroomy) roof, a fire chimney, a few wooden chairs scattered around the well-kept green grass lawn before a simple door.

"Pretty colors, same question," Heather asked out of nowhere. "Where—"

"Godhome," was the very questionable answer, as Bastile knocked.

But there was no answer.

"Who should be opening this particular door?" I asked. "Your godmother?"

"The hand of astronomy, daughter of Aestella, my godmother, yes," Bombelle said to me. "The planetarium's location is unknown, even to the caput himself. We're here for a map, or at the very least, some eyes."

"We should have seen eyes by now," Bombelle said, looking around.

"That's what I'm saying," Elyia said, and we all turned to him. "I heard there was an outbreak, a few weeks back. I heard the last died not even a day ago, the sole surviving elder of the city, of course she held out the longest. Is your godmother's name… Lady Armanda?"

"I knew I felt thunder," Bastile said.

He stopped moving. The horses did too. For a moment there wasn't a sound. It was clear skies, I didn't understand. Then we heard the cold metal of Willa's sword being unsheathed, and watched her put it against Elyia's back, still on a horse together, the tanto-bladed edge holding steady against his spine.

Oh. That kind of thunder. Where I came from, it hardly ever rained.

"How do you know that name?" Bastile said, with his back to us.

"I think we're past that, caput," Elyia said, hands up, a sword at his spine.

But it wasn't surrender. It was a sign. We were silent when the shapes started coming in. From the dark, dense jungle enclosure, they came from above, from below, even from the houses we thought empty. They were wearing tattered rags if anything, a few of them almost completely naked. Tall, short, men, woman, it varied, but the lean lack of muscle and scarred, blackened bare feet didn't. These weren't dirt drones. They weren't enemies. But it wasn't just a guy in a hogtie, it was at least fifty, some taller than us sure, but skinnier too, not that it was comforting—together those traits made a bad combination. A nothing-to-lose kind of combination. Each looked wild and strong, with an arm reach that easily outgunned ours. And each were people. Homeless, traumatized, ex-military, dangerous and scary sure… but just people, just like us.

That might have been the worst part.

"This is the opposite of Jerico's prestigious warrior elite," I said, frozen.

"Stop narrating," Heather said, frozen harder.

"We were family once," Bastile said to the surprise vanguard, seeing the same bleak future as me. "I told you I wouldn't harm you. Should I promise it?"

"You could, but we are going to try that promise, immediately, and to the grave," Elyia said. "Fifty of mine against your nine. This should be simple."

"It's never simple," Willa said, her eyes set.

"Then don't make any more promises you're too weak to keep," Elyia said. "It's not stealing if they're dead, right?"

"It's… that's worse than stealing," Bombelle said, looking to Bastile with all the worry in the world.

"Tell me you're joking," Bastile said, not even acting surprised, as the rest of our jaws—you know. "Tell me there really was an outbreak."

Elyia shook his head. "We do know our poisons. But we both know anyone living in Titan Arum was too smart to be taken by something that simple."

And that was it. Something changed in Bastile's eyes.

"We trusted you," Willa said simply, her sword arm not moving an inch.

"Did I earn it?" Elyia said. "Or did you want me to?"

Bastile narrowed his eyes, his arm dangling at his sides for the surprise, the wristlet coming off again enough for us to see the scar… the one that meant survival, and a lot of other things too.

"Get off this horse before I kill you," Willa said softly.

"Funny, I take that as mercy," Elyia said, swinging off the horse. "For you."

"It is," Willa said. "If I let myself move, I'll have all your blood on me."

Her face contorted, every vein in her arm about to explode for holding the sword motionless where Elyia's spine had just been, unmoving. He danced back to the small army waiting for him, where someone handed him a small contraption that looked like another crossbow.

"Where are the bodies?" Bombelle demanded.

"At the bottom of the ocean," Elyia said.

Bastile made a sound. He had both his hands over his mouth, forcing himself quiet, but he was shaking, with rage, with tears.

"Same, love," Bombelle said, closing her eyes to the shapes in the forest like they weren't human anymore. "Astral. We are engaged."

"And farther from home than the twins," Elyia said, not backing down.

"Don't do this," Xero said, tears unstemmed. "Please. Family, old or new."

"You will never again see a home in our jungle," Bastile said, reading my mind. "Not after taking this one away. Anyone who wants to surrender, do so quietly. Otherwise meet me."

"I'll meet you."

There was something funny happening around the edges of my vision, almost like a lightning vignette. I saw the fervor of the jungle men (and women) sitting on the edge of that first meet, walking the edge of a razor, waiting to see what Bastile would do, as a single, scrawny soldier came swaggering forward with a spearpoint aimed right at Bastile's fists. Even though only one side bore weapons, if it came to it, neither was going to miss. Both were ready to kill. All I could think about was how much I wanted everyone to survive, and I willed it to the mountaintops, expecting my powers to kick in regardless of the storm season, regardless of how much I'd already accepted that they were gone.

But nothing happened.

I wasn't the answer. I didn't immediately get my superpowers back like I had in the Vempire. I couldn't will this one to life under the rules of the Jerico. Whatever closer source had seen us through last time, this wouldn't be the same. So I tried something else. I tried hope, holding the word in my brain hard, hoping as hard as I could that just maybe, for once, I wasn't the answer.

And that worked.

Just as my heart was about to fall, just as the frenzied veteran soldier in the jungle was about to put his blade through Bastile's heart… we heard the most vicious, air-ripping, earsplitting roar of the jungle I'd ever heard in my life. The horses stalled, the people froze, even Heather's face turned white for a moment. It wasn't a lion or a tiger. It wasn't a bear. It was… a clouded leopard that sometimes spoke to humans, oh my.

Now *that* was power.

Sophia landed before the charging veteran, Bastile doing absolutely nothing in the aggregate, just standing still with his fists by his face, and a four-foot jungle cat with paws bigger than dinner plates taking his side, stopping the homeless guy's blitzkrieg in barefoot tracks. The spear wavered, trembled, then dropped, as Sophia opened her jaws, letting that foot long canine show.

"The horses," Bastile muttered behind us.

"Stop making bets you can't win," Lynn said, patting Seanderthal gently.

The horses took a few steps away, but did not bolt. Once again, Lynn had spoken for these jungle animals better than their handlers ever could.

"I mean take the horses and run," Bastile said.

Oh right. Perspective.

"We can help," Derek said. "We can fight."

"You will do no such thing," Bombelle said. "If your butts leave those horses, you can walk back. That's an order."

"You can't be serious," Lynn said.

"Try me," Bombelle said. "Prove you can obey an order. Prove you're not children. Prove you can be more."

"Not fair," the scrawny, spear-wielding guy said, properly wary of how much muscle the leopard had on him. "This was a duel to the death. One on one."

"When did we decide that?" Bastile asked.

"Bastile, get up here, we can still make it out," Willa said, tossing him her shorter sword (I just realized she had two).

"Right," Bastile said. "Thanks, kitty."

"You better not be talking to me," Willa growled.

Sophia growled too, like she was saying *chill, girl.* Bastile took a step back to the horse—but then there was a click of something in the air, and he turned around swinging a sword for the first time since I'd met him. He moved fast. There was a rush of sound as he spun backwards, as the feathered back half of a crossbow bolt hit the ground in front of us. But the front half…

"No," Bombelle almost coughed, seeing it before we did. "That didn't—"

I didn't understand the voice she was speaking in… until Bastile turned to us with the front half of a thick crossbow bolt sticking out of his ribs. It was high on the left side, either the lung or the heart. That was a bad place to get stuck. Sure he'd slashed the thing in two, cool and all, but… momentum…

"CAPUT!" Xero screamed.

He jumped off his horse and ran for the caput as Willa notched her bow/sword and sent an arrow through the night. She had warned him twice before. This time, she took the shot. Elyia hit the ground at the same time as Bastile.

"Damn you," Willa said, close to tears.

Bastile was struggling, coughing and already breathing with a rasp, but Elyia wasn't moving. The silence that followed was the worst sound I'd ever heard. It may as well have been the blast of a gun, the start of the race, the official sound of a thing starting that couldn't be stopped. In that moment, in that cadence, both sides looked from their wounded (or worse) to the other side. For all the talk of rehabilitation, of respecting the other side, at that moment, I heard and felt nothing but rage. Anger. Hatred. Resentment was corrosive. I felt it. I hated it.

"For BASTILE!" Astor shouted.

"For KYUDO!" The jungle shouted.

Ollux and Willa jumped down off the horses, their weapons held high, running to cover Xero, as he took rocks and pieces of sharp wood in the back trying to scoop up Bastile. The homeless forest army surged forward, the scrawny spear-carrier running point, now that Sophia wasn't there to hold him back. All the men and women of the forest roared, seizing our moment of confusion as only a military could, and they leapt on us, literally, some of them reaching at least seven feet in the air off the trees and roots around. I saw Xero smash two of them aside with a wheelkick, but as he tried to carry Bastile back to the horses, he hadn't gone five steps before there was a small jagged rock blade in his leg. Xero roared at the guy who'd stabbed him, and head-butted him into the ground so hard the knife stayed in Xero's leg. Then he held Bastile limp over his head as his body was tackled (but not really) by four of the smallest jungle veterans at once. Xero only looked down, stretched out his legs, and went to work, one at a time.

Willa was dancing around three barefoot jungle bruisers, using the blunt edge of her sword to knock as many heads as she could, wasting no time, just dodging spears and rocks, lashing out when she could—then one of the guys on the ground grabbed her leg and she stumbled just enough for someone to get a hand on her throat. He was two feet taller than her, she was on her back fast, but she found a way to anchor the sword at her side, angled just enough to catch the guy's side the closer he got, and his hands were suddenly much less white-knuckled around Willa's throat.

"Get OFF ME!" Willa shouted.

She shoved the guy off her just in time to see another round of six men charging. She cracked her neck and flung her sword into the nearest tree trunk where it landed point first, sticking and shaking like a throwing knife. And speaking of, Willa barely had time to replace the sword with two small tactical knives as the oncoming men tackled her back to the ground. Then the screaming started, and it wasn't coming from Willa.

Ollux and her brother held the ground behind Xero, facing off against the densest part of the mob. Ollux was smart enough to ride the edge of the forest, all she had to do was kick someone into the trees and the claws of a leopard would do the rest, dragging the body out of the clearing. That leopard was being as brave as she could be, I would take it. However, Astor was the exact opposite of everything that came before—the moment my eyes found him, well, that was the moment the wooden handle of something came flying out of nowhere and hit him right in the forehead. He toppled over, and landed facedown at Ollux's feet.

"BROTHER!"

"Behind… you," Astor said, before his eyes closed.

A dozen homeless slammed into Ollux and dragged her away screaming, lashing out in defense until she started taking blow after blow in the head, the mouth, the nose… and both wonder siblings were lost to almost the entire attacking army in a moshpit circle around them. They were quiet. Bad quiet.

"Can we help now?" Heather said through clenched teeth.

"No," Bombelle said. "Still, you doubt us. Look."

Xero had fought his way to Garunde holding the leader of Jerico in his bruised, bleeding hands, and Bombelle helped get Bastile's wheezing body up into her lap. Xero found us staring at the carnage, absolutely frozen. Behind us, the small army was doing its worst to Astor, Ollux, and Willa.

"You think us done for," Xero said. "Bastile, is survival your only order?"

"At all costs, old friend," he said before collapsing again, Bombelle sighing in relief hearing him speak.

"You heard that?" Xero called out.

"Yes sir!" Came the unified, confident, voices of Willa, Astor, and Ollux.

And at once, they rose up off the ground, each one of them wiping the blood off their faces, easily throwing off any hands that still tried to hold them. The homeless army looked worried, seeing the warriors of Astral turn on them like they'd been holding back this entire time.

They had been.

"Get someone to talk before there's no one left with teeth," Bombelle said, sounding like she was finishing Bastile's orders—or speaking for him. "Meet us at the waterfall. And Xero. Everything they did to you, return it."

“That’s not what Bastile—” Lynn started.

But Bombelle slapped Garunde so hard the thing ran right into Seanderthal, who stumbled and followed without a second thought. Sophia Sabretooth stepped out of the jungle to snarl once at Ekapian, and suddenly we were all hauling ass, straight towards what looked like a full forage wall of leaves, then the horses had head-butted through it and emerged out on a dark, backroad leading away from the crazy curved trees of Titan, taking us far out into the wilderness literally, with no thought to map or path.

“Was that supposed to happen—” I started.

“You want to be free or WHAT?” Heather shouted.

She was right. She was scared, and so was I, but she was right. I shut up, and we galloped until the incline started going crazy and a shrouded lake came up out of nowhere, with a small but sparkling, short rock waterfall at the other side of it. There was something ancient about the lake, the mood was mist, the shadows, the beams of light hitting the edges of the water. Then—

Bombelle signaled the halt, and her horse hadn’t even stopped moving when Bastile fell off. She couldn’t hold him, she could only slow Garunde until Bastile was close enough to a big, curvy stump of a tree next to a big fern that didn’t look too poisonous, and he fell to his back in the grass, the half arrow still sticking out of his ribs.

Everyone dismounted but me. Bombelle had Bastile in a cradle, but there was no blood. She opened his shirt to see.

“You bastard,” she said, weeping, crying in relief.

Bastile’s eyes were somewhere in between closed and open, looking us over. There was a notebook with an arrow in it, the edge of the arrowpoint still visible on the non-skin side of the notebook. That meant it hadn’t even stuck him as bad as we thought. Maybe a quarter inch, at most.

“I’m… fine…” he said. “You saved my life without trying.”

Derek only held his hand out. Bastile wrenched the arrow and notebook out of his body and handed my brother the more deadly of the two.

“You can keep the arrow,” Derek said, stuffing the notebook down his pants, right where it belonged.

Bombelle laughed in the desperate relief, holding her husband all over, his hands reacting to hers without seeming to notice.

“I underestimated things,” Bastile said. “I believe Titan has been compromised, from root to stem. Bombelle, what distance did we put between?”

“Not enough,” came a voice.

It was Ollux. She led the others, and in one look they were all accounted for. Willa, Astor, and Xero came up on their horses looking far off into the distance, not even excited to see us. Rude. Willa dropped down from her mount, alone now that Elyia was gone, and walked straight for the lake. As she passed I could see… she was covered in blood. Not a little bit. Xero was the same, Astor and Ollux almost worse, seeing as they’d acted as Bastile’s shield. All of them were in the water and silent before we had a chance to say hello.

“You’re alive,” Xero said, seeing Bastile on his feet.

“You’re alive,” Derek said back. “And the horses.”

"As commanded," Willa said, her eyes heavy. She'd seen some stuff.

"Do us a favor, give the hand of Jerico a moment with their commander," Bombelle said, with a sad wink to us.

Understood. We didn't speak. It wasn't a moment for us. Bastile and Bombelle walked right up to their soldiers and settled into the water with them, knees in the silt, the water coming up to their shoulders. Bastile put his arm on Xero and Willa, and Bombelle held Ollux and Astor. Connected, they drifted in the water as one. It was the four of us there in that small clearing by the lake, pretending there was no one else around. The light was barely there, what else was new? The forest had screamed claustrophobia for a good day at this point, so bring it on. For a moment, the moment settled. The journey had taken a halt. The brakes had come on, but so had the jet takeoff at the same time, weird that we'd gotten both. We'd chosen flight, and now (at least if you were me) we didn't know here from anywhere. We were still lost. We were still stuck. Something big would have to happen in order to give this dark moment a bit of light. And whether it was coincidence or the other thing, that's exactly what happened.

From nowhere… came light.

"Hey now," Lynn said, the first to realize.

"What's just turned purple?" Bombelle asked.

It was us. Four amethyst necklaces were glowing a brilliant, shining purple over our dark grove. I thought that wasn't supposed to happen in the territory. But now, this far from the gates themselves, so close to a part of the island that was maybe not so subject to storm season…

"How far have we come?" Lynn asked, a hand on her neck.

"I guess we're gonna find out," Bastile said, his head on the edge of that stump, watching us closely, curiously.

"We're headed for the Planetarium, the one we believe is contributing to the area of anti-electrics," Bombelle said. "Something like that would have to be outside the kill zone, right?"

"I recon so," Lynn said.

She held her hand out and let the necklace hover off her chest, rotating in the air, the colors dancing across her face as the soldiers in the water looked up to the light with what might just possibly have been… hope.

"That rock is flying," Willa said, blinking.

"We all do," Heather said. "Before we lose the chance, do we do the thing?"

"Absolutely," Lynn said.

"What thing?" I asked, innocently.

"Get him," Heather said simply.

Then she grabbed me by the good leg and yanked me off the horse in a free fall, and Lynn was right behind her, pinning me to the ground.

"No!"

2.8

PLANETARIUM

"NO!"

James was thrown off his horse so hard he shook the earth.

"Dudettes!" I yelled, watching his foot and splint hit the ground.

"Too bad, hold still," Heather said. "Lynn, you know what to do."

"I actually don't, I'm just following you."

"NOOOO!—"

Before James could finish that scream, Heather and Lynn were on the forest floor next to him, their hands hovering over his bum leg with a focused prism of purple light coming out of their palms, aimed on that splint.

"You get it now?" Heather asked, her eyes never wavering.

"Go on," was all James said, without a note of the usual pain in his voice.

"The HELL is going on?" Willa called.

She was in the lake up to her hips, the first of the hand to see us, and then they all did. Even Bastile and Bombelle's long faces turned when they saw the pretty lights. One by one they walked out of the water, all brooding replaced with child-like wonder (I hoped), and they circled around us, the smell of wet hair and fresh lake already better than jungle armpits.

"A little warning, sirens," I said shaking my head.

"A little help, Reaper," Heather said, again not even looking at me.

She wasn't asking. Wait did she just call me Reaper? What a day.

I slid to my knees by my brother where he'd fallen (or more accurately been ambushed and Yoshi slammed) to the ground. I didn't know what to do, the girls seemed to have it covered, but my necklace was lighting up and levitating off my chest the same as theirs, the point of our crystals pointing straight down to James. I had no idea how they were controlling this madness, but I wasn't about it—except I probably was, so I put my palms on Lynn and Heather's shoulders, and felt the energy flow out of me the same as I saw their light double in lumen.

"Did it work?" I asked. "Am I helping?"

"You actually are," Heather said.

Score one for instincts.

"So much for the inconspicuous escape," Bombelle said.

She squinted her eyes for the brilliant purple light, trying to see past this part of the dark forest we were lost in, as James only looked up and saw us all over him, doing everything we could, the first chance given, no other thought to it.

"You sir..." James said.

"You sir," was my only answer.

"What are you doing?" Bastile whispered/shouted. "Can't you hear that, there's something in the trees! You've made us!"

"No, the girls made us," I said.

"That's probably true but not what I meant," Bastile growled.

Too bad. We didn't stop until the light did. Until James looked down at his splint in wonder, and outside the open-toed covering... his toes moved.

"No way," my brother said, his voice back to normal, whatever that was.

"Guess who's back," Lynn said. "And not just you."

The necklace from her father glowed true, the ground at her feet trembled, and Lynn Lyre took to the air like she was defying gravity. Because she was.

"What is this..." Bombelle said.

"You know it, we just haven't seen it in years," Bastile said, his eyes still in the trees, but alive, with something that looked like... hope.

Then as something huge and powerful roared at us from the treetops above, I saw in slow motion my brother putting both feet on the ground, one still wrapped in that splint, and with the sound of the crutches clattering over, he stood. On feet. As we all took a line in the dirt, my brother was there with us, back on his own legs, hands up, the rocky armor swirling around him like a cloak, until it solidified against his un-broken body in a jumble of chunks and sharp edges. Eh, he was out of practice. But—

"You're standing," I said, the relief indescribable.

"Back again," James echoed, with a grin.

And as a proper together for the first time in the Jerico, we faced down whatever was out there waiting to ambush us. The growls came again, the creaking of the tree branches, the rustling of leaves as Sophia poked her head out of the lowest ferns, walked head-first down the trunk, and made for the water without hesitation, covered in patches of blood.

Just like the Astral had.

"That cat saved me nine times," Willa said, her voice lower, calmer for her animal instincts. "That's my favorite number."

"Yeah, because you're a six," Bombelle said.

It was so deadpan I didn't get it for a moment. Then Willa clutched her pearls, Heather bit her lip, even Lynn closed her eyes, trying not to laugh. Sophia grazed Willa's entire side as she walked powerfully past her and up to Bastile. The caput frowned, held his ground, and held his hand out too. Sophia had a small leather bracelet around her giant canine, and she let it gently slide off onto Bastile's hand.

"I..." Bastile said, looking at Sophia like she was his own. "I made this for my godmother, ten years ago. Did you... know that?"

Sophia's nose flared. She could probably smell a godmother on a wristlet.

"She says yes," Lynn said. "She says her scientific hypothesis would be...

it's not good. The trail ends at this river."

"You mean lake," Bastile said.

"Cat says river," Lynn said. "The ocean Elyia spoke of. It's this."

Bastile wiped a tear from his face with the wristlet, paying no mind to the leopard slobber. He took a deep breath and pulled it over his free wrist, now wearing a wide bracelet on each arm like Wonder Woman—or shackles.

"Our eyes in the trees," Bastile said. "They're... signed off."

"We've come this far to find nothing?" Willa said, angry, but hollow.

"We've come this far for a cat to help us more than kids," Bombelle said. "Sorry, just calling it like I see it."

"You'd be right, if you weren't wrong," I said. "What's the problem, you really don't know where the Planetarium is?"

"We really don't," Bastile said. "I was going to exert every ounce of executive and crisis privilege for the coordinates. Without my... without Lady Armanda, I don't know what to do. This is all my fault."

"Not to us," I said.

"With all respect—" Bastile started.

"Don't tell me what to do," James said. "That... was not your fault. Don't you dare think for one moment it was."

Bastile looked at him. "I... said that."

"We both said it," James said, walking up to Bastile and putting a hand on his shoulder, for the first time free to do so. "And we both mean it."

"Smart boys," Bastile said, fondly, before the frown returned. "I still don't know how we're supposed to find something we're not supposed to find."

"I do," I said. "That's what we do best."

"That and losing things we shouldn't lose," my brother added.

"What are you talking about, little one?" Xero said. "We're halfway to Silka without a map. It'll be a miracle if we can return to the Oleander before leopard season—I mean nightfall."

"I thought you were Jerico's elite," I said.

"Yes and now this has gone far beyond a single casualty," Xero countered. "And we don't know where we're going."

"To the Planetarium in Titan Arum, right?" I asked, a hand on my necklace.

"Why are you repeating everything I say?" Xero barked.

Suddenly all four gemstones hovered up off our chests. All chains were pulled taunt around all necks, and we all took a single step forward in the direction the rock was pulling, trying to un-choke ourselves. But we'd all taken the step in the same direction, left of the lake, down with the flow of the river, as everyone else took a step back.

"Witches, every one of you," Willa said, her sword separating us from them.

"Not denying it," I said. "But Planetarium's that way. You coming?"

"He does listen," Heather said to Lynn, impressed.

"What was your role in this unit before being here, Derek?" Bastile asked.

"The map," I said. "Although right now, I put that on the Vema. If you still want to get there and back again by nightfall, keep up. Lynn, you want a break from a horse?"

"Never," she said, smiling at me. "You go out ahead. We'll need a ride home, I'll keep her under rein and reign."

"I know you will," I said. "James, you know what it is?"

"Yeah, what it do," he said.

He was smiling from ear to ear with a single finger pointing up. Yep.

Together, we spread our wings and flew into the small, leafy world, mostly around the clear space over the water that admittedly was starting to seem more like a river than a lake. I couldn't see an end to it, not even from all the way up here, too many trees. But that didn't matter, not after a few days of solid ground. I was good with endlessness. There was no fishbowl big enough for me.

"How's the leg brother?" I asked, already seeing him whip around on a dime, the splint tearing apart in the wind around his working legs.

"It feels GOOD BROTHER!" James yelled.

He yanked the thing off his foot and threw it into the sky. Then he caught it, because littering. But his voice was back to full volume, no more tinge of pain behind every word he said, and we flew into the swamp together, if not the sunset, just glad to be finally back on the same level, whatever level it was.

"But... the fodder... they're flying..." Xero said, amazed and just a bit frightened, looking at us like he was seeing the horde for the first time.

"Yeah, well, the fodder are doing a lot of whatever the hell," Bastile said. "Although I do think we've found our path."

"Our map," I corrected.

"Correct," Lynn and Heather said at the same time.

Their horses pulled up next to each other, both necklaces glowing and pointing out the direction as clear as day, as the head and hand of Jerico mounted up behind, as boy and brother flew overhead, darting through the trees, hovering over the horses, as once again Sophia stuck her tongue out, like she was laughing. Once again, we were moving. Together. Because when the jungle gives you a long, twisting jungle lake, you follow it, by sea, sky, or land.

We held the waterside for a half hour, our necklaces following the ripples to the wave so perfectly that we may as well have taken to the lake/river instead of wearing out the horses. All we were missing was a—

"Is that pontoon big enough for all of us?" James asked.

I was flying a good fifty feet in the air, a vantage enough to see far down the river in both directions, but the bounty of the banks was mostly hidden by long overhanging trees and brush. I hadn't seen the thing until I was on top of it, half-buried in the mud, a wooden construct next to the ancient remains of a well-built, but rotting, completely unusable dock.

"Depends on how much of it's buried," I said. "But good catch."

Through the treeline, I had manifested something. Or you know, someone had been here before me, with the exact same quandary. There were only so many ways to travel a river.

"I don't know how we're ever going to get that out of the ground, brother," James said, with a small grin.

Right. Sarcasm, from the world's newest Reaper, besides the rest of them. Without another word we dove, our hands glowing, not really knowing what we were doing but willing to try—and the vessel moved, sliding out of the mud and onto the water like something was controlling it. But it wasn't us.

"Faster than you," Heather called up to us from the solid ground, coming out of a gallop to a skidding stop on Ekapian. "Even without wings."

"Aw," I said.

I landed beside the emerged pontoon, glowing wings folding back into suspenders, the power of invisibility at my fingertips, and still upset. Kind of.

"Ew it's all muddy," Bombelle said.

Okay it wasn't just me.

Heather sighed and lowered her hands, and the entire vessel dunked itself under the water, coming up wet and slick, but clean. Awesome. The horses stopped beside the boat of destiny that Heather had willed in and out of the mud like the savior of everything she already was, and more. Willa smiled, the first sign of emotion from her since she'd come back from Titan.

"I love how this is normal to you, but microwaves aren't," I said.

"It is a forgotten normal," Bombelle said. "One we thought gone forever. I don't think you truly grasp the weight of what you've done for the Vempire."

"I can assure you we don't," I said, Heather nodding hard behind me.

"Paradigm shift," Bastile said, unhorsing himself, feeling around his ribs where the arrow had (barely) got him.

"Truer words," Lynn said. "After you."

"Hey thanks," I said.

Heather had a muddy underwater grip on the pontoon, and she didn't just bring it close to shore, she moved the dirt around the thing so there was no difference, holding the wood on the water literally rock steady for boarding. Even the horses didn't think twice. They should have though. Bombelle gave me a single touch on the shoulder as she walked onboard, her hands graceful, her fingers just so soft. Man she was beautiful—not that it changed anything, it just made speaking and breathing around her harder. Then all horses and soldiers were accounted for, all wings stowed, all claws retracted. Gemstone necklaces still going crazy, all pointing in a unified direction down the river.

So down the river we went.

"What a lovely family heirloom," Willa said, staring at Heather's chest.

Lynn laughed. She was back in regular Lynn mode, which meant she had a contingency ready for everything that could possibly happen to us—out here, at least. It meant she was relaxed, maybe even… calm. Like the bomb.

"You speak of our normal, this is yours?" Willa asked her, sensing a much bigger change than a gemstone.

"This is half of normal," Heather said, with a proper wink, mysterious and cute at the same time.

James tried to return it and nope, both eyes closed. He couldn't do anything.

"It's not though," I said. "Do soldiers usually talk when something happens like… what we all went through, twenty minutes ago?"

"We do," Bastile said. "Though I would say we've been talking this whole time. For once, just tell me what you want."

"The order not to help aside," James said, as ready to cut to it as any. "We weren't even done with David. You were going to have his body recovered, and delivered to his family. Can that still happen? On our way back, when it comes around? No matter what, no excuses, no reasons why it's too hard?"

I thought on it, and I agreed. We could come back to a lot of things but this one took priority. James had summed up the feeling—the feeling of not being able to do anything except what we could do given reality, given the past was the past and we couldn't change it, no matter how fast we ran. Ever.

Bastile nodded. "I promise."

"I believe you," I said, holding him to it.

And so we floated, down the misty lake, trees so thick on either side all we could see was a few yards of dew soaked grasses after water's end. The fog was only getting heavier, settling on the river itself. The horses kicked a bit at first when the world was enveloped in mist, but Sophia yawned, sounding like she was spread out on the wet wood at full chill. Then the horses were calm too. The water was zen, but the vibe was shot. We could barely make eye contact, each of us thinking the same thing—pirates (if you were me). Then, out of nowhere—

"There," James said.

"Where?" I asked.

But James only hit his wings, which I realized had been half-extended this whole time, holding him upright, not really letting him puts any weight on his legs, and he flew into the mist before I could object. Poof, gone.

"Hey man," Heather said.

"I said stay together," Bastile growled.

"Sorry!" James shouted back through the fog. "We're here. It's—"

"Pirates, it's the pirates!" I shouted, looking for my slingshot.

Suddenly there was no more fog. We had emerged through it like the white nimbus that separated a mere mountain ridge from the glory of cloud city. And where we were was closer to cloud city, I'll give a jungle that.

"Let the truth be told," Bastile said quietly. I'll elaborate.

"Holy batman," Lynn stammered.

Well said.

No more trees, for starters. The fog had cleared, the lake had turned, both without warning. This side of the thicket, we floated naturally to James, standing on the sandy, grassy banks of a long stretch of treeless land to the river's left. Beyond that dawned on us all the sense and scale of the side of the cliff we were clearly on. You didn't get a view of the ocean like that unless you had mountains to stand on, and baby, up here, we had all the mountains. But it wasn't only the falloff past the river, the shore's end (as it were) only thirty yards behind James that caught our eye. There was only one thing keeping this place from its natural beauty, and that was the clearly unnatural gigantic lens cap hanging off the very end of a gigantic telescope leaning up against shore's end in front of us. And even though it was as decrepit and derelict and decommissioned as a thing covered in a decade of vines and jungle moss could be...

It was still pointed straight at us.

"Telescopes do one thing," I warned the group. "Heather, can you make a ship invisible?"

"It's already seen us," Heather said. "Also no, honest answer. I'm not a car."

I was confused for a moment. Right. Flight pattern—woah.

"Land," Bastile said lamely.

I couldn't tell if it was an order or an observation, until Heather moved her hands slowly and our pontoon ate the beach, the waves not even a factor in our landing, not for a river. Smooth wasn't the word, not when the landing was calmer than the entire journey by a factor of infinite. Again the horses walked off without nary a second thought of the moving ground or the giant man-made machine over yonder. But speaking of water, a river, or an ocean.

We'd reached an end of the island. I wasn't sure which end it was, but that was the actual ocean right there, behind the giant telescope with nature growing on and over it. The spacious, scenic cliff overlook, the perfect break on both sides to the otherwise endless jungle, the sun high overhead and nothing but water in the photogenic distance, this place had wedding reception potential—unless it didn't. I wasn't the one to put up a parking lot in paradise. But clearly someone had already put something up here, a telescope the size of a roller coaster, probably. If the very top of such a construct was all the way up here, the rest of it was probably far off, founded from a ground a long ways below, right?

"Where ARE WE?" I asked, for the sixth time.

"The territory Planetarium in Titan Arum" Lynn said softly. "How we didn't account for a telescope..."

"We don't have to be invisible, but we can stop glowing in the dark," Heather said.

She made sense. Our necklaces must have been listening, because together, and out of command instead of force for once, the light went out. All of our lights went out. It was as clear a sign as any actual sign. This wasn't Jerico, this wasn't Vema. This was strangerland.

Which meant... we were here.

"Perimeter check," Bastile said. "Astor, Ollux, deploy. The rest of you..."

We crept forward slowly, towards where the sidewalk ended, through the single long stretch of beach separating us from a telescope that was angled perfectly for clambering down an otherwise vertical cliffside falloff. Bastile led us closer to the edge, his eyes darting all around, and he finally got close enough to shift his weight to his back foot, creeping forward...

"Take a look," he said, and we took the last few feet forward, to see—

"No way," I said.

"Is that—" James asked.

"Sanjos Cove, first ocean this far north to be considered within Silka City territory, yes. We've come far."

From up here, it looked like a natural divide between mountains, marked by sand, waves, and a cove beach the size of two football fields on end. We looked down on the beach from our side of the cove, and there were cliffs as high up as us on the other side. No one down there could have ever seen this far up to us. I knew that because I'd been down there before. I knew this beach, from childhood, and from a certain sea conch story.

Memories… with pincer claws.

"If we fall down, we'll be home," James said, his face red, but eyes set.

"We need you here," Bastile said. "Don't fall, that's an order."

Don't say it, my brother screamed at me with every clenched muscle in his body. Fine. I wouldn't talk about that day on the beach—anymore. But just as I thought that, I remembered the reason we were here. A telescope the size of a small space station wasn't in my memory from any of our day trips to Sanjos. There was more to the cove than the beach, so I looked closer—literally, to the bluffs below me, and saw a secondary ridge about as wide as the width of Crete's mountain range ridge valley carved into the mountains below us, still a hundred stories over the beach. That's where even the vines and trees and ivy couldn't hide the clear building-shaped constructs at the base of the telescope, carved and crafted straight into the side of the mountain itself. From up here, falling down and not hitting the Planetarium would be hard. I wondered how deep into the mountain it went.

So that's what was below us. Home, and also something stranger.

"We go home when you do," Lynn said, reading my thoughts, because everyone was.

"Well said," Bombelle said to Lynn. "I understand you grew up with the wayfarer—I'm sorry, with Crete Magellan, the master crafter. Did he prepare you for the demands of a building of such literal scope?"

"Absolutely not," Lynn said. "You're sweet, it is usually me who does everything. But if you're on about a telescope, you're asking the wrong twins."

"I'm not asking twins," Bombelle said, frowning.

"Well you should be," Lynn said, bowing, giving way to…

"You twins?" Bombelle said, blinking, looking at my brother and me. "Oh right. Telescope."

"That's like the only thing we can actually offer," I said, meekly.

"You, the fodder?" Bastile asked, blinking. "Not the woman more mysterious than Issaic's twins and more dangerous than the Reaper? Not the girl who spent years under Magellan, the girl who talks to LEOPARDS?"

"I have to say, I'm offended you didn't automatically assume I was an astronaut," I said.

"Are you?" Bastile asked.

"Yes," I said.

They stared harder.

"Where'd the confidence come from?" Bombelle asked.

"From the girl who talks to leopards, personally," I said.

"You're making it hard to decide who watches the horses," Bastile said.

"We're kind of a package deal," Lynn said.

She was perfect.

"Perimeter secured," Astor said, as he and Ollux emerged out of the trees—I hadn't even seen them leave. "All three of us can confirm."

"Three?" Bastile asked.

Ollux nodded to something up in the trees; a long, grey and black, clouded tail swinging powerfully over our heads. Kitty.

"Right," Bastile said. "Bombelle, Astor, Ollux, stay with the horses. Your only job is to make sure we have a way home."

"Yes sir," Astor, Ollux, even Bombelle saluted him.

Right. We couldn't rely on our Reaper abilities, no matter how dope they were, not if they couldn't see us all the way back to safety. Once we were back within the electromagnetic perimeter of the Jerico jungle, horses meant home.

"Willa, and Xero, enter at risk," Bastile said. "Fodder, stay close behind. We have no intel on what may be inside, but we'll worry about that. You worry about anything trying to follow. Could be Infinite, could be snakes."

"I'd take the Infinite," I said, shaking my head.

James smacked me. "Don't put that into the universe. Take snakes. Right now. Wish for them harder than you've ever wished for anything."

"I wish… for snakes?" I said.

"Damn right you do," Lynn said, backing James. "Now. About a way in."

"Sails down!" Heather shouted.

And she was the first to jump from the edge of the cliff onto the very top of the telescope, instantly sliding down slow enough to guide her descent—until she got the speed wobbles and fell to her butt, her two perfectly working wings fluttering in the wind, forgotten behind her.

"WOOO!—"

"I said behind," Bastile growled.

"You crack that cookie, you let us know," was all I said.

I got a big nod from James, Lynn, even the horses behind us.

Bastile sighed. "What did she say, sails down? That's the vibe. Let's GO!"

And with surprising enthusiasm, he leapt down after her, keeping to his feet as long as he could before the speed took him to the butt too. He was followed by Xero and Willa, as Astor, Ollux, and Bombelle gave them an honorary salute, and the courtesy look-away when they inevitably took the telescope to the—

"Ah!"

"AH!"

"MY B—!"

"Back soon horses," Lynn said. "Don't leave us, we'll die. Okay bye."

And with one final pet, she joined us in the air, and we levitated down to the bottom of the telescope with wings and ease, to find a party of Jerico and Heather already breathing hard.

"I forgot about—" Heather said, looking up to us.

"You forgot about your wings," James finished for her.

"Does anyone else's butt hurt?" Xero asked, the bravest, in so many ways.

Nods all around.

"Well now what?" Willa asked, from her back, Xero's legs on top of her.

"This isn't real," I said.

But it was, especially from this angle, from the domed top of the construct to a telescope that could maneuver wherever it wanted up here. As much as this looked like roof, it would move on us if that telescope chose to move position. At least, that's how the Silka City Observatory was built, and we knew—we'd spent a day on hands and knees and ladders and crawl spaces, in engine rooms and server bays, on top of the dome by the telescope *just like this*, where we'd used a window entrance to a ladder leading directly down into the main control atrium, right over where our mother had sat over the thirty foot super desk in her wheelchair. But this wasn't that. Or was it? Because that hatch outline in the dusty, dirty dome was right where it had been at the Observatory…

I kicked the leaves off, smacked the dirt gone, and Bastile's eyes widened when we all saw the clear four-sided frame of a trapdoor, exactly where I'd expected to find it. Maybe trapdoor was a bad choice of words. It was a hatch, and nothing more. So far.

"How did you know that was there?" Bastile asked.

"Easily," I said simply.

He stared at me like a bull breathing slowly, I stared back like a red cape.

"Can it be opened?" Xero asked, with bated breath, like he'd forgotten he was part of this movie. "Oh right, I'm me."

He grabbed the door and wrenched it open so hard the metal bent. Leaves fell into the opening, as dark as anything, the rust creaking, winces all around.

"Should I ring the doorbell too?" Bastile asked, annoyed. Xero gently set the door down and we shut up, and rightly so.

"I'll go first," Bastile said, holding his hand out. "Rope."

Heather smacked his hand away.

"I won't tell you to stay behind again," Bastile said.

"Good," Heather said, as her necklace roared to life. "I got you. Top to bottom, T to B. Speaker for the Reaper, right? We walk loud, and talk louder. But let's get one thing straight."

Bits of rock traveled around her in a mist, a swarm, until she was donned head to toe in a different kind of armor, a dark grey granite much sleeker than before, with the amethyst of her necklace sending ripples of power throughout it, amplifying the light so much she might just be a fire. Better than rope, for sure.

"I'm not your soldier," Heather said. "I'm mine."

"You're still nothing without backup," Bastile said.

"I've got backup," Heather said, winking at us.

And without warning, the fire (Heather) fell down the open hatch, landing a few stories down on her feet in the dark atrium. We peeked down; her claws were out, the light reflecting off the blades, throwing different colored purple auras around so bright that we could see the entire command station, abandoned, empty, and best of all, no snakes.

"You should have waited for the rope," Bastile said.

"Well I'm waiting now!" Heather called back up, in a low, hushed voice.

Bastile smiled. "She may save us all."

"Only if I help," Lynn said. "What were you saying about backup?"

She too threw herself sideways down the hatch, and Bastile's eyes went wide again—until she hit her wings and hovered down to Heather. Bastile wasn't talking so much anymore. Xero and Willa tied a rope to the telescope and threw the length of it down into the hatch. Bastile was adamant about going first to test the strength of the rope, and so he did. My brother and I followed, but not by rope, landing down in a mossy, humid, sulfur-smelling dwelling of brick and mortar, a large domed atrium with not much in the way of lights, a few hallways offshoot on any side, the works, the entire thing screaming underground. It was by the gentle purple light from four necklaces that the room was illuminated from corner to ceiling. We stood back to back, all seven of us—claws out, eyes up, head first, can't lose.

"Contact," Bastile said. "We'll call this room alpha."

"'We could have flown you down," I said.

"That would make our ascent reliant upon you," Bastile said. "We all need a little something. Hope, an escape rope, whatever."

"Understood," I said. "Contingency plans don't usually assume the best."

"They do not," Heather said, realizing the contingency plan was for escape without us. "So. Ancient secrets, modern day nerds. What now?"

Bastile shrugged.

"You... really don't know?" Xero asked, for the first time sounding like us.

"I really don't, champ," he said. "Something brought us here. Whatever it is, I never imagined it would be subtle."

"I hate subtle," Willa agreed.

I looked sideways to the light switches on the walls, and decided not to say anything. I didn't even know if they worked. Besides, Willa already had torches lit a few feet down each hallway, giving us a little view of a lot of ground. Primitive, but effective, enough to settle a nerve. There were four hallways in total connected to this room alpha. Between the memory of being here before, between Willa and the sword, Xero's silhouette almost filling out the hallway, I actually felt confident enough to turn to the tables in front of me. And that's when all the familiar feelings hit me, all at once. I knew these tables.

"Okay," Bastile said. "Down the telescope, through the hatch in the roof, into a big dumb table room with mirrors on the walls. Think like a lightning man..."

"Those aren't mirrors," I said. "If it helps."

Looking up made us all feel small, here on this side of the wide, battle station desks, spanning thirty feet wide, with no less than seven monitors looming over us. The one in the middle was bigger than a car, right now just a dark frame with dust all over the once high-definition lcd screens. The dust was so fine I couldn't fault Bastile for thinking mirrors. It was another world, through the looking glass, past the mirror dimension, beyond the quantum realm, but then I looked down to the computer interfaces on the mega-desk and once again saw something I'd seen in the Observatory. In the exact same place and everything. No way...

"The lights..." Willa said, her pupils straining. "Who built such a thing?"

"Clearly the same person who built the Observatory," I said.

"I can vouch for that," Heather said. "That means my father should be popping up for that long overdue family reunion. Any moment now."

"For your family's sake, I hope that doesn't happen," Lynn said sadly.

"Fine, then prepare for death by surprise missile," Heather said.

"Much more relatable," I nodded.

"For everyone's sake I hope THAT doesn't happen!" Bastile said, alarmed.

"Teresa Nite was here? I mean… she was here?"

"She was," I said. "But so were we. And Hector got us out in lightning speed. He either had time to get her too, or wait. What if…"

"Say it," James said. "Please say what I think you're thinking."

"Maybe our mother didn't need him," I said. "If Hector went from wizard to flashpoint in a nanosecond, maybe she did too. Maybe all she needed was…"

"A distraction," James finished for me. "It's worked for us."

"The building?" Willa asked. "Was it empty? Were there people on the observation deck less tethered to the destiny of the island? Did innocents die?"

I was about to go there. We'd seen definite signs of chaos as we ran up the hill to see the scorched remains of the observation deck. The wheelchair on its side in the flames. But then a strange memory hit me in the… memories.

"There were people there," James said, his eyes the same as mine. "There was a family, the Alders. They were supposed to be burned. But they turned up later, far from the Observatory, safe and sound."

"Was that Hector?" Bastile asked. "Or was it maybe… not?"

I didn't want to believe it, but it was the most logical proof yet. If Hector hadn't stepped in and saved young Jesi and the Alder parents, someone else had. And the closest person there would have been…

"It's hypothetical of course," Bastile said. "But anyone who knew Teresa Silk, or Teresa Nite post marriage, knows her real name. The Always Soldier. Not the good for a while then blown up in a freak accident soldier, not the soldier with the broken back—"

"Supermom—wait, did you say Silk?" James blinked.

"Here's what I'm saying," Bastille said. "We're way in over our heads, we're up against a system that we know not about, and I'll be damned if you can actually live up to the expectation that you know how something as big as this comes together. I bet you're still thinking about—"

"You said Silk," I said.

"I also said it wouldn't be confusing, a man can be wrong," Bastile said.

"You said they weren't the same, it was purely symbolic," I said.

"I did," Bastile said. "But clearly… family names stick around sometimes."

"Look, they're learning," Xero said.

"Are you saying our mom was… that we're…" James asked.

"I am," Bastile said. "The world does not revolve around you, but on this island, the history of humanity revolves around your mother and her ancestors. You need to know where you came from, in order to understand why you're here. Why all of us are here."

"It is all for our mother, isn't it?" I asked.

"It sure seems like the exact opposite," Bastile said, his eyes narrowed for all our talk. "At least the plan understands itself. Now answer me this, small children of destiny. Why is nothing in this control room working?"

"Because you can't control this place from the control room," James and I said in unison.

Bastile backed off. I'll give it to him, twins were creepy.

"Sorry," we said again at the same time.

"AaAH!"

I held my hands up, and my brother gestured for them to follow. A very curious Willa, Xero, and Bastile followed him to a certain panel in the walls that was all wonky, instead of on the level.

"Of course," Lynn said, smacking herself in the forehead. "If this was built during the founder's age…"

"It would come with the Silk trademark hierarchy of control, accounting for all before the one," I finished, my face pale. "Check it."

"Hardware and software," James said, pointing to two of the readouts.

"Power, and release," I finished, standing at the other end of the panel. "We need all of these readings re-calibrated from their source locations—that is, if we want a telescope working again. Do we?"

"I don't know," Bastile said honestly. "We're here for Jerico, not for telescopes. What do you think we should do?"

"You're serious?" I said, staring.

"I left three of the hand watching your horses," Bastile said. "You are here because you said you could help the territory. Can you?"

And it hit me. Maybe it was the look in his eyes, and how it wasn't even the first time I'd seen it. I'd seen that look in Sand. In Crete. In Elin Mare, and Aunt Elma. The look that we might be the answers, to questions we still didn't even understand. Sure thing, we saved the underland, we could totally just do it again here—right?

"I have a hard time believing I'm anyone's answer," I said, no filter.

"We all do," Bastile said. "But when our name gets called, we stand. No matter what's waiting for us."

"Well the dark earth did say my name," I said.

"A jungle animal said mine," Lynn joined.

"A flying car said mine," Heather agreed.

"A mysterious girl from memories, at night in dreams—" James started.

"Man you kids are weird—how is this any harder than any of that?" Bastile said, as Willa and Xero laughed. "I don't expect you to do anything but try."

"We have to try," I said, snapping the notebook closed. "But you aren't ready for this answer."

"I'm ready for a lot," Bastile tried to argue.

"I'll remember that," I said, smiling. "Oracle, you there?"

"Always."

For the second time, Bastile was suddenly silent. Willa darted to Heather, like she was going to hide behind her, then caught herself.

"Flattered," Heather said, as Willa went red.

"System… online. Conducting identification. Holy shengcun."

The others started, looking up in the air.

"We're not alone," Willa said, the sword in her hand as I blinked.

"Voice unknown," the Oracle said, her voice coming over us at a low volume, a gentle knock instead of a blaring doorbell. *"By the accent, assuming three high-ranking warriors of Jerico Territory."*

"A computer knows me?" Willa said, the thought scarier than any enemy.

"A computer is designed to," the Oracle said.

"Hi Oracle," my brother said, delighted.

"Hi James," came the obligatory response. *"I see you have not changed."*

"Never," he said. "We were wondering about all this, if you have a moment."

"But of course."

"But who the hell?" Willa said.

"She speaks to us," Xero said. "Is this technology?"

"This is Oracle," I said. "She tends to meet us at places like this."

"She can travel technology?" Xero asked. "Is she of the island?"

"No, she's not real," I said.

"Hey now."

"She's a program," I said. "Artificial intelligence, the power of a super computer, the voice of, well…"

"I would know that voice anywhere," Bastile said.

He hadn't spoken since Oracle had started talking. Xero and Willa were skittish, and looking all around for the source of the voice, but Bastile had stood silent the entire time, his eyes unblinking, unbelieving.

"My program was created from a vocal database supplied by Teresa Silk Nite, yes."

"What does that MEAN?" Bastile asked, more sad than mad, a sort of hopeful frustration that broke my heart when I realized he was looking at us for the answer.

"It means it's her… but it's not," I said, the bittersweet feeling at full force. "It means… we take what we can get, and hold on."

"I have underestimated you," Bastile said, no filter.

"I think he means that," Willa whispered to us, just as moved, and stunned as Bastile.

"I think we're wasting time—Oracle, is the telescope operational?" I asked.

"It can be."

And the entire last few days of being in the technological dark were done. In a collective, colorful snap, the rope behind us moved, the roof did too, the house lights came on, and monitors lit up from wall to wall. It was easy to see the moss and grasses overtaking the metal floors, even the ceiling. Even more, from behind us the ground moved, the floor panels melting away to reveal—

"I knew we were missing something," my brother said. "Specifically—"

A suspended, circular platform that hovered off the ground like a gravity-defying motorbike. A seat, a backrest, feet and hand controls, and a viewfinder that connected with a part of the ceiling that dropped down to meet it, into a telescope the size of a giant's baseball bat. The roof started reflecting, the external sensors kicked in, and the entire domed ceiling turned into a perfectly visualized representation of the sky.

"What are we thinking, captain?" Xero asked.

"Best case scenario," Bastile smiled, no filter. "No power tools, huh?"

Willa's jaw hung open.

"I'm not usually this assertive," James said.

He sat down first on the viewing chair before we'd even rock-paper-scissored for it. I threw my hands up the in air. James looked at me, trying to find the words to say in a code only we'd understand.

"I'm looking for more secret letters from Mom," he said simply.

"I think you already found a big giant one," Xero said, his eyes on the ceiling, still looking for speakers.

I winked at James, which meant I blinked at him. He grinned, put his eyes to the viewfinder, and saw…

"Nothing."

My heart dropped.

"I got nothing but the sky, the cliffs, Astor doing some kind of handstand…"

"Astor's are the best handstands in the territory," Xero said. "Put it on the screen."

"Yes sir," James said sadly.

And the world above us moved, as the telescope shifted its focus, and settled on the horses and the rest of our crew in the cliffs. Astor fell over, the others jumped and stared, they all thought about it and then… waved. We waved back. But they didn't know. It was a one way thing, here and there.

But speaking of coordinates.

"My turn, get off son," I said.

"Ah!"

I pushed a brother out of the chair and he tumbled down in a flash of light.

"Why?"

"I'm following up," I said.

I had the coordinates memorized. I had only seen them every-time I'd opened my notebook in the last two weeks. The buttons beeped, the dials in the telescope ticked away, and the viewfinder zoomed in on something impossible to see, but not by operator error (I hoped). For the first time in all the two minutes we'd known this thing, there was static on the screen. It didn't register as anything but annoying, and I zoomed past it to clearer skies, settling the telescope on something in the atmosphere that was… just a bunch of air. But that's not all that happened. There was something obscuring part of the coordinate, so I pressed my eye closer to the viewer to see—no way.

"There," I said frantically, hoping everyone was looking up. "The last known astral coordinates of the Observatory telescope, the picture of space it was taking when it died. I've been waiting for weeks to plug this into something and figure everything out, but now… I…"

"It's nothing but sky," Lynn said gently.

"Exactly why I'm looking," I admitted. "Future monsters, right?"

In the distraction my hand almost went unseen as I folded the small piece of white paper into the notebook in my hands, like I was turning a page. I was. No one else was looking for it, except for James.

"If not the satellite, what did you expect to find at those coordinates, Derek Nite?" the Oracle asked, almost playfully—I mean ominously.

"I don't know," I said. "I thought it was important, I still do. That's why I wrote it down and put it in my pocket. Heather, you can read the stars right?"

"I can," she said. "What year did the Observatory go down?"

"Hector said it's been decades," James said.

"I need an exact number," Heather said.

"I know we do, I'm saying I don't have it," James said.

"Why?" Lynn asked, curious.

"Because of the oldest astronomical event known to man," I said, and Heather nodded, like it was allowed. "The universe is constantly expanding. Literally, we're not getting any closer to the stars."

"We're not?" James asked.

"To the contrary," Heather said. "The stars are getting farther away. Blame it on the expanding universe, not that we can do anything about it."

"That's what you meant," James said, the lightbulb finally going off. "I was nodding along like I understood but you said it Derek, all you needed was some time, and some books that will probably be impossible to find, but you might be able to match up the constellations with where they'd be today. It would still be an unknown—"

"But it would be a consistent unknown," I finished. "You listen too."

"Okay, well your own notes say forty years at least, right?" James asked. Then his smile dropped. "Wait. You also said you had evidence that the Observatory shutdown was electromagnetic. You said the words brother. EMP."

"I did," I said, blinking. "Holy shengcun."

"Language. Don't be like Lynn."

"Sorry," I said, as Lynn threw her hands up.

"You've seen electromagnetic weaponry within Silka City?" Bastile asked, edging in on the conversation. "Specifically within the last forty years?"

"Since before we were born," my brother croaked out.

"EMPs, last forty years, checks out," I said. "I mean… we have the tech."

"Infinite has the tech," Heather corrected. "Issaic Nite's Infinite, to be—"

"We get it," I said, just as the power flickered around us again.

It was too on-point for us to feel cool about it. When the lights came back on, they found every one of us in a fighting stance, instinctually taking a circle, watching outwards and upwards at every angle. Almost like a proper fam—

"Surge detected in the server bay," the Oracle said. *"It's probably nothing."*

"She said, before they all died," Willa said, even dark for Heather.

2.9

SAD SONG

"You are walking towards your own death, Nite," Bastile said.

"Or towards the reason this entire place was running on ten percent power," I said. "If the telescope isn't going to show us anything without a bunch of math I don't feel like doing, let's keep looking. Besides, the Oracle would give us a warning before dropping us off the falloff."

"She would," Lynn agreed.

The Oracle did not object, almost like it was another clue, or a nod to the voice log, and anyone who might be listening in on us even now. Hmm.

Bastile sighed and took one last look up to the sky and stars we could see through the modular projector roof, as we left the atrium and walked down the hallway towards the server bay.

"I feel it in my skin," Xero said. "The goosebumps, they're back."

I felt it too. Science with Xero—I meant an electrical hum, echoing harder the farther down we walked. The walls were derelict wood and mossy concrete. There were signs of damage at the floorboards. Half a trash can sat in the corner with a mound of dirt and rocks around what looked like a closed door to a bathroom, and finally the hallway ended in a small staircase that curved us down into a large computer room.

"You hear that?" Derek said, stopping suddenly.

"Not really?" I said, touching my necklace again.

The purple light swept out from the top of that five-stair, and we could almost see the entire room from up here. The ceiling wasn't more than twelve feet high, the length of the room was between a warehouse and a recording studio with an open-floored control desk station close to the stairs, before the madness of the machinery started. Some of the servers towered over us, making the back of that room a small maze, easy to get lost in, easy to hide in—either way, the claws came out. Bastile looked around in wonder at all the blinking lights, the quiet hum. Bombelle had her head in a swivel, keeping an eye on the unknown for her wondering, wandering caput. Xero put his hand on a big, space-grey slab of a processor, feeling the hum, the heat, looking at the thing like it was alive. It was, kind of. Willa hadn't left the staircase, she looked spooked, and ready to bolt.

"So the software's working," Derek said, looking around.

It was true, for every big mechanical block, brick, tower or desktop, I could find at least one little glowing light. These machines weren't making much noise, but they were on, and doing something.

"But working what?" I asked.

"Check it out," Derek said.

I looked—below the stairs was a huge input bay, where the computers were supposed to be connected to the rest of the telescope. I knew that because we had spent hours re-soldering some of the loose ports back at the Observatory, and Hector had shown us which color and which connector went to which wire. We had single-handedly re-routed the Observatory servers, and we were ready to do it again here. But it wasn't only mis-routed. There was a roughly chiseled hole in the wood underneath the patch bay, and through this narrow, but twenty foot wide hole, every single cable ran outbound, instead of connected to the professionally installed bay just above the hole.

"Hackers," I said, frowning. "That means the telescope was operating without a single network connection?"

"Of course. I wouldn't have let you touch it otherwise."

"Oh good," Derek said. "For a moment I thought someone might be following our path to nowhere."

"Isn't this why we're here?" Heather said. "Why shouldn't I just slice through every one of these cables right here and now?"

"If you want to take the shockwave of a geomagnetic storm, go for it," I said. "It'll probably feel like a solar flare."

"A solar flare..." Lynn said, her eyes flashing at the thought for some reason.

"I'm not stupid, I have plans," Heather said, and a cloud of earth floated up to her, sculpting itself into a rocky outline of her own hand. She took a claw glove off and put it on the rock hand, suspended in the air, a good ten feet away from her. When she moved her bare hand, the rock drone claw moved in tandem.

"Again, why are we seeing this for the first time now?" I asked. "You promised you would teach us the secrets of the Reaper!"

"I promised no such thing."

"It would be polite to try," I said lamely.

"But that sounds boring," Heather said, moving her claw like a telekinetic fan of blades.

"Girl's a lot of things, but boring isn't one of them," Willa said.

"Stand down Reaper," Bastile said, as the claws in the sky got closer to the cables. "We can't risk it, not yet."

"Fine," Heather said, and the dirt drone fell away, her glove fitting back over her hand, all telekinetic. "This is your one. I still think cutting these bad boys in half is the answer."

"Let's figure out what these bad boys do before the raze," Bastile countered.

"Deal," Heather admitted. "Sorry for saying bad boys."

"It happens," Bastile said.

"I feel… cold," Willa said, standing on the rail perfectly balanced, looking out into the small studio sized maze of the servers and computing towers.

"Technology runs hot," I said. "Whatever this is, it's more important to someone than astronomy."

"I never expected this to end up being about astronomy," Willa said.

"I did," Derek said, tapping his notebook.

"Sorry starboy, those cables aren't going up," Heather said, looking closer. "Check this out."

She put a hand on the wall above the mess of cables disappearing into it. Her necklace instantly responded, in fact they all did, if you were the four of us. They hovered together off our chests, slowly, aiming hard at the floor.

"What?" Lynn said. "But the underland… the usual access…"

"Bastile, does the Jerico have their part of the underland?" Heather asked.

"We do," he said. "We have not been able to contact the Vema since the Blitz of Silka City. Are you saying the island is opening up again?"

"I'm saying it's more connected than once thought," Heather said, thinking.

Willa dropped down, and walked around a long table with a few computers on it. As she passed them her chest lit up.

"Hmm," Willa said suddenly. "That is a very cute cat, I have to admit."

"What?" I asked.

It was something about the blue light on his chest triggering a red flag in my brain. I walked/stumbled over to her in a flash to see—

There was a small laptop on blue light filter mode, it had its back to us the entire time and was on such brightness control we hadn't seen it but—it was on. There was a file pulled up and everything. I couldn't believe it. The dust, the dirt, the lack of lights. No one should have been here. I looked down, and saw the footprints, everywhere. Not just from where we'd come from.

"What is it?" Bastile demanded, as Heather and Lynn went quiet, hands up.

"It's… on," I said. "The computer is on."

"It's technology," Willa said. "It's supposed to be on, right?"

"Yes but this is someone's personal computer," I said, panicking.

"So what?" Bastile asked, arms in the air.

"So that means we aren't alone," I said, quietly, claws at my side.

And suddenly it was even colder in that dark sub-basement, even with all of the lights on. We tensed up and took a few steps closer together.

"We should get out," Xero said. "Right caput?"

"Right…" Bastile said, no sign of moving yet.

But while they were talking, I was doing something we hadn't thought to do yet. I lowered myself to the floor, looked under the desk… and found a man. He was skinnier than any jungle vet we'd seen, like emancipated, captive skinny, with glasses thicker than his bones, a dirty pair of cargo jeans that looked stuffed with tools (or worse), and the remains of a white button up shirt that he hadn't even bothered to button. I stared at him, and he stared at me. His eyes dashed to a big red button there underneath the desk with him, and he saw me see it too.

"Don't do it," I said.

"What's happening?" Derek called, the first to understand. "Oracle?"

"I detect only the eight of you," she said.

"You're wrong," I said, looking down at the guy, already sweating.

He looked at me with a mixed expression, fear, and pain, or hatred, something poisonous like that. He held a weird gameboy-like device in one hand, but I didn't really care about that—not when his other hand was already reaching for the big red desk button.

"No!" I shouted.

And then someone picked the entire desk up with one hand. Xero. The guy underneath threw his hands over his head, as the eight of us circled him with everything from swords to fists to claws aimed upon him. Bastile kicked his hand so hard the gameboy-like device tumbled out of his hands and right towards me, as Willa pounced on him with rope before he could scream. He was outnumbered and tied up, on his stomach on the floor with a length of Willa's chainmail dress fabric stuffed in his mouth so hard he was already bleeding.

"Found you," Xero said, towering over the guy, holding the metal desk in one hand. "Willa, get that out of his mouth. I want to hear him—hey."

And just as I was shaking my head (and pocketing a weird gameboy-like device), we heard whistling from up those stairs. We froze, torn between the guy on the ground and the footsteps above.

"What is this?" Bastile seethed.

The captive on the ground shoved Willa away and spat the fabric out of his mouth—before she landed on him, pinning his head to the ground. He cried out as the metal stung his cheeks, but his cries turned to a wicked laugh on a dime.

"All a game," he said, the first words we'd heard from the skinny, half-clothed hiding guy. "It's all about the game."

I was stunned, but just like my mission to decipher a bunch of star charts, there was no time. A figure emerged from the hallway, cutting our only exit off. It was clearly a young male in a full bodied Infinite supersuit, the kind I'd seen Alcyon and delta unit wear, not at all like the more blue-based slimlines that we usually wore. He wore a full facial shield, a dark covering from forehead to chin, ear to ear, making it impossible to see who was behind it.

"And you are?" Xero asked, the weight of the desk nothing to a Champ.

The figure's answer was to blow through the metal railing to rush Xero, the rods coming apart at his sides and legs. Xero swung the desk just in time, sending the figure into the wall beside us for the momentum. Xero followed up by throwing the desk after him, taking out an entire side of the wall.

"That's impossible," Heather said. "Even the Reaper—"

"I am not Reaper," Xero said kindly.

Right. The only soldiers that could ever match the Infinite, and barehanded to boot. Talk about shirts and skins (we were skins). With a roar, the Planetarium creaked, sunlight poured in, and the Infinite soldier was gone—for the moment.

"He'll be back, move!" Xero shouted.

We leapt to it, Bastile grabbing the tied up guy on the ground and slinging him over his shoulder like Xero had done to Elyia.

"YOU'LL NEVER TAKE ME ALIVE—wait why is this so comfortable?"

"JericoOO!" Willa shouted, losing no time.

I grabbed the laptop on the way out, seeing as we had the owner in tow too, and we bolted up the stairs. Lynn and Heather were the last, and they looked over the banister to see the Infinite super-agent come blasting back through another wall, glaring at us with some kind of blue thunder rolling in his eyes, hovering off the ground until even Xero had to acknowledge it.

"Go!" Xero shouted.

He squared up against the guy, his hands empty but balled, his feet spread, weight ready. Horse stance. Heather cried out for him, but Lynn had her by the hand and didn't let go. Then it was the agent's turn to shove Xero through a wall or two, and with a blast, they were both gone.

"He'll DIE IN THERE!" Heather shouted, yanking against Lynn's hand to no avail, finally succumbing to the all-out retreat.

"He won't," Bastile said quietly, on autopilot, or just focused. "But we will."

We sprinted back through the halls and didn't stop until we were back in room alpha, racing towards the rope dangling from the ceiling, closer every moment, wait too close—

"Trap," I said, blinking.

"AH!" Willa shouted.

She was hit in the face by the rope as it was thrown into us by another figure standing in Infinite attire, waiting for us in a combination of stationary dread and a blurring canon of an arm. Bam. So much for an escape rope, or hope. Willa threw the severed rope off and skidded to a stop in time to dodge the blur of a blade as it slammed into the ground right where her next foot would have gone, and she looked up to see another. Same suit, same facial shield, I would have assumed misdirection, if not for Xero still shouting and smashing things behind us.

"You're fast," the figure said.

"Thanks mate," Willa said, her hand twitching over her sword, all but frozen.

"Who are you?" Lynn shouted, her claws up.

The guy only looked sideways at her, and stepped away from Willa as she unsheathed her sword, as the Infinite agent pulled a gameboy like device out of his pocket—just like the one I had in mine. Interesting.

"Ready?" He taunted.

"Bet," Willa said, holding her ground.

"No!" Lynn shouted.

Too late. He pressed a button, and suddenly the lights were flickering, the screens dashing in and out of static, the world sinking smaller. Then our necklaces roared to life harder than ever, turning the world an emergency purple, as our wings fought to stay unfurled, the struggle sending shudders and spasms down my back, until—it was over. The electricity of the place was gone. The lights were dead, it was only the purple glow from here out.

"That sucked," my brother said honestly, but we stood our ground.

"Interesting," the guy said, throwing the gameboy to the ground, taking his sword with both hands. "So that's why we couldn't trace you. Al natural."

"You make it sound like we're going commando," Derek said.

"We're not?" Heather asked. "That sounds badass."

"I'll explain later," I said to her.

The agent advanced, the power in his jet boots coming at us at thirty miles an hour. My claws came up, one regular, one sideways, and together they made a pretty good shield. I caught his blade as the wings came out behind me for leverage, and I didn't give an inch. I flew my body weight forward and shoved the guy back so hard he tripped over his own feet, the jets firing at the absolute wrong time, and he sent himself into the wall.

"I guess I'm the distraction," I said.

"Can you handle it brother?" Derek asked, Willa jumping into his arms before he had to say another word.

"Always," I said. "I'll meet you at horses."

"I'll hold you to horses," Derek said. "Let's go Killa."

"Thanks hope," Willa said.

"What is my command?" Bastile asked, seemingly to me.

"Survive, sir," was all I said. "Hands up."

And before he knew what was happening Lynn was there, not even landing, just scooping Bastile up in his rugged rock arms and flying him out in a blink.

"Aaaah!" Bastile cried (but held on tight) all the way to the hatch, and out.

And they were gone—just as the Infinite was back.

"I could have sworn I counted different," the agent said, looking around.

"Right here," I said, bringing the eyes of the agent on me. "All you get."

"They won't get far," he said. "What have you done, James?"

"Nothing yet," I said. "Honest. You didn't give me enough time."

"Time is not your friend," the agent said. Then he proved it.

With a crack, with a motion blur that warped the world, the lightning came down on me. I barely hit my wings in time. I arced high into the air, smashing into and off the ceiling as the lightning followed, destroying two of those high-mounted monitors, and as the glass and sparks rained down in the atrium, I took a hallway (any hallway) and flew off at maximum effort into a darker part of somewhere I hadn't even been yet.

"YOU CAN'T RUN!" the lightning shouted behind me.

"Bet," was all I said—quietly, of course.

The figure flew just as fast as me, shaking the already rotting wooden walls in our close-quarters race, the hallway shrinking in size as we sped deeper, my wings starting to clip the edges of the wall, the Infinite starting to catch up.

"Come ON!" I shouted, taking the turbulence, forcing myself forward—

And the walls closing in on me were gone, a light had come and went, and the room opened up into an underground cave with size enough to fly over the machines, as long as I avoided a few fuselage hoses coming down from the ceiling.

"Still ended up in the generator room," I said, nodding, soaring over it in just the slightest bit of wonder when—

Bam. A white hot bolt of something chipped a section of rock armor away from my leg, the impact like someone had taken a baseball swing at my leg.

"No wonder no wonder!" I shouted, the fear up, the lightning right behind.

I focused every bit of energy into re-expanding those bent Reaper wings to full tilt, and then I was blasting off again, zig-zagging through the machines, sideways through two parallel towers, through the energy hoses of what looked like a two story vacuum; soon enough I had a bunch of weird machines between me and the soaring sound I was hearing at my back.

At least I was drawing him away. The others would get out. The distraction would work, the distance would help. As for me?

"I need to hide," I said to myself. "Wait—really?"

I should have expected the hand on the arm. Of course. I'd thought my flight plan unpredictable, I'd made a decision without asking anyone else, which totally meant that she had been here with me the entire time, just a single, much smarter step ahead.

"Turn out the lights," came the invisible voice of Heather.

Right. Power of suspenders—I mean invisibility. In a flash, I was no more. My body disappeared, and in the purple outline next to me only visible to those who wore the necklace, I saw Heather beside me—just in time, as the Infinite figure darted out over the machine I was standing behind. He looked all around, he scanned the grounds around us and over our heads like there was nothing to give us away, he even touched a hand to that huge facial visor screen and we heard the beeps from all the way down here. Because this was normal.

"YOU CAN'T HIDE!" The suit shouted.

"Who we up against?" I asked, keeping it short.

"Infinite," Heather said. "But they seem inexperienced. Must be young."

"Too short for Odd, too stocky for Hannah," I said. "This is something else."

"At least we've got you back for it," Heather said. "Bout time, yeah?"

"I HEARD THAT!"

And we split apart just as a laser blast burned a hole through whatever huge mechanical device it was we'd been hiding behind. There was a groan that shook the entire building, but nothing exploded—yet. Heather closed her eyes as we grabbed each other and launched sideways, ending up twenty feet from the blast and closer to the agent than before, but we were still invisible. All we had to do was keep quiet and stop sweating. We were holding each other harder than we ever had before (actually this might have been a first), basically twenty feet underneath the furious agent, his palms still glowing with electricity, looking everywhere for us as we just tried not to breathe.

"Okay maybe you can hide," the agent said, taking a deep breath, touching his wrist and speaking low. "Agent to agent. Full honesty, I think I've lost the twin. Where is the giant?"

"On route," the response came, clear as day. "Full honesty, I was just about to ask you for help. He's not going down easy."

Heather was right. Whoever these two were, they reminded me of us. Not me and Heather, but me and Derek. Two young, inexperienced minds in two omnipotent supersuits. It didn't always a good combination make. And just as I was thinking about unparalleled destruction—

Boom. The wall we were closest to burst apart over us, as Xero flew out and slammed into some unwieldy machine, screaming to wrench himself loose. I saw the other agent follow him out of the hole in the wall, as the one above us looked delighted to see Xero stumbling up, his torso bloody, his hair damp already, looking like that machine wasn't the first thing he'd hit.

"Okay so we wait for the opportune moment and get him out, simple," I said, before blinking. "Is it snowing?"

"Worse," Heather said, grabbing my hand.

The agent over our heads was looking straight down, at the debris crumbling around the unbroken outlines of two small figures. Us.

"Found you," he said.

He fired at a small coil by the machine closest to us, which just happened to be like, comically full of motor oil. We were instantly pressure-pepper-sprayed with enough black dye to render invisibility moot on any level.

"Oh come on!" The agent overhead shouted.

He flew backwards, covered in the stuff himself—which probably saved our lives. Xero fell to his knees in a growing puddle, gasping on the ground, as both agents landed over him, free of the oil spray. I had to do it. I pressed a hand to my gemstone, and watched my body blink back into the visible world, soaked in gross black oil from head to toe. I didn't care too much—until I saw the streaks on Heather's face, in her hair and down her arms.

Still, we looked worse than we felt.

"You good?" I asked.

Heather nodded, and spat oil onto the ground. I did too.

"Me… first," Xero said, struggling to stand in the slippery puddle.

"Fine," one of the agents said, stepping down on Xero's back without mercy, smashing his head into the slick floor. "James Nite, Heather Denien. You are wanted in the city of Silka, and that was before all the trespassing. You have proven unworthy of arrest, by way of deception and escape, multiple times."

"He's right, we don't do handcuffs," I said.

"You're proving our point. We have no alternative to bringing you in dead."

"What if we surrender like, I don't know, twelve percent?" I asked.

"We don't negotiate with traitors," the taller agent said.

"You're assuming Issaic Nite is okay with this," Heather asked, hail mary.

The second agent brought his hands (lasers) up. "He'll understand."

"Liar," Heather said, standing her ground, as I was lost, for the moment, I was frozen. The wrong moment. I saw the white light.

"I said… me first."

Suddenly the biggest warrior here wasn't struggling. He lashed out with both feet in a move that ended up with both agents on the ground and Xero flipping to his feet, towering over them both. He leaned down with a terrifying, slick, black-toothed grin, grabbed them both by the collar, and easily threw them both back through the hole in the wall he had made.

"James, need you now," Heather said, her hand on my arm, right—

"Here," I said, officially snapping out of it. "How'd you know he was—"

"I can tell when a man's lying to me," she said. "He'll kill us James, he wants it so bad he's willing to spite Issaic to get it. Whoever he is, he's more dangerous than your father."

"Okay Xero, let's get out of here. Put your hands up, now."

"You're going to teach me how to fly?" The Champ asked.

"I don't have to," I said, willing four rocks out of the ground with all the heart I had to muster, holding them steady in front of Xero. "Hold on."

"I'd slow you down too much," Xero said, pushing the rocks aside. "I'm a big guy, if you haven't noticed."

"A big buy with a big heart," Heather said, her eyes blurring over.

"I'll say two things," Xero said to us. "Thanks for showing me how to be a hero. Now get the hell out."

"Don't you dare," I said. "You hold on, right now."

"You let go," Xero said, looking at me fondly, sadly. "Right now."

"Not like this," Heather said, starting to panic, very slightly. "Xero—

"Right now," he said.

He was staring up at the sun, like maybe he wasn't even talking to us anymore. But the time for maybe was gone. The oil was releasing around my body, every ounce of the material coming off me like reverse rain. Heather was the same. She frowned to me, as the ugly tar-colored liquid hit the ground all around us. Then—in that moment a few things happened. Before we could heard the crash coming, the agents had blasted out of another section of the wall and came roaring for Xero. Heather grabbed me by the shirt, only it wasn't Heather, it was Lynn. She had us both by the shirt.

"Don't make a sound," Lynn said.

I didn't have to look back, I was facing back. Lynn had given us no choice but to bail, to soar upwards at whatever speed she chose for us. Xero didn't look around in confusion, he didn't scour the air, he simply looked straight at us like he could see us… and he smiled.

"Not like this," Heather said, yanking herself free, letting her wings—

But it was too late.

Xero was still smiling when a hand from each agent lit up in the opposite of light, in a focused beam of dark energy that took the big guy from both sides, back and chest, so powerful he was lifted off the ground almost ten feet. Heather was free but she stuck close to us in shock, as silent as Xero, both of them refusing to scream, as the blasts found their way out of the opposite sides of his body. The next thing I knew, I was invisible. I didn't chose it, maybe Lynn made it so, maybe we'd flown far and fast enough for most of the oil to air off. All I knew was my mouth was about to betray the sole purpose of invisibility, but then Heather was back, and she had her hand over my mouth, and hard. I put a hand up to counter, but she grabbed that too, and squeezed it tight.

"Mhm," I cried into her hand, the best I could do. It meant—

"I…" Heather said, as low as I'd ever heard her. It meant…

Unseen to the visible world, we watched Xero hovering there in the crossfire until the blasting stopped, the agents holding their hands out like they were burning, and the giant man fell ten feet to his knees, looking back at us (again, with an alarming accuracy given the sheer distance and now invisibility), holding something in his hand. A single, lit torch.

"That's not FAIR!" One of the agents shouted.

I didn't know what to do. I wasn't sure if there was anything I could do. My eyes filled with tears. I knew what was about to happen. I knew what I had to do. It was the absolute opposite of what I wanted. Lynn, Heather, they were only doing everything they could to get us out of there. I think it was time I let them.

"Xero…" I said, looking at him like a child.

"Live, little ones," were Xero's last words.

"NOOO!" I shouted, breaking the whole point of invisibility.

But there was nothing we could do. The agents fired again, Xero dropped the torch, and both sides disappeared into the explosion.

Boom.

"It's not happening," I said.

"ARE YOU TRYING TO DIE HERE?" Lynn shouted to us.

Xero's body was lost in slow motion to the flames that only grew larger as they consumed one oil-soaked machine after another, engulfing the two agents and already thundering towards us up the hallway as Lynn easily (while roaring and cursing) still dragged me by the collar up and over towards that ceiling access/hallway exit out of the generator room. We narrowly made it through at mach 1.2, Lynn was shouting something at me, the fog was keeping her words from getting through, all I saw were Heather's dirt and claws and wings tearing through the world, watching her like I was sitting backwards on the crazy train—what else was new? Then I blinked for the first time, and Lynn's shouting came through, as did the raging winds of the hallway, and the absolute breaking going on behind us.

I was back—ninety eight percent of me, at least.

"We gotta go," I said.

"YOU THINK?" Lynn and Heather shouted at me from all sides.

I stopped resisting, the hallway expanded out towards the atrium, and I took to the sky (tunnel) like we were trying to outrace armageddon (we were). For a moment the hallway behind us seemed normal. Then there was a rumbling, and the warmth was being sucked out of the air as we flew.

"Bad," Lynn said.

"Faster," Heather grimaced.

Then the fire came out of the ground itself, taking out the hallway brick by brick, the same firelight glow coming out of the other hallways, and we were screaming as we were flying, dodging the falling rocks and freezing the boulder-sized pieces of metal in place that otherwise threatened to bury us.

"It didn't happen," I said to myself, shaking.

"FASTER!" Heather shouted to me.

Detritus came down on our heads yet still, somehow, we raged out of that hallway, back through room alpha, and up the escape hatch without stopping, anywhere away from that rolling thunder about to break, but we were fifty feet in the air before we realized the gigantic metallic telescope was following our retreat angle, and starting to shake something terrible. We couldn't catch a break. Even up here in the air we felt the vibrations of the Planetarium as it shattered from the ground up, sending out fireballs that skimmed our feet no matter how high we flew.

"It never happened," I said.

Lynn gave me a single worried look among the flight. Heather must have heard too because she stayed close by as we outflew the explosion in close pursuit behind, as we arced far enough over the cliffside banks we'd come from us to finally see it all, from a single, bird's eye perspective.

"Say goodbye to the beach," Lynn said, through the tears.

It was true. Both the Planetarium and the cliffs it was built on were destroyed, but that wasn't it. All that destruction needed somewhere to go, and it had chosen that perfect crescent cove below the mountains. Down there, the water was black and boiling, and sharp bits of metal littered the sands, the shore, as far out as the coral probably. Above the beach, the cliffs were a massive fireball and cloud of smoke, the world's worst signal fire. I had no doubt the smoke could be seen from Silka. I actually was about to scream, when I saw something else that stopped me. It was Derek.

He waved at me, from the ends of the once solid thirty-yard banks of a certain jungle river. Now the cliffside edges were starting to come apart from the rest. Best guess, a fireball had crashed into the base of the mountain and started a landslide. The entire slope was giving way, and Derek was pointing to a certain part of it. The horses, tied to a shaking tree, and half of our group, already far from the horses, already about to fall off the edge of the new world.

No rest. Not over.

"DOWN!" Heather shouted.

She flew off to pluck Astor up by his own suspenders, as Derek shot by for Ollux, who was holding onto the trunk of the tree closest to the horses. He shredded the lashes with claws and the horses cried in terror, bolting for the water out of fear and instinct. Derek was right behind them with Ollux in tow. Lynn dived low for Willa.

"Lynn, where is he? It's all crumbling into the ocean, WHERE IS XERO?"

"JAMES!" Bastile shouted from the ground.

Right. He was falling down, sliding on a piece of land already almost vertical, a single hand stretched out before it went tips up—but in a flash of rock and wing I was there, and flying away with his wrist in mine, his feet dangling until they wrapped around me in an extremely inappropriate fashion. I didn't break, I shot for the horses and joined the mad dash to avoid the breaking, by galloping, sprinting, or flying. I saw Bombelle waiting for us, standing guard over a small guy in a hogtie, which meant all were accounted for… save one. Then the mountains gave way, burying the remains of the Planetarium in less time than it had taken for my mind to comprehend it happening.

Ash in the air. Fire in the sky. The burning, the smell of rubber, the shock, the accounting for all but one… it was back.

"It's happened again," I said, finally finishing the thought killing me.

Astor, Willa, and Bastile crumpled to the ground, but Heather, Lynn, and I crash landed, our wings barely retreating in time, the dirt around our limbs slowly eroding, pieces scattered here and there for the smashing.

"This has happened before?" Bastile asked, a hand out to me on the ground.

I took it and stood up, letting go of her hand in favor of Heather's. I found her shaking behind me, literally watching the world burn. The edge of it, at least.

"Where is Xero?" Willa asked again, turned away from us.

"He…" Heather couldn't speak.

"He… chose us," I said. "He saved us. I didn't expect him to."

"To seize the moment?" Bastile said quietly. "He knew his mission, it was to protect you to the end. We couldn't have asked for more. He was always a hero."

"And now he's dead," I said, my mind slipping. "And any chance of finding out what was happening here…"

"Burned to the ground," Heather said, looking down the edge of a new cliff, a good fifteen yards closer now. "So he did his job. Is that a win?"

"How could it be?" Bastile said, sad as ever, seeing no victory in anything.

He wasn't the only one.

SAND FREEDOM

3.0

THE STRENGTH TO GO ON

I moved dead trees from dawn until dusk, and I still had another day to go.

It was the same soldier that kept coming up to me. The someday soldier. Not that he would never be one, but he hadn't been yet. Not a single face was familiar, but all were fresh-faced and hopelessly outmatched, all somehow thinking they were different. They were watching me, from the trees around the crash site. They would talk to each other every time another one had a go. One time they even grouped up, four of them, as if they'd forgotten I had a big pile of sticks to my back. Once the battlefield was defined, taking four down at once only took for times as long. Four seconds. As for me, I would simply carry the fallen soldier(s) to the third pile, look sadly back at the others, and carry on.

I didn't see it as them interrupting my penance. They were the penance. My work wouldn't be over when that tall pile of tree branches and dead leaves was moved. I would forever be figuring out just what to do with that third pile.

"Excuse me," came a voice.

It was a woman. An old one. She was close, and I hadn't heard her. She looked up at me with a small, sad smile. She was trying her best. I did the same.

"Ma'am," I said. "Do we fight?"

"Not yet," she said. Honesty. So rare.

"Did I kill your kid?" I asked.

"Not yet," she said. "He came home yesterday with a split jaw. It'll take weeks before I hear his sweet voice again."

"I remember the split jaw kid," I said, wincing. "I should have caught him."

"He said the same, or less," she said. "The rock got me. Not the Sand."

"I'm sorry," I said. "He seems like a smart kid. You're a lucky mom."

"Aunt."

It was all she had to say. The weight was back. Not like it had ever left. Everyone who came into this forest to find me, to fight me, had lost someone close in the war. It was almost comforting, knowing that even in death, the living still stood strong, that those who left us weren't even really gone. Everyone who stepped into this grove was doing so for someone else. Because the ones I had actually wronged… they weren't here to fight me for it.

"So I killed one of his parents," I said.

"You did them both," the woman said. "Do you have kids, Freedom?"

I looked down. How could I answer that?

"That's a no," she said. "Some advice from a woman who used to be a sister. Don't talk about things you don't know. Kids, family, least of all, brothers."

And suddenly she was a step outside my reach, holding a loaded bow and arrow at my chest. I blinked, and stood there, between a bunch of leaves, a pathway my bare, bleeding feet had carved into the jungle, and... the third pile. I looked lamely at the leaves behind me, the part of the forest that used to be a forest, before we'd let Issaic and his dogs crash us here, of all places, in a world trying to heal, an old fool with a fake name trying not to cause any more hurt...

"You are doing this because you know in your heart you don't belong," the woman said. "You gave all that up long ago. For the rest of my life, when I hear that boy speak, I will remember the day you almost took that away from him."

I didn't move. I'd seen it in her eyes. Her mind was made up. The arrow loosed, the wind raged, and the metal spearpoint stopped against my chest at the first serrated tip. It got me, but only by a centimeter. Man I was getting old.

"You..." the woman said.

"I," I said, holding the arrow in the fist I'd caught it in. "No weapon can break me, though I'll admit you and your son have now collectively gotten closest. Maybe I can have my personal medic pay your family a visit."

"Just us?" The woman asked, looking over at all the boys helping each other limp out of the grove, the jungle gift that kept on giving.

I growled, but nodded. "Fine. You get the collective ego of Jerico's young soldier men in check, and I'll have Magellan himself make the rounds while I finish up here by tomorrow, so we're all ready for the next nine hundred and ninety nine times an old fool breaks his spaceship off against your trees."

"I think my job's harder than yours," the woman said.

"I think we're both equally capable of anything," I said.

She lowered her bow. "You know the trees are not our problem with you."

"I know," I said. "I'll make it right. Before I die, I promise I'll make it right."

"How long do you think you'll live, Freedom? How can someone like you grow so old, when so many others have died so young?"

It was a good question. I looked up at the sky, then the ground, and around, at the very apparent lack of anyone here with me. Friends, acolytes, weird mysterious twins, they were all elsewhere. Story of my life.

"Let's put it this way," I said, for some reason choosing honesty to a stranger. "If I could die, I already would have. But I can't. Not yet. There's one thing I have left to do before I give you my death. Until then, no bow and arrow can stop me. No Jerico can stop me. Nothing on this island can stop me."

"Not even Nite?" The woman asked, her eyes holding mine curiously.

"No," I said, putting something into the world that for the last half century had only been a thought. But for the first time, I was confident enough to stand by it. I meant it. Every word.

"Not even Nite."

PART III

3.1

WHO THIS IS FOR

Willa was on the ground.

"He's..." she said, unable to finish her own thought.

She had been our rock steady, now she was as close to the edge as she could be. We all were, the edges had literally gotten closer. Willa's face was locked on the smoking crater, her eyes stinging for the ash in the air—or more. As much as the sides of the mountain had crumbled, the landslide hadn't gotten far enough to reach the river, thankfully. How bad would that be, if we diverted the entire river by blowing up a beach—which we hadn't, but so much had crumbled into the ocean, leaving actual burn marks on the sand, it was enough wreckage for the next few crash sites. From up here, looking down to first an inferno and second a blue lagoon on fire, it was too much. It was like seeing a glimpse of paradise right on the other side of hell. And they were both burning the same.

"It's not fair," Willa said, wiping her eyes and standing up.

"I'm not arguing," Bombelle said.

She and Willa held each other in the quietest breakdown I'd ever seen. The fact that they weren't bawling was somehow worse. They flinched when Bastile came up and put his hands around them.

"I... thought we were family," Bastile said.

Those were Xero's words.

Ollux sniffed, and nodded. She and Astor joined, their heads down, as Bastile awkwardly tried to comfort four people at once. His mistake was thinking that was his job. Somehow, the group found itself, and collectively, they were going to be as okay as five people could be.

But that was just the Jerico. As for the strangers (that was us), I was less sure. I had the ringing of a thousand bad guitar chords in my ears. The rock armor had come off and left me feeling lighter and smaller than I'd ever been.

"I can still see it," James whispered. "The way both agents switched tactics in a blink, choosing to pool their power, using it to cut down the more offending enemy, no hold back, no arrest. I can feel... the beams of light carving through him. I can see him standing, with that torch. I can hear him..."

"Hear him use his last breath to keep us alive," Heather said, barely a sound.

"How many…" I said, my voice breaking worse than Willa. "How…"

I thought I was going to cry, my throat had closed up so quickly. Then I felt a hand on my shoulder, and someone hit the grass next to me. It was James.

"How many have died for us?" He asked.

"None like him," Willa said, staring at us, trying not to hate us, I could see it.

"Every one too many," I said.

Willa disappeared back into Bombelle's shoulder, shaking.

"I can't repay it," James said. "He saved my life, I can't even thank him."

"If you died for me James, would you do it for a thank you?" Bastile asked.

"I don't know," James said. "I don't know what a hero would do."

I saw my brother, but I saw something else too. Someone who was doing a much better job of processing his feelings, or at least keeping his head on straight while subjectively drowning in them, like we all were. Like I was.

"Is it enough?" I asked. "Is what we're doing so important that this is okay?"

"No," James said. "None of this matters, no numbers or letters are worth it."

"Agreed, except for one part," Bastile said. "This all must matter. Those numbers and letters must be worth it. He died for something."

"We'll see," I said. "I'd give them all back for him."

"You can't," Bastile said, sadly.

I could make all the bargains I wanted, but unless I was going to rewind time, Xero wasn't coming back. He had died in the planetarium, but the two agents probably hadn't. That was just coming from experience. There was no longer any reason to be here other than to get caught (or worse). It wasn't like help was on the way. It was just us, and there was only one thing I could do—keep thinking about what I could do. Nothing else.

"Heather," James said, suddenly. "Speaking of what we can do."

She looked at him like someone needed to slap her back to life, which of course Lynn did, gently, because she was in tune with the universe. Heather nodded, and we all walked to the edge in arms, literally.

"I can sense the body," Heather said. "I could make a rock tomb around his… remains. It would be the size of a coffin. I could levitate it back up the river but after that, it would be on us to carry it back to Oleander."

"Does he have family in Oleander?" I asked.

"Everyone who knew him enough to care at his passing is here," Bastile said. "Speaking as someone who knew him…"

"He always wanted to be buried at sea," I said.

Willa's eyes flickered. Heather's hands summoned a purple aura that defused around her on that clifftop. No one spoke, we just watched the dirt move, searching over the exposed hallways and down through the foundation like there was a fire raging just below the surface—until the fire stopped, and a rock rectangle emerged from the ground. It was as long as Xero had been tall, hovering up to us over the exploded remains of the planetarium.

"That's close enough," Willa said.

Heather held.

"A hero's end. Nothing less. Nothing…" Bastile said.

I thought he was being wise, but the next thing I knew he was fully doubled over Bombelle's shoulder, crying louder than any of the girls had, as Heather only tried to keep her hand from shaking the rocks in the sky. It was our turn to rally around the captain, and in true fashion James remembered not to leave Heather out, with a hand on her arm, right where Lynn always took mine. We stood there in the purple sunset, watching the dirt fly farther and farther away from us, out into the ocean, where it was finally far enough away to collapse, hitting the crystal clear water with no sound, not delayed, not ever. We were too far away to hear it.

And that was it.

There was a lot of silence that came with the slow walk back to the horses, the emotionless boarding of the river craft, seeing the empty saddle aback Ufwelle who somehow seemed just as sad as the rest of us. We turned our backs on the calamity and sailed away upriver in slow motion just as the first of the rain started, light at first, then a downpour. But the river flowing against us was nothing compared to whatever rocky hold Heather had the ship in. Lynn walked over and held her hands the same as Heather. Heather moved her right wrist sideways, and Lynn's necklace lit up to match Heather's. They were learning.

We sailed in silence until we were looking at that small rocky waterfall, the one we'd rallied around after the attack in Arum. It was so familiar it almost wasn't. I almost couldn't believe I'd been here before.

"Hey."

I didn't have to look. I could sense James next to me on the black-bodied Ekapian, already in step with the coarse brown hair of Seanderthal. The girls had gone from river pontoon to flying, enjoying the last of the air before it was over. We had taken the horses. For some reason, I didn't feel like flying.

"You weren't there, you deserve to know," James said. "Xero's last words. They were… live, little ones. He was talking about us."

"Did you think it didn't hurt enough?" I asked.

"I know that's sarcasm."

"Yeah," I said, shutting up. "What happened in there?"

"We didn't fight," James said. "We didn't even try."

We were a different kind of quiet after that. Until—

"Hold," Heather said.

She and Lynn landed suddenly in front of the horses, who didn't seem to mind in the slightest. It was the first she'd spoke for a few miles.

"We're nowhere," Bastile said. "Why hold?"

"You see that half stump right there?" Heather said, pointing low. "I knew the second I crossed it I was back. That stump is the line."

"What about it?" James asked.

"I need to decide if I can do more good here or back in Vema," Heather said, looking at that stump. "On one side of it, we can do anything. On the other…"

"What could we do in Vema?" James asked.

"Find some actual help," Heather said.

"Wasn't that the one thing we weren't supposed to do?" I asked, sadly.

"So you're saying a message could accomplish the same thing," James said.

"Yes, and yes," Heather said. "But the Vema are far fashioned, and old away. I don't know how the young people are communicating these days."

"Easy, tiny scrolls tied to trained seahawks, I got you," Lynn said, holding a hand up in jest, but then a literal messenger hawk landed on her hand.

No joke. No metaphor. That bird was a bird.

"No way," Willa said, sniffling a bit, but her eyes coming back to life.

"Not even," Bombelle scoffed, but looking like she was ready for… hope.

"Is someone messing with us?" James asked the jungle.

"Well the joke's on you, because I forgot all my tiny scrolls," Heather said.

The hawk made a sound, pooped all over Lynn's hand, and flew away. We all saw it. It was everything but an answer. But it was the first time we'd laughed in an hour. I was counting chuckles and curved lips as laughter. I could read a face.

"Heyy!" Lynn complained as she made a beeline for the lake, elbow first.

"Was that a joke?" James asked.

"If so, it was a crap one," Heather said. "Or it got scared."

"Should we be scared?" I asked.

"We're not birds," Willa said. "Lynn, don't make us leave you behind."

"Right."

Lynn was back, holding a wet hand out to me on the horse. It was the same hand that… too bad. A girl was asking me for help. I answered the call.

"Hold still," she said, wiping her arm off on the back of my shirt.

All boundaries crossed. I shivered, but got over it. Her crap was my crap, apparently. Was that a metaphor? If so, it was a crap one. Okay done, promise.

"This isn't normal," James said, looking around us. "Heather never asks for favors unless they involve other people, she's earned the right to phone a friend, Lynn was only sticking up for someone who's proved worthy of sticks. I'll ask again, is someone messing with us?"

And the jungle replied, with a sound like laughter. As magical as that would have been, there was still the matter of it laughing at me. Then I realized the laughter was mechanical. It was engine exhaust, not words. Those came next.

"Someone is."

The headlights hit us at the best time—if you were familiar. But the hand of Jerico roared in defense and had weapons aimed at the light before we could blink. Then the car honked once, a blaring alarm in the jungle, and both Bastile and Willa dropped their swords. Yes.

"Meet car," I said.

"Do we fight?" Ollux asked, hands up.

"Unnecessary," Lynn complained, with a small smile, and a wet arm. "Are you here to save us again?"

"Everything apart from flying off into the sunset," the Oracle replied.

"That voice," Bastile asked. "She's here too? But the Planetarium is gone."

"So is the initial response team."

"So they got away, to come after us again, and harder, one day," I said.

"One day? I've thrown them off your trail twice in the last hour."

"This thing is… aiding our retreat?" Bastile asked. "This is normal?"

"This thing usually is our retreat," I said, frowning. "Why no sunset?"

"You are needed right where you are. Infinite is still miles behind. They're looking for horses, but it's hard not to change course when a flying car almost runs you over, in the air, in the jungle. I am needed where I am too."

"Easy to say when you're a talking, flying supercar," James said. "We cross that stump we're back to claws. Again."

"Then claw your way out of it. Again."

"I've read about cars, I just never knew they were this wise," Willa said.

"Please, wise and noble machine," Bombelle said, putting her hands together like she was praying. "Did our efforts at the planetarium… was there a reason… do I just wish upon you or what—"

"I'm still decoding every last readout from the Planetarium, but I don't need a code to detect a shift in the territory's magnetic field. Again."

"Again," Bombelle said, thinking back to her polestar hypothesis. "For the second time in—"

"Fourteen days," Caput and computer said together.

Bombelle's eyes went wide, Bastile held his hand out for the car to sniff it.

"I knew she was the brains."

"I always liked you," Bombelle said, a single tear in her eye. "Teresa."

"I take it as a compliment. But I am not her."

"We sure about that?" Bastile asked, looking sideways at the car.

"Speaking of decoding things," I said, nudging James in the side, and he untucked the laptop from his shirt, the one we'd taken from the underground server room.

"For me?"

"Mmm!"

Right. The laptop probably belonged to that very tied up, muzzled captive worker man, currently trying to shout/bite through the gauze in his mouth. We paid him no mind, he was hogtied on his stomach to the same horse the soldier Kyudo had been, Willa's wild Jeff. He wasn't going anywhere.

"Excellent. Put it in the glove compartment for scanning."

"Keep it," I said. "Jerico would just strip it for parts."

"Hey," Bastile said, eying me. "You're right."

"Mmm!"

"Sorry bro, should have mercy-deleted your browsing history," James said.

"MHMM!" The guy on Jeff cried, shaking his head.

"That bad?" Heather asked, patting him on the back.

"What was he doing to the Territory?" Bombelle asked.

"And Vema," Lynn added. "I felt the pull, the door was open. Something about that place was drawing from the underland."

"To be fair, that's the only way the polestar works," Bombelle said.

"There was a leviathan source of underland power coming off the Planetarium before it was destroyed, yes," the Oracle confirmed. *"However the readings were not calibrated to Jerico. They were set to… something else. Something much bigger."*

"The sun," Lynn said, her voice weak. "I… knew it."

"Precisely," the Oracle said, as all heads turned to her. *"Wait. How—"*

"This isn't about Jerico," Lynn said sadly. "Your polestar picked this place up because it's tapped into the heaviest magnetics readable from the surface of a planet—its sun."

"She's right," the Oracle said. *"Magnetics this massive, instruments set to such stellar coordinates… this man is studying the fallout of a—"*

"A solar flare," Lynn finished with the computer.

"You keep DOING THAT!" Heather asked, afraid, kind of impressed.

"It's a flare?" Bastile said. "He's not aiming some sort of electrical impulse cannon gun on us? He's studying the gun? What could humans do with a flare?"

"What we do to everything in nature," Lynn said, like she's seen a ghost. "Control it like a conduit, or brandish it like a weapon. Most likely, both."

"Oh no," Willa said, paying attention. Ollux, Astor, and Xero looked lost.

"It's possible for such a thing to be… a thing," the Oracle said, trying to make sense of it the same as us. *"What it means for Jerico, that research starts now. But for now, here's what we know for sure."*

There was silence.

"You were waiting for Lynn too, weren't you?" James said.

"I was."

"I'll say it," I said, white in the face. "We're only up against the power of the sun, and those capable enough to harness it. To direct it at places."

"Or away from places, I don't know," the Oracle admitted. *"Right?"*

"Right," Lynn said, all eyes on her.

"What's the word I'm thinking of?" I stammered. "Superflare?"

"Is that a superhero name or a disease?" Heather asked.

"Dibs, wait—ew, nevermind," James said, just reacting, speed of thought.

Lynn looked between them. "When did you two get on the same page?"

"Chapter two," James said bluntly. "Destroy and search."

"Why?" Heather asked.

"Technically we've known her longer," I said, shrugging, Heather beaming.

Lynn took her hand off my arm. I hadn't even realized it was there. Damn.

"So that's what had you thinking backup," James said to Heather.

"That was before the superflare," Heather said, scratching her head. "Now I'm thinking super backup."

"Do you have a request for leader Mare?"

"Two," Heather said. "The dragon scouts Sasha and Volf."

"That's it?" Bombelle asked.

"We're not at war," Heather said. "We don't need an army—not yet. We need confidantes. I need the Vempire to see there's more than one build going on."

"I'm starting to think we still understand each other," Bastile said.

"Right now our nations are half-formed at best," Heather nodded. "We'll need help to finish that form. When did we ever not understand each other?"

Bastile stared at Heather with pride, clear as day.

"Sasha and Volf alone. I don't understand, but… understood."

"They are to meet us at Southern Arbor tomorrow morning," Heather said. "Jerico may welcome them all they want, but they will have a guide waiting for them at the north western end of Commander's Pass, where the maple trees meet the lava rock. They'll be edgier than usual. You'll have to stay sharper."

"Are you telling me how to open a door?" Bastile asked.

But then we heard it. Far off but not that far behind, a splash.

"Six approaching by air, three miles out. Heading up river. I'm sorry. If you want to live, I have to go."

"So do it," I said, with a salute.

The car's headlights blinked, and it was gone. Zoom. Out of the forest, out of our lives. No rescue, no easy way home. The horses wouldn't have fit anyways.

"Was that… a good sign?" Bastile asked.

"Maybe so, maybe not," I shrugged. "What are we deciding, Heather?"

"I'm not exactly sick of you, yet," she said, wheeling on a stump. "Let's go."

"Before we go, does anyone need anything magicked?" Lynn asked.

"You're not kidding, are you?" Bombelle asked.

"We aren't anyone's answer, usually," Lynn said quietly. "Anyone?"

"We're good," Bastile said, looking back to us fondly. "You are too, right?"

"Always," James said. "Let's get back and decide for ourselves if we've accomplished anything. Man, if Sand had dinner ready right when we got back… can you imagine?"

"Don't remind me of food," I said. "How much longer till topline?"

"A few hours," Bastile said. "Here."

He handed James a small pouch, damp with sweat, but clean on the inside, and full of fruits and nuts. We were hungry, it was instinct. James had a handful, and man it looked good. But then I looked closer, and put my hand on my brother's wrist, calmly, almost like no one had seen it. Because they hadn't. When James looked at me funny, I only shook my head.

"Mmm, food," I said loudly.

It was innocent, but Astor looking right at James wasn't. He saw his hand clenched around the fruit, the bits of glowing blue just visible through the nuts and berries, like a fine, powdered coating. My hand on his wrist. Then he looked back at how close we were to that stump. Or more accurately, how close he was.

"Yeah, don't eat that," I said.

"Why?" James asked, his hand an inch from his mouth, but very afraid.

"Get him," Lynn said, a step ahead of both of us, like usual.

And she bowed over on that horse, letting me spread my wings and take the sky for Astor in a flash. I grabbed him by the throat with both hands and let my wings push us up into the air, his fingers desperately clawing at the rock armor coming over my wrists. I pushed him hard into the first tree on this side oft the stump I could find, took that tree to the ground, and slammed him into the dirt so hard the leaves came down on us like snow. Then as everyone collectively realized what was happening, I punched him in the cheek and followed through, holding my fist to his face to the tree. Bam.

"WOAH!" Bastile shouted.

"Derek!" Astor yelled, flinching at the surprise volatility. Good.

"Another move and the claws come out," I said.

"I have to ask what you're doing to my brother," Ollux said, her hands up, the only one of the group moving towards me.

"I'm wondering the same," I said, my eyes never leaving Astor. "I was going to fly us up into the trees for a little talk. I no longer trust a single one of you. That includes you, Ollux."

"That's not how it works," Ollux said. "We agreed to trust each other."

"We agreed that either was capable of killing the other, and codified not to," James said, looking at the poisoned trail mix in his hand.

"Derek, you're hurting me," Astor cried wolf.

"I should hurt you," I said. "You just tried to drug my brother. Again."

And that was it. Something changed. I saw it in Astor's eyes. He was caught.

"You didn't," Ollux said, her arms at her sides.

"He did," Lynn said, sniffing the pouch, then she rattled it high in the air. "What, you've never had a cat?"

And like magic, Sophia Sabretooth landed before Lynn, straight out of the trees. Even Ollux took a step back. The sabretooth wasn't walking with a swagger this time, now her shoulders were hunched over and tense, as she took each step with her eyes locked on Astor. She put her giant nose up to the pouch, to James' hand, gave the palm a lick, then gave Lynn a small growl.

"Blueblood," Lynn said.

"No," Bastile said, looking at the crumbs on our hands. "I... my dear..."

"We both, my dear," Bombelle said. "Astor... what have you done?"

"What needed to be done," Astor said, in a different voice.

Like I said. Something changed.

Sophia walked over, as close as possible to Astor's face. He tried to look away but I pushed my fist harder into his cheek, as Sophia opened her gigantic jaw and let out a sound I would never forget. It started as a low rumble, like a jagged purr, then it grew into a drone with demonic vibrato, into a sine wave that had Astor shaking. And that was just the leopard breathing in. As the drone came to an end, Sophia let out a roar more bloodcurdling, earsplitting, heartbreaking, and terrifying than anything these wildlands had ever heard... I hoped.

"What she said," I seethed. "Thought we'd forgotten? Thought enough time had gone by? Did you know my brother came to me at night, in the rain, asking me to help keep him safe from THIS EXACT THING?"

I let my fist off Astor's face, and I realized how tensed he had been. He understood the claws enough to feel fear, I'll give him that. Good.

"Who are you, Derek Nite?" Astor asked. "Who are you, to think the death in the hand is just another casualty? Your glorious purpose just cut a family at the knee. Whatever you're here for, I hope you never—"

It was a setup. I had him by the neck, but his desperate fingers form a fist, and he sent knuckles to my face faster than I thought possible from that angle.

"AAHH!"

I was still on the good side of a stump. My rock armor shielded the side of my face just in time, and though I didn't feel the punch, I felt his bones crumple against my guard. Astor screamed, no longer acting, his neck bulging, and for all he struggled I only rose us up into the air again as he hit me over and over with his other hand. But wherever he touched me turned to rock. I felt nothing.

"What show is this?" Bastile said, looking at me sideways, not at all rushing to Astor's defense, instead watching my armor, my focus.

"Ollux, HELP ME!" Astor cried, feet off the ground, hands on my wrists.

"Not a chance brother," she said, sad and angry at the same time.

"He killed him, THEY KILLED XERO!" Astor cried. "They didn't fight for him. They didn't try to save him. They let him die."

"They did no such thing," Willa said.

There was no one on Astor's side. I knew the feeling. I let my hand go, he took one last unsupported swing at me, and by the way he fell… I could just tell. Both hands were either sprained or broken from his attempts to get through rock. Once he was on his side, he wasn't moving. He hadn't broken his fall, he was still cowering from Sophia… he was done. His ability to harm my brother had been… lessened. It should have been neutralized, but that would mean causing more harm than we were facing. If I took this too far, I would become the bad guy. Simple as that. Sometimes, logic sucked.

"What do we do?" Willa asked the universe.

"Babe," Bombelle reached for Bastile, weak. "I'm hearing colors."

"Who said that?" Bastile said, his eyes glazing right over Bombelle's head, staring at a tree behind her. "Oh. It's just you, blue. Good wood this jungle."

For crying out loud.

"You've drugged the captain," Lynn said, stunned. "Heather, he's drugged the captain."

"How is this happening AGAIN?" Heather said, staring at the adults who now needed help sitting upright on a horse.

"Purposefully," I said, glaring at Astor. "Bastile, I know you're in there, give us one last touch of reality."

Bastile struggled to look around, finding four strangers, a traitor, his wife, and a very apparent lack of a certain hero. Then he saw Willa and reached out for her face like she was within reach, and not a few horses away.

"Wildfire," he said. "I bestow the command of the caput onto you for the next twenty-four hours. Get us home however you can—the best you can. That's my final order. I can feel it, I'm almost gone. I need you. We need you."

"But what about… him?" Willa asked, her eyes huge.

Bastile started to whisper, leaving Willa no choice but to steer her horse up to his. He leaned his weight onto her shoulders, and Willa's eyes went wide.

"Helps to know what?" Willa asked.

Bastile touched his nose, then Willa's nose.

"What about him, what about US?" I shouted, then caught myself. "Sorry. Probably not helping. Not simple."

"It's not going to be simple," Willa said, growling, holding Bastile up with one hand on his horse. "Okay. A lot just happened. I thought we went through it together. Now… I'm not so sure. But after losing Xero, I can't be the reason we lose anyone else. I'm asking for mercy here, for all of us. Can you do that?"

"Meaning can we make it home alongside someone who's tried to kill us, or worse?" James asked, looking at me, and hard.

"Of course we can," I said, looking right back. "Right?"

Astor slowly held his head up, blinking.

"You can?" Willa asked. "How?"

"Experience," I said, grimacing. "This week."

"James, I didn't know, I'm so sorry," Ollux said, kneeling over Astor, just far enough away to make sure he wasn't going to lunge at us.

"Not so sure about that," my brother said. "You're supposed to be our host, but twice now you've let that guy inside my head. You are no guard."

"Well that's only the worst thing you could say to a host, and a warrior—"

"It's not personal," James said. "Not yet. But if we get back alive, if there's a Jerico version of the old reset button, I would ask that of your leader—you know, when he's done tripping. Sorry, I guess it is personal."

"A bit, yeah," Ollux said. "I understand. We can have that conversation."

"We just did," James said.

"Ollux, take the scientist and ride point, so I can watch every move you make," Willa said. "Astor, take the rear with Quixote. We won't leave you out here, as much as I want to. As of now, your service to Jerico is ended."

"You can't do that," Astor seethed.

"Yes... she... can," Bastile said, staring at him, never blinking. "I would have left you. That's why I gave it up. Just in time. Not for me. For you."

Astor was silent as he mounted up, at Willa's direction.

"Good," Willa said. "Derek, with Lynn, all eyes on James. You seem to be his best chance, good job taking the reins for once in your life. Do it again."

I wanted to argue, but she didn't really give me a choice. I let Lynn's foot guide me back to Seanderthal's saddle. But just as I was settling in—

"Lynn, sit backwards and keep an eye on our frenemy," Willa ordered.

"Yes Ma'am," she said.

And while still sitting farthest up in the saddle, Lynn turned around, her legs thrown over mine, couldn't avoid it. Somehow this was better.

"I meant back to back goddamnit—"

"Yes MA'AM!"

"Good?" Lynn asked, the backs of our heads close together, if nothing else.

"I got mad just now," I said, feeling out of body.

"And you looked very tall and strong doing it," Lynn said. "We need that. If we don't look after each other, we'll die out here."

"You're saying next time, bring the claws out sooner?" I asked.

"No," Lynn said. "I'm saying, next time we might not be able to."

She was right.

It was the worst formation imaginable. Bad vibes on all sides. Ollux was the woman who'd welcomed us into the Jerico, and we'd basically just told her to get bent. She was either holding in a hurt unlike anything we'd ever known, or she was in on the gambit and just a better actor that Astor. We couldn't be sure. I kept the trail, Lynn kept eyes on Astor, doing his best to hold onto Jeff's reigns with his busted hands. He was glaring at me the whole time like a fight had started, but hadn't even ended yet, never even blinking as we galloped over the lands from which we'd come, leaving behind all semblance of the team that had gotten to the planetarium. The team that wasn't coming back. The survivors of that team let Ollux lead them (us) through the forest, careful to take the long way around Titan Arum, for fear reasons.

"On guard," Willa called as the path became grass, and grass the path. "We don't know what's out here. Unless you see hunters, don't stop moving."

We galloped harder than ever. Everything else was a blur until the gates of Jerico rose up before us, already opened, not a soldier in sight. We passed through them but did not dismount. As the colossal gates shut behind us, Sophia snuck in at the last moment. I was more interested in that leopard than the spectacle of the wooden wall moving on its own. Priorities. And even though we were within the gates, it wasn't over.

"Hold!" Willa shouted.

We'd passed the gates and come upon a long clearing by a small river. Now that the fauna was trimmed and the ground wasn't full of ferns and trunks trying to trip us, it was obvious to see the body, laying in the leaves, and an old man standing over it—it was the only thing besides the bare tree trunks for a hundred yards. Then the strangest thing happened. I heard wings above us. Not leaves.

"A right commander you make," Ollux said, as her horse skidded to a stop.

"Watch your mouth, and for bears," Willa growled.

I blinked and looked around the grove, scanning for what could have made that sound. Then I saw it, and wished I hadn't. The giant owl had been about to take off, but its gigantic neck swiveled down to face me and we started off, both wings deployed and a single clawed foot raised off the tree branch, its entire body as grey as charcoal, with a face like a ghost.

"Tyto," Lynn said.

It was magnificent. It was also completely terrifying, with ashen wings and a head almost as big as the rest of its body. The face was a single element with two tiny slashes for eyes, the beak so narrow and low profile that I didn't see anything but those eyes on an otherwise mouthless, noseless face.

"Ghost owl," I said.

"Barn owl," Lynn corrected. "But you're not wrong. Here's demons."

"As long as I'm not wrong," I said, eyebrows disappearing into my forehead.

Willa got off her horse and walked towards the body. It was facing away from us, spotlit by a single beam of sunlight coming down through the canopy. But speaking of canopy.

"Please," Willa said, raising a hand to the trees above us.

We were back within the Gates, and so the platform came down out of nowhere, landing right next to the body. The old man standing over it didn't move. Oh right, he was there too. I'd been distracted by the tyto.

"When the jungle cries, we cry," he said. "Tears of crystal—hey, it's you."

"Fellow moonman," Bastile saluted.

"Ah. The blueblood," Owl said, smiling, reading Bastile perfectly. "Enjoy the trip. See you next time, caput."

"I'd better not," Bastile said with a bigger smile.

Willa looked back at us, unsure of what to do. "Is your name Owl?"

The guy nodded.

"No last name?" Willa asked.

"What, like… Owl Capone?" the guy asked.

Willa frowned. "I mean…"

"How about Owl Pacino?"

"Stop it, I get it, you're all there. Okay Owl. What are you doing here?"

"Waiting for you," he said. "I know Bastile. I knew he'd be back. It took you a day. Was it your day?"

"Not really," Willa said.

"Well the jungle is a jungle," Owl said, putting his hands together respectfully. "If it helps to know, Xero is at peace, surrounded by every other hero and heroine we owe this island to. He is home."

"I…" Willa said.

She couldn't finish the sentence. She turned away and wiped her face, as Owl gently put a hand on the body and moved it onto the platform in one go.

"How could you know that?" I asked Owl.

"Intrinsically," he answered, staring me down. "Why?"

Did he know things we didn't? He was speaking our language and everything. I mean anyone with eyes could see the lack of Xero among us, especially someone who'd seen us leave the Oleander with him. Xero was kind of hard to miss. But how on earth could Owl know anything else? Was he saying it for us? Trying to make us feel better? Or could it actually be…

Above me, the wings of the giant tyto owl came over me again as the thing moved branches, swooping low to a small knot of branches only a few yards over our heads. The owl stared at me, like it knew exactly what I was thinking. No way… right?

"I know he's a sore subject, but Kyudo said that David still had family in Ravenna," I said, my eyes on Owl, my thoughts still as stuck on David as they had been since the bridge.

"Thank you Derek," Willa said. "I couldn't quite remember. I had a life in my hands, and in that kind of trance, it's either real easy or real hard to focus. Help me get these two to the hospital with that big red roof, and I'll help you get David home."

"Deal," I said, holding my hand out to Willa.

She helped me down off the horse and we bowed to each other at the same time, accidentally, but it was cute, like soldier and commander cute. Lynn threw her arms up in the air for some reason.

"Ollux, I'm going to need you to tie Astor's feet together," Willa said.

"Um, I already can't feel my fingers," Astor said. "If I fall—"

"How it's gonna be," Willa said. "I already went through the list. Can't send you up early, you might sabotage us. Can't leave you here, you might escape. Can't stop now, you might call for backup."

"What makes you think I won't do all three on the platform?" Astor said.

"Because James is coming with us," Willa said. "And you want what's in his head? Hard to do that when he's dead."

"Also a leopard," Lynn said, as Sophia fell out of a tree as much as she sprinted down it, head first and all.

"Anyone wants to explain, I'm right here," James said, his hands out.

Astor sighed. It seemed like the threat (of Sophia) had worked. "Fine."

"Then less talking, and more goodbye horses," Willa said, from the platform.

"Thank you, wise and noble horses," Lynn said as the rest of us dismounted.

Heather and Ollux maneuvered Bastile and Bombelle, Lynn pet the gigantic Seanderthal on the white nose one last time. Her horse made a happy sound, and then all the horses stomped their feet once, every snout in the room aimed at Lynn, before rearing up and galloping off freely back into the wilderness from which they came. Lynn motioned for Sophia to take their place beside her, and the leopard obliged. She sniffed at James as he walked by, but then James took a knee next to the big cat. I hadn't seen him do that yet.

"Thank you," he said.

The leopard made a low growl, then put its face directly onto my brother's, dragging its cheek across his neck and head. James didn't move his hands, he just held his head there as the cat face mashed him like they were siblings.

"I feel love," Lynn said, wiping her eyes, letting Derek steer her onto the platform. "Heather—you too?"

"I love… animals…" she said, her eyes just as misty.

"And away," Willa said, her eyes dark, the burden of command apparent.

We were ascending. It was a smooth, controlled ascent—for once. We didn't rock and roll, we didn't even need to hold onto anything. One moment we were eye level with those horses that had seen us through everything, the next we were higher over their heads than the birds in the lower trees. Then we were higher than the gates stood, then higher. Lynn and James held Bastile and Bombelle tight, we were already way too high for the loonies. Willa stood alone, thinking, her face stone. I felt what she felt. Not really, but kind of. Actually, not at all.

"Hey Derek," my brother said. "I can walk again."

"I noticed," I said.

"I couldn't walk yesterday."

"Well damn James, it's not like we can do this without you," I said, honestly. "Glad you're back man."

"Me too man," he said.

There was more to be said, but we were within arm's reach of everybody.

"Kiss him!" Heather said, her face a wreck. "That was the sign!"

Ollux was the only one to laugh, a small sound, and she stopped when she saw Willa's closed eyes. Shut down. But truth be told, I had felt like laughing too, if just for a moment. Finally a single bridge platform walkway made itself seen, at least four hundred feet off the ground, and I saw the chipped, stained skateboard leaning against the tree, right where we'd left it. It was the first thing we all saw, but no one said a word about it. James silently took it from the tree and held it at his side, as we walked the road… not home.

It was safe to say that the magic of walking a single, man-laid bridge through the upper later of the jungle was lost on us. Our leaders were silent. The mission and all its glory wasn't worth discussing, not in the current… climate. At some point, the singular focus had turned to getting home. It meant shelter for Bastile and Bombelle. It meant regrouping for Astor and Ollux. It meant Sand and Crete, for us. There was no point denying it. We weren't running home. We had sensed danger, called it out, punched it in the face, and now we were running towards our much stronger friends.

"Almost there," Ollux said, taking point without having to be asked. "When we arrive home like this, will it be a step forward for the Jerico?"

Willa thought on that as we walked, no more horses, no more skateboards. James had two feet on the ground like the rest of us. Was that a step forward for the Jerico? Or was it just for us?

"It was a step somewhere," Willa said. "Only Bastile can tell us what's next. I'm saying this one time, for everyone to hear it. If Bastile doesn't make it through the night, the investigation will start with our own wonder twins."

"You're not talking about us," I said.

"She is not," Ollux said.

"As for the brother twins Nite," Willa said. "You're getting close to what some in the Jerico consider kanaka. That means Ohana, and Ohana means—"

"We know what Ohana means," I said. "We're so close to the end of the journey, what's left between us and all that dinner Sand has ready for us?"

"You have a lot of faith in Freedom," Willa said. "There's one last thing. One tradition of the Jerico we haven't… how do I explain this?"

We ended the pathway, and were at the tops of that long inclined descent that would lead down into the back of Oleander's ancient Solar Temple. We were here. We were back. The circular watering hole, the shouts of the warriors in the trees rushing to put the storm shields up, the grey, black, angry swirling clouds in the distance, wait a minute. We were home, but it was about to—

A horn blasted at the far edge of the Oleander. Yep.

"Storm coming," Lynn said, beating me to it.

"Ten minutes to fall," a voice came.

And for the gigantic shadow that stood up from what looked like a cross legged prayer, my heart leapt. The height, the shoulders, the clothes…

"Xero!" I shouted.

Then I saw the face. It wasn't him. It was a man the same age, with the same mask and clothes, speaking around the same tone. It was different in every way, most of all in the way that he had died. What in the ghost—

"Xero," Willa said, a lump in her throat, but looking at us like she was in charge (she was). "Glad you escaped the landslide. About time you caught up."

"I heard the territory still needed me," New Xero said. "Wait a minute."

The voice wasn't Latin at all. He made some sort of salute to Bastile, who only flickered his eyelids at the guy, from bent over Heather's arm.

"The territory has put me in charge until they recover from the psychoactive effects of the blueblood," Willa said.

"How much of that is true?" He asked.

"All of it," Ollux said. "Were you hoping a man would respond?"

"No, just validating," New Xero said. "Who drugged the caput?"

"That would be me," Astor said, waving an elbow, his hands didn't work.

"My faith in men wavers," New Xero said.

He got in line, as the rest of us were shaken to the core—except for Willa, who kept moving like nothing was wrong, like our mouths hadn't hit the wood.

"We…" I said, unable to go on. Literally.

"Say it again," Heather said, her eyes still wrinkled, and puffy. "Tell me you're the same man who gave his life to four kids he'd known ten hours."

"I am not," New Xero said. "Do we have less problems now? Can we fight for the territory that gave us the bridges we cross, the clothes we wear, and the roof you are retreating to? Or should I give up the decade of my life that got me here for your own… comfort?"

"Yeah, get 'em!" Bastile cheered the new Xero on, in the opposite direction.

"This isn't right," Lynn said. "Xero was… damnit."

"He was," the guy said. "That's why I'm here. That's why I'm not…"

"We know," we all said, sadly. It made sense, in a stupid way.

"Then as we were, the party that left," Willa said. "We're home."

But neither of those were true. Heather and James supported Bastile, Lynn and I helped Bombelle, as Willa and the new guy kept watch on Ollux and Astor. Before I knew it the wooden incline had become stone, the incline ended, and we were walking back into the atrium of the sun temple. All of us. I wasn't about to scream it from the mountaintops, but I still didn't quite understand. I guess I wasn't shy about it. My face was my book.

"It's not a person," Willa said sadly, reading me, seeing I was following without following. "The warriors of the hand. Ollux and Astor the siblings clandestine, Xero the Leviathan, Wildfire Willa, and Lady Bombelle. The brigade does not always serve Bones, but they serve. For hundreds of years the territory has had these names to protect them."

"No one lives hundreds of years," I said.

"People don't," Willa said. "But names do. A warrior that outlives a man, what do you call that?"

"Legend," I said. "Here I thought we were out of the war business."

"Wars aren't won by legends," Willa said, her eyes far off, like there was more to the story. "But people are. Remember who this is for, Derek Nite."

3.2

ALL THE TREES

Legends. That's what this was all about?

No. *Remember who this is for.* That was the last thing Willa left us with, as we walked back into Oleander in a trance, my eyes not even flinching as the low light got even lower. I was used to walking in a world without the sun. Weird.

"They're back," came a familiar voice.

It was skinny skateboarding Shane, the first of the figures in the hallway.

"Is that a casualty?" Bryan asked, stepping up next to Shane.

"He is deceased," Willa called out. "Bring a cart, no emergency."

"You heard her!" Shane shouted.

A few soldiers in the back turned for the atrium, a hundred yards away. The rest of the crowd parted as we walked through, catching open eyes and curious stares as we passed.

"We could use a few emergency carts for Bastile and—" I started.

"I am seeing them to the hospital myself," Willa said, staring at us. "No rest. Not over. You know?"

"Hell," Heather said, looking at her with a step back. "I do."

"Why is the warrior Astor in ropes?" Bryan asked.

"I've been duped," Astor said as he passed, his eyes furious at the judgement. "This is a kangaroo court, I demand trial by fire—"

"Overruled," Bastile said, held up by Heather and Lynn, holding his head up long enough to mime a zipper over his mouth. "Zip."

"Caput…" someone said.

"Explain," Bryan said folding his arms and walking alongside.

"Warrior Astor has been compromised," Willa said sadly.

The group around us blinked, looking for the leader.

"I'm sorry, did you not leave under the command of Bastile?" Bryan asked.

"Our leader has been subjected to the blueblood, at Astor's hand," Willa said. "I am in command of the territory until he regains full function."

"By who's order?" The guard asked.

"By the last conscious order of Bastile himself, would you be asking this if I were a man?" Willa shouted.

And the guards saluted, none faster than the one standing in our way.

"Better," Willa said.

"Not yet," Bastile said, unzipping his mouth, his eyes bloodshot, his pupils wide. "Wildfire speaks for me. I am using every ounce of energy I have not to speak at all, in fear that I'll tell you all about my greatest fears. Chocolate with nuts. That's all of them. Damnit. Zip."

He zipped back up.

"Astor did this?" Another guard asked, a shorter but lean woman with a buzz cut, more worried than angry. "Can we… ask what happened, your grace?"

"You can, but the answer will not be simple," Willa said. "And don't call me grace. If anything, I'm mercy."

"What's the difference?" Heather asked.

"Grace is given altruistically," Willa said. "It's goodwill without qualification. Mercy is goodwill INSTEAD of the other thing you could do. It takes power to give mercy, like not killing you at the gates. Grace would have been food and shelter regardless of who you were or how well you could fight."

"Sounds like we don't deserve either one," I said. "Just being honest, since that's your whole thing."

"You're learning," Willa said.

"What happened out there?" The buzz cut woman said, her hands up. "We felt the earth shake, we heard something from the edges of the territory, now there's another category-three cyclone coming out of the northern capes, and our leader can't stand on his own foot—why?"

"Did you find the Planetarium?" Shane blurted out. "Did we make a step towards a day in the light?"

"You mean a night in the light," I said.

"He's right," Bryan said. "Are we free of electric prison? Or did you just muck everything up worse?"

The weirdest part was… I didn't know. But there were a whole lot of heads staring at us, waiting for any kind of answer.

"I don't know," Willa said. "My only command was to get us home. After that, I have no orders, so I will give none."

"What about Astor?" Bryan asked.

Bad timing. Or perfect, if you were a hallway full of people. Willa sighed.

"The blueblood will take a day to leave Bastile's system," the buzz cut soldier said. She hadn't given her name yet. "It's a bit longer for females."

"That's sexist, come on mushrooms," Willa shook her head.

On cue, Bombelle came walking into the group like she was blindfolded, taking huge steps, both hands in front of her face.

"Where am I?" She asked. "Is this Rome?"

"Rome fell," Willa said sadly. "This is Jerico."

"Will we fall too?" Bombelle asked.

Heather put her hand gently back over Bombelle's mouth. The leader seemed to accept it, and her eyes closed, her body swaying on her feet with Heather's other hand on her back. For lack of a better word… she was sleep-dancing.

"Ma'am," Shane said, his eyes blurring over for a moment. "Her too?"
"Her too," I said, staring at Astor. "Be a pal?"
"I can be a pal," Shane said, nodding hard.
"I know I said I wouldn't give any more orders," Willa said gently. "I guess I'm just asking for a friend. Take Astor and his sister to their room, guard the doors and windows, please. Find another room for the scientist—for the tied-up guy on Jeff."
And all she got were salutes. Shane and Bryan led the load-out. Ollux went willingly, holding Astor by the shoulder as they were led away by twenty warriors, leading the horse Jeff along with them, and—
"MHMM!"
"You don't owe us every detail, but we need something," the buzz cut soldier woman said as the others left down the hall. At this point not knowing her name was bumming me out. "Twenty four hours? Then storytime?"
"What are you talking about warrior Dawn?" Willa said. "You're with me for the debrief. Personal guard or whatever. Leave them, sound off."
"Yes MA'AM," Dawn said, trying not to smile too hard.
"The territory thanks you," Willa said, blinking, like she wasn't expecting it.
"The territory still needs you to tell it what to do," Heather said, leaning in.
And man, we watched it hit Willa hard. There was still a hallway full of people waiting for the next 'order'. That tended to happen in moments of crisis. She couldn't see it, but I could. I was looking at the present and future leader of Jerico. I was feeling every single soldier in that room accept Wildfire—I mean Willa—as their crisis leader.
Bombelle mumbled something into Heather's hand.
"She says *what about me?*" Heather translated, wiping her hand off.
"I'm not leaving your side Belle, you're the better part of Bones and we all know it, I'm only keeping him alive so we can all keep pretending you don't run this jungle," Willa said.
"That was the nicest thing a wildfire has ever said to me," Bombelle said smiling, then waving her arms and blowing at Willa, trying to put her out. "Now stop talking flames."
Willa's face froze on the grin she'd given Bombelle, right before she had started talking. Heather gently put her hand back over Bombelle's mouth.
"Zip," she said, seeing it coming.
Heather looked sad at their half-awareness. It was painful to see them completely useless, vulnerable, trapped in a pain we couldn't cure. Hard to believe a handful of that mushroom coated trail mix had done this to them. That state was meant for me. Literally.
"I've got you," Willa said to Bastile. "Hospital. Just a few trees more, sir."
"I built that hospital," Bastile said, his eyes a wave.
We all picked up our feet to keep up, four strangers and fifteen soldiers.
"Soldier Soltis," Derek said, seeing a familiar face help him with Bastile.
"When the jungle calls, the jungle answers," he said, simply. "All the trees."
"Now I feel thunder," Willa said, ominously.
We walked among the vanguard to a new, small army. Willa hadn't just been

put in charge, she'd been accepted as it. When she looked back and saw all that she was leading, she growled, a low sound, barely there. But she carried on.

"I see we have a new old face," Soldier Soltis said.

New Xero nodded over us, still holding the body of David in his hands.

"You don't even know," I said.

"I don't," Soltis said. "But he must have gone off only so we could go on. That's all this man is here to do. Don't forget that, Nite."

"I... yes sir," I said.

New Xero looked at me, for the first time with nothing between us.

"Sorry," I said. "It's just... you're—"

"I am nobody," New Xero said. "The old me was somebody. I'm here to give the territory everything I have. You don't have to worry about my story. It's simple. I can either live up to his name, or die for it. Either way, I'm doing one."

"Sir," I said, giving New Xero the salute I'd seen the rest of the Astral give. The one Soltis himself had taught Derek, in topline boot camp.

"Look at you," New Xero said, smiling. "You've got him in base?"

"I don't have him at all," Soltis said. "He showed up himself, at 5am, two days in a row. That was before Astral drafted an eighteen year old kid into a mission so dangerous it involved the caputs themselves. I got two days with the most promising cadet of the summer, what was I supposed to teach him?"

"Everything," Willa said. "How many days do you need? Four?"

"For another of my proteges to end up... a hero?" Soltis asked, his voice somber. "Was he at least—"

"Buried at sea, yes," Willa said, her face heavy. "I can take you to the burial site, sir. Once this is all..."

"Don't," Soltis warned her. "But yes. One way or another... I'd like to see a hero's final resting place. I think I'd like to know the ocean as he did."

Got it. That meant take me there in life, or bury me there in death. I was catching on to the macabre, just part of growing up apparently (?).

"SHENGCUN!" came a voice, and a flipped table.

Bits of electronics and trinkets rained down on our heads as we finally emptied out of the hallway and found Crete in the atrium, working on a long table with some very precise pieces of machinery and wood laid out everywhere. Of course as soon as he saw us, he flung the table upside down and the pieces went everywhere.

"Loud," Willa said, pulling a lego out of her hair.

"You're WALKING!" Crete shouted, stepping over the broken, upside down table to get to us like he had absolutely no awareness of his own destruction.

"I can do anything, on my own, without girls," I said, my face emotionless.

Heather threw her hands up.

"You look great, but terrible," Crete said, holding his hands out to Lynn, expecting her to run into them after a bad day like usual.

But Lynn was staring so hard she didn't see the hands. "Crete. We're..."

"You're back," he said, arms down. "I knew you'd be back, what happened out there? We felt the earthquake, was that you? Were you the earthquake?"

Our numb silence… that was a yes. When were we NOT the earthquake?
"Was that Arum Planetarium?" Crete asked eagerly, all but shaking me (because Dumbledore NEVER EVEN—).
"Yes," Lynn said, just as blankly.
"DO YOU KNOW WHAT THIS—" Crete said, as he got shushed in every direction. "Sorry, I am so coming with you."
"Great, but wait," I said.
The entire temple of people watched me as I left Derek with Bastile for a moment. I walked over to the wall where all the ancient artifacts were displayed on long floating shelves, and returned the skateboard to the shelf. It was covered in blood, and not just my brother's. Xero was a part of that board, for always. It belonged here. It was also the metaphorical end to skateboards being the answer to anything. Kill the boy, right?
"I'll explain later," I said, not really feeling like sharing.
"As you wish," Crete said, looking at the giant among us with a sharp eye as he got in line with us. "Actually, if you don't mind, this city's not big enough for two leviathans. If you don't mind…"
"I do mind," Xero said, as Crete took the body of David from him. "Hey! Commander, control this… guy!"
"That man is one of Jerico's best… guys," Willa said. "Xero, the hand needs to keep clear of this city for a month, to let the transition… settle. Your hands will guard Astor's door until the sun comes up. If we still find him in his room tomorrow, you can keep them. Don't leave the temple."
"Seems harsh, Ma'am," he said, looking at his hands, like he loved them.
"I am expecting a coup in the next twenty-four hours, either led by or including Astor Akoura," Willa said. "You give your heart and soul for the territory, for the good of every single person alive under the canopy, then we're good. You betray us, we're not good. Simple?"
Neo-Xero stared at her, then nodded hard, and saluted. "I like simple."
"Me too," Willa said. "Not that I ever get it."
She hadn't even broken stride for the front doors. We followed her, and the path was familiar. If we were going back to that giant red roofed hospital, that meant down the temple staircase, left and up the western edge of the Oleander towards the arborist community of platforms and bridges carved into the tree trunks. I had a bunch of Bastile's weight on my shoulders and an entire journey hanging on my clothes. This couldn't be over soon enough. The only thing that kept me going was the trance…
"You four, details," Crete said, turning to us. "Now. What did you explode?"
"Everything," Derek said sadly.
"And our friend?" Crete asked, looking down to the guy in his arms.
Willa shot us a look. Of course. I sighed, and stayed quiet. Derek was the same, a bit too late, but whatever. To Heather, this was normal. But we started the story from the beginning, as we took to the wooden, bridged, and platformed body of connected constructs among a higher level of ground than even the Oleander had provided. Just treehousing it.
"So this guy right here," Crete said, looking at the body of David in his

hands.

"Yep," was all I said. "He looked at me, said *Issaic, no,* then jumped."

"From the kingsroad..." Crete said, wincing, realizing. "That's a fall. And because of..."

"Because of the Blitz," I said. "Because of whatever my father did to anyone who wasn't Infinite that night. You know anything about that night, Crete Magellan?"

"Come on, Crete," Derek said, turning the turn tables. "What did you explode?"

"That list is long," Crete said.

"And overdue," I said.

"I'm sorry to interrupt," Willa said. "It seems important."

"Yet someone like you is always right on cue," my brother said.

"Too bad," Willa said. "You'll have your talk. But we're here. Doctor."

The doctor met us at the door with a small army of nurses, male and female alike. And standing beside her was another familiar white coat—Seath, MD.

"Hey Dawn," Claire said, and buzz cut waved.

"No carts?" Seath asked, only clinical. "Are they—"

"Physically unharmed," Willa said. "They've both ingested the blueblood. Thought walking here would give their bloodstream a chance to circulate."

"That's actually not a bad idea, with non-toxins," Claire said, looking down, lowering her arms. "Glad they had a walk, they'll be horizontal for the next twenty hours. This cure is time, and vigilance."

"Don't say it," one of the nurses said, lowering his head.

"If you're wearing scrubs, you're spending the night," Seath said, turning a deaf ear on all the complaining with a coldness that was probably pretty valuable in the medical field. "Commander Willa, do you have any reason to believe the next hours won't be peaceful?"

"It's not like anything happened out there that would have dire consequences for the territory, is it?" Claire asked, very directly. "Let alone the traitor Astor?"

"We're working on it," Willa said. "But no. No credible threat. Yet."

"Qualifier," Claire said, shaking her head, as the army of nurses descended on the leaders. "One room, three beds. You're not going anywhere, are you?"

"I am not," Willa said, nodding to Ana.

"That's a soldier right there," Seath said. "Come on in."

Claire sighed, but gave the nod. The rest of the nurses moved for the doors, but Willa took a single step and stopped against the tide rushing into the hospital. She looked back at us. The four of us, five including Crete, six including David. We'd just through a thing with her. A lot of things.

"Something tells me you aren't needed in Ravenna," Lynn said.

"I'm not," Willa said, her eyes narrowing at us. "But we had a deal."

"I'm breaking it," I said. "Lynn and I know the way."

"You'll find Sand there," Willa said, already accepting. "He hasn't left. I hear the crash site is almost cleaned."

"Great, be right back," Heather said.

"I'm hoping you won't," Willa said. "I'm hoping you'll get the rest you deserve, so you'll be ready the next time we get blasted out the canon together."

"You're using our words," Lynn said, a tear in her eye.

"Love is a beautiful thing," was all Willa said. "I'll never command against it. I will… never forget you. I'm not saying goodbye. I'm saying go on. Finish what needs to be finished. I'll be here until Bastile walks out. After that…"

"We all will," Derek said. "See you on the way back, with Freedom. The only way we're saying goodbye is together."

"You…" Willa smiled, sensing a losing (and very winning) fight. "Aloha."

"Kanaka," my brother said.

Willa nodded, and touched her lips with two fingers. "Kanaka."

We watched the hospital doors close behind her. I was impressed with Derek. He really was learning.

"Start the clock, loverboy," Lynn said, annoyed for some reason.

Why? She was kanaka too, she knew that right? Girls could read minds, that's why they always expected boys to do the same, right? Eh, it would be fine. But just as I had that incredibly (and dangerously) peaceful thought, the wind died in a momentary flurry, bringing our attention to the sounds of the trees, the whistling in the air left behind. It almost sounded like… peace.

Would that change tonight?

"Crete," Heather said.

We all saw. He'd been carrying the body of David so long, there were a few red lines of what could only be blood flowing down Crete's hips and legs.

"It's… his blood's on you," I said.

"It is," Crete said. "Let's get this guy home, then the same for us yeah?"

Agreed.

"So where now, Ravenna?" Heather asked. "How far—"

"Not at all as far as Titan," I assured her. "We're almost there. Lynn—"

"We're up the arbor," Lynn said. "We can gap the northwest pass right there, then it's past the giants nest, around the devil's knot, and over the gates. Twenty minutes to topline. Derek, lead the way."

"Yes Ma'am," he said, putting the notebook away.

Crete continued to carry David, as we turned from the hospital and faced the wide open world of jungle treehouse city. For all the questions we could ask each other… we didn't. No talk. A few bridges later, we were at a particular part of the tree-path that simply ended in a block of wood, overlooking the gates below and a large patch of open canopied jungle at the far end of a dual cable system tied into the higher trunks above us. That could only mean…

Wee.

At this point the trees were just moving around me, whether I was flying, galloping, walking, or zip-lining. The journey was long, and long was the journey. Crete, Heather, and I were all star-fished into the platform, freaking out with every slight change in angle. Lynn and Derek were holding David in their hands, feet planted on the platform, moving when it did, trusting the physics at work to get us down safely—and they did. The platform slid gently into the grass, the wooden ground stopped moving around, and Crete stood up first to take David off our hands. We were here.

In a weird clearing, with a long, well-walked pathway up a hill through the trees to the north side, and not a whole lot else at all. There were two huge circular clearings in the grass, like something huge and heavy had been there. Then we saw him.

A man, on his back in the middle of those two circles.

"Are you done?" Crete called out.

The man raised a single fist, a thumb sticking out. "No!"

"Duality, not confusing," Crete said, and he lifted the guy out of the grass.

It was Sand. He spit leaves, and shook the moss and ferns off his shoulders. His forearms were covered in callouses, his knees were shaking, but he looked at us like the day was new.

"You aren't dead," he said.

"You weren't sure?" I asked.

"Did you just actually send us out on a mission without keeping an overwatching eye on us the entire time?" Derek asked, his mouth open.

"I did," Sand said. "Was it not a success?"

Then he saw the literal body in Crete's hands.

"Nope," Sand said, scratching his head. "That's no win. Who's this?"

"Warrior David, four hundredth guard," Derek said.

Sand's eyes snapped back into his head for a moment. "But the four hundredth was… I mean, it doesn't matter. Did you—"

"Nope," Crete said, shooting Sand a look that had *later* all over it. "Derek, no talking. Sand, we're taking this man back to Ravenna, where he might still have family to see him through."

"Well then we're but a hill away," Sand said. "Boom. Easy journey."

"Nope," the four of us said at the same time.

Sand frowned. "Did some part of your secret mission through the jungle go wrong? James, you're walking again, yes?"

"I am," I said. "We'll talk about it later. Let's just… do this first."

"Alright fine, mister opposite of brightside," Sand said. "That's the hill you couldn't walk up this morning. You first."

He pointed up the hill at the path more taken, leading up to a few buildings through the trees. I remembered the girl in the trees who'd thrown us a canteen of water. Should I have tested that for poison too? Man my trust was shot.

"That's it?" I asked.

"The village has been helping me with the drop-off," Sand said. "In return, I have been given access up to the gates. I have climbed that hill a thousand times, but beyond, I am not welcome, and I do not blame them. The plane almost…"

"It almost," Crete said. "I see no plane. I see a field ready for cultivating and re-planting. I feel like before we leave for good, let's cross those gates."

"Let's not and say we didn't," Sand countered, then he looked sideways at Crete. "You've got blood on you."

"We both do," Crete said.

"We come with the world's worst welcoming gift ever, what could go wrong?" Heather said, taking a step up the hill before any of us could bail.

Sand almost sighed, but given the gravity, he only held another shaking thumbs up. We walked up the path, the six of us, headed somewhere that so far only Freedom had gone. And not a moment after the trees had closed in over our heads, at the top of that hill, out of sight of the clearing… there it was. Through the trees in every direction, a single fence, like a miniature, very jumpable version of the gates of Jerico, and a small village behind cleared of trees.

"Freedom," came a voice by the fence, the figure cloaked in shadows for the moment (ooh, ominous). "Your arms are empty."

"No they're not," Sand said. "I have… a final request. Will you allow it?"

Sand bowed as Crete walked forward with the body of David in his arms.

"Is this a game?" The man said.

And suddenly there were figures looking over the fence all around us, creating a single walled line of people, every one of them looking at us like we thought we'd get through that gate.

"Someone needs to explain," the man at the gate said, sounding angry.

"One shot," Sand said, looking between us. "Don't miss."

"We were on the kingsroad, traveling from the Oleander to Arum," Derek blurted out, breaking the cadence, as all heads turned to him.

He could do this. I thought a single thought. Become the notebook…

"Six assassins were waiting," Derek said. "We subdued every one—I guess Bastile and the hand of the Jerico did, but then I tried to talk to one of them. I got too close, he saw my face, said my father's name, then he screamed and ran for the edge of the bridge. He was falling before we could make a move. After it… happened, the leader of the ambush told us his name was David, he had lost a son in the Blitz, and he may just still have a surviving son in Ravenna."

"Hell," Sand said, looking back at Derek.

"I think my name, my face, what my father's done to this island, I think that's why he jumped," Derek said. "I made us stop on the way back for his body, I'd already sworn to return it. I don't know anything, except that whatever ceremony this man would have gotten from his home town, he deserves that more than being left forgotten in the forest, forever. I didn't kill this man. But I still feel responsible for his death. Let me return him to you. Because that is literally the LEAST I could ever do for him."

The guy stared at David, then at Derek, then at the rest of us. Crete gently laid him on the ground, and turned him face up. Luckily… it was all there. The man looked the same as I'd known him, for all of five minutes.

"David Volle, four hundredth guard," the guy said. "Of course we know this man. His family lost him, then he lost his mind. Unfortunately by now, his family is also gone. They moved out of the territory a year ago, I think they had relatives in Mylo. We can try to contact them, and at least now the village can stop wondering. My only question is this. Is he at peace?"

"He is," I said, no matter how much I wanted to cry. "An owl said so."

And the fence of people shook. The leader looked at me curiously.

"What is your name, sir?" Derek asked. "It's just… I'm tired of not knowing who I'm talking to."

The man nodded. "My name is Nari. My family has given their lives to Ravenna village for centuries. This is my home Nite, not Oleander, not Jerico.

Just here."

"See, that's why I asked," Derek said. "Usually it's a one sided thing."

"Your name sends no shockwaves here," leader Nari said. "But your actions are… memorable. You seem at ease with our culture. Are you faking it?"

"I'm faking the confidence sometimes," Derek admitted. "But I never talk of anything I don't know. That's the combination."

"Is it?" Lynn asked, folding her arms at Derek.

"I don't know, who cares right?" he said, all cool.

Lynn blushed. "Right, totally."

"Oh Lynn," Heather sighed, as I laughed my head off in the background.

Nari, the guy by the gate, motioned for a few neighbors behind him to collect the body of David Volle. Crete's arms hung heavy at his side, covered in… yeah. His job was done. Was ours?

"Is this about the plane?" Sand asked.

"You were barred from us forever because of the plane," the leader said. "It is not because of you we open our gates. You can thank these meddling kids."

"I'll take it," I said, my eyes swimming.

The guy silently motioned left, and we saw it—the village Ravenna, less than ten houses total. We were going on a tour, apparently. We walked inside for the first time, to find the smallest town square I'd ever seen in my life. There would have been eyes on every side of us, if the town already wasn't. Every house's front door was open, the steps in the dirt leading up like my memory was trying to give me a heart attack. We were steered into a large meeting hall, something out of a medieval banquet fantasy, and sat at a circular table while the rest of the town sat opposite us. Forty men and women, a few kids, a few teens.

"I'll stop talking about a plane once I ask the question I've been trying to ask for two days," Sand said, getting right to it. "I take full responsibility. The crash was my fault. Did I kill anyone?"

There was a long pause. Nari turned to us, that razor thin eyebrow not wavering an inch, that beard as still as the air. Then—

"Your ship fell out of the air without even a sound," leader Nari said. "The canopy was thin in that field. We had a daughter of Ravenna out on the branches, just looking up into the sky, marveling at the moon. She was eleven."

The guy motioned behind him, and a scared, quiet little girl came out, her tiny hands clenching her father's long coat.

"I know you," Derek said.

"Thanks for the water," Lynn said, winking to her.

The girl smiled, her knuckles almost white on Nari's coat.

"She doesn't look dead to me," Sand said.

"She would be," leader Nari said, as the girl took a single loud step away from Sand. "Hey. You okay? We talked about this. I told you didn't have to, you don't have to do anything."

"You also said that I can do anything, Dad," she said, looking out at the group, the dim lights, the tension, the aura of things about to break out into fist-fighting any moment.

"You can," her father said—but Lynn had said it too, at the same time.

"You're pretty," the tiny girl said to Lynn with a dreamy look in her eye.

Lynn fell back against the table like someone had hit her. She smiled. "You're prettier."

And the girl's face lit up.

"She is, isn't she?" the father said. "Tell them what happened Lily."

She nodded. "I was up on the branches. I didn't hear the ship. I only heard the growls."

As Lynn stared at the girl, her eyes dilated like crazy, like she was suddenly seeing the situation through the same kind of huge, adorable eyes cats make in the dark.

"As soon as I realized something was coming, there were shredded leaves in my face," Lilypad said. "A cloud cat got me by the back of the shirt, I saw the ship come in like a comet right where I'd been sitting, and then—we were upside down."

"We watched the cat grab her in midair, climb with its head face down running vertically down the trunk, and land on its back with Lilia in its mouth," her father said. "It looked like the beast had her ready to… but in truth, it used its own body to help her absorb the landing."

"The cat landed on its back," Lilypad said. "That's not supposed to happen. Then the ship landed and the trees were coming down all over, and the cat was there. I reached for it, got my hands around its neck, and it ran so fast I didn't care that my feet were dragging across the grass. It got my necklace and we never saw it again, but…"

"We all saw it," an elderly woman by the door said, and the townspeople around her nodded.

"It's something I can't explain," Lily's father said. "None of us can. That makes us wonder if you can."

Lynn got off the bench and took a knee in front of Lily. She dug into her pocket and pulled out the necklace she had found on the tooth of Sophia, back in the pre-mushroom days.

"I believe this belongs to you," Lynn said, handing it back to its owner.

Lilypad looked down, stunned, her mouth dropped open. Then she composed herself and looked back at Lynn.

"That's the wrong necklace."

"But whaaat—"

"I'm just kidding," Lilypad said, grinning, and swiping the thing from Lynn's hand. "Wasn't there an emerald here?"

"Yeah but… it kind of got crushed by the killer canine of a sabretooth tiger," Lynn said. "I don't know if you find that cool or…"

"Wicked cool," Lily said. "I mean, the OCD's gonna kill me, but—"

"How about I replace that gemstone with a piece of the moon?" Sand offered. "It'll glow green in the night, that's basically an emerald, right?"

Lily's jaw dropped even farther. She nodded, hard.

"I don't know what to think of you, Freedom," her father Nari said. "I thought we did. We were going to kill you the first night until we got dr… until we thought twice. Thought maybe we owed one actual face-to-face with the strangers before judging them without reason—you know who's idea that was?"

"Lily's idea?" Lynn said, like she wasn't surprised at all.

"It was LILY'S IDEA!" The leader Nari shouted, choosing not to have heard Lynn. "We have decades of casualties between the leopards and us but this summer, not one. That's unlike the jungle. What happened to my girl is unlike the world. Every single one of us saw it happen, and the same day, you're here. Silka doesn't clean up their own messes. But you're here. Animals don't save small children, they eat them—but again, you're here. We aren't mad at you over a few trees, you already remedied that. We aren't mad at you over David Volle, somehow you returned him to us when we thought him lost. We are curious to just who in the world you actually are."

"Are we going oldest to youngest?" I asked.

"We know Sand Freedom and Crete Magellan," Nari said. "They are responsible for much more devastation than a single jet could ever cause. Why do you think they are bearing such consequence? For trees?"

"I thought trees was kind of a big deal here," I said, a hand on my head.

"Leading trees to their death is," Nari said. "Answer me this Derek Nite, does Sand command an aura of leadership, while at the same time refusing to actually lead anything?"

"He does," I said, my eyes wide. "Why is that?"

"Because he can't stand to ever lead again, not after the last time went so… well," Nari said. "Finally, we have something in common. Neither of us knows who we are."

Sand was frozen. He wanted to fight. He wanted to flee. He did neither.

"Yes Freedom," I said, my eyes unblinking. "Who are we?"

"Seath said it was your penance," Lynn said. "For what?"

"For everything," Sand said. "Good enough?"

"Not even," leader Nari said. "Hah. Everything. That would be a start."

3.3

STORM SEASON

Thankfully, the citizens of Ravenna were not cannibals. We could now say that from experience. The next thing I knew, town hall lost interest in us, Sand took to an open door like James to crutches, and we were heading back through the arbor. That could only mean one thing. Wee.

"Hell Derek," Sand said, holding on for dear awesomeness.

He hadn't said anything since the village hut in Ravenna. No one had.

"I didn't know that," Crete said. "Not all of it."

"That's not all of it," James said.

"And now you have the smallest perspective into how we feel," Sand said. "Sometimes it's hard to tell the story to someone who wasn't there."

"We can try," I said.

"But that would just be more talking," Sand said, sighing. "I would do something out of character, I would offer a group hug. But just this once."

"Say it all," I said, and I jumped before the offer was taken back.

We held each other, Crete crashing into us from the side, for a moment. It was just us. Just the strangers, with the only things like parental protectors we had. We were back. We'd survived splitting up. I would think twice before doing it again. Maybe this was a horror movie. Maybe we were all still about to die.

Eh, who cared.

The platform landed us back at that rainbow road platform edge, and from there it was just another walk through the trees until they revealed the ancient, mysterious hospital built into and around a huge trunk, supported by the even more massive circle platform around the hospital. Ancient secrets, not so hidden.

"So you were military?" I asked Sand, tentatively.

"I still am," Sand said. "But yes. I have a bit of combat experience outside Infinite. And now, so do you."

"But we didn't… ask for it," I said. "Did you?"

Sand thought on that. "No. The things I've been through, the people I've lost along the way… I never asked for any of it. The burden was carved into my heart before I was ever born. All I can do is carry it on."

"What kind of burden is it?" I asked.

He didn't respond. I touched the part of my waistband where the newest note was tucked away. I hadn't even looked at it yet. Someone who just might have been our supermom had passed along… something. We had already thought there might be something for us to see out there. Something in the sky. Was it a coincidence? Crete didn't make a sound, he just watched us. But we were busy processing the most information Sand had ever trusted us with. Meanwhile we'd arrived at the hospital, and when Sand pushed the doors open, his hands had never shot up faster.

"Surrender," he said loudly.

"You offering or asking?"

Fair. Sand had his fists by his face like a boxer as we were met by the open lobby of the hospital, a sea of blades and fists and angry Jerico warriors. Surrender, my butt.

"You will let Sand Freedom through this instant," Willa called from farther down. "And guests."

"MA'AM!" Said a crowd of sheathing swords.

Suddenly the light was twinkling less. There were fifty of them, all facing towards the gigantic double doors and the glass windows of the hospital. We walked through them, and found a single operating room in the back, with a glass paneled monitoring room beside it. But there was no one in the operating room. Here, the torches were low, the room was wide and empty except for a few wooden folding chairs by a wall without a window, as Bastile and Bombelle laid in two adjacent gurneys, seemingly aware enough to toss and turn. Willa sat next to them on a small couch, as Dawn stood with a sword in each hand, a statue, motionless as the window in the room.

"And now we wait?" I asked as we entered.

"And now we wait," Willa said, nodding to us. "Have you—"

"Yes," was all I said. "Thank you for… thank you for."

"You're welcome for," Willa replied. "It's finished."

"It's over," Lynn said. "But nothing's finished."

"Your instincts have been right, so far," Willa said. "Don't ever think they're a burden."

"Don't ever think you're not a leader," I said, using those instincts she was talking about.

Willa blushed. "Deal."

"Storytime," Sand said.

It wasn't a question. He and Crete leaned on us, Dawn pulled up a chair facing the door, and together we went over the chapters Sand and Crete had missed. Willa nodded along, Dawn tried not to gasp, and Bastile and Bombelle slept soundly only feet away. If they had been conscious, they would have collaborated everything we said (I hoped). The hours went by as the story did, only stopping for the few times doctor Claire knocked on the door with trays of water and food. Dawn always sensed footsteps and met her at the door, our internal signal to shut up until she was gone, which was always quick. As nice as she was, she did that doctor thing where they asked you how you were doing as they were already walking away.

As for me, I was just hungrier than I was willing to admit, in a world where we had started to examine everything we were handed. If I saw Crete eyeball something, nod, and send it down to the stomach, I would to. Hey look at that—we weren't alone. But the story was long, and I was tired. If not for James I don't know if I would have gotten it all in order. The next thing I knew I had woken up with a start, some sort of image of a house on fire in my mind, before it was lost in the fuzzy memories of dreams that seemed to disappear the more you tried to hold on to them. I'd fallen asleep. I wasn't alone.

"Bleh," I said, wiping the drool off my chin. "Yo."

"Coffee," my brother said, starting in his chair next to me.

Lynn was still sleeping, leaning back precariously on her chair, her head on the foot end of Bombelle's mattress. Heather was on the floor, stretched out on her back like a cat, looking the most comfortable of all of us. I looked around and saw someone wave at me through the glass between our room and the monitoring station. It was Sand. He was awake, with a cup in one hand, Crete and Willa deep in conversation beside him. There was something else too. The torches were gone, but I could still see. There was light, all around us. That could only mean one thing.

"We did it," I said.

"It's morning," Sand mouthed, shaking his head.

That too. Dawn opened the door into the observation room for us with a nod, and we left the girls asleep with the leaders. Crete and Willa turned to us, both had shadows under their eyes.

"How long?" I asked.

"All of it," Crete said sleepily. "Twenty hours on the dot."

"We slept for twenty hours on folding chairs?" I asked.

"In ergonomic folding chairs made from pulp wood more moldable than memory foam."

I didn't know that voice, but apparently James did.

"Foe," he said.

"And co," came another voice, a guy beside Foe. "Try cracking your back."

I swung my hips around, but there was nothing to crack. Wait. Really? Not waking up with back pain for once…

"Okay now I KNOW this is science fiction," I said, moving my hips around without a single twinge in my back.

"You're welcome," Racket said.

"How ergonomic is your floor?" My brother asked, for Heather's sake.

"How do we feel?" Sand asked, ignoring us.

He was quick to hand us two cups of coffee before we answered. Smart man.

"Better," I said. "Still wondering how much of this pain led to something."

"All of it," Sand said, his head bent over some map on a table.

"Aw, you were battle planning without us," I said.

"We were actually," Crete said, looking at me weird. "We filled in the builder co, if you don't mind."

"I don't know these people," I said, looking to James.

"They're cool," he said. "They were going to teach me to build anything."
"We still are," Foe said, staring, reaching out for a strand of his hair…
"Don't study a man without permission," James said, swatting a hand away.
"Should I not have taken these then?" Foe asked, holding up a few vials of…
"You can't be…" I started.
I was already looking down at my hands and arms in a panic, but there was no sign of a needle—then everyone was laughing except for Doctor Claire. She had poked her head through the door just in time, and she stared daggers at Racket until he put the vials back in a tray on the counter that was clearly marked *Eleutheria*. Weird.
"Are you afraid of what we might find in your blood?" Racket teased. He had a dark sense of humor, I'd remember that.
"Uh yeah, I'm afraid of it, you should be too," I said honestly. "Back up a bit, who are you?"
"They're friends as old as—" Crete started.
"Bad," I said simply.
"They're the first friends I made in Jerico," Crete said. "I met more than Freedom here. I was twenty three, and had just lost my parents. The more time I spent in that giant mansion all by myself, the bigger it got. I didn't like feeling small, and I'd always heard the northern men could make anything out of trees, and all without electricity."
"Did you have to fight your way in?" I asked.
"No," Crete said. "I'd been accepted long before. My parents were known in the Territory, and back then we had different rules for children. When I got to the gates and the warriors of the living leaf saw me without my parents, they opened up without so much as a word. A young perimeter warrior named Tomas Bastile Bones introduced himself to me as a host. When I told him I was here to learn to fix my heart, he took me to his friends Racket and Foe. That's when I learned how little I knew about fundamental engineering. No circuits, no electricity."
"He stared at a screwdriver for a good minute," Racket teased. "How long did you spend trying to plug that thing into the sun, the ground, the air, anything that might give you a charge?"
"I'm sorry if an electric screwdriver was the best present my father ever gave me," Crete said, touching a part of his pocket out of instinct, finding nothing. "Actually I'm not sorry at all. Because of him, I can build anything."
"Because of us, you don't always need electricity to do it," Foe reminded. "We had some good years in the Evergreen. Then you met Sand and the next time we saw you, you were wearing a onesie and complaining about not being able to fly in the jungle—which is a pretty milestone accomplishment, the man who invented flight. Then the NEXT time we saw you—"
"Meeting wasn't the best thing for Jerico," Sand said. "But you can be assured it was the best thing for the island."
"You can't possibly know that for sure," Foe said, frowning up at Sand.
"That's the only thing I know for sure," Sand said, staring back. "Although right now we should focus on what's best for Jerico. One undoing at a time."

I could get behind that.

"So you've had a day to catch up and talk about us behind our backs," I said. "How far behind are we?"

"Not far," Crete said. "Infinite already knew we were hiding in the north, now they'll be closing in. We need more eyes in the trees than ever."

"We can double the topline," Willa said.

"That means less defense within the inner arbor," Foe argued.

"That should be okay," I said. "If the Infinite get here, they'll be here for us. We'll surrender before you make a single soldier defend us."

"No you won't," Crete said.

"Yes we will," I said back, not even willing to argue about it. "You said it Sand, we can't bring our problems here. We can maybe hide from them long enough to be ready when they come knocking."

Sand frowned at me. "If you're just going to remember everything I say, what's the notebook for?"

"Giraffes, mostly," I said. "And songs about tonight being the night."

"And no more heroes," my brother said, heavy.

"Agreed," Sand said. "Good morning."

"Don't look at me," Heather said, ready to kill—until Crete pressed a cup of coffee into her lead jab hand. "Okay. You can look at me."

Lynn was still sleeping, precariously leaning back a full fifty degrees, the back of her chair just catching Bombelle's bed enough to keep her levitating. It looked like she was snoring through the glass, but I couldn't hear it. I smiled.

"We are prepared for Infinite," Willa said. "Now about a star temple, Issaic's justice for it aside. The jungle knows what you are trying to do for her, and we stand by it. All of us. All the trees."

"A world without electricity," Foe said. "Imagine… the complete opposite."

"I usually do," I said, my hands out like the scarecrow.

"Of course you're awake," I said, turning to see the girl at the door.

"Yeah, well, you're loud," Lynn said.

"You really think that?" James asked her, bright-eyed.

"I always have," she said. "You do one thing it seems. You fix things."

"We break things too," I said. "Or the people we come from already did that, in a past we know not of."

"We all, it seems, have a bit of that going on," Crete said, with a hand on Sand's shoulder.

"You think what, the numbers and letters we came back with—" I started.

"They're the answer," Willa said. "To everything the Jerico has thought impossible for centuries."

"Because they are or because they have to be?" James asked, honestly.

"Because now we can," Willa answered, staring him down.

"Oh good, I haven't missed anything," Lynn said.

I handed her my coffee, and she took a sip without a second thought.

"Our understanding is this," Foe said, putting something on from a shirt pocket—were those GLASSES? "It seems the magnetic positions discovered by Bombelle's radar system are indeed symbolic of something. Each of the four represents a signal path of massive solar magnetic interference—except the fifth, which points to a small teenage boy."

"Same difference," Heather said, scratching her head. "We think."

"Come back to me," James said, waving us on.

"Thanks to, um, the other teenage boy, the readings we have on both the Observatory and the Planetarium both confirm their instruments were calibrated to something in the north," Crete said, looking at my brother in a way that very much agreed, we'd definitely come back to this one. "What's unknown is why they are practically aimed on the sun, and whether or not their position on the island is contributing to the electromagnetic dampening over our territory."

"That might stay unknown, seeing as both places are dirt," Willa said.

"It seems resorting to complete destruction is a pattern," Racket said, thinking. "Is there any other consistency?"

"There is," James said, looking at me. "I'm right, aren't I?"

"Well, we lost James," Heather said.

"We didn't lose anything," I said, staring a soldier down. "He's right."

"So what?" Heather asked. "We just… do it again?"

"And lose all possibility of staring at the stars," James said slowly.

Sand didn't move. He knew. The Silka City Observatory, Arum Planetarium, these places were our eyes to the skies. Were we ready to lose them? Personally, for origin reasons, I was absolutely not. Just in case there was any confusion. I still didn't know why, but I had coordinates to find, and I'd gone zero for two so far. I'd even plugged the same day-zero coordinates from the Observatory into the Planetarium, and nothing had even happened—yet. Whatever was out there, it seemed like I had two more chances to find it.

If there was anything for me to find at all.

"So you're saying… there's a chance?" James asked. "And it's because of what we blew up—I mean did?"

"Yep," Crete said. "How's that for simple?"

"I think it's more than what we blew up," Willa said. "What we did there, as a team, if only for the moment… I am starting to feel less empty about it."

I could hear it. It was something that usually came with risk. It was hope.

"I wanna feel less empty," I said, blinking. "How'd you do it?"

"No, how did YOU do it, Nite?" Willa said. "How did you know exactly how to engage that sort of mechanism, how did you arrive without tools and STILL make the telescope move, when generations have been unable?"

"Mom made it seem easy," I said. "She taught us once, we just repeated it. I've learned from experience that we all live the same world. It's my fault I didn't know this existed. But that doesn't mean I'll always know how to fix it."

"From experience, that's not true either," Lynn said sleepily.

"Incredible," Heather said. "We found a people outside of capitalist society, living in harmony with nature, and the one thing they want is power. How—"

"Different kind of power, but I get you," Willa said. "There are cities within Jerico pledged to life without technology, no matter the future. The culture we have been forced to adopt will survive. I do not fear for the Jerico. I only wish them the same choices in life that those willing to put them down have."

Heavy. She meant Infinite. She was essentially saying… know thy enemy.

"Okay, moving forward, understood," Lynn said. "Has anyone before Bombelle ever shown interest in this sort of thing?"

Of course she was in my brain.

"Not really," Willa said. "She was an anomaly long before making Bones her husband. It's not his job to worry about these things, not when keeping a territory alive is a daily task to itself. But together, well, look where we are."

"So where's your man?" Heather teased.

"I…" Willa said, her eyes fluttering, looking up at me. "Maybe him?"

"I was kidding," Heather said, wincing.

Lynn only made a sound, and her face turned red. I was probably the same.

"Fair," Willa said, with a shrug. "I shot my shot, no regrets. I don't have a cute backstory or canonical history with any of you. I can't compete."

"Then stop trying," Heather said. "You know I was kidding, you don't need a man to lead, and even if you did, you wouldn't turn out like Bastile and Bombelle. You're right, they're cool. I like them, and I hate most things. You feel like you can't measure up, I would point out you've kept them alive for a day without help. You'll be the reason they survive this, not me, I was sleeping."

"You twitch like a bunny when you sleep," Willa said, smiling. "It's the cutest thing I've ever seen. Really took the fire out of your dragon."

Heather looked mad enough to throw Willa into the sun.

"There she is," Willa winked. "Before you kill me, check it out."

"Is somebody talking about me?" Bastile said, rubbing his eyes, sitting up in his bed with no weird gyroscopic tilt to his head, a hand instinctually reaching over in bed for Bombelle.

"My neck, my back, and my kidneys," Bombelle complained, sitting up holding her head against a pillow. "My dear. For why?"

They were awake. We all ran inside.

"For me," James said. "You took a psychoactive attack aimed at me. I think."

"At least you're thinking," Bastile said in a sarcastic, loving tone (I hoped).

He was back. They were both back. To say we were beaming…

"ASTOR!" Bastile shouted, loud enough to carry out into the lobby of the hospital.

The guards trembled. The room did too, come to think of it. Willa didn't move, every word she'd said suddenly validated by the man who commanded immediate respect. It wasn't an interim commander thing. It was an alpha thing, and this alpha was back on his feet. For just a moment, even the sun outside the building got brighter.

"Are you okay James?" Bombelle asked.

"Am I—are you?" He stammered.

"Course," Bombelle said. "Did they get anything out of you?"

"They got nothing," Heather said, her eyes dark.

"You'll have the entire territory standing as guard between you and those two," Bastile said. "I promise this. I must admit, I gave Astor the benefit. From now on, the benefit is yours."

I didn't know what to do, so I bowed, like I'd seen the cadets do around him.

"Not only our own people but, to think… our soldiers," Bombelle said to me. "I just can't believe them. That's… that's not us."

"What happened to Xero, that's not us either," I said.

"We know that," Bastile said, looking around. "Where—"

"Astor and sister are waiting for you at the sun temple, along with the captive Arum engineer," Willa offered, bowing her head.

"Don't you ever bow to me again, your grace," Bastile said, standing up.

"You must mean the other thing," Willa said.

"I don't," Bastile interrupted. "I'm sorry. Last time I ever interrupt you."

"You can speak to me however you wish, I take no offense," Willa said.

"How about as an equal?" Bastile offered. "Honorary Caput, starting now. This way when I die and the job's yours, it won't be a surprise."

Willa froze. She started tearing up, we all saw it.

"Say yes, girl," Lynn whispered.

"I… won't let you down," Willa said, and she grabbed Bastile in a hug. "I thought we lost you sir. I thought my best wasn't good enough."

"You thought wrong, first and last time," Bastile said, patting his new co-leader on the back as she laughed with relief. "What now, Ma'am?"

"Polestar," Willa said.

"Naturally," I said, holding my hands out for more.

"A fresh reading from Bombelle's ingeniously invented magnetic floor chart," Willa said. "Whatever role the Planetarium played in this, that's an awful lot of charge to be detectable from the jungle."

"True," Bastile said. "Now that it's gone, I'm curious what's changed."

"We all are, that's literally—nevermind, welcome back sir," Foe sighed.

Sand was first out the doors. We could talk about leadership all day long, but he was always the first to know, first to go. What would you call that?

"An inventor does not seek credit, but she appreciates it," Bombelle said, smiling at Willa as we made through the hospital lobby, none of us even on crutches. "There's nothing not to like about you."

"So far," Willa corrected.

"Was that a threat?" Bombelle blinked.

"I'm only human, Willa said. "Don't be upset when I can't get you stars."

"Then I won't ask for stars," Bombelle said. "Simple. Oh sorry, I forgot you have a thing with simple."

"I wish I didn't," Willa said.

"And that's why you've got us," Heather said, throwing her arm over Willa's shoulders as the double doors of the hospital entrance opened on us. "Oh wait."

"As far as consolation prizes go, you're not bad," Willa grinned.

"So far," Heather corrected.

"They LIVE!"

And as Bastile and Bombelle walked on their own out of those doors, the evergreen erupted in cheers. We didn't have to go far to see the people, and not only the perimeter guard, Soltis and Xero holding the line themselves. They were everywhere. Left, right, up, down, they were shaking the trees, kicking the leaves, letting their roars of relief be heard. Bastile smiled, Bombelle took his hand, and we all made for the nearest platform to the nearest tree. The people followed us all the way through the arbor, from that red roof hospital to the edge of the Oleander clearing until it was nothing but a fifteen foot drop down to the edge of the grass. The masses were still clearly coming with, so Willa kicked the edge of the platform and a small wooden staircase un-tethered itself from somewhere, anchoring itself in the dirt, like stairs had always been an option.

"Where have you been my whole life?" James asked Willa.

She shook her head, but walked ahead first, trying to hide the smile. There was no thought to the blades in the grass, not when the sun was high and only getting higher. It was early morning when we returned to the first of the steps of the temple, from the front this time, and saw all the other soldiers standing above and around us. Bastile walked forward, and all saluted. He opened his mouth to spread the word of victory. But instead of a man speaking, a sky did.

Boom.

The territory flinched, like all of them, all the trees, as the sky opened up in a rolling blast of thunder that settled into silence and destroyed it at the same time. It felt more like a warning shot than a storm breaking.

"Say it all," Bastile said, smiling, looking up.

One by one the raindrops came down. But one by one, the citizens put their hands to their hearts, finishing the salute. No more kneeling, every single one of them stood, even as the rain started to come down. Bastile stood there returning the salute just long enough for it to engrave itself in my heart forever, then I heard the shouting/changing far over the heads of the crowd. When I looked up the trees were already swaying, the ropes and canopy system coming online thanks to the same topline system that had platformed us around this territory all week. It was calculated.

But nature could be calculated too.

Our blissful mid-summer morning had turned as dark and grey as any port in the night, without any warning besides all of them. The first bolt of lightning caught the makeshift water-catching canopy in the middle, and that's where the fire started. It looked like it was burning through the sky itself, until the cloth split in the middle with a roar of steam and smoke, and fire followed the canvas back to the trees, where the screams and sounds of leaps of faith and panic were all we could hear. But that wasn't the biggest problem.

"Everyone INSIDE!" Willa shouted, her first order as caput. Aw.

The grasses were alive with another retreat, a desperate sprint for the largest indoor building around. Bits of fire were landing down like a mad movie poster, sure, but the rest of the cloth canopy wasn't a threat. Then I saw it, and was less worried of the trees catching on fire. Fire wasn't the enemy, not here. I suddenly realized why the canopy had been a thing.

"So this is storm season!" I coughed/garbled, as the water hit.

This wasn't rain. This was river. I was on my butt for the torrential force in a moment, fighting water up to my knees to stand. But I was still about to drown on two feet, I had to put my hands over my mouth and nose to get a good breath in, and that meant the water was bounced into my eyes like mad, no matter where I turned.

"THIS WAY DEREK!" I heard someone shout.

I made myself open my eyes and it was like seeing underwater, without the salt sting. I followed the stairs on all fours, until the doors of the temple were behind me and I could breathe, see, and walk on two legs again.

"I made it," I coughed out. "And with all my dignity…"

"Great, now make way for everyone else," came the voice, and a hand that dragged me sideways.

It was Heather. She threw me into James and pushed us along the crowd, towards the end of the atrium, where Lynn was holding onto a pillar and waving. I shook the water out of my eyes and saw the bodies surging into the sun temple, by the hundreds. The storm had cleared the grass in a moment, and I couldn't blame them. We were pushed farther and farther into the sun temple until we got to Lynn, and as the storm raged outside, the doors closed on Willa and another crew she'd scrapped together without meaning to.

"How did she save…" one of the soldiers she dragged through the door said, wet from head to toe.

"Every single one of us…" his buddy said, his hat upside down, his shoes in his hands, leaking water like a sinking ship.

Boom. The doors were closed, the storm was shut out, the world was quieter.

"I remember this place less crowded," Willa said, walking straight through the crowd, everybody parting for her until she saw us in the sea and nodded. "I need you and Bombelle at center mast. Where she at?"

"Oh captain," came a whistling call, and Bombelle waved over the crowd of people. "What can I lend you?"

"Your height," Willa called out.

"Everybody SIT DOWN!" Bombelle shouted.

And here, in her own home (temple), her voice was louder than any storm known to man. Suddenly the room got shorter, as the heads of everyone but Bastile, Bombelle, Willa, and the four of us sat down. Bombelle made her way through the crowd of parting, crab-walking bodies until she got to the small recess in the floor. There were a few people half sitting on the three half-stairs, but one glare from her and they sensed the sacred nature of what they were sitting on. But most eyes were on Bastile.

"Were you worried about me?" Bastile suddenly said, turning around on the steps, only high enough to project his voice.

And then the cheers came in full. As far as I could see temple, I could see people. From the floors, from the rafters, the second story balconies, the stairs, on anything they could climb, they were pressed in on every side to see and hear their leader.

"What happened sir?" Came a voice from the crowd.

"I assume topline command is on their way here right now to answer that," Bastile said.

"No—I mean before that, yesterday, when you came home a loon."

"Oh," Bastile said, looking at Willa. "Short answer… hmm…"

"We took a preliminary excursion to a suspected point of magnetic interference, hoping to understand it enough to one day counteract its effect," Bombelle said.

"How did this one go?" A man on the ground said, like he wasn't surprised.

"We blew it up before we could understand it," Bastile said honestly, looking sideways at Willa as he gave the people nothing but the bare naked truth.

"Instead of the other way around?" The man on the ground said. "Not bad. Does that mean you mean to do something about... the situation?"

Bombelle smiled. "The situation. The simple answer is... we have been searching for a solution since before you were born. Is anyone mad at that?"

"Of course not," the guy said, blinking, not seeming that happy to finally be involved. "Transparency is always appreciated. You got close, didn't you?"

Willa smiled. "We got closer."

I didn't know what was louder, the storm outside or the energy in here. No one leapt to their feet, no one sang our praises, and why would they? The north wasn't a trap for tourists. It wasn't a camp for prisoners, or worse. And it wasn't a safety zone—unless you were us. Jerico was a way of life, and as much a part of the island as it could be, just like this. What I felt from the heads and shoulders on the ground was... the opposite of judgement. A cautious acceptance. It was almost like they were open to the idea of saving... but they had been disappointed before. Weird energy.

"I assure the heartland," Bastile said. "The lightning is coming. It will be up to you whether you want your land plugged in or not. But thanks to the leadership of Lady Bombelle, and the aid of Wildfire Willa, I can promise you this: it will happen in your lifetimes. In this lifetime."

"Maybe sooner," Willa said, standing up by Bombelle. "I have an idea."

"Your idea is to use my idea," Bombelle said.

But she had her hand in the pottery before we could blink. The people around that clock compass system scattered, as the grains fell as they would... into three lines.

"What... what is this?" One of the folks nearest it said, clutching his heart.

"The closest thing we have to a storm-o-matic," Bombelle said. "It tracks changes in the magnetic fields that have broken over Jerico for centuries. Some might call it a radar. James, which one are you?"

"Let's see, sorry, watch it, coming through buddy," he said.

James was already on it, moving clockwise around the room, stepping over people left and right who had no idea what he was doing, while the ones closes to the compass looked at him in wonder.

"He's a line?" Someone asked.

"We've been through this," Bastile said, sounding much more dangerous.

And suddenly the crowd was quiet. Bombelle clocked the only magnetic line that was moving in a path clearly orbiting him, simple enough given a single moment of focus.

"Got it," she said. "Accounting for James... there are no more magnetic signatures pointing anywhere towards Silka City."

"Were there?" A voice came out from the crowd.

"There were," Bastile said, taking center stage. "And those days are... maybe done."

"Like beating the boss before the minions," Shane said, under his breath.

Bryan gave him a fist pump. No one heard but me.

"With the help of our four newest, the hand and I traveled outside the territory, on target to the end of what used to be the fourth line," Bastile said, still speaking. "What you know is that I came back under the influence of the blueblood, with Wildfire in command. What you don't know is that we found the end of the readings pointing us west. It was indeed a machine, just outside our farthest boundaries, plugged into a part of the lightning city's ocean shore."

"Lights and all?" One guy asked. "At the click of a button?"

"Yes," Bastile said. "I also saw... computers."

The murmurs started. I blinked. Right.

"Of course that meant the Infinite were there waiting for us," Bastile said, almost quietly, and the crowd died down at once to hear the rest of the tale. Nice. "The only way we survived... it was the four of them."

"The kids?" A voice called.

"They're not kids," Bastile said for us, before we could rage.

"THEY faced Infinite?" Another voice came, and suddenly a lot of shirtless people were looking at Heather, and Lynn, and me.

"They... did," Bastile said, nodding at us, reading the room. "And they held like stone. Meet you the newest four warriors of Jerico, to take the Hand's place if ever they are gone. Derek Nite, the historian. James Nite, the guardian. Lynn Lyre, the polyglot. And Heather Denien... everything else."

"Polyglot?" I asked.

"It means someone who speaks all languages," Lynn said, then she clasped her hands to her mouth. "How did I know that?"

"Dead on captain," I said.

"I know," Bastile said, trying not to smile.

He was telling the truth. Of course there was the whole Vema rock power part of it, but Bastile was leaving that out for reasons. I wondered what they were. Was he trying to protect us? Trying to give us a secret weapon to fall back on later? Trying to keep the Vema out of all things Jerico for the sake of simplicity?

Or quite possible all of the above.

"Okay great, but what does this all mean for ME?" A voice came out.

I swear, if a person could die from keeping the laughter in, that was it. That was my moment. At that moment, I was one with the universe, realizing that every once in a while, no matter what town or state or nation I was in, there was probably at least one person around thinking EXACTLY what I was thinking. Thank the world for people like that—and hey, all the other people who weren't thinking like I was, thank the world for them too.

"Wanna rephrase?" Bastile said, scanning the crowd.

"What does this mean for the Oleander, and all her inhabitants, sir!" The same voice came out of the crowd, as a few around him laughed.

"Don't laugh at him," Bastile said. "The future will come, but first the storm.

We must either ready the Oleander for her to get worse before better or…"

"Or?" The voice called out.

"You know what or," Bastile said. "The caves of Pluma Petra have given us shelter for generations. If that fails, we'll have to relocate deep into the evergreen. I'm not saying it will happen. But when you return home, the first thing you must do is prepare to leave it forever—or just for the caves, I'm not sure which yet. Either way, take only what you can carry."

"Simple, right?" Willa said, her eyes closed.

Then we heard the horn, somehow making its way through the closed doors, the wet rooftops, a long blaring note that almost shook the shelter.

"A bit late, but I'll take it," I said, shaking my head.

"Grey cloud signal," Bastile said. "Good news, there's your warning."

"Bad news, big storm," Bombelle said. "The caves it is."

And suddenly to everyone sheltering inside the sun temple… this sucked.

3.4

NO GIRLS ALLOWED

No more temple. Good old cabin.

I was in the shower, thinking about all the usual shower stuff; life, love (and lack of), and making sure I'd gotten all the soap in all the places. But as nice as it was to leave my problems outside the shower like dirty clothes, only the clothes were gone when it was over. I had something on me I couldn't wash off. I also had no clothes to cover it up, bad combination. But I'd been through worse, so I tip-toed through the cold stone ground wearing only a towel and my waterproof Reaper gemstone necklace, back to the warmer, hard wood floors of the bedrooms under the loft—and realized at the worst moment that tonight, our little cabin on the side of the Oleander was more crowded than usual.

Bastile and Bombelle were at the table by Sand and Crete. Willa sat by the fire with Heather, beside the sideways body of a sleeping leopard. I heard noise from the kitchen, must have been Derek and Lynn, which didn't bode well for dinner, or wait, was it technically breakfast? Didn't matter. Thankfully only the closest eyes at the table snapped to me.

"My pants disappeared," I said, suspiciously.

"Laundry day," was all Crete said.

I sighed, grabbed a leather belt from the bedside table, and strapped the towel down over my waist. Shirtless was the norm here, right? I sat down at the table next to Sand.

"Is that the source of everything you are able to do outside the territory?" Bombelle said.

She was either looking at my necklace or the six chest hairs. I would guess—

"It's more about the person who gave it to me," I said, holding the still wet stone, clear as day to see without a shirt to cover it up. "But yes."

The smooth, but asymmetrical thing was heavy in my hand and pulsing with my heartbeat, almost like it was trying to say something. Bombelle noticed, her eyes narrowing at my hand.

"Where's your backpack?" Sand asked me.

"In the room next to Lynn's," I said, sadly. "Do you think it still stands?"

"I don't know," Crete said. "Does it matter?"

"My stuff is nothing compared to… your stuff," I said. "If it burned—"

"It's just stuff," Crete said. "I would build and burn a hundred houses for another minute with my parents. Storm's going mad though."

And like the universe had heard, the sky broke in rolling thunder, so loud it was like the roof was—oh good, Crete had put the roof back. Even if it wasn't, the sky was too dark to see exactly what was going on up there, but we all knew what was coming. Spoiler alert, it was a big giant super storm. Still, even shirtless in the wind, I hadn't been cold once in Jerico.

"Is he staying?" Bastile asked, his arms folded at me.

"I can go," I said, in a high voice.

"Hell you will, we were just wondering about a storm, and the polestar," Sand said. "I mean… we have the coordinates."

"We have a line in the sand, it's a miracle the first two only went so wrong," Bastile said, speaking angrily, and freely. "How about you sacrifice one of your own for the next one? Is that why James is here?"

"Seriously, I can go," I said.

"That's why we're here, James don't move," Sand said. "I am not willing."

"We weren't either," Bastile said.

They were speaking in a code of command, I understood (also I didn't).

"If we're right, it could be over in two moves," Crete said, his head low.

"If the storm doesn't let up, or worse, gets WORSE, then it's a different kind of over," Bastile said. "I can still send my people in two directions, to the frontlines or to the caves. What would you have me do?"

"Ask anyone but us," Sand said, his head still low. "Sorry. I'm…"

"I know what you are," Bastile said. "Crete?"

Crete put his hands up. "The resources can speak for themselves. James?"

"We're not fodder anymore?" I asked, blinking. "Now we're… resources? Does that mean we have value?"

"It means what it means," Bastile said. "And you are only being used as much as my soldiers are being spared."

"And I'm okay with that," I said, thinking it over. "Side of life, right?"

"Right," Bastile said, looking at me funny. "What's it gonna be, Nite?"

"Simple," I said. "You've got two problems, you're trying to solve them together. Firstly, get your city in the caves, until storm's end. Women, children, soldiers and scouts, all of them—no one asked for us to change the weather. They don't deserve this. Tell them we'll do our best to make sure they have a home to come back to."

"You'd have them safe?" Bastile asked. "You saw what waits for us down this path, how easy it could follow us back, if it hasn't already—"

"I can't bring my problems here," I said, looking at Sand. "And we don't ask for soldiers. We brought our own."

"No offense…" Bastile said, classy enough to not finish the sentence.

"You'd be surprised," I said, holding his eyes as steadily as I could. "Now, the part where we might have duped the scales of perfect island magnetic balance and what it means for Jerico? That's the second problem—I don't have a clever answer for that one yet."

"I do," Bastile said sadly.

"That's us to you?" Heather asked. "Soldiers? A shield to the jungle?"

She and Willa came up to the table. They'd clearly heard everything the boys had been discussing loudly not ten feet away.

"I never said it wasn't," Sand said. "Is that a problem?"

"Nope," Heather said. "It's about time they get a shield."

Sand nodded along. They understood, who this was for.

"As long as you aren't talking about me," I said.

"And if we are?" Willa asked. "I see you, James. You are becoming a leader for the right reason, for the same reason Derek is becoming a fighter. For that which you never wanted."

"You have yet to be wrong, Wildfire, but…"

"Are you laughing at me?" She asked, hurt.

"I'm laughing at myself," I said. "The thought that I could ever be something to someone like you, without my supersuit, it's just funny, that's all."

"How funny is this then?" Crete said, motioning to me, and I saw he had something spread out on the table before him.

My supersuit. Pants and shoes, a shirt, a watch. That was it.

"That's it?" Bombelle said. "He puts that on and can destroy planets?"

"I can fly," I said, my eyes high. "Just curious, you saying that out of folklore or experience?"

"How much do you know about planets?" Bombelle asked, like she knew something I didn't. "Do you know what we called the first man in the sky, flying like a shooting star? We called him Moonbreaker. A man like that was so extraordinary to us, it didn't seem that impossible that he could fly up to the moon, break it in half, and throw the pieces down on us. He was the end. The Infinite Soldier is still an extinction level event waiting to happen. So yes, that is what I am looking at, right here on this table. The power of all the bombs."

"What are you doing with them, Crete?" I asked.

"Derek told me what your dad said to you in prison," Crete said simply.

"Right, because tons of great inventions started like that, no red flags—"

"It was something about taking the guidance array out of the laser," Crete said, all defensive for some reason. "It's a good idea, I'm doing that."

"You're taking advice from Issaic, seriously?" I asked.

"I'm taking the threat seriously," Crete said. "I built these things, I'm just checking them over for signs of sabotage. So far nothing, which is good. Next is removing every part of a thing that accepts a two-way handshake with the island-wide… super wifi."

"You're cutting us off?" I asked, in simple speak.

"Just at the hands," Crete said. "Until we find a way to turn them on without immediately waving to the Infinite."

"But how can we be Infinite without Infinite?" I asked.

"You tell me," Crete said. "You keep ending up fine without it, James. Maybe we should acknowledge that, an advantage so extreme it's hard to comprehend, just so long as we can figure it."

"Oh we can figure it," I said. "But that would mean…"

"Everything," Crete said. "We all saw you underland, James. You're making me change my mind about everything I've ever thought about the island."

"Imagine that," I said sarcastically.

"Imagine a power superior to the aggregate of everyone to ever put on suspenders or a supersuit, outside any command but yours," Crete said.

"Imagine—that means you haven't made it work yet, have you?" I frowned.

"You're learning," Crete said, touching my nose. "I have to make thirteen thousand microscopic receiver arrays do the exact opposite of the only thing they were ever designed to do. I could use a hand."

"You could use a hand factory," Sand said. "Wait, you're not Derek."

"Still here to help, since day one," I said with a smile. "Nothing changed."

"Prove it," Crete said. "Six hands, a thousand micro cuts, and maybe, possibly, the lightning city won't be a candle on us."

"That's not the saying," I said.

"Well all I'm saying is if what happened in the underland really happened, and if we can make it happen again… you'll be something else," Crete said. "Are you ready for that?"

"I wasn't ready for something," I said, looking at my feet.

Then, as I was wondering where something's dinner was, I got a bell sound instead. Bastile and Bombelle looked up like a missile alert had gone off. I took my cue from them and clenched everything. Just in case.

"What is it?" I asked.

Heather and Willa joined us, their faces a bit ashen from sitting so close to the fire, but they looked warm. Derek and Lynn did too, wearing aprons and oven mitts, Lynn's claws sticking out of her left mitt. Bastile didn't speak. He only got up and walked to the sliding door, and we followed with a worry in our feet. The sky was as dark as night, so from the front porch all we could see was a single torch, barely visible over the Oleander, coming for us from the north.

"Is today—" Bastile started.

"Not for a month," Bombelle said.

"What is it?" I asked.

"The northern pass," Bastile said. "One of our trading roads is, for the first time in centuries, being used for not trading. I wonder why."

"That whole Infinite tracking us down thing didn't take long," Derek gulped.

"Are they here for… us?" Heather asked.

"You wanna go ask?" Bastile said, giving some sort of look to Bombelle, who returned it, high over his head—as the torchlight turned into a soldier running down the path towards us, meeting the leaders by our door.

"Sir, Ma'am," the soldier wheezed, standing straight up. "It's… an agent."

"Just one?" Bastile asked.

"Likely not," the soldier said, breathing heavy," he said, trying to keep his eyes away from Lynn and Heather for some reason. "He's waiting a few miles down, but that means he's already crossed through Yonder and Arrowstar. He's… asked for the twins. In his words, this isn't about the Planetarium, or Jerico. Just send the boys, and the boys alone. No… no girls allowed."

"Why, because of sexism?" Heather asked.

“Designated survivors,” Crete said in a low voice, leaning over to Heather. She was suddenly much less pissed, and much more concerned for us (I hoped).

“Dismissed,” Bastile said. “Wait, I take it back. Continue to the sun temple, and arrange with Xero teams to confirm our sister villages still stand.”

And the way the guard saluted, I could tell it wasn’t sarcasm. He again took up the torch and ran, this time down to the temple. He was replaced with Sophia, walking around the closed cabin like she was looking for dinner (join the club), almost frowning at the tension. Meow?

“This is textbook,” Crete said. “This is political retaliation. A summit before they lose another building to the crossfire—oh my stars, this is peace talks.”

“He’s right,” Heather said. “This could be a good thing, I can’t afford to miss it for something as stupid as gender. Lynn, draw a mustache on me.”

“That’s not going to work, because, experience,” Lynn said heavily, a hand on Heather’s shoulder. “But no one said anything about leopards.”

And Heather’s eyes shut tight as Sophia paced at her legs, pressing her cheeks against everything in sight (adorable, terrifying, the works).

“Heather, draw a mustache on her,” Lynn said.

“Not even,” Heather said. “Okay Sophia, those boys right there are about to do something stupid. Maybe if you’re with them, they might stay alive longer than ten seconds without us.”

“What are we about to do that’s stupid?” I asked.

“You’re gonna go,” Lynn said.

Derek grimaced. “She’s right.”

“That’s not enough; *why* is she right?” Heather asked, arms folded by Lynn.

“Because every one too many,” I said. “We’re not hiding behind a tree. Any tree. If we’re what they want, we’re gonna go. Thanks for not trying to stop us.”

“Stop you?” Heather said, laughing. “We preemptively came up with a way to keep you safe on the path before you even realized you were on it. That’s what we call, you’re welcome. Lynn, would you like to add anything?”

“I would not,” Lynn said, her arms matching Heather’s, down to the attitude. “But thanks for asking.”

“You owe them all the planets, you do know that right?” Crete said to us.

“I know what I know,” I said. “Do we have time for this?”

“Do we care?” Derek asked.

He was right.

“I hate everything about it too, but we’re past that,” Lynn said. “If anyone’s going to talk to the voice of the jungle, it’s you. It’s always you. Just do it before the storm gets… you know what, I’m not going to finish that sentence.”

“Jinx,” I said.

“Why would you jinx me right now James?” Lynn said, hands in the air.

I sighed. “Unjinx.”

Sophia growled and made for the door like she was saying *let’s go already,* like she knew dinner would have to wait. Sassy cat, I loved it.

“James,” Crete said, throwing something into my bare shoulders.

“Clothes,” I said. “Thanks.”

“Go easy on him,” Sand called out, but for some reason I got the sense he wasn't talking about the Infinite agent.

"Sure," I said. "Heather, how about you? Any last advice?"

"Kill him," she said, without hold back, without hesitation, without sarcasm. "Wait, who are we talking about?"

And that was it. We left the temple to make our way up the curving, slightly uphill path through the Oleander in silence—if you were us. Bastile and Bombelle were talking amongst themselves up ahead, we were just following behind by the light of the torches and all the—uh oh.

"The sky is still stars," Derek said, his head tilting up, drifting the rest of his body left, nooo—wait it was morning.

"Focus brother," I said. "Or no more stars."

It was dark enough to see the stars in daytime, this was true, but thankfully Derek kept the path after that. Even after sleeping for a day, it had already been a day. Bastile and Bombelle only stopped once we came to a natural path leading out of the grove, back into the woods. No platforms, no treehouses this time, just a big, giant, endless green exit sign (kinda). Bombelle stopped at the path, kissed Bastile on the cheek, then bowed us on. She was staying, for secret reasons, or no girls allowed reasons. I gave her a small fist bump as we passed, and she watched us leave with something between worry and wonder in her eyes.

"No backup?" I asked.

"No girls allowed," Bastile said, turning to the leopard following our every step. "Before this, what was your purpose in the group?"

Like he would get an answer. Sophia bared her long fangs in a yawn, and I heard no voice inside my head. Finally. We kept close to the trees lined with torch holders, walking a clear pathway as wide as a city street, but it didn't take long to lose sight of the grove. Sophia walked directly between James and I, her head just about rib level to us. We were surrounded by lights and leaves now, and forward was the only option. Until—

"Halt!" Bastile roared.

I heard a fluttering in the trees behind me, the smallest sound hidden in the wind, and a single figure was there. A lone man, face hidden by full body Infinite armor, up to the hood worn so low we couldn't possibly see a face yet. Add the shadowy torch light, the nighttime, and the dense forest, I felt the danger more than saw it. But as soon as the guy spoke, I knew him.

"That's a big dog," he said.

Alcyon Akoura. Something tugged at all the heartstrings, or well, at least a few of them. Him? Here? Why? I should just listen…

"You are within Territory grounds," Bastile said. "For years the Army has kept their honor. I wish to know why you break it now. Before we break you."

Sophia let out a roar that shook the entire forest, literally. Whatever was about to happen, let the world know how the forest felt. That cat had said it all. And yet, the agent stood his ground. His suit was every bit as threatening as it looked… but was it? He couldn't possibly have power. That meant—

"Unclench, Alcyon," I said. "No one's gonna hurt you."

He obliged, removing the hood, as Derek gave Sophia a hand, letting her sniff him, but also saying *stay back*.

"I know this man," Bastile said, suddenly lost.

"You don't know me," Alcyon said.

"Then it must be the onesie, and the violent disregard for any rule but yours," Bastile said, full focus. "Infinite. Here. Tell me why."

"You tell me, Bones," Alcyon said. "You may have taken the Cove. But how many did you send to the Crossroads?"

Alcyon held something in his right hand. I didn't know what he was talking about, but Bastile's eyes hadn't blinked. I thought about it. There had been more than one of Bombelle's compass lines to track down. Our only mistake was thinking solving all of them was our problem. Maybe the mission for the second outpost had already begun.

"You didn't," Derek said, looking back at Bastile. "When?"

"When we left for Titan," he said, turning to agent Alcyon. "Four."

Alcyon nodded. "You are an honorable dead man. Just like them."

He wasn't talking about us. Alcyon opened his hand and let four bracelets fall. Each one hit with an earthquake, a visible shock to Bastile, his eyes shaking, closing, then settling as he stood his ground. No blitzkrieg, no rush.

"I wanted the boys," Alcyon said, moving along like he hadn't just admitted to murdering four people. "But now you are the only Jerico commander in a hundred years stupid enough to provoke Silka City, twice, in the same lifetime. End the excursions you old fool, while your forests still stand above the sea."

Bastile stopped breathing, just for a moment. Then he was back.

"Prove it," he seethed. "For once in our lives, we're on equal grounds. You don't have powers here, makes us even. Why should I honor your request when you don't honor the dirt we're STANDING ON! This road is sacred. For centuries it has been a place of peace, even in war. But if you're trying to keep me out of my own forest, then maybe today's the day a bridge burns."

"We'll burn more than that," Alcyon said, sadly. "Tell him, boys."

"We'll burn everything."

The voice had come from somewhere behind Alcyon, along with a glowing light in the trees. It was so far off it wasn't that useful for vision, just threatening. It was hard to see in the dark when something was burning the night vision out of you. But that was another voice I'd never forget.

"Odd," I said, under my breath.

"Miss me?"

"Not a single bit, no," Derek said. "Doing just fine without you showing up to set surprise fire to another—wait."

"Is that the one who tried to blow up Avila Road, only setting fire to an ancient depository buried by the Vema founders, a bio-char ready to be burned and returned to life, the very super soil that made life this far removed from society possible in the first place?" Bastile said. "He's the dark earth?"

"No we are!" I complained. "Top marks for the summary, but that guy sucks, he tried to kill us."

"Several times," the voice in the trees reminded me.

"Several times!" I echoed, hands in the air. "And for why?"

"Because YOU infiltrated Infinite under fake names and no mustaches, destroyed the most valuable weapon in our possession, and blamed it on me!" The trees shouted. "And that was BEFORE you lost a small army to the Vempire using Infinite technology to undo ten years of their captivity."

"Top marks for the summary, still both your fault," Derek echoed.

It landed. He had reasons, sure, though I didn't know him. I couldn't pretend like I did. But I was standing in the dirt, and he was somewhere, hidden. Kind of like the dozens of Jerico in the trees behind me at this very moment. It was touching. Bastile was fresh off the mend, but he was a leader for a reason. Infinite had given him one command, and Bastile had done whatever the absolute hell he'd decided was necessary, command be damned.

"Just a note to everyone hiding in a tree right now, the dog can climb," I said.

And I heard sighs, and rustling from behind Alcyon. No one made themselves known on the path, but there was movement backwards, along the edges. I saw Sophia's nose in the air, clocking the smells, but she didn't exactly share the tactical information with me.

"He seems like pressure," Bastile observed. "And pressure makes… things."

"You mean diamonds?" I asked.

"Or squished rocks," Bastile said, challenging us. "It took lighting a fire to wake the Reaper. Don't underestimate a fight, if you know what you fight for."

I looked at Derek. "Has fighting Odd ever helped us?"

"That's too early for this deep," Derek said. "Or wait—reverse those."

"It's dark noon," Bastile said. "And we're done waiting."

He didn't even have to say what for. We all knew. Alcyon took a step forward, and Bastile would have done the same—but Sophia reared up on her back legs and put her massive paws on Bastile's chest. He was stoic, he didn't flinch, but I could see his leg muscles tensing as tight as they could go. Sophia only looked at him, and he at her. He didn't pet her, she didn't lick him. But Bastile let his head drift closer to her mouth, until she dipped her forehead to his. Alpha to alpha. Then she melted away and Bastile stepped back.

"Choose," he said.

"We go," Derek said, no hesitation at all about it.

Simple as that. No guarantee we'd be back, just belief. We had made a promise to Lynn to say goodbye to her before leaving, and we'd broken that promise exactly two times so far. I wasn't going for a third.

"We'll be back," I said, no doubt at all about it.

Alcyon smirked, but Bastile nodded. That was that. I flexed my fingers, both hands gloved in that cloth that meant claws, but I didn't need them yet. Bastile was becoming… something resembling hope. So of course we immediately walked away from that concept, until the path grew brighter, until the caput himself was gone from the fleeting glimpses over my shoulder that haunted me like a tick, tick.

I realized why the light was getting brighter. We were farther down alright. Alcyon took us off the path, towards the glow, and only a few hundred yards through the rough brush, we came to a clearing. There was a fire, I could see that by the smoke, by the smell. It was wonderful. For as much time as I'd spent at the beach, we'd rarely gone camping, and it was a crime. There were even a few long logs around the campfire, perfect for sitting and reminiscing, or ghost stories, I didn't really know, I get it, I should have camped more! But then I saw the figure sitting by the stone-ringed fire and I… remembered why we hadn't.

"Is this the part where you tell us what you actually want?" I said to Alcyon, every bone in my body telling me to deflect.

"Um, no," Alcyon said. "This is the part where I wish you good luck."

And that was it. He was gone, and we were suddenly speechless, looking at the fire, the flames, the smoke, the silhouette, the head turning towards us, the body snapping to attention…

"I made you fire," the silhouette said, his arms open to us.

Suddenly I couldn't breathe. I felt my heart skip a beat. I felt a lot of things in that moment, the biggest one being… fear. For the walk, for the brave face in front of Alcyon, forget it all. My hands were shaking, but I was still standing. So we walked forward, past the last of the trees, and into that center clearing. As we did the silhouette was illuminated farther by the fire, and yeah, it was our father.

Issaic Nite, wearing a dark overlong peacoat that went all the way down to his feet, almost like a full body blanket, complete with a thick hood, and a smaller version of that full beard we'd seen in pictures over fireplaces. It was too dark to see the color of his eyes, only the whites of them.

We found a log, and sat down.

"First, my demands," he said.

The fire roared.

"I'm kidding," he said, making his best attempt at a smile. "That's a joke. I'm a father meeting my kids at eighteen for the first time, I have no demands."

"How about some ground rules then?" I said.

"Like?" Issaic said.

"I don't know," Derek said. "We can talk. But if this is going to end in handcuffs—"

"It's not," Issaic said. "We're past that."

"In a forgiving way?" I asked.

"In a… blame shifting way," Issaic said, looking around. "I'm in a forest right now. I have the sky and sea at my command, and twice now I've found you at the edge of Infinite ability. First the Vempire, now the Jerico."

"You say that like we should be ashamed for getting culture," Derek said.

"You should always know what you're doing," Issaic said. "And of that, I am confident, you do not."

Strike one. It landed, and hard. He could see through me like jello.

"Trust, but verify," Derek said. "First lesson of strangerland."

"The things they said about you are clearly not all true," Issaic said, looking almost pleased at the big boy answer.

"We'll take the compliment, but the things they say about you—" I started.

"Are nothing on what Infinite is right now saying about you," Issaic countered. "I don't have any memories of you as a kid James, so I have no idea what you could be talking about. I don't care what happened ten years ago, I care about what you've done the last two weeks. Answer me a simple question, are you trying to take Silka City down from the inside?"

"NO!" I cried out, my brother right there with me, hands up. "There's literally SO much else we want, and none of it's that."

"I believe you," Issaic said. "See? That alone negates the need for handcuffs, at least to me. But to literally EVERYONE ELSE... not so much. Hard to cry innocence into a sea of shouting judgement, no?"

He wasn't shouting, but we got it. Again, as much as we knew we were fighting for what we thought was right... his words kept landing heavier than I expected them to.

"Strike two," I said, hanging my head.

Issaic had us introspecting, and he saw it. He also saw how we weren't fighting, or taking the immediate offensive. We were scared out of our minds, at least I was.

"I didn't... see, this is exactly what I'm talking about," Issaic said. "We've got work to do, but whatever definition of good goes for passing around here, I can see it in you. Okay screw it. How about this for ground rule number one, no shop talk. We owe each other that, right?"

"I don't know if we owe you anything," Derek said. "But you might."

Issaic looked ready to counter, then he shut up and nodded.

"I might," he said.

It was... the first sign of submission we'd ever gotten from him. It hit. The silence followed. James shifted on the log, we heard the creaks. Then I couldn't take it anymore.

"Are we adopted?"

Issaic looked ready to laugh. He caught himself, just as Derek elbowed me.

"What? We look nothing alike brother, it's weird," I argued.

"Who cares what we look like, ask him where our damn mother is!" Derek shouted.

"You are not adopted," Issaic said, as his smile faded. "But I was going to ask you that."

"You don't know?" I asked.

"You don't?" Issaic said. "I wasn't sure which elephant in the room to set on fire first."

"I heard a different story, and that's not the saying," Derek said, tensing up on that log.

"Whatever happened on that hillside, there actually is a beautiful and tragic love story behind it," Issaic said. "But I can read a room. I don't know if you want me talking about—"

"For ridiculous planet ending reasons, you have permission to talk about Teresa Nite for the next ten minutes," I said, my heart beating so loud I was afraid Sophia would go after it.

"Okay," Issaic said, his hands up. "For the record, I appreciate it. Star and I—sorry, I mean your mother and I... let's just say this island was a wonderful place before it wasn't."

"You saw it change?" I asked.

"I made it change," Issaic said. "Silka's still the same, but creating something like the Infinite, and making it last, it took everything. Things Star wasn't willing to give."

"He said, egomaniacally?" Derek asked.

"He said, with deep regret, and sadness, at yet another failed attempt at love, to no one's fault but my own," Issaic said, and for a moment I think he meant it. "I made my choice. She made hers. It ended everything—a marriage, a partnership, it almost broke Infinite in two and the city by proxy. And then a month later, just as we'd figured out how to survive, biology made a different choice. An awkward one. Or rather… two."

"Oh no," Derek said, his eyebrows high.

"Yeah," Issaic said. "I know you won't believe me. But I tried, and not just once. She made it clear. Any roof you were sleeping under, I was not welcome. Not for a day, not for a minute. As she said… I'd already made my choice."

"This doesn't make you sound that good you know," Derek said.

Issaic shrugged. "Isn't honesty kind of the thing here?"

"As long as it is," I said, with a deep breath. "You should know she never made you sound like that. She only said we had a father who was alive, and one day we might meet him."

"And he wasn't around because of reasons we might one day understand," Derek said, his feet digging into the dirt like a tick…

"Reasons I still keep close to the chest," Issaic said, nodding. "But yeah. I can do a lot in these clothes, but against the wrath of a woman like Teresa Nite, my options were obey, do nothing again forever, or die."

"Why is that so familiar on so many levels?" I said.

"Because you're a guy," Issaic said.

"Nice," Derek said. "We should take a strike off for that one."

"That's… not how baseball works," Issaic said, with a sigh.

I made a fist, ready to explode. Issaic got the memo and held his hands up.

"Right, estranged father ground rule number two, don't talk about baseball," Issaic said.

"You THINK?" I said, shaking my head.

"See, that I can understand," Derek said, thinking. "She gave you the boot."

"It was a bit more complicated than that," Issaic complained.

"Nope, she's supermom," Derek said. "She never did a thing on this world without a purpose. That means she did love you. Letting go must have been hard. Good on her."

"That's it?" Issaic said, frowning. "The journey of your paternity ends there?"

"This is going to sound harsh man," I said. "But the idea of love lasting forever ended the day we realized you weren't around."

"Yeah, you're about thirteen years too late on the fairy tale love story ending making sense," Derek said. "We kinda figured something had gone sideways."

Issaic was quiet, sweating in the spotlight.

"I was… only creating an army of super human soldiers capable of defending the island from the next millennia of threat," he said.

"I thought we said no shop talk," I said.

"You know what the crazy thing is?" Issaic said, like he hadn't even heard me. "Even knowing she was somewhere in Silka raising you herself, I was so sure of my purpose that I thought... I thought I was giving you the world you had. For eight years I worked, and every day I thought I was doing you proud. I thought what better father, than the one flying so fast over the city that no one ever saw him? What better parent than the one who kept danger so far away from you that you never needed to know his face?"

"You've got father and fighter switched, man," Derek said.

"Every day you'd come home from school and sleep safely through the night, that was a twenty-four hour shift for the perimeter guard," Issaic said. "I would be with them, as far from the Engineerium as possible, my eyes on the island, my back to the city, but my mind thinking... they stop here. If anything ever came for the city, you would never know it. And you never did."

"Until we did," I said.

"The Blitz," Issaic said, nodding. "That was the first day I ever doubted what I'd built. It only took three nations working together and rising up against me to do it. Even worse, for another first, I saw the damage around the Engineerium. I know you had been through it, I failed to keep it from you. Not only did those nations attack my city, they went for the heart."

"We're your heart?" I asked, sarcastically.

"I didn't choose it," Issaic said. "Sometimes... it just is what it is, right?"

I kind of got it. It was a sad thought to admit. But I guess we were both doing it.

"So everything they say you did after the Blitz... you're saying it was justified because it was for us?" Derek shot back. He clearly had other issues.

"For the family, yes," Issaic said, darkly.

"Why do I get the sense that you're talking about the pure-blooded when you say that?"

"About the lightning city Silka and her original mountaineer descendants, those who proved themselves by crossing the island?" Issaic said. "I don't have to explain war to you! It was Infinite on one side, and on the other, Reaper scouts, Astral warriors, and Mylo's water warriors, whatever they decide to call themselves later, all working together by sea, sky, and land, both over and under! We should have DIED."

The wind snapped through us, the fire blew strange shapes in the air.

"And now for the second time, I find you among a foreign nation, among soldiers and locals known and implicated in the Blitz," Issaic said, and it had the aura of a lecture coming about it. "You undid the most complicated plasma bind system I've ever thought up, by exploiting the only takedown measure I programmed it with, a DNA detector—yes, I get the irony, you're right, shut up. No, you are not adopted, James Nite. You are very much my own blood. I know that because... you've already learned how to use it against me."

"By necessity," I said, taking a step back, afraid of everything.

"You think staying alive is surviving?" Issaic said. "Only the most powerful creature on earth truly survives. The rest of us only live only long enough for the food chain to do its job."

"I think we have different definitions of survive," Derek said.

"Mine means to outlast every other city on this island," Issaic said. "I mean to survive this island James. That means to get off one day. That's not going to happen if you've got four entire nations fighting over a raft."

"Then we make the raft big enough for everyone, it doesn't seem that complicated to me!" I said, my hands in the air.

Issaic only shook his head, and relaxed. "I'm not laughing at you. I was just thinking… there's a story I could tell you, about what happened the last time we tried to fit everybody on the raft, so to speak. A story about overpopulation, some boats, and the man we named this island after. It's a long one."

"We're already in the middle of a long one," Derek complained, arms folded.

"And time has never been our friend," Issaic agreed. "I only mean to say… I see the desire to help in both of you. So far, you have done nothing we can't undo. With the right amount of penance, I don't see why we can't get you back to Silka tonight. Give this a full start over, no more forest, no more underground. You can even help restore the superfecta."

"Superfecta?" Derek asked.

"Like trifecta, but four," Issaic said, folding his arms.

"Penance?" I said, making sure I'd heard him. "You want me to atone for the fact that a thousand children are eating every day again, and a thousand more might see electricity for the first time?"

"Uh yeah, none of those children are even from Silka, so I don't care about them," Issaic said. "But us, we're family. It's time we start over. No handcuffs."

"No, just prejudice in the form of invisible laser barbed wires," I said, sadly.

"We aren't going anywhere," Derek said. "The fact that you want us to, instead of seeing the forest through the storm… wait a minute. You said superfecta. You ARE controlling the weather?"

"Don't be ridiculous," Issaic said. "We can't control the weather, we don't need to. We just need to control the magnetic fields created by all the geomagnetic storms, and stop them at the gates. It's simple."

"We just—"

"At least, it was simpler, before you brought my superfecta down to two," Issaic said, his face scary dark again. "But don't worry—you haven't visited the Observatory once, you'd be surprised at the progress. Arum Planetarium is also being rebuilt as we speak. We'll get those electric storms breaking over the north again, don't you fret."

"Don't remind me of guitars," I said.

"You play guitar?" Issaic asked, blinking.

"I…" I said, my voice cracking. I didn't know what to say to that.

"Why would you do that to a territory?" Derek asked, his hands on his head.

"You think I invented this?" Issaic said. "I inherited it, from centuries of the island surviving on the edge of a knife. I didn't take anything away from Jerico."

"You're not giving it back to them either," I argued. "So this is the way it was meant to be? This is how the island works? Keeping an entire nation in the dark? AGAIN—"

"That is how it has always been," Issaic said. "You've seen the borealis, what did you think? Did you think it was ejecta from a terminal superflare that would cover the island if we let it past the north, and radiate us all in the same lovely anti-electricity as this barbaric torch and sword city? Because if so, then congratulations, you're caught up—to our ancestors."

"I thought they were pretty lights," I said. "Okay so you do control the—can't we break the storm over the ocean instead of a quarter of the world?"

"As I understand it, the technology doesn't reach offshore," Issaic said. "But imagine if it did."

"Yeah well, imagine if there was a way off this island," I said.

"Imagine if we were in control James, when that day comes," Issaic said, staring at me through the blurry heatwaves of the fire. He had learned our names. "Or imagine undoing every step of progress that's seen us survive this far, and we never make it there. Is that what you want? To turn out every light on the island? Because if so, by all means, continue doing what you're doing."

His tone had switched in a second, but there was a word for trying to brainwash someone into thinking the world was a certain way. That word was gaslighting. Issaic was trying too hard, for a stranger. See that's why I was questioning the guitar comment. Either my father was trying to bond with me, weird, or it was all just another… distraction.

"So whatever can we do?" I said, only a bit sarcastically.

"You can come home, right now," Issaic said. "Leave this place and we won't even have to burn it down."

"So for all the borealis, right now Silka's totally fine?" Derek asked.

"Of course she is," Issaic said. "Let's go, boys."

"Not even," I said, making it clear we saw through him.

"We're going home," he said, dangerous now.

"You're going home," I said. "You can take your agents and get out of the jungle. Whatever you wanted from us, multiply it by about a thousand. That's what we wanted from you. So excuse us for giving you nothing."

It was harsh.

"I thought I was the speech guy," Derek said, softly.

"It comes and goes, depending on the situation," I said, sounding like someone who was sitting in a big awkward silence (I was).

Issaic thought on it, then stood up. We flinched, he had been so still for so long. He was taller than we'd remembered, and the light of the fire didn't do much for zen. He looked like he was weighing the options. Like he was about to grab us both by the arm. If he did, there wouldn't be much we could do about it—until Sophia rose in front of us, not growling, not snarling, just slowly coming out of the shadows in a way that reminded us how big she was. Issaic saw it.

"Your hellhound doesn't scare me," he said.

"The disrespect," I said, petting Sophia once under the ear, once she'd seen my hand coming. "How about the jungle, Issaic? Does that scare you?"

I'd been completely bluffing, but all the same, the trees around us started to shake. Like, all the trees. Aw.

"I thought I said…" Issaic said.

He stepped back as the rustle of boots on the ground started behind him, and though the eyes of the jungle were looking down at Issaic from every angle, his gaze never left us. His towering, empty, terrifying black and white eyes…

"I said no handcuffs," Issaic said. "I meant it. I'll give you two days to change your mind. I won't lie, I want you home. If I have to burn down every place you could hide to get it. If I have to move the mountains, or turn the world upside down—again, I'll get it. You'll come home before it's over."

"Will you?" I asked.

Issaic kicked a wave of dirt over the fire angrily, then snapped out of it.

"Teenagers."

And he was gone, leaving us in a dark grove, with nothing but the rustling around us of people leaving. Sophia grazed against my knee, the trees shook with relief, like they'd been the ones frozen in fear, not Issaic.

"How'd we do?" I asked my brother under my breath.

Derek patted me on the shoulder.

"Good brother. Bad, but good. Kinda like—"

3.5

CHAOTIC GOOD

We sat there in near pitch darkness, just for a moment. All I could see was the slow-moving body of Sophia through the embers of the fire. But I wasn't thinking about a cat. I was thinking about what we'd just been given. Not peace, not at all. But for the first time in my life, I had insight. I would be wary of the exact words he'd given, he was too good at manipulation for me to take it as gospel. But though we didn't exactly have answers, at least we had… reasons.

"Long way to go," James said.

"On our way though," I said, taking a deep breath.

"I mean back to cabin," he said.

"Oh," I said. "I thought we were still being symbolic."

I got up off the log and held a hand out in the darkness. Sophia found me with her nose. James took my other hand, and we were careful not to trip on a root as she led us through the now absolute pitch darkness, back out the small off-path of trees we couldn't even see until the back of a leopard was slinking around them, until we finally saw the far-off illumination of a single lantern. As we got nearer that one lantern turned into a pathway lined with them. We were back on that trading path, still in the middle of the forest, but practically home.

If that's what we were calling it.

Bastile was alone waiting for us where we'd left him, the Infinite already far retreated down the path from which they came. We didn't stop walking for a moment, ready and itching to get out of the trees.

"Thank the jungle," he said as he saw us. Sophia yawned, almost like a hello, as we walked down the lamp-lined trail back to Oleander. "What happened?"

"We just talked to our father, with no one else around," James said.

"Did he hurt you?"

"Nah, just the old two-day ultimatum, come home or fire, or worse," I said.

"Did it help?" Bastile said. "Was he less of a warmonger in private?"

"Not in the slightest," I said sadly. "He's got a warped sense of what we want from this world. Seems he takes the banishment of every other nation as the thing that's let us grow up in paradise."

"Bad," Bastile agreed. "That's negative reinforcement. Every day you live is another day he chalks up to the military island of Issaic."

"The irony is our mother's the only one who did that," James said, shaking his head. "I don't think we live in the same world as that guy."

"Well he does have the power to set us all on fire, so we do," Bastile said. "You can't block him out, boys. You'll have to face the man he's become, before his madness takes the island, or worse… you."

"Why us?" I complained.

"Because the heart," James said, sighing. "Like it or not it's the truth. We're tethered. Ancestrally, biologically, both ways."

"Why can't we be non-metaphorically tethered to still having a mom?" I almost cried.

"Right, Teresa, did Issaic have anything to say about that?" Bastile asked.

"No," James said. "In fact, he asked us. I got the feeling he was trying to write her off. He didn't even mention her after that."

"Issaic and Teresa," Bastile said, wincing. "I don't think he's ever given anyone the real truth. I know it hurt him more than he lets on."

"You're telling us to hold back?" I shouted. "US?"

"Yeah," Bastile said. "You were denied the chance to know Issaic as a father. Maybe you can try to see him as a human."

"Maybe we'll know it when we see it, like a ship at the bottom of the sea?"

"How did you know about that?" Bastile said, eyes narrowed.

"Because Sand said it was a metaphor for answering a question, why?"

"This isn't the sea," Bastile said. "I have to ask, what's your plan? Just out of curiosity, wondering if my ancestral home will still be here in two days."

"Of course it will," I said. "If Issaic wants us that bad, we'll go. Or…"

I looked down at my hands, at the gloves, my bare feet. This wouldn't do. There was only one way we stood a chance on our own, without a misfortunate army of faceless soldiers behind us. One way we could drive the Infinite out of Jerico without sacrificing ourselves to them, or letting them harm the territory.

"Or we won't," my brother said. "Or we'll fight. Not you, just us."

"Even with the wayfarers, that is still six against Infinite," Bastile said. "How could you possibly be enough?"

"In the sky, that's how," James said, reading my thoughts. "How about it brother? You tired of walking?"

"I was born tired of walking," I said. "We've gone far too long without supersuits, this is unacceptable for science fiction."

And I meant it. Mostly. Of course this was about more than superpowers, if that wasn't clear by now, then I don't know what to say. But when you usually have all the power to solve all the problems, then when that power's taken away, that's how you get a really long series about friendship instead of a short story about lasers. Either way, we were already back to our cabin, and I was ready for Crete to have all the things all spread out in that cabin, with every tool at his disposal ready to work, ready for action. But instead what I got was a flurry of packing, and a heavy metal bag thrown straight at the door behind me.

"Take it easy!" I said.

"Great, you're alive, help us move our crap into the caves," Crete said.

"But we just got here," I said, blinking.

"Storm's coming, the guy with the horn said so," Crete said, pointing up.

And like he could hear us, another far away horn started, low at first, then I had to drop the bag and put my hands over my ears.

"Second warning," Bastile said, his eyes set. "We've got five minutes to maelstrom. Grey clouds can last days, so say your goodbyes to the sun now."

I thought Sophia was complaining, but it was Heather, actually growling like a cat, as she came down the ladder while Lynn threw things off it.

"The sun seems to be a trigger for you," Bastile said.

"Losing it has become a pattern for me," Heather said. "And patterns are boring, that's why I have rocks for wallpaper. Hey look, the twins survived."

"Good to see you too," I said, shaking my head.

"They're back," Lynn said from the loft. "Derek, your father, what—"

"You can talk about it in the CAVE!" Bastile shouted.

And another horn went off, this one already noticeably muted by a rolling thunder in the sky. The storm was coming. Right. —

Sand and Crete came running out from the back of the loft with two big bags in each hand. Lynn jumped the eight feet from the loft as Heather passed us another bag each. We assumed it was every earthly possession we had left behind in that cabin (it was), then Lynn was on her feet and we were off, joining the mad dash of people making for the part of the path that rose up on the right side, away from the quad, into its own mountainous valley that continued so far north there was probably an ocean on the other side.

Cave Pluma Petra, Bastile had called it.

Then as the horn sounded out a third time, the sound was completely lost to something else. The rumble had become an ocean, the darkness creeping in had swallowed our heads in a blink, and those dark grey clouds looked ready to lose a twisted, angry energy over the jungle… because they were, and they did. We all watched as the rain came in a blanket, like a wave over our heads, a physical thing as clear as an actual wave, just… sideways.

It was a monsoon. Coming heavy…

"MOVE!" Bastile shouted at the top of his lungs, his voice cracking for the strain but still we barely heard him.

We ran the last of an uphill incline towards a huge open faced, carved door in the otherwise sleek and tall mountain cliff before us, already higher than I would have ever been able to see just from the path itself. Bastile doubled back to help a few final stragglers with their huge bags and small babies, and just as the last of the men threw themselves inside—the water hit. It wasn't rain. One moment we were watching the guy limp inside with the grove, Oleander, and mountains behind him, the next it was like we were behind a waterfall. In an instant, nothing could be seen through that thick of a raincoat. The opening was angled in our favor, and the sloped ground took the water away by design and nature, but for a moment I felt more fear than I had in that grove with Issaic.

"You… weren't kidding," I said.

"You'd drown in ten seconds out there," Bastile said, nodding. "And we can't risk our second canopy, not against this downpour."

"What about Issaic and the Infinite?" James asked.

"A reminder to stick to the trading schedule," Bastile said. "But the trees will diffuse the tempest. Their path will end safely as long as they retreat. It is the open-aired grove cities like Oleander and Yonder that are at most danger."

If I hadn't known any better, I would say we were back underland. As endless as the mountain had seemed from the outside, it was almost more than that within. It was a weird kind of warm, with a crisp wind coming from the entrance—like driving with the heater on and the windows down. The entire thing was hollowed out, and I could see a good few football fields away from us, a few falloffs where the ground clearly gave way to a lower level, a few higher ridges and levels already full of people, some even sitting on the edge with their feet hanging off hundreds of feet above me, and above even that, a sloped ceiling that did come to a centerpoint a good ways away from us, the only reminder that there was supposedly a single peaked mountain around us.

"So this is your storm shelter," I said, looking around. "Bloody convenient."

"Bloody necessary," Bastile corrected.

"You talked to your dad, what did he say?" Lynn asked, staring at me.

"We did Lynn," I said. "It was… weird. Hollow."

"Like this mountain," James said, looking around. "Single peak. Naturally excavated interior. Warm wind coming out of the ground. Am I crazy or—"

"Is the only thing missing the lake?" Heather said.

"Are we *inside a volcano right now?*" I asked, in a higher voice than—

"Dude, there's kids around," Bastile said. "Keep the V word low, you know? But technically yes, and also technically it's still… the A word. Why'd you think it was so warm?"

Suddenly the concept of shelter was broken into a thousand pieces. Boom. A cave for a home didn't mean much for two twins who had spent this entire journey already searching for home, we knew this place wasn't it. We'd know it when we found her. When we could ask our mother just what in the hell was all this all about, and hear it from her why we'd chased her to the stars and back. I'd start rebuilding that house over the Engineerium right now if it meant we could get back to it one day. Brick by brick. But for now, we found ourselves following Bastile back to Willa, waiting for us with wet hair.

"Everyone in the temple accounted for?" Bastile asked. "Including?"

"They are waiting for you around that big rock," Willa said, nodding. "You want the fodder with you for this?"

"They're no longer fodder. But no, not at first," Bastile said, turning to us. "Give a captain a moment with his soldiers?"

"Oh," I said, realizing who they were talking about. "Astor and Ollux. Of course. Not exactly ready for that, not without another cup of that sweet kona."

"The cave is rationed," Bastile said, folding his arms. "Right now, this is survival. You'll get your coffee when you fix this DAMN—I mean, when the storm goes to sleep."

"If you're looking for the wayfarers, they're around that other big rock," Willa offered.

She wasn't totally focused on us, but there was something like comfort on her face as she turned away, pointing to a piece of obsidian obscuring a part of the underground. We nodded, bowed, and turned around the black rock to find…

A black blade at my throat so quick I almost walked into it. So not coffee.

"Help," was all I said.

"You're clean," the voice came.

It was Sand. He lowered the makeshift sword and let us turn the corner.

"Didn't realize you were a door, would have knocked," James said.

"Can't be too careful," Crete said. "We're doing science in here."

"You didn't say the storm shelter was an active… shelter," James said.

"You're still expecting simple?" Crete said, like he wasn't worried. "The thing hasn't gone off for a hundred years. We have trigger sensors that'll give us a month's warning at any change in temperature. Lots of things to worry about, I get you, loud and clear, but trust me. The volcano isn't one."

I rubbed my ears. "Sorry. Just, first time, those words, that order, you know."

"Let's worry about those two days Issaic gave us," my brother said.

"Oh great, because that should be just enough to bring a nation out of the stone age—again," Heather said, sarcastically (if that wasn't clear).

"Two… what?!" Lynn shouted. "What did your dad even talk about?"

We told them everything. It was just us and a small worktable in an alcove lit by the torches Heather and Lynn were holding, the light flickering and moving around as they did. On the table surface were our Infinite supersuits, as well as three small devices covered in small fabrics. Right. The parts of the plane we weren't supposed to have kept. It was hardly a secret though, right?

"So our… he… so Issaic basically told us we're messing with some ancient magnetic stasis system, something that's been keeping the island alive for centuries," I finished. "He said as much as this… the four systems keep the balance, and we've already taken his superfecta down two pegs."

"A classic bifecta," Sand said, nodding. "Two strikes, two days."

"Glad someone thinks it's simple," I said. "Meanwhile I'll just keep falling asleep to the idea of nuking the island being all my fault."

"Or…" Lynn said, hoping.

"Or the downpour clears, the shelter is called off, and my brother and I turn ourselves into the almighty power of the lighting city," James said. "Where will these people go, if we don't?"

"You would what now?" Lynn asked, blinking, losing hope fast.

"Pick a jungle," Sand said, pointing his arms in all directions. "But let's not worry about that. As for turning yourselves in—"

"I'll put them in a cell of my own before that happens," Heather said. "Or…"

"Or we put our heads back down and end this in two moves," I said, looking right at Crete. "And no one has to do anything but dry off. That's the plan."

"But you're not leaving, right?" Lynn said. "Promise that's not the plan?"

"Promise," I said. "Unless that changes."

Lynn wasn't laughing. "I decide if that changes. Promise me that."

"I like you Lynn," Heather said, cutting me off before I could reply. "But you can't make that decision for the greater good. I can."

"Why can't—" Lynn started to argue.

"The greater good doesn't include us," Heather said. "Any real objections?"

Lynn looked around for help, but she got none.

"Then I shall be the law of the land," she said, her eyes glazing over, born for the job. Then she focused. "Wait, what are the two moves?"

"In a perfect world, we put those on, and they work," my brother said, looking down at our supersuits on the table. "In this world, the other two polestar positions, probably. By the way, no objections here to military state Heather. Any progress, nerd?"

"Yes, and thank you," Crete said. "It'll take a while but your suits will be completely self-contained. They won't have the Silka City source to power them of course, so they won't work without a barely explainable and self-perpetual, god-like energy connection, the likes of which the boys could only hope to explain. I'm hoping you can take care of that part?"

"You hope correct," Lynn said, looking at us with that look in her eye.

"I've never built something to run on hope before," Crete said. "You do understand this is uncharted territory?"

"Why do you think I'm mapping everything?" I said. "Of course we aren't expecting this to work. If it does, it's admitting we understand nothing."

"We haven't already done that?" James asked.

"You have," Sand and Crete said at the same time.

"Well… get ready for us to do something about it," I said lamely.

"Like what though?" James asked. "Blow up more astronomical centers? What about what Issaic said, how the solar magnetics could be pushed over the entire island? What if we accidentally bring the darkness to Vema? Or Silka?"

"Remember what we said about Issaic," Lynn said. "He's been word-manipulating things since the moment he opened his mouth."

"Right," I said, blinking. "Maybe that's what he wants me to think."

"So what do you think?" Lynn asked.

"Nothing at all…" I said honestly. "Is that bad?"

"It's a start," Heather said. "We aren't going to doom humanity by changing the winds a bit. But if last time was a template, then we need a new template. We don't know what's at the end of the next polestar coordinate."

I bit my lip, only Lynn saw it. "We actually do."

That's when we all heard it, fighting, crying, scuffling coming from the front part of the cave. Crete and Sand stayed behind, never taking their gloved hands away from their microscopic tasks. We turned the corner to see—woah.

"Please," Bombelle said.

Her hand shook as she held four pieces of leather. Willa silent by her side, hands behind her back, tears running freely down her face, as small group of people stood in a crescent moon before Bombelle. An older woman with greying brown hair was holding point, wearing a cross hatch pattern poncho, and just punching a lady caput in the chest over and over, as half-hearted as could be.

"Keep them," the woman said. "They'll remind you, you sent him to die."

"I sent myself and my husband out against the same risks, Robin," Bombelle said. "But it's true. We've lost Ivy, and three of the senior division with her."

I couldn't breathe, just for a moment. Did she say... I clenched everything. I knew helper girl Ivy. I only hoped the other three weren't... right, that's exactly how that small mob must have felt. I could join them in turning on the caput, but that wasn't the side to be on right now. I stayed quiet.

"Who were the other three?" Robin demanded.

"Rose Aida, Dalle Daud, and... I believe he only went by Fawn."

Come on.

"They followed our polestar to the Crossroads, and the Infinite say they did there find the end of their mission," Bombelle said. "But... they died there."

"How did you survive the path, when they didn't?" Robin asked.

By now it wasn't just us that had gathered around, it was an entire volcano. The way echoes worked, you couldn't really miss it.

"I'll say it again, it was four four newest territory—" Bombelle tried.

"The lightning children," Robin interrupted. "You mean the sons of Issaic? Them being here is the only reason any of this is happening in the first place. They'll turn the lights on and we'll burn in them Bones, you know it."

"You didn't see what I saw," Bombelle said. "You didn't see the Reaper."

And I swear, my gemstone moved with my heartbeat. Like it was listening. I pulled my necklace out from under my shirt to see—it wasn't listening.

It was glowing.

"Do I have purple on my face?" I asked.

"You do," Heather said, looking down. "What in the fall of troy—"

"I think I would have felt something about my family's most ancient heirloom, if it were to—wait look at that, he's right," Lynn said, suddenly cutting herself off as she pulled the front of her shirt out, looked down, and her face lit up. Literally. In purple.

"Sure, the Reaper came to you, in your need," Robin was still shouting, just staring wooden daggers at Bombelle, at us, at everyone. "Why not ours, here and now? Who's to say we're not next for the burial?"

"That's not happening," Bombelle said, to the approaching crowd.

"What is happening?" Heather asked only us, her voice a whisper.

"As long as they're within our gates, that's the only thing destined to happen!" Robin cried. "We can't fight the Infinite here, that's why we turned the lights off. You turn them on and we're on our own, and no one's coming to save us. Not your lightning children. Not even you."

Bombelle looked to us for help—or maybe something else.

"Come on, speech boy," I said, in a stupor, the crowd edging closer.

"I told you, it comes and goes," James said. "Heather?"

"Incoming," she said, blinking. "I mean, speaking for the Reaper—"

And whether the answer was something else or all of the above, it didn't matter—that's when the rumbling started. Something was happening to the ground below us, mostly, it was tearing itself apart. But the eyes of a small mob were locked onto Heather like they'd found a witch, get her.

"What?" Heather asked, stepping back. "You didn't feel that? And Lynn?"

"I'm only saying this a fourth time girl, you NEVER TAUGHT US—"

"CRETE?" James called back to the rock behind us.

"T'isn't me," Crete said, sticking his head out from behind the rock hallway (or whatever). "The shaking is local. The epicenter is close. That's not nature."

"Well this isn't a mountain," Willa said under her breath.

"You sure about those sensors sir?" I asked in a high voice.

"I am," Bombelle said, confidently, standing as confidently as a woman could with an active volcano between her legs. "Heather, what did you mean by incoming?"

Heather only held her hands up in the air, and then it happened. Boom.

The ground split in two, a rift in the dirt no wider than a few cars, but the entire mountain (volcano) wrenched with the divide. The people (mob) closest to us screamed and scrambled away, making for higher ground immediately. Then a light erupted up through it, catching only those of us leaning head-first over it—so the four of us, classic. But in the light we saw everything, especially the gemstone around my neck giving the floor a run for its money, so white-hot I almost fell over. James was the same (I hoped). At least I didn't panic.

"I'M BLIND!" I shouted. "I CAN'T SEE, AND, I'M DYING!"

The light finally faded enough for a human to see, right about the time Sand poked his head around the rocky corner and saw all four of us shining in a brilliant, unmistakable purple glow, next to a still ripping hole in the earth. He frowned at me. I gave him the sideways thumb, not bad, not good, he nodded, and was gone—just as the supernova went out, taking the cave torches with it, and all that was left was the glowing, slow-burning, almost crystal bright purple light from whatever was coming out of the ground. I guess in an underland sort of way, the lights of a cave had come back on, no harm done. But when they did, I wasn't wearing tan fabric any longer.

We'd gone far too long without supersuits.

"What is… happening?" Bombelle said, sounding like she'd been a lot angrier a second ago. "Am I still hallucinating?"

"You are not," Willa said, the only one who didn't look surprised.

I looked to my brother and the sight made the hairs on my arm stand up.

"Oh," I said. "I thought you were mad about the light."

"I'm not actually mad at anything happening here," Bombelle said.

"Hell," James said, in shock, but the good kind. "Yes."

James was covered up to his neck in a perfectly molded, shiny, obsidian coat of layered armor. Very humanoid, still uncanny, definitely scary. From toes to neck a purple energy seemed to illuminate the obsidian, but it didn't reflect exactly where James moved, it came and went as it pleased. My only complaint was it looked heavy. Then I brought my hands up to see the exact same armor on me, and it felt like a leather jacket at worst.

"By stone, brother," I said.

I moved my hips around, did some leg stretches, played some air guitar, the armor didn't give me an inch of grief. I thought claws to myself nice and loud, and I felt the rocks respond. Wings, same thing. Good lava, this rock.

"Nice digs," Willa said.

I had to agree. I gave her a razor sharp salute, each claw sticking out over my fingers a good two feet. I got the sense they could extend as far as I wanted them to. I made a fist and they were retracted before my fingers ever touched, faster than a blink of the eye. Meanwhile Lynn was looking down at the same sleek obsidian body armor, in a smaller fit. Still she looked like us, a mermaid in sharkskin. But not Heather—not with that purple hair and matching aura around her obsidian, this girl was on fire. Like ultraviolet, dragon-breathing fire.

One of these things was not like the other.

"This is normal?" Bombelle asked, blinking.

"This is thank the stars for, never thought we'd see it again, stone cold normal," Heather said, nodding. "I am finally yours. All those things you wanted from a living Reaper, we don't get more alive than this. My only question is the usual question."

There were hundreds of eyes on us. Our faces were uncovered, above the coolest lava rock armor I'd ever owned—and yes, the only one, that too. But it left my face vulnerable, although here's the thing... if there was anything I didn't feel like, it was vulnerable. I felt great. I felt like I could do anything, in a place where up until now I hadn't been able to do much but tag along and stay alive. This was different.

"Why?" Bombelle asked. "Why here, why now? Is it the storm? What we did at the Planetarium? The cave? Or is it... something else?"

"I think you're looking at your something else," I said.

And together, carefully now, we all stared down into the divide. The lights hadn't calmed a bit. It made it hard to see, but we still did it. Staring at the sun...

"It's... endless," one of the men by the edge said, a hand over his eyes.

"Thank you for not saying infinite," Heather said. "There's still incoming, I just can't tell what. It's definitely—"

"Don't you dare say something," James said, as we all looked down.

It wasn't only a never ending view of a tunnel that got brighter the farther away it fell, like there was some sort of natural illumination coming from the sides of the walls. Right, lava, that would do it. But it wasn't red, or pink. It was shades of purple, like EVERY shade of purple, from mauve to eminence to indigo. Even though there was only a soft wind here in the cave, as we looked down over that divide, Lynn's hair was suddenly defying gravity, then Heather's, and James' too. And that wasn't even the best part.

Only by the beauty of the light could we see the coming shadows.

"Purple, and out of the dark earth," James said, putting the pieces together.

"You'll get there brother," I said, with the world's biggest smile.

"Is that what I think it is?" Lynn said, her eyes absolutely soaring.

Shadows coming up out of the ground bathed in purple crystal luminance, and in our line of work? Always a good thing. Out of the tunnel, a few climbers on claws were scaling up the sides of the earth itself. If the shadows could be believed, they were absolutely hauling. They quickly got close enough for me to see the figures themselves, the sleek obsidian full facial helms and shoulder armor to match, claws as thick and sharp and long as... well, us. Willa was the first to take a stance, holding her greatsword out over the divide, only for it to be met by another much larger, silver edged broadsword coming out of the ground with a force so hard it lifted Willa off her feet, only a fist visible behind it.

"Finally," Willa said, nodding at the size difference. "A challenge."

"So can I come in now?"

Willa nodded, both swords retreated, and Heather was the first to kneel by the rip in the world and hold a hand down—only to pull a girl out of the ground. It was priestess Reya the Red, guardian leader of Eclipso, first defender of volcano lake mountain, the good old VLM. She was the same tiny ball of fire, less than five feet tall, the same bloody red brilliant armor and half-cape, the same smile, the same swords in both hands.

"Where am I, and how the hell is swords my welcome?" Reya asked.

"Get out of my HEAD!"

Like I wasn't already jumping towards her for a hug. Reya lifted me off the ground for a moment too, girl was strong, then my brother crashed us all to the ground.

"How the hell are you here?" James asked.

"We got an SOS from a car," Reya said. "Hard to ignore a thing like that."

"We?" Heather asked, with, dare I say, a smile on her face? "I don't remember asking for you. I also don't remember what I was thinking."

"We thought it for you," another voice came, and it was slightly less familiar.

"That's synergy right there," Heather said, as pleased as punch…ing a guy.

It was the Reaper scout Sasha, and yep, behind her, partner guy Volf. He was actually kind of cool, they both were. They'd gone from secretly tracking us under order from the head of the dragon, to leaping at the opportunity to aid Heather and us in the new plan for ascension. I didn't have a single personal problem with them. They were more than just this thought, but they both seemed to only do what they were told. Soldiers, much more, but also nothing more. Heather gave them both a small fist bump and a salute, and then a group hug.

Yeah I really didn't know them at all.

"Any other surprises?" Heather asked, jokingly, but their faces fell.

"Just one," Reya said. "You left something in the Vempire, and when he discovered we were setting out for you, he made it impossible to leave him behind. He's your problem now. I mean—there he is, you made it, aw GOOD!"

A scared, anxious Benjann Matthews climbed up out of the ground as it sewed itself back up after him, hands up, eyes locked on the silver sword Willa held aimed at his throat. I was a statue, staring at Benjann, thinking that we could run from a lot, but we'd finally been outran.

The past was getting better at catching up.

"Who are you?" Willa asked simply.

Benjann made a mouse sound. I couldn't blame him. That's how I felt.

"He's… with us," Lynn said, the first to speak (like usual).

But no he wasn't with us. He hadn't seen the message. He'd been on the underground side of a force field when it went down, he'd probably gotten lost among the swarming, stampeding crowd of Reapers coming out into the sunlight for the first time in ten years. He couldn't possibly know why we'd flown off to Silka because we never told him. He'd lost a week to the underland, same as us. The only difference between him and the other Infinite who accompanied us down into the Vempire was where they'd ended up after the battle for Reaper.

And just maybe… he was still alive for it.

"Where am I?" He asked, so innocently, so unknowing, it was too much.

"Pluma Petra, one of the many storm shelters within the jungles of Jerico," Bombelle said. "You still haven't given us a name, my boy."

"Benjann Matthews," he said. "Honorary Reaper. In training."

"Is that true?" Bombelle said, looking straight at Heather.

She nodded, without emotion or hesitation. We all did, out of pure instinct. Speaking of the ascension. Benjann had not only chosen the side of life, he had fought for it the same as us. He was an orphan kid in his teens and his first battle, and man he'd given us everything. Every ounce of trust. We could give that trust back to him, sure, but we could also give him the worst news we could imagine giving somebody. So there was that.

"He's a study alright," Volf said. "No fight, but he can wrestle. Don't let him get you on the ground, or it ends, no matter how many times you call uncle."

"I told you that's not my tap-out word," Benjann said.

"And I told you I'm NEVER calling you daddy," Volf said, retracting his claws and lunging at Benjann, who dug his feet into the ground.

"Is this—" Bombelle said.

"The vay of the Volf, yes," Sasha said. "Red and I have no sparring setting. If our fists come up, someone's dying."

"Can you believe it took saving a world for us to meet?" Reya said, butting up against the much taller Sasha so hard she almost fell over.

"We should really do it again sometime," Sasha said. "Are you happy now?"

"I am," Reya said, looking around. "Pick a volcano. I'm home, I love it."

"You were much more… stabby last book," I said, my eyes on Benjann.

"Food," Sasha said.

"No, it's something more," I said.

"I've eaten every other day for two years, it's food," Reya said, smacking her abs, seeming to hurt her hand more than her stomach. "I am literally twice the woman I once was, and she was already the commander of a castle on the volcano lake mountain. By that logic, all your base are now—"

"Nerds, every one of you," Heather said. "But thanks for believing a flying car enough to make the trip. I owe you an SOS."

"So what's the action?" Volf said, on his back in a headlock with Benjann squatting over him, trying to get him to tap, Volf absolutely refusing.

"The action?" Bombelle said. "Stop talking that way this instant, and get up. It isn't takanakuy for another two months. Whatever you're fighting, you do not have the territory's blessing in combat for your hatchets to be truly buried."

"What if we didn't bring hatchets?" Benjann said, looking up while keeping his weight down, just as Volf tried to escape. "Nope, go to sleep…"

"I don't care what you do, you're grown boys," Bombelle said. "But you are strangers in sacred grounds, and we have rules for strangers."

"I promise you, they're worth it," I said. "We'll be their hosts, if that helps."

"No, just," Willa said, smacking her head. "Damnit, Derek."

"Strangely enough, that does help," Bombelle said, grinning. "You read my mind Derek. Four strangers, four of you. I believe you know what to do."

"Oh no," I said, as it hit me, in the gut, heart, all the places Ollux had…

"Oh Derek," Lynn said, realizing what Willa meant. "You… fool."

"Why?" Sasha asked, curious.

"It's a simple initiation ceremony," Willa said. "It would have been a lot simpler if Derek could learn to keep that big mouth shut. Before anything else, they must become one with the territory."

"I know," I said, hanging my head. "Who do we want?"

"You leave that to me," Heather said.

"You can't be serious," Reya said, almost smiling, the oldest among them even though she was thirty at the most. Maybe she was familiar.

"I don't want this," I said, as my hands came up in claws opposite Reya, who drew her swords. Yes, plural.

"We're here to help, damn," Benjann said, eyes locked on Heather, who only dug her feet into the ground and held her hands out.

"Try to get me on the ground," she dared him.

He gulped. "Volf, if you maybe get a minute…"

"I don't see that happening," he said sadly, looking at Lynn hovering off the ground with a small swirl of rocks around her slowly forming a full facial helm.

That left James with Sasha. She raised her fists, and I remembered what she said about them. To his credit, already fully helmed in the rock armor, he held his hands up as Sasha walked towards him with no sign of armor on her skin.

"Do we allow this?" Crete asked from the sidelines.

"We step back, for sure" Bastile said, appearing by his wife's side out of the blue, and suddenly there was nothing but a big giant clearing for the eight of us.

"Losers do laundry," Reya said.

"I already did laundry," James said.

"No you didn't," Crete called from behind a rock.

3.6

FIRE FROM THE GODS

It was quiet on both fronts—unless you were Reya the Red. She crossed the distance between us in a blink, and it took all ten of my brother's blades to stop her sword. Derek was shoved about twenty feet backwards, and she was already sprinting in for another blow.

"Jungle attack!" I heard Lynn call, and she rushed Volf.

"AH!"

Sasha and Benjann still didn't get it. They only watched Reya dive down with her huge broadsword, easy enough for Derek to dodge, but he didn't see the other one coming in sideways. Still, it caught against the obsidian armor and there was no contest. Without that armor, he would have been a half boy. But the reality was somehow worse—for Derek. Her smaller sword shattered into a thousand pieces against his obsidian, leaving a foot of broken iron, a handle, and a shocked, slighted priestess of the volcanic underland.

"Oh no," Derek said.

"You broke my second favorite sword," Reya said.

She took her broadsword with both hands, the blade still sunken into the ground. The thing must have weighed fifty pounds, but she wrenched it out like it was a toothpick and aimed the flat side of the blade at him like a baseball bat.

"I mean… it looks like you have a—"

He didn't get to say spare. Derek went slamming across the ground so hard, the next thing I knew, he had hit the crowd and taken out a lady.

"Sorry lady!"

"A challenge indeed," Willa said, nodding in clear approval.

"Oh I get it," Sasha said. "James, prepare to die."

"You… first," I said, lamely.

Her fists solidified into an extremities-only obsidian, skin meeting more, metal as hell. I shrugged and threw a punch, expecting her to counter—not to catch my punch in a single dark hand, like I had thrown myself into the ether.

"Uh oh," I said.

"Mine," Sasha said.

She turned her hand and forced me sideways. I buckled like a belt. Then her foot came up and I saw the solidification just before—I got the boot.

Boom.

I flew, same distance as Derek, even landed in the same part of the crowd too. He pushed a few people back just in time for me to take the landing on empty cave floor, bouncing painfully over butt and back in the dirt, as he kept the crowd safely behind his arms.

"You're learning," I said, catching my breath.

"You forgot about your wings brother."

"Yeah well… you did too," I argued, as he pulled me to my feet. "Derek."

He followed my eyes, just in time to see Reya, coming in hot.

"I'm tired of being a tennis ball," he said.

No one had told Reya to stop, so she came in sword-first (again), as Derek flexed his claws out a foot longer than normal and caught her swing with his hands crossed over each other, letting both feet slide over the ground instead of trying to stick it. It took both Reya's hands to keep the pressure on, but the sword was coming down right in the middle of his crossed hands, so hard that if he couldn't hold, it would take both hands off in one blow.

"No Derek, not criss cross, never criss cross!" Heather shouted from the ground, with Benjann in a leglock only a few yards to my right.

"Why are your legs so strong?" Benjann roared, doing everything a wrestler could to break the hold, but he couldn't do it.

"I'm TRYING!" Derek shouted.

At the last moment he gave an inch, like a game of tug of war, and it was enough to wrench his hands down and out, as half of the sword disappeared into the ground again. Reya was smart enough to let go and dance away as Derek came for the hilt with all ten claws. Of course he didn't get anywhere near her, but she was bare-handed for once, and she knew it.

"Derek."

Then there were two brand new swords sliding across the floor. I saw Bastile smack Willa on the shoulder, but Reya already had one, so Derek took the other.

"Fair fight, right?" Willa asked (Bastile only grumbled).

Reya and Derek held their sword tips towards each other, as the rock armor crept over their entire bodies, head to toe. Reya even took the blade and ran it over her obsidian covered forearm, the sound was horrible.

"I'm not trying to kill you," she said.

"I have to see you try," Derek said, holding his ground, and sword.

She lunged, he countered so hard she almost fell over. She looked at him like they had found a way to communicate, soul to soul. She looked like she knew him, he looked like he knew what he was doing. After that, well, they danced a dance of swords. Bottom line—Derek was fine, back to me.

"Danger, James Nite," someone said behind me.

"Where, robot?" I asked, looking back to see—

Right. Sasha had settled back into her defensive stance, not taking a single step towards me—but still less than three feet away from me. I got up and looked at her. At all the room between us. At Heather and Benjann in a standing stalemate, both of their arms around each other's heads, just trying to wrench the other to the floor. At Lynn and Volf, both on wings flying low to the ground in a violent and relentless clash of claws, their fight by far the most entertaining, but the matchup the most predictable.

"HELP!" Volf shouted as he did his best to escape the wrath of a winged Lynn Lyre.

"Get back here and take it," Lynn said, zipping by, in control of damn near everything, because normal.

Reya was dancing dangerously around Derek, they were acting like two swords could only act. But I was supposed to be the shield, and right now it was Sasha standing her ground, calm as the bomb, not a single footprint in the dirt around her. She kicked me the hell out of her ground. I could learn.

I wiped my nose and circled Sasha, carefully. She didn't move. I put my fists up and stood my ground, just outside her reach.

"You gonna stay there?" She asked. "Two metapods, harden versus harden?"

"I've seen that fight, I can't believe you have too," I said.

"I won't say it again, we have television in the Vempire," she said.

"What's television?" Came the voice of a young boy in the crowd. Right.

"Two shields, no swords," I said. "Just these."

That's when the claws came out, and I took a running leap at Sasha, taking a chance at the offensive again—really not my style, but counting on that. She didn't even use her own claws. She only brought her forearm up, the obsidian rock armor hardened up to her shoulder, and she caught my blow like I had sliced into wood. We clashed and stuck together, sparks flew, but the momentum hadn't changed. Yet.

"Don't do it," I said, looking down, too late—

Boom. The boot, the damn boot again, and I went flying back into the crowd. For the second time, she had kicked me out of her reach.

"How do I win?" I asked, dazed.

"You're not supposed to," someone said.

Suddenly there were hands all over me, picking me up and putting me back on my feet facing Sasha. She had her hands up, and for the first time she even took a step towards me—but then she stopped, looking at something behind me with a face that said it all. It was the entire crowd around me with their hands up at their faces, in a fighting stance not even behind me, but at my side.

"This is normal?" I asked, looking around.

"You've done the job of any host," one man said close to me.

"You're not supposed to win this fight, you're supposed to engage the stranger enough to uncover their true colors," said another. His hands were at his face while mine were already hanging by my sides, as I caught my breath. "Jerico is only the strongest. She fits the bill. You aren't supposed to stop until the crowd intervenes for you. We're doing that."

"We just started fighting!" I complained.

"Yeah well, you're bad at it," the first man said. "And she is not."

"And so I have value?" Sasha said, listening, putting her hands down. "My looks aren't enough?"

"Oh she's funny too, she'll fit right in," the second guy said.

And he waved over to Bastile, who walked over to us. Even Sasha felt the weight of the reverence as the leader of the territory looked over us, weighing the decision… then he held his hand out.

"Welcome to Jerico," Bastile said. "Looks have nothing to do with it."

"Finally," Sasha said, taking the big man's hand. "Scout Sasha Green sir, first guard to the head of the dragon, hand of the royal blood of the Reaper, captain to the army of the underlord."

"Caput Bastile Bones," he said simply, blinking.

"Bastile—wait, Tommy Bones?" She cried out.

Bastile blinked.

"We can't call you that," I complained. "How come she can call you that?"

"It depends how she knows that name," Bastile said, looking down at her.

"From Portia Pass," Sasha said, looking up at him like we had this whole time. "We fought in the Blitz together, on the eastern banks of Cotillon. Remember the water? We thought it was rain, but it was—"

"Stop," Bastile said, looking at the hand in his. "I remember the water we thought was rain, every night in my nightmares. I remember you, Reaper. But I never saw you again—did your battalion make it through?"

"Of course not," she said sadly. "Yours?"

"Of course not," Bastile said. "A painful beauty, this life."

"Did everybody but us fight in the Blitz?" I asked, my hands in the air.

"Yes," Bastile said.

"Is anyone going to explain it to us, like ever?" I asked.

"That story… once again, that would be up to Freedom," Bastile said.

"Sand?" I asked. "Literally the first person we ever met on this mad path? He could have just told us everything from the beginning?"

"Yes," Bastile said. "But he didn't. For whatever status Freedom has lost on the island, he still commands respect. To defy his mission means death."

"Of course, to accept his mission also means—" Sasha said, all sass.

"A long life full of happiness?" I interrupted, suddenly white in the face.

"No, the opposite," Sasha said, pulling a not so small knife out of a strap on her leg with an inscription carved into the blade. For Freedom.

"That's poetic for a warrior like you," Bastile said, then he blinked. "Wait. That's not figurative."

"It is not," Sasha said. She wasn't turning into a villain or anything, she was just, I don't know, introspecting. "Speaking of death, will all due respect to the faithful Volf, how has Lyre not killed my guy yet?"

"He's faster than he looks," Lynn said as she swept by low on the chase.

"Don't kill him Lynn," I said quietly, watching the flight, my brain on crash.

"Go AWAY LYNN!" Volf shouted.

He was just a hair ahead of her on their mad dash through the cavern, as the youngest kids chased after them in delight on foot.

"Sixty seconds without a scrape from Lyre, that's another win," Bastile said.

He held a hand in the air and the crowd cheered Volf's name so loud that Lynn had to slow down. He landed heavily at Sasha's back with Lynn only a moment behind him, retracting the claws she already had primed for… winning.

He peered over Sasha's shoulder, all but hiding from Lynn.

"Aw," Lynn said, leaning up against Bastile. "Next time, wolfie."

"Absolutely not," Volf said. "You're dangerous Lyre. You don't fly like you lost ten years to the lightning city. You move steady, like rock. Like Reaper."

"Is that a compliment?" Lynn asked.

"Do you consider being Vema a compliment?" Volf asked. "I thought you left the empire for reasons."

"Eight year old girls don't really have a say over what house they call home," Lynn said. "I did what my father told me to do. But for ten years I've been a half girl. You calling me whole is indeed a compliment, Volf. I am Reaper. I am also—"

"Much more than that," she and Derek said at the same time, as he and Reya came limping over, too exhausted to continue.

"I was rooting for you two," Volf said, with a wink, a proper one.

"I don't know what to say to that," Derek said.

"Then don't say anything," Sasha said.

Man, dating was starting to sound dangerous.

"Her rightful owner," Reya said, handing Willa back her sword.

"It is enough," Bastile said loudly to the chamber. "The ceremony is officially ended, with welcome to all. For the love of the jungle, stop fighting, you too Heather Denien, speaker of the—wait what am I seeing right now?"

"A physical miracle," Benjann said. "Quick, take my picture."

Heather only growled. Somehow she was on her back on the ground in a full leg-locked cradle, Benjann holding her so hard we all saw her hand tap-out on his leg. The crowd around her moved in but he was already standing up, punching the air in victory.

"Is the universe broken?" Lynn said, blinking.

"He's pretty good on the ground," Volf said. "I've got forty pounds on him, and he always puts me in the same lock. He calls it the little baby."

"It's because you're a little baby," Benjann said, winking at Volf.

The crowd even clapped for Benjann as he got up and ran over to Volf for a fist bump, a chest bump, an air-bump, they were close, we got it. Heather meanwhile walked towards us with what could only be described as… a limp? On HEATHER?

"I would say don't say it, but—" she started.

"He got you in the little baby?" I asked, my smile absolutely ear to ear.

"I had the shot," she said, with a face that said it all. "I didn't take it. I could have… and maybe I still should… but I couldn't do it alone."

And the smiles was gone. Right.

Heather versus Benjann, one side had a major reason for hold back. The shot she could take on him… she was talking about the one we collectively owed Benjann. The truth about Ana. What was and wasn't waiting for him back in the lightning city, how it was worse than he was ready for… how it was all our fault. So there was that. We were realizing it now, Heather had to figure it out from her back with the adrenaline coursing through her. She had never tapped out before.

"Sorry," I said, my eyes low. "I'm stupid and I'm sorry…"

"I know you're sorry," Heather said. "But you're not stupid, and he deserves to know. Just, don't make me do it alone."

We'd had enough, and so had the audience. The four newcomers bowed to a still cheering crowd, and that was it. Willa walked over carrying a small wooden box on a strap that was just packed to the brim with irony—I mean rations. Bread, nuts, a few orange slices, some waters all around, and we were good. Still no coffee though.

"I believe we are now officially your problem," Reya said, her head on my brother's shoulder, swords on the ground, just catching their breath.

"You are accepted under grand tradition, the lands and ancient secrets of Jerico are now yours to experience, great, moving on." Bastile said.

The crowd was still curious, but the excitement was gone. A few of them stayed, but most eyes turned away from us, now that the 'ceremony' was over. Most obviously, Sand Freedom was nowhere to be seen.

"Been a while since I done kicked the leaves," Volf said. "This jungle looks different. Looks like obsidian. We got kids around?"

"Yep," Sasha said, looking up. "Memories."

Right. We'd been to volcanos together before. I didn't know what I didn't know, but Volf and Sasha had been following us for almost the entire time underland, invisible as the sulfur air, from Galan to Cauldron to Eclipso. They were Heather's contingency plan—actually, we were her contingency. Tapping in the head of the dragon was always her play.

"This is not a tree," Bastile said. "Storm season's something else this year."

"Why are we here?" Sasha asked. "The car did not elaborate. For a decade the underpass has been broken off, but today the rock moved aside for us like the era of the original Ocarina might just be back upon us."

"Have the barriers between nations eroded?" Volf said. "Is this traveling?"

"You know the four pillars of astronomy?" Heather said.

"Course," Sasha said. "Our most important international achievement, the literal symbol of how coming together in pursuit of survival is possible even in the wake of a ten-year long fracture."

"We're nothing without our future," Volf said, folding his arms like we'd insulted his intelligence. "Those four pillars are hope for every man woman and child on this rock."

"We broke two of them," Heather said, wincing.

"You did what to hope?" Sasha asked, staring like we were setting fire to art.

"The Observatory in Silka, and the Planetarium in Jerico," Heather said. "Gone to this world, until Infinite can rebuild them of course."

"You don't know that," Volf said, still mad. "Infinite can't fix anything, they never have."

"We're not on that," Sasha said, her eyes drilling into Volf with *shut up man* all over them. "But okay, no need to wonder. Volf, stop baring your fangs."

"I'll do what I want," Volf said, uncrossing his arms. "I mean yes dear."

"You mean yes Ma'am," Sasha said, blushing for a split second.

"I mean what I mean," Volf said, and he put a hand out for Sasha. She took it, and looked at him, stunned. "She's right. We were at the Crossroads ready to lose power when the ground opened up for us. In that moment, the choice, the fork in the road, when until now travel has been so impossible, it was beautiful."

"The Crossroads?" My brother asked.

"What was beautiful?" I asked.

"Real freedom," Sasha said, still holding Volf by the hand.

"On our own terms." Volf said, still looking only at Sasha. "I've never been so willing. All it took was a touch of the familiar in strangerland, you know?"

"A sense of command," I said.

"An air conditioner in a flying car," my brother said.

"The ability to bring my culture's most ancient tools of safe travel into a place where for centuries we haven't, that's worth more than air to me," Volf said, narrowing his eyes at me. "That's more than a spark. A whole new—"

"Copyrighted!" I said. "Well you're welcome for activities, it's what we do."

"Are you bragging about destroying two of Ocarina's oldest and most iconic constructs, the closest thing we have to national monuments?" Sasha said, her hands on her hips. "Is the Mercurial next? Do we have to worry about the Mylotic coming after us?"

"What's a mercurial?" I asked.

"Mylo's floating, astronomical epicenter, it makes parabolic reflections out of spinning mercury and points them at the stars," Bombelle said.

"And/or kelp," Sasha said.

"Science by the boatload," Volf said.

"Literally," Bombelle said, nodding to the Reapers, thinking hard about her polestar (probably?). "It goes without saying that none of you are going to lay a finger on the Mercurial, let alone step foot in Mylo."

"I thought I was going to have to say it," Volf said, nodding at Bastile like an equal. "The port city is off limits. We can't bring our problems there."

"Uh oh," I said.

My brother smacked me. I didn't care. This might be preemptive… but sorry Mylo. One day, we were going to show up on the shores of the port city we never knew still existed. Probably wet, and hopefully with all the answers, but more likely with all the problems. But not right now.

"We would never," Heather said. "I can do math, that's three out of four devices, and three out of four nations. It almost seems like you're about to tell us the forth would be somewhere in the Vempire."

"The polestar detects overland," Bombelle said. "Sorry to break the cycle."

"We haven't done that yet," Lynn said.

"You shouldn't need to blow things up to do that," Reya said.

"We were actually hoping you'd help us blow the next one up," Heather said.

"No you weren't," Willa said. "You said you wanted them here because one day soon, the Jerico and the Reaper would have to work together again. That's already happening, nothing is on fire."

"No, just drowned worse than the seven continents ever were," Bastile said, his eye on the outside of that cave where the rain was coming down like metal.

“Two days of this and Issaic won’t have to burn us out. If the fields flood, the Oleander will be unsustainable. We might be next in line for the burial after all.”

“Unless…” Lynn said, sensing marching orders.

Bastile rubbed his forehead, and we faced him as one.

“Four of our best gave their lives attempting to infiltrate the Hexoscope, unless they didn’t,” Bastile said slowly. “Your immediate assignment is following up. You have no orders to do a single thing to the construct, this is, hopefully, a humanitarian mission. The truth, and the cost, wait for you at—”

“The Crossroads,” James said with Bastile. “I’ve been waiting to do that.”

“Good job James,” Bastile said, shaking his head.

James beamed. Then his smile fell. “Wait. The Hexoscope?”

“It’s a three day ride from the gates,” Bastile said. “It was supposed to be, in technical terms, a layup.”

“And what, in those same terms, was ours?” I demanded.

“A moonshot,” Bastile said. “I don’t have to remind you which failed.”

“Both,” I agreed, thinking of heroes again for some reason.

“We all thinking the same thing?” Sasha asked. “Big giant silo center, about ten miles east of Commander’s Pass?”

“You’re right,” Reya said, blinking. “We flew over it, it still stood for the bombs that put us underland. I was wondering why.”

“Wondering over,” Bastile said. “But caution. We have encountered Infinite defenses at both ends of our polestar positions.”

“You see enemies, that means you’re going the right way,” I said.

“Great, we go?” Lynn asked, looking around.

“Seems so,” Bastile said, looking at me like he could finish a thought.

“Come on, you’ve got us,” Willa poked at my side. “What could go wrong?”

“Literally an infinite number of things,” I said. “You think you’re coming?”

“Starting with, how’s Willa going to keep up?” Lynn asked.

Reya nodded, unclipped her suspenders, and let them hit the dirt. She kicked the thing over to Willa, letting the fabric get dusty and dirty.

“You would… share your supernatural?” Willa asked, almost unbelieving.

“Why not?” Reya said.

There was so much more she could have said, but somehow, she’d already said it all. Willa put her hand to her heart and bowed to Reya, who blinked awkwardly, but didn’t seem to mind. Then Willa jumped to the suspenders like a kid on Christmas morning, dust, dirt and all.

“Thanks for not letting the lack of flying disqualify me,” Willa said.

“Skyfire,” Derek said, grinning. “The most dangerous kind of fire.”

“I’ll be good, I swear,” Willa said, giving her shoulders a roll. “To think, the hand of Jerico and the freedom of the Reaper combined. This must be a first.”

“I’m keeping the necklace,” Reya said. “My father gave it to me. I’m not much for material things, but this leaves my body when I leave this world.”

“What she said,” Lynn said, holding a hand to the rock around her neck.

“Great that’s Skyfire, what about Red?” I asked, looking at Reya without wings. “You’re not planning on keeping up, are you?”

“No,” she said. “The unburying is still undergoing. There are parts of the

Vempire that do not yet know they have again the option to live overland. Every day is progress, I can't afford to miss it. If you need us, we will be there."

"You're talking about the city of Eclipso when you say that, right?" I asked.

"I am talking about the nation of Vema when I say that," Reya said. "From Avila to Galan, Zentri to Zadaa, Eclipso to… Oran, who have treated my new command with more grace than I could ever deserve. Still, I am no Balin."

"What he did for us can never be repaid," Derek said, eyes down.

"What we owe you is just as impossible," Reya said. "But we have to try."

Reya the Red held her hands out and a small ringlet of rock came over each of her limbs, like four bulky bracelets. Her necklace shone bright, and she levitated off the ground by weird rock power alone. She was even able to salute us, before the ground opened up beneath her again, and she was gone, headfirst into the purple glow that stopped as soon as it started.

"Well good for her," Heather said, turning back to us. "We leave in, now."

"Now *that,* I was ready for," Volf said, on his feet and stretching. "Finally."

"And where are we going?" Benjann asked, innocently.

We stared at him. All of us. At the same time.

"You been paying attention?" Willa asked. "Anything, last ten minutes?"

"Not really," Ben said. "I was thinking about my girlfriend. It's been ten days since I've spoken to her. She must think I'm dead. Please. I need to get back to Silka. That's what we're doing, isn't it?"

Sasha sighed. Everybody got up, ignoring Benjann. There were a lot of us.

"What'd I miss?" He asked, innocently.

"That's a big no on Silka City," I said. "Believe us, we didn't ask for you. But you're not leaving our sight, that's the only way we can make sure you stay alive. Unless you'd rather stay here and cooperate from the sidelines?"

"I'd rather die," Ben said. "Thanks for the benefit."

"No damsels," I said, giving him a fist bump. "No benchwarmers."

"Just thrown into the mix without knowing why, lest the road in the rearview catch up and perish me," Ben said darkly. "Hey look, I'm you."

It was kind of true.

We faced the exit hole of the cave, where the water was still coming down in sheets. I saw Heather don her reaper rock armor and step out into the downpour, holding an armored hand up in the rain, her entire face covered by a sleek obsidian facial helm. She must have liked our chances.

"It's not getting any lighter," she said.

"Hope you know what we're doing," I said to Volf as we walked past him.

"I don't," he said, frowning. "But the car said you've already had Jerico casualties. I'm guessing I'm here to make sure that doesn't happen again."

"Even if—" I started.

"I know my place," Volf said, and the way he looked at me then, I could tell he meant it. "Have you found yours?"

I didn't know.

"That's a no," Volf said. "That's good."

"How?" I said.

"Means you need to stay alive long enough to find it," Sasha said, coming up on my brother's side. "From here on, that's your only job. Do it."

"Yes ma'am," we said.

"Call me Sasha or die," she said.

"Safe travels," came a voice behind us.

It was Crete. Sand was nowhere to be seen. I waved back, then my necklace lit up and a coat of transparent obsidian overcame my head in all directions. I was in rock mode, and so was everyone else.

"Get our real hope machines working," my brother said to them. "If anyone could do it, it's you. You give us that one thing, and we'll take care of the rest."

"Deal," Crete said. "Hey James. Someone's gotta step up. Be a leader."

He was right, even if I hated it. But I nodded. "Alright. Flight pattern astral."

"Pattern what? Speak Reaper, city boy," Sasha said.

Crete laughed out loud as I sighed, smacked my suspenders, and became invisible—because normal, remember?

"Oh that pattern," Sasha said, and then she disappeared. Everyone did except Willa, but she was watching us, and she smacked her chest all the same.

"Holy…" Bastile said, as he held Willa's eyes until they blinked out of visibility.

"Shengcun…" Bombelle finished, at his arm.

"Language, both of you," came the disembodied voice of Wildfire Willa.

I winked at them, then remembered I had a rock helm covering my entire face, then remembered I was invisible. Always something.

"Wink," I called out to the world. Wait why hadn't I thought of that before?

The rain never let up. It pushed us down and sideways, but only as much as water could move rock. Yet over time, that's where sand came from. Wait. Interesting that once the Reapers had shown up, Sand had disappeared. Maybe he'd taken over the suits for Crete, or maybe he didn't want Sasha recognizing him from Portia Pass, or Cotillion, or any of the other places I'd never even heard of. I couldn't worry about it. All the mystery about Sand Freedom had wrapped itself up into a nice box and bow in my brain, a single thought outweighing everything else—he'd tell us when we were ready. Somewhere between not having a home to go back to and all the fantastic damage that had followed, we'd learned one thing about him. There was a lot to learn about him, and any ground gained on that usually included crazy things for Derek and me. Maybe taking it slow was the best thing for our limbs and ligaments, for our already fragile sanity. Maybe we were simply too young to understand him—that I could understand.

For now, it wasn't about Sand Freedom. It was about Lady Bombelle and the first working navigation system to come out of Jerico in a decade. It was about the first team Bastile had sent to this particular direction—the team he didn't tell anyone about—and how they had never come back. Sure there was a part of me that hadn't really come back from the Planetarium, but that was different than dying in the field, an hour at top flight away from your home. The best case scenario for them was that Infinite had imprisoned them, and taken them alive as captives, to at worst be… interrogated.

"How do the soldiers of Jerico hold up under… interrogation?" I asked, sensing Willa on my right, the most turbulent of all the fliers.

"Till death," Willa said. "They will give Infinite every reason to kill them. To us, the only thing worse than torture is betraying the secrets of our nation."

"Of course it is," I said, rolling my eyes (since no one could see me). "You junglefolk can't be selfish for one second."

"No we cannot," Willa said, sounding like she was smiling.

I couldn't see her, but I could sense everyone. Those yellow tinted eye covers made a sparkling purple outline easy enough to follow into the night. The only problem was that no matter how high we flew, I kept seeing branches and leaves coming at me at the last moment.

"Stop it tree!" I shouted, after the third leaf smack to the ear.

"Your necklace!" I heard Heather shouting. "It knows the land. Use it!"

I closed my eyes and thought the word MAP as hard as I could, feeling something building up around my armor. Then the rock around me unleashed a burst of purple energy, lighting up the land and trees like a wave of echolocation in all directions. When it was gone, the imprint of the trees around me was burned into my facial screen, and I could use it like a map. Wait just a minute.

"THAT'S what that is?" I asked.

"Light up the night!" Heather said. "We're not a fighting people James. We're survivors, doing a whole lot more than just surviving."

"Why are you more honest when you're invisible?" I asked.

"Easily," Heather replied. "I get to smack you upside the head with the truth, and not be reminded by the peach fuzz that we're all just kids."

"Well we are what we are," I said. "And we wouldn't be here if we couldn't help. If we take anything from this territory, let it be the honesty."

"I'd rather die," Heather said.

"You said I couldn't go home yet," Benjann said, reminding all of us he was there. Right. "You said you had to keep me alive. What was that about? Why am I flying over a part of the island I've never been to, instead of making sure the one person I care about is okay? What if something happens to her while I'm out here?"

The similarities were similar.

"Here's not really the place for that," I started, as I felt the eyes of Derek, Lynn, and Heather on me. "You know Pilot Mara gave her life for the Vempire?"

"I know," Ben said, his eyes low. "I saw her. I watched it happen. She and Jett, they just... never stopped fighting. Until they did. What about the rest?"

I winced. Of course.

"Everyone who fell off the falloff..." Derek said slowly. "Geran and Laurel were beaten half to death by Hannah. Noah and Mikael were left in our prison cells, dead. The only one who isn't dead or willing to kill for Issaic is... you."

"What..." Benjann said, his head heavy. "All of them? Why, because we were underland for FIVE SECONDS? I'm the only one of them who did a damn thing to help the Reaper! Why did they have to die, why NOT ME?"

It was hard to argue with that. Mara the pilot, the interim commander, the kindhearted, stoic face of Infinite, so unreadable that we had doubted her true colors until the very end, until she had made herself perfectly clear. Jett, the young, teenage leader of the unfortunate crew of Odd-abducted Vema agents. Two people who'd met on the other side of an invisible line the universe had drawn, before either were ever born. It wasn't our fault we had come into Infinite (and then Reaper) with a complete lack of preexistent knowledge and immediately drawn all the suspicion. Or maybe their deaths were exactly our fault, and we should stop expecting the win by jumping into a thing headfirst, butt last, eyes closed. It was a good way of drawing swords to necks before knowing why. But maybe there was a lesson in there somewhere, about how when a world was already so messed up, the only way to come together again was by coming together against outsiders? Could that be us? Then how do you explain Ana? She was a doctor working for Infinite. There was no logical reason to put her down, except for maybe the contents of a single, one-sided video message, sent to Lynn at a girl's darkest hour, unanswered by the only ones who could have helped her. I felt like screaming again. On one hand, the people of the Vempire were finally free. On the other, the memory of those bodies in the dirt… my brain was already actively trying to block out what I had seen. That was trauma. But here I was, thinking about myself, like always.

"I… know the feeling," Derek said, his words heavy, but quiet.

"My head wants me to remind you this is a covert mission, but my heart can't stand it either," Sasha said, suddenly swooping in on us. "What you are feeling… I won't pretend I know what it's like. I won't compare it to something else I've been through. I'm just sorry Benjann. I'm sorry you feel you should have died, when everything I've ever seen from you tells me otherwise."

"Same," Heather said, coming in from the other side. "I've been trying to figure out how to say it, and she just said it all. Now get out of my brain."

"Make me," Sasha said.

It was… familiar. I guess Sasha had probably spent the last few days with Benjann. It was more than we ever had.

"That's some apology," Ben said, sounding like he was breathing normally again. "If what you're saying is true… it's not worth finding out on my own, if the same is just going to happen to me. I won't question you again."

"The day you stop questioning is the day you are truly ended," Sasha said. "Just, you know, maybe save some for the post-op. We're kind of on a jungle doomsday deadline here."

"I understand," Ben said. "Thanks Sasha. For not leaving me behind."

"Never," Sasha said, sticking her tongue out at me (I imagined).

He'd said it himself, that was some apology. Why couldn't we just do that?

We flew farther out into the night, so far that we eventually got to the end of the rain, except not. That was sarcasm. The farther we flew, the more we realized this was no localized storm. It was a summer system that was probably going to make its way across the entire island. We could count out the possibility of being not wet. Another summer with athlete's foot…

"Keep your armor tight!" I shouted out. "We're far from that beautiful lava rock, anything on the ground will be as wet as mud. This obsidian armor is the best chance we'll ever get, don't you dare forget it!"

"NO SIR!" Seven voices shouted back.

"Any part of that accurate?" I heard Derek ask the purple sparks to his right.

"All of it," Heather said, impressed. "Hell, James. Also we're here."

That was fast. But it made sense, we'd been at full tilt invisi-trooper mode for a while. It was time. The edge-line of the green sea finally made itself clear(er) through the heavy rainfall. It was hard to see through the veil of rock lens and then the nature of it all, the rain so thick it was hard to see a hundred yards ahead clear, and anything after that was just mist. Except—

"Is that it?" Derek shouted out through the rain.

"That's what flying does!" Heather s shouted. "Takes the travel out of it."

"That's usually when we find out the most about each other," I said sadly.

"No, traveling without superpowers is just universally boring, that's what gets us talking," Heather said. "I wonder if we'll still be friends, now that we're not forced to be boring?"

"I need to take a class on how your mind works," Lynn said.

"Strike one, school's boring, so are you," Heather said.

Lynn thew her hands up, but we were laughing behind her. Lynn Lyre was anything but boring. And Heather was right. We were here.

We started our descent among the thunder and lighting, coming down to a small hill a few hundred yards up and away from a long stretch of land that didn't end in any direction we could see from up here, the only thing standing out was the structure. It was a small containment site, with fences and utility trucks and piles of materials scattered around the circular, single story perimeter building. Inside that ring was the main hub, a box building at least two hundred feet high, a good six stories tall. There was no telescope sticking out of this building. We had the part of the world that became trees and nothing else about a hundred yards behind us, we were back to open air.

No problem for the invisible, but still, it was time for a plan.

"We need a plan," I called out, surprising myself (and everyone else) again. "Two objectives, infiltration and backup. Heather, you're with me, Sasha, and Benjann. Derek, take Lynn, Volf and Willa inside. Your our eyes."

The group was quiet. I saw most of the purple outlines looking to my right.

"How is this happening?" Heather said. "He's right. Again. Any questions?"

"No ma'am," seven voices said, including mine.

"Then we all know why we're here," Heather said. "No more heroes."

"Godspeed brother," Derek said, and we hugged once in the air, unseen, but for a flash of purple and blue sparks from where our rock armor met.

"What's the point of invisibility if you're going to sparkle all day?" Volf asked.

"That's why we're splitting up," I said.

"I still can't remember the last time this worked," Derek said.

"You two are the only ones who speak telescope," Heather said. "We can't risk losing you both, not until we know what's waiting for us. James knows it."

"I… do," I said, realizing it in that moment.

Derek thought on it for a moment, and nodded. "For all the enchiladas."

I couldn't help it, I had to laugh. The rest of the team(s) didn't need such ceremony, they were actual soldiers. They dropped low and soared invisibly over the plains towards the structure. They were on their way.

"So how we feeling tonight?" I said in a low voice to Sasha, Heather, and Benjann. "I know Heather said no more heroes, but you can't always get what you want. Is everybody ready to change the world?"

Grumbles. All I got were grumbles.

3.7

KINGDOM COME

"Careful now," I said.

"That changes everything," Volf said sarcastically.

The four of us flew as fast and invisible as the wind, keeping no higher above the ground than a front door. On Infinite jet boots, the stars weren't even the limit but on these wings, well, I could only remember the first time I had seen the red Reapers of Eclipso defend their castle against the hordes of dirt drones. The way Reya's warriors had flung themselves forward in a gallop, their bodies fully sideways, taking the enemy head on. It was almost like they were faster on earth than above it. Made sense, because rocks.

"We gotta get Willa some claws," I said.

"There's no time," Lynn said, somewhere on my left. "We're here."

"Where?" Volf asked.

"We don't really know where here is, most times," I said, scratching my head. "We're just... here. There's only one thing I know for sure. The last four soldiers to set foot here, they never left. Bastile and Alcyon told me that much."

"Alcyon?" Volf asked.

"He was in one of the jets," I said. "At Cradlesong. You fought that name."

"That means you did too Derek," Volf said.

"So he can fight?" Willa asked. "I never doubted Lynn, he's in boot camp."

"I'd say you were wasting all of our time, if we weren't here," Volf said. "They're not kids. Don't make that mistake, I already did."

"Thanks Volf," I said.

"Thank me over dinner, when this is all over," Volf said. "If we make it out."

"Kingdom Come," I said, the thought gripping my body. "And never leave."

"Get it together Derek," Lynn said. "It looks deserted. We got this. Still... maybe everybody keep an exit in sight."

I could feel her unease. That was never comforting. Too bad.

We never even landed, we only flew closer and closer to the scaffolding around the structure, the invisibility our only safeguard. I didn't know how radars worked, I just hoped they didn't. We passed the piles of supplies and followed a clearly paved, curvy road all the way up to a part of the structure that looked the most like a front door, or at least a thirty foot clearing at the end of the worn path. As we got closer, the walls responded like they could see us coming, and on what was clearly an electric tread, they slid open.

"Who's that?" Willa said.

"Hold," a voice came.

It was Lynn, sounding like she already had her head stuck through those doors. Because she did. It was time to kill the wings, and I felt the wind around me calm down as one by one we landed. Something bumped into my butt.

"Who's THAT?" Willa said again.

"It's a me," I said, putting my hands around in the air until I found a pair of shoulders. "You good Willa?"

"I haven't been this invisible since high school," she said.

"Even you?" I said. "High school must suck for everyone."

I couldn't see it, but I had a vision of the entire group nodding along.

"Okay all clear," Lynn's voice came.

We all passed through the open, sliding door of the one story structure. We flew in and landed on the inside of an open door. I thought there would be a few hallways between us and the high rise room but no, once we were inside, it was all open space, a ceiling two hundred feet high, and a huge honeycomb structure in the middle of it, twenty feet up on a boxed platform with stairs all over. It was a rocket science launch chamber, just without the rocket. The walls were covered in soundproof panels, the space around them home to screens and desks and support pillars, spare parts and roller carts, and the fuselage that were all connected to the main hexagonal-patterned device in the middle of the room.

"What is this?" A voice came behind me. "A room for bees?"

"That's no honeycomb," Lynn said. "It's a three mirror anastigmat."

"How do you know that?" I asked.

"Because speaking of stupid high school, it looks just like the one Crete and I made for science fair," Lynn said. "Just a hundred times bigger."

"But those words you just said…" Volf said, confused. "Three mirror what?"

"It's a telescope, designed to correct and capture light from the deepest, darkest parts of space," Lynn said. "This isn't just astral. This is… cosmic."

"Speak up, can't hear you," came a voice from over by the Hexoscope.

"Sorry, I was just saying about a—" Lynn started, then we all froze.

That voice wasn't us. I tensed up, sensing the others doing the same, feeling the heat on my back as we instinctually moved closer together.

"What was that?" Lynn said.

"Just… me," came the response, again, not from any of us.

It was dark in the launch chamber, but for a single glowing blue light in the corner, making its way around the box taking up the middle. It was moving towards us. It was a person, holding a palm up, the light enough to see a small box shaped device in their hand. It kinda looked like—

"Out of here," I whispered, the wings coming out again—

But then the doors slammed shut, the lights around the ringed walls flickered on in sequence, and the figure in blue pushed a glowing blue button on the thing in his hand that looked like a gameboy—and our invisibility flickered out. So did our wings, and all manner of Reaper powers. Power shift.

"What?" Lynn shouted.

She looked down at the rock armor dissipating from her body, leaving only skin and tan Jerico rags for protection. I was the same, straight dusting away. We'd been caught by the light. And as soon as we were seen, twenty feet from the middle of the room, the figures emerged from the shadows, from railings and platforms overhead, from up on top of the beehive structure itself. There was motion in every direction, there were agents all around us. I turned for the closed door, but when I looked back at it, there were two other agents standing in front of it, with their arms folded. We'd been had.

"Did we plan for this?" Volf asked, his armor in a pile of dirt at his feet.

"To be honest?" I said. "No."

"On and off again," the first agent said, holding the device in his hand, another familiar (and unexplained) thing from the Planetarium.

"Your monologuing needs some work," I said. "I don't even know who you are. I don't know how much I should be afraid."

"I don't want you afraid," the agent said. "I want you to feel like me. Betrayed by someone you called friend not even that long ago. All used up and nowhere to go. How's that for monologuing?"

The agent took off his hood. I was expecting Troy, or Alcyon. Maybe Odd or Lukas. But it was worse than I thought.

"Jemeni?" I said, actually blindsided.

Not only the oldest kid from that room of misfits back in Infinite Blue Panel, but the one who'd come closest to understanding us. He was clearly the leader of that small group, clearly the only one looking out for the orphans of Infinite, clearly their only lifeline to a stable existence. But that also meant…

"You killed him," I said.

The memory of Xero hit me in the face, trying to come out of my eyes in tears. This meant we had watched Jemeni take a life, right in front of our eyes. I wouldn't give him the satisfaction. I wanted the satisfaction.

"You killed her," Jemeni said.

His eyes were red and furious, no hold back, as the memory of Ana collided, my brain officially overloaded, neither of us wrong…

"We didn't," I said. "We have it on—"

"On your conscience for eternity, I'm familiar," Jemeni said.

He helmeted up, looking at us through an actual physical bodysuit with metal protection all over it. It wasn't online, but somehow medieval Infinite had me more scared than the usual. There was something that looked like a police baton at his hip. It gleamed like metal. Heavy.

"I was going to say we have it on camera," I said, not backing down.

"So you bugged us, that's why you allowed yourselves pranced through every inch of headquarters," Jemeni said, nodding behind us, and agents on the ground started forward, as those up on the railings started down towards us using stairs and ladders, not grappling hooks or jet boots.

"You're as cut off as we are," I said, realizing.

"It's still five on one," Jemeni said, like he didn't care.

"Gonna need a miracle for this one," Volf said, his hands up.

"Should we call in a miracle?" I said.

"I wasn't… damnit Derek," Volf sighed. "Information is ammunition."

"I heard that," Jemeni said. "Search the perimeter. Remember, only the twins are off limits. Everyone else can die tonight."

"SIR!"

Eight of the twenty ran outside, their full bodied, metal armor clearer than ever in the sprint. From head to toe there was protection, if you were them. For us, we were back to Jerico fighting. Nothing but fists and feet, skin and flesh exposed. Barely any weapons, not even a skateboard in sight.

"Three on one," Jemeni said, shrugging, turning back to us.

He was right. Lynn's hands never left her face, but Willa was still staring around at the circle, her sword untouched at her side.

"I don't want to fight you, child of Infinite," she said.

"Then stop aiding and abetting Silka's most wanted," Jemeni said. "Look at that, too late."

"What happened to two days?" I asked.

"That line was crossed when you opened that door," Jemeni said. "You're here to alter the geomagnetic currents over Ocarina, we can't let you do that."

"Why not?" I asked, innocently.

"For reasons," Jemeni said. "First rule of energy, it can't be destroyed. Where do you think all that anti-electricity would go, if not the north?"

"We've been here before, wherever it's going NOW!" I shouted. "What's so wrong with that? Why do you keep trying to take the modern world away from any place on this island that's not Silka City?"

"Because they're quieter that way," Jemeni said darkly, his eyes narrowed at me. "And I can't remember a louder group of kids than you."

"I don't think we've had the pleasure," I said, my hands up.

"Yeah well I'm taller and stronger, this should go quick," Jemeni said.

I could do this. He was a few inches taller than me, but we were probably the same weight. That meant his limbs were longer and leaner than mine. He turned sideways and became even smaller, holding his hands up like a boxer.

"I'll give you the first—" I said.

Bam. Punched in the face.

I took the blow but there was another behind it, and I still hadn't gotten my hands up. The fist broke across my ear and I got wrung like a bell. I staggered away and yanked my foot out from underneath his, and thankfully he stumbled for just a second—bam. I'd sent the foot at his stomach without even putting it down first. He groaned and I came down in a hammer arm but he dodged it and I almost fell over. My ears were ringing. I was already breathing heavy, I was at full tilt just trying to stand straight up—

"Derek calm down!" Lynn shouted.

"You'd never say that to a woman!" I shouted back, full nerve ending, until realizing—she was right.

Jemeni was looking at me like a crazed bull, but I couldn't return that energy. It wasn't me. I took a breath, my entire body shaking with the adrenaline, feeling like I was about to cry, or burst with emotion—truly, calming down took more discipline than the fight. But I did it.

"Calm, like the bomb," I said, taking a deep breath in.

My teeth locked, watching Jemeni come in with a curved right hook, narrowly stepping back in time, then jumping forward and letting my elbow smash across his shoulder and neck. It didn't hurt as much as last time, but he was still wearing metal armor. I would feel that in the morning. The worst thing was... it was a good hit. It would have taken anyone down, if they weren't coated in steel armor from head to toe. As it was, Jemeni spun with my blow, caught me landing, kicked out my front foot, and then we were on the floor. That's when it happened.

"No," I said, feeling the legs tense up, Jemeni already making sure the majority of his body weight was on top of me.

"Don't tell me you can't wrestle," Jemeni said, flipping his body around and slamming my head into the ground at the same time.

I saw stars, but it was nowhere near over. I felt something on my neck and legs, then my back hit the ground with Jemeni sitting on my stomach, cracking his knuckles.

"DEREK!" Lynn shouted, racing forward, right into another agent with a rusty metal rod in a hand, and Lynn hit the ground before her head was taken off in a swipe.

"You'll get your turn," Jemeni said.

He motioned to the other two agents watching our fight. They wheeled on Lynn and suddenly we were cut off by no less than six huge male soldiers between us.

"I don't wait," Lynn said, and she flew to the attack, claws out, sparks flying.

My hands came up, but he wasn't aiming at my face. Jemeni could fight, fair and cruel. My shoulders and biceps took two sharp-knuckled charlie-horses right in the deep muscle, and I screamed as I felt the ligaments move, as my own hands smacked myself across the face, because I couldn't lift them anymore.

"It's DEREK, HELP HIM!" Lynn shouted, swinging two pieces of a broken bo staff at six fully grown men, somehow hitting every single one.

"Right!" Volf said, kicking a cloud of dirt up in a line towards the closest agent. He ran for them and smashed them into a wall as they were busy blind.

That's all I saw before Jemeni started hitting me in the face. The first one didn't even hurt, it was just a shockwave while I was trying to watch the rest of the movie—I mean fight. Then the second time was so much worse it wasn't even worth comparing. Bam. My nose screamed out, the blood flowed freely, I tasted acid on my lips.

"DUDE!" I shouted, the words slurred for the fat lip.

My arms hurt too much to move, there was too much weight on my stomach to break free, and my face was ringing so hard I could barely tell sky from ground. Jemeni got off me, which was good, but then he pulled me up by the shirt and hit me again, which was bad. Somehow I stayed on my feet this time, my only goal in life at that moment, besides putting ever ounce of energy into lifting my arms. But I just couldn't do it. One of my gloves fell off my useless fingers and burst into claws as it hit the ground. Jemeni saw it; I tried to shove him away as he came closer but he only kicked my kick away and punched me in the face for the seventh time. I was bleeding into my eyes, I still couldn't raise my hands, and then Jemeni had picked up my claws, walked around me in a circle, and kicked my leg from the back, forcing me to my knees.

I might have lost this fight.

"Come on man..." I wheezed. "We're not... your enemy. You don't need..."

"You don't know me," Jemeni said, holding a single claw to my neck. "You don't know how long I've been waiting for this. For some part of this miserable life to make sense. I don't know how you came into Infinite, I don't know how you've gotten away with it. But if a kid like me can be all it takes to stop you, it must not have ever been that important."

"It's funny," I said, breathing as deep as I could with half a nose. "Odd said... the same thing. That's your... side?"

"Side of winning, yes," Jemeni said. "What side are you on?"

"Side of life," I coughed out, the memory of a certain Infinite captain coming over me, her ghost telling me to be strong, to fight, for us, for them...

"You chose wrong," Jemeni said. "I see that now. Thank you Nite. You've given me everything I've ever wanted."

Then he had me by the hair, and yanked my head back. He brought those Vema claws up to my throat and I saw it in his eyes.

Fight Derek, I thought. But for all my will... I just couldn't.

"When you see her, tell her I'm sorry," Jemeni said. "Tell her we miss her, and we'll never be the same without her. Can you do that Derek?"

I would have hung my head if he didn't have it pulled back so hard. It felt like my scalp was already on fire. But I couldn't think about Ana right now. I had one image in my mind, and it was the three of us sitting at our kitchen table by the window. Just two kids and a mom, in a house on a hill, under a bright and sunny day. It was quiet there. It was peaceful there.

"No words? Fine. I'll have to trust you," Jemeni said, his eyes flashing as he dug his feet in and pulled the claws back, ready to—

"DEREK!"

I knew that voice, and something in Jemeni's eyes told me he recognized it too. He stopped, the claws wavering only millimeters from my skin, and my mind snapped back to reality, the house on the hill fading far into the distance. It wasn't Lynn, she was held to the ground by three agents all holding pieces of that bo staff. It wasn't Volf who had a single agent by the neck with a sharp piece of rock held to his spine. It wasn't Willa, who was frantically spinning in a circle as six soldiers came at her from all sides.

It was James.

He had an entire building of eyes on him. Even Jemeni looked up at the sound. James was standing at the door with Sasha, Benjann, and Heather, no trace of any of the eight Infinite agents Jemeni had sent to hunt them down.

Sasha had some dirt on her clothes, and Heather was holding an iron stake, probably from the piles of construction equipment around the building. But it wasn't the weaponry that caught my eye, it was what James had in his hand.

It looked like another gameboy.

"I didn't…" Jemeni said. "Is that from the Planetarium?"

"We grow our own," I said.

And through a bloody smile, I pulled out the device I had stolen from Jemeni at the first takedown. It looked like the same thing James held. We were counting on it. Jemeni frantically patted himself down. If he had any brains at all, he was just now realizing that I had wrestled for three years in high school, and that all the close-combat ground work that he was supposedly in control of was all a big giant perfect stupid working…

"Distraction," James said.

Okay maybe Jemeni didn't realize all that. Didn't matter, gospel truth.

"You… are unbelievable," was all Jemeni could get out at me.

"That's the nicest thing you've said to me all day," I said.

And I smashed his device into the stone ground as hard as I could, as James held up the one we'd found at the Planetarium and pressed the hope button.

"NOOOO!" Jemeni screamed, throwing himself forward at me.

But he was too late. In a purple flash, the lights of the building blinked off, and the magnetic powers of the Reaper returned to us. Symbolically, it meant we had finally found the literal deus ex machina button, a real, tangible effort to employ the supertechnology of various islanders, probably in pursuit of ultimate power, whatever. But right now, it meant this fight was far from finished.

"Wanna start this over brother?" James asked.

"I think so brother," I said, as the obsidian rock armor came over me in a flash, just as Jemeni came running in at me like a linebacker. Cute.

My wings extended like an extra pair of arms pushing me off the ground, my armor came back in a blink, and I body-slammed into Jemeni with everything I had. The sparks blew from his armor as it came apart in pieces in the blast, his head whiplashing back as mine stayed right in place, and then he was tumbling backwards until the constructs in the middle of the room stopped him. He hit the bottom of one of the staircases, the metal bent around him, his helmet flew off and his head snapped back—he was down for the first time.

"How did that work SO GOOD?" James shouted in victory, just as an agent broke a wooden chair off against his obsidian armor. "Hi there."

"Monster," the agent said, backing off. "Jemeni, what do we do?"

"Get me out of this mess, Joe!" Jemeni shouted, clearly in pain, the stairs cutting into his skin wherever they weren't bent around his body.

"Jemeni?" Came a voice that made even the agent in front of me pause.

"B… Ben?" Jemeni said, slowing lifting his head to see…

Benjann standing next to my brother, in claws, suspenders, wings to boot.

"What are you doing?" Benjann asked, looking at the blood on my face, the bruises, and Jemeni entangled in the broken metal teeth of the staircase.

"You're alive?" Jemeni said, half horrified, half relieved. "What are you wearing brother? What have they done to you?"

"They saved me, I thought," Benjann said, confused.

"They did not," Jemeni said, fighting against the metal so hard he left skin behind as two agents helped him finally stand up, but he didn't care.

"Did they tell you why brother?" Jemeni said, almost crying. "Did they tell you what they've done to us? To—"

No.

"Shut up," I said, realizing the tension, sensing what was about to happen. "Ben, we were going to tell you."

"Tell me what?" Benjann said.

"I knew it," Jemeni said, shaking his head. "They needed things from you. If you knew the truth, they wouldn't get anything from you. It's simple."

"What's he talking about?" Ben demanded, wheeling on us.

"Ana," Jemeni said, before we could say a word.

"What," Ben said, his face fading, his fight… gone.

"Dude SHUT UP!" I shouted, about to punch Jemeni in the face again, and I would have if not for the look on Ben's face.

"What about her?" Benjann asked, his eyes locked on Jemeni. Not us. Not anymore.

Jemeni held a hand up, and the other agents stopped fighting us, if just for the moment. Jemeni was smart enough to see the battle was continuing on a different plane. He was smarter than Odd.

He was more dangerous than Odd.

"Lynn?" Ben said. "What's going on?"

Lynn flinched. Maybe it was the memory of what she'd found in her prison cell, before Heather had rescued us from the wretched. Heather only turned away, shutting Benjann out. It was my brother and I who gave us away. Our sadness must have been transparent. We'd never been good at being invisible.

"Why are you looking at me like that?" Benjann asked, slowly. "Derek, you left me in the Vempire—which is doing great by the way, but I saw you fly off to Silka, what was it? Another satellite crashing? Didn't we win? Wasn't everything we did in spite of Issaic—what's going on? Where's Ana?"

"I…" I said.

I wanted to tell him. I mean I didn't want to, but I couldn't lie to the guy. But I also couldn't get the words out. Like, physically, they would not come.

"She's gone," Lynn said.

Benjann was quiet. He looked at Lynn on the ground, at Heather's turned back, at the two of us unable to take our eyes off him. He took a breath.

"She's what?"

"Issaic…" Heather said.

"Don't," Jemeni cut in, his eyes burning into Heather. "We lost Ana to the injuries sustained when YOU blew apart half the hospital trying to get to Issaic. She had glass in her lungs from what you did to her. Don't put this on Issaic."

"I will, when it's the gospel truth," Heather said. "He killed her."

"Take it back," Benjann said, retreating like we were going to hit him too.

"I wish I could," Heather started, looking at me for help. "She's—"

"She's dead, because of you," Jemeni said, bitter as anything. "Reaper."

"That's not TRUE!" Heather and I shouted at the same time.

This time I did hit him, and harder than I should have, right across the cheek. But seeing Jemeni on the ground didn't make me feel any better.

"Ana recorded Issaic letting Odd out of jail," Lynn said, numb. "She recorded him telling Odd to forget the lost Infinite crew and to hunt us down underland. Our entire plan for ascension was based on the assumption that Issaic and Odd were working together. Our plan worked because they were. Ana's message confirmed what we already thought. Now, because of her, it is that which we know."

"That which we know," Benjann said, his face empty. "That becomes the girl. Nothing more. That's what we get from..."

"Ben..." Lynn said, her face breaking.

"You're telling me... she's dead?" Ben cried. "You saw her body?"

It was Lynn's turn for her face to go white, and it was the worst answer she could possibly give. The one that went unquestioned. The only answer Benjann could accept, the only one he didn't want.

"I was... I wasn't..." he said.

Benjann sank to his knees. Even Sasha and Volf were quiet. The rage had come and gone in a single hopeful crescendo. The only thing left was the loss.

"How old was Ana?" Willa asked, the only one willing to speak.

"Younger than me," I said, barely able to get the words out.

"Hell," Willa said, and she hung her head in respect.

"We wanted to tell you," Heather said, looking away. "I didn't know how to do it. I guess none of us did."

"But you could have," Benjann said, looking at my brother, stepping away from him. He was horrified. "That's why you left me."

"To confront Issaic the moment we saw that footage, yes," I said. "We should have told you. We can't take that back."

"You can't save her either," Ben said, resolute.

It was what his mind had arrived at. James was standing too close, wondering what to do, how to comfort him. But Benjann wasn't looking for comfort. He was looking for agency, to make something out of the pieces of his life. Looking back, I have to give him credit. There weren't a lot of things he could have done, and with one move he made a pretty big statement. It was so simple, so perfectly avoidable, we really should have seen it coming.

Benjann made a single move, a swipe of his hands, and knocked the gameboy device in James' hands across the floor.

"Oh Ben," was all I said, my heart sinking in a flash.

James reacted a moment too late, diving into the air after the thing, fully sideways, but a heavy metal boot came down on it at the last second. As the thing cracked apart between boot and rock, James crashed into the ground like a plane falling out of the sky. Just like that, the switch had been switched. Power shift—again. Whatever the opposite of the hope button was, it had been hit. This time, we were the ones who'd gotten caught monologuing.

"Welcome back, agent Matthews," came the voice of an agent on my right.

"No..." I said.

"Yes," the agent said.

He shoved me backwards into the waiting arms of Jemeni, who was very much not on the floor anymore, and madder than ever. I saw three agents rushing James as four more were forcing Heather to the ground, as others from outside the structure rushed in and Sasha tried to run, anywhere. She made it a few steps, but then there were four agents pulling her to the ground. Only Willa was able to keep to her feet—then suddenly something cracked against the back of my head and I saw stars. It was either superhuman strength or a big metal pole. I slammed across the floor and only stopped when I skid into Lynn. She screamed and pushed me off her, holding her ankle.

"Was that me?" I asked.

"No, it was shoulderpads," Lynn said, unable to stand. "We can't do this."

"Not alone," I said, looking around, thinking this was maybe the last time I would see some of these soldiers alive.

"But you are alone," Jemeni said, walking right past Lynn, eyes on me.

He grabbed me by my shirt, by the front this time, and continue to pummel me. In the neck, in the chest, in the face, not just once. Bam. Each punch was starting to hurt my nose more and more, so much I shifted my face so he wasn't always hitting the same spot. My great defense. It was all I could do, that, and realize he was leading / beating me towards the middle of the room.

"STOP IT!" Lynn shouted.

She tried to stand but couldn't on her ankle. The two agents standing over her didn't need to do a thing but watch her struggle.

"For Ana," Jemeni said.

He shoved my hand away from my face and hit me again, this time right in the forehead. I felt something in my head light up and knew he had broken the skin. That blood on his right hand wasn't his. And he wasn't stopping.

"For Silka," he said, as he hit me for the twentieth time. "For Infinite."

"I'm… all of those things too…" I said, the words slurring again, my lip now completely busted open and bleeding as much as my nose.

"I don't care," Jemeni said.

There was no hold back. He would do this until I was dead. I guess we didn't know each other that well, or at all. James and Benjann were close to wrestling, James doing everything he could to keep off the floor. Heather and Willa were holding off a few guards trying to get to Benjann's side. Lynn had her face pressed to the floor by the back of her head, Volf wasn't any better.

"Derek," came a voice.

It was Sasha. She was on her knees with the jagged end of a metal pole at her throat, held by an agent walking in a smug circle around her.

"It's over," Sasha said quietly.

"It's not over," I said, my heart beating so hard, like it was going out in a blaze of—

Bam. Again in the head, so hard my vision was going out. No one was helping me. The entire team was compromised, we'd relied on the Reaper powers to see us through and they hadn't even gotten us halfway home. No one was coming to save me. Sasha was right, even if I didn't want to admit it. This was either over, or going to be over. Then—

The world roared.

Every Infinite soldiers stopped at the sound. I could barely see through the blood in my eyes again, but there—at the top of the ceiling, half hidden by the shadows of the loft. It was her. For a moment the agents stopped moving. A few even stopped breathing, gasping at the wild animal only twenty feet away from us, an easy jump for such a creature.

"The jungle answers," Lynn said, spitting blood, holding her fists up.

"That's a big dog," Jemeni said, his eyes fixed on the creature. "Everybody steady. I've got this."

"Reverse that, maybe," I said.

"Dog?" Lynn asked. "You got eyes in idiotland?"

"Boom, roasted," I coughed out, spitting blood over Jemeni's chest.

"Just like we planned," Jemeni called around.

Like they planned?

"Boss!" someone shouted.

An agent threw the four foot piece of a broken bo-staff to Jemeni, right as the big cat leapt down from the ceiling, claws out, headfirst, those canines aimed right on top of us.

"NO!" Lynn shouted.

I saw it too, but when I opened my mouth to scream Jemeni put his forehead in my teeth, head-butting me to the ground. He swooped down to his knees as I landed on my back, and anchored the staff in a rock in the ground as I slammed hard. Then… the cat did the rest.

"NO!" Lynn screamed.

Her face was already white, the tears hitting the ground as I did, as Sophia did, right on top of the staff. The sound that cat made… I don't ever want to remember it. It was the sound of an animal that knew exactly what she'd done, how hard she'd messed up. She'd landed with Jemeni within striking distance, both claws and jaws. He even stared her in the eyes, close enough to feel the heat, somehow not afraid. But he didn't have to be. Sophia had impaled herself on the staff. She knew it. We all did.

"The jungle dies," Jemeni said. "And you will too. Remember that, Nite. See you in two days, in handcuffs."

And as the cat sunk to the floor, Jemeni left me there with her, staring into the eyes of our clouded leopard Sophia. They were already calm, and accepting of what had happened. She was barely breathing. No need to live in pain. For a moment, I saw the future in those eyes. Then I remembered she didn't have one.

"Sophia…" I said.

My arm resisted, probably broken, but I reached out to her so slowly that by the time I touched her nose, Lynn had rolled over on her busted ankle, dragging herself across the ground to get to us.

"I'm sorry," I said, trying not to cry, for the pain, or the emotion. "Lynn…"

"Just don't," Lynn said.

She held Sophia with one hand, and reached out to me with the other, her fingers trembling around my face until I grabbed her hand and held onto it.

“They’re retreating,” Volf said, spitting something to the ground that sounded like a tooth. “Why?”

“Because we failed,” Sasha said, limping over and falling to her butt behind my head. “The structure stands, the magnetics are clearly under control.”

“We could still blow it up, if nothing else,” Volf said, sounding like something was still off. “Why’d they just leave us here? Where’s the boy?”

“Benjann?” Heather said, looking around. “Looks like he went with—”

“I’m not talking about Benjann,” Volf said.

And something about it was enough to break my focus. It took every ounce of my willpower to pull my eyes away from Lynn’s tears, to push my head off the ground. The rest of my body wasn’t working, Heather had to help me sit up.

“No,” she said, looking around.

“Hold up,” I said, following her gaze, searching everywhere, seeing nothing.

No Benjann, no Infinite army, no reserve troops waiting to finish the job. But there was something much more obvious missing. Someone we’d come here with. Someone I knew better than myself.

“They weren’t here for us, or for the building,” Heather said, blinking. “It was all for something else. That’s why they retreated. Did we see where they went? Anyone?”

“I saw nothing,” Volf said, angrily. “The cat… I was… distracted.”

“We all were,” I said, looking down at Lynn.

And even distraught, she had been listening. Through blurry eyes she looked up, and saw the same thing we were all seeing. Or rather, the lack of him.

“Where is he?” Lynn asked, her voice quiet, but scared. “Where’s—?”

3.8

MOONBREAKER

"JAMES!"

But no one answered.

I dragged myself all over the interior of that stupid box building, finding my own blood almost anywhere I went, at least in the main room. I took every stair to every level around the thing, a sharp pain in my knee sounding off with every step. I didn't see anything up on the platforms, so I limped back down to the ground level, looked out the exit and found... nothing.

"But it was so many stairs," I said, on the edge of crying.

The wind hit me, fast, free, invisible, all the things we couldn't be right now. There was nothing to see, but it was midnight. Maybe if I had that Infinite facial screen, I would have been able to detect the escapees taking off in the night with my brother. Maybe if we had the glow in our necklace gemstones, they would have pointed him out. But no. We'd gone through a few power cycles with those little gameboy devices, but whatever dampening system was being used to monitor and inflect the magnetics over us, they had been left on.

In other words, I was human, and nothing more.

"They're gone," I said, to the world.

The world did not respond. But yeah.

"We have to go after them," I said, in a panic, in a trance.

"We have injured," Heather said. "It would be a lousy chase."

"It's James," I said. "Do we really not go, and now, and—"

"Calm down," Heather said. "Try to smile. You look tired. We got this."

"Four things you'd never say to a woman," I said, all fired up—

"See you're still there," Heather smiled. "Don't worry Lynn."

"A little late for don't worry," Lynn said.

I found myself drawn back to the blood-stained, smashed up ground we'd been falling and fighting all over not even five minutes ago. I was the one limping this time. We were still in that open room with instruments on the scaffolding overhead, but there were plenty of tools and heavy pieces of wood and metal around us on the ground. I didn't have a sword, but I could see pick up sticks, and I was ready to crutch all over the forest to find James if I had to.

But Lynn was still on the ground. Willa was holding her head and hair in bloodstained hands. Sasha and Volf were sitting together and talking low, Volf's eyes up and darting around as they did, watching Sasha's back and never stopping. We weren't broken, but we were definitely bent. Speaking as the one who'd gotten the worst of it—sabretooth aside.

"They knew what they were doing," Lynn said, her voice still in pain, and not only over the ankle. "If they left us alive there was no reason to kill Sophia."

"Except as a distraction," Heather said. "They got us. You put an animal in pain and teenagers lose their minds. We paid more attention to the cat than our own James. We let this happen."

"I think we did," Lynn said, sounding furious, ready to sob, all at once.

"It wasn't just the teenagers," Volf said, wiping his eyes. "The loss of such an animal is the death of nature itself. What did Jemeni say? The jungle dies."

"Everything dies," Sasha said.

"Not everything dies by Infinite," Volf said, matching Lynn's fury.

"True," Sasha said. "This was planned. And their purpose was James."

"Then we gotta go now," I said. "They could be halfway to Silka. Come on, we can't be that hurt. I'll… I'll lead."

"I wish you could see yourself right now Derek."

Heather was the only one who didn't look traumatized. She tore a piece of my shirt at the sleeve with nothing but her fingers, and pressed it to my face.

"Ah," I said, as nose, forehead, cheeks and lips lit up with pain (that meant they were all bleeding).

"Stop, let me help," Heather said, pushing the fabric over my eyes.

"I can't—"

"You can," Heather demanded.

She was right. I took a breath, holding a piece of cloth against my face, the darkness settling in, the panic of another ambush versus the breathing of my team around me, all as scared and shaken as I was. I'll admit it, my face was covered, it was the perfect time to stop fighting that feeling behind my eyes. The tears came, silent, raging, while I stood still with my face in the dark like I had buried my head in the sand. But I was no ostrich.

"Not alone, you're not alone," I reminded myself.

"Never alone," Lynn said. "James is the priority. But we'll never—ah!"

"It's your ankle isn't it?" I asked, still blind (still crying, just a bit).

"Yeah," Lynn said. "Not as bad as James. But you're limping, and I'm on the ground. Even with crutches—"

"We can't do this on foot," Heather said. "Not without… help."

"Their suits didn't work either," I said, blindly. "They just figured out the opposite of a purple volcano miracle, quick. How far could they have gone?"

"A few of them came for us on horseback," Heather said. "It took a while to ditch them and sneak up to the hex, even longer with Benjann."

"Ben," Volf said, remembering everything, all at once. "Damnit."

"So they came with horses, and we did not," Willa said, looking over her suspenders in disappointment. "I've never been farther from home with less."

"You flew though," I reminded her.

“I… did,” she said, sounding like she was holding her head up. “For a moment. But I put my safety in a supersuit instead of myself, and I flew myself all the way to the edge of the switchblade. I’ll never make that mistake again.”

“Poetic,” Heather said. “But the world keeping our power from us is literally what it means to be Reaper, so it's my turn to welcome you into the Vempire.”

“Oh,” Willa said. “I didn’t… I just love horses.”

“Me too,” Heather said sadly. “Yet here were are without them. Asses kicked, skinny twin kidnapped, no way home, and no heading. I miss anything?”

“The skinny twin?” I asked, my eyes still covered, the frown unseen.

“What did you call your volcano again?” Sasha said.

“Pluma Petra,” Willa said. “It’s Latin for feather rock.”

“What’s feather rock?” I asked, turning to the part of the darkness Heather’s voice seemed to be coming from.

“Around volcanoes can form a porous rock that some plants can live decades in, no dirt required,” Heather said simply.

“I’m sorry, you can grow flowers out of lava?” I asked.

“Of course we can,” Heather and Willa said at the same time.

“I don’t even like flowers,” Lynn said. “But lava flowers, that’s just dope.”

Mental note taken.

“Okay great, names,” Willa said. “On foot, Pluma’s a few days away. We can do it, but not if we’re walking into the maelstrom. There’s no way we could cross back into Jerico the way we left it, not without…”

“Say it,” I said, blindly.

“Without super help, or horses,” Willa said. “The jungle is dangerous enough in the dry season. On foot, in the depths of the season, it’s a death sentence.”

“So what, we’re stuck here until the storm dies down?” I said.

“What if we’re halfway home and see grey clouds?” Willa said. “We need two days of clear skies, we haven’t had that all summer. It’s not happening.”

“Then James isn’t headed that way,” I said, thinking. “They aren’t stupid, they’re in the same storm as us. That means none of us are headed anywhere. Damnit, we were supposed to stop shooting us out the canon. How do I look?”

I took the fabric off my face and quickly folded it up so I wouldn’t have to look at the blood.

“Better,” Willa said sadly, wincing, with Sasha bent over her, trying her best to stem the blood-flow from a cut on her forehead.

“I said hold still,” Sasha said, looking white in the face.

“What’s around us?” I demanded. “Where could they go?”

“There’s nowhere to go,” Volf said, bluntly. “The Crossroads stretches a hundred miles in all directions between the four nations. To this day it's still unpaved. The only way through is aerial.”

“A lot of that used to be Vempire,” Heather said. “Before… the bombs.”

“Issaic’s bombs?” Lynn said, her eyes flashing.

“I’m thinking if it happened once, it could have happened a hundred times,” Heather said. “Anyone here have a reason to keep people from settling the middle of the island?”

"Yes, blasphemy," Willa said. "You surf, right?"

Heather laughed. She actually laughed. "Seriously, Skyfire."

"No reason we know of," Willa said. "It's every nation's dream, to be the one to settle the Crossroads. But for the strength of the Infinite, the cunning of the Reaper, the skill of the Jerico, or the purpose of the Mylo… none have."

"I thought you were going somewhere else with that," Lynn said.

"Like where?" Willa asked.

"Like if all four could come together… it might be possible," Lynn said.

"Is that possible?" Willa asked.

Lynn didn't answer. She didn't have to. None of us knew, that was the truth.

"A brother for a leopard," I said, frowning, looking up at the beehive—I mean three mirror antistigmat—in bitterness, but still wonder. "There should be a city here. But instead, we have you."

"Derek, are you talking to the Hexoscope?" Lynn asked, rubbing her ankle.

"This is the second biggest telescope on the island, and that was before we blew up the other two," I said. "This is it, they all are, they have to be."

"Have to be what?" Lynn asked.

"More than telescopes," I said, thinking hard, zen riddle…

"This is a telescope?" Heather asked, looking up at the center structure.

"Three mirror antistigmat," Lynn said.

"WHAT did you just call me?" Heather demanded.

She wasn't wrong, she had just missed Lynn's initial explanation about the thing in front of us, standing on a boxed platform and taking up the entire height of the room. Lynn started from the beginning as I limped over to a part of the metal staircase that wasn't ruined. I had searched every level and platform above us and every inch of the interior, but I hadn't given a moment to the colossal feat of engineering that had brought us here in the first place. We'd been too busy playing with gameboys.

The first level was a full control box. I found a small chair by a big desk, complete with a three monitor viewfinder. I had lost sight of Lynn and Heather and the others, I had a smaller kind of beehive in front of me, and the controls were as small as the device was leviathan. No matter how far back I tilted my head, it seemed as physical as things came, the entire construct an exoskeleton of wires and rods, all supporting a football field sized array of folding, curving hexagons wrapped in reflective golden material. No screens, just gears and mechanics. That was the above. Below it, down here with the ants, the triple viewfinder was strictly analog, just the recessed, flat end of a glass prism system. All I had to do was wipe the dust off and I saw it.

"Up is down," I said. "Where do you think we are, Vema?"

The viewfinder was clearly the upside-down negative of something at the end of a scope system. I could see a sky like the ocean, but this wasn't a city built into the ceiling—as much as that wouldn't have surprised me. I searched around for the controls, finding only knobs and dials. I knocked something against my knee and the image moved like a free rotation tool had been unlocked—turns out it yep, I had found a rotary knob under the desk, and in a few tweaks I had the image stabilized, right-side up, and—

I fell off the chair, and backed away from the thing so quick I almost fell over the balcony too. As it was I slammed my back into some metal and grabbed it like a lifeline. I was at the edge of the boxed platform. Everyone could see me.

"We lose you too?" Lynn asked, looking up to me.

"It's my house," I said, staring. "This thing is aimed at… my house."

"Prove it," Heather said.

"Lookit," was all I said, slowly walking back to the prism viewfinder.

I did my best to see anything else, but it was as clear as midnight. Those houses, that slowly curving, inclined street down to the creek on one side and grass on the other, the sloped front yard and huge backyard until it me the cliffs at the edge of it, the lack of a two story house between them, instead just a big hole on the side of a hill, almost like something had been there before, like a certain house a certain pair of twins had grown up in.

"I liked you better upside down," I said to the screen.

But the screen didn't answer. I didn't know how far we were from Silka, either half an island or closer to the full thing. Yet this viewfinder looked no farther away than we'd been when we watched the Odd squad blow up our house. I hadn't been this close to home since… well, since we lost it. I tore myself away and searched the console frantically, looking for notes, etches, scribbles, anything at all that would help me figure out why a machine that looked like it cost more than the sun was pointing itself at the window I never even snuck out of, not once. I did spend a lot of time looking out of it though. How long was this here? How much had it seen? And most importantly—

"Why?" I asked, the feeling of dread slowly coming over me. "Why me?"

"Because of course you, that's why," Lynn called out.

"Okay so it is a telescope?" Heather asked, from the other side of a machine. "Any way to turn it back off so we might have a chance of a quick flight home?"

"I don't know Heather, I haven't found the big red button yet," I said.

"Even if you find it, let's take a committee approach to big red buttons from here on, yeah?" Lynn called out.

I nodded, then remembered she couldn't see me. Why did that always happen in that order? But she was right. It was a scary feeling, finding someone had zoomed in on your childhood home. That kind of thing cut right through to the heart. I touched my heart, like I was clutching my pearls—then remembered.

"Oh my…" I said.

"What is it this time?" Lynn asked. "Another secret note from your mother?"

"I just thought of something," I said, ignoring them. "We haven't actually destroyed anything. I didn't shoot the Observatory, and I didn't burn down the Planetarium. What I actually did was tune their telescopes to the same coordinates, because that's all my mother told us to do."

"Wait a minute," Lynn said, thinking about it. "Heather, you thinking what I'm thinking?"

"Think so," Heather said. "If you were going to have a big red button without actually having a big red button…"

I raced back to the chair and sat down, and found the array of gears with small hand-written notch marks next to them. It was tricky with the delayed movement of the hex panels, but even though the sky didn't immediately light up when the telescope clicked into place, something else did. Me.

Power shift.

With a mechanical roar and a light show like the underbelly of a rainbow octopus, the world raged. I tensed up with the sudden flashes but that only meant the rock came up to save me like a blanket, wrapping itself around my soft baby skin and smoothing away this time into something that had definition, like that obsidian armor had taken my clothes as inspiration. Finally. I watched my arms, wrists, then fingers be overcome by the crystalizing dirt, the wings folded out like always, and the claws, well, we almost lost all the monitors to the surprise. As it was, hell, even the best baseball players went one for three.

"Ah!" Willa said, dancing away from two halves of a television screen smashing into the floor not even a yard from her feet. "Flatscreen, retro."

"Derek, what the WHAT?" Lynn shouted.

And for once, just as the killer light show died, it was enough for me to tear away from the computer and round the machine on the raised platform with a hip level railing all around it, sort of like a boxing ring.

"Okay so, here's the thing about what just happened," I said, leaning over the railing, ever eye in the room on the light from my necklace. "It happened."

"Boom baby!" Lynn shouted up at me from the ground.

And everyone who wasn't Heather cheered. She only looked at me with a small uptick in the static line that was her lips. That was Heather's way of smiling. Or trying not to, either way, good. I thought I was in trouble. Then Sasha jumped all the way onto Heather's shoulders and she was suddenly part of the celebration, like it or not.

"That's what I'm talking about, now LINE UP!" Heather said.

She put a hand up, Sasha took it, flipped off Heather's shoulders, and landed landing gracefully, somehow still holding Heather's hand, but bleeding through a cut on her wrist. Heather didn't respond, she just clamped down on the handhold they still held, and there was a small aura of purple light between them. It was over as soon as it started, as soon as Sasha had the sense to jump away from the small supernova. But her wrist wasn't bleeding anymore.

"I could have done that myself," Sasha said.

"Then why didn't you?" Heather asked.

"Because… I didn't exactly let the guy off unscathed," Sasha said. "He's probably still bleeding. And I'm not. That's not exactly fair."

"You know what Sasha?" Heather said, looking at the exit, the open world beyond. "If they came back, right now, and asked for help… I'd give it to them."

I wasn't crying. But some part of me was drawn to the edges of what had been a battlefield fifteen minutes ago. We'd done some damage. If there was anyone left behind, hiding, this was their time to come on out. But no one did.

"Mare would be proud of you right now," Sasha said.

"Bastile would share the feeling," Willa said. "You too, soldier."

Volf walked up to them quietly, and nodded from their side. He was still keeping an eye out, still quiet, ready for the next attack

"Your forehead is still bleeding," Volf said.

"Damnit," Willa said, wiping the blood away, and putting herself in between Sasha and Heather. "I'll still be beautiful, just fix me up doc."

"Hold still," Heather said, her lips fighting that same fight they always did.

"Your default is to trying not to smile," I said. "Wherever you learned that, doesn't matter. We'll beat it out of you."

"You think you can?" Heather said, and speaking as the epitome of it, that wasn't sarcasm.

"What's going on today?" Lynn said, her hands in the air.

"Right. Let's make this quick. It's only your face, lots of room for error."

"WHAT?"

"I said hold still Skyfire!"

Another purple aura came and went, Willa gasped, and it was over.

"Heather," Lynn said, sitting up on the ground, transfixed on Willa's face.

"I did my best," Heather said. "Sorry if that's not enough. Here Willa, for the blood. I took an extra piece of Derek's shirt."

I knew it. My back was never this cold. I reached back and yep, skin.

"Damnit Heather—" I called down.

"Thanks, I guess," Willa asked, her head buried in a piece of brown shirt by the time I looked back. "Battle scars are sexy, right?"

Then she took the shirt off her face, and besides the blood left on her hair... the cut had not only healed itself, but repaired the skin without any sight of scar tissue.

"They are, when you've got them," Lynn said.

She motioned to the sword on Willa's hip. Willa frowned, but she unsheathed it, and stared at her reflection in the polished metal. I didn't want to be rude, but in STRICTLY medical terms, damn.

"I..." Willa started, but she couldn't speak, she could only stare at herself in the sword. "It's nothing?"

"Nothing," Lynn said.

Willa crashed into Heather, almost taking her to the ground, but something (about Benjann) had Heather keeping her weight low, and she only slid backwards in a perfectly balanced stance, taking the hug sideways from a slightly shorter, but much more muscular Willa.

"Thank you thank you thank you thank you," Willa said, her head buried in Heather's neck. "Sorry about the blood."

"I like blood, it means we're alive," Heather said, hugging back, if just for a moment. "And you've got enough scars for a soldier. But a full face scar, come on. Not happening. You're too young."

Willa suddenly couldn't speak. She must have been that angry.

"How about you, Volf, we good?" Heather asked, blushing.

"You keep doing you, don't mind me," he said. "I like this Veman."

"I... like her too," Willa said, stepping aside.

Heather took a knee over Lynn's ankle, propped up between two rocks.

"Okay Lyre. Last for best, sorry."

"That's not the saying," Lynn said, smiling. "Be honest, you're just putting dirt in our wounds, aren't you?"

"It's good for you," Heather said, her hand over Lynn's ankle.

"You're good for you," Lynn shot back, then frowned, then thought about it, then nodded. "I said what I meant."

Flash of light. Purple glow. More cliches. And then it was over, and after all the super nonsense, Heather was holding a hand out to her friend on the ground.

"I'll take it," Lynn said, letting Heather pull her up by the hand towards two feet. "Trusting you… nice."

"All good?" Heather asked, watching her move on the ankle she'd been holding off the ground for fifteen minutes.

"All good sister," Lynn said. "You're the best, but I'm not last. Derek?"

"It's okay, I think most of the bleeding's going to stop on its own soon," I said, my eyes on the screens and not moving. I'd seen something.

"Don't make me come up there," Heather warned. "Wait I take that back, I want to see the computer."

"There's just the one chair," I complained, my eyes still glued to—

"Too bad," Lynn said, standing up, shaking her ankle out, nodding, then racing up the stairs and over to me, as the rest of them followed suit. "Derek, let's see it. Show us your face."

"No, just ten more minutes—"

"Show us your face!"

The next thing I knew—

"Hardly a fair fight," I said, somehow being held over the railing by three girls at once, while Heather walked up the stairs shaking her head at me.

"I'm going to need you to follow the light."

And in a flash, I had come and gone, and when I returned, my face hurt a hell of a lot less. I heard a rip, and then there was a piece of cloth in my hands.

"Heather!"

"Let him be useful Lynn, damn."

I could feel it, I was shirtless, again. But when I took what was left of my shirt off my face… I didn't have to squint to keep the blood out. Progress.

"You… okay?" Lynn asked, taking a step towards me.

"I feel better," I said, blinking. "Why?"

"Because you took a beating like that and still walked every inch of this place, then found… all this weirdness, and figured it out too," Heather said. "Are you wired right?"

"I dunno," I said honestly.

"We all saw it right?" Heather said.

Lynn nodded hard. " I'm not mad, but what on earth, who does that? You almost fell down the stairs twice. What were you thinking?"

"That I have you," I said. "And if I die, they have you."

"But I didn't do anything," Lynn said, blinking.

"Neither did I," I said. "And yet… look around. Look at—"

"You could have died," Lynn said. "Even Heather couldn't have saved you without… superhelp. But you knew that."

"He did know that," Heather said, frowning.

“Derek,” Sasha said from the top of the stairs, joining the party. “How did you know… to know that?”

“To not go anywhere without Lynn and Heather?” I said. “I like living.”

“They’re partners, Sasha,” Volf said, from the ground, keeping an eye on the exit for us. “I wouldn’t go anywhere uncharted without you. We die together, that’s the deal, right?”

“You went from light to dark just lightning quick there,” Sasha said. “But he’s right. The pack lives. The lone wolf—”

“Finish that sentence,” I demanded.

“The lone wolf is James, and he needs our help,” Sasha said, looking down.

“Thank you,” I said. “So can we GO NOW?”

“What is this place to you Derek?” Heather asked.

“I’ve never been here before in my life,” I said. “And I wish I’d never come. You have five minutes to figure out what parts of this benefit my brother, then we’re leaving for his rescue.”

“I agree with that, before our powers are gone again,” Heather said.

“Seconds,” I said, blinking, holding my head. “I meant seconds.”

“What is this technology?” Willa asked, her eyes wide at the contraption.

“This is gears and mirrors,” Heather said. “But I can sense a current. It’s strong. It’s coming from somewhere to my right.”

“Heather, your claw is on a live panel,” I said, looking down to the sparks of electricity that were making the single extended claw of hers red hot.

“Oh, come on me,” Heather said, moving a claw, the electricity fizzing away.

“You didn’t feel that?” I asked.

Heather made a rocky, gloved fist. “Electricity doesn’t affect ground.”

“I thought that was just Pokemon,” I said lamely.

“I’m going to forget you said that,” Heather said.

“And I thank you for it,” I said. Then I remembered something. “Heather. The thing you said about healing an Infinite soldier. How’d you find the peace to say something like that?”

“I didn’t,” Heather said. “I didn’t find anything different than you, I haven’t seen anything you haven’t. I just realized, here, for the first time, that if there’s a peace so strong it could mean actual freedom… then that’s what I want, I know that for sure. But I understand the pursuit of peace is less dramatic than the pursuit of war. I’m only wondering if my… personality has a place.”

“If you ever change, I’ll burn the world down,” I said.

“And I’ll help,” Lynn said. “How’s that for peace?”

“This,” Heather said. “Whatever this is. I want this.”

All purple glows ended, all defenses were down. She grabbed both of us. Lynn was surprised but she didn’t fight it. I not only let her, I grabbed back, my arms bringing her as close as they could with her face in my neck, and I could feel the relief in her shoulders as she fell into Lynn and me.

“Are they seriously—” I heard Sasha start.

“Don’t you dare ruin this,” Volf said.

“Thanks Volf,” Heather said, picking her head up. “But we’re missing one.”

"Voice identification complete."

Lynn grabbed me, her eyes lighting up. She didn't even have to say it.

"Hell yes," I said, to the absolute shock of Willa, Volf, and—

"Who what now?" Sasha asked.

"Two factor voice authenticated. Name updated, Heather Denien Veman."

"This place knows your name," Volf whispered.

"See?" Willa said. "Veman. It is known."

"I'm never getting used to that," Heather said, shaking her head.

"Hi Oracle," I said.

"Hello Derek. Where is James?"

"We'll get to that," I said. "How are you here? Isn't the building—"

"Your attempts to understand the island are adorable. Those coordinates you entered into the telescope system triggered a contingency plan of the old guard. It has done nothing but enable a sort of... Night Mode. The Infinite source is connected, but the geomagnetic dampening system is crippled."

"Was that the purpose?" I blurted out. "Is that it, an off switch?"

"An incredibly well designed, secret off switch, yes," the Oracle said. *"Even now, at the Arum Planetarium, the Infinite are realizing what's been done, and how deep the damage goes. I would say something out of character for a computer. Good work."*

"Thanks Oracle," I said, feeling Lynn's hand on my shoulder. "I'll take the step forward. But I need to do it with my brother, and right now, we don't know where he is."

"Do you need something from me? You know all you have to do is ask."

"Trust me, I'm about to ask for stars," I said. "Oracle, you're a talking supercomputer, and you're really helpful a lot of times, but I gotta say it seems like we're always doing the heavy lifting. Can't you just take this one?"

"This one?"

"James is somewhere out there, without me, probably scared out of his pants. If all I have to do is ask, then can you just find him, and rescue him for us? Because I want that. I want that so bad."

"You want someone else to do the rescuing for you, or you wish it was this easy?" The Oracle asked.

"If it was that easy, I'd do it myself, every time," I said. "But I'm sort of in a big red button mood, and you seem as calm as the bomb, so can't you just you know... just once?"

"Derek, you're asking a computer for—" Lynn started.

"I know I'm asking a computer for," I said. "But where I come from, computers can do a lot you know?"

"I understand," the Oracle said. *"Okay Derek Nite. But just this once. And only because the coincidence is too perfect."*

That's when a figure came through the front doors. For a moment I thought we'd died and gone to the good place. It was a horse. A single white horse had pushed through the doors and was walking up to all of us, all but emerging on a rainbow and a cloud of sparkles. The sticks in my hands hit the floor.

The horse hadn't come empty... horsed.

"Did that just happen?" Heather said, unbelieving.

"The service in this jungle," Lynn said, her eyes wide.

"I must express just how much that wasn't me."

"You certain about that?" I said, sarcastically.

"I am always certain. Aren't you?"

All I'll say is… if you really know what you want, sometimes it doesn't hurt to ask for it.

3.9

PIECE OF MIND

I woke up on the hardest ground I'd ever felt. It was worse than obsidian. My head was pounding like a guitar, my thoughts weren't quite all pickle yet. But I was alive. And… was that the sky?

"Ben," I said, my first thoughts of vengeance. "BEN—"

"Right here," came the voice, and I was relieved—until I wasn't.

I expected to see him tied up like me. That wasn't the case. He was standing over me with a jungle behind him, with two other pairs of feet aimed my way. No restraints, and no expressions. Then the memories came back, seeing him and Jemeni squaring off, being manipulated between us, as much as our manipulation had good intentions behind it, it hadn't really given us an out.

"Hooray," I said, suddenly much less enthusiastic about it.

We hadn't told him. We'd let someone else control the information, instead of getting ahead of it. And it had landed me back in the jaws of something. This time, it seemed like a cliff to my back, a jutting outpost of rock with the forest behind that line of feet, and only a steep falloff behind me. Sharp rocks at the bottom? Most likely. Bring it—

"Where am I?" I asked. "Why did—"

"Careful," came the familiar voice. "Lest you fall off the world."

And I understood. I was facedown, closer to the edge than I had realized until I tried to put weight on my back foot. There was nothing there.

"Come on," I said, scrambling forward in the dirt, only to find a foot on my hand. I bit down and wrenched my fingers out, not letting myself cry out in pain.

"You come on," Odd said. "Big Ben here just did something we've been trying a week to do. You should be thanking him."

"I've never given a genuine thank you on command," I said, only for another foot to come down on my other hand. "You—"

Yep, it was him, and even worse, next to him was… him. No Hannah in sight, in fact, there wasn't a single girl among us, only worth noting because it was actually pretty rare around these parts. And it had me scared. The three of them stood with their arms folded smugly beside Benjann. It was chilling seeing them together. The Reaper spy Lukas, our old Infinite nemesis Odd, and the new

Astral warrior Astor. Not to mention their puppet, poor Benjann.

"Whatever you've done, it can be undone," I said desperately, to the only one of them who might still be listening.

"What about what you've done, James?" Benjann asked. "I gave you time to explain, and you never did. I guess we aren't as close as I thought. Or maybe they're right, and you do think yourself above us."

"I never did," I said.

"I can't trust you," Benjann said. "I only trust my voices in my head."

"And what does these voices say to you, at night, in dreams?" I asked.

"Let the truth be told," Benjann said. "One way or another. Right?"

"Right," Astor said, looking at me like he was counting down to something.

That's when I saw the neon blue glowing around us. There were mushrooms on the edges of this cliff. No way.

"You'll never..." I said.

I felt it on my lips. There was some sort of liquid on my chin, almost dry, like someone had forced it down my throat while unconscious—yep, I'd been reverse drugged.

"You bastards," I said, blinking. "Why is my tongue so heavy?"

"Time to talk," Astor said, taking a cross-legged seat in the dirt, and Odd did the same. "You have something we want, James,"

Then the lights went low and the feeling started in my head. I couldn't stop it. I tried to bite my tongue but suddenly I couldn't really feel my teeth. I wasn't in loonyland, this was worse. This was concentrated.

"Woah," I said. "Astral plane James."

"We gave you a double," Odd said, holding a water bottle in his hand that was glowing more electric blue than a powerade. "You should be deep enough by now to remember everything."

"I am, and I do," I said numbly. "What do you want from me?"

Jemeni looked at me with something like victory his eyes. He'd wanted this, and he was getting it. But Ben was side-eying the vibes coming off him, Odd and Astor. They weren't good vibes. But it reminded me of something.

"Correction," I said. "What does Issaic want with me?"

Odd tensed up. Even Astor clenched his neck, and I saw it.

"Common denominator," I said. "That guy falls out of the sky, and suddenly all the rules change on me. That means we've found the guy who made them. I'm right, aren't I? That means Astor... that means Infinite knew everything."

"You have gained an inch, we have gained ten years," Odd said. "I don't know how they've survived all this time in exile, but Sand Freedom and Crete Magellan are names we will NEVER forget, not to any of us who fought for Silka. Even Teresa was injured—in the end, it all came down to Issaic. If not for him, we wouldn't have had a city to come back to."

"So Silka didn't really win the Blitz either?" I asked.

Odd looked at Lukas, who shook his head.

"We all walked away from the Blitz broken," Odd said. "For ten years we've had no clues, no hints at what may have happened, and then you showed up. Two kids who grew up Teresa's own house..."

"Ten years?" I asked. "That's a long time to not solve something. I hope it doesn't take me that long to find mom."

"Is that your primary objective?" Lukas asked, cutting in like the bad cop.

"There is nothing in this world more important, every step I take is for her."

"How about taking down Silka City from the inside, where's that rank on your to-do list?" Lukas asked.

"It doesn't, and seems you're doing that for me anyways," I said. "Why?"

"The blueblood doesn't allow for deception," Astor said, studying my face. "He's telling the truth."

"You don't say," Odd said, sounding amazed. "How about the solar flare system?"

"Phrasing," I said, scratching an ear.

"The literal proof that the four nations can come together, our most important international astronomical advancement, the four pillars containing and island-sized fallout zone to the northern jungles," Lukas translated. "You're trying to weaponize the sun against Silka City, aren't you?"

"Am not," I said, offended. "Just trying to turn some jungle lights on, I don't even know what they'd do with the them. Don't know if they even need it."

"We don't," Astor said. "But the old fool in command is right, we'd appreciate the choice."

"Great, then as far as the secret jungle lands go, same page," I said. "The lightning is coming Astor. Hope you'll be alive to see it—if that is actually what you want."

"I don't know what I want," Astor said, blinking.

"You know we can't allow the containment to breach, not in this lifetime," Lukas said. "Are you still a part of this, Astor Akoura?"

"Alcyon Akoura," my mind said, before I could stop it.

"You do know that name," Astor asked. "Akoura is the name I bring to the warrior Astor, that part of my name is real. You know my brother. Is he alive?"

"Of course he's alive," I said, not understanding. "Alcyon and us… there's a long story of a short history there. He's helped us escape—twice now, actually."

"He let you escape?" Lukas asked. "Are you sure? How?"

"Redundantly," I said.

"Why would Alcyon risk exposure for a teenage kid?" Astor asked.

"You pronounced treason wrong," Lukas said under his breath.

"Exposure?" I asked, ignoring Lukas. "Alcyon is an agent of Infinite."

"He's not, actually," Astor explained. "He's been installed within Infinite for going on twenty years now. My brother Alcyon is the most accomplished veteran of combat in the entire territory. He was hand selected for infiltration, whatever actions he has taken amongst the Infinite have landed us exactly in the position we are in now."

"We're still a bit new to that information too," Odd said, scratching his head.

"I'm sorry," I said, wringing my ears out. "I thought you just said the Jerico have people inside Infinite."

"We do," Ollux said. "Why?"

"No way," I said. "I get to ask that question."

"Oh I forgot, were you part of the twenty generations that grew up in the forest without a single iota of electricity?" Astor said. "We know what we're missing. But the north is our home, and we aren't leaving. We're a practical people though, and when we see a problem, we send soldiers out to try to fix it. Sometimes that takes playing the long game. But you saw for yourself the difference in how one man treated you, versus an organization."

True. That was true.

Alcyon had… been hard to read. And we thought so much of him from a single shot he had taken at one of our friends. But there was something else going on. I knew there were people inside Infinite that wanted me bleeding on a cliffside, I knew there was foul play going on, I knew there were conflicting interests, not just the Infinite soldier mentality. So why was Astor bragging about another person inside Infinite? Was this double agent different than the double agents who were beating me up for memories? Was help on the way?

"I still don't understand what side he's on," Lukas said, like he was reading my thoughts.

"Did you plan on executing them inside headquarters?" Astor said, annoyed. "No? Then maybe we all take a big calm down on the T word?"

Lukas glared up at the jungle man through a two foot height difference… and nodded. "You're right. I did want to do this myself. Now I can."

"I didn't hear a thank you anywhere in there, captain underworld," Astor said, rolling his eyes, but turning back to me. "So. James. Not Alcyon, not Issaic, not Derek, just… you."

"What do you want from me?" I echoed, nowhere near as afraid as I should have been.

"I would say everything," Astor said. "But it's not that. It's just one thing. Simple, right?"

"Probably not," I said. "Probably the exact opposite—"

"You are the son of Issaic and Teresa Nite," Odd said. "Here you are, deep in the territory, climbing branches and bridges all over the arbor, in search of reclaiming a long lost ancient power. What if I told you we were doing the same?"

"You're not talking about Jerico though," I said.

"No we are not," Odd said, nodding. "You catch on quick, Nite. This is less about the Jerico, more about the lightning city. I wonder how much you know about the source of Infinite's power."

"Don't need it, I know a closer source," I said, my head swimming.

"And that's exactly what we want to know," Odd said. "Because that's a ridiculous answer, James. We kinda thought something like was going on, what with you glowing in the dark and all."

"You can't handle the light?" I asked.

"You ask another question and you go over," Odd said, looking to the edge of the cliff, still only a few yards away from my feet. "But no, we can't. We turned your fire off, and still you won't stop burning."

"You can't stop a rock—" I started.

"We're not talking about Reaper," Lukas said. "We can account for a rock.

What we can't account for is you. You're clearly rocking some hand-me-downs, there ain't nothing factory fresh about your supersuits, but still—to fly, to run, to see the world from the clouds, anywhere the source can reach, that requires a connection to the source machinery."

"A source machinery?" I asked.

"Less machine, more… fire from the gods," Astor said, taking over, his eyes calm, and why wouldn't they be? I wasn't in control. "The original source machinery, Silka's original breakthrough mechanism, literally the reason Silka was settled so quickly. Whoever commands that fire, commands the island."

"I don't have it," I said plainly. "But I'm supposed to help people, my mother taught me. Okay I'm in, let's take over an island."

"Where have you been my whole life?" Odd said, like he'd found religion.

"We'll get there James," Astor said. "You were a kid for the Blitz, so you couldn't possibly know this, but that night—"

"You lost your godfire?" I asked.

There was silence. Only the wind spoke.

"How could you possibly know that, Nite?" Odd asked, slowly.

"I didn't know I knew," I said, honestly.

"He's pulling our—" Odd snarled.

"No, it's the blueblood," Astor said. "Watch. James, which of you is older?"

"No," I said. "Not for you."

"James, you're embarrassing me in front of my co-workers," Astor said.

"That answer is for me," I said. "There are a thousand little things and one big thing you could ask for you. Those I will answer."

"Then be that way," Odd said, his eyebrows furrowing furiously. "Yes James. The night of the Blitz was the night someone stole our godfire."

"Technically that's the only way to get godfire," I said.

"This isn't Prometheus, this actually happened," Odd said, angry.

"Oh so this isn't even about storms or strangers for you," I said.

"Not to us, no," Odd said. "It took a while but to this day, we are operating on a duplicate generator, but let's just say it was never meant to be a permanent solution. Let's just say that if we'd found whoever stole our godfire, Issaic would have come back a whole lot sooner."

"Issaic…" I said, thinking of how long he'd been gone, just damn near Blitz years. "He was out… all this time… just looking for—"

"Ten years of stalemate, no victory," Odd said, ignoring me. "No one claiming credit. But with that power back in our hands… all we have to do is find the titan who took it. You don't happen to know who that is, do you Nite?"

"I know who took it," I said.

"Again, how could he possibly know that?" Odd shouted.

"Easily," Jemeni said, stepping up to us for the first time in a while. "If you know the last known location of the generator—I mean godfire. It was Teresa Nite's own house, on the hills above the Engineerium district."

Lukas and Astor looked at him funny.

"You talk loud," Jemeni said.

"And that, my friends, is the first step forward in ten years," Astor said, his eyes flashing, proudly? "I told you I saw something in him. I told you patience would be rewarded. You barely gave me two days, I delivered this."

"Impressive," Lukas said, sounding like he hated to give it up, but he had to. "Okay James. Tell us everything. Take us there."

"Okay," I said. "My first memories were of the girl falling out of the sky. It was also the night my mom turned into a superhero. But I remember first waking up with the explosions."

"We know this, just pick it up from the prologue," Odd said, waving his hand.

"Which prologue?" I asked.

"The MOST RECENT ONE!" Lukas shouted.

"Loud!" I almost cried.

"That's not how we do this," Astor said, shooing the rest away. "Give us ten minutes, alone. Now."

"Fine," Odd said. "Reaper, children, this way."

Lukas growled, then obeyed. Jemeni and Benjann followed without a word. Astor sat on the ground next to me and handed me a a small steel thermos.

"Rainwater?" I asked. "Or more blue?"

"Rainwater," Astor said. "It's just me and you James. I'll keep the others away best I can, but I need to know everything. From the beginning, now go."

"No problem," I said, and I took a sip of fresh, cool, clear water.

Astor drank too, then took my hands and I saw the aura come over us both. He was right, this was much more calm. My brain opened up, and the memory came at me like the expanding universe. With no brother to pull me out of the void, I fell into it. I was always weaker alone.

Zoom…

-

Ten years ago… an eight year old Kira had just kissed me on the cheek, quicker than I could react.

"So do I just…"

"You just," I said.

I walked backwards through the force field to our backyard. Kira was looking at me with a smile as she walked up and disappeared into the blue light. Just before she fully crossed, I could see her eyes wide and taken by what she was seeing. Then the energy flared and I closed my eyes for the bright lights, losing the feeling in my hand, not knowing if Kira was still holding on to me. Then the energy flared down, and I opened my eyes to a world of white, until my pupils could adjust enough to see, blinking madly… nothing.

"How… where…" I said.

Kira was not on this side. Not turned to dust, not fried to bits, just not here. Gone.

What…

"Hey now," I shouted, looking around, my head feeling like it was being twisted in a vice, my voice shaking. "What just happened?"

I ran forward and held my shaking fingers out to touch the force field. The blue lights fazed over me warmly, but I revolted at their touch, no longer enamored by my own ability to use it like a door when the ONE person I was trying to save hadn't been able to cross through. No force field for her. No ending to our rescue op. And she had trusted me. And I…

Wait the front door was open.

To my own house, to be clear. A red flag came up, seeing it ajar. It had been closed for sure a moment ago, I had seen it behind the blue light filter myself. The ashen footprints on the porch were new too, and tiny. Like, eight year old girl in a parachute tiny.

"K… Kira?" I asked, my eyes wild. I mean wide.

Actually, both.

She must had made a beeline for our house so quick that I thought her disappeared into the ether, or beamed up, or… whatever the force field did to not the strongest. The only thing keeping me from assuming the worst was… man those footprints were identical to the ones I was leaving behind me. Something my size had this way come, I was sure of it. I found myself following the footsteps into my own house without realizing it, Derek in the backyard without me. I should have called for him, I should have went for help before the chase.

But I… didn't.

There was a war going on behind me, bathing my house in oranges, then darkness, then fire reds, but I paid the colors in the clouds no attention. I was busy following those footsteps on my own, just a great call from an eight year old. But this was my house, my mom's house, and she was off fighting to keep the city safe, or something. She had told us to be heroes. Actually, what she'd said was be exactly who you are every day. So that's what I did.

It was easy to find where she had gone. Through the landing room and past the grand piano, to the living room, past two couches and a modular coffee table, down the stairs towards the underfloor. Every door was open—regardless, I may as well have been following a dark grey line of arrows on the ground. The house loomed over me without my mom around to keep the emptiness away. I must have turned on every light in the house as I walked through, every shadow something terrifying until… click.

I took the stairs down to the garage and past, only stopping at the second landing to the second garage, in front of that big rusted metal door that was always bolted shut. I wasn't allowed past here, and to this day I hadn't so much as tried to touch that door—but now it was open, and something was calling me. Fate, mystery, quite possibly masochism… or was it a girl?

Let's be honest, it was a girl.

I took a breath and braced for the stairs—but that red metal door held no stairs on the other side. It was just an offshoot of the garage, a room the size of a warehouse, clearly built deep underground, so deep it had massive carved pillars holding the ceiling up. But I couldn't see past what was going on not twenty feet from me.

"K… Kira," I said.

She looked up, only a few workbenches and huge machines away from me.

There was no light in this room, I hadn't found the click switch yet. But I could see at least what she was doing. Kira had her hands on something that was glowing, sending off blue wisps of energy and white sparks that were clearly landing all over her arms and legs as she clenched her teeth together for the pain, her hands slowly turning the light down, the ball of glowing energy getting smaller and smaller…

"We're not allowed in here," I said to her, lamely.

She looked up at me without any emotion. "Why not, James?"

There was no stutter. No shaking legs, no holding my hand. Her voice was the same, but it wasn't. It was deeper. Darker. Or maybe she had let go of the princess crap for one moment and I had assumed her a villain—bad James, very bad.

I had one chance, I could see that. I racked my brain. What could I say? What did I want? Why was I here?

"Whatever's going on, and believe me I have NO idea… I don't care. After you rob us, can we still be friends?"

Kira stopped. Her hands were close to connecting, the room was growing darker as she did, and the look on her face was the last thing I remember. She was either trying not to laugh, or smile.

"I'm not robbing you. But yeah. I'd like that."

"Friends forever?" I asked. "Promise."

"I promise," she said.

That was it. Eight year olds cutting to the chase. Also the ball of energy was vanished, the palms of Kira's hands lit up one last time, and the reflection of that blue light in her eyes was all there was before… darkness.

Except not, because the world whipped around me, there was some kind of pressure on my back and neck, and in the time it would have taken me to jump and land, my feet touched down on the grassy sideyard of my own house, back right within the force field, looking back at a very closed front door, with no marks of ashen footprints anywhere to be seen. My hair flew up in the wind… but there was no wind. It was leftover momentum, that's what that was. But I couldn't think about why, not when all I could think about was the girl in the parachute.

It had seen so simple. Not that I had any thought to what would happen after we got back home, but I hadn't imagined her blinking out of existence. There was no excuse, I had made a mistake. I didn't know what I should have done differently. But I couldn't possibly hope to know her story in one night.

That being said, I had been really into the story.

"You… you promised," I said, to absolutely no one.

No one answered, until someone did. My brother. He was screaming my name.

-

…Unzoom.

My head snapped back and the memory was done. I remember looking around through a huge fog by then, like the mushrooms were on the verge of shutting my body down. Whatever I'd drank, it was concentrated. I'd had that thought before. I was going in circles. Astor was looking at me funny. He couldn't speak. I wondered how a simple story could have such an effect.

"That enough for you?" I asked. "Too much? Not much enough?"

Astor looked like he wanted to throw up.

"We forgot about the girl," he said, his voice as thin as ever. "ODD!"

"That a good Odd or a bad Odd?"

"It's something else," Astor said, deftly dodging the question. "James, you've been perfect. I always knew you were worth keeping alive, if only for a short time, but by my count boys, I think our time's up."

"So you got what he wanted?" Odd asked.

"I got all there is," Astor said (again with the non-answer). "Anything else we need from him in this state, before I bury the evidence?"

"Before WHAT?" Benjann said, suddenly full of something. "You can't be serious."

"Uh oh," Lukas said, turning on Benjann.

"You said he was cool," Odd said, wheeling on Jemeni.

"He is," Jemeni said, taking a step to meet Odd head on like we'd been forced to, countless times, again, the similarities. "Don't do it in front of us, that's all."

"I didn't realize my freedom came with your censure," Odd said. "You know what I call that? An oxymoron."

"Call me whatever you like," Jemeni said. "I'm not here to be your friend, Odd, so do your worst, but do it to people like me, who can take it. Personally, for lots of reasons, I think you should still be in jail."

"And I—" Odd started.

"You don't want to say anything right now," I said, the words so sudden than even Odd shut up.

Jemeni looked at me, and looked away. He didn't say anything. But I felt it.

"By all means, speak more, and tell us all," Odd said, with a fake bow to me. "Last words Nite. Make 'em good.

"Benjann," I said, turning to him in full honesty. "I failed you. I only ever came into your life hoping to help people like you from people like me. Your part in this is the worst possible stereotype there is, that in true war, the true innocent are always the first to feel the consequences. If these are my last words then you know I mean them. I'm sorry for everything we've put you through and I'm sorry for not telling you sooner."

"I... you say that and I think there's a world we can survive together," Benjann said.

"Watch it," Jemeni said, taking a step closer to Benjann.

"In this world I would still let you die if it meant my own survival," I said, again under the omnipotent control of the mushrooms. "I understand that you probably think the exact same. We're both either monsters, or just people. People who haven't even had a real chance to be friends yet, I know it."

"Heroes neither, clearly," Benjann said, looking like he might cry again. "I wouldn't die for you Nite. You are nothing like they say, maybe neither am I. But here's the difference between us—I actually do want you dead. You deserve this, so take it."

And the others only smirked in the background as it was Benjann who came forward, ready to kick me off that mountain. But as hard as his feet came in, there was a look in his eyes that told me everything I needed to know.

Help me James.

"I got you," I said.

It was instinctual. Universal. I didn't know how or why I knew it, but if a man asks for help while he's trying to murder throw you off a steep, snowy mountain, you help him. I guess that was the saying, right? In that moment, even under the blueblood, I just had this crazy instinct that I wasn't the one in danger. I knew it from the tips of my toes.

Survive, Benjann Matthews.

I stepped backwards, my foot catching the edge of the edge, sending rubble down onto—the head of someone climbing up the mountain. I shuffled away just as the climbing gear stuck down right where my foot had been. Benjann's eyebrows froze as the figure climbed up next to me in full on snow-gear, down to the goggles.

"It means shengcun, Benjann Matthews," I said, full smile, blueblood reality.

"Well, we lost James," came the voice, and the goggles came off.

It was my hero. Sand Freedom, his mouth open, his face frozen. He'd heard everything. But he wasn't racing towards me, he wasn't saving me. He was staring at me like I'd just sprouted antlers.

"She's alive?"

"Who lives?" I asked.

"Kira," Sand said, and hearing the name from him was the last thing I remember. "Did I hear you straight, James? Did you say Kira Command is... ALIVE?"

"Last time I saw her," I nodded.

"You SAW HER?" Sand shouted.

"You listening, anything, last ten minutes?" I smiled.

"Who's down there?" Astor asked, frowning as he leaned over the mountain to see what was up. "Damnit—IT'S SAND, RUN FOR YOUR LIFE!"

I think I'd hit the end of my truth serum—all I remember is touching my nose and pointing, and the look on Sand's face as he shifted his furious focus to Odd, Astor, and Lukas, who all collectively looked ready for the bathroom in his wake.

"Jemeni?" Odd called, looking around.

"Outa here!"

We caught the far-off sight of Jemeni holding Benjann by the shirt as they jumped off the mountain side, sliding on their butts down and out of sight before I knew they'd even left.

"It's... him," Odd said, Astor the only one left by his side. "We're doomed."

"Just us," Sand Freedom said, cracking his knuckles. "James, you good? James!"

And the last thing I remember... I forget.

4.0

THE LITTLE BROTHER

"Prepare for landing, agent Akoura."

I was a minute out from the waterfall when the red light started blinking.

"I know how to land a plane without you waving your arms at me."

"Great, do it yourself then."

And the radio clicked off. Sorry Troy. I left the radio on, my end on mute.

"System, night mode."

"Cameras and microphones in four seconds," came a voice (not Troy).

The cabin went dark. Not literally, just in all the ways that mattered. I was alone in my jet, the one I'd flown since before anything like the Blitz happened, and now after that fact too. Alone, I touched the red light on my watch.

"Two to one, come in one," came the voice from tiny speakers.

"Hello sister," I said. I'd know her voice anywhere, even over the static of a communicator watch as old as, well, me. "I assume something's happened?"

"Everything's happened you idiot!" came the much harsher male voice of, well, my big brother. "His stupid brother caught me the first chance I could try, now the hand's all over me."

"How about Ollux, she clean?" I asked, almost without a care.

"Barely," she said. "Infinite was supposed to be there, did they get our—"

"I definitely did that," I said, leaning back into my seat with my free hand on that spot in my forehead that was always bulging out like a balloon.

"But you sent TWO KIDS?" Astor shouted. "Are you completely useless?"

"One of the brothers drew Infinite power underland!" Ollux shouted through the watch. "The girl talks to animals, the Reaper does things we haven't seen from the Vema in centuries! We were expecting the Infinite envoy yesterday."

"The jungle is thick, and hard to cross without power," I said, thinking quick.

"Then switch to Reaper tech," Astor said. "If Infinite can't get this done, we can wear the enemy's clothes—if we have to. We still have the valley Reapers locked away in the underground prisons, yes?"

"Two of them," I said. "Trevor and Ronan Akoura. They share our last name, you could call them more than Reaper."

"It's the oldest name on island, bound to happen, who cares?" Ollux said.

"About FAMILY?" I asked, throwing my hands up.

"We'll come back to it," Astor said. "Right now, even once Bastile is out of the way, we've underestimated them since you brought them into headquarters, Alcyon. If Issaic hadn't returned, we might have lost much more than Odd."

"I know it," I said, thinking hard on that coincidence. Except it was no—

Then there was a tap on the jet window. Of course it was Issaic, looking at me like he'd caught me with my hand in the cookie jar. I gave him the thumbs up, clicked the red button (and my family) off, and stepped out of the jet.

"I still don't understand why I can't talk to them directly," Issaic said.

"Plausible denial, sir," I said. "Unless you're actually ready to take over the island yourself, there are reasons to keep us around. Are you?"

"Close, but no, not yet," Issaic said. "I've been gone too long, I was sure the world I left behind would keep. I dreamed of it every night, coming home to Silka, flying over the endless wasteland of the Vempire without a single cretin in sight, watching the entire island go up in flames starting with your infernal jungle, the ashes mine alone to rise from—I mean ours. Ours to rise from."

"Do we really have to start from… ashes?" I asked.

"Not Silka," Issaic said. "Not the lightning city, she's just as perfect as I left her. There was never room on this island for the rest. But speaking of the north, surely you've heard?"

"Sorry sir," Alcyon said, thinking hard. "Still nothing. I haven't heard anything from my siblings. It's like they're out of service. And don't call me—"

"Copyrighted," Issaic growled.

He gave me a wave and walked out the door, like always. He never gave anyone more than five seconds, if he knew they didn't have what he wanted. I wiped my forehead, and went back to thinking. Mostly about… what on earth was I doing?

Then, without warning, the electricity went out. Not just on the ship. Everywhere. In the last flash of light I saw the silhouette of Issaic Nite stop and turn to me. Then it was just us and the darkness. The electricity hadn't gone out in Silka City since ever. This meant… victory, in the smallest sense of the word.

Let it be known, that for the first time in a generation, a Nite had listened

"Alcyon," Issaic said, his voice much closer in the pitch black than I'd remembered. "Tell me this isn't what I think it is."

"I…" I stammered. "It can't be."

But it wasn't just the lights. We were in a utility tunnel halfway between the heart of headquarters and the city above us. That's when, from the city side of the tunnel came the cold, the smell of rain, the sounds of the wind picking up. The lightning cracked and I saw Issaic lit up for the flash, looking past me, out the tunnel, at what was coming over Silka.

Spoiler alert, it was a big fat storm.

PART IV

4.1

ANIMAL SPIRITS

All I'll say is, if you really know what you want, sometimes it doesn't hurt to ask for it. Coming through the door was none other than Sand Freedom, with my brother James draped over the white horse below them. My hero, my brother.

"I must express just how much that wasn't me," the speakers said.

"I have gravely underestimated the power of technology," Willa said.

"No, horses," Sand said.

"Where'd it go?" Sasha said, patting herself down. "Anyone seen a knife?"

"Not now dear," Volf said. "I mean ma'am."

He took her by the shoulders and faded into the background, as we scrambled over to help Sand with his luggage (my brother). One fistful of shirt and yep, I could tell he was alive. A bit bruised and bloody, especially around the face, but I probably didn't look any better. We were twins after all.

"James?" I said, still not really getting it. "Here? You?"

"Out, get out," Heather said, walking up and lighting up both hands in that purple heal glow, ready for the works. "How dead is he?"

"Not even," Sand said. "No real damage, I saved that for them."

Another horse walked up behind, tied on a long rope to the makeshift saddle beneath Sand like this was medieval times—and speaking of, lashed to it sideways were Odd and Astor, looking as miserable as I'd ever seen them.

"Oh I can do better than this," Willa said, walking towards the second horse with a knife. "Permission, Wayfarer?"

"You don't ask for anything, Skyfire," Sand said. "But that's not my name."

"Well that's not mine either," Willa said, shrugging, as she flipped the knife between her fingers. Then—

"AH!"

Astor and Odd were suddenly upright on the horse, still as tethered as ever. But now, the way their bodies were slammed together and their hands lashed to the reigns, they looked like lovers.

"Can we laugh at that?" James asked, through a familiar fog.

"It's for the horse's sake," Willa said. "Center of mass and all."

"I've… been through worse," we heard Odd admit.

Astor shrugged behind him. “Same.”

“All’s well,” Willa said, shrugging. “How about James? What happened?”

“I found him by the cave on the edge of the mountain, with Astor, Odd, and Lukas,” Sand said. “Benjann was with them, and another kid I didn’t know.”

“Jemeni,” I said. “He… I thought he was cool.”

“The four of them force-fed James the blueblood, not that cool,” Sand said. “He stopped talking a few minutes ago.”

“He is going in and out of sleepytime,” James said suddenly.

“And talking in the third person,” I said.

It wasn’t just me, Sand took a step backwards like James was possessed, until he was quiet and still again. Heather had jumped too. She carefully came back forward, moving her shiny hands all over him.

“Heather,” Sand said. “Your… aura. It’s glowing.”

“Nicest thing you’ve ever said to me,” Heather said, her eyes never leaving James. “You missed the part where it went out and came back, twice. Infinite’s got more than a head start on a Reaper killer, it’s a miracle called Derek Nite that the connection to the Vema still stands.”

“You’re gonna need to explain that again,” Sand said, looking at Heather with something like hope in his eyes. “But if it does… and it’s in his blood…”

“Then I got this,” she said, hopeful. “Everybody stand back. And Lynn—”

She came up eagerly.

“Take notes.”

“Aw come on,” Lynn pouted. “Derek, take notes for me.”

“Yes dear. I mean ma’am. I mean—”

“Uh oh,” James said, turning to us with both of his eyes closed.

“Shut up James,” Lynn said.

One of us was trying not to blush. Maybe her, maybe me, who knew?

Heather took her necklace in her hand and whispered to it, or kissed it, she did something with her mouth, that’s all I could see. Then the thing was shining brighter than ever, and a stellar, spiral of light was coming out of her hands, in waves that enveloped us all, the sky, the ground too.

“Out to lunch,” Lynn said, looking around.

Heather never wavered, she held that glowing aura until James’ necklace lit up in the same pattern. The lights doubled around us, but in the sphere of here, I could see everything. Inside the purple crystal around my brother’s neck, there was a pea-sized, neon blue gem forming.

“Is that what I think it is?” I asked, in wonder.

“Derek,” Lynn said, pointing to the chain of the necklace.

There was blood running down James’ throat. The small silver chain around his neck had latched onto his skin and seemed to be cutting into his neck.

“Ugh,” I said, convulsing. “Look at that neck! UGH—”

“Are you five?” Heather asked.

“I trust you,” I said, answering the real question.

Heather bit her lip, and the glow lessened a bit, as the healing was redirected to my brother’s neck. My brother’s body convulsed a bit, but we all grew up and moved on with the otherworldly, demonic saving ritual. And speaking of, just then, the lights flashed, and we all saw something that looked like his soul (or heat waves) at the edges of his body. He moved one last time as the lights of the glowing dome around us flashed again, and off.

Then everything was still. Absolutely still.

Heather let her legs give out, but she still held her hands out over James' chest, until his necklace rose up in the air towards her hands, and the neon blue stone moved through the purple amethyst like water. Finally they were separated, Heather took hold of the tiny, shiny blue stone, and fell over sideways into the dirt, exhausted. But James' eyes blinked back open as his necklace hit his chest, as purple as before, and he sat up like a spring.

"Ben?" Were his first words, before a breath. "Wait. Where—DEREK!"

"You're back buddy," I said.

"Derek," James said, grabbing onto my arm, looking around. "I'm… here? Back here? Was that all a dream? Is that a pegasus?"

James was looking all around like he hadn't registered a thing before, under the blueblood. I'll admit Sand and his giant white horse kind of stood out.

"How'd you know her name?" Sand asked, petting the horse's nose.

"I got here on a pegasus…" James said, probably living out his best day—until he finally saw her on the ground. "Heather! You better be alive, you hear me? If you died for me, I'm going to—"

"Here," she said, giving a shaky thumbs up from the ground, a blue stone held carefully between thumb and hand. "You wouldn't last a day without me."

"Is that what I think it is?" James asked.

"What kind of notes were we supposed to take?" Lynn said, sounding small.

"That was kind of a first for me too," Heather said, awkwardly holding the blue stone out for James. "Only right you keep it."

"You pulled his blood out like a splinter," Lynn said. "I've seen you heal skin and bone, but if you can reach into blood and pull something out…"

"What do you want from me Lynn, a cure for cancer?" Heather said.

"Have you tried?" Lynn asked.

"Of course I haven't," Heather said. "Maybe we should come back to that one. James you got a pocket or what?"

"Actually don't," he said.

"Then give it up," Heather said.

James shrugged and reached for his shirt, Heather only held up a hand, and a small piece of obsidian broke off her armor. We all watched as the blueblood stone moved into the obsidian, the pressure around it forming a sphere, until the entire thing was a marble enclosed in lava rock with a small top hook. Heather willed the entire thing onto my brother's necklace, just moving the rock around the chain instead of bothering with clasps or latches. Suddenly he had two gemstones on that necklace, when everyone else had one. Lucky James.

"I'd say thanks," James said. "But that's not exactly enough this time."

"How did you show up at the exact right place at the exact right time Sand?" Lynn said, looking up at Sand like he had ridden (rode?) in on a white horse and solved everything (he had).

"For the first time," Sand said. "I believe in really long leashes. But I told you once. Whatever path you take, wherever you will go, whenever you decide to lead, I will follow."

So close. Those were song lyrics, and it was *leave*, not lead. But maybe Sand knew that.

"So you're following us," Heather said.

"When am I not?" Sand smiled. "I owe you more than a tail."

"Don't remind me of…" Lynn said, her eyes low.

Sand got off the horse and that's when he saw it. Her.

"That's not fair," he said, frozen in front of the body of Sophia Sabretooth.

"That's how they got us," I said, back to clenching. "We were distracted over the cat, while they were kidnapping my brother in the background."

"Don't blame the cat," James said, eyes closed, taking deep breaths.

"I blame myself," I said. "It doesn't make it better."

"It doesn't," Lynn said. "That was the thing connecting us to more. I felt it even before the gates. She was special. She made me feel special."

"She made you talk to animals, that's more than special," I said.

"But for why?" Lynn said. "What was trying so hard it broke through nature itself to get to us? To me? And why isn't this even the first time?"

"And why is it not just you?" James asked, his eyes heavy.

"Something is calling you," Sand said. "I don't know if it's related to what I just walked in on with this one, but James has something he needs to tell you."

"And what might that be?" James asked, innocently.

Sand looked back, making sure Astor and Odd were out of earshot. "Really? I was climbing a thousand feet of vert, I only caught the last few moments. You went full orator back there, let's have the story again."

"The story of what?" James asked.

"The GIRL IN THE PARACHUTE!" Sand shouted/whispered. "Why can't you just finish a story for once?"

"Double standard," I said, pointing right back.

"Because of prologue reasons, probably?" James said.

"What does he mean?" Heather said, looking at me. "What more is there? I thought you made it through the Blitz together?"

"We did," I said, scratching my head. "Mostly."

"And Kira too, can't forget the girl in the parachute," James said.

"I hate kids," Sand said, his face in his hands.

"What," Sasha said, not questioning, demanding. "Kira what. Say it at the same time."

"Kira Command," we said at the same time, as requested.

Sasha took a step back. "Witches."

"Just twins," I said, scratching my head. "Bells?"

"All the bells," Sasha said. "Volf, you were right."

"Boom, baby…" Volf whimpered, not sounding too happy about it.

Sand held his hands out at James, then me, and the others nodded along like they couldn't believe us either. What in the what?

"Why?" I asked. "What's so bad, so maybe we know Kira, why's that—"

"You keep SAYING THAT NAME!" Sasha shouted. "Do you know what it means Nite?"

"Finally," Heather said.

"Of course I don't!" I said. "I can't imagine it's important except I'm sure it is, so go ahead and tell me about it so we can all STOP YELLING!"

"You really don't know?" Lynn asked softly.

Her too? Judas. Wait, I already knew that. We'd just… never talked about it.

"I don't know anything, gospel truth," I said. "And I have no way of knowing, you haven't even let me get to that part yet."

"Then how did the name Kira Command just come out of your mouth?" Sasha asked.

"Because she fell out of the sky and James jumped off a roof to catch her!" I shouted, my hands out. "He saved her, I only helped. We were eight."

"WHAT?" Everyone shouted at us at once (literally).

"Loud," James said, rubbing his ear.

"But we did get split up for a moment," I said, remembering. "When the bombs came down and our mom flew for the first time. I went through the blue. I was going to turn around, but then I saw the helicopter land on our back lawn and five soldiers brought my mother out on a stretcher."

"Oh," Lynn said, looking away. "I didn't know that part."

"We haven't gotten there yet," I said. "There's… more to the prologue. I mean story. We've been really stretching it out, if you haven't noticed."

"I've noticed," Sand said.

"We did it," Heather said, shaking her head. "We watched Bastile do it, and it's for the same reason and everything. We came in hot, our bad. I forgot… how much of this is about your mother. I forgot—"

"Who this is for," I said, my lips as thin a line as Heather's ever were.

"All the trees," my brother said, still half in a trance. "But her first."

"Yep," I said. "Sorry not sorry. What I saw on that backyard, by myself, I was kind of… that was kind of it. Next thing I knew, I was screaming for James, and James answered. But only James."

"What happened to Kira?" Sasha demanded.

"I don't know," I said, honestly, looking at James as hard as the rest of the group. "We never talked about it, it was kind of a rule we had, seeing as our Mom asked us to do one thing, we did the opposite, and she never walked again. I never pressed, he never offered, and to be honest I've never given it this much thought in my entire life. Whatever the truth is, it's in James' head, not mine."

"Well," Heather said, looking between us. "Good thing there's two of you."

"We might have a chance in hell," Sand said suddenly.

"We talk when you do," James said, staring daggers at Sand.

"I'll tell you everything," he said. "It's time, it's beyond time. I know I don't deserve it. But can I ask… can we just… I don't think I can do it on my own."

"Damnit, again with the relatable," Heather said, deflated.

"Do you want to phone a friend?" Lynn said, smiling.

"Crete," Sand said. "I need him to do this right. I've always needed him for that, more, and everything else. We go back, and we talk. Deal?"

"Well as long as there's more talking," I said sarcastically.

"How do we get home?" Lynn asked.

"How'd you get here?" Sand asked. "Just turn around. And don't leave me too far behind this time."

"Uh, same," Willa said. "Just remember, nobody fly over the gates. I'm looking at all of you."

"I can't fly, I'll let you know if that changes," Sand said.

"Have you tried?" I asked, lamely.

Sand froze. Then he held his arms out, and we all heard the wind whistling in underneath him. Saw his body lift off the horse just a bit, and as we were about to really panic—

"Just kidding," Sand said, falling back down on his horse. "No I can't fly. I've always been good at whistling though. Are we all good on a Hexoscope?"

"All good," I said. "Let's just say, we got what we came for, except not at all, and them some we didn't want. Please let's just go home—I mean not home—"

"I know what you mean," Sand said. "Let's go, not soldiers."

And everyone but Willa was back in that rocky obsidian armor, head to toe, including a full helm of tinted rock. Willa sighed, and her measly suspenders emerged into a half-formed wingsuit. It was enough.

"I'd say it's been real," I said. "But..."

"Don't," Lynn said, taking one last look at Sophia Sabretooth. "Just..."

We left that place, flying high over a galloping white horse and the prisoner cargo behind, back up the incline and towards the far off trees. There wasn't much else out here. With every moment the horses only seemed to run faster. Before long, we were putting on the speed to keep up.

"What did I say?" Willa shouted out from behind us.

But we could hear her, more than we'd ever been able to hear words shouted into the screaming wind at breakneck speed. My armor was sleek and streamlined, almost like the dirt knew we were not only above ground, but airborne. Clearly the Vema were never meant to live just underground. Whatever this magnetic gemstone nonsense was, it was for more than digging holes.

"Trees," Lynn said, pointing, and I was ripped from my thoughts as we watched the horses approaching the absolute wall of trees, not so much as half a path anywhere in sight.

"Slow down Sand!" Heather shouted.

"There's no path this far out!" Willa called out.

"Yes there is, I made it this morning," Sand shouted back. "Now FLY!"

His white horse slammed into the tree line and disappeared without so much as a leaf out of place. Maybe path? Hopefully path. We pushed forward frantically, keeping over the canopies of trees that were only fifty feet tall out here, and yep, I kept getting glimpses of something snowy dashing around trunks, over small bushes, never losing speed, the rider never losing balance. All things considered, it looked like a smoother ride down there.

"Okay then, jungle madness," I said. "Willa, where are we?"

"Closer to Ravenna than expected," she said. "We can take the topline in."

"But Willa, we're flying," I said.

"We are," Willa said. "But we don't… we can't fly over the gates."

"Um, yes we could, and easily," Heather argued.

"But we won't," Willa said. "Nothing's supposed to get through, no matter what. It's the only way our people can truly tune the island out and forget what's been done to us for centuries—that's the deal. If they see us flying over, the illusion is over, and those gates lose their only purpose in the Territory."

"It's not just us," Lynn said. "Anyone could fly over those gates."

"Anyone, like the Infinite Army?" Willa asked.

She had us all figured out.

"You think that's possible?" Volf asked quietly. "I mean, what we did at that complicated beehive, you don't think, that maybe more than just the Reaper—"

"I don't think so," I said. "If the Silka City source had gotten through, Sand wouldn't need a horse."

"Or maybe he's cut off in the same way we are," Lynn said.

"No," I said. "I've seen him fly without a shirt. He's… different. Crete is too. Besides, if Infinite could bring their power here, all the trees would be on fire."

"They'd start with the gates if they had any brains," Willa said. "Right?"

"We don't even know the rules," Lynn said. "How are we supposed to play this right?"

"By instinct, I guess," I said.

"But we've been here before," Lynn said. "We let James get got, again. We knew from the start Astor wanted something in his head and we let it happen. How's that for instincts?"

I didn't know what to say.

"Here," Willa said, and we dived, straight over the tops of those trees that were now easily over two hundred feet above the ground, even as we flew into the incline of the northern edge of the island.

"Oh that's clearly a volcano," I said, looking into the distance at the only thing rising higher than the treetops, the leviathan, mountainous end to the north.

"Best beach on the island, on the other side of it," Willa said.

"The best beach?" I asked. "And you're just mentioning this now because?"

"Storm season," Willa said. "But I'll take you, when this is all over. When it can be summer again. When we can be friends, instead of… whatever this is."

"Soldiers?" Heather said, simply.

"No," Willa said. "The Jerico has soldiers. I am still willing to die any day for my territory, but I am no longer expendable, and you never were. We're not quite soldiers now are we, Reaper?"

"I guess, we're not," Heather said. "Not soldiers, not scouts, not agents or warriors. And not—"

"Whatever the Mylo decide to call themselves later," Lynn finished.

"Not that either," Heather said, with a smile. Not a hint of one, a real one.

"Does that mean that we might actually be able to decide for ourselves what we could and should be, without the chaos of everything that's come before us, no matter the family ties?" I asked, in a single breath.

"It might," Willa said. "You want?"

"Sign us up," James said.

I took one last look at the misty, far off edge of literal strangerland, but this time I didn't see a volcano. I saw the best beach on the other side of it, or at least, that's what I wanted to see. I hoped I would get there. A lot of this island had made itself part of us recently, the actual strangerland was running out. That's when I realized I wanted to see the world. Or at least the island. Every single part of it, and decide for myself if it was the way it should be.

Normal thoughts, right?

"How about it Lynn?" I asked. "When this is all over, and we can actually start that map?"

"I'm there," she said. "I'm so there it's not fair."

"Rage," Heather said. "That means me too. I haven't… all this time, I still haven't touched the ocean. Wait that's not true, I did once, but only because a man had just fallen out of the sky."

"Right, that's me," I said. "Good at catching people falling out of the sky, bad at figuring out why, or where they came from."

"Well good thing there's two of us," James said, shaking his head.

"Then one of you, catch me, if you can," Willa said, folding her arms together, her wings followed, and she plummeted through the soaked leaves.

"Ah!" I shouted. "Not cool Willa. For trauma reasons."

She'd left me no choice but to recall my own wings and drop through the trees like a bomb, leaves and water and branches smacking me all over. For all the jostling I had my eyes open behind that rocky face covering, and twenty feet over the ground was all I needed to hit my wings, catch my fall, and slowly come to the ground as the moss, dirt, caterpillars and leaves caught up with me like rain—also, with as much water as we'd knocked loose, there was actual rain for a few moments. I looked up and around through it, but Willa was—

"I'm going to remind you of something that sounds sad, but it's just the truth," Willa said, standing her own ground beside me. "You don't need to save me, Derek Nite. You have too much else to do."

"I… will," I said lamely. "Why's the ground so soft?"

"Cool, clear water," Willa sang. "We're lucky the maelstrom has calmed. Let's hope it holds."

"Hope," I echoed, like a prayer.

The others fell through the canopy and spread their wings at the last second, coming in hot but landing gracefully on the dirt and tree-bark lined grasses, with trees behind us and a small hill in front of us, the gates nowhere in sight. Not yet. But that wasn't it.

"I know this clearing," I said.

"Crash site," Lynn said. "It looks… better."

It did. I could see the stretch of open land, but with no piles of detritus towering over it, and after a good rainstorm, there was nothing but green grass and the clear signs of plants growing back. On top of that, I could see the ten foot planter kits of what was clearly going to be four new trees. Right now they were comically far apart from each other, but that was by design. In time, they would grow hundreds and hundreds of feet all, and as thick around as a mansion. They would fill this clearing, even if it took a hundred years. But that wasn't all. There was a small raised patch of dirt with a wooden well built around it. It was the landing point of a certain topline platform zipline construct, and the running wire was still attached to a wooden pole at the ground, lifting up and away over the treetops, disappearing into the fog.

Willa walked up to it and put a hand to the sky. There was no answer.

"It might take a few minutes to descend," she said.

So we waited a few minutes. But that wire never moved, never started vibrating with an incoming platform, nothing. Willa frowned, took out a sword, found a beam of light coming in over the canopy, and angled her sword under it until she had a beam of light reflecting (refracting?) up into the tops of the trees. Still, nothing.

"There goes that," Willa said. "Strange."

"Again, we could just fly, it's so simple," I sighed.

"It's never simple," Willa sighed harder. "Okay, plan Ravenna. Their village is on a hill, it gets wet, but they're safe in their homes. They'll have horses."

"Higher ground physics, I like it," I said, nodding. "Wings out."

"No," Willa said. "We might scare them into attacking. I'm begging you."

"Straight walking, got it," Heather said. "We can be normal, Willa."

"Can you?" Willa said. "Or do you just want to be?"

Heather lost her swagger. "So it's like that."

"I'll believe normal from you when I see it," Willa said, then her eyes narrowed at something up the hill. "Wings down."

Straight walking. Of course it was uphill. But even as the wet dirt gave in like sand with every step, we made it to the top of that hill and came upon a soaked, soft wooden fence, until we could see the length of a small plateau, with exactly nine buildings all across it, the largest still a single story barn, the others smaller, individual house units. One door opened across the way, and the silhouette of a very small child looked out at us.

"Lilypad?" Lynn called out in hope.

"LYNN?"

The door slammed shut, then opened again with a much bigger figure being pulled along by a tiny child. It was Nari, the village leader, all bundled up in a puffy hemp sweater and a knitted beanie, with gloves to match. Lilypad wasn't even wearing shoes, she dropped her father's hand and ran halfway to the fence.

"I was going to open the gate, but you could just jump it," she called out. "I'm gonna get shoes, be right back."

"I told you," Nari said, shivering.

Heather didn't hesitate, she was over the hip-high fence without an ounce of effort. We followed.

"That fence isn't for humans," I said.

"Wild boars," Nari said. "They tear up the ground something awful. Why—"

"We need horses," Willa said.

"I thought you might," Lilypad said, coming back around the house with four horses behind her, no reigns, just following her. "They were standing by my shoes, they followed me as soon as I opened the pen. That never happens. You must need them. I will allow it."

"You can't be serious," Nari said, turning on his daughter.

"I'm sorry, who trained the horses?" Lilypad said, standing her ground.

"You did," Nari said. "Okay fine, as long as you know what it is you want."

"I do," Lilypad said, looking at Lynn. "I want to be like her. Right now she needs horses, and I have horses. Simple."

"I love this child," Willa said, proudly.

"I do too," Nari said, even prouder.

Once again, I found myself horseback, but this time Lynn was in front of me, and I was pressed into her back.

"Closer, for balance," Sasha said, as she and Volf rode past us on another horse, their bodies pressed together from shoulder to waist.

"Sorry horse," Lynn said.

"What did you call me?" I said.

Lynn backed up into me. Like... shoulders to waists. Why was it so comfortable? How was her skin so soft? I didn't say that out loud right? No...

"Better," Volf said, pointing right at me. "Don't make work for the horse."

"Yes sir," I said.

"I can feel your heart beating Derek," Lynn said. "Why is it so fast?"

"Just for all your normal planet ending reasons," I said. "Why?"

"No reason," Lynn said. "Something's different with the animals this week. I'd be more okay with it if..."

"I know," I said. "I can't imagine what it's like. I'm sorry Lynn."

"I am too," she said, softly. "For..."

"Where's the clouded leopard that saved me?" Lilypad asked, looking up to us with nothing but excitement on her tiny face. "Sophia, where is she?"

"For..." Lynn said, blinking.

Talk about bad timing.

"You know what... we had to let her go," I said, seeing the look in Lynn's eyes as I lied. "She's out there in the wild right now, and she's happy."

"She's... happy?" Lilypad said. "I'm not five. Don't lie to me, trust me with the truth."

"I'm sorry," I said, looking down. "Honesty, or worse."

"That's not a saying," Lilypad said, folding her arms at me. "Lynn?"

"I want you to do more than just live, little one," Lynn said. "I don't know if that means keeping you innocent or treating you like an adult. I don't know that answer yet. What happened to Sophia... it's a big answer. Lily, she's—"

"Okay he's not kidding, that's enough," Lilypad said, holding her ears closed. "I've changed my mind. No matter what, it must have been hard, to let Sophia go. Really hard. If she's out there in the wild right now, I believe that she's truly happy. And if for whatever reason, if there's a world where she isn't, then there's gotta be one where she is, right? If only in our hearts?"

"Are you doing the Schrödinger's cat thing, to me?" Lynn asked, smiling.

"Maybe," Lilypad said. "She found us for a reason Lynn. She saved me from the ship on fire, she got so close to me I swear I heard her—nevermind. If you ever figure out why, maybe let a little girl know, yeah?"

"I love this child," Lynn said, blinking.

"I do too," Nari said for the second time.

"To the gates," Willa said, rounding on us with Heather behind her on the third horse. "Thank you… little one. Keep your village safe. The storms are far from over."

"And yet, we're still here," Lilypad said, saluting Willa like no one else in the village had. "Caput."

"We don't… do that here," Nari said, looking down at his girl. "Wait. Wildfire, is that true? You'll be in line, after Bones?"

"It is," Willa said. "And I have no objection to your independence. I won't forget your help. If I can ever return it… wait a minute. How'd you know that?"

Lilypad froze, her face turning red. "You wouldn't believe me."

"Answer me, devil child," Willa said.

Nari stepped forward, a hand on Lily's shoulder, his eyes staring daggers at Willa, his other hand holding a dagger at Willa. Willa didn't even see it as her hand quivered for a moment over the handle of that sword at her hip… then she lowered her hands.

"Sorry," Willa said. "You are clearly no eight year old super spy, I'm putting my faith in there being an even crazier explanation. Ready when you are."

"If I told you, you wouldn't believe me," Lilypad said, blushing.

"It was a bird, wasn't it?" Lynn asked.

Lilypad stared back. "How did you know? I mean no… I mean okay yes, that's exactly what happened. Damn, Lynn."

"Language, Lily," Willa said, arms folded, all smiles.

"Sorry," Lilypad said, bowing.

Nari dropped his dagger and looked at his daughter. "A bird told you what?"

Chirp.

"What?" Nari asked, going white.

"See!" Lily said. "Told ya. Hi bird."

Chirp!

A small yellow canary had landed on Lily's shoulder. It seemed to shake its head and feathers once at Lily, as it hopped madly across her shoulders and sang a beautifully annoying song of sharp chirps and rolls.

"But I like them!" Lilypad said to the bird.

The bird was on her head, still hopping and chirping away.

"Fine!" Lilypad said, exasperated, looking annoyed at being the messenger. "The bird wants you to leave."

"Of course it does," Heather said, bowing to the bird, half sarcasm, half non-aggression.

"The bird is not alone," Nari said, looking at us like the much more complicated thing we'd ended up being, instead of just horse-borrowers. "What do you want with Lily?"

"Absolutely nothing, we're leaving right now," Lynn said. "Keep listening to animals when they talk to you, Lilypad. Anybody in this village calls you crazy, just write their names down for me."

"I will," Lilypad said, her eyes beaming again as she looked up to us on horseback. "I know all their names."

"That's precious cargo, that Lily," Volf said, staring Nari in the eyes as we started to turn for the hill. "Don't you dare let anything happen to her."

"Don't be the reason anything happens to her," Nari said. "Or us. When you get to the gates, keep the horses. Add them to your herd. Wait—what's that?"

We had officially overstayed our welcome. Nari froze, looking at a figure walking up from the side of the small village. It was a single man wearing a dark cloak, and mittens almost identical to Nari's. He wasn't with us. The bird on her shoulder shriveled up behind its wings, and pressed itself into her neck.

Chirp…

"Uh oh," Lilypad said.

"Get down, or the horses die first," the voice said.

"Dad?" Lilypad said, looking up to her father.

Nari wouldn't look at her. He only nodded to the figure in the middle of the courtyard.

"Oh," James said. "So it's like that."

"Yeah," the figure said, a hand out, clearly pointing up. So we looked up…

"LOOK OUT!" Heather screamed, and we hit the skies, leaving our horses behind in a—

Boom.

A fireball had blown through the trees, leaving a ring of growing fire spreading even as my eyes were still vibrating in my skull. I was airborne somehow, probably instinct, but even that wasn't fast enough to stop the shape descending in a single line in front of me. I brought my claws up like a shield and bounced off something so hard I almost impaled myself. I fell out of the air and hit dirt, my armor coming over my body at the last second. When I sat up, my head was ringing, and the world was on fire, or at least half of Ravenna was.

"The houses, put them out!" Nari shouted, and the crowd moved around us, but not for us. "You said you'd keep the village safe, Nite!"

"I said no such—" I started.

"Wrong Nite," the figure said, and he lowered his hood.

Through the fire, I saw it was a man, and that man was my father. Issaic.

"Am I dead?" James asked/shouted.

"I asked if you were trying to harm Silka," Issaic said, and it was only then I felt his hands on me, felt my feet leave the ground. "I tried to help. I gave you a chance. You lied."

"What is this?" I asked, head still ringing. "A father for ants?"

"The storm," Issaic said. "It's unleashed Derek. What did you do?"

"I don't know what I did!" I shouted. "The Hexoscope still stands, nothing's on me, wrong guy, I'm a CLEAN BOY!"

"In your words," Issaic said, before he dropped me out of the sky… and wheeled on my brother. "It was you twin."

"Wait, I take it back," I said, my hand out, the claws coming halfway, my vision hazy…

"Not guilty," James said in a high voice, Issaic already holding him in one hand by the throat, a brother ready to take the fall for me. "Derek, what did we do to the Hexoscope exactly, while I was being drugged on a mountain?"

"I'll answer that one actually—you ordered the destruction of your OWN CITY!" Issaic roared at us. "I don't know how you did it. An hour ago the Hexoscope launched a program that's overridden a geomagnetic deterrent system that's stood for generations, and right in the middle of storm season."

"So WHAT?" I shouted at him, as James coughed, not breathing probably. "Why's Jerico gotta take the fallout, why can't we let nature BE NATURE?"

"Where do you think the storms will go after the north?" Issaic said, quietly.

"I don't know man, how about WHEREVER THEY'RE GOING NOW?"

Issaic was quiet. Willa hovered above the ground with a tree to her back, Heather and Lynn around him, Sasha, and Volf at the trunk of the tree, fading back in from the background.

"Wherever they're going now," Issaic said, shaking his head. "Right. Without the northern deterrent, as agreed on by the island before there ever WAS AN ISLAND, the storms will now pass through into the other three nations of Ocarina—as is the natural way of big storms and small islands. These winds will strike everywhere from the sands of the southern Vempire to the shores of Silka City—again, like they always do. But thanks to Derek Nite, now they will carry on their currents the same remnants of a terminal solar flare, one Infinite's been studying since, well, before there ever was an island. You thought you were so noble didn't you? Congratulations Derek Nite. You've saved Jerico from anti-electricity... by passing it off to the rest of the island."

"No," I said. "That's not true, you'd be flying. How are you even here?"

"The topline," Willa said, her eyes blinking. "What have you done?"

"Did you expect us to take the silk roads again?" Issaic asked. "You thought gates of wood could ever keep us out? Did you forget about fire?"

"But this isn't your city!" Willa shouted in panic, her eyes darting up, and up again. "How dare you..."

"My city, to be clear, is evacuating as we speak," Issaic said. "The storms will descend on Silka in less than an hour. We are preparing for an immediate city blackout, not exactly something we're used to. I wonder how long that perfect city's going to last before the looting starts. I give it twenty minutes."

"No," I said.

"He's bluffing," James coughed again.

Issaic only squeezed his fist harder around my brother's neck.

"Aw come on," James wheezed, and there were ten claws around Issaic's hand. "Unhand me... before I unhand you."

Issaic must have taken the threat seriously, because he set a brother down.

"I could work with almost anything," he said, shaking his head. "There were a hundred things you could have done we would have forgiven. A hundred ways to disappoint me. In all those ways... this is worse. Poetically so. You have successfully conspired with the jungle to level the power of electricity against the lightning city. Am I supposed to ignore that?"

"That's not what happened," I stammered. "It was just for them, just for Jerico. Not against anyone, I mean, it wasn't supposed to—"

"That's not how STORMS WORK!" Issaic said. "I mean you don't even understand what it is you were doing, that's WORSE, YOU GET THAT RIGHT? Either you ARE the greatest threat to Silka alive today—or there's somebody else behind you, pulling your strings just enough not to break them."

"That's not true either, you suck at truth!" I shouted.

"I do not, I've decided," Issaic said, full irony, nothing funny about it.

"Is Silka really about to… go dark?" James asked.

"It is," Issaic said. "But remember, that also means Jerico's about to light up. You have set the storm on a path never before taken, you think I'd miss it?"

"Miss what?" Lynn said, her fists coming up, expecting the worst.

"The next time the shade line crosses us…" Issaic said, pointing off…

Up to what was clearly a break in the clouds, starting far off in the distance over the canopies of trees, coming towards us like the light in the dark it was.

"The clouds," Heather said, staring at the sky.

"They're clearing," Lynn said.

"For the first time in hundreds of years, the Jerico are about to see the light," Issaic said. "I wanted to watch your reaction, as you accomplished the thing you set out to do. Congratulations boys. You have successfully liberated the Jerico Territory. You've saved them."

"From safety," I said, only starting to realize what we'd done.

And even before the light show all around us, I felt it. The hair on my arms stood up. The wind roared just a bit louder, and I could see everyone sway like a pressure wave had hit us all. Then the shade lifted, and a single light-pole in the middle of the village flickered on.

"That… who set that curvy glass aflame?" Someone said behind us.

"No one," another said. "It's been there for decades. It's never aflame."

I hadn't even noticed it before, but now with the light, I couldn't miss it. But even though I shouldn't have stared straight at it, I did, until I could confirm it wasn't fire. It was something much better, but much worse.

It was a dusty old lightbulb. It was electricity. It was running. That meant—

"Oh no," Heather said.

"Oh yes," Issaic said, as the lightning danced in his hand.

And one by one, in absolute horror, we turned our eyes to the sky, to the twinkles in the trees, almost like stars. All around us, in every direction.

Then all the stars exploded.

4.2

RAVENNA

No they weren't real stars. They were just human-sized flashes of light, all around us, turning fake midnight into a brighter fake midnight. It was worse.

Unlike that very symbolic (and convenient) legacy lamp post in the middle of village square… these weren't lightbulbs. These fifty, shocking, blinding sparks of light went off in the trees above us, over the ground behind every village house, above the fence and down the hill, even at the edges of the crowd around Nari. Places only people could get to, or animals. Sparks flew as the very human figures erupted into fireworks, the dazzling light leaving behind…

An army. Of people, to be clear, not animals.

"The power of the source, this far north," Issaic said, flexing his arms, a current of electricity flowing over his clothes, morphing them into something living, not a single crease left in the full body fabric. "For the first time in our history. I never thought I'd say it, but you do have my deepest thanks."

"No," Willa said, looking around, Issaic not even the worst of it.

There were fifty fully armored Infinite agents around us, and we weren't talking about chainmail and aluminum underwear. This was the army I knew too well, all fully plugged in, all hovering in midair, dressed head to toe in the cloud blue supersuits of Infinite. They must have been here waiting for us. They were too high up in the trees, and all without their power, just waiting on a switch.

"I know it's a bit late, but with all due respect, I think this is a trap," I said.

"We know it," Willa sighed.

The village of Ravenna had lost its charm. It was about to lose much more.

"You wanted electricity, I'll give you electricity," Issaic said.

He punched his fists together, sparks flew, the sound like two chainsaws colliding—and from every angle, the Infinite army descended on us, as half the villagers ran for their lives off into the forest. A blast of something white-hot came at me from the left and I hit the dirt to dodge it. It missed, but a two-story wooden cabin on the far edge of town burst into an inferno. Three people had been sprinting for the front door, now they were watching it melt.

"Dad!" Lily shouted, holding her father's hand. "What did you do? Who are they? Why is that curvy glass on fire?"

"That's not fire," Nari said.

He was staring at the light-pole like his entire world had been turned upside down. Then another laser blast went off over his head and he turned to Issaic as the world got much brighter—and darker, at the same time.

"You promised," he said, as Lily closed her eyes. "You PROMISED!"

But the second time he shouted, it was over his shoulder, while he was running away, Lily doing her best to keep on her feet as he tugged her along.

"What did you think was going to happen?" Willa shouted to the villagers as they screamed and fled. "Who's idea was it to listen to a single word from—"

"From me?" Issaic said, suddenly holding Willa by the throat, having crossed the distance between them in a single blast of blue energy from his feet.

"Really?" Willa choked out. "All that power... you went with blaster boots?"

Issaic glared at her as his palm lit up with the power of a hundred suns—

"And LASER HANDS TOO? Seriously? Any other cliches? You got a mustache and a bad attitude too? Where's the damsel in distress?" Willa said.

"Apologies, you see I just now realized you were a woman," Issaic said.

"That's cold man," Willa said, like his words found a way through her armor.

Then, I hate to say it, but his fist found a way through her face. She took the blow like a champion, tumbling fifty feet back and right into a weak wooden fence that barely caught her. Still, she held her head high, and turned to a few villagers cowering behind the fence.

"You going to let him talk to your new Caput that way?" She coughed out.

"We don't call you that out here," one of the men said. "That being said... you could use some help."

"I'm asking for it, and not for the Oleander," Willa said. "We'll never get out of here without you."

"That's kind of the point, right?" Another of the guys said. "It's you or us. And we're us."

Judas. The guys outside the fence hesitated, and Willa's shoulder's dropped. Then they were grabbed by Issaic, and he flipped her around to face him.

"Fine," Willa said, cracking her knuckles even as Issaic roared and started lifting her off the ground by the neck. "I'll do it myself."

And her hands came down on Issaic's wrists. His elbows buckled and they were suddenly much closer when Willa sent her other elbow into his face. I saw his nose move, his eyes closed in the pain. He dropped Willa and she wasted no time in assembling that bow out of her sword, loading a single arrow, and sending it into the sky so hard it blew through the trees and leaves, leaving a red dust behind almost like clay, until we heard it punch through the canopy. From somewhere in the trees, we heard a single laser shot, then two pieces of broken arrow came back down, making a sound in the trees above us, but they must have stuck themselves up there because no pieces of arrows came down on us.

The red smoke hung high in the sky.

"What's that?" One of the guys over the fence asked, staring up.

"A signal," Willa said, staring at them. "For actual soldiers."

"Damn you," Issaic said. "I thought this was going to be silent."
"Now the territory knows where we are," Willa said, standing strong.
"They'll know where to find your bones," Issaic said.
"Prove it," Willa said, swinging her sword with her eyes never leaving Issaic. "You'll have the entire Territory here in sixty seconds, they'll find what I want them to find."
"Big words from the Jerico, after our last meet went so well," Issaic snarled.
"We've never met, not us," Willa said, holding her sword on a swivel as they circled each other. "You thinking what I'm thinking?"
"You and me?" Issaic said. "Infinite versus a tree? When I have the whole jungle at my fingertips?"
"You've committed so many crimes against this island that right now, I wouldn't care if everyone else just disappeared," Willa said, her sword up. "Yeah Issaic. It's you and me."
"Been waiting for it all day big bird," Issaic said. "I could use the practice. I've forgotten how it feels to kill a Jerico."
He was fully distracted by the fight in Wildfire, but he had brought fifty other fighters, he could afford the distraction. We could not. I was starting to like Willa's idea about disappearing. Wait a minute. I saw Lynn give me the smallest of nods. As long as we didn't give it away… it wasn't an idea, it was the plan. Willa turned her hips to Issaic, holding her sword out. Issaic shook his head.
"A shame," he said.
Issaic even gave a small bow, as his hands lit up at Willa. But before he fired, she angled her silver sword so the light bounced off the blade and hit Issaic right in the eyes. He couldn't help it, he closed his eyes, and his hand wavered blindly for half a second before it went off, missing Willa by centimeters.
That's when we disappeared.
"JERICOOO!" Willa shouted, hitting the dirt in a forwards roll, coming up with her blade at full force, the blade about to take Issaic through the chest before he could open his eyes when…
"No…" I said, fully a beat behind.
Willa had delivered the perfect counter, but it just hadn't worked. Her blade had shattered against his chest into a thousand pieces, big and small, and she cut her hands open on the pieces of breaking sword in the follow through, until she was pushing the hilt into the armor where blade had failed, until it fell out of her hands as they were as useless as—
"Did you think that would work?" Issaic asked, looking up to find—
Nothing. We were invisible.
"It did," Willa said. "And you know it."
She was smiling when he grabbed her by the throat again, when his hands lit up again. I wanted to scream, but that wasn't what being invisible was all about. So instead… I did nothing. And I'll remember that choice forever.
Issaic had Willa, point blank. She stared him down the barrel, both her hands bleeding so bad it might as well have been the end. From Issaic's perspective, it

was going to be. Then someone broke the invisi-spell, and it wasn't me.

"NO!" Volf cried.

In a flash he was there, right at Issaic's side and wrenching his hand away, or trying his best, putting all his weight on the guy and barely moving his hand an inch. But it was enough. It was more than enough. He was there, and I wasn't. He had sacrificed his invisibility for a teammate… and I hadn't.

Boom.

Willa flinched as the laser went off in the dirt right where she had been, before she'd been tackled sideways by someone flashing in and out of focus as they tumbled across the ground, pitched up, and started flying away. It was Sasha. Some team they made (no sarcasm).

"Hell YEAH WILLA!" Sasha shouted.

Willa only hollered in victory as she let Sasha swoop them through the air with eight Infinite soldiers already on their tail. And oddly enough, some of the villagers were hollering with her. Willa noticed it, traveling backwards and all.

"Fight for me!" She shouted at the villagers as she was flown away. "That man betrayed you, he'll set your home on fire! Fight for your families! FIGHT!"

And below her the shouts actually started to grow louder in response.

"You're very inspiring but your hands," Sasha shouted to Willa, dodging laser blaster fire.

"I'll be alright sister," Willa shouted. "Send me!"

Sasha threw Willa into the air like a pumpkin, and Willa extended her wings just in time to veer off through the trees, taking five of the Infinite agents with her into the deep forest. Sasha curved around and eventually plunged into the trees right where Willa had, bringing even more agents after her. But the last was caught, by a man who'd taken to the hip-high fence and leapt six feet off it at the slowest flying agent, bringing him to the ground with muscles that rivaled super strength, the fence breaking all around him as they landed.

"What are you made of?!" The agent cried, as four seven foot tall men leaned over him in the grass. "Don't touch me!"

"Don't kill him," the villager said. "Just make walking away real painful."

"AAAH!"

It was on. At least fifteen men from Ravenna jumped to our side, which against the remaining forty Infinite, well it was almost even.

"Get off me Reaper," Issaic said, staring at the Volf on his arm.

"Obliged," Volf said.

He dodged an elbow from Issaic and threw himself to the ground in a somersault, as Issaic held his hand up to see a glowing purple grenade tied to his wrist with a shoelace. Tick, tick…

"You—" Issaic said, looking up before—

BOOM.

And the figure of our father went flying into the trees to disappear into the foliage at mach ten. Volf winked at all the soldiers staring at him, then disappeared as the lasers came in.

"GET THEM!" One called.

"WE CAN'T SEE THEM!" Another shouted in protest.

It was true. The Infinite were aimed anywhere except on us, and shooting at it. The world was full of the kinds of sounds I'd only heard in bad movies. The constant barrage, the wooden cabins exploding, the nearby trees catching fire, the unrestrained terror in the eyes of those agents, setting fire to everything just because they couldn't find us. Even those fighting for us were screaming and looking all over for us in horror, but they couldn't see us either. That was the problem with invisibility. What were they fighting for? Nothing?

"Stop," Derek said. "We have to stop this. It's not right."

"The horses," I heard from my right. It was Lynn.

I saw more than one of Lily's horses scream and collapse under the scorched dirt being unearthed by all the terribly aimed lasers, penned in by fire in all directions. I wanted to help, I did, but suddenly I'd taken a glancing hit and my foot was on fire. Rude. It took all my focus to build up that obsidian armor around it, smothering the flames.

"Not good," I said to myself, backing off, the wings coming up, my body hovering into the air before I'd realized I was doing it.

"We need a plan," Derek said, swooping beside me.

He was just as out of sight. Literally. I didn't get a chance to answer, I hit my wings before thirty different laser beams hit the ground where I'd been a moment earlier. I hoped Derek got out too. But did he? I couldn't see, not him, not anything. Only enemies. This sucked. And just as I was about to panic—

"This sucks," her voice came from not even two feet to my right.

"You THINK?"

It was Willa. Now that I was looking for it, a dense purple outline could be seen around both my brother and a few faint shapes behind him. I took a chance and landed on the backside of a sloped roofing, on a two story building on the edge of town—and to my unspoken surprise, the purple shapes followed me. We landed low on the roof. One of the shapes came over where I'd heard Willa's voice and pinned her to the ground. It must have been Heather.

"Hold your hands still if you want to keep them, Wildfire."

Yep.

"We gotta go now," Sasha said.

"I agree," Lynn said. "Do we… should we use the distraction to flee, to save ourselves, to just leave these warriors and their village behind?"

It was quiet for a moment. We were all thinking it. But we were thinking something else too.

"Ohana," Derek said.

"Nobody gets left behind," I said.

"Or forgotten," a purple shape said to my left. Lynn.

"Disney prince Derek," Heather said, with what sounded like a smile. "Same as badass Derek, weird you can pull off both. Welcome to the—"

"Don't say party," Lynn and I said at the same time.

And it wasn't hard to break off in five directions, as invisible as the wind. Sasha and Volf had a constant barrage of attention at them, it wasn't hard to hover in quietly, then send the blunt end of a full paw of claws into the unsuspecting face of an Infinite agent. The tricky part was flying away faster than the lasers that came in after.

"THERE!"

Bam.

"MY FACE!"

"Sorry, move next time—THERE!"

Missed me.

I soared low through the fight, trusting the wings and rocks to keep me from slamming into the homes and houses. I felt the ground move as I flew over, as my necklace lit up in purples and pinks. Right. My default was flight, but there was another option. Something up my sleeves other than claws, almost like a real Reaper. I had moved the dirt only once before, to unbury myself from the detritus of a hundred-foot cave in, for living reasons. I didn't think I was ready to wield the earth itself as a weapon against my fellows and foes. I'd leave the more fantastical of the fight to my friends from the underland. Another thing that separated them from me, in combat. There was no hold back in the Vema.

I passed an agent who never saw the gigantic boulder of rock coming for him. Even I was almost taken out by the boulder, Indiana Jones style and all. I grabbed my hat and hit the trees just in time, as the thing slammed into three agents like half a house in a hurricane. But though they were thrown far into the jungle, the boulder dusted itself before hitting a single leaf of Jerico. Instead of slamming like a meteor or peppering the jungle like gunshot, rock turned to pebble, then, dirt, then minerals and sand. The leaves of Jerico only got a nice brushing, probably taking off a good layer of spider mites in the process.

Hmm. Maybe the Vema came with some hold back after all.

"Someone's been watching too many movies," I said, as I traced the boulder's trajectory back to where it had been thrown from, passing a purple outline in the air only by pure chance.

"You got time to talk, you got time to die," came a purple flash between us.

"Is there an in between?" I blinked.

"Please," Volf said. "Show us how it's done, Sasha."

The wind whipped around us and she was gone. But then there was a rustle up in the trees above us, and three Infinite agents fell out of the tree, all barely catching themselves before slamming to the ground, hard. Then the wind whipped around us again.

"Was that how it's done?" I asked.

"You noticed," was all Sasha's voice said.

"You saved Willa," I said. "You kept Issaic from taking her head off. While I did—"

"Exactly as you were told, because that's what soldiers do," Sasha said.

"You kept her alive plenty, let us help," Volf said.

"But I'm not a soldier," I said.

"And you'll never need to be," Sasha said. "It doesn't take a soldier to fight when there's a greater cause to fight for."

"What does it take?" I said.

Sasha said. "A hero. Not everyone can be a soldier. But anyone can be a hero. It's not exactly an ideal future in this context. But someone who lives and dies for the greater good, what would you call that?"

"I didn't think I was doing this for the greater good," I said. "I couldn't even save Willa."

"Don't take this the wrong way," Sasha said. "That girl doesn't need saving. Not by you."

"How could I take that the right way?" I complained.

We only had the break because of the village. Even though they didn't live inside the gates, the fifteen helping us were at least seven feet tall, and like wrestling, once an agent had lost the speed and height of flight, the Jerico warrior could hold him (or her) against the ground long enough for a pack of four men to come drag them away to the big tree they were tying the rest of the agents up against. The trunk was about six feet thick, plenty of room for the ten agents already tied up on it, and more. I found myself drifting back to that first roofing, just for a moment, just a single break from the flames, the ashen faces, the screams. It must have been a communal feeling, because as my feet touched down again on that thankfully unscarred, unburnt, still standing rooftop, I saw the auras around me like they'd never even left. It was tricky because invisibility. But it was me, my brother, Lynn, Heather, Volf, Sasha, and Willa. We'd come for horses, we'd gotten nonsense. Also a small army in the people of Ravenna, twenty men and women who were more than capable of dodging laser blasts and crippling the agents in the air. Even a fully armored Reaper drone wasn't capable of such a thing. Taking on a flying super soldier alone, that took an experienced fighter, like those of the dragon—a place that still offered no explanation, but was the common denominator of Sasha, Volf, and Heather at least. They had no problem wielding the earth as a weapon, or more accurately, a home. Aww—

"We've got this," I said, for one moment feeling all the feels.

"Who you mean by we?" Heather snapped.

"All we," I said. "They we, us we."

"We just might," my brother said.

But… alas.

"Do I have to do everything myself?"

The voice came from the edge of the town. It was Issaic. He took one look at the tree with all his men tied around it and shook his head. The world stopped in that moment. I knew he was pissed, we all did. The only question was… what was he going to do?

Issaic took a step away from the tree and looked for a place above the tops of his tied up agent's heads. They shook as they looked at him, or maybe I was the one shaking, either way the next thing we knew he was spinning, his feet blurring faster than the blue light they kicked up. Then my head snapped back with the sound wave, like standing next to a thunderclap, and the tree above the agent's heads split in half where Issaic had, I don't know, wheel-kicked it? What would you call kicking a tree in half, besides terrifying? But that wasn't all. The tree wasn't a tree anymore, only an eight-foot stump remained as the other fifty feet slid dangerously sideways, right into Issaic's hand. And somehow the tree stopped there. Issaic bit down and we saw the sleeve against his forearm tighten.

But the rest of his body didn't move. He was… the tree was…

"Bad," Lynn said, her hand on the back of my neck, then head, then shoulder. "That's really, very—"

Yeah. Issaic was holding a tree. It wasn't one of the hundred foot titans, this was a mere fifty feet of a sapling, but talk about weaponizing nature. Issaic was wielding it like a one handed sword, when we all knew it weighed at least five hundred pounds. Behind him, his agents looked up to much less stable imprisonment system than before, with freedom only one good synchronized jump away. But of course they only shouted and climbed over each other and shimmied up their ropes until they were freed from the top of the now stump. But that wasn't what I was looking at.

I was looking at the guy holding a tree over a village.

"Mutiny," Issaic said, holding the tree over a cluster of brown and blue houses to our right. "Is this level?"

"NO!" One of the attacking villagers screamed, falling to his knees in front of the blue house.

"So a bit to the right?" Issaic asked, moving the tree over the brown house, over an outdoor stable, only to stop atop the red brick barn at the top of town.

"NO!" Another villager said. "Jessie, Caleb, GET OUT HERE!"

A rustic red barn door opened to a host of people hiding towards the back, the sounds of animals all around, all in distress. They could tell. It was first a young boy and girl who took a strong step outside… only to see the tree trunk over their barn, ready to take out the village in a single swing.

"I…" the boy started, losing his voice to the lip quiver.

I knew what was coming next.

"MOM!" He screamed, in perfect time with the young girl beside him.

"Don't do it Issaic, I'm begging you," the villager said, hands up. "We… all are."

"Everybody hear that?" Issaic said, waving his tree trunk around like a sword, the village shrieking as it got too close to the tops of a few houses. "Right? You begging over here too?"

"WE ARE!" One of the villagers closest to him shouted out.

"So this is the level," Issaic said.

He swung the trunk violently up and an entire village screamed—but Issaic only slammed it into the ground by his side. The earth shook and some of the wood burst. Issaic had set the thing at least six feet deep into the ground. But at least it was vertical.

"Two things," Issaic said, with a village at his attention, with his agents regrouping behind him. "First, I hope I'm talking to nobody. I hope you escaped given the moment, instead of hanging around, because that would only mean you actually consider these outsiders part of your team. I do hope you can't hear this. Secondly… just on the off-chance you can. Do you want to join Ravenna in the consequence of what just happened, or should I just take it all out on your brothers and sisters in arms?"

The world was quiet. But it wouldn't be, not for long. Nobody gets left behind.

"I—" I started.

Issaic's head caught the words like a ghost in the wind, and he looked around for the source. He would have gotten it too, if it weren't for whoever had their hand in my mouth. I almost gagged, I didn't know who, or why, I tried to pull their hand off my mouth and she grabbed me from behind, pinning one of my arms between our bodies and keeping the other one under control with her free hand. *Get off of me,* I tried to say. But I couldn't. I tried to mumble and she pivoted—suddenly she was blocking my mouth and my nose with one hand, suddenly my mumbling was broken. Try it.

"I wish I could say I didn't hear that," Issaic said, sighing.

Someone smacked me in the back of the head. I couldn't help it. I was looking down at twenty men and women on their knees in front of Issaic, their only crime being helping us, helping Willa. This was on the orders of the new caput, and Willa usually knew what she was doing. No. Not usually. She ALWAYS knew what she was doing.

I stopped struggling, and found the invisible wrist of the woman who had me by the mouth. My fingers walked over the leather armband, and I gently closed my hand around it. I felt Willa respond behind me. She was shocked. But also…

"Yes James," she whispered into my ear, finally taking her iron fist out of my mouth. "Trust me."

I did.

"Alright, they're clearly still here," Issaic said, his hands up, until he turned and made a motion to the soldiers behind him. "I believe this is why I brought you along, agent scout. Where are you anyways?"

"Right here boss."

And the light shimmered by Issaic's right side. It was Lukas, dressed from head to toe in Reaper rock armor that looked two upgrades behind ours. But his necklace was every bit as purple as mine.

"You chose the right side, I'd say," Issaic said, looking at the tree stump he'd hammer smashed into the ground on his left like it was nothing.

"I was actually standing right there," Lukas admitted. "But I… moved."

"Thrilling," Issaic said.

"No," Heather said. "He'll know."

"Not if you shut up," Lynn said, as Issaic looked our way again, frowning.

Lukas held his hands out like they were a magnet, or a meter. He closed his eyes and clenched his fist. Suddenly that faint purple outline around us was seeming much more of a shining dead giveaway.

"Oh they're here alright," Lukas said, his eyes closed, his nose to the wind.

I wanted to roll my eyes, but even with his closed, his eyeless gaze kept getting closer to us. We held our breath, staring at him, all thinking the same thing. Lukas had to go.

"Trust…" Willa said, almost indecipherable.

"How's he doing that?" Heather asked, too loudly.

Then it happened. Lukas steadied his closed eyes, but his face was looking right in our direction. Forget holding our breath, I'd stopped breathing. It didn't help.

"I see them," Lukas said.
"And so much for flight pattern astral," Lynn said.
The world was fire in front of us, and lasers powering up.
"Where?" Issaic demanded.
"Hold…" I heard Willa whisper/shout.
"Right…" Lukas started, his hand coming down…
"You better have a plan, Wildfire," Heather said, biting her lip.
We did nothing but cling to the invisibility (and rooftop) like it would withstand the absolute arsenal being aimed pretty accurately at us. If there ever was a hope machine, I was going to run it into the ground. And just then… right before Lukas's hand came down on us… we all heard it. It wasn't a bell. It wasn't a horn.
It was a whistle.
"Am I dreaming?" I asked.
"I'll be damned," Issaic said.
I was not dreaming. Every agent in the air stopped in their tracks, faced with something behind us. Lukas's hand was frozen, every laser in the jungle had stopped making weird sounds, no one could move. They could only watch.
Sand Freedom had ridden into town on his white horse, with the younger faun behind him, Astor and Odd still lashed tightly to him.
"Found you," Sand said to Issaic (or quite possibly us).
"Stand your ground," Issaic said to his army (or maybe to himself).
He wasn't moving a muscle. The showdown was real, the high noon staring contest, it was as clear as the midnight moon, these two had history. Issaic looked like he wanted to take a step to Sand, like he wanted it so bad… but didn't.
Then something unexpected happened. It started to rain.
"Is this a bad thing?" Came the calls around us.
"It might be," Issaic said. "Let's kill them quick, before we're stuck here in the next storm. Wait."
Issaic blinked, finally having looked over Sand's shoulder.
"Is that…"
"Astor and Odd," Sand said, as the two of them had fresh gags in their mouths and couldn't speak.
"Give me back my toys," Issaic said, sounding mad. "Exile."
"Make me," Sand said. "Xenocide."
"You said you would stop calling me that," Issaic said, sound even madder.
"Yeah well… so did you," Sand said.
"It's a guy and a horse, I've got this," one agent said, as the rest stared.
"I wouldn't," Issaic shook his head.
Too late, a single Infinite agent soared headfirst for Sand, his hands powering up with blue energy as he descended—only for the horse to rear back and launch Sand up like a pole vaulter. He dodged the Infinite laser and kicked the guy in the face completely upside down, stopping the flier and sending them both back the opposite direction. The agent was unconscious as Sand followed through, arced in the air, and landed on his feet holding the unconscious agent

by the shirt, and only once they were back on solid ground, did he let the guy hit the dirt.

"Next?" Sand asked.

"It's Freedom," came the calls around us, the agents stepping back in fear, staring at Sand. "Everybody re—"

"I said stand your ground!" Issaic shouted, in complete contradiction.

"Hell we can boss, it's him! We can't stop Freedom, if you can, GO AHEAD!"

Issaic growled, staring across the grounds at Sand. And as their eyes met, just as Issaic was opening his mouth to say something, something else happened. The horn sounded so loud we felt like screaming. It was that loud because it was right behind us.

"Ah!" Lukas said, jumping hardest of all, his face falling as he did. "Damnit! Wait—"

From the crest of the hill around Ravenna they started coming. From the trees high above us, somehow already on all sides, like stars, they started descending. In a flash, the village was full of bare saddled horses, warriors with swords and bows, shields and axes, and best of all—

"Defend Ravenna to the end!" Bastile shouted, the first to settle into a fighting stance aimed at Issaic. "No attack without cause, now hold Jerico, HOLD!"

"HOLD!" The warriors of Jerico shouted, from every angle, from horseback and treetop alike, the jungle shook.

"Bones," Issaic said, staring at the captain. "I know you."

"I wish you didn't, Nite," Bastile said, his entire body clenched.

"We've been here before," Issaic said, looking between Sand and Bones, like they were some kind of old friends. "We were FRIENDS! Why do I keep finding the ones closest to me on the opposite side of the sword?"

"I never wanted to hurt you," Sand said.

"What are you all planning without me," Issaic said, sounding tortured over it, confused, even overwhelmed. "And WHAT ARE YOU DOING WITH MY BOYS?"

"Your what now?" Sand asked, a scary kind of calm.

"I'm not talking to you right now," Issaic said. "Bastile Bones, Jerico elite. I know you, you attacked my city."

"Yeah, well you attacked my island," Bastile said, holding up his right wrist, lifting the armband. "You won Issaic. Remember that? Remember when you branded me? Here it is. I have to look at it every day and remember when we lost, when you rounded us up and branded us. Like—"

"Say it," Issaic said. "Branded you like what?"

"Never," Bastile said. "This isn't your mark any more. This is my home, not yours. And I don't need to fight you, not if you leave."

"That sounds like diplomacy," Issaic said. "I heard there's a new Caput in town. Shouldn't we all make this very diplomatic decision together?"

The arms around me lessened. She was about to take off.

"I reckon no," Bastile said.

And the arms around me settled. Willa would have leapt to something, if he hadn't said that, I felt it. But as it was... I still had her by the armband. The same armband as Bastile wore, hiding the same scar. A winged, lowercase letter a.

I stood up on the rooftop we were cowering behind and made sure I still had a strong hold on her. The village stared at Issaic and Bastile, each with a small army behind them, only an entire village full of houses hiding women and children all around them.

"With all due respect Issaic, which is none," Bastile said, stepping up and sheathing his sword, standing with two feet pointed at Issaic but nothing else. "Get out of our jungle."

"That's your diplomacy?" Issaic asked, feigning shock.

"That's my warning," Bastile said, turning on Issaic. "You have a problem with us, you bring that problem to the gates of Jerico. This is a FARM TOWN Issaic. These people—sorry for saying these people—are civilians. I don't care if you manipulated them, I don't care if you set them up to trap Derek and James, it's not their fault, it's ours. Jerico has so much to offer it could never truly be kept behind closed doors. We're here for them even if they want nothing to do with us. So get out of Ravenna before we really make you regret EVER thinking the tribe would let this happen to the tribe."

"For Jerico," Nari said, his hand in the air, staring at Bastile, his back to Issaic.

"For JERICO," Bastile said, meeting Nari on his feet, as the rest of the villagers stood up, as more warriors dropped down from the trees to put their bodies in the middle of the fray.

Even I was impressed. Issaic was not.

"Touching," Issaic said, sarcastically. "But here's the thing. I'm not Jerico. So again, I kinda feel left out."

He took one step towards Bastile when it happened. Another horn let out, just as loud as the first, just as earsplitting. Even Issaic stopped, the knife in his hand frozen in the air a few feet from Bastile. But this time... it was no horn.

Issaic froze. His feet didn't move, only his head looked left to see...

"Kitty," Lynn said.

"How can I say this?" I said, thinking hard.

It was an elephant. It looked a bit like the dwarf elephant we'd seen a few days ago on our way in from South Arbor, but I couldn't be sure. It was louder, for sure. All I knew was it towered over Issaic, staring right at him, somehow through all the dense trees only a few feet away from him. That gigantic trunk was closer to smacking Issaic than his knife was from stabbing Bastile.

"I..." Issaic said.

"Say it," Bastile said.

"I should get out of the jungle," Issaic, staring at the elephant like something had been triggered in his eyes.

The elephant seemed to agree. They had a pact. Mutually assured destruction, by stomping.

"Hey man, I can get tied up all day, but no one said anything about dinosaurs!" one of the Infinite agents shouted. A few around him smacked him, which made me feel better. "What? You want to fight that thing?"

"They're only extinct in the east," another agent said. "Hey Reaper, how about the underworld? You got monsters like elephants down there with the rest of your monsters?"

"You must mean the underland," Lukas corrected. "We don't have monsters, we barely have bugs. And no, we don't have elephants either. No mammals really, not even rats."

"No rats?" One of the agents said. "How'd a bunch of cavemen figure that?"

"We ate the rats," Lukas said simply. "Can we go home now Issaic?"

I got the feeling he was being bullied, being the only Reaper in the army.

"We can go," Issaic said, eyes only on the elephant. "Slowly."

And it wasn't without ceremony. One by one the Infinite realized they'd been ordered to retreat, and they obeyed Issaic without hesitation. The village saw, and doors started opening around us. The big barn by the southern house, the cluster of six buildings all sharing a wall, from the roof of a few two-stories at the edge of what used to be a fence. They weren't exactly cheering, but they were staring up in awe of the perfectly timed elephant, as the Infinite ascended freely, no ropes, no trees. Just flight.

Hold up. The Jerico had just stood their ground against Infinite at full force. And—

"Did that actually go our way?" Volf said under his breath from behind me.

"Yeah," Lynn said. "It did. My stars and also my pearls, it did."

"I'm sorry," Nari said, approaching Willa, and taking a knee. "I'm sorry."

"You fought for your village today," Willa said. "That's all I saw."

"But I… he made me keep talking, buying the time until—" Nari said.

"May you live long enough to right your wrongs," was all Willa said. "I hope the same for myself. You're not alone. You're never alone."

Nari's head was on the ground. He couldn't bow any lower, or he was trying to hide the crying. Lilypad came up behind him and put her hand on his neck.

"You're in so much trouble dad," she said honestly. "But I still love you."

Nari laughed so hard the tears started to stop, then they came right back as Lily grabbed him in a hug. He hugged back.

"That curvy glass though," one of the neighbors said, as a small group gathered around it.

"That is electricity," Willa said. "It has returned. Leader Bombelle has led us to this light, no one forget it."

"I mean, she had some help," Bastile said, proudly looking at caput Willa.

"It comes with a cost," Willa said. "You just saw all the power we've always heard about. We beat them one way, together. If there was ever a time to rejoin the interior, it's now."

"I won't lie, I've been thinking the same since the moment he landed here," Nari said. "I figure even if the gates burn down, we can give them the same bootstrap crossover hell we all just pulled out of our collective—"

"Shengcun," Bastile said, holding his hand out.

"I was going to say asses," Nari said, shaking it.

The villagers cheered. It was so beautiful, it made me stop and stare. Then my eyes drifted over the neighbors and I realized I wasn't the only one staring. I thought Infinite had faded out of sight. Most of them had. But of course, just at the edge of town, a single figure had remained, alone in the fog, staring at Nari and Lilypad. It was Issaic, and I could just feel the hatred coming off of him, the same as I could feel the love coming from the other side. I froze. I was invisible, no one had seen me yet, but I felt Sand react on the ground like we shared goosebumps, and his head whipped to Issaic like he knew exactly where to find him. The others saw, and one by one they went quiet.

The village froze, from citizen to soldier to outsider to us.

"You forget how to leave, Nite?" Sand called out.

"I..." Issaic said, looking up, then back at us. "I'm thinking."

"About what?" Sand shouted.

"About how long it would take the Scarlet to get here, traveling around the perimeter of the storm," Issaic said. "Tell me again, what are fifty jungle warriors worth against a super jet? Oh that's right. A hell of a lot of digging."

Sand went quiet. The village noticed. The pieces of blue sky we could see through the green canopy were suddenly much more ominous. He was right. If the Infinite source was here, then... what else was?

"Before I have her open fire, I'll say this," Issaic said, looking around for elephants. "If Derek and James do not leave with me, I'll burn this village to the ground, and then the gates. If they really think they're still doing this for the Jerico, then prove it."

"He's bluffing," Heather said, way out of Issaic's earshot.

"Where are you?" Bastile shouted up to us.

"Oh right, we never even stopped being invisible," Sasha said. "Should we?"

"Depends," Volf said. "No way we're letting Derek and James leave her with Issaic, right?"

"Hell no," Lynn said. "Better just make ourselves known and decide together with Bastile?"

"Think so," Willa said. "Back to visible in three, two, one—"

They all materialized on the tops of that rooftop. It was funny, even this far away, with every one of them connected to the Reaper power the same as me, I could hear them.

Even from way over here.

"There you are," Bastile said, counting and frowning. "Where are—"

"Look at that," Derek said, an arm's length away from me. "No choice?"

"Nope," I said, and together we looked up to see Issaic, a yard away from us.

"DEREK!" Lynn shouted, a football field away from me and Derek.

"Good choice," Issaic said to us, as Lynn's words echoed in the far distance. "You truly have chosen to save them, instead of yourselves. Too bad they'll never see it that way."

"JAMES!" Heather shouted from afar.

"Whatever it takes, to keep them safe," I said. "You wouldn't stop for anything else."

"BOYS!" Sand joined in.

“Who says I’ll stop for this?” Issaic said.

“I do,” I said. “We go with you, you don’t touch this place, ever again. That’s the level.”

The others were closing in. Issaic’s army was airborne. He looked at us... and nodded.

“Deal,” he said, looking at the two girls leading the charge towards us, Lynn and Heather. “I know what I’m giving up. Those two girls especially. One day they will fight for Infinite, or they will stop fighting. Tell them that, from me.”

“Don’t tell us what to do,” I said.

They were on us. Lynn looked at us like we were about to die. Because—

Heather took a lunge at Issaic with all claws out, but Lukas dropped down from the sky with a hand up. Suddenly the rock around Heather stopped moving. Issaic reached out for her claws, almost frozen in time, and pushed the razor sharp edge of one claw with his gloved finger. The claw broke down against the glove, folding back on itself like a string, never once breaking Issaic’s fingertip. Again, the message was clear.

Lukas had to go.

“You aren’t doing this alone,” Heather said, struggling to make a move against Lukas’s hold. “What have you done?”

“Whatever necessary,” Lukas said, staring her down, until Issaic took a step back and they both released their energy, Heather falling to her knees, Lukas barely keeping himself in the sky. “You tried to kill him—”

“I said retreat, Lukas,” Issaic said. “It’s the nature of the Reaper. Born killers, every one.”

“That’s it?” Lynn said, one hand on Heather’s back as they stared up at us. “We’re letting this happen?”

“He’s the killer,” Heather said, the rest of her body as still as stone.

“There’s no way we get to go back now, not without them setting the forest on fire,” I said sadly. “We’re all he wants.”

“Correct,” Issaic said. “As for you Sand, old friend, we’ll come back to this.”

“I thought we might,” Sand said. “Next time, leave the jungle out of it.”

“The jungle started it,” Issaic said, not backing down an inch.

Then he grabbed us by the shirts and we were rising up in the air, away from the horses, away from the warriors of Ravenna and the forces of Jerico, far from Freedom.

4.3

WINGS DOWN

There was no ancient, traditional path out of Ravenna. There was sky and ground. Issaic flew us up, past the tallest parts of the village, up to the break in the canopy, past it, and suddenly, we were looking at the jungle the same way we'd found it. From far, *far* above.

"You know they'll follow," I said.

"Not if I give them something else to do," Issaic threatened.

I didn't know what he meant, not until we got closer to the red jet hovering at twenty thousand feet. That's when we saw the crew, a small team of flying figures in the turbulent sky, quietly loading missile after missile into the under-chamber of a big giant canon on the side of the Scarlet. I stared at them until one of them stared back. It was Benjann, there was no mistaking it. I saw his throat clench up, I saw the figure next to him turn around and see us. Jemeni scowled and pushed Benjann around, motioning to the missile they held, instead of the bomb that was us.

No.

"You can't be—" was all I got out, before we were swarmed.

Four agents on me, four on Derek. They'd come from the ship itself when we'd been distracted by the pretty lights underneath. They had hands on us from all directions before we knew what was happening.

"So you CAN stop talking," Issaic said. "Let's start from the part where they get in the ship. As for the rocketeers, we'll come back to it—but in like a minute, make sure they're ready agent Jemeni."

"Sir!" He shouted, glaring at us as we passed.

We got in the ship, or more accurately, Issaic and his army hovered us up to the part where a door slid open from the inside, and eight people threw us in hard. It was metal, the ground we bounced off, barely saving our heads from concussion city. A bit of my rock armor chipped away and was lost out the open window, and this high up, there was no getting it back. I didn't think much of it… until I saw who we were sharing a plane with.

"Holy—" came a voice from the small command station in the back of the jet.

"I'm going to say this once," Issaic said. "I don't want to hear it."

We were back on an airplane far quicker than I would have liked. But this wasn't just any airplane. Not even counting the rocket launchers attached to the undercraft, this was a bunch of bad, and about to get worse in all the ways. Hannah gulped. Troy blinked. Odd and Lukas growled. Astor looked away... and Alcyon only closed the pilot's cockpit door on us, his face stone. Jemeni and Benjann were literally loading the canon.

The only enemy missing was... no, they were all here.

"First things," Issaic said, shaking his head at the stunned crew. "Hannah, the honors."

Issaic motioned in the air and we heard a small grunt, and a loud mechanical snap. Something lit up from the back of the plane, there was a whirling in the air, and my necklace made a single, fleeting bounce off my chest... before going out again. Glow and all.

Not again.

"As it comes, it goes," Issaic said.

He watched our faces fall, as well as our obsidian rock armor, leaving behind the tan shorts and shirt for me. Derek didn't even have a shirt on. We were both staring, standing in a pile of rock and dirt. Thank the stars for underclothes. A press of the deus ex Reaper button had once again been levied against us. In other words, wings down. In other words, damnit.

"Worse," Derek said. "Really? How did this get worse?"

"I was lying about the two days," Issaic said.

"Were you not lying about anything?" I asked, sadly.

"Of course I wasn't," Issaic said, thinking.

Damnit.

We hadn't moved yet. We were hovering at stasis in the queen jet of the Infinite, the Scarlet, thousands of feet above the canopy, once we'd broken through. But speaking of breaking things, like words. Words from a man we knew had been word-manipulating things since the start of the start. And if Issaic was lying about the two days, he was lying about not setting the jungle on fire.

"We saw the cannons," I said.

"And?" Issaic asked, unconcerned.

"Last time an Infinite megalomaniac threw us in the Scarlet and took us to the star charts, this jet didn't have canons," I said, staring at Odd with every nerve in my body.

"So stop me," Issaic said. "By all means, which remember right now, are none. You know what kills me, you didn't think twice at the Hexoscope. Thanks to you, now we know a dense enough magnetic field can kill a Reaper. The power of the underland, gone in a single click—or rather, three! You had THREE chances to think maybe something else was up, and you didn't once look outside the scope of your own selves. That, boys, kills me."

"How about that backup gameboy, brother?" I asked.

And for a moment, Issaic looked up, almost proud, almost ready for the challenge—

Derek shook his head, hands out, and empty. He was shirtless in shorts, there was nowhere he could be hiding anything.

"We're out of aces brother. And don't call this a game, boy. It isn't even close."

"I wish I could disagree," Issaic said, sounding... dare I say it... disappointed.

I pushed my claws back and took the gloves off, throwing them in my pockets in a huff.

"Isn't this a good thing boss?" Came the voice of a girl who wouldn't survive her next encounter with a certain Lyre.

"It's excellent work Hannah," Issaic said. "It's just... you ever have a thing work too well?"

"Can't say I have, sir," Hannah answered honestly. "Why?"

"Forget it," Issaic said. "How's the portable version going?"

"It's... not going."

Hannah looked up at us in goggles from the back of the plane, standing next to a huge spinning machine, glowing and pulsing neon colors.

"Woah," Derek said. "That's what's disrupting my magnetic field? Look at the size of it. You think you can ever make that much power portable?"

"The Infinite figured it out, why not me?" Hannah asked, almost like she was serious. "Wanna help?"

"Absolutely not," I said. "I'm all for shields, but when no one's even attacking, that's no shield, it's a kill switch. That's anti-power."

"And what are you?" Hannah asked.

"Powerless," I said.

"So how are we different?" She asked.

"I'm not actively trying to take things away from people," I said, standing my ground.

"If Lynn were here she'd kick your ass," my brother blurted out.

Hannah opened her mouth like she was going to respond, then clenched it shut, shrugged, strapped another pair of goggles over her goggles, and turned around with a wrench.

"Smooth," I said, smacking my brother on the shoulder.

"Don't smack me," Derek said. "We're a team, he's the one who turned a plane into a prison cell. Where's the trust, old man?"

"It's not there yet, to be honest, small boy," Issaic said. "Something about the impending, unending dusk for half a million people, every piece of electricity in Silka City on the brink of going dark."

"Except the part that lets you fly around all Infinite-like," I said.

"And the part that powers the Reaper killer," Issaic said, pointing to the shiny machine at the back of the ship.

Damnit. Actually... noted.

"This is not my first blackout, in my life as a superconductor," Issaic said, reading my face, as the flash of hope faded as fast as anything. "I know my priorities. Don't worry about Infinite, worry about yourselves. Even head to toe in that ridiculous dirt armor, two rocks aren't nothing, and I damn sure haven't seen your Infinite supersuits, not after we cut you off at the source. Now we could do handcuffs, or we could do cool. You feeling cool, Derek?"

"What choice do I have?" He said, taking a deep breath.

"I just explained your choices," Issaic said.

"Then I choose cool," Derek said. "James?"

"Cool as anything," I said. "Just wondering why I'm here, and who's gonna take the first swing at me, the usual thoughts, when surrounded by Infinite thousands of feet in the air. Why?"

"No one's going to swing at you, that's an order," Issaic said.

"Except maybe me," Odd said, speaking up for the first time.

"Except nothing, don't speak again," Issaic warned him, and Odd powered down. "We have one objective, and that's the fifty mile perimeter of Silka City. I don't care how we do it, but we're stopping this storm before it passes by Silka."

"What's wrong with just letting it pass by?" Hannah asked.

"The warm tropical waters on literally every side of Silka," Issaic said. "If this thunderstorm makes it to the ocean… all we can do is pray the winds are blowing the other way."

"And if not?" I asked, afraid of the answer.

"Then the thunderstorm returns a cyclone, or worse, a hurricane," Issaic said. "Derek and James, you made this mess, everyone on board this ship expects you to fix it, or you die. Everyone else, same thing. Ready?"

"SIR!" Everyone else shouted.

"They didn't say it," Odd said, pointing at us.

"Odd I swear to—" I said, shaking my head. "You're kidding me. I thought you were just going to kill us right here and now."

"Nope, there and later," Issaic said. "I don't want you dead. I want my city safe and not wet. You might not believe me. You will."

"Damn," I said. "Okay, well full speed ahead, what are we looking at stopping—"

"Oh no," Derek said, his eyes already glued to the window. "See this brother."

"What, all I see is grey," I said, coming closer. "Oh. That's the storm. All of it."

"How is this not a hurricane?" Derek said.

"Only scientifically," Issaic said, sadly.

The ship rocketed in a long arc over the island. We were probably on course to arc around the storm and re-join it at the head, but there was no getting around this. The entire left of our tiny ship was like staring into the heart of the universe. Dark, swirling, angry clouds, the light breaking through like stars. It was a massive thunder system making its way over the northern jungle canopy line, leaving a bright and sunny day behind where it came from, which just so happened to be more and more of the Jerico Territory as the system made for Silka.

"The Vema?" I asked.

"Underground," Issaic said. "First time I've been jealous. We crushed every underland entrance in Silka, including the forgotten tunnel you breached us through, from the Engineerium. I shouldn't have told you that."

"We're not trying to breach you," I said. "But it would give the people somewhere to go."

"He's right," my brother said, blinking. "Forget the underland, you can shelter the city in headquarters."

"Headquarter?" Issaic asked. "You mean Infinite?"

"We already use that word too much, you know what I mean, through the waterfall and down the—"

"I know what you mean," Issaic said, rubbing his chin. "You're saying I should assemble my entire military into rescue hero mode?"

"I… yeah, a bit," I said.

Issaic nodded. "Not a bad idea. Send two agents to block the waterfall, come to think of it stop the river too. Make it a priority for the wharf, an option for the historic downtown… and prepare the interior city for a hurricane level surge."

"It's not even a hurricane yet," Hannah said, blinking. "It's just a thunderstorm. We'll probably be putting fires out all night but—"

"You know for a certainty they can fix this in one try?" Issaic asked. "You don't want to maybe plan for two?"

"Of course," she said, nodding. "I'm sorry."

"Don't apologize, just keep making sure that machine does the thing I pay you to make it do. The rest of you prepare to keep the people as high up as the underland allows, I know it's a complete paradox but for the love of our city just DO IT!"

"Sir!" Troy said, and he jumped back to his computer screen on the big desk behind us. "Come in Headquarters, this is Orange, I have instructions from Issaic. All agents are to open up the historic downtown entrance to the Infinite underland for emergency evacuation of the city. Prepare for refugees in the… tens of thousands."

Troy's voice shook as he wiped the sweat off his forehead and kept his eyes down on the communication station, putting a hand on the window next to him to block out the view of the storm, barreling down on Silka City, daring us tiny humans to do something about it.

"So we're teaming up now?" I asked. "Ironic."

"How, Alanis?" Issaic said, wheeling on me.

I shut up. Issaic only had eyes for the storm. For the moment, for the first time in the world… we weren't on opposite sides. It was a fleeting feeling. But it had happened.

"What's it gonna take to break you?" He asked under his breath, his entire face pressed against the window.

"How'd you ever keep something like this confined in the first place?" I asked.

Issaic glared at me.

"It's a long ride man," Derek said. "We can… talk."

"You know what a faraday shield is?" he said.

"Yeah," I said. "The cork and can experiment. Full electric stoppage, not a tesla gets past, like the outside of a microwave oven—wait a minute."

"What did you think the gates of Jerico were for?" Issaic asked. "To protect the barefooted arborists? Those gates aren't for keeping us out."

"It's for keeping the solar fallout in," Derek said. "It's that simple?"

"It's not simple," Issaic corrected.

"But we didn't touch the gates," I said.

"It's not just gates," Issaic said. "They catch the flare head on, but we'd still be flanked by fallout on either coast—if not for four generators in perfect position, two in the west, two in the east, all calibrated to confine the stratospheric winds over Ocarina to the north, invented by the best minds on the island, in what was maybe the second time we've ever actually come together to solve a problem. It was perfect. Then you—"

"Meddling kids, we know," I said, trying to sound flip, like my brain wasn't working overtime. I had an idea. But for it to work, I needed more than wings. I needed a girl.

"The storm will land," Astor said, walking back from the cockpit. "Silka will spend this night in the darkness. Can your city survive?"

"The lightning city is about to earn that moniker," Issaic admitted. "She was built for the seasonal thunderstorm, hopefully she can take a hurricane. Silka will survive if the people do, even if by candlelight."

"Should we prepare to lose connection, sir?" Troy asked.

"No," Issaic said. "That won't be happening. Even if the entire city itself goes dark, the gen—I mean, the source is designed to survive. It's, let's just say, not exactly magnetic. But Silka will need Infinite more than ever. Your abilities will not be compromised. Use them for survival, those are your only orders."

"I'm missing something," I said, blinking. "No, I've got something. I don't know which."

"You're sundowning," Derek said, a hand on my shoulder.

"If we have indeed moved the system away from the Territory, can we use this opportunity to explore the changing seasons?" Astor said. "I know this isn't about Jerico, but if there's even a one percent chance we could change the—"

"You're right," Issaic interrupted, forcibly. "This isn't about Jerico. Pilot, make sure we haven't left sight of the gates."

"Confirmed," a familiar voice came through the speakers.

"I thought we were on the roundabout," Troy said. "I assumed storm."

"You assumed wrong," Issaic said, holding Astor's eyes in his without blinking. "You should have assumed consequence."

He was deadly serious. Derek's face was just like mine. Absolutely terrified at what was about to happen (twins right?).

"You can't be serious," I said.

"That's not consequence, it's a preemptive strike!" Derek shouted.

"Tell that to THAT!" Issaic roared, his hand out the window at the storm. "What good is a hundred-mile shield, if enough radiation to kill a continent can just GO AROUND IT?!"

"I seen it," I pleaded. "We still have a chance to stop it. To undo it. If we can do that… what's the point of wasting a perfectly good faraday?"

I had an airship full of eyes on me. Even the pilot was listening (I hoped).

"Target a section mile," Issaic said, staring me down, standing his ground. "On my mark, sixty seconds to launch, no exceptions. Status?"

"Ready to fire sir," came a voice through the speakers.

"Are you SERIOUS RIGHT NOW ISSAIC?" Astor shouted. "You PROMISED! For once in your life, listen to—"

"Finish that sentence," Issaic said.

It was not an invitation. Issaic walked up to Astor and put an armored Infinite shoe on his bare foot, and while no one was flying away, we all heard the sound of his jet boots powering up.

"I get it," Astor said, holding back the pain. "You don't care. You just want to watch me burn."

There was smoke coming up off his foot. The cabin bell went off.

"This is your pilot speaking; we're twenty thousand feet up in a pressurized, hydrogen powered anti-gravity superjet. No smoking please."

Issaic's boots powered down, but he stepped down even harder, finally squeezing a single wince out of Astor.

"Why?" Astor said. "What did we ever do to you? Why can't—"

And mid-sentence he sent a single right cross at Issaic's face… but Issaic caught it.

"I was wondering if that was ever coming," Issaic said.

Astor's face contorted as Issaic took his hand and turned it over, revealing that lowercase letter 'a', the brand of an Astral warrior caught in the Blitz.

"I thought so."

"It's the mark of my people," Astor started. "People you're about to—"

"It is the mark of a Jerico caught in the siege against my city," Issaic said. "And you think you get to have ideas? You're lucky I let you live, from ten years ago until this moment. You've conspired with these boys for a week."

"I HAVEN'T!" Astor roared. He was almost crying. It was heavy. Issaic had him not like a captive, but like a friend he'd turned on at the last moment.

"Then what have you done, besides nothing?" Issaic said, his eyes flashing, pointing out the window to the rest of the north. "You know who actually did something? They did. The unaided, un-manipulated Jerico. Your legendary caputs, all the king's horses, all the queen's women, all the trees in the forest, they did this. Maybe that's why you're on this side of the firebomb, maybe that's why it's aimed at them, and not you. You're so useless you ended up on the right side without trying, without helping them or us or ANYONE, at all. I mean come on Astor, you said it yourself, the answer was in his head. That's the only reason I let you live, and even in your complete and utter failure, I'm still doing it. Aren't you the least bit grateful?"

Astor slumped over, doing his best to not reach for his foot, but every muscle in his leg was tight, just bracing through the pain. Hold up. Was Issaic playing another game, or had Astor really not told him anything?

"What happens now?" Astor said, slowly.

"Those who survive the fire will return to their anti-electricity as soon as we can rebuild our astronomy centers," Issaic said. "This is nothing but the misguided attempt of children, don't think it means anything else. In a few days, Silka will be restored. In a few years, maybe your trees will start growing back from the charcoal remains—dark earth and all, right? In a few generations, maybe you'll outgrow the brands I'm going to put on every surviving human with a heartbeat. The day that mark fades from your people, we'll talk."

"That'll take a hundred years," Astor said, blinking.

"I know," Issaic said, almost fondly, like he was picturing the peace. "Now I'll only ask this once. Do you understand what's about to happen to you?"

"I understand perfectly," Astor said, staring at my father. "Will you get off my foot now?"

Issaic stepped back, and we could all see the red, swollen skin on Astor's bare foot. He didn't seem to mind though. Then Issaic kicked him, and it was as hard as it was cheap. Astor took it on the chin, literally, soaring off his feet, smashing down hard a few yards away.

"I told you," Issaic said. "You don't get to have ideas. You don't get to want things. You will do what I tell you to do, and then you'll die. You signed that contract ten years ago, when you attacked my city. I understand you've had a bit of a free rein in my absence. That's over."

I was stunned. So was Astor. He was on his butt, looking up at Issaic with the strangest face on his… face.

"She… she knew it," Astor said, shaking his head. "Ollux told me not to trust you. She told me this could only end one way. This way. She was right, about everything. She told me this would happen, and you know what the strangest thing is? I believed her. For all the things I've done to Derek and James, I did something else too."

"What did you do?" Issaic said. "You're looking at me like you're about to take a shot at the king. You do that, you better not miss."

"That's why I didn't aim for you," Astor said, still sitting down in front of us. "I aimed for the pilot."

And we all saw it. Issaic blinked. It was quick, it was perfect.

"On some level, hell yeah," I said, ever the fan of chaos.

"Wings down," my brother reminded me, solemnly.

"Wait you did WHAT about the pilot?" I asked in a panic, and I snapped back to reality—just as the plane jolted.

"What did you do?" Issaic asked.

Troy raced past us to the cockpit and pulled the doors apart to see Alcyon tumbling out of the doors to his back, looking up at us with some sort of blue liquid on his lips.

"Oh hell," Derek said.

"Why is everything upside down?" Pilot Alcyon asked, through a haze.

"It's not," I said.

Then the ship hit a pocket, spun out of control, and we were very much—

"WHY IS HE CLAIRVOYANT?" I screamed from upside down.

"ASTOR!" Issaic shouted, madder than hell or honey.

But all we heard was a door slamming, and then the body of Astor soared out of the airship windows, a parachute extending out at the last moments before his body hit the canopy below. All I could think was how in the hell he'd fit a parachute in those pants.

"My ship!" Issaic shouted.

We were all spinning when he stopped, finding the ceiling of the plane and putting both of his open palms against it. Suddenly Issaic had the Scarlet steady from the inside and we all hit the deck harder than we had any right to.

"Nice save," my brother said, sitting up, his head spinning like a top, not like I was any better.

"Who's got eyes on that traitor?" Issaic said, both his hands busy… carrying a plane.

"Odd's out," Lukas coughed out, pinned against a half-shredded seat and the lifeless body of an unconscious agent Odd. "I'm not much better."

"Occupied," Hannah shouted, using her whole body to keep the glowing mechanical machine in the back of the plane from falling out of its already broken frame.

"I am upside down," Troy said, holding his head, his legs in the air against a wall.

Then there was a metal crack as Issaic's hands started pushing through the mechanical frame of the airship. Alcyon's feet were slumped against some part of the trust controls, Issaic was fighting a plane that wanted to take off and spin out of control, all at once. He wasn't going to be able—

"I can't even do everything myself," he said, shaking his head. "I don't care if you're unconscious or upside down, everyone out of the ship and that's an order! Those rocketeers go off and we won't have a Scarlet to save! Everyone get in there and grab a part of this timebomb, just maybe don't squeeze too tight! Clear? Objections?"

"SIR!"

He called for doom, they had answered. Loyally, I'll give them that.

"Troy—clear the cockpit!" Issaic shouted.

Troy took Alcyon's torso with both hands and dragged him to the emergency exit door closest to the cockpit. He kicked the latch down with his foot. Wait.

"You can't be serious," Derek said.

Issaic's answer was to look at us with nothing but hate in his eyes.

"You don't know me," he said, in a tone that screamed last words.

Then in a flash of white light Troy kicked the door open and dumped a lifeless Alcyon into the stratosphere, as he and the agents shot out into the sky, leaving Issaic holding the plane. No one bothered to close a door behind them, everything in the jet was strapped down—except us. Nature could be cruel.

My brother went first, here one moment, then head over heels out the open door and already a hundred yards away by the time the shouting started. As for me, I was taken by the raging winds and shot out of the cabin right behind him—until I got a couple fingers on the doorframe, ready to tear them off before I was thrown out into the open air. I didn't recognize what I could see of the ground, a long way away, but getting closer. For a moment Issaic was right beside me in the air, flying as I was flailing, the five Infinite agents doing their best to keep up with an out of control plummeting starship, waiting for the opportune moment to grab it.

"NOW!" Issaic shouted.

The agents around us screamed for their lives as they charged the plane, wrenching it out of its doomed descent in such a sharp jolt that I lost my half hand hold as the ship buckled. I was ready for the rocketeers to go off, and so were Odd, Troy, Lukas and Hannah, judging by their screams. Yet as the ship came to a controlled descent in the hands of the Infinite, no bombs lit up the night. They had done it. But as soon as it was apparent, Issaic turned on me, soaring off to save his ship, as I tumbled through the air head over heels. Wait.

If they could catch a plane in their bare hands, they could—

"HELP ME!" I shouted through the sky.

"You'll figure it out," was all Issaic said.

"YOU SAY THAT!" I said, seeing nothing but sky, ground, sky, ground…

At around a hundred yards from the ship my necklace lit up again, the wings deployed only a few hundred feet away from the green sea, and I flew. Instinct caught me, or more accurately, wings did. I knew they would eventually… but still. I had dropped a few cloud layers, and for the moment, I couldn't see Issaic. I was closer to Jerico than him. And speaking of—

"Rude," I said to the open world around me. "Where am I? Besides strangerland?"

"It's always something," my brother said, coming in to hover just out of wing-tip range, staring at me with something new on his face.

I wasn't even surprised. We just needed a bit of space from the Reaper killer in the back of the Scarlet, and it was wing city. It happened to me, it would happen to my brother. Keep up.

"What happened to—wait," my brother said, squinting through the clouds.

"I seen it," I said.

The army only had eyes for their out of control Scarlet jet, but Alcyon was still falling through the air seemingly unconscious, with not a single Infinite breaking orders to help him. It was only right to shoot forward, pluck the falling guy out of the clouds, and let the momentum take us both down, closer to the dirt and tanbark than a conscious Alcyon probably would have liked. I was expecting the Reaper wings to die any moment, with every inch closer I flew, but it seemed like Hannah's anti-magic machine didn't have that wide a radius.

"Thanks, birds," were his first words.

He was clearly out of it.

"Dude," I said. "You got the blueblood?"

But Alcyon's eyes were as clear as anything. He put a finger to his mouth, then pointed down. I frowned, trying to decipher the riddle.

"Check it out," Derek said.

We were hovering over a small divide in the green sea below. Only this close could we see an unbroken strip of land stretching out to the left and right below us. It was the small section of cleared land around the gates, that's why it extended so perfectly curved in both directions. But we were high enough to see something else waiting for us over even the gates. It was a cleared playing field, with a single tree trunk in the middle of everything, and a small amphitheater of seats all around it. I could almost hear the cheers. Stranger…

"Southern Arbor," I said. "He almost set fire to Southern Arbor. Of all places. You think it's a coincidence?"

"It doesn't matter," Derek said. "All that does is… how do we take away the cannons?"

"From a man who's determined to fire them?" I asked. "I don't know if we can. Pilot?"

"It's funny you say that," was all Alcyon said. "Look."

The clouds moved, and we saw a sight in the sky alright. They were small and getting smaller, but we could hear Issaic shouting orders to five agents who all had hands on the still roaring engines of the Scarlet, pushing against it for all they were worth.

"They can't see us down here," he said. "Land, now."

Derek snapped to attention, I'd heard it too. It didn't sound like Alcyon was hallucinating any more. Could it all be for show?

"You didn't drink it," I said, realizing.

We landed, back at the jungle half-way point, staring up at two hundred feet (or more) of gates that now seemed alive, almost buzzing with the electricity in the air (they were, apparently). Derek followed me down and we stood Alcyon up on his feet, a massive tree trunk behind him for stability, a canopy cover miles wide in any direction.

"But your mouth…" Derek said, staring.

"I like blueberries, okay?" Alcyon said. "Always have."

"Blueberries?" I asked.

Alcyon threw a handful of metal objects into the ground at our feet and quickly buried them with his foot and some dirt.

"What kind of blueberry is that?" I asked.

"The firing pin kind," Alcyon said.

"How many?" Derek asked.

"All of them," Alcyon said. "You didn't see anything. When the time comes, you have to sell it. Trust me."

"Why?" I asked.

"Because I'm not the one trying to burn an island down," Alcyon said.

"You mean a territory," I said.

"I do not," Alcyon said, looking through me somehow, far past my soul—

"But what about Astor? Why do all that, and then help us?"

Alcyon didn't answer. Not that he didn't want to.

"Issaic made us a promise."

We started, and looked around. The voice was only coming from the trees around us, his body unseen. It wasn't even the first time.

"He just broke that promise," the disembodied voice of Astor said from the trees, all the trees. "I wanted Jerico free of the burden. I wanted the lights, and he promised them. All we had to do was…"

"Enter the void," I said. "My spiraling mind, the den of scorpions, the falloff of all—"

"Yes," Astor said. "Issaic can keep us from freedom. That's his choice to make. And I can see it in his eyes, he's desperate this time. He's still looking."

"For what?" Derek asked.

"The same thing he was looking for last time, when he burned Evergreen to the ground," Astor said. "But he has twice now gotten nothing from Jerico, so he… prepared us for your arrival. Ollux your host, and I… your judgement."

"So he knew?" I said.

"He suspected," Astor said. "Nothing more."

"The Hexoscope," Derek said. "It was aimed on our house brother. Someone's looking for something. That doesn't mean they've found it."

"So what did you tell him?" I asked, face white.

"I told him nothing," Astor said. "I told him I found nothing. For that lie I am proud. For the others… I'm not. I'm sorry."

"I believe you," I said, strangely sincere. "But did you find it? In my head?"

There was a pause. The forest was thinking.

"I might have found something," Astor said. "But that doesn't matter. What does is… will you?"

And that was it. The voice in the trees was gone, and when we looked sideways, so was Alcyon. They had disappeared together, the agent and the warrior, into the very trees from which they came. The Akouras.

"They don't act like brothers," Derek said.

"Do we?" I asked.

I shrugged. It was a complicated shrug. I thought I knew Astor. He had found his own way into my brain, that I would never forgive him for. But what he'd uncovered there was… something. Something we'd forgotten, something we might have gone the rest of our lives never remembering. And somehow, it seemed that information hadn't quite made it to Issaic yet. Interesting. But before we could say anything else, someone else had dropped down between us on wings as big as ours. It was Lukas, in his half-assed, jagged armor and unprotected face. His eyes were closed until he touched down.

"There you are," he said. "Thought you'd booked it. If I were you—"

"There's nowhere to go," I said sadly. "Where's the jet?"

"At the end of the forest," Lukas said. "There's a ridge, it's just a hill, you'll see it once we get clear of these trees. But that ship's not flying anywhere. We go on wings and blaster boots from here."

"I thought the whole point of a superjet was to beat a storm," I said.

"It was," Lukas said. "And it would have, if Issaic hadn't tried to half-ass two things at once. We should have beelined it for Silka, we would have had a chance."

"And now we don't?" I asked. "You don't sound that upset about it."

"I can't keep up with blaster boots," Lukas said. "They'll leave me behind like you. Good thing, otherwise… someone might have heard those trees."

There it was. Side of—

"Who are you?" I asked.

"Someone who wanted you dead for your last name," Lukas said. "But… that was before Cradlesong."

"We didn't do anything to the—" I started.

"I know what you did to the Reaper," Lukas said.

"Well… you say that, you're fighting on the wrong side," Derek said.

"I'm not fighting for anybody but myself," Lukas said, stepping into the sky on Reaper wings. "Around that guy… I do as I'm told. He's killed for less."

And he took off, trusting us to follow. We did, leaving the gates of Jerico behind, up and out of the canopy, hovering around the first cloud layer until the green ocean below our feet started thinning, eventually turning into the low grass plains around the northern side of Silka. The valley started pretty much on the other side of the jungle, and Lukas was right, I saw a big ridge, it was the only noticeable feature in the plains for a few miles. The remains of the Scarlet were wedged into the incline, looking like it might just slide down the entire thing, if not for the agents keeping a hand on it.

And on the other side of that hill was my home.

Hannah was the farthest away, with the Reaper killer machine having rolled down into the valley on the other side of the hill. She must have been a mile out, but the night was bright, and full of cliches. In the distance was Silka City, surrounded on all sides by cliffs, mountain ridges, what have you. And in between, moving over the long expanse of unbroken farmland, was the scariest cloud monster I'd ever seen in my life. It was unbroken, both behind and before us, a huge bulging head, crazy shapes that went a good six to seven miles high, spread out in front of me in different colors like I was watching planets form. It felt cosmic, not atmospheric. The storm system was coming in from the north, so much so that I could still see the very front of it, the dry and shining land right in the path of such horror, the parts of the land that had yet to disappear into the ground fog and merciless rain that touched the ground like the cracks of thunder and lightning touched the sky.

"The jungle did this," Issaic said, staring at his ship, almost in pieces. "Troy, were you able to recover the payload?"

"Only one of them sir."

"Well why haven't you fired?" Issaic said.

And at the click of a canon, I remembered Alcyon's words. Trust me.

"NO!" I shouted, feeling my body jumping in front of the gigantic thing.

"DUDE!" Derek screamed. Then—

I was hit in the side by a car. A flying car. Our CRV was back, and it had slammed me out of the way, taking chunks off my rock armor, leaving a spray-pattern of dents and scratches on the hood, but slamming me out of the way of the rocket that—

Never even fired. With a hiss, the missile broke apart inside the canon chamber, and the pressure was only released as a small scream of air. Derek was on his knees, I was upside down, and the car…

"The car!" Derek shouted. "Thank the blue—wait what just happened?"

"It's critical," Troy said, sinking behind the canon. "Issaic, I'm sorry, the rocketeer program is—"

"Save it," Issaic said, looking at us. "You just jumped in front of a missile. I said it from the beginning, I knew these two weren't behind this. They didn't know it wouldn't fire. The car didn't either."

"You promised," I said. "The level. We help you, the Jerico lives. What part of that don't you get?"

"The part where ANYTHING I want has any prerequisite," Issaic said.

"I think that's where you went wrong," Derek said, shaking his head. "James, how about you never do that again?"

"No promises," I said. "But I think we just found a way to keep up."

"I've seen that car before," Issaic said. "That's Star's car."

"You mean our mother, yes it is a hand me down," I said, annoyed. "We're not ten anymore, we grew up man. You can't skateboard everywhere."

"You… skateboard?" Issaic asked, again sounding just a bit relatable.

"Not anymore," I said.

"Not exactly true," my brother said under his breath.

"Come on Issaic," I said. "You want to waste whatever time we've got left on fire? I thought this was about Silka."

"It is," Issaic said. He looked out to the jungle, to the forests, the canopies, all of it. "Fine. Leave the ship. Every agent back, full speed. Protect the city. Or at least, do whatever you can, against the storm."

"Sir!"

And one by one, his stars shot towards our city at an impossible speed. They easily out-flew the storm, we could see their light descending on Silka even from a good ten miles away. Issaic looked back at us, and the flying car.

"I'm not carrying you," he said. "So be it. Meet us atop the Engineerium. The outpost hill that used to be the Observatory. I'm sure you know the one."

"I do," I said.

"How do I know you won't bail?" Issaic asked.

"It's my city too," was all I said.

The driver's door opened by itself and I got in. Derek flew over the hood and folded his wings up, coming in through the moon roof. Bits of tree branches and leaves fell down on us as he closed it, skylight style. Right. We were out in the open, but the car had followed us through a good amount of the jungle.

"I'll give you sixty seconds," Issaic said.

I flashed the headlights, car talk for yep. The heat wave came over his body, and he was vibrating—then he was a dot of light, already miles away from us in a single push. We were here, alone for a beat. But we didn't have much time.

"Where are they?" I asked the car.

"Turn around," came the Oracle's reply.

And I did, my head whipping around in the driver's seat to see—

"Heather, get your foot out of my face!"

"Oracle, keep this flying vehicle at stasis!"

"Now it's in my mouAHTH!"

It was Lynn Lyre and Heather Denien, tumbling over themselves in the empty trunk, big enough for them to both kneel side by side as the car finally leveled out, their arms flung over the backseats for support. I looked hard, but detected no more invisible people in this car.

"We saw it, we saw everything," Lynn said, looking out the window to make sure every Infinite was gone. "The Jerico saw it too, they're all gathered at

Oleander, watching you through Crete's thousand foot television."

"His what?" I asked, blinking.

"He works fast," Lynn said. "Everyone saw you jump in front of that canon. Most thought moving pictures was witchcraft, some were impressed. How on earth did you think that would end?"

"I had… a feeling it wouldn't," I said, looking out the window, but in the direction of the jungle, where I knew a certain stadium was hanging hundreds of feet over the gates. The stadium where we'd been accepted into the Territory by our host, Ollux.

"Sorry Ollux," I said, shaking my head. "We missed you."

"We haven't figured audio out yet," Lynn said.

"I thought Crete worked fast," I said.

There was a warning horn from a half a mile away.

"He can read lips, man," Lynn smiled. "Wave to the jungle. Now."

We waved, and on the crazy winds and roaring static in the thunderous air… I swear I could almost hear the cheering in response.

"I can taste the jungle," Heather said, her eyes closed, still pawing at her tongue where Lynn had left a footprint and everything.

"You said you saw everything," I said. "So you saw Alcyon swipe the firing pins out of the canons? You saw Astor fake-blueblood his own brother, the pilot, and crash a superjet full of killer agents just as Issaic was about to give the order to burn the gates below Southern Arbor?"

"No we missed all that," Lynn said. "Okay so what does it mean?"

"I don't know," I said. "We don't have the whole truth, we never do, but I know for sure Alcyon and Astor Akoura just saved our lives and the jungle in one go."

"Well… damn," Heather said, scratching her head. "That means—"

"Not enemies?" Lynn asked, her eyes lighting up.

"Not even," I said. "But Issaic's out of canons. Maybe… we can forget about the jungle."

"Not sure how likely that is," Heather said.

"I mean maybe Issaic can," I said. "We brought him here, as much as we don't think we did. I think… if we want to really keep the Jerico safe from him, we shouldn't hide behind their walls and guest rooms anymore."

"Ah man," Lynn said. It had hit her too. "He's right. Objectively, we can't stay. Absolutely, we should move on, first chance given. If that. You're only wrong in one way James."

"Only one?" I said. "I'll take it. How?"

"I could never forget about the jungle," Lynn said.

"Me neither," Heather said.

"Get out of the trunk," Derek said. "Sit like people. This car is your car."

"Then get out of the driver's seat," Lynn said.

"I have no problem with that," I said, and Derek and I fought to climb over each other into the backseat, as the girls clawed their way over us for the front.

"Much more accurate this way," Heather said, pushing the hair out of her eyes. "Okay boys. Wanna hear what Lynn and I came up with, while you were, I don't know, making peace with the siblings clandestine?"

"Very yes," I said, no hesitation.

"Great, then pay attention," Lynn said, picking up from Heather. "We've got a whole bunch of different island super powers and just as many reasons and ways for them to be turned on and off again. It's going to get confusing."

"It already wasn't?" Heather said.

"Let's just do this without superpowers then, we've come this far haven't we?" Derek said. "All in favor? Back to solving our problems like people? Power of friendship against the storm?"

Everyone looked at him. I was the first to break. Then we were all laughing. It was short lived, but it was necessary.

"I haven't laughed that hard in weeks," Heather said, wiping her eyes. "It's a geomagnetic solar flare with the passive power of a nuclear bomb, in storm-form, a hundred miles wide. Of course we need superpowers to stand a chance. That being said, as a wise young man once said… I think we got this."

"We do?" I said, stars in my eyes, the hope machine dialing up.

"We've got once chance to get it," Heather said, as confident as the day we'd met her—and every day after that. "Here's what we do. It's *so* simple."

4.4

BRIGHT & SUNNY DAY

Our flying car came in for landing at the crest of a gigantic cliffside overlooking the valley side of Silka. From here, opposite the southeastern end of the Engineerium, we could see the mountains rising up even higher to our right, the start of the Valley of Edna. This was somewhere between the underland and cloud city. Maybe a thousand feet up, with so much below, it was hard to describe, and that was before we landed. Issaic glared at us as we opened the doors and got out. No Sand, no Crete, no jungle backup. Just us.

"You've multiplied," Issaic said.

"You're asking for a miracle," I said.

"I'm asking you to think, before you touch an ecosystem again," Issaic said. "You want more eyes on you when the city realizes this is your fault, go ahead. Let's see how long they stand beside you, when the flood turns to people."

"You wouldn't still be trying to pull us apart, now?" Heather asked.

"I'm trying to pull certain people away from certain other people," Issaic said, not even looking at her. "By all means, Reaper, run your wings into the ground saving my city."

"We will," I said. "But even that would work against us. You've left the city scared, Issaic. We won't get anywhere close to done, not like this."

"Do you maybe see that's my point?" Issaic asked, rubbing his eyes.

"I don't care what people think of me," Heather growled. "Let them fear me. I'll save them all, no matter how hard they scream."

"I should like you, remind me why I don't?" Issaic said. "Right. The part where you lived up to that fear before I ever knew your name. Terror is all they know of you, Reaper. You deserve to be feared."

"I deserve to be loved, all the same," Heather countered. "You disagree?"

And it was so out of nowhere we all stopped breathing for a beat.

"I… don't," Issaic said, again sounding honest. "You're what, twelve?"

"Eighteen," Heather said, her eyes narrowed.

"Same thing," Issaic said, through the wrinkles on his face. Sixty? Seventy?

"There's an easy way around clothes," I said. "We could change. All of us."

"I see what you're getting at," Issaic said. "No."

"We were that obvious?" I said, scratching my head.
"Lynn, the plan didn't work, what do we do now?" James said.
"You don't have to SAY THAT OUT LOUD!" Lynn whisper/shouted.
Issaic shook his head. "Since you brought it up so unceremoniously. There's no one on earth I trust with the power of my city less than you. Specifically you. You will do what you came here to do without a single iota of help from the lighting city. You have access to none of our resources, nor my soldiers. You may as well use what you brought."
"Can we at least get a friendly fire warning?" My brother asked.
"I'll spread the word," Issaic said, barely moving his head.
"It doesn't seem like you will," Lynn said, sadly.
"Well it doesn't seem like you can stop a storm," Issaic said, looking out over the only thing we had in common: impending doom. Always something.
"How about we all agree to surprise each other?" I said, meekly.
"Deal," Issaic and Lynn said, far too quickly.
For a moment, we didn't know if Issaic was going to kill us or salute us. Then he blasted off, on a curving jet-stream for downtown Silka—before he course corrected in the air and took for the ports, the sky already as dark over the eastern edge of Silka as the storm coming in from the northwest.
"That guy," Lynn said. "Just…"
"Sucks," Heather finished.
"Work to do," I said. "Lynn, we need a miracle. You said you brought one?"
"I brought three," she said, pulling a blanket out of the trunk, revealing—
A change of clothes. Three of them.
"Yes," James said. "Was Crete able to—"
"In theory," Lynn said. "Presenting the sword, storm, and shield supersuits, minus any kind of power. We assume."
"I thought we were done assuming," James said.
"The classics," I said, distracted. I let the Vema armor fall away, and pulled my Infinite supersuit on over the Jerico boxers. How cultured was I?
"Wait, only three watches?" Heather said, hoping.
"You're our contingency," Lynn said. "If we don't work, you have to."
"I was planning on it," Heather said, sounding disappointed.
Lynn smiled. "If it helps, it's waiting for you on my dresser."
Heather punched the air in victory.
"Adorable," I said. "I still can't believe the plan depends on a watch."
"Pressing a button is the easy part," Lynn said. "As long as James—"
"I am James," he said, brain so full of confidence it was out of room for words. "Leaves Derek on rescue mode, sorry brother, I know you want to fight."
"I don't want to fight, I have to be a fighter," I said.
"Why?" James asked.
"So that the next time we're sitting on the outskirts of a city on fire, it can be me who risks his head to save everyone, and not her," I said.
"We've been here before, I'm not leaving you behind—" Lynn started.
"Lynn you can do anything, we all know it. I just wish… for once…"
"For once what, you'd finish a sentence?" Lynn asked, her hands in the air.

"Nevermind," I said. "Oracle, how many people are we looking at out here?"

"There are a hundred and eighteen citizens farther than a half hour outside the waterfall," the car said.

"Lucky farmers," Heather said.

"Aw," Lynn said, smiling. "You care."

"I've always cared," Heather said. "I'm still growing up, damn."

"Me too," Lynn said. "Don't change too much though. We good with this?"

"We have to be," Heather answered. "I wish we had time for specifics, instead of relying on, again… you know…"

"It's almost like having friends is going to keep you alive," Lynn grinned.

"Almost," Heather said, again with that half smile. "Okay byee."

"Don't diee," Lynn said, again, almost sarcastic.

Heather got into the CRV and closed the door. James was in the driver's seat without another moment to waste, but we didn't say anything else to each other, not just then. There was too much. We just gave a final nod, and I closed the hatchback. It was hot, more than machinery, it was alive. So was I.

"All the queen's men," I said, slapping the taillight.

And as the car took off into the sky, heading straight for the storm, I saw James' eyes on mine through the driver side mirror. They stayed on me until the car was lost to the clouds. Somehow, I knew what he was thinking.

Survive.

"We're counting on a miracle, Derek," Lynn said, her voice breaking as soon as we were alone. "This isn't crazy, it's worse. It's witchcraft. We're—"

"Not witches," I said. "We're not counting on crazy, we're counting on everything he's seen, heard, talked to and been confronted by through macrocosmic unconscious slumber. It has to make sense, it's science—and it was your idea by the way. It's going to work."

"And if it doesn't?" She asked.

"Then… hell, I don't know," I said, holding out my hand. "Small steps?"

"I told you," Lynn said. "It's a long way man, we aren't going to hold hands the whole time."

But unlike last time, she grabbed my hand anyways and dug her fingers in. Then we were flying, because she was flying, and I was being swept off my feet literally for once, instead of just figuratively. So much for not holding hands.

"I have wings, Lynn!" I shouted up to her, through the world's biggest smile.

"Then USE THEM!"

And with superhuman strength, she flung me up into the stars, our hands letting go at the peak, my momentum carrying me high like she had shot me out the canon—which she'd promised she was done doing. But I didn't mind.

"Woo!" I shouted as I flew.

I was weightless in the sky, even free falling for a bit until I felt my wings extend out from the shoulders. Then I was really flying. Something I had been able to do, ever since meeting Lynn Lyre. I flew myself over mountains and plains, into the empty stretch of land before the final destination of Silka City in the distance. Together we soared on wings not of leather, but thinly textured magnetic rock. It had taken me far too long to figure that out. But what we were flying towards…

"Pretty lights, coming fast," I said.

Lynn didn't say anything. She knew I wasn't talking about us. The city in the nearing distance was cut below and around the natural rising mountains of the valley, and behind that was more ocean—I knew that from childhood reasons, and prison reasons too. Overhead the sky was dark and full of clouds, because tropics. That was normal. But making its way through a sky devoid of stars was something… green. Beams of borealis lit up the night to herald the coming of the cyclone, in colors of soft pastels, almost like ice cream. Sorbet yellow, a touch of pink and strawberry red—once I got ice cream in my head, that was it, usually. This time was different. Because this time, below all the beautiful northern lights, a spherical monster cyclone followed, as big as the island.

Pretty colors, aposematic monsters, you get it.

"This is… my fault," I said, almost unconsciously.

"Our fault," Lynn said. "Hell of a weather."

The thing could swallow Silka in its wake, from port to farmlands, but the crazy thing was how fast it moved. I was at top wingspeed and just barely staying ahead, speed shakes and everything. It wasn't the first time I had imagined the citizens leaning out of their car windows, standing outside on their terraces, climbing up on their roofs to get a better view of the colors. I hoped they could see the storm behind, the tornadoes and bolts of lightning and sheets of rain and hail just slamming any tree it passed into the ground, not even a trunk left in its wake. But then I didn't have to imagine people, I saw them. The night was so dark from the storm, and so were the houses—right, the electricity was down, even all the way out here.

"Hey Derek," Lynn called out.

"I seen it," I said.

My eyes caught a light blinking off in a house not even a hundred feet from us, before I saw a figure inside close the curtains on me. But we were past curtains. I dove down on wings of rocks and let my claws hit the roof before anything else. In seconds I was in a very dark, fire-lit living room, with a man and wife cowering before me, holding each other and screaming.

"I'm here to—" I started, but then the wife threw a spoon at me. "Ouch."

"AAHH—"

"Not enemies!" I said. "Look!"

I pulled open the curtains in front of a window, where there was nothing but a beautiful, bright and sunny city through them (the midnight version).

"You have a lovely view," I said.

That's when Lynn Lyre smashed through the curtains on the other side of the living room, taking them all out, leaving an open sight to the dark fury of the oncoming cyclone.

"AAAAHHH—"

"No time!" Lynn shouted, grabbing the woman by her hand, and she leapt them out the broken second story window even before all the glass had settled.

"ELEANOR!" The man shouted, and before he knew I was going to grab him too, he'd left off the balcony after her.

"My dude!" I shouted.

I flew after him and lowered us both down to the side of the road by the house, where a group of neighbors was swarmed around a dark pick up truck, pushing it as hard as they could, trying to get it to start (it wasn't going to start).

"Should have given you a heads up, my bad," Lynn said, as Eleanor rushed into her husband's arms.

"You... are the heads up, aren't you?" The guy said.

I nodded, just as the gigantic mouth of the storm cracked open in thunder, and the air around us got colder. Most of the guys gave up on the truck, looking at us in our wingsuits in wonder. More were coming in, down the road. I saw a lot of confusion, a lot of fear. But no instant rage at the Reaper (me). Good.

"What's your name?" I asked. "And how many neighbors do you have?"

"Rob," the guy said. "A hundred something. Not all as nice as me."

"You have to trust me Rob," I said. "If you don't... they won't."

"REAPER!"

And there it was. The shouting started, the truck was forgotten (finally) as the small circle grew around us. Good. I wanted it as big as possible. An older guy stepped up, fists first. I cut off any armor above my neck and faced him.

"You're just a kid," Rob said, blinking.

"And you're just about to die," I said.

"Because of you?" The older guy said, pointing up. "What is THAT?"

"Listen," I said, louder than anyone else, the only one not looking up. "That storm's already hit Silka with the electromagnetic fallout of a solar flare. Nothing electrical can work, and Infinite isn't coming. Put those together on your own. You want to stay, good luck, but we're the last ride to higher ground."

The storm broke again, something Lynn and I had gotten familiar with after a week in the Jerico, but there was only one farmer who didn't jump, the same farmer who had a hand on my shoulder. It was Rob. Eleanor grabbed Lynn. It did everything I hoped, meaning it turned a bunch of angry eyes into confused eyes. I would take it. I wasn't going to turn the stigma of the scythe around in one night. The survival instinct was strong in farmers facing the end of times.

"We have to try something, Torin," Rob said to the older man before me.

"Fine," Torin said. "I suppose, thank you, baby man. But there's only two of you. What do we do, form a line and cross our fingers?"

I refused to answer. He could have been talking to anyone.

"Close your eyes," Lynn said, smiling, giving a small salute to the sky.

No one closed their eyes. Why would they? Didn't matter, I felt the rock around my neck lighting up all the same, to the point of—boom. A radial shockwave of pure light emerged from the gemstone itself, not me, just like James said it would. For a moment, I saw Silka only in purple lighting. Then came the map—if a map was a hundred flying, clawed, armored scouts of Vema.

"So that's where the confidence comes from?" Torin asked, on his toes.

But actually. From the light around us came the invisi-soldiers of Reaper, as the only proper backup we'd brought made themselves known in the air above that rusty old pick up truck and thirty farmers. Friends, and in low places too.

"Infinite can't help you now," came the ominous voice of Sasha, the first to land by the truck. "That's why we're here."

"Thought that was going somewhere… darker," Torin said, eyebrows up.

"We're going there," Sasha said, pointing hard to the middle of the city. "The storm's twenty minutes out. We can spare exactly half that making sure we get to everyone in the district but not a second more. I need everyone's help to check on the neighbors, then we can all get back to drinking. Understood?"

"MA'AM!" The farmers shouted, somehow already on the same page.

Sasha grabbed the closest farmer's hands and forced them onto her shoulders. The guy didn't look that upset about it, until the wings came out and he screamed—but held on. With her leading the way, the scouts flew off in every direction towards any structure in the storm's way, left, right, and center. In a moment, every farm and barn house we could see through the night without light had at least a pair of soldiers on their way. There were easily two hundred Reapers in the air, the best of Eclipso, I could tell by the ruby reds, their armor the color of the firelands.

"Hold on Rob!" I shouted, gladly joining them in the sky.

"Best order Heather ever gave," came the voice of Volf, swooping out of the air by my side, carrying a small boy in one hand and a smaller dog in the other. "Do whatever Lynn does. I get it now."

"Shut up," Lynn said, only half serious. "Takes both of us."

"Where's Heather?" Sasha asked, hovering over with a woman on her back.

"Short answer, eye of the storm?" Lynn said.

"Order among chaos?" Volf said. "I know her, she'd choose chaos every—"

"It's not just Heather," I said. "It's James too. They're going to give us a way out of this storm, without it ripping a roof off the city."

"What if we're too late?" Volf shouted to us over the roaring winds and screaming farmers, both only getting louder, as the swarm of refugee-laden Reapers grew denser around us. "What if the roofs are as good as ripped?"

"There's safety in the caves, take the people there," I said (stole from Bastile). "Which by thunder we're already doing, imagine that."

But we didn't have to imagine thunder, not when the sky opened up in lightning. From the dirt itself to a few hundred feet above us, it was all alive and amplified in the worst way, one moment we had the storm at our heels, the next it had overcome us. We were losing this race. But then something funny happened—we were caught up in the flight response so hard, we were flying so fast… I felt the winds on my face change temperature. It was either the lightning, or we'd found a sweet spot of low atmospheric pressure at the edge of the storm. Like really low pressure. Suddenly flying got easier, with the air rushing upwards faster than it could come down, I felt it on my wings.

"Speed hack," I said.

"Not even," Volf said, sniffing the air. "You know what that is? What happens when—"

"GO!" Lynn shouted.

And together we surged forward, over the first paved, curving road of the city and up the incline that would eventually lead into the hills at the far side—

waterfall, Engineerium, you get it. There was a reason the Oracle had told us to start with the farms. Actually there were a hundred and eighteen reasons.

"Do we know if we got everybody?" I shouted over the breakneck winds.

"You did," came a voice over my shoulder. In the rock armor, Rob didn't weigh a thing. To a farmer's credit, he held on.

"You don't know that," I said, my face white, and wet.

"I do," Rob said.

I got the feeling we were having different conversations. Then I realized his words were coming from my left, and Lynn was on my left. He was staring at his wife, using her beauty to block out the storm all together. To him, she was everybody. Cute, but more work for me. A head count it would be.

"We're not even there yet," I reminded him.

"We're closer," Rob shrugged.

True. We were flying over buildings instead of farmland for once, over the populous downtown city sector, a hundred blocks of apartments, shopping streets, historic parks and communal centers. The valley was rounding out in front of us in glorious waterfall and Engineerium fashion, with the equivalent of main street absolutely packed with people all making for the falls.

"Lots of windows, lots of people," the woman on Lynn's back said. "Look!"

We weren't even five roofs in when we saw the shooting stars of white light in the rain, racing over the rooftops and city streets, doing whatever the Silka version of super-evacuation was. One white light landed below us next to a couple of kids on a rooftop, then he saw us above, flying as fast as lightning, Lynn and I leading the charge towards Silka, leading two hundred Reapers and a hundred farmers (and some good family dogs) towards the center of the city.

"What in the…" I saw him mouth.

Then the thunder cracked and the agent was in the air with a young boy and girl in his arms, holding each other as hard as he was holding them. The storm roared, the rain got worse, the thunder almost split our heads open, and we flew together, all the way until we landed close enough to the waterfall for the young couple in the agent's arms to jump down and join the surge of people being guided slowly through a break in the water, where a trio of guards hovered in the air, blocking the falls with their shoulders. A dozen more hovered over the line, overwatching the trickle of citizens being flown in personally by dark shapes, so dark they were almost invisible… almost.

"Is that… my butcher?" The agent we'd flown in with asked. "Rob?"

"We out here," the guy on my back waved as we touched down.

"Explain yourself, before I explain my foot through the flying kid's face," the agent said, standing tall despite being outnumbered a hundred to one.

"Don't you dare, a kid saved a life," Rob said. "All of our lives. Did you have a different plan for the farming district? Or any plan?"

"We… were getting to it," the agent said, as white in the face as the clouds in the sky used to be. "Is anyone else seeing this? No? Just me? Oh good—"

It wasn't just him. The growing group of Reaper scouts wasn't even a hundred yards from the most vulnerable of Silka. Around twenty agents had noticed, and they went from a pattern over the refugees to forming their own line, lighting up their hands together to make no mistake at the small army from the Vempire that continued to grow. But with every Reaper scout came a Silka citizen, that was also clear.

"Get inside, butcher," the agent said, furious that he couldn't attack us, and madder still at the reason. "That was no invitation, Reaper."

"You pronounced thank you wrong," I said.

"Thank you," Rob said, as he grabbed his wife off of Lynn's shoulders. "Get yours safe. I'll handle mine."

"Deal," Lynn and I said at the same time.

His wife gave me a salute, then took her husband's hand, and led the charge towards the waterfall. A bunch of old hunchbacked farmer-dudes and dudettes followed them, all surprisingly agile (and thankful) for their age, as others continued to arrive from the trail of scouts behind us, arriving progressively wetter and colder. The water continued to break against the heads and shoulders of three fliers, as thousands sought to escape the storm through a gap in a waterfall only the size of a small house. But the agents were looking at something else. The purple necklaces, the rocky armor. Us.

"You… shouldn't be here," one of the agents said, blinking.

"Issaic, we've got Reapers," another said into his watch.

"Did they help?" Issaic's voice came through for all to hear.

"It… seems so," the first agent said, completely confused.

"Are they done helping?"

My heart sunk. Not in fear. I wasn't mad, I was just disappointed. But as the last of the farmers faded into the rest of the retreat behind that line of super soldiers who still couldn't really tell how many of the underland stood behind Lynn and me… we finally had silence. Until—

"LYNN!" One of the Reapers shouted out, coming forward.

I knew that face. It was Steve. One of Lynn's friends from childhood, when she lived in overland Galan with her father. They'd grown up together, they were close. I didn't like Steve.

"Are there any others to save?" Steve asked. "The storm's getting intense, we can take it, just tell us where to go! There's no reason to fight this fight, not when we don't have to—how can we help Silka?"

Okay maybe I liked Steve.

"There's no help now," Sasha said, her hands up. "This will be for what they did at Cradlesong."

And unfortunately, I saw too many nods around to breathe easy.

"No it won't," Lynn said loudly. "You want to help, either of you? Prove it. Burrow away from here."

"On who's orders?" Sasha shouted, looking back at the army.

"What you've done has been very… public." Lynn said. "Any more time in the spotlight, you'll burn in it."

"Don't quote Hannah," I said.

Sasha was going to scowl, but we saw it at the same time—a glowing light inside the waterfall. Lots of glowing lights. An army of them…

"Last chance," Lynn said. "Underland. They've killed for less. Don't let another Reaper die here. Please."

Sasha gave us the evil eye… then nodded. "Wouldn't dream of it, boss."

"Oh thank the undergods," Steve sighed in relief. "This was her plan?"

"Course," I said. "I wasn't willing to put the Vema up for collateral."

"Neither was Heather, but she did," Lynn said. "Means she trusts us."

"Means she trusts James, crazy voices in the dark, and talking animals—"

"After Sophia, I get it," Lynn said. "I heard what I heard, no matter what anyone thinks. Except maybe you, Derek."

"I think you heard what you heard," I said. "And going by experience, you'll hear it again. All we gotta do is listen. Wait why maybe me?"

"You ever feel like, maybe we were meant to meet?" Lynn asked, softly.

"Only every day," I said, honestly.

"Keep her safe man," Steve said, turning away for some reason.

"She doesn't need me," I said, surprising even myself.

Lynn blinked.

"Well then… find another way to be useful," Steve said.

"I can do that," I said.

Steve was cool by me. His necklace lit up, the ground at his feet started moving, the others copied him, and he nodded to us, like words were enough.

"Home, brothers," Steve called, to hundreds of claws and wings around him.

And as if on cue, the Infinite Army exploded out of the waterfall, taking to the skies like shooting stars in reverse. One by one we watched them clock a massive army of Reaper scouts standing not even a hundred yards from the line of refugees, but just as Lynn and I waved up to them innocently, Steve and the scouts around us melted into the very ground, taking to the rock itself, and willingly. I remembered the tunnel caving in around me again, the feeling as I emerged, the slightest barrier of a dirt armorsuit and that purple necklace somehow being all I needed to avoid being buried alive. Again I wasn't ready to revisit that particular power of the Reaper. But before a hundred agents could decide what to do about two hundred scouts, they were gone. It was just Lynn and me, standing in the rain, as a hundred agents changed course and headed for us, instead of all those poor innocent civilians. Bad distraction—as they shot off for a fight they wouldn't even get, they left the water gate to close and send a hundred pounds of waterfall down onto the heads of the evacuees.

"AH!"

"It hurts," I said. "I know because I've got a head. Wait—"

Then something hit me in the back, side, and face all at the same time. Right. No sense worrying over water now. Not when the storm was on us all. It was rain, snow, and hail all at once, and ocean winds faster as anything I'd ever sailed through. I looked behind me and saw the gigantic green and pale pink solar storm coming in from the north, growing stronger as it swept over the land.

"I see you've multiplied," I said, still not thinking.

"Don't quote your father," Lynn said.

"WHAT IN THE ABSOLUTE—"

"You need help or no?" I asked, not in the mood for questions.

"Well not no," the first agent said, looking between us and the endless downtown, signs of life everywhere. "Was that a small horde of Reaper—"

"How about we evacuate the city first and storytime later, so we go, and NOW!" I shouted, taking off without waiting for permission.

"You know WHAT?" The agent shouted up at the storm (and me). "Fine."

Half a hundred agents scratched their heads, then turned for the line of evacuees instead of us with little more than shrugs. Good. If there were hands in the air, they were grabbed and flown through the waterfall, no questions asked. The line was thinning, but there was still a steady stream from the city streets of downtown, I saw the first agent following it back, all the way down main street, as he drifted up after me.

"Thinking about getting ahead of it?" I shouted through the rain.

"Exactly," he yelled. "Gamma Unit, half here, half with me, to the city."

"SIR!"

"You really aren't here to end us all, maybe you come too," the guy said, as he recurved with his Gamma Unit, trusting us to follow.

We would.

"That's my words," Lynn said. "Why did you—"

"I just thought they were worth remembering," I said. "It's like I said Lynn, you ever think we were meant to meet, or something?"

Lynn smiled. We left the watery grounds at the base of the waterfall behind, both following and leading those small jet streams left behind by fifty agents. It was a small flight through the open historic park between the waterfall cliffs and the actual shops, streets, and eventual high-risers in the background where the city got the densest. There was no fight here. No great plan to win the day. We weren't fighters tonight, this was rescue, and we would be done when everyone was safe. The farming district was a win—not for us, for life. Next, well—there, almost eye level in the distance, atop a building at least thirty stories tall, a figure waving, just low enough that the rest of the army was too high to see.

"I seen it," Lynn said, her eyes never moving from mine. "Hey Infinite."

"By all means," an agent said, without looking at us.

He took the cluster of agents around the building, leaving us to come up alone on the edge of the silver skyscraper, broken windows on every side and floor for the bomb cyclone. It was a big building for two kids, a thought that caught in my mind just as we cleared the stadium sized roof of the thing. But as we neared the edge of the roof…

"Lynn," I said, the hair on my arms standing up. "You feel that?"

"Something's off," she agreed, frowning. "Some hum…"

As the seemingly empty roof came into view our necklaces both picked up together and pointed (hard) to the source of that weird hum, to see something shimmer into focus, straight out of the invisible plane.

It was an invisible plane.

"The Scarlet," Lynn gasped.

"Half of it, at least," I said, my voice breaking. "The back half."

"I thought portable was a pipe dream," Lynn said.

I didn't know what she meant until I followed her eyes, down to the girl by the back half of a plane, cut in jagged angles by Reaper claws, next to—

"Define portable," Hannah said, as she clicked the machine on—the one that killed our Reaper powers.

The next thing I knew… she killed our Reaper powers. Boom.

The Infinite cluster (Gamma Unit) overhead laughed and spread out, as our irreplaceable obsidian armor blew away on the wind, gone, in all the directions. The world snapped, my necklace burned my neck before flashing out entirely, the claws died, the wings dropped, and Lynn did too. Thankfully the last push from our winged arc dropped us ten feet over the roof, right to legs and butts. There was no armor this time, it was skin on cement—but rooftop, not sidewalk. I took a hit to the hip but rolled the rest off; I saw Lynn's shoulder snap back but she tensed up enough to keep her head an inch away from the ground. We were bodied, but we would live. Then someone else hit the ground next to us.

"Got… you…"

Lukas had fallen too for some reason, ghost-white and face-first into the ground beside me, no hands to catch his fall.

"But did you?" Lynn said sadly, holding her shoulder.

"What did you call it?" Lukas asked the roof, making me flinch away from his face-down body (but glad he was still alive). "Flight pattern astral?"

"We asked Heather to make a ship invisible," I said. "She said no."

"I should have said no," Lukas said softly.

I got the feeling he was talking about more than this. His bloody face was in the ground, wheezing. It was only as interesting as it was macabre—apparently, like everything, the power of the Reaper had its limits? It was sad, but the Scarlet showing up out of the invisible dimension here was less sad, and more planned. That meant we were the target. I had seen a lot from Infinite, but using a Reaper to hide a Reaper-killer, and then sacrificing him to it…

"This is all you'll ever be to them," I said. "The tool that makes the change engine possible, and the first victim of their new world."

I thought I saw something in his only open eye… then he was out.

"He's… breathing," Lynn winced, standing up. "Score one for some bull—"

"What on island do you think you're doing?" Hannah asked, pushing the machine across the roof towards us.

"Equal parts proving our worth and serving penance by mitigating the worst of a storm we caused by being stupid young and handsome, why do you ask?" I said/coughed out, a sharp pain in my ribs. "We have ways, you mad?"

"We all saw the Reaper," Hannah said. "How close they got to the waterfall. If that's your help, you officially have too many ways."

"There's only one sun, why can't we just see the same light?" I pouted.

Some part of Hannah wanted to fight me, I could see it. But then her eyes snapped up to the skies. I felt the wind too. I clenched my teeth. I knew he was coming, I just didn't want to see it. I thought this was our fight; Hannah and Lukas versus Lynn and me. That I could handle. What came next, less so.

"You're asking the wrong people," came the voice.

"What if I'm asking you?" I said, my back still turned.

"Easy answer," Issaic said slowly. "I don't want the light."

We were so high up the clouds were surrounding us on all sides—or maybe that was the storm. Either way, it had found a way to get worse. Issaic had landed on the open rooftop with as much subtlety as a king cobra. I felt Lynn take a step towards me, or maybe it was the other way around.

"What if you don't… what?" I asked.

"You heard me," he said. "Even if you were actually able to put an end to this natural disaster, we'll see it again. And again. This city will now survive without electricity the same as we've survived with it, at the will of the Infinite."

"So all the talk of the city," I said. "That was lies too?"

"Silka will live," Issaic said. "The people, well, they come and go."

"But not you," Lynn said.

"No," Issaic said, shaking his head. "I'm too important. Silka needs me, whether she knows it or not. Now… well, I'll be everything to her. I reckon thirty days in, she'll forget any other way, but—"

"Your way," I said. "That's what this is about? Right now? You're really gonna go for terrible supervillain bingo—"

"WHO ELSE BUT ME?" Issaic roared.

"Bingo," Lynn said sadly, quietly.

"Who else can protect the legend of the city from threats like *you?*"

"A city isn't made of legends," Lynn said, louder. "It's made of people. You gonna let us continue the evacuation effort or not?"

"I am not," Issaic said, coming closer with every step, because that's how walking worked. "I have no doubt you would contribute to the effort. But I can no longer calculate what that contribution might look like."

"Easy, fire-breathing, talking elephants," Lynn shot back.

"Maybe," Issaic growled. "Wouldn't be surprised. You first son. If it helps, I'm sorry."

"Me too. About what though—ow."

There was a foot in my stomach before I realized what was happening. I swear my eyes saw the shoe, my heart registered it was my own father who'd kicked me, and only then the pain shot through my chest, as my back hit the black granite of the rooftop.

"Not about that," Issaic said. "About this."

"Hey man," Lynn said.

I was on my back. He had kicked me so perfectly, I felt like a knife had me by the spleen. I tried to look up but my abdominals screamed at me, and I had to crane my neck as far as possible to see.

"DUDE!" I said/coughed.

Issaic was backing Lynn towards the edge of the roof. Hannah was on one side, Lukas on the other. She had nowhere to go. Her necklace was quiet, her claws a roof away. She put her hands up but Issaic sent a bolt of white lighting so close to her head I saw a piece of hair burn up like an electric current, and for the first time ever, like *ever*, I saw Lynn flinch.

"Um…" she said.

"My sons are my own to figure out," Issaic said. "I don't know why they've chosen the path of arrant betrayal, but I do know it started with you."

"I only want the best for them," Lynn said.

"The best a Reaper can do is not enough," Issaic said. "Not for a Nite."
"This another pureblood thing?" Lynn shot back.
"It's a contamination thing," Issaic said. "Your days of manipulating your guilt into my sons are over. I understand what this looks like, but it's better to remove the contaminant early. Any objections to what has to be done?"
"No sir," Hannah said, like she was ready for the entire world to die.
"Lukas?" Issaic said.
"I... no sir, of course not," Lukas said, looking down at the ground.
"Less hesitation, next time you lie to me," Issaic said, glaring at Lukas.
"It's okay Lukas," Lynn said. "Survive."
"Ironic, as far as last words go," Issaic said.
Before I could respond, Hannah stomped on the back of my neck so hard I saw stars. My lip and nose were dashed on the ground, the blood was everywhere, even in my eyes. Gross. But I couldn't look away. Issaic stepped within arm's distance of Lynn, her back foot on the edge of the roof.
"Don't..." I garbled. "Stop..."
"It's too late," Issaic said simply.
"It's never too late," Lynn said, maybe just to spite him.
Then Issaic picked Lynn up by the neck and threw her off the rooftop. She tried to grab onto his hands but it wasn't enough. Her hair defied gravity as she left the edge, and her wide eyes stared into mine—until they were gone.
Lynn.
"LYNN!" I shouted, blood flying, body moving in ways I wasn't controlling.
"Let her go son," Issaic said, his hand coming so close to my collar—
But I dropped to my knees and slid past his hand, the edge of the roof coming and going in the same flash, and then there was nothing but the open air of the city to take me down. I didn't know what I expected Issaic to do. Would he shout my name? Would he soar down after me and swoop me away? I guess we learn the most about people in times of crisis. As I fell away from the rooftop with both eyes locked on Lynn, I saw him give the smallest motion to Hannah, and that was it. The city ate my vision on all sides.
In complete free fall, I only blinked. This just didn't make sense. Was Issaic giving me a way out? In a few seconds I'd be far enough from the sliced up Scarlet, and my Reaper powers would kick back in enough to join Lynn somewhere up in the air. All good. I could even see her, only a few stories below, staring up like she wasn't even surprised to see me. Then her eyes went wild. I mean wide. I mean both. She pointed to something behind me, and that's when I heard it. It was something big. It tumbled off the rooftop, crashing into window and concrete, sending a dust cloud of detritus down with it. It was a giant glowing machine, the very one we'd called the Reaper killer not a minutes ago. Even worse, Hannah and Troy were shooting back up into the air above it—they must have wrenched it out and dumped it down after me. After us.
Not good.
"DEREK!" Lynn shouted, less calm for some reason.
I felt the wind on my back like I was free-falling towards the hard concrete ground of the paved street above the shopping center of Silka City (I always

was, but I'd just thought, you know, wings). Without wings, it was a thirty story drop down a skyscraper, and that wasn't happening. I put my head to the enemy's gate (down), and felt my body moving faster than machine, until I caught up to Lynn and would have slammed into her stomach if she hadn't caught me and danced our body weight around. It still hurt, but I was in shock anyways.

"WHY?" I shouted, looking between her and the Reaper machine.

"I don't know," she said, looking between me and the sky and the city. "But we've got the rest of our lives to figure it out."

"Or he does," I said.

In that moment I realized either we would both hit the ground and die, or James would figure it all out in the next ten seconds. And given those odds, I knew what was more practical. I had all the faith in the world in my brother, but if I was going to die, at least it would be with—

"We were meant to meet," I said to Lynn, like they were my last words. "We weren't meant to die alone. We'll die together, or not at all."

"The second one sounds better," she said, seeing how close the ground was rushing towards us. "But if this is it…"

"Don't look down," I said. "Look around."

"Look at life," she said.

But we were only looking at each other. Our heads drifted closer, I saw her eyes look down. I leaned in, she did too, and just as our lips were about to touch, the sky over the Engineerium exploded in the biggest bolt of lightning I had ever seen. It lit up the night so suddenly that it was no longer night. With only a hundred feet left to fall, the midnight was illuminated like nothing I'd ever seen before. For a single moment, it wasn't night any longer.

It was a bright and sunny day in the city, with a beautiful girl in my arms.

JAMES NITE

4.5

THE FALL

"Back off James, you don't know what you're doing," she said, claws up.

"We don't usually fight but I'll die for this," I said, not afraid.

She gave up, I pushed the CD in, and got a good five seconds of soft 90s grunge-rock in before someone turned the volume down, and for the sake of our friendship, gladly, it wasn't Heather. She had both hands on her ears.

"Is it over?" Heather shouted.

"Hi Oracle," I said (grumbled).

"Hi James. I will ignore the attitude."

"Given the trauma," Heather and I finished for her.

"Yes. You learned to speak computer? I'm impressed."

"We learned to learn," I said. "And we need something from you."

"That is why I exist. Go on."

"Go away," I winced. "Just for a minute."

There was a pause. Matchbox Twenty was faint, but there.

"You've got a supercomputer scrambled," Heather said.

"I'm asking her to go radio silent, when she's supposed to protect me the most, especially from strangers," I said. "It's not fair to ask her do that without a reason. That reason is... she's not who I need to talk to right now."

"Damn," was all the Oracle said.

"Language."

"Sorry. Can you explain, James?"

"Most of it," I said. "I mean, the part that's all me, at least. The good thing is, it's never been just me, right Oracle? This car did some super human things underland, where not even the Infinite source can reach. You and I have always had that in common."

"I didn't think about it that way. I am an emergency protocol, built decades ago by Teresa Silk. I was awoken by a technology similar to the Infinite but... hold on. You are correct James Nite, I am no longer powered by the Silka City source. I have a log of a... shift."

"You have a log of a shift?" Heather asked. "Is that code?"

"That's not surprising," I said. "Ten years ago, you had access to something.

Something you don't have the same access to anymore... unless we do."

The CRV jolted, the lights went off, inside and out, just for a moment.

"One bombshell at a time, please."

"Tactically inaccurate."

"Memories aren't war, Heather," I said. "I'm going on the roof."

"But it's storm season!"

"Then I'll take a jacket," I sighed.

"And a helmet?"

No. I slid the moonroof open and pulled myself out on top of the car. The wind was so intense, I had to keep one ankle hooked tight around the opening.

"WHAT ARE YOU DOING?" The oracle said over increasing volume and choir, until she remembered to turn the cd player down.

"I'm seeing about a missing connection," I said. "Something so unreal, it has to be real. Something that sometimes when it's quiet, I can talk to."

"Okay James."

And that was it. Heather closed the moon roof up against my foot, the Oracle turned her volume down. It was just me, talking to the sky, or a ghost, or maybe nothing. But hopefully...

"Okay world," I said, taking a deep breath. "I just made a pretty big bet on myself. I'm not even unconscious, I'm wide awake. But I gotta say, between you and me, I'm kind of new to this whole believing in myself thing. If I could ever use a miracle, it's now. I'm ready to talk. What's it gonna take?"

But no one answered. The universe was silent, the cadence all I had to bear. A bit of hail was falling, some the size of golf balls. Maybe a helmet—

"Caw!"

There was no way. I was starstruck, looking up at the rain/hail, but that noise hadn't come from the angry heavens, it came from the rubber coping on the far edge of the roof. The entire surface area up here was a small rug, it was easy to see the bleach white body, the sunken black eyes, the peppercorn black spots on its wings and tail-feathers. I knew this bird. It was the tyto of the falcon, the killer of the north, another bird with ghost written all over it. It was one of the biggest falcons in the world. The rare gyrfalcon. No typo, yes way.

"You're real?" I asked. "You're—"

The gyrfalcon pecked its beak curiously at the blue stone on my necklace.

"Here?" I said. "Now? Is it too late for the helmet?"

The bird shook its head and stabbed me in the wrist with a beak like a blade, then went back to trying to eat my necklace. It hurt, but I got the message. I held my hand out and the blue sphere shot off my necklace and into my hand. I was about to throw it down my throat—when the falcon snatched it off my hand and swallowed it. I stared at the bird.

"Dude, rude. Sharing is—"

"Finally."

And I had never been closer to falling off the roof of a flying car in a storm. But something else happened too—my right wrist was burning, like the on fire kind of burning. Like someone had put an invisible brand onto my arm.

"AAAHH—I thought you was on the mend!"

I grabbed my wrist in pain. I knew what it was, it was the slashing I'd gotten from the first supersonic bird at the beginning of it all. It had literally died trying to keep itself latched onto my wrist, and to be honest I hadn't looked at it since the first wrap. Now I tore the wrap away and saw…

"Nope, none of this," I said. "What are you, gyrfalcon the spirit bird?"

"How'd you know my name?"

On my wrist was the clearest hallucination I'd ever seen. The scars on my wrist were settled in the lowercase letter 'a' of a Jerico caught in the Blitz.

"How'd that get there?" I said.

"Focus James," the bird said. **"You took a bet and sided with witchcraft, it's time for your trust to pay off. You really haven't given up on me."**

"Might not have planned it that way… but no, I haven't," I said. "Whatever you did to me underland—"

"I got you," the bird said. **"Last time your suits were screaming out for connection, right now something's different. You've severed any server signal that ever originated from the lightning city. You're a blank slate. Retro, I like it—except for the part where you forgot the charge."**

"The what?" I asked.

"You're starting from scratch, which is great, everybody loves an underdog, but the power I'm about to transfer into you is planetary. Your gear is more capable than it looks, but it needs to work before it can work."

"But that's a catch twenty—"

"I know what Matchbox Twenty is," the bird said. **"Trust me James."**

"I'll do it," I said. "What is it?"

"I need you to wait for the bomb cyclone to break. At the updraft the lightning will be the most powerful."

"Okay and then what?" I asked, eagerly.

"I need you to get hit by lightning."

"Oh just that?" I asked. "Just me?"

"Just you."

My face fell. The bird could tell.

"You can take it," the bird said, walking away from me now.

"I can take it?" I asked. "Have you EVER seen me fight lightning?"

"It won't be just you. I watched every move Crete made. He did those clothes justice, so put them on and trust him. All they need is one good jolt. I mean volt."

"You MEAN—" I said, on the edge of panic.

"I'm just asking for a little kiss."

"With a bolt of lightning," I said.

"You ever want to talk to me face to face again, it starts here."

"Is… is that all?" I stammered. "Wait. Starts? This isn't even the end?"

"It's not even our beginning. For that, I'm gonna need you at full tilt."

"To do what?" I asked, suspiciously.

"To save me, without killing everybody."

"Who everybody?" I asked, more suspiciously.

"Wait, switch those two."

"WHAT?"

"JAMES!"

That wasn't bird. It was human. It was Heather, her head popping up through the sunroof, just in time to see the gyrfalcon spread her wings. It hovered in the air, riding the currents over our car, just a flex, purely symbolic.

"Wait," Heather said, pointing. "Bird."

"You know what it is?" the bird said.

"Yeah, what it do," I said without thinking.

Heather dropped her jaw. The bird curled its wings tight against its body and was flung away into the night, on the updrafts of something truly terrifying. Two storms, for the price of—

"Help," I said, my ankle finally slipping.

"I gave you literally five minutes," Heather said. "Who's the polyglot now?"

"Me…" I admitted guiltily.

She grabbed me and dragged me back down through the sunroof. I collapsed in the backseat as the sunroof slid closed and for once, the storm was quiet. The car was too, except for the acoustic interlude in the background.

"I actually like this one," Heather said, nodding her head to the music.

"Can I talk now?"

"Please," I said, numb from the head down.

"What just happened?" Heather asked. "Did you—"

"Yep," I said.

"Okay isn't that a good thing?" Heather asked. "What did she say?"

"She wants me to get struck by lightning," I said, looking down at the change of clothes at my feet. "She says I can take it."

"I'm sorry, who said what now?"

"It's a long story computer," I said sadly, and the Oracle went quiet again.

"She wants…" Heather started, looking at me, then at the clothes, then back at me. "But you're so short. I mean short. I mean sh… small."

"This time… no arguments there," I said. "I can't do this, I'll die. Let's just throw the clothes into the storm, won't that work?"

"It won't," the Oracle said. *"Assuming my spectral analyses are correct, and adjusting for all possible ampere influx… Kira's right, you can take it."*

"I thought you'd try to talk me out of it," I said, then I did a double take. "How do you know a bird?"

"How do YOU know a bird?"

"Circles," I said, as Heather gave me the look.

"You were talking very loudly," the Oracle said. *"The voice recognition had a single match, from a person of interest marked missing in action, ten years ago. A young girl, the only child of Pierre Command. Her name was Kira."*

"Her name IS Kira," I said.

"Damn straight," Heather said, like she had her own reasons for—yeah.

"I would be delighted to update my internal files to mark her alive and active. Do I have permission?"

Heather looked at me. She sort of frowned.

"Maybe just… active," I said. "We haven't really seen her yet, we've only spoken. Assumingely. Over great distances. Through every method of human communication but normal."

"I understand."

"No you don't," Heather corrected.

"I am beginning to. The variable my supercomputer was missing, the power to deploy the lightning in a place where it shouldn't have been possible. The only question is... how in the world is a missing teenage girl in command of this much power to begin with?"

"I don't know Oracle, I don't have all the answers about girls," Heather said sarcastically. "Besides, it's not like James has a personal childhood memory that would explain exactly that."

"That'd be nice though."

I was waiting for Heather to be sarcastic, but she nodded along with the Oracle. Right, I hadn't gotten to that yet. The story was either as fresh as spring flora in my mind, or an underwater painting I couldn't see for the tides. I remembered every moment of what I'd said, but the imagery that the blueblood had conjured into my mind, that was brand new—yet, I'd lived it all.

"Weather report. It's bad."

"How bad?" I asked.

"Hold on to something bad. Like, NOW!"

Right. The sky opened up before us and exploded in lightning from every angle, because storm season. We barely had time to grab each other. We were each other's somethings. Aw—

"We're GONNA DIE!" Heather shouted, already upside down.

The car drove itself, we could only hold on and be ready to roll or dodge with no warning. I had one hand on the seatbelt and the other around Heather's head. The car slammed us right into the window and I took the brunt on my back but didn't feel it, I could only see a nightmare outside the window I'd just cracked, the electric bolts curving slightly in the after-burn, clearly following our car before fading out completely. Wherever we went,8 we were drawing lighting closer and closer. It could only mean one thing.

The flying metal car was a perfect lightning rod. Of course.

"At least we're making this easy for you," Heather said to me.

"How is any of this EASY?"

"Level," the Oracle said, as she stopped putting us through g-force training.

Finally. I realized how hard I had Heather in my arms, and I let up—only to not budge an inch. Something about sudden death had taken the breath out of me. Now that I needed it back, I couldn't breathe. But before I said anything about it, I looked down at the girl with her head in my neck, her hands pinning us against the door, holding the seatbelt as hard as she was holding my back. For all the short jokes her entire body was on me, her legs were in my lap and everything. I had never seen Heather dive for cover before. I had never seen her throw her life in my hands either. Yet... she'd just done both. Like maybe I was somebody who could do something about it.

Like maybe I could do this.

"Strategic," I said. "A single point of potential energy."

"Crash protocol," Heather said, her words vibrating my chest.

"The threat is passed," the Oracle said. *"You can disengage crash protocol, if that's what this is."*

"Yeah," Heather said, lifting her head up for the first time. She slid off my legs, but not by much. Our arms were the last to leave, and she looked at me, weird. Like she was proud of me. For something I hadn't even done yet… wait.

"Yes," Heather said.

"Yes to what?" I asked.

"What you're thinking right now," she said. "You're wondering if we're thinking the same thing. We are, I'll prove it. I think you can take it too."

"How could you know that?" I said.

"You're here for a reason. I think it's this."

"You're just saying that so you don't have to get HIT BY LIGHTING!"

"I'm saying it because it's true," she said. "You have a problem with truth?"

"You know WHAT?" I was ready to argue, but I couldn't. "No. The truth has done me dirty about eleven times this summer, but I still wouldn't change it. It's what got me here, I have no problems with the truth. If what's true is true, and if you can't change the truth, both of which I believe, then the only ones with problems are the liars."

"You… talk like that more often," Heather said, looking at me even weirder.

"Yeah well I…"

I wanted to kiss her.

I had never had that urge before. She was holding eye contact with me and literally leaning in, I felt like, I don't know, wasn't that the signal? What was I waiting for, the actual bat-signal? We were in the backseat of that car together, it would be easy. But it would also be complicated. And just as I was about to make a decision, Heather put her forehead against mine. Her hand was on my shoulder, her hair was instantly covering my face. It wasn't a kiss lean, it was even better. She was using my face as a crutch, leaning on me for support. There was no way I would let her down.

]This was better than kissing. What had I missed? Who lied to me?

"As long as you're being all honest and sweet and all," she said. "I am glad I don't have to get hit by lightning. I'm so happy it's you, and not me. I'm from the underland man, I'd rather be buried alive."

"But I already did that too!" I said, laughing into her hair.

"You did? When? Where was I?"

"After we got Lynn out," I said, the memories coming over my head like, well, a cave in. "We got the breakdown end of Odd's secret tunnel. They saw the light, we saw what the Reaper was really meant to do. You and Luthor were—"

"That's why you were so dirty," Heather said. "I just thought, you know, boy. How'd you get out?"

"Jett—"

Then I realizing what I was saying. My throat closed up, I literally choked on the next words. Heather's hand was slowly exploring my neck. I didn't realize it until we stopped talking. I felt her fingers tense up, then they held onto me hard.

Not like she was trying to hurt me. More like she wasn't letting go.

"He died for us," she said. "I don't know if his family knows. I don't... I don't even know if he has family."

I saw his body in my mind, lying there in the endless bowl on the downside of the extruding half-cliffs of Cradlesong. He had every claw out, but they weren't moving, as he lay beside the ended body of agent, leader, and pilot Mara Stone. None of us had seen what happened. No one had taken responsibility. But it wasn't about who had decided to take their lives. It was about what they had done with the last minutes of them. One was Infinite and one was Reaper, but in the face of the end, they found a way to fight together. Even if it was forever.

"We did all we could," I said.

"We did everything," Heather said. "The Reaper live. Ten years of desolation undone, the sky the ground, the sun the limit. I don't know how anyone can die more of a hero, except maybe eventually, us. But the younger the greater, when it comes to martyrs—I mean heroes, right? And he was so tall too..."

"He's... got me there," I admitted, remembering Jett was our age. "You sure the lighting will reach me all the way down here?"

"You aren't short," she said. "I'm trained to attack, that's my default."

"But I'm not even your enemy!" I said.

"I know that," Heather said. "If you want me to say it I'll say it."

"You don't have to say it—"

"I don't want to see you dead, that's it, the end," Heather said. "That's my only setting for positive emotion. Is that not romantic? Have you not seen the black and white version of The Notebo—"

"I got it," I said.

"I know you do, I'll prove it right now," Heather said. "Would you let me take the hit for you, if I offered?"

I thought on that. For all her sarcasm, for as much as I knew this was just hypothetical. The answer was the same. Interesting.

"Never."

"Why?" Heather asked, unsurprised. "Because I'm a girl? Because you're trying to out-hero a dead guy and his very tall—I mean long legacy?"

"Neither," I said. "Because this is my past—I mean future. Actually both. You helped us find a way to keep the Jerico out of this fight. If I'm learning from the best, then I have to do the same. I can do this."

"Say it," Heather said. "And believe it. Believe in you, James. I do."

"I can take it," I said, quietly, then my eyes snapped into focus. "All that, just to make me—"

"You had to," Heather said. "Glad you figured it out in the car. Otherwise I was going to kick you out, if that wasn't clear. Tough feet, tough love."

I finally realized. She wasn't leaning on me, she was pinning me against the door, her right hand on the handle. So much for crash protocol.

"That's not the saying," I smiled.

"You're not the saying," Heather said. "You gotta be all mature for some reason. Big man, too good to get kicked out the door."

I smiled. "I spent half of this story talking about skateboards. When I grow up, you'll know it, I hope. Get off me—and don't peek."

"I have to, if you're losing your obsidian armor, I have to make sure you don't waste a speck of dust," Heather said, backing off (but only kind of). "We're a mile up in the air, rock's a valuable thing. Don't be shy."

I stared at her, thought hard about whether or not I still had clean(ish) jungle underwear on under all this, decided to roll the dice, and in a single move my necklace lit up, Heather's did too, and the polished black stone around my body gave way to skin and—yes, thank the universe, clean boxers, the good kind of brown (they came that way). But nothing else. Heather wove her hand around the dirt and formed it all into a sphere of black obsidian the size of a soccer ball, as I pulled some light blue socks and pants on. I felt a rush of nostalgia putting shoes on again, we had gone so long without them in Jerico—but these were the speed shoes, maybe the first step we'd ever taken into the world of what Infinite was capable of. There had always been a vibration to them, a reminder that they were ready to break the sound barrier, just say the word. Right now the shoes weren't giving off that vibration. They were unconnected, just like us. I knew if this plan worked, they would all come back online like in the beginning, when there was nothing we couldn't do, no mountain too high, no valley too low—

"Someone forget the shirt?" I asked.

"Must have," Heather said, staring at me. "Well, we take what we can get."

"It's underneath the rear left seat cushion," the Oracle said. *"I wonder—"*

"Damnit—I mean yeah, weird," Heather said.

I pulled it on. As expected, nothing happened, except for the memories.

"We didn't have to carve out half the suit for it to work underland," I said.

"This is not underland," the Oracle said. *"I take it you don't want the army tracking your every move, or controlling your on and off switch?"*

"No," I said.

"And am I correct in assuming you are again counting on a connection outside the Infinite's control?"

"We are," Heather said.

"I am continuing to understand. That could only mean... overridden."

"Excuse me?" I asked.

"The results of that computation are overridden. Overridden. I'm not saying overridden, I'm saying overridden."

"And you wonder why we're going off the grid," I said.

"Not anymore," the Oracle said. *"I was not aware of any limitations to my programming. Allow me a minute to decrypt this sh—ensitive information."*

"Okay great," I said, taking the door handle myself. "Oracle, whenever you're done hacking yourself, identify the strongest lighting clusters, and take me there. Make sure to get Heather out safe before anything gets too hot. Then… I guess just stay close enough to catch me, if it all goes to—"

"Understood."

"He meant me," Heather said.

"I did actually," I said.

"Are we going to have problems?"

Heather screwed up her face. "Overridden."

"Can we not?" I asked the world, shaking my head—and my everything, as the car flew on so fast the seats started rumbling.

What happened next was the buildup to the fall. I could sense the plan, everyone knew it, everyone had agreed to it. The car flew up higher and higher, Heather only holding me against the seat for the turbulence, until it seemed we were over an entirely new planet. The world below was wisps of wind and barrels of rain and swirling, raging electrical currents. It was endless.

"Get me close enough," I said.

"Holy..." Heather said, blinking. "Will do. Wait—"

I saw them at the same time. There were all sorts of flying figures in the eye of the storm, almost like they were waiting for us. I counted fifteen soldiers in the background who slowly pulled their facial screens and longsleeve hoods up over their heads. There were two in the front, already ready for war, covered head to toe light-blue, crackling superwear, with the metal bulges of what I was sure was an under-layer of bulletproof armor.

"They were waiting for us," Heather said, her eyes out the windows. "Here, where nobody can see what happens. James... it's a kill squad."

"It's the same two from the Planetarium," I said. "It's Jemeni. It's a trap. We're trapped like—"

"Rat bast—" Heather seethed.

"LANGUAGE."

And all at once, all seventeen agents hit their jet boots and rocketed towards us with their weapons and/or palms aimed at us.

"If it's all the same... I'd take that helmet now," I said.

We clicked in our seatbelts and just in time—the car was upside down a second later, dodging the blaster fire and oncoming bodies at mach 1.0, whipping us around like the car was a fighter jet. I saw three agents get slammed out of the sky by the doors and sunroof opening hard whenever a soldier got too close. The centrifugal force of an upside down loop slammed the car into our backs, then the seatbelts caught us as the car flew out of it backwards. I looked out the windshield to see ten agents soaring to us with their hands outstretched like Superman. They only shouted louder, the car only reversed faster.

"ANY IDEAS?" I shouted to Heather, the blood rushing to my head.

"Always," she said. "Give me your clothes."

Maybe it was the clear mind of being seconds away from dying, but I knew exactly what she meant. I looked down to the roof of the car where a certain obsidian soccer ball-sized piece of rock was rolling around the ceiling (we were still upside down). I reached, but my fingers were just out of reach of the rock. I was glad Heather hadn't seen me fail the first time, she had her eyes locked on the assailants out the windshield. All I knew was she needed that soccer ball, and that soccer ball used to be my clothes. I thought about drawing the rock around me for the simple purpose of armor—and the rock ball shot to my hand, defying gravity and momentum, snapping to me like a magnet. Small steps, small victories. I had just moved the dirt. I handed my prize over to Heather, she held up (or down?) her hand and the soccer ball of rocky road armor from the backseat levitated out of my hands and into hers. Then she smashed it out the window and stared through the windshield at the oncoming agents.

"ALL OVER MY FLOOR!" I shouted.

My hands covered my head, bits of glass hitting me in the face, just as easily being blown out the rotating window, with no consistent ground to fall upon, neither seats nor ceiling.

"No talk back," she said. "It's glass, find the minerals and move it like sand."

"Oh," I said. "It's that easy—OWW!"

I sent a single thought-command to my necklace, get the glass away from me. It worked, I moved glass like loose pebbles, but that meant all the little shards in my neck and arms came out too. From places I didn't even know had been stuck. A hundred needles, all at once, that's what it felt like.

"Always hated glass," Heather said. "Now you know."

"I liked not knowing!" I half cried, angrily sending all the loose glass in arms reach out the open window. I moved dirt and glass for her, she couldn't press a window button for me?

The answer was no, like usual. Not when she was keeping us alive singlehandedly, like usual. A piece of rock shot off the soccer ball and slammed the point agent in the face. The rock molded over his facial screen and pulled him down like a heavyweight, the agent screaming and flailing the entire time. I saw the horrified looks on the next few agent's faces, as they saw their comrade yanked down to the dirt by the dirt, as they realized they were next.

"No, NO!" One of them shouted. "NOT LIKE THIS!"

Heather clenched her fist, the rock flew, and suddenly the windshield was clear of enemies. Ten for ten. Not bad.

"I knew you had it," I said, trying to be nonchalant in the face of battle.

"It took your armor," she said, looking serious. "You have nothing now."

"I have everything now," I said. "But that wasn't all of them. I counted ten down, seventeen total."

"I had seventeen too," Heather said, looking around. "Where—"

"Get in!" I shouted.

I yanked her away from the window, pulling her arm back into the car just as a bolt of plasma sliced through the air right where it had been, glancing off the hood of the car. The car spun upright and my butt finally touched back down.

"I… totally saw that coming," Heather said.

The car sizzled, and a light blue force field could be seen for a brief moment around it. Then I realized there was no damage to the hood. No scorch mark, no dent. That meant we had enough of a shield to be advancing, not retreating.

"You can't stay in there forever," came a voice.

It was one of the full-suited Infinite agents, flying alongside the car, a hand on the broken window, the wind screaming through. The agent lowered his facial screen, it was Jemeni alright.

"Watch the glass," I said unconsciously, my mind numb.

"I know we found something," Jemeni shouted into the car. "But the next time you conspire against the city together, tell Astor this from me: well played."

I couldn't think of what to say. What to give away. How much information to let Jemeni walk away with. He was dangerous, I wished he wasn't.

"Stammer much?" Jemeni said, putting his hand through the window, letting us all see the glowing palm glove, powering up with the most cliche of superpowers. "Pull over or I'll—AAAHHH!"

Jemeni screamed, as Heather molded the last of my rock armor around his wrist and put as much torque into it as she could (without completely disintegrating the bones). As it was, his wrist was already broken, the palm turned all the way around to face its owner at an impossible angle.

"Take your shot," Heather said, ice cold. "After all, you already know everything, don't you?"

"You can't be..." Jemeni's voice quivered, staring his own canon down.

"Stammer much?"

"You're CRAZY!"

"You don't say that to a lady," I said, making sure to duck.

"NOT LIKE THIS!"

Jemeni barely got his facial shield back on before his own hand blaster went off, slamming him in the face with the redirected power of the sun. Bam.

The car was thrown sideways with the explosion, I felt the heat even with Heather in between us. Jemeni flew off towards the ground with no life in his free-falling body, and another white shape dived down after him. I hoped it was whoever had backed him up at the Planetarium, we still weren't sure of a name. It couldn't have been Benjann, he crawled up from the underland with Reya.

"That was for Sophia, the best indoor pet I never wanted," Heather growled. "I should have killed him."

"I'm glad you didn't," I said. "That was perfect Heather. Tactically, ruthlessly perfect."

"Thank you James," she said. "That... means a lot. What now?"

"Easy," I said, taking a deep breath. "Oracle, we're going backwards."

"Are you sure James?"

"Absolutely not," I said. "But we have to try."

"Seconded," Heather said, looking at me weird. "Do what he says computer. We run from no one."

"Yes Ma'am."

The car pivoted on a dime and suddenly the winds were less, as we started flying back towards the center of the storm, instead of seeking refuge in the clouds, where the rotations were much less forgiving. This time there weren't so many figures in the sky waiting to take us head on. This time, there were none.

"Approaching the center," the Oracle said. *"Ten seconds to optimal launch."*

"See," I said, dazed. "I got everything."

"I have a hard time believing that," Heather said.

"That's the key," I said. "You gotta believe."

"James," Heather said before I opened the door. "I'll believe, as long as you don't miss."

I looked down into a nightmare, worst case scenario. Damn you imagination.
"How could I miss?" I said.
BOOM.
"Incoming."
I knew that alert. I looked out the window to see a single Infinite agent hovering only a few thousand feet away from us. He had the back half of a rocketeer launcher in his hand, and this one clearly wasn't missing a firing pin, because it was already out of the gate, and on course to torpedo into us at twenty thousand feet. But the explosive rocket locked onto our flying car wasn't the worst part. The worst part was the face, no longer hidden behind any facial screen. It was another long forgotten friend from superball, from blue panel.
It was Eve.
"Not you," I heard myself say.
"Tough feet, tough love!" Heather said, claws down, legs up.
"NO!"
Too late, I had a car window in my face and two feet in my back before I could say ow. Heather kicked the door open with my face and shoved me out, right before the Oracle shut it so hard it broke what was left of the window behind me. The air took me immediately, there was already a hundred feet of nothing between us. The world slowed to exist in a blink, the wind in my ears, the missile in slow motion, but not, entering my peripheral vision almost invisibly fast—then it missed the hood of the car by inches, making its way up and on course to fly over the storm entirely. Recurving itself towards what could only be… the great wide north.
"Gotta go," Heather said while we were still close enough to fall apart.
"HEATHER!"
Too late. The car sped off on course to intercept the missile, both of them aimed directly down the path this storm had come from. The missile wasn't for us. It was just Issaic's longest ranged attempt at setting the jungle on fire.
"Please jump out," I felt myself saying, right before the car caught up to the missile. "Please—"
Boom.
I felt the ash in my lungs, or maybe it was just the shockwave. I watched as the car either sped or fell away with Heather inside it, the entire thing a flaming fireball with thick black smoke trailing it wherever it went, losing altitude about as fast as I was as I plummeted, free falling, with no backup plan. The car could take a laser, but a missile, clearly not. And there was nothing on the wind or in my ears. No flying car. No wings. No purple haired girl who challenged everything I'd ever thought made up my moral compass, making me better, or maybe just more informed and educated, just by being around her.
"SURVIVE!" I shouted desperately. "YOU HAVE TO—"
And that was it. My vocal cords tightened, the air in my throat suddenly stung. I had thrown my voice out in four words. I couldn't talk, I couldn't even cry. I clenched my shoulders but there were no Reaper wings to take me into the sky—mine nor Heather's. She was gone and I was alone, both bad. I kicked my shoes, the jets didn't work. I had always been able to fly. Now, when I needed it

the most, all I could do was fall, my hand outstretched to the car like Heather would be able to grab onto it.

And that's how I fell into the eye of the storm. Upside down, broken, past the edge of panic, in control of NOTHING, reaching out to something I couldn't hope to touch. I couldn't even cry, my throat hurt too much. It was almost silent. Almost. But the view was better this way. I watched the clouds get farther away, letting all thoughts of the actual ground escape my mind. I was clocking those electrical currents in the sky, sensing the charge in the humidity around me. Until I knew Heather was alive, I wouldn't be myself. But whoever I was at that moment, I wasn't giving anything up. For crazy reasons, and just maybe, problem solving reasons. Any normal person, any normal car, they would have been gone for. But me…

"I'll believe normal from you when I see it," Willa's voice rang in my ear.

Heather was a lot of things, but normal, no. It wasn't the her I was worried about. Not the sky, nor the ground. It was us.

"Let's do it," I thought to myself, my teeth clenched shut. "Do it now, while there's still time… to save her. Fire from the gods, yeah? Prove it."

The sky proved it.

At once a hundred lightning bolts lit up around me. No warning, no arc, one ear-shattering moment they weren't there and the next, they were. My eyes watched that flaming car on its careening descent into the farmlands until my eyes were alive with electricity.

"AaaaAAAHHH!"

I felt every tinge of thunder in my bones. I coughed blood in between spasms. That was the only thing I remember doing, because the rest of my body couldn't move. I hadn't gotten hit by lightning, not by a single bolt. I'd been hit with at least four. They had all coalesced into a single explosive strike in the middle of my chest. My heart was in shock, my body the same. I couldn't move. I wasn't falling anymore, the pain was enough to hold onto.

"You did it," came the voice. **"It'd be weird if I turned out to be the villain, right?"**

"Please don't…" I said, in a different kind of shock—I could talk. My throat wasn't tight.

"Never. I'm not boring."

"Don't… let her die," I finished.

"How is that on me?" the voice argued. **"Do you know what you're about to be able to do? Here's the short answer. Everything. Why are you still afraid of anything?"**

And then my feet started vibrating. That sounds so weird, it was just the super shoes. But I could feel it. I felt the goosebumps all along my body as the fabric folded into itself, shirt into pants into socks into shoes, creating a single, unified body of Infinite superwear, just like we'd started with (and then lost a bunch of times). It didn't matter. This time would be different.

I'd make sure of it.

4.6

NOT SOLDIERS

From the fall, came the flight. Boom.

Something invisible snapped over my head and suddenly the wind wasn't tearing into my eyes. I could see again, I could blink radars and relay screens into view again. But this time, there was no hood. My head was exposed, it was the rest of me that lit up—as the ground came up fast, closer than ever. And my feet were vibrating. That could only mean one thing: all the things.

"Outta here!" I shouted, trusting Lynn to hold on harder (she did).

A hundred feet away from the bottom of the cliff, with the exoskeleton of half a super-ship and a glowing Reaper killing cube about to bury us from above, Lynn wrapped her legs and arms around me. I let my feet rotate one last time, then I gently pushed us left, out of the plane's plummet, and took off at enough speed to avoid slamming into the ground, arching (arcing?) us back into the air like it was nothing. Talk about timing. Talk about half a plane smashing into a thousand pieces against the concrete of main-street, while we flew away on the power of friendship.

"I LOVE YOU BROTHER!" I shouted to the world.

It was over—the fall, at least. Lynn was right there with me, shouting her head off in relief, both heavy and absolutely weightless in my hands, but there was no way on island or earth I was letting go. I was flying. We were flying, and it wasn't on wings, and that wasn't a metaphor.

"You did it," she said, looking at me like the sun.

I unclenched. Everything. The light danced across Lynn's face, lighting up the curve of her nose, the dust on her forehead, the perfect skin across her cheeks and chin, the black eyes that were determined not to break, the brown hair that had admittedly seen better (and less humid) days. I should have been thinking about how much she meant to us and our little family. I should have been thinking about how many times she had saved my life without making a big deal out of it. But all I could think about was how beautiful she was.

"You saved me," Lynn said. "Instead of the other way around, for once."

"Just once," I said, sounding all emotional about it, instead of cool.

Lynn looked at me weird, like usual. Then she kissed me on the cheek, so sweetly, so quickly, I didn't have a chance to blink. But I felt the spark. The world did too, I saw it. The lightning flew, the storm raged, and when she pulled away, Lynn's hands were alive with yellow electricity. Her clothes were primed, we both watched the raw static come in tiny, curving, crackling bolts from head to toe. Yeah, she had taken the connection. But this time—

"My router," Lynn said, with a smile on her face, and a small sun in the palm of her hand. How could I say no?

"I guess...scientifically speaking," I said, hoping my face wasn't too red.

"But it was just a peck," she said. "It wasn't even on the—oh."

"What?" I said.

"Nothing bad," Lynn said, turning away. "You must... really like me."

I didn't know how to respond to that (except by nodding hard). But before I could, we came in to land back on that skyscraper roof facing Issaic down, the very one he'd tried to kill us from. No rooftop for romance.

"I'll be damned," Issaic said.

"You are," I said. "We're fine, by the way. What were you again?"

"The man with all the questions," Issaic said, a darkness in his eyes, as he held his hand out to us in a flash of light—

That James blocked, his watch emerging into a gigantic shield, powerful enough to stop even Issaic's attacks. He had dropped from the sky in a nano second right between Lynn and me, and when the lasers stopped, the shield did too. But when the shield fell, the sword took its place.

"I love you too, brother," he said, without looking at me. Yes.

"Perfect timing," I said sideways, blade first. "What happened to the car?"

Beep.

Even better. The smoking remains of a CRV with no windows rolled out of the fog, from where the rooftop ended. The passenger door opened and Heather took a step out on shaky legs, her entire face ashen with dirt and minerals.

"It's got aluminum in it," Heather said, her head twitching, until James held a hand out to her, she flinched, then took it. "Am I dreaming, dream boy?"

"Aw," James said, touching his heart.

"You're alive, so no," Issaic said, rudely.

Right. The part where that guy... sucked. I stood in the only stance I had ever seen get close to overcoming Issaic's style of combat. The sideways horse stance of Willa the Killa. Issaic was smart enough to do a double take.

"I'll admit, I saw this ending differently," he growled.

"Then see better," James said to Issaic.

It was so sarcastic, I was so proud.

"What if I don't want to?" Issaic said.

"Then how come you're always in our way, man?" I asked.

"I'm NOT!" Issaic shouted. "You're always in MINE! I ask you not to destroy a city, you show up in Infinite superwear with an army of Reaper scouts, what AM I SUPPOSED TO DO?"

"Nothing," Lynn said. "We told you before, we got this. We also agreed to surprise each other. But dropping me off a roof—"

"He did what?" James asked, blinking.

"I had to be sure," Issaic said, his eyes dark.

"Sure about losing your only end to mad season?" Lynn said.

"All I see is a teenage girl shouting at me," he said. "What can you do against the—"

Lynn held her wrist out, the words on the watch as clear as day to read.

Storm 1.0.

"Well that's just… convenient," Issaic scowled.

"Hell… yeah…" Heather coughed from the car.

It was perfect. It was convenient, Issaic wasn't wrong. I knew my watch was capable of producing a razor sharp sword out of absolutely nowhere, but I'd started drawing one with a dulled edge, better for whacking heads instead of slicing them off, because ew. James' watch was able to put a shield of any size between himself and anyone else he chose, objectively dope, a defense for an offense, who could get mad at that? Lynn however, still seemed to fight with fist and foot, sometimes going so hard she drew yellow lightning out of the air itself. Was that her watch, or her? She'd only used her app once that I could remember, to draw a cloak of thunderstorms behind us as we escaped the Infinite underground in a certain, familiar flying car.

"Are we sure?" James asked.

"Absolutely not," Lynn said. "If that could stop us…"

"We wouldn't do anything," I finished.

"Get… a… roof…" Heather coughed from the car.

There was yellow energy around Lynn. It wasn't lightning, it was a softer glow. Again the only thing my stupid teenage could think of was the power of the sun, in the palm of her hand—before she shot up into the sky. For a moment the small crowd of us on that roof only watched her take off like a space launch. She was faster than she'd ever been on wings, leaving a single pillar of light behind her for a jet stream. In seconds she had broken the storm clouds above us and disappeared with as much fanfare a single water droplet in the ocean.

"Takes care of her," Hannah said, shaking her head at the sky.

"You think?" Issaic said.

Hannah dropped her eyes. "A girl can dream…"

"You haven't been paying attention," Issaic said. "Please tell me there's less dreaming, and more going after her. Someone. Anyone."

"Aw, don't worry man, she's got this," I said. "But thanks for the concern."

Issaic sighed. "I wasn't talking to you."

"Oh," Hannah said, like we were about to battle (because duh). "Yes sir."

"Still?" James asked sadly.

"Am I still in control of everything?" Issaic asked. "Then yes, still."

The shooting stars were back. They came up quick from the ground streets of Silka, passing us up on that skyscraper roof at a thousand miles an hour, all trailing Lynn as fast as they could.

"If this ends by pushing a button, I'd should be the one to push it," Issaic shouted. "Bring me that watch, in one piece or a hundred! NOW!"

"YES SIR!"

"No rest," James said, shaking his head.

"Not over," I said.

"That way," Heather said, pointing up, and falling into the car.

James and I shot up into the sky, disappearing into the whirling, flashing clouds of the cyclone. The facial shield upgrade did its best, but I could feel the weight of the winds pressuring me from every side, even if I couldn't feel the ripping air over my skin. This was nuts.

"LYNN!" I shouted into the tempest. "Fancy clothes, find her!"

"Target acquired."

It was as simple as that. I heard the voice, I saw a red flash in the distance, and flew until it got close enough to turn into a girl.

"Go away Derek, I've got this!" Lynn shouted.

"Maybe tell that to them," I said.

There were figures emerging around us, here in the densest part of the storm, the winds and shadows raging all around. I trusted the sensors in my suit. A burst of light came in from my right and my body ducked around it. Then the guy behind the blast hit me from the right. I barely had time to get my sword in between us. He was lucky his sleeves held.

"Find someone in the city, and help them," I said. "Don't come back here. We're not worth it. Not when you could live, and do something good."

"Whatever you say man," he nodded so hard he cut his chin on my blade.

He was gone, but the others came in his place. Like Sand in that crash site clearing, I would let them come. I took the edge of my sword and ran it against my sleeve, metaphorically dulling the edge. I didn't know if it worked, but it would do, something between a shield, a pad, and a crutch. The first guy flew at me head first, I caught him by the shoulders and let him push us backwards for as long as it took to get my feet on him. Then, he was blasting off again. The next was a pair from either side; I ducked right, let them collide, and whacked them in the side of the necks with the dull sword as hard as I could. I felt them feather away. They would hit the ground, and hard, but they would live. I felt hands on me, all sides, and I swung again, using my suit itself as leverage, the suit and armor version of a death roll—trusting my sword to once again lose the real edge. Smart sword.

"What are you, a cartoon?" Came the low voice of an agent with a full blown tornado at his back.

"I'm Derek," I shouted over the winds. "What are you, a tornado boy?"

"My name's Mark," was all he said. "What did you call me?"

I shot forward, flipped my body around at the last second, and was about to mule-kick the guy in the stomach with both feet when I thought about it. He looked at me in fear, then over his shoulder real quick.

"Were you about to kick me into the tornado?" He asked, all fear.

"I was," I said. "But I'm better than that. How about you and I just—"

"Tough feet tough love!" James shouted, zooming in and kicking the guy in the chest, sending him helplessly careening straight into the tornado behind him. Mark disappeared in a shout and an outstretched hand, the last part of him to disappear into the swirling vortex.

"AAAHAaaahh—"

Then tornado boy was gone. Maybe I was a cartoon.

"I was handling that diplomatically," I said, all smiles (sorry Mark).

"We have no friends here, brother," he said.

It was a mood killer for sure. I saw his disapproving look, but it didn't stop me—I flashed forward with every inch of power in my suit, and was back in less than a second, holding a very wet and confused Mark in one hand.

"Did you just—"

"I did," I said proudly. "I'm officially tornado proof."

"I'm not!" Mark complained/coughed water.

James did his best, but couldn't stop the smile, until he could. "It was Eve, Derek. The second soldier, it was her."

"That... sucks," I said, honestly. "Jemeni and Benjann, Ana and Eve. We split them up, what were they supposed to do? Not this, I mean damn."

"For what it's worth, I actually agree," Mark said quietly, as the air screamed above me. Or maybe it was the guy. I knew a distraction when—

"AAAH!"

And before I could look up James had a shield held high, smashing into the head and shoulders of an oncoming Infinite agent who'd been dive-bombing us. He crumbled against James' shield and another flier rushed in to grab him out of the air before he fell from mountainous heights. The others looked at me, then James, then Mark. I threw him into the air, catch and release at worst. Mark hovered away with his hands up, waiting for the catch. No catch, not with us staring him down, along with the only agents brave enough to fly this far up. One by one they floated down and out. Finally. For the first time in forever, we had intimidated someone into not fighting us. It was just me and a big storm, thundergirl was somewhere around here, and—

"No fair, what about our big fight scene?" James complained.

"Already got it," I said. "Just not together. I'm just happy you're walking."

"But Derek," he said, blinking. "I'm flying here."

"Aren't we both," I said, smiling. "Time to end this, you think?"

"It's not even our beginning," my brother said, before shaking himself out of the demonic possession. "Sorry. Time to... whatever you said, brother."

James followed me, as I flew where my facial tracking systems told me to go until I saw her silhouette again, the girl in the storm, the only other flying human this high above the island, in what HAD to be the worst strangerland yet. The winds were worse up here. Lynn had drifted a good hundred feet up. I flew freely up to her, looking over my shoulder the entire way for assailants, but there was nothing there—except for my brother, the always shield, keeping an eye on my back. It was just the three of us. It had always been.

"Issaic still trying to keep us from helping?" Lynn growled.

"He wants Silka to lose power, or order, or both," I said. "I don't know why, but we can stop him here, stop everything here. Please tell me you've got this."

"Are you asking or hoping?" She said.

"I'm asking," I said. "I know you can do it. I know it's only a matter of time. I'm just wondering how many more soldiers I'm going to have to scare the cartoons out of before—"

"None," Lynn said. "Not if I can do something about it."

"Prove it," I said. "But before you do. I want you to know that whatever happens—"

She pressed the button on her watch. She didn't even wait for me to finish.

Storm 1.0.

We froze, holding our breath, but nothing happened for a moment. I blinked. Looked at Lynn. She shrugged. I almost laughed. Then the sky changed colors, and so did the girl. Her face went white. So did the sky around her, as what looked like all the wind and water in the air around us was redirected towards us, somehow spinning and raging even faster and closer than ever before.

"HOW IS THIS NOT A HURRICANE?" I shouted.

"We just passed a hundred and forty knots, this is literally a double hurricane," the Oracle corrected.

Right. I had the Oracle in my skin again. Think clean thoughts…

"She can't do this," James said.

"Are you asking or hoping?"

"I'm—damnit," James said.

"She's got this," I shouted. "James, get clear!"

"WHY?"

"Designated survivor," I said, my throat almost closing up the first time saying that and meaning it. "That got heavy. I just meant—"

"I got you."

And he was gone. In a blink. Without arguing. It meant the world. It meant he knew this wasn't goodbye. It meant he trusted me.

"No… on… gets… left… behind," I seethed as the turbulent air turned my every movement to molasses. "LYNN!"

I was so close to her. I tried to put a hand on her shoulder but I couldn't. There was something repelling every muscle in my body. I saw her going through the same trying to turn her neck, trying to reach for me too, but the closer our hands got, the more the pressure built. I was giving her everything I had, trying anything I could, I just couldn't. Because I didn't need to. She was enough. The only light in the sky as big as a storm, and still growing.

"I'm… okay," Lynn called, her body lost among the clouds. "Is it working?"

But either I was too close to the change machine or part of it, and without warning the sky imploded and changed colors again and I was falling, butt-first, both hands stretched out to the girl in the clouds. The pressure had broken and sent me an entire layer of atmosphere away. I caught myself in the air around skyscraper height, with the soldiers and civilians on their roofs all around downtown. But that wasn't all. From the portside to the Engineerium, over the waterfall and all around the valley cliffs, Silka's higher grounds were full of faces. We could see all the way through the city again.

"What a lovely view," I said, the hair on my arms standing up.

In silence, the city agreed. The air was clearing. Anywhere there were people, there were eyes to the skies… watching the storm disappearing. Slowly the light from the full moon overtook the grey clouds, then the clouds were barely there. The yellow glow faded too, then there was nothing in the air but midnight, moonlit skies. The water turned back to blue, the white caps slowly lapping back into a crystal clear, calm ocean. And best of all—

"Please tell me you—"

"I seen it," I said.

It was my turn to see the girl come falling out of the sky. My turn to be the one to race after her, albeit this time as weightless as a bird, with enough time in the free-fall to gently pluck her out of the air in a controlled descent. All that to say she leaned against me as we recurved into the sky above Silka, as dead weight as she could be, but very much alive, then she opened her eyes to a world without a cloud in sight. It was just us, and the stars.

"I'm tired," she said, closing her eyes, a small smile on her face.

"Lynn…" I said. There were no words. I was just proud.

"Is it…" I heard one of the agents close to Issaic said. "It's… the moon."

"She's on our side right?" A suit flying over Issaic said.

"Wrong," Issaic said.

"Aw that's not good…"

Issaic scowled, but that's when from waterfall to skyscraper to headquarters, the cheering started. The very last crash of the rain was overtaken by a wild chorus of clapping, stomping, jumping up and down on soaked rooftops, hollering at the tops of their lungs for the returning of the light, crying over the safety of their families.

"You got dirt all over you," Lynn said to me, numbly, the last in the lightning city to open her eyes. "Didn't see it before. Must be the light. Wait. The light…"

I couldn't help it, I was laughing.

"You did it," James said, hovering over to us.

"You pronounced we wrong," Lynn said, holding my shoulder as we all stepped back onto a very specific rooftop by the edge of main street.

"See?" Issaic said. "Solution. I should be awarded."

"Not over," I said. "What about the lights? Should we figure that next?"

"It's already figured," Issaic said. "The lights stay off. There is no way to repair the city's electrical grid during a tropical onslaught."

"No way for electricity to find a way?" I asked, looking over my brand new superwear.

"You know very well I prefer it—" Issaic started to rage, then he stopped. "Why am I hearing an echo?"

"That might be the broadcast," I said.

And we all looked over to the beat down, scorch-stricken flying car on the roof beside us.

"But the city's down," Issaic said.

"The city is not in the city," I said. "Most of the city are taking shelter within the Infinite headquarters. All her refugees have been seeing this through the screens and speakers of a place that is clearly still running on something."

"Since when?" Issaic asked.

"Since it's got aluminum in it," my brother said. "Whatever source is letting you fly around in the blackout, you're going to plug the city grid into it. It's time

Silka ran off Infinite, and not the other way around."

Issaic considered it, arms still folded. "Fine. Reconstruction on the Planetarium and the Hexoscope will begin immediately."

"What?" Lynn said. "But that wasn't the deal. Oh wait."

"It's a better deal," I said, folding my arms, staring Issaic down.

"I don't suppose the city will give me a few quick months of complete electromagnetic shutdown to figure it out?" Issaic asked, facing the car now.

"They will not," James said. "You're gonna have to share, Issaic. At least until the building's done. Consider us your new storm deterrent, as long as you hand over to the city what you've been sitting on for years. All the power."

Issaic glared at us. He knew what was going on. He knew we weren't bluffing. We were counting on Infinite keeping their own lights on at all costs. The entire plan to get everyone into headquarters had been beneficial to the city, and to us, but not to him. In other words…

"I've been duped," he said.

"Little bit," Heather said, proudly.

"Scorched earth," Lynn said, almost bragging about being alive.

They were the best.

"You may call this your victory, but all I care about is the survival of Silka City and clearly… so do you, if only a little bit," Issaic said. "Of course I will share the power of our ancestors with our people in this newfound state of emergency. What on earth makes you think I wouldn't?"

"Life, memories, everything I've ever seen with my own eyes," I said, looking up, giving the camera exactly what it wanted. "Dad."

"We've a long road to walk before you call me that again, boy," Issaic glared, almost flying off the handle—

We heard the gasps. Literally, half a city and a waterfall away. Then Issaic remembered he was on camera. Realized who I was talking to. Why I'd said what I'd said. It was all a show.

"Well played," Issaic said, his teeth clenched. "Impressive, boys. Time to plug the city back in."

"You're welcome," I said, staring him down.

And even all the way up here, I swear we could almost hear the cheers coming from the land underneath the waterfall. But Issaic winced as he turned on us. There it was. Strike one. We could have thrown him to the wolves, but personally, I was done letting our meddling hurt the innocent. I didn't think tonight was the night anyone should be forced to learn the truth about Issaic Nite. Not when I didn't know that yet myself. Why had I let Issaic know he was being recorded? Maybe we were hoping for some good karma? A kickstart to the old hope machine? I didn't know.

"Off the record?" Issaic said, his back still to us. "Before I take the roof off this skyscraper when I go?"

"Disconnected," the Oracle said through the open door speakers.

"I know that voice," Issaic said. "I know this car, someone's messing with me. That's Star's voice."

"It's your own AI, you should recognize it," I said.

"That's not ours, and that's not why I recognize it," Issaic countered. "You don't know as much as you think. Our source generator was already operating inside a fifty year sundown. The entire Infinite army just barely taps into that power, but you plug a city in, that's a different story. You are asking gods for their godpower, to run space heaters and kettles."

"Then maybe you work fast," I said. "And maybe we think twice before… next time. You know we didn't mean for any of this to happen."

"I—" Issaic started, then stopped. "Was that… an apology?"

"Don't apologize to him, Derek," Lynn said, grabbing me by the arm. "Can we close the door now?"

"For now," Issaic said. "We'll see how long it takes until you're knocking."

"You say that like we don't have an entire island of doors," I said.

"Go," Issaic said. "See what an island thinks of you now. You didn't save this city. You didn't even save the Jerico."

"We were never supposed to," I said. "That's why this happened. Never again."

"Not in Silka," Issaic said, looking at us like he was the one shutting the door. "Maybe this time you don't come back. Maybe you never set foot in the lightning city again, and we'll have that peace you always talk about."

"Are you asking or hoping?" I said, numb.

Issaic didn't answer. He fell off the roof and flew off into the sky. Hannah and Troy left followed a word, only worried looks to us before mirroring Issaic's deadly quiet footsteps. We were left on a rooftop, with a burnt car and the smell of rubber behind us. It was just us. The same four it started with.

"Did that just…" Heather said, through the ash on her lips.

"It's over," James said. "Done? Done?"

"It's not over, but it's over," Lynn said from the ground, holding a hand up.

I grabbed it and pulled her up. Easy as that. We stood on that roof, watching the shooting stars descend back into headquarters, following Issaic like it was all they ever did. The farmlands showed the worst damage—there were upturned construction vehicles and pieces of roofing everywhere, fences and small trees uprooted all over the place, but the city had taken the cyclone and the hurricane like it was built for danger. I didn't see a single broken home, at least not down here in the valley. There was some damage in the Engineerium, but nothing the neighbors couldn't rally together and fix in a week—even without power tools.

Right?

I didn't really know my city. It hit me hard, for the first time. I knew more about the Vema and Jerico at this point. I'd gone a month of summer without talking to a single person I'd ever known in my home city, besides my brother. Could they fix a house without power tools? Could I?

"Be honest," Lynn said, a hand on the door of the CRV, wrenching the side mirror up to see herself. "Who looks the worst?"

"I feel better than I look," Heather said. "Hey Lynn. All that storm's end stuff you did without any help at all… that was cool."

"Hey Heather," James said, as Lynn's eyebrows were lost in her hair for the surprise. "Next time you take a rocket for me… don't."

"It wasn't for you," Heather said.

"I know," James said.

"Aw…" Lynn said quietly, pointing at us all. "Team…"

I blinked myself away from the sky where my father had disappeared into, and turned around just in time to see it. James had walked over to the ashen car, and was using his brand new, freshly cleaned, light blue sleeves to rub the dirt off Heather's face. For half a second, Heather was speechless, looking slightly up at James as he wiped the dirt from her face.

"Hold still, flygirl," James said.

"As long as you're offering," Heather said, helping herself to his fabric, wiping her hands, nose, face and neck all over my brother, using his brand new clothes like a human towel. James let his body go limp, trying not to laugh.

"Am I beautiful now?" Heather asked sarcastically, whipping her hair up and pretending to take off the glasses she didn't wear.

"Give me back my glasses," was all James said, and Heather smiled.

"What am I missing?" Lynn asked, confused.

"The part where we did all we could do?" I said.

"I was there for that," Lynn said.

"Okay great," Heather said. "So what's next? Leave and never look back starting now, or wait on this roof until Infinite arrests us for the third time? Or?"

We were all thinking it.

"I thought we couldn't bring our problems to places any longer," James said.

"But we never even said goodbye," Lynn said.

"True," I said. "I feel like this ends in the jungle. Anyone else?"

"You're carrying enough power to squish the sun," Heather said, arms folded. "Crete did this. He incapacitated the receptors on a legacy supersuit and made a connection with a third party source, outside of Issaic's and Infinite's control. The only territory on-island without regular access to electricity did this, he and they should witness the weight of what his work hath wrought. You're goddamn right this ends in the jungle."

"Exactly," I said. "You just… said it better."

"Well as long as it's like that," Lynn said, looking up to the stars.

"Like that?" James asked, looking down at his hands. "We just accepted the kind of power that kills continents. The things we could do with our hands right now… it's endless. Uncountable. I know a girl just saved the lives of every single citizen in the city, a real hero, hooray Lynn whatever—but is running away REALLY the first thing I'm gonna do with all this power? AGAIN?"

"We're not running away," I said. "We're going home. To the guest house were we left all our stuff, anyway. What we're not doing is causing any more harm to the ecosystem. Sometimes… we can bow out."

James looked up from his hands, to the four of us in light blue superwear, all ready to hold our ground against any physical threat the island had to offer.

"You put it that way, I can hang," he said, cautiously.

"Okay great," I said. "Then—"

"We run from no one," Heather said, her eyes staring out at the horizon. Then she flinched. "What are you guys talking about?"

We stared at her.

"Can we go?" She asked, oblivious, maybe just hungry.

"Come on girl," Lynn said.

And we were flying away, the five of us, including the car. The city would survive, we would be watching the weather report, ready to send Lynn in the next time something bigger than a light shower passed over the city. Stormwatchers, maybe. Friends, more likely.

"They're not following us," Lynn said.

"Confirmed," James said, by the radars only inches from his eyes.

There must have been some sort of head facial screen protection stemming from the neckline of our supershirts, but I didn't build them. I didn't know.

"Can I ask a supercomputing, flying car to double up on that?" I asked.

"You can," the Oracle said. *"I'm with James. All readings clear."*

"We thought that last time," I said. "What about Lukas?"

"What about the tracker pill Crete forced down his throat?" Lynn said, blinking. "Is it time for that to pay off, or are we going to forget about it more?"

Heather laughed.

"I'll be damned," the Oracle said. *"If this is the tracker you're referring to, I beg you, pay it off now."*

The red dot was coming from inside the car. But this time, I was enclosed from head to toe in an impenetrable suit of armor capable of space travel. I was less afraid and more curious. Heather stopped laughing.

"Should I initiate shock protocol?"

"NO!"

The voice hadn't come from us.

"This is one of those times I wish I wasn't right," Lynn said, her eyes closed. "I'm going to open my eyes, and there isn't going to be a frenemy Reaper stowaway in the hatchback. One, two—damnit."

Lukas crystalized into sight, frantically rolling down the window and holding both hands up through it. Our nonchalance felt more menacing than curious, as we slowly circled the car.

"I beg you, wait, hold on," he said, before letting out one good cough. "Finally. That's better, something weird in my throat. Take me home, or kill me. Anywhere but there. Please."

"Anywhere but my car," I said.

"Oracle, what the hell?" James called out, not even mad about it.

"He's really light, and invisible," she said. *"Definitely malnourished."*

"I'm sorry," Lukas said. "I'll get out."

"No you won't," Heather said, pushing the door closed where he tried to open it, right in his face.

"Not like I was using that nose," Lukas said in pain.

"What are you thinking, speaker of the Vema?" My brother asked Heather.

"I'm thinking… Oracle, keep the doors locked please, and take this man to Reya the Red. Tell her it's a gift best opened in Eclipso, far away from Cradle… from our new world initiative. Once she can confirm he is not a timebomb, or a portal to another dimension, I will meet you at the volcano."

"Best ultimatum ever," Lynn said.

"Understood. But... you think the boys are good without me for a minute?"

"Probably not," Heather said honestly. "But it is what it is."

"I trust you, Veman."

"High praise from a flying car," Heather said, fondly. "Hear that Lukas? You're off the fishhook, but there's a compromise. We'll get you underland, but the first stop is the volcanic prison system of Eclipso. You're up to anything, the good old volcano lake mountain will burn it out of you."

"I... was born in the firelands," Lukas said, something like relief coming over his face. "You're sending me home to the briar patch. Thank you Heather."

"Thank us?" Heather asked. "After everything you've done?"

"I know what I've done," Lukas said. "None down there in that lightning city quite know what you've done. Not yet. But I don't care. I don't want to fight you anymore. I don't want to make sense of it, I don't want to justify it. I just want to leave."

"Prove it," my brother said.

We gave Lukas one last look, something between anger and peace, atonement and judgement, fight and flight. This wasn't over. He wasn't absolved of anything. But maybe for once, we could just be cool. For one damn second.

Just cool.

"No one's talking, I must have missed a cue," the Oracle said. *"See you soon."*

And a flying car exited cloud right, blasting off, becoming just another flash of light in the night sky.

"Not mad, but why did you do that?" I asked Heather.

"You don't know what Odd put us through," she said. "How do you expect him to hold up under Issaic?"

"He still threw us into the fire a whole bunch," I said.

"We just did the same to him, welcome to Ocarina," Heather said. "And for all the fighting, no one came out on the right side of anything. All we did was stop the storm we started from destroying Silka. No side won but one."

"Side of life," Lynn said, blinking.

"Let's see that side through when it comes to Lukas, yeah?" Heather said. "What would Mara Stone say about Infinite versus Reaper?"

"She would say... there is no versus, and no threat from one side of those two," I said, my throat closing up for some reason.

"Boom," Heather said. "You're welcome."

"We're free," I sighed. "Like actually free."

"Because we finally lost our shadow?" Lynn said.

"Because hope, Lynn," I said. "Hope."

She looked at me sideways as we flew through the air, only sweetly. Then her eyes frowned, and I felt something on my back.

"Hold still brother," James said, with a foot on my neck and the small of my back. "I'm surfing here."

Lynn bit her lip and soared away, doing circles and loops with Heather as my brother and I surfed through the air.

"Hey Derek," Heather shouted over the clear skies. "Be a kickflip."

"That's not the saying," I said, grinning from ear to ear.

I rotated, and sent myself forward as fast as I could go, feeling my brother's feet landing on my back, holding on until he just couldn't. And that's the way we left Silka City. In complete denial of having just been kicked out. There was the whole part where we'd just saved the city too, and the memory of those cheers, the farmers looking at us for help, the look in Rob's eyes when we flew away. I could see past the threat, itself just another refusal to deal with the real world.

We would come back to it. As sure as I lived and breathed. I was born here, to the port city Silka, on the east coast of the island. I would call it home again.

I'd make sure of it.

4.7

ASTRAL

That wasn't a win. But the dangerous part was… it kinda felt like one.

There was something else on the air as we flew away from the rooftop where Issaic dropped Lynn. Where I'd watched her fall, thinking I was too beat up to do anything about it. Where I'd felt myself surging forward on pure instinct, and from my bad knee no less. I hadn't accepted a world without her, not while I was still breathing.

"Whatever we just did…" Lynn said, reading my thoughts because of course. "Can we all agree that good or bad, for better, worse, or whatever… it worked?"

"It almost didn't," I said. "You almost…"

"Everyone almost," Lynn said, without looking at me. "I'm not special. I'm just glad we survived splitting you two up."

"I can't believe it worked, except of course—" Heather said.

"I can't stop seeing you falling off that roof," I said to Lynn.

"Well I can't stop seeing you in that satellite," Lynn said. "Ask Heather. I cried my eyes out."

"She did," Heather said, nodding in the air. "Which time?"

"I thought you were dead," Lynn said.

"I told her you were," Heather said, nodding. "Again, which time?"

"I only stopped crying when I remembered," Lynn said, ignoring her.

"Remembered what?" I asked.

"That I believe in you," Lynn said. "You got the same hope machine going for me, right?"

My mouth hung open, because the words had literally caught in my throat. She'd flipped a switch in my brain.

"I was going to stammer something," I said, feeling unusually at ease. "But that answer has been yes since coffee. That doesn't mean I still don't worry about you, I still see you falling, your hands reaching out to me before I'd even followed you down—wait."

"Okay if you've got, like, some sort of photographic memory and haven't told us…" Lynn frowned.

“Like Cam Jansen?” Heather asked. “Click?”

“She was about to die, I was in hyper-focus mode for *some* reason,” I shook my head. “ That means you knew I’d follow.”

“Without hesitation,” Lynn said.

“And that James would make it in time?”

“Total fluke,” Heather said.

“I’m RIGHT HERE” James shouted, flying closer.

I laughed. Heather chased James away, while Lynn flew closer. We were going fast, but for once we were in control. Or maybe just I was.

“I really like… that you care,” she said.

It was her turn to stumble over the words. It seemed like she was going to say something else, and recurved. In another world, or maybe just another time, she might have finished that sentence differently. She still could.

I’d make sure of it.

“Always did,” I said, repressing every urge in my body to wink. I was bad at it. Simple, right?

She gave me another weird look, then took off faster than me into the night. I followed, because of course. Heather and James were right behind. We flew loops around each other until the jungles of Jerico were all our eyes could see, and then flew farther, looking for a certain rising rock formation in the distance, the most obvious volcano known to volcanos—when suddenly there was a data screen in front of my eyeballs with a rotating pinpoint of directional lasers and the words *searching for volcanic rock 9*under them. All of this without that very logical hood to neck facial shield/screen we were used to.

“You’re in my head again?” I asked the world. “No hoods, upgrade?”

“No hoods, upgrade,” the Oracle confirmed, almost sarcastic about it too (maybe the reinstall had worked). *“Welcome to the future.”*

“Wait I heard,” James shouted in surprise, even forgetting to finish the sentence. “And we have navigations again? Why are we not using them?”

“Don’t need them,” Lynn shouted, looking to me. “We have Derek.”

I swear, I never cry…

“There!” Heather shouted.

“Oh come on that was CLEARLY MY MOMENT!”

Heather was doing her best to keep up, flying the lowest of all of us, and breathing the hardest. Someone had forgotten to share the new source with her. But she was right, the green sea below us was finally broken by a ring of trees with the sight of open dirt between them. It was a rare break in the behemoth that was the rest of the jungle, only visible from a bird’s eye view (thank you, the gift of flight, still to this day one of my most outlandish fantasies made not just real but NORMAL). It wasn’t as big as the Oleander. This was the still-uncovered crash site near Ravenna. We had left Jerico through this village on the hill, it only made sense to make sure it wasn’t on fire on our way back in. We landed among the open ground, and saw something new.

“The opposite of fire,” Lynn said, impressed.

Four saplings had been planted. They were surrounded by carefully ringed dirt mounds around each, accounting for the massive size they would one day become. Right now they were four small trees swaying in the wind, not exactly goliaths yet but titans all the same, and reaching for the sun. And best of all, the spacing of the mounds took up the entire open field of the once crash site.

It was on the way to healing.

"Are those plants a metaphor?" I asked my brother.

He shook his head, and held both hands out pointing in opposite directions.

"You're just going along with it," I said. "That's your secret."

He put a finger to his lips. "Shh… circle of life."

"They're very pretty," Lynn said, taking one of the four saplings by the trunk, her hands almost weightless as they felt the plant over from stem to leaf. "And healthy. They will grow strong enough to block out the—"

"Heads UP!" Came a voice over our heads, and speaking of the sun.

We looked up to see a huge platform zip-lining down towards us at breakneck speed. I dove away from the sound of hydraulic brakes, the platform stopped in a perfect deceleration, and a group of warrior cadets got off, all holding buckets or shovels or other cleaning supplies. But like normal cleaning supplies. Like electric vacuums and working flashlights.

"Where did that come from?" I said, blinking.

"Derek?" someone said. "Where did you come from?"

"The sky," I answered, logically. "Why?"

All fifteen of the cadets from the platform were in a solid sprint up to Ravenna, there was only one guy looking to us with his back to his own team, his jaw in the dirt.

"Same," he said, flustered. "We watched you over Silka not ten minutes ago, we saw the storm's end, we saw everything! Look! Wait, CRAP!"

And as he pointed to the team he was supposed to be a part of, halfway up the hill already, I realized why it was bright enough to see them all the way over there, at such an hour. There were single bulb lampposts lining the crash site, as well as the path up to Ravenna. They were so dim I hadn't realized it, or maybe I was just used to lights, and had forgotten where I was in the world.

Probably the second.

"Soldier Crete is riding a motorized wooden cart all over Jerico, planting these sun sticks like trees," the soldier said, already backing away from us, about to run off. "Can you believe it? It's the middle of the night, but I can see you like it's day, just look at this! Look at you!"

"Get that flashlight out of my face," smiling. "I see the path, who's it for?"

"It's for cadet Caleb to catch up with his unit," came a voice.

"SIR!" Caleb shouted, as he raced up the hill, last of his unit, but by the looks of it the fastest. "Wait for ME!"

The man sighed. It was Sand Freedom, with Ravenna's leader Nari at his side and a young girl running circles around both of their legs.

"I'm a helicopter I'm a helicopter I'm—LYNN!"

"Hey you," Lynn said, dropping to a knee as Lilypad crashed into her.

"You came back," Lily said. "Can we talk about the animals now?"

Lynn's eyes welled up. She almost laughed, but just hugged her harder.

"You know, back in the old world, there used to be a storytelling stereotype about girls who could talk to animals," Lynn said.

"I just watched Mulan," Lilypad said. "I'm no princess. I'm a dragon."

"I thought you were going to say queen, or a warrior," Lynn said, tearing up.

"I have a dragon in my soul," Lilypad said, her face so intense I felt the heat.

"If she were a real dragon, she would be strong enough to carry her own bags," her father said, his arms loaded with luggage and packs.

Lilypad just shrugged. "I'm a little dragon."

"Smart girl," Heather said. "Leader Nari. What is this?"

"Ravenna is relocating to the Oleander," he said. "There's seventy six of us total, I'm told there's room within the gates."

"More than room," Sand said. "A whole new world."

"I thought that was—" Nari grinned.

"Context is everything," Sand said. "You're doing well by your tribe."

"Change comes," Nari said, with a deep breath. "Change can be good. I'm willing to try. I just… don't know what's wrong with ladders."

"You do this, you can do anything," Sand said, with a grip on one of the four ropes attached to the topline platform.

"Okay but hold my hand," Nari said.

"Weird but whatever," Sand said, no hesitation.

"He was talking to me," Lilypad said.

She pushed Sand aside and dragged her father onto the platform.

"Wait," Lynn said. "I thought the topline crew was…"

"They were," Sand said, holding back with us as the rest of the Ravenna boarded the platform. He spoke low. "There's no good way to say it. Twenty kids, none older than thirty, shot from the back with some sort of poison dart, maybe blowgun or bow, we don't know, then…"

"Found out and transported to the big red roof hospital in plenty time?" James asked, hopefully.

"Not our hospital, but an emergency medical cluster in Arrowstar, yes," Sand said, looking down. "They'll be fine. They're lucky to be alive of course, but—"

"That's better," Heather said. "I mean horrible. There wasn't even a fight?"

"No way Issaic would let an unplugged agent anywhere near a cadet trained for topline," Sand said sadly. "That fight's no fight. Issaic knew the stakes and circumvented them. Admittedly an effective strategy if you and your army are all cowards. And if it's wartime."

"Well then this is war," Heather said, as angry—and tired—as all hell.

I was quiet. I had a name for every one of those topline soldiers. It wasn't fair. We hadn't even seen what was up there, at the peak of the trees. I looked up and somehow my suit responded, my vision zooming in past leaves, trunks, and hundreds of feet. Then, at the very top of the world, I saw it.

"Is that…"

"You noticed," Sand said. "You coming or what?"

We could have flown, but we… didn't. We stepped onboard, and Sand followed us, giving a salute to the sky as he stepped on. The platform started rising in the air. Nari screamed, and Lily laughed. But I had my eyes glued on the top of those wires that seemed to disappear into the trees.

"Hey Steve," I said.

"What?" Lynn asked, looking up. "I'll be—"

"Yeah," Sand said. "The loss of our summer topline warriors was a nonstarter. You are looking at the solution, the Vema volunteers. They arrived here an hour before you did. There is no taboo of the Reaper in Jerico. That's Issaic's thing. They arrived to cheers and crying, offerings of home-sewn tapestries and armor, coins and goodies, and just all sorts of snacks."

"Oh come on," I said.

Trying to ignore my stomach (and bladder) was normal at this point.

"I will say, it's a smoother ride than expected," Nari said.

He was holding onto one of the ropes with every muscle in his body, but looked surprised at the speed and stability of the topline. There were twenty people on that platform with us. Lilypad and her father, fifteen other Ravenna faces that looked sort of familiar, and us. Sand was looking at us like he wanted to laugh, or smile. I couldn't tell.

"What?" I finally asked.

"You're offline," he said. "Yet returned with the power of a continental electrical grid, without any connection to the only island source that even comes close to providing that level of command."

"They're what?" One of the passengers said, his eyes wide at us.

"And?" I asked.

"AND?" Sand blinked. "You're as powerful as the sun, you had a city booing you, the first thing you did with that power was give it back to Silka?"

"Should we have taken separate lifts?" Another passenger said.

"Why don't you just say what you're actually thinking?" I asked, hoping for a life-hack.

"I'm proud of you," Sand said. "There. Happy?"

I was. Unexpectedly so.

"I know I am," Nari said, wiping a tear away from his face. "Don't be fearful. You should be honored to share this flying plank of wood with such wonder-kids."

"He's right, we're in control for once in a blue moon," I said. "Good, because I've kinda had it on the running away. It never works."

"It was a nice intro-superpower," James said. "But from now on… what did you say back there Heather?"

"We run from no one," she said. "I thought it would be a good band name, or a chapter title, something dumb."

"I think Issaic ran away this time," Sand smiled. "Specifically from Lynn."

"I need to thank your programmers," Lynn said, still numb over what she'd done up in the troposphere. "A fruit basket, a coconut cake maybe… unless Crete's allergic."

"You pressed a button called Storm 1.0 and fixed everything," Heather said. "That's worth more than cake."

"That button's been there all summer," Lynn said. "I never needed it before. I'm just… glad we figured it. Now my only question is the usual one. Why did it work so well?"

"James, you want to take this one?" Heather said.

"I mean… no," he said. "I still can't explain what I can't explain."

The platform leveled out and a small Jerico medic unit in waiting went crazy over our new friends from Ravenna. They were covered in blankets and had scientists poking them on every side as they were led off to the Oleander. The rest of us stepped off the platform so it could dive back down for the next group from Ravenna. Lily waved at us as she was directed off with her father and her neighbors. I hoped I waved back, but I was too shook. Also, there was this.

"You," Volf said.

He was leaning against the massive tree trunk that carried on farther up than we could see, a single hand held out to maneuver the rocky handle of a spinning system that was doing all the rope-pulling work for him.

"You look comfortable," Heather said.

"I told him to work smart, not hard," Sasha said from above.

She fell out of the canopy and Volf scrambled up to attention as she landed, on wings of Reaper rock, like it was nothing new.

"Did it work?" Sasha asked. "Everything we did wrong, did you—"

"We did," Lynn said. "But I told you to go home."

"And where's that?" Volf asked.

The rocks still spun behind him, the rope slowly descending, not forgotten.

"Good question," Lynn said sadly.

"Sasha, Volf, the jungle needs you," Sand said. "Everybody else, follow me."

"Right," Volf said, returning to the edge of the trees. "See you around, wonder kids."

"It's been… an honor," Sasha said, before flying up into the green.

"You know these woods," Heather asked Sand, as we looked around at the twisting turns of the tree branch walkway before us.

"I came up in them," Sand said. "That was a long time ago."

"Seems like a lot happened a long time ago," I said.

"You know more than you know, I'll prove it." Sand said. "Why are you here?"

Lynn and Heather looked at me. My brother shrugged.

"To get our stuff?" I offered.

"Awareness," Sand said. "You know we're moving on. How?"

"We?" I asked. "You didn't escape Infinite prison and flee to the Jerico expecting asylum. That was us."

"This time, maybe," Sand said, shrugging.

"THIS time?" I asked.

"Maybe you, maybe we, time is linear," Sand said. "We'll see."

We crossed through the arbor district without seeing a single person in any of the exterior constructs. It made sense if they were all still hidden inside Pluma Petra, but the storm had passed hours ago. Maybe they were all waiting for the day. Either way, we dropped down into the Oleander without the need of a platform or a ladder (unless you were Sand). It was still midnight, and the grass was swords. We could have flown over it, but we didn't. A long path around the grass it was.

Ten minutes later we were outside the cavern walls and single story door entrance to Pluma Petra. It was dark though, and we could hear nothing but snoring from inside. Sand looked to us and shrugged. Everyone was asleep. We didn't need to ring the bells and wake everyone up, what we'd done would keep until the morning. So we continued down the path until we were outside the sliding front door of a familiar guest house.

"Crete is out planting solar lamps," Sand said. "I think I might join him."

"Why?" Heather asked, curiously.

"Because… I love—" Sand started, lamely, predictably.

"That's a joke, not an answer," Heather said.

"Okay well I'm not the ones who stopped a storm and a war tonight," Sand said. "If you were my top soldiers I would give you the night. A vict… an ending this grandiose, the debrief can wait until morning."

"Thank you for not saying victory," James said.

"Did you just compliment us?" I asked, again, so tired I could barely—

"I'm offering you the house, do you not want it?" Sand said.

"Is that your way of telling us to all get a room?" I asked.

Sand wasn't amused. But he wasn't mad. Not exactly.

"You know…" he said. "This goes for all of you… if you had a place on or under island in mind… we could build you a house. Not a guest house, a real home. It doesn't have to be in Jerico. You could design it yourself, you could even build it. I can't do a lot for you, but… you deserve more than a house."

"That was almost… sweet," Heather said.

Sand winked. He didn't have to say another word. He trusted us to trust him, that it would all come later. The four of us entered, the sliding door closed, and like a switch had been finally pressed, like coming home after a long day at work, we all knew we were done. At least for tonight.

"Finally," I said. "No parents."

"Serious question," Heather said. "Do we need to flip for the bathroom, or can two guys let a couple of—"

"Ladies first," I said. "Is that sexist?"

Heather and Lynn were gone before I finished that sentence, and the back door underneath the loft mysteriously slammed shut.

"Apparently, doesn't matter," I said.

"You think they're as hungry as we are?" he asked.

"Only if they're human," I said.

We found ourselves in the kitchen, moving slowly, looking over every wooden construct between living room, kitchen bar, stool, desk and diner patio with reverence. It was probably the last time we'd ever see this place this way.

"Now I really don't understand the strawberries," I said.

"She put one in her mouth and we… shared it," James said, his face red.

"I get it," I said. "Did you… want it?"

"I wanted it," James said. "You and Lynn have this cat and dog thing going on, Heather and I are more… misery loves company."

“That’s bittersweet,” I said.

“I’m working on it,” James said. “Being able to walk again went a long way. But after straw—after we almost kissed, she said the sad thing. That what we’re doing is too important. We’re here for a reason, and barely hanging on as it is. There’s a hundred ways we could screw this up, and we’re also teenagers. The only thing we can do is…”

“Is control our every emotion down to the heart?” I asked. “Maybe they teach you that in Reaper school, but I’ve learned this; either I confront a thing head on, or bury it deep and hope it never rears up, which it always does.”

“No pain worse than real love lost forever,” James said.

“No punishment worse than knowing it was all my fault,” I said.

“Get out of my brain brother,” James said, commiserating. “But also don’t.”

I nodded sadly. I was right there with him.

“So what do I do?” He asked.

“I think you and Heather need to confront some things,” I said. “No more strawberries. Either kiss her or don’t.”

“It’s… not that simple,” James said.

“What I mean is talk to her or don’t,” I said. “Whatever you want from her, or her from you, you’ll figure it out. Just don’t forget to let each other know.”

“Oh,” James said, blinking. “I mean on some level, it is that simple.”

“And that’s the level,” I said, as a door opened underneath a loft.

“Go on then, show me how it’s done,” he dared me.

My face betrayed me. Damn these owl eyes. The girls were back, that meant the bathroom was open. James and I hip-shot a quick rock/paper/scissors under the kitchen counter. He threw scissors. I had thought… thematically… this was one of those times when a notebook didn’t beat a sword.

“A good time for a long walk,” James said, nonchalantly, bowing out.

“What’s this?” Lynn asked, as the girls walked into a mess of a kitchen.

“Our last night in Jerico,” I said. “I was doing my best at putting together one of those, what do you call them? Sean Connery boards?”

“Did you just… what?” Heather asked. “What are you, country club without the golf? You think we’re doing brunch by the fire?”

“Well there is a fireplace,” I said, looking left. “I know what we just did, I was there too. We almost died, and we’ve been up another full day again without trying, this isn’t celebrating, it’s surviving. Cheese?”

Heather still found a way to glare at me so hard that I could see her hulk-smashing me into the ground all around this place.

“It’ll do.”

“Okay great, because I was looking for jam but all I found was fig,” I said, shrugging, like I was sad about it. “I guess I’ll put it next to the sopressa.”

“Remind me why we’re leaving?” Lynn asked.

“How about you remind me of that in eight hours,” Heather said. “You can keep your fancy cheese, what’s for dessert?”

“You tell me,” I said, motioning to the freezer. “There’s more ice cream in that coldstone than Coldstone.”

Lynn made a fist in victory, and the girls made for the freezer together.

“There’s literally no tomorrow,” I said. “If you don’t eat everything, I will.”

“Acceptable,” Heather said.

A minute later, we were up on that loft, a sprawling surface as big as the cabin itself, fifteen feet in the air. Lynn lowered the roof, and in the rare clear skies, we could see all of the Oleander as she slept, as well as the lights slowly moving through the forest canopy beyond. We were on our backs on the two beds up there, all four of us sideways, our feet hanging in the middle.

“I don’t mean to throw the bad vibes around,” I said. “But with all those lights up in the topline… I can’t see the stars.”

“Means you’ll crash into things less,” James said.

“Maybe,” I said.

James took a drink of orange juice out of one of the cleaner plastic cups we’d found in the pantry. We’d wanted glass, but he’d refused for some reason.

“Cap the reconstruction at a hundred days, at worst,” Heather reminded us. “Then back to the way it always was.”

“That’s still a hundred days more than if we hadn’t… you know,” Lynn said.

“I know,” I said. “We won’t pay for those hundred days. Silka will. Lynn, I don’t know what your schedule looks like the next three months but—”

“I’m there,” Lynn said. “I just… like to think I have more of a purpose in this life than sometimes pressing a button.”

“You do,” Heather said. “If your app can do it, Crete can do it. Have him program an automatic response to the shifted storm season. That’ll free you up for the next book—I mean adventure.”

“Hmm,” Lynn said, thinking it over. “I’ll admit, your way I wouldn’t have to be all self-aware and existential. Okay I’m in. I’ll just take my one defining power and turn it back over to a male character.”

“I didn’t mean, wait I thought you said you didn’t have to be so—”

“I know who I am,” Lynn said. “I can’t control the weather, that can’t be my thing. I’ll gladly put that power right back where it belongs. Whoever, whatever. Please and thank you.”

“What if it belongs to you?” I said quietly.

“What are you saying?” Lynn asked.

“If you had to… would you do it?” I asked, trying to keep my face from betraying myself. “Would you become thundergirl?”

Heather laughed—another thing as rare as dirt in the green world.

“Shut up, that’s a terrible superhero name,” Lynn said. “You wanna talk about the level? The level is zero. We have too much power to rise above that zero with anything other than benevolence. From here on out, what we do has to mean something, it just has to. Otherwise—”

“Otherwise it means nothing, and by proxy, so do we,” I finished.

“Was that sarcastic?” Lynn asked.

She turned her neck sideways on her bed and I did too, our bodies a good five feet apart, though somehow it felt much closer.

“No,” I said. “I meant it. I know you did. I need this to be for something too. I don’t want it to be easy, and I’m not just looking for a fight. I’m looking for something…”

"Not temporary?" Heather offered.

"To the end?" James said.

"And over," Lynn said.

"All but never ending," I said. "Funny, there should be a word for that."

"There should be," Lynn said. "But there's not. Not yet."

We were all quiet. None of us dared say infinite. It was too easy. And somewhere, somewhen, that was it. No more ice cream, no more fancy crackers. No dreams. Not symbolic, not otherwise. Just sleep.

The next thing I knew… it was light.

I pulled the pillow off my face and sat up from sideways over Lynn's bed up in that loft, in the brightest part of a guest house without a ceiling. I stumbled to the only edge and peered over, seeing Crete Magellan standing in the living room, his left hand on the roof-sliding mechanism, his jaw on the ground.

"The sun," I said, my first words.

"I can take it away…" Crete said, blinking.

"Don't you dare," came a voice from the bed behind me. A girl's voice.

I hadn't dreamt. I hadn't even felt my head hit the pillow. I had slept at least eight hours solid, straight REM, sideways on Lynn's bed with my feet hanging over the edge, with her curled up at the head of the bed. I was the same as before, I just felt better. And thirsty.

"Check it out," she said. "Aw."

I barely saw Heather move her legs off James' before they both woke up from opposite sides of her bed.

"Coffee?" Lynn and I asked at the same time.

Heather rubbed her eyes and looked at us. "New rule. We don't make each other breakfast. Crete does it for us."

"You do know I'm standing right—"

"I know," Heather said, winking, making it look so easy, until her necklace flashed purple. Then she was flying. Then we all were. Finally, back to normal.

"So there's that," Crete said, taking a step back.

All four of us flew down the height of the loft above us. No ladders required, yes we had slept in our clothes. Clearly someone had told Crete we were back. That could only mean—yep, Sand walked inside right behind Crete. They were both out here, this far from the cave storm shelter, almost like they knew exactly where we'd be. I was wondering how, until I saw Sand. But I almost didn't see the canary on Crete's shoulder.

"What are you doing here?" Heather asked. "Did you know?"

"No, I was planning on spending the next thirty hours on the solar-powered lamp post planting drift car, but I got distracted wondering about a bird," Crete said, his eyes narrowed. "The bird led me back to the Oleander, I found Sand at the Oleander. He made me give you the night, fine, but that's the sun I see right here right now there, right over there. Now I'm wondering about… all this."

"Good to see you too," Lynn said. "You haven't slept in how long now?"

"Thirty hours, why?" Crete said, and his eyes went wider—somehow. "It worked? Good job beanbug."

"Hey, thanks," Lynn said.

"You're welcome, okay great—except not, you brought me here for a pat on the back?" Crete asked Sand. "We knew this would be the result, we have a reckoning with the lighting city to face, but for as long as the north accepts electricity, we can accomplish so much I shouldn't even be here right now. They can dig ourselves out of this tomb, they've done it before—as for me I'm wasting build hours not building anything. I wouldn't be here if not for this damn canary. What's up Sand? Here, and now? Like this? Why?"

"She's alive," Sand said.

"You're telling me, she ate all my sunflower seeds," Crete said.

"Not the bird," Sand said.

"Then what?" Crete asked.

"The girl behind the bird," Sand said, ominously.

"Behind all the birds," Lynn said, like the words hadn't come from her.

"Don't say it," Heather said, looking the canary straight in that tiny face. "Don't you dare say caw, or chirp, or do anything else cute or adorable."

Crete looked at the canary, and the bird looked up at him. The bird almost shrugged, but stayed silent. Sometimes silence said it all. The bird took a single hop across his shoulder and nuzzled its tiny head against Crete's cheek.

"I warned you," Heather seethed, as the bird simply ignored her.

Crete stopped moving except for the single step back he took, like a bird had shoved him.

"Don't give me hope," he said slowly, his eyes about to tear themselves out of his head for staring at a bird without moving his neck.

"Not without reason," Sand said. "She lives, brother."

"It's been years," Crete said, his eyes as big as we'd ever seen. "It's been TEN YEARS Sand. Now? Why?"

"Why else?" Sand said, pointing to us, knowing we were the answer without knowing why.

"It's really…" Crete said, staring at Sand. "It's…"

"Not over," Sand said.

And Crete fell to the floor, but Sand holding Crete in a hug before either one actually hit the floor. I'd never seen two grown men hug each other so hard. Then, as our attention was duly shifted, the canary let out a single chirp and flew off, making a small circle around Lynn before it was lost to the jungle.

Or home in it.

"So we're crossing that bridge, and without coffee," Crete said, his voice cracking. "Is it time? Will it hold?"

"It's past time," Sand said. "I trust them. Every one of them. They'll hold. But no, not without coffee, don't be ridiculous. I've got it."

I could only look at my brother. His face said it all. The hurt, the healing, the journey, the ending. The longing for coffee—I mean answers.

"Okay," Crete said, turning to us as Sand stumbled for the kitchen. "No more secrets. Only honesty. Honestly, you might want to sit down."

"I've been sitting down my whole life," I said.

"Fine then," Crete said. "Just remember one thing. Kalopsia."

"Welp, we lost Crete," James frowned.

"Kalopsia?" I asked. "Is that a word or a stroke?"

"It's a delusion," Crete said. "It's the Greek words for beauty and sight put together, but it's more than that. Some can see beauty where there shouldn't be, and some just want to. Neither of those is real. Kalopsia is the delusion of thinking life is more beautiful than it really is."

"So I'm gonna find that word in the dictionary?" I asked, sarcastically.

"You can internet it," Crete said, full zen, until he wasn't. "Under every inch of the paradise you grew up in, there are the bodies and bones of buried soldiers who gave their lives to make the grasses and flowers. All I'm saying is..."

"The grass is swords," I said, eyes wide.

"Sacrifice holds up this island," Crete said. "Every time you see a pretty color, remember it was painted in shades of blood."

"I'll... do that," James said, frowning. "But ew."

"Again with the doom," Heather said. "Ever heard of a bright side?"

"I gave up on a bright side named Pierre Command seven years ago," Crete said. "I've been carrying the weight of him and his daughter ever since, like it was a normal thing—because it was. I only know how to fight, and move forward. I've forgotten what it's like to... hope. Is that normal?"

"It's not just Command," Sand said, coming back to us with all the coffee. "We've been fighting our entire existence. It defines Ocarina well. We fought to get here. We fought over the resources. Over power... for it, and against it."

"Against it?" I asked. "How was anything we just did against anyone?"

"It wasn't," Sand said. "It was for everyone. You just helped the city you were born to, the father who never knew you, the enemies you've survived ten times over, and the friends you've made along the way, all at once. You just carried the best interest of Vema, Jerico, and Silka on the backs of your wings. All I'm saying is... not everyone is like you."

"We didn't hack our supersuits to work off belief, that was you," I said.

"Yeah well maybe we all have our strengths," Crete said.

"And just maybe our similarities," Sand said. "You're not the only ones in this house to command a multi-national army."

"We did what?" I asked.

"We're not what?" My brother asked. "What's dangerous enough to bring the island together, if not the exact thing we're all thinking right now?"

"It's complicated," Sand said.

"Don't know how it could get more complicated than waking an eight-year-old up with bombs," I said.

"I know how," Crete said sadly.

That was our first clue. The first time the world stopped with the revelation. The crack in the armor. The idea that...

"What are you saying right now?" I asked.

"That if Kira is really alive, I don't think I can tell you how much that means," Sand said. "I thought... I've gone ten years thinking we failed. Thinking that the consequences suffered by Vema and Jerico were for nothing. Every soldier I've had to bury. For the thousands of men and women who died following me into battle. For the loss of the greatest army the world will never know. For every single soldier of Vema… and Jerico… and Mylo."

"Wait," I said. "Follow… you… and all those names… where were you leading to?"

"What the hell are you talking about?" Lynn asked.

"You know," Sand said.

"I've honestly never had a SINGLE reason to put the two together, so come on man… don't tell me this is true…" James said, stalling.

"Why not?" Sand said. "I thought you were ready for the truth."

Lynn almost fell over. It wasn't only quiet. It was cold.

"Don't be afraid," Sand said. "I'm not your enemy. I never will be. I'm just a guy who knows what it's like to lead. Who knows what it feels like to assemble anyone I've ever met, liked, and trusted, to bring them together in secrecy, to send them off at the gesture of a hand… to their deaths."

"Accurate," a voice said.

It was leader Bastile, leaning against a very much open front door, listening. We weren't even mad, I was even glad to see him. Tommy Bones, back again.

"What did they call that battle, Sand?" Bastile asked calmly. "The one you promised us we could win, the one you said would be over so quick we'd feel it on our faces like the winds changing direction? What did they call it?"

"The Blitz," Sand admitted.

I heard the words in slow motion. Was it the same Blitz?

"The Blitz of Silka City?" Lynn asked, almost crying.

"Y… yeah," Sand said.

"No…" James said, so innocently it made my throat close up. "You… were Infinite that night. You had to be. The night ended with Issaic handing the reigns to you, before Odd took them over."

"It didn't start that way," Sand said.

"No," Heather said, her hands on her head, then on Lynn's head.

"Wait a minute," I said, grabbing my brother's shoulder. "He's right. Sand… how could you be there… if you were… there?"

"Fate, or masochism," Sand said, shrugging.

"My stars… or my pearls," Lynn said, slumping off her chair completely.

"It's a long story," Sand said. "But I think it's time to tell you how I commanded the Blitz of Silka City. From both sides."

4.8

WHO THIS WILL HURT

And to be honest, it was not that chill of a thing to say.

It hit me in the gut. It forced me into confrontation. It made my brain feel like someone had it in the vice again, talk about build hours on this one.

"From both…" Lynn said, blinking.

"Midnight…" Derek said.

The damage was done. The revelation set in like a whip. I saw my eyes white out for a moment, the memory still only a reach away. The bombs, the lights, the soldiers coming in from the ports, the swarms downtown, blue light filter…

"The Blitz," I said. "It was you."

It wasn't a question. It was an answer. For ONCE.

"It was me," Sand said. "Ten years ago, I brought every kind of super soldier on the island to rid the Infinite of only one thing, a single thing, one I watched lead them down the hateful path they still walk today. Then I went to bed in Blue Panel and acted surprised when the alarms went on throughout headquarters. It wasn't a targeted attack against Issaic Nite, or Infinite, or even Silka City, it was only supposed to look like that. Because here's the thing. The Blitz, the actual assault from sky, sea, and land, that wasn't the game. It was all one big… say it with me now…"

"Distraction," Derek and I said together, horrified.

"Yep," Sand said. "Our target wasn't Silka City, nor Issaic Nite. At least…"

"Not until it was, very recently," Crete said. "But that's the post-game."

"Call it a game again, see what happens," I said.

Someone hit me on the shoulder. It was Heather, who nodded at me with respect as I tried not to cry. It must have been a good-on-you punch. Ow.

"You're not leaving me with lots of ideas about why this even had to happen," Derek said. "You enlisted the jungle before?"

"I did," Sand said. "They're worth two agents each, without armor."

"You led Reaper too?" Heather asked, torn between repulsed and impressed.

"They're wonderful people in person and absolutely terrifying in combat, of course," Sand said. "What are you getting at?"

"Who were you, to pull so many favors, all at once?" Lynn asked.

"You don't know my story," Sand said. "You don't even know my real na—"

"But why?" Derek interrupted. "What could have brought so many defecting forces together? What could have possibly been worth risking the city—"

"Godfire," I blurted out.

"Welp," Heather started, but then Lynn had a hand to her mouth. "Hmhey."

"He's right, like always," Crete said, looking like he'd underestimated me. "How'd you know that James?"

"I... know what I know," I said, holding my necklace tight. "You know?"

"We know," Sand said. "If you knew the story of the original Teresa Silk, you'd know the reason James calls it the godfire is scary accurate."

"Her story?" Derek said. "The founder of Silka City, the first to cross the island from Mylo Port in the west? They say she lost half her original expedition party searching for the right lands, and only found them around the oasis that became Silka. They say she found fire from the gods here and used it to plug Silka in. What? Why's everyone looking at me like—"

Then his words caught up to him. "Oh my godfire."

"Yep," Sand said. "Before the Breaking, before the truce that brought the armadas of the world here, this was the power that united the old world, if *literally* only for an afternoon. This is THE fire stolen from the gods, the original technology taken from the Infinum Collective and used to transition the survivors of the old world to the only inhabitable part of the new one."

Sand stopped, seeing our faces had turned from curiosity to terror.

"Oversharing," he sighed. "It's always been my weakness."

The irony was...

"Keep talking, for ONCE IN YOUR—" Lynn shouted.

"Long story short, our founders, our ancestors, they always possessed the original supertechnology," Sand said. "It's been used to create the Infinite agent, the Reaper scout, the Astral warrior, the list goes on."

"Does it?" Lynn asked. "Or does it stop there?"

"It can't stop, it's a never ending, self-perpetual clean energy machine," Sand said. "Even captain Mylo himself had no idea this thing made it to the island."

"What thing?" Derek asked.

"The source?" I said. "Like, *the* source?"

"The Infinum Generator," Crete said, his eyes narrow.

He waited for us to gasp. He even looked around in the awkward silence. "I thought you were going to—"

"We're not gonna!" I said.

"The Infinum what?" Heather asked.

"Generator," Crete said, shaking his head. "An engineering marvel that took humanity centuries to perfect. Indestructible, unsinkable, incapable of being turned off, ever. The only reason the Arks—I mean the island—ever lived."

"Actually both," Sand said, thinking.

"This isn't about the Breaking, this is about the Blitz," Crete asked, his hands folded in front of him. "One nuclear disaster at a time, please."

I mean, clearly we'd come back to that.

"You aim high, I'll give you that," Derek said.

"For all the moons," Crete said, backing Sand up in his own weird way.

"If you had gotten it," Lynn said, thinking. "Wouldn't that have taken the Infinite power away from every agent in Silka?"

"It did, beanbug," Crete said.

"So that means… Infinite isn't operating off their original source," Lynn said, reading Crete's face, slowly. "They never were. As long as I've lived."

He winked. "On the nose."

"Hence some kind of copycat engine below headquarters?" I said, realizing.

"On my other nose," Crete said, turning to me with respect.

"I'm only going to say this again," Derek said. "Underground is already underground. Oh wait you mean underland. That actually makes sense."

"I'm not sure about that," Crete said. "These days, the Infinite source seems to come from above, no matter where in the city I'm positioned. I hate to say it, but we might be dealing with another—"

"Don't say it," Derek said, shaking his head.

"What, distraction?" Heather said. "That doesn't make sense."

"Satellite," I explained, sadly.

Heather's eyes went wide. "Oh. Yeah that's worse."

"For traumatic, city ending reasons, please don't let it be that," Lynn said.

"Not up to me," Crete said, hands in the air.

"So let me guess, this copycat engine is about Blitz years old?" Derek asked.

Sand and Crete nodded at the same time. Ew. Twins were creepy.

"And let me guess, you made it," Lynn said.

Crete looked away like a child… but nodded.

"He never could do a thing half assed," Sand said, mad and proud at his friend at the same time.

"Teach me," I said.

"I will James," Crete said. "I'm going to force you to have an actual summer first. Then I'm taking you to school, and hard."

"Cool," I said, too excited to speak.

"Ignoring the nerds," Derek said. "That means the original supertechnology had to have disappeared in the Blitz, or maybe repurposed, relocated…"

"We tried to get rid of it, one way or another," Sand said. "You could say we got our wish."

"You tried to steal?" I said, folding my arms. "I'm putting build school on hold until I know you aren't war criminals."

"We needed the generator out of Issaic's hands," Sand said. "I saw a pattern emerging, one that became exponential in the aftermath of the Blitz. I didn't want the power for myself, which is why I didn't send myself. I sent the best of us. His name was Pierre Quinney Command."

"And who… exactly was important enough to be in command of a thing, when Pierre came for it?" I asked, already afraid of the answer.

"Historically it has belonged to the lightning city," Crete said.

"But the attack didn't exclude my neighborhood…" I said.

"You're right," Derek said. "Where exactly were you looking, when you were trying to find this this strange and magical object?"

"We were looking at the last known coordinates of the generator, once the Always Soldier sent them to us," Sand said.

"The…" I said. "That nickname…"

"Yes James," Sand said, shooting me a look.

"Correct," Sand said. "In the years before the Blitz, the island received intelligence that the source, thought to exist unilaterally untouched under the foundation of Silka, had gone missing. Infinite had not reported anything of the such. Our contacts within Silka and even Infinite validated this. There was one prevailing theory as to who would be bold enough to hold the city, the Infinite army, and the rest of the island hostage so. You are correct James. The Blitz was not aimed at Silka nor Issaic. It was not even aimed at Infinite. It was aimed so prophetically, like you said, like a throwing knife—"

"At the godfire," I said, not even surprised at this point. "So here's the part where someone does control the weather."

"Well… whoever holds the generator… controlling the weather would only be the easiest thing to do," Crete shrugged.

"You neglected to tell us literally every part of that," I said, wheeling on Sand—

"Is our dad really…" my brother started—

"Your father is a complete enigma, even for us," Crete said. "None of us truly know him, not even you Sand, as much as you always said you did."

"He isn't evil," Sand said. "You don't know Issaic Nite, you only know his ego. The day he turned around and saw a hundred agents behind him, he was never the same. If you want to talk to your father, if you want a real word, you'll have to fight for it."

"I hate that," I said. "But speaking of one on one, I'm going to need to take a peek at this very mysterious generator you speak of."

"I just told you we staged an entire war over recovering it, and were not successful," Crete said sighing.

"You didn't mention that last part," I said.

"Because it's embarrassing," Crete said. "We angered the gods, we poked the lighting city, destroyed buildings and caused terror… for nothing. That's the part of the Blitz that hurts worse than all the fallen. No one has seen the thing since. To this day, the attack was for nothing. Pierre and his daughter died for nothing. We had one chance to recover the generator—or to steal it, same thing, same outcome. Until today, our nothing has cost everything."

There was silence around that weird clock magnet platform. We could all see each other, lamenting, thinking the exact same thing—what the absolute hell.

"But we had a backup plan," Crete said, his eyes flashing. "One we'd have absolutely no way of knowing if it worked, until we did. That plan was called The Kira Command."

"Your plan was an eight year old girl?" I asked.

"Not my plan," Sand said suddenly.

"Our plan was Pierre," Crete said. "But someone else had another idea. In a world of suspicion, the youngest would pull the most hold back. To use children as agents, that was never my plan. The Always Soldier herself suggested it. The very idea of preparing Kira for the worst… that came from your mother."

"Seems she didn't stop with one," Derek said.

"Please tell me you're not talking about child soldiers," I said, face white.

"Good thing we're not soldiers," was all I could say.

Sand gave me the same look he'd given me the day we'd met, when it was just a rustic, ancient looking door and a head sticking out to see my brother and me with no bags, and the smell of the first explosion still all over us even after the showers. It was a look he didn't want to give, but knew he had to. His first words came back to me.

"I'm sorry about your mother," Derek said. No blueblood. Just memory.

"What?" Crete said. "What's that?"

"Literally the first thing I ever said to them," Sand blinked. "Who remembers something like that?"

"Derek does," Lynn, Heather, and I said all at once.

Crete threw his coffee on the ground. It wasn't helping.

"Were you comforting orphans… or in total awareness of what was about to happen and apologizing on her behalf for the impending doom?" I asked.

"Both," Sand said. "The only thing harder than saving the world is growing up. I would never ask a kid to do what's been asked of you."

"Good thing we're not kids?" I said, echoing what my brother had just said about soldiers.

Sand looked up just as sad as before. It was warranted. He had meant it both ways, and we all understood. We no longer could afford to be boys. We weren't kids. We weren't soldiers. So what were we?

"We were never meant to overpower the lightning city," Sand said. "My friends from every nation on Ocarina. Mare Veman, head of the dragon himself, and the Vema battle unit so feared they were told never to land, to stay in the sky unless engaging, for the sake of the other soldier's sanity. Bone's Brigade, led by a young Bastile himself, a thousand Astral strong, Jerico's finest warriors, barefoot but armed to the tooth with diamond coated wooden weapons. The Myloian by sea, the armada Kalopsia at the best the port city could spare, only a fraction, because that's all that was needed. I'm forgetting something."

"The Infinite defectors, soon to be exiles, at best," Crete said, like a soldier who would never forget.

"Right," Sand said. "I led them all. I had the peace among nations I'd always wanted, it only took war to do it. We stormed the city at midnight, we were the biggest threat the island has ever seen. I knew it would take us all. One look at what was coming and all logic had to be gone for. That was the distraction. That was the Blitz, for every soldier but Command."

His eyes teared up in the light, just for a moment.

"I thought you were going to say something else there," Derek said.

"I was waiting for that too," Lynn said. "You brought my father."

"Mine too," Heather said, getting madder. "You said it was WHAT?"

“A distraction,” Crete said. “We would hold the attention of the city, and the island, in a way that would give Pierre the window he needed. He wasn’t supposed to… you know… he promised us he would live—”

“He was supposed to return with the Infinum Generator,” Sand said. “But he never even got the chance. He went radio silent over the cliffs. I only found his plane a week later. His body took longer to recover, we got there… but we never found the daughter. If she survived, even if her father died in front of her, she knew what was at stake. She would have at least tried to make it. Now I’m wondering if she did more than make it. Here’s where I really wish I could press a button and make you repeat everything I heard in that cave.”

He stared at me, and for a moment I saw him on that cliff again, holding on by a single hand at the last step of all the rock climbing, choosing to hang on still enough to hear my entire story before they found him out. I went to touch the second stone on my necklace and found nothing, because a bird had taken it, duh. Instead my fingers found my heart.

And as they made contact, I remembered everything. Also I fell over.

“Well, he found the button,” Derek said, pulling me back up. “You good?”

“Who?” I asked, fists up, looking around, whipping my hair back in place. “Sand. I remember.”

“What do you remember?” Sand asked.

“Everything,” I said. “It worked. If your plan was Pierre, that didn’t work but if Mom’s plan was Kira, then great, good plan. She got out, she definitely got in, I mean the front door was open, I followed, I found her downstairs, we agreed to be friends forever, and she teleported me to the backyard.”

“Maybe she just ran you really fast,” Crete asked.

“Woah. Maybe,” I said, shoulders high. “I don’t know, I just know I saw her, she was there, she knew how to get where she wanted, and I never went back to check but I’m pretty sure she took the weird glowing magic ball too.”

And if silence could get quieter.

“I’m sorry, did he just describe the Infinum Generator?” Crete said, dropping his backup coffee, the thing bouncing all over the ground (because Jerico pottery didn’t break).

“He describe a glowing sphere of light,” Lynn said.

“That’s what the Generator looks like,” Crete said.

They all looked at me.

“I mean… you’re serious?” Heather asked.

Sand watched Crete’s reaction. He stared at me, blinking in the dark.

“You could not know that,” Crete said. “You did not know that.”

“I could have seen it in a cartoon,” I said. “But I saw it in life. There was a lot lost young and it all seems important, sorry it took until now for answers.”

“And?” Sand asked.

“And, that’s it, I’m out,” I said. “I hope I’ve helped. If you trust me, she still exists.”

“If you don't trust him, trust me,” Sand said, with a smile.

“James,” Crete said. “Why did you never say this?”

“Because YOU never ASKED!”

"A sharp point," Crete said. "Sorry friend. I told you so, even before the satellite, we bring them in full."

"We agreed to half," Sand said.

"HOW IS THIS HALF?" Lynn shouted, her eyes never leaving me.

"What if I knew where to find her?" I asked.

The world stopped moving. Literally, the wind outside stopped. Bastile was still leaning against our front door, just listening. Sand and Crete both looked to my brother like this was new information.

"The past is one thing," Sand said. "Now's the part where you explain the present."

"I can't explain it," I said. "I'll have to show you. Isn't that right Lynn?"

"Isn't that right, all the birds?" She called, passing along the request.

Derek blinked, like his brother had lost it, again. Then he saw the trees moving—all the trees. In a completely controlled, sing-song flurry, a hundred birds in every color known to man descended on us. We were so shocked we didn't react when they started landing. Lynn was the only one to hold her hands out like a scarecrow, the rest of us wore birds from head to toe in a blink.

"The birds say yes," Lynn said.

She sounded proud of us. I felt like dancing, but I couldn't move. I had birds all over me.

"If she's alive," Crete said. "If the Generator is too, there's always the synthesis theory—"

"It's not a theory anymore," Sand said. "They became one and the same ten years ago. That's why we never found either one. James found both—or, possibly more accurately—"

"Both found James," Derek said, looking over at me, carrying the weight of more birds than anyone else. "This power found us underland. It's the reason the Vema ascended. It's how we survived tonight without sacrificing a city, or two. It's a good thing."

"Are you sure of that?" Sand asked.

"We were sure about you," I said. "Cautious optimism."

Sand winced. I wasn't giving up on him, but I was disappointed. Which was code for mad. You keep the details of your involvement in armageddon from me, I tend to get a bit cranky. The birds were nice, but like all things, they had to go. And just as I had that thought, all the birds lifted off and up into the air again. We watched them leave in wonder.

"So what now," I asked.

Sand didn't answer right away. It was the heaviest question I had ever asked.

"Now you decide if you want to fight," he said.

"I was afraid of that," Lynn said.

"We aren't charging the castle," Sand said. "Not as long as we stand a chance against the Infinite Army, when the day comes."

"What day?" Heather asked. "Not today? You want us to fight by not fighting?"

"I want that very much," Sand said. "But I'm a bit burnt out on the leading thing."

"But you never even told us the mission!" Derek shouted. "What if we do it, what if we stand a chance against the Army, what then? What would you have us do?"

Sand narrowed his eyes at us. "Survive. That's it. I wouldn't ask for war, I wouldn't enforce my peace. I would just have you live long enough to see this world for the beauty I know she can be. You're what, eighteen? I'm sixty-six. You have NO idea what I want. What I've given up."

"We kinda do now," Lynn said.

"Okay great, you still don't understand who this is for," Sand said. "You couldn't. Not unless you'd seen…"

"Seen what?" I asked. "You said it before, you said you'd seen something though a telescope and then what, everything changed when the fire nation—"

"The best you can do right now is survive, to grow stronger, so that when the day calls, we might stand a chance against the real storm," Sand said."

"And that's not this?" I asked, eyebrows high.

"You'll know international warfare when you see her," Sand said.

"Is that coming?" I asked.

And it was Crete's silence that really got me.

"Come on now," Heather said. "Fists up?"

"Not immediately," Crete said. "But what we just did to the Infinite, and the retaliation against Jerico, we have no way of knowing what's coming next."

"So more like backpacks up?" Derek said sadly.

Crete touched his nose. "That is, if you're not already about to run screaming from us."

"We've done that," I said. "Maybe give us a beat to process, we'll be fine—"

"Of course," Sand said, wincing. "But given what you've seen of Issaic—"

"We're thinking," Derek said. "Leave it."

"Of course," Crete said, bowing.

Two figures came up to our front doors, Bastile and Bombelle. They looked at us in mid-conversation/argument like we might shoot a neighbor. Never. Crete motioned for us, and we met them on the terrace. It was a beautiful day, why stay indoors? Out in the sunlight our superwear was obvious, the small technical glitches and sparks and LEDs all over it. For a moment no one could speak, they could only stare at Lynn, my brother, and myself.

"I must admit, I'm here to bring you to temple," Bastile said.

"Give us a minute and we'll bring our things too," Lynn said to him.

He nodded to us. Both sides knew what it meant. The boot was coming.

I walked to the bed under the loft. I carefully made the bed one last time, I touched the necklace around my neck, and realized that was it. There was nothing left in this place that was mine. I turned around and ran into Derek, Heather, and Lynn all looking down.

"I… got everything," Derek said, both of his hands free, the notebook back down the old—

"That didn't take long," Bastile said. "You never even got the chance to live here, did you?"

None of us answered. We all knew the answer was no.

Bastile led us down the curving pathway against the grass quad, all the way to the gigantic center-pole to the Oleander district. We walked up the stairs and I felt my body physically react when we passed the platform where I'd opened the top of my toes and bled over the wood and wheels of a stupid skateboard. I swear I could still see the drops of blood staining the wood. I smiled. Memories. Then we were inside the temple and the door closed behind us. Only when I looked back did I see the massive crowd of people following us in, that Willa closed out with a look and a gigantic door slamming shut.

"As if I didn't already like you," she said, turning back on us.

"Had to do it," I said. "He was serious about burning Ravenna down. Burning everything down, really."

"We saw," Willa said. "The storm hadn't even passed and Crete was rolling out a thousand foot television."

"You spent the entire night planting sun sticks," Bastile said. "Please, learn to delegate."

"I have a hundred days," Crete said. "I will give every single second of that time back to the land that made me, and I'll do it my own damn way thank you. Even if the electricity doesn't last a season, what we can build together will last decades."

"What if Jerico needs no improvement?" Bombelle asked, testing him.

"Opportunity comes to the fortunate and unfortunate alike," Crete said. "Only the foolish ignore it."

Bombelle bowed. "Crete, your all access pass to Jerico comes with but one condition. You must be rested. Get some sleep."

"Not without someone in my place," Crete said. "Bring me Racket and Foe. They taught me everything, let me pay it back. Wait, is that them—"

"They commandeered your mechanical horse about sixty seconds ago," Bastile said, shutting a wooden window on our right. "They will carry your efforts on to the farthest reaches of the territory. Now will you sleep?"

Crete nodded. He quietly sat down on the floor, fell to his back, and fell asleep. Right there, right then.

"Easy," Bombelle said. "What's next, not so much. You want to tell them honey?"

"Together," Bastile said. "By witness of everyone in this room, we'd like to give you the good old heads up. After what's happened this week, you know we elected a new caput. Wildfire Willa—"

"That's not my name," Willa said. "I'm okay with Wildfire, that's just dope. I was born in Norther Arbor to the best parents in the world, and I was raised to fight for the beauty of the jungle. I earned a place in the hand by being the closest thing to warrior Willa the green world had ever seen. But my real name is Waylilla. My mother said it means music to fight to. Takanakuy, you know?"

"Let's just say… sure," I said, mouth open.

"I was born for this," Wildfire said. "I've lived my entire life in the jungle. I know change when I see it, but I see responsibility the same way. Part of me wants to run off into the sunset with you four. But another part of me knows her place in the jungle, and what it takes to be a warrior. I'm not making decisions for only myself anymore. If I were… maybe this would be different."

She looked back at Bastile with hope in her eye, but he only shook his head.

"I feel like Ollux should be here for this," I said, looking around. "She started this. She brought us into this forest, her and her brother—"

"Astor has not been seen inside the gates for a day," Bastile said. "It is likely he will never return. He assaulted a guest within the territory, accepted by all, possibly under the duress of the lightning city itself."

"It was definitely under that," I said. "He had the chance to turn me in. He chose to save me. When it came down to it, he trusted me not to burn his world down. I'd never do that willingly, so he repaid the favor. It's likely he won't survive lying to Issaic Nite."

"What are you saying, Nite?"

"I'm saying if they turn up, don't kick them out for us. Maybe give them a home before Issaic shows up for the endgame, even if it's only for a while."

"I'm afraid that's the issue," Wildfire said, sadly. "I couldn't have said it better."

"Uh oh," Lynn said.

"Correct," Bastile said. "Whatever endgame Issaic is playing at, we need it played anywhere but here."

"I see you brought your bags," Bombelle said, sadly.

"We did," Heather said. "Had a hunch, you know."

"As much of a futurist as my wonderful wife is, none of us saw the weight of this last week," Bastile said. "Our advancement just came at the cost of an island-wide spotlight cast upon us, only amplified by the personal connections between the source of the spotlight and… certain people in this room."

"Are you talking about the people in this room capable of tearing the moon in two?" Sand asked.

"Maybe," Bastile said. "We just wanted lights in the bathroom, maybe some television, but noo. With you, there's no lightning without the thunder."

"We came here to help," Lynn said.

"That's not true," Heather said, wincing.

"Okay, we came here FOR help, and you gave it to us," Lynn said. "We were four people and seven legs and you made us better. We didn't come here to help you, but we stayed to. I like to think we did a few things right along the way."

"Me too," Waylilla said, her eyes gleaming. "But this isn't about us. Even if you've found yourselves on some epic adventure with the grand fate of a small island at stake… this is Jerico. We have only ourselves, and the biggest opportunity in centuries. We can't afford to lose focus. We can't afford…"

She trailed off. She didn't want to say it. I could tell, by the tears.

They couldn't afford us.

"Here's how we repay you," Heather said. "You don't have to say it."

"As newly appointed leader of an entire nation, she should say it," Bombelle said, softly, but not too soft.

"We'll all know it," Lynn said, on the edge of tears. "You know she means it. We do too. Look."

Derek held the notebook up. Lynn and Heather let their Reaper rock armor dissipate, revealing the cut up concert frays and perfectly spaced hemming of their Jerico brown clothes. I pulled his pockets out, revealing nothing.

Willa smiled. I mean Waylilla. "You got everything."

"We are standing in the same room, yes," Lynn said, a tear on her cheek. "We came back to say goodbye to the best friend we've made in a while."

"You and I both," Waylilla said, and she bolted for Lynn.

We joined them, gently group-hugging the life out of Wildfire, let whatever Bastile thought about it be damned. She laughed as we let go, then shook it off, her face going stoic again.

"Good enough?" Bastile asked, his eyes innocent.

Bombelle sighed. "Fine. Just this once. We hired her for the fire and the flames, not these weak knees."

"How DARE you," Waylilla said, turning on her heels towards Bombelle.

"There she is," Bombelle said. "Also… kidding."

"You weren't a minute ago," Waylilla said. "But a queen forgives."

Lynn and Heather burst out laughing.

"Would it be out of line to say… we'll be back?" I asked, shooting an emotionless half-look to Sand and Crete.

"I hope you'll be back," Bastile said. "Once you can arrive in peace, instead of the other thing. No one's ever done what've you done. Give us more than a single season to process it. Maybe this time next year, we'll beg your return."

"You never have to beg," Lynn said, still holding Waylilla by the arm. "We're yours."

"You are so cool," Waylilla said, about to burst into tears again.

"If I may," I said. "We're about to leave your lands. But Willa—I mean, Waylilla, she made us a promise. Once this was all over, she'd show us the best beach on Ocarina. You don't just forget something like that."

"Waylilla is a grown ass woman, and I'm not in charge of her anymore," Bastile said. "What say you, caput?"

"I'd say, a promise is a promise," Waylilla said, her eyes sparking one more time. "Can we fly?"

"Can you what now?" Bastile asked.

Waylilla was in the air on a pair of working Reaper wings, in the middle of the Oleander, before the rest of us could blink.

"That's not… traditional," Bastile said, frowning.

"That's why we hired her," Bombelle said, taking his shoulder. "Let her go."

"But—"

"Just let her go, dear," Bombelle repeated.

We were already in the air. Sand and Crete were on the ground, Crete still snoring, Sand still smiling.

"We'll come back to it?" I called down to Sand.

"It's like seven am," Sand said. "Go enjoy the day. We'll meet you there."

"Soon," I said, smiling, saluting. "Sir. Ma'am. Thank you for everything."

"You're welcome for everything," Bastile said.

Waylilla shot off into her green wonderland, and we weren't far behind.

4.9

THE BOTTOM OF THE SEA

We flew as a team of four, plus one. That extra spot was usually reserved for a flying car alongside us, but in this case, it was a girl with a future. Waylilla the Wildfire, head of the hand.

Not some old couple who sort of got us, not this time. Bastile and Bombelle were nothing like this girl—sorry, woman. She was closer to our age, that's all. We'd never met anyone like Wildfire, except perhaps the Reaper Reya, who'd already proven she could pop up at anytime, anywhere, anyhow, probably from underground. But we and Willa had started a story, and we all knew we'd be stopping it here. I could only hope the ending was as open-ended as Reya's.

Wildfire led us high over miles of Jerico treetops we hadn't even seen yet, until the mountains in the north really hit us, a single peak that screamed volcano instead of a series of ridges. We never even saw the top of it, as the heavy white clouds kept that hidden from us. At the end of the green sea was another mount Olympus (cloud city), great, good to know, we'd come back to it. Today wasn't about the volcano. For the first time this sad, sweet summer, maybe today could just be about nothing.

Yeah right.

Waylilla sped us around the right side of the craggy cliffs, and in the same moment we all gasped in disbelief. The single mountain was nowhere near as big as the green sea, it basically ended as soon as it came, then for the first time the trees did too, and like we were looking at the entire portside of Silka City—

Woah.

"I've never seen so much sand," Lynn said.

It was the beach. Like, *the* beach. The one you think about in your head, a crescent moon shaped shore, with the scenic uphill cliffs and palm trees and grasses at the back of it, and nothing but open, crystal clear water before it, devoid of any rocks except the ones in a small wall about two football fields out, the best natural wave breaker a man could ask for, even if the surfer in me was ready to tear every one of those rocks out of the ocean by hand (or Heather).

"You deserved to..." Waylilla said. "You deserve to be here. You shouldn't have to leave us. You are us."

"Metaphorically," Heather nodded. "In reality, we all have... places to go back to."

"Thank you for not saying homes," Derek said.

"You have a home here," Willa said. "Just... maybe you close out your business with the Infinite before the decorating. Speaking of."

She reached into her pocket and pulled out four leather wristbands.

"No," Lynn said. "If those are what I think they are—"

"They are from the four lost to the Crossroads, while we were barely surviving our breach of the Planetarium," Wildfire admitted. "Bombelle and Bastile have given their blessings. They—we, want you to hold onto them."

"For guilt reasons?" Heather asked.

"Metaphorically," Willa shot back. "You did not kill our soldiers, that was Infinite. But you also cannot replace our soldiers, you are Infinite."

"So why even give them to us?" I asked, my eyes welling up.

"So that maybe you can be something more," Waylilla said. "So that maybe the next time you show up limping to our gates, you won't have to do the whole pretending you can't fight thing. Looking at you, Lyre."

"I know you're talking to me, but my surname gets confusing," Lynn said.

"I know, I heard it when I said it," Waylilla said. "I'll just call you friend."

"Aw," Lynn said. "Girl..."

"It's not a supersuit, and it's not a necklace, but it is a sign of of the times," Waylilla said. "Maybe next time, this way, the entire Jerico will be as willing to help you as I am. As I will always be."

Now I was really tearing up (which was guy-talk for straight crying in front of everyone). They were as slim and scratchy as the rest of the Jerico clothing, just slightly more elastic than the rest. They fit perfect. We pulled them on.

"It hides my scar," I said.

"That's the idea," Waylilla said. "Wait what scar?"

"The locked in the car scar?" Derek asked.

"No."

"The hand in a Pringles can scar?"

"No!"

"How many scars do you have?" Lynn asked.

"Yes answer," Heather said, staring at me.

"That's not—well more now," I said. "The bird scar."

Waylilla's eyes froze as I held my left wrist out. Like the very clothes I wore were made of nanotechnology (they were), the fabric melted away into itself, revealing bare skin from the elbow down. I guess between bandages and supersuits, they hadn't seen my wrist in a while.

"That's a new one," Derek said.

Waylilla traced the new scar tissue on my wrist, a clear lowercase letter 'a' with either a wing or lighting pattern (?) on the right side, then she held her own wrist out and moved the armband that covered... the exact same pattern on her.

"Okay why are they the same?" Lynn asked, the last to notice it.

"At least it's not on the hand-shaking hand," I said. "I'm saving that for my rockstar tattoo."

"What's that?" Lynn asked.

"The right wrist," I said. "You put something there when there's no more need for first impressions."

"The very nature of that scar defeats that sentiment entirely," Heather said, pointing.

"Only in Jerico," I countered.

Derek nodded. We were both thinking the same thing, that shaking hands with our father was still *technically* a possibility.

"At least it's healing," Lynn said. "But why is it the same as Willa—as Wildfire?"

"We didn't even brand you," Waylilla said. "We were only talking about it."

"Talking about it?" Heather shouted.

"Did you do this yourself?" Derek asked, looking at me like *what the—*

"Maybe on some level," I said. "But no. A bird done did this to me."

"It's frighteningly accurate for a bird," Waylilla said. "You three better not show me the same thing."

"We can't," Derek said, holding out his own wrists, no brands or scars to talk about. "We saw that happen. It was before the ankle. We just didn't... see it."

"Me neither," Waylilla said. "I guess... we really aren't that different, Nite."

"I never thought we were," I said.

"I never thought you wouldn't think we were," Waylilla said, sweetly. "Glad you don't."

"Never," I said, smiling, while everyone else scratched their heads. "Lynn, you pretended not to hear that bird. I think we need to know what you actually heard."

"I told you," Lynn said. "I heard... turn back."

"From what, our purpose in life?" Heather argued.

"No, from... Silka," Lynn said. "The bird said turn back. It said... you're going in the exact opposite direction. Turn around, turn back, try again."

"So what's the opposite of Silka?" I asked. "The Vempire?"

"Metaphorically," Lynn said. "But geographically, the opposite of Silka, if we'd turned around and flown west... that's the harbor town. Mylo Port."

"You mean Mylo Command, at Strangerland," Heather said. "Where humanity came from, says nerds."

"The nerds who wrote all the books that you clearly read, you big giant reading nerd girl," Waylilla corrected, as Heather doubled over laughing. "Truthfully, you've got an easy map to Mylo from here, just fly shore left."

"You turned that around fast," Lynn said, her face falling the smallest bit. "You really want us gone."

"There might be an ulterior motive to this beautiful beach, one that benefits the entirety of the Territory, yes," Waylilla said, her turn to turn away from us. "I want you here. I just... don't every time get what I want."

"No one cool ever does," Lynn said.

And in that moment, I felt closer to all three of them than ever before. Also in that moment, a particularly perfect wave hit the shore not fifteen feet from us, five heads turned to the beach, and five teenagers remembered where they were.

"Never end on a sad song," my brother said. "You coming or what?"

"What do you—oh," Wildfire said.

Derek pulled his shirt off (or told the Infinite suit to chill or whatever), and was back to the Jerico shorts, racing for the water before we could blink.

"I mean," I said, looking between this heaviness and the ocean. "Bye."

And my feet didn't touch the ground for the next hour. But we weren't flying. We were laughing and swimming in salt water so buoyant we barely had to tread. It was so warm I needed the endless cove winds blowing through my hair to keep cool.

"Look around," Lynn shouted to me, rising five feet in the water with a new set.

"Look at life!" Derek called back.

He'd swum halfway to her before I came crashing out of another wave over his head, and everything was water. I had ten feet of crash above my head, and even though it stung, I had my eyes open like always, and just in time to see the glowing yellow eyes and rocky helmet of the Reaper swim by, rotating like a torpedo. But there wasn't any armor over the rest of Heather.

"I think I like the ocean," Heather said, her words in my head even with the water around us.

"Good," was all I said, the bubbles following me up the surface.

We played in the waves like we were kids, the shore so forgiving it was nothing to tumble into the sand after getting pitted head over heels underwater. I came up laughing from one particularly rogue wave and saw Derek panicking, raising his watch out of the water and pressing a button—suddenly his Infinite clothes came alive and covered him from neck to toe. I stared at him.

"It happened to me," was all he said. "James, it happened to me—"

I was laughing so hard I didn't see the next wave coming.

An hour later we walked out of the water together, drenched head to toe, me in my brown shorts, Derek wearing Infinite from the waist down, Lynn and Heather in the same shorts just cutoff and the Jerico equivalent of sports bras (?), and Willa fully naked. Just kidding. She walked out of the water just like she'd flown out of Oleander, dressed in the slim but sturdy ceremonial armor she always wore, sort of a martial tunic and half dress. She'd left the sword in the sand though. As we came back up the shore she swung the blade through the air and returned it to the sheath at her side. It was such a part of her it almost disappeared, only visible because her clothes were wet and sticking to her, instead of billowing around gloriously in the wind. And since I didn't see any towels around, I joined a sword, throwing my wet butt and back straight into the sand, letting my hair take the grain, down the pants too…

I loved the beach.

Heather's head landed in the sand next to me. Her body was the other way, and then Derek and Lynn hit sand, and Waylilla too. We were all on our backs with our heads in the center, some sort of hippy trust circle nonsense—

"So you're really… off the grid?" Waylilla asked.

"Let's see," Derek said. "Oracle, lasers please."

"Finally."

And the darkness came over us even though the day was bright and sunny. It must have been a facial display thing. Once again the connections to any unphysical light and sound were displayed like lines coming and going, up and down. We all had a purplish, pinkish light coming and going from our necklaces, all except for Waylilla, her clothes seemed paired to Lynn's somehow, like bluetooth, weird. But other than that, the only light in the sky was a yellow downstream connecting from the clouds to my brother's heart. Not his clothes, not his watch. From his chest, the same yellow electricity flowed to me, and from me to Lynn—this time from watch to watch.

"Once again, I feel left out," Heather said.

"I knew I forgot something," Lynn said, throwing something to Heather.

It was a watch. A superwatch, similar to ours in every way.

"You tried to give this to me before," she said. "Thank you for trying twice."

"We're learning," Lynn said, smiling. "Put it on."

"You think I've ever had a watch before?" Heather asked. "What is this double clasp system bull—oh. Well that was infinitely harder than it had to be, and it doesn't even fit."

"For the love of—" Lynn said, leaning back over, showing her how to be fancy.

"Oh it gets smaller, that's just good engineering," Heather said, shaking the loose wristlet Waylilla had given her around her other hand.

Waylilla threw her hands up.

"That's like the one rule with nice watches, you're not allowed to use them to be condescending," Lynn said. "You're still just a person."

"I didn't know that either," Heather said, dropping her head. "I supposed it fits. Am I online? I didn't feel the spark. Why am I not a firework?"

"Based purely on experience and previous events..." I said, grinning, just watching my brother's face turn red.

"Superpowers on standby, fine with me," Heather said, blushing.

"For now," I said. "Until we need more from us, I mean from you, I mean—"

"You mean like maybe once in forever you stop talking and kiss me?" Heather said, blinking, still blushing.

That was all it took. Without any horn warning, the sky opened up above us one last time, and a single bolt of lightning dissipated straight into Heather's watch. The actual electricity was completely contained by the watch, that was no worry—it was just the thunder, the sound of an island tearing itself in two, so loud it shook the ocean, like all the ocean. But then we looked up to see the yellow laserlights connecting us all, from me to Derek to Lynn to Heather. No one was left out (except for Wildfire, obviously).

"Rude," Waylilla said, to an already bright and sunny day.

"Did that just happen?" Derek said, scrambling away, somehow throwing more sand into my face because WHY NOT—

"Shengcun," Heather said.

"You pronounced dope wrong," Lynn said, smiling, then frowning. "Wait, did you just play us for power?!"

"Not even," Heather said. "I kissed James twenty chapters ago. Kind of. There was a strawberry, that's all I really remember."

"Same," I said, logically.

"There was a block, and it wasn't you," Heather said. "It was me. I needed to do more than strawberries. It's supposed to be simple, but for me it's the hardest thing in the world. I'm not supposed to get the happy ending. I'm dragon born and Silka's most wanted."

"For all the right reasons," Lynn said, shrugging it off.

"I will end you, right here, right now," Heather threatened.

"You won't," Lynn smiled. "You like us."

"Wrong," Heather said. "I love you."

Lynn stopped smiling. But somehow, in a good way. The best way.

"What, you think there's a better time to say it?" Heather said, still red in the face. "I don't really have a family, none of us do. I'd rather be right here than anywhere on the island. Am I alone?"

"You're never alone," Derek said. "We're stronger together. Like a jungle, instead of a tree. Like—"

"We love you too," Lynn said.

"She speaks for us," I said.

"Always has," Derek said.

And they sat up and jumped into each other's arms, throwing sand all over the rest of us. I sat up and spat the sand out of my mouth, chose peace instead of violence (or more talking), and succumbed to the group hug.

"Tell me why I could die happy right now?" Heather said.

"Because you're home," Lynn said. "We all are. And there's no dying in our house."

"Our house is the beach?" Derek said.

"Whatever he just said," Lynn said, without even looking at me. "We need you Heather. Right here, right now. No rest."

"Not over," Heather said.

"And no prisoners," I said darkly, making my eyebrows match Heather's.

"That… was never part of it," Lynn frowned.

"Let's hear the guy out," Heather countered. "He's talking about scars and tattoos and prisoners now, I kinda like this new James—"

"I wish I could come," Waylilla said. "I don't think you need the help. It's just… we just got television."

"You do now," I said. "A hundred days? Start with Scrubs."

"Staring Zach Braff?" Waylilla asked, her eyes full of hope.

"That's a good show," Heather said, and Lynn nodded, the only one not surprised that Heather knew about—nevermind.

"You're all welcome," I said. "Least I could do. But I command you all to stop thinking about television. It's not hard. This is the best beach I've ever seen. It's like the definition of vacation, at least from this angle."

"You should see it from about a thousand feet," Waylilla said, her eyes suddenly colder. "You might eat those words."

I looked at her. "Speaking of words. What was it Bastile whispered to you, when he was under the blueblood?"

"Helps to know," Willa said, blinking. "He said, keep them talking, because it helps to know."

"Helps to know what?" Heather asked.

"Friend or foe," Willa said, shrugging at me, like she was saying sorry.

"You have nothing to be sorry about, Wildfire," I said, taking a chance.

"Thank you, Nite. You neither."

And the rest went unsaid. For now.

We took a step away from Jerico's new leader and blasted up into the air, with the Territory at our back and the ocean floor as clear as day going on seventy feet from shore. The water was so calm, clean, and blue it was hard to see anything else but living coral, the sandbar falloff, rainbow reefs, and—wait.

"Guys," Derek said, frowning.

"Is that…" Lynn started.

"Well, I do love a good downwards spiral," Heather said.

Together we stared through the transparent waters and shallow sea floor to see a ship the size of an ocean liner sitting at the bottom of the water, almost like it was waiting for us, taunting us. It was a ship at the bottom of the sea, only bigger than any vessel I'd ever thought possible, bigger than any vehicle I'd ever seen. I'd heard the word before—ark. If this wasn't that…

"Kira?" I said.

I swear, I heard something bang against the inside of that ship, calling for me as hard as I was calling for her. It was her.

It had to be.

EPILOGUE

<u>KIRA COMMAND</u>

5.0

LIVE, LITTLE ONES

I breached the surface and took my first real breath of air in six minutes. It tasted like life. But it still smelled like a ship at the bottom of the sea.

"How fare they?" begged the coxman's voice.

"Not even a towel?" I asked.

"Is my sister alive?" he asked, staring at me so hard—

"They live," I said. "The bread got a bit wet, nothing she isn't used to."

Coxman Connor cried, bursting into tears with a hand over his eyes, as six men waiting for me by that sinkhole sighed in relief. We all had family down there, some more than others. It was, as my backup team was want to say, heavy. But no one was coming forward with a towel, so I rolled my eyes and vibrated my body at superspeed like a dog until the water was evaporated. The men took a step back, I saw the sweat on the Coxman's forehead. They were afraid of me.

"The navigation unit lives," Connor said.

"For now," I said. "They've got a day before their own breathing turns that air bubble to poison. If we're to avoid the same, we need to shut a sector down."

"You're certain about a key, before we turn that lock?" Connor asked.

"I'm pretty sure," I said.

"I can't put thirty thousand lives on the line for pretty."

"Then you haven't been at sea long enough," I shot back. "What I know for absolute sure is I can't get us to the surface alone. We'll need either the entire navigation team, a capacitor room that isn't flooded to the high heavens, or… something else."

"Even navigations is down to reserves," Connor sighed. "We've lost too many to the underwater repairs, when all this time you've been sleeping in your shell—"

"Someone rigged an entire nautical sector to convince me I was still underland," I shot back. "That I was ready for. This… not so much. Also thanks for calling me a diamond."

"That's pearls," Connor frowned.

"Diamonds of the sea, even better," I said.

“Seems you lack even a basic understanding of the most ancient—”

“Would you rather I wasn’t here?” I asked, tired of the jokes.

“I’d rather see your potential in actuality, for once,” the coxman said. “If you’re a literal living legend, why are we still living off rats?”

“Because we’re in a ship at the bottom of the sea!” I shouted. “There’s a million tons of water pressure on top of us! I know I’m the living embodiment of an entire civilization’s technology, but I’m only a girl man. Overcoming that much weight would take, I don’t know, five of me at least, what do you want from me, a miracle?”

And that’s when I saw the colors coming through the water towards us. Four of them.

“Much obliged,” I said to the universe. “Coxman, ready the ship.”

“For what?” He asked.

“For ascension,” I said. “I stand corrected, or validated, or something. Doesn’t matter, today’s the day.”

“It doesn’t MATTER?”

“Today’s the day,” I said, shutting him up like usual, by pointing a single finger his way. “There’s your miracle.”

“That’s…” he said, looking out the underwater window to the same four figures I was seeing. There was no denying it. Together six aquaneers, their captain, and I stared out that window, just watching the figures fly through the water without pause. It was him. It had to be.

“You found me,” I said. “I only did everything. But you still found me.”

“You’re still talking to yourself?” the coxman sighed.

“I never was,” I said. “I was talking to them, the whole time. Who’s ready to meet Derek and James?”

The ship was silent. The faces gave away the hope, the tiniest spark in the old hope machine. Then one man spoke up, and even on shaking legs and a raspy voice, he said it all.

“Who the hell are Derek and James?”

"…unless it's replaced by something more permanent… which becomes more intangible."

-Rodney Mullen

ABOUT THE AUTHOR

David William Olivas is a 29 year old Newhouse graduate from the San Jose bay area. He is an alumni of University Union, and as Director of Cinemas he brought digital cinema projection to his college theaters, as well as co-created the Syracuse University Film Festival. He presciently quit a journalism job at NBC Bay Area in 2016, and moved to Los Angeles to work in the music / film industry. Now, he helps run a music company for film and television composers, and manages a catalog that hundreds of artists all across the world contribute to. His hobbies include skateboarding, recording music, and guitar.

Made in the USA
Monee, IL
13 August 2022